# THE PREPPER'S SON

A novel by
Joel Gallay

FIRST EDITION FEBRUARY 2019

Copyright © 2019 by Joel Gallay

*Pre-Cover Art Edition*

This is a work of fiction. Names, characters, creatures, inventions, businesses, places, events and incidents are either the products of the author's imagination or used in a fictitious manner. Any resemblance to actual subjects, actual persons living or dead, or actual events or places is purely coincidental.

**Furthermore, the actions, attitudes and behaviors of the characters depicted in this work of fiction are by no means condoned by the author or the publisher.**

All rights reserved. All characters, settings and depictions are reserved by Joel Gallay and Gallanic Media, respectively. This book or any portion thereof may not be reproduced or used in any manner whatsoever without the express written permission of the publisher except for the use of brief quotations in a book review.

Published in the United States by Gallanic Media, Prescott, AZ. Originally published electronically in the United States through Amazon Inc. Kindle E-Publishing, February 2019.

## Table of Contents

### ACT I: A MINUTE TO MIDNIGHT
1:4  2:10  3:13  4:16  5:19  6:23

### ACT II: PARADIGM
7:28  8:32  9:44  10:50  11:54  12:63  13:69  14:77  15:84

### ACT III: PILLARS OF SALT
16:89  17:99  18:103  19:113  20:118  21:121  22:130  23:140  24:150  25:159  26:167  27:173  28:182  29:192  30:203  31:207  32:216  33:221  34:227

### ACT IV: BAPTISM
35:232  36:240  37:250  38:258  39:264  40:270  41:279  42:285  43:289  44:294  45:298  46:305  47:313  48:321  49:327  50:335  51:340  52:348  53:354  54:363  55:367  56:371  57:373  58:380  59:385  60:390  61:396  62:401  63:405  64:412

### ACT V: GRADUATION
65:424  66:429  67:433  68:435  69:438  70:444  71:449  72:460  73:465  74:471  75:478  76:482  77:485

### AFTERWORD:493

# ACT I
# A MINUTE TO MIDNIGHT

**Chapter 1**

I'm sitting alone here. Taking in these slow, subtle moments of stillness inside the muffling canopy of the car that made the rest of the world quiet, watching the front door of that simple, unassuming house for a long while until it slowly cracked open. I sat back in the driver's seat, feeling my wordless, subconscious reaction to watching her exit that front door, backpack over one shoulder as her mocha eyes met mine for a split second, as if a silent conveyance of her exasperation this morning, bags of sleeplessness beneath her eyes. I witnessed the front door slam in silence as she pushed it closed, and I simultaneously pressed a button on the dash, opening the passenger seat. I heard her footsteps under the sound of the newscast playing on the holographic windshield of the vehicle, as she circled the front of the vehicle around to the other side, opening the passenger door and throwing the bag down towards where her feet would soon be as she sat down with an unceremonious grunt. She pulled the door closed by herself before I could push the button, and it latched closed, the console beeping and entombing us in a strange silence, with only the news to be heard.

"Hey, Maria," I said quietly to her, as she looked over to me, brushing her silky black hair out of her face. She looked at me with her deep brown eyes, soiled by weariness, bagged beneath them.

"Noah," She remarked groggily, with us hardly sharing a split second to look at each other. She leaned in to kiss me on the cheek. It was too early for me to reciprocate, still half asleep in my own way before she sat back and fastened her seatbelt, clearing her throat.

"All right," I ordered. "Let's go."

"Of course, Noah," the onboard computer said. The engine started up, whirring ceaselessly in near complete silence. Aside from that, the news was still playing on the front windshield's holographic screen, filling the cabin with voices sound, a welcome alternative to icy silence.

"Special report," I suddenly heard the news bark out behind exciting music as we listened half-mindedly. "Are radicalist groups becoming more and more common closer to home? From home-grown, far-right and far-left militias in America and Canada, and Texan and Quebecoi separatists-"

"Ugh," Maria interjected. "Why is the news always so dark? It's always terrorism or war or murders or something depressing," She said, and I changed the channel with a swift hand motion on the holographic display, the sensors picking up the subtleties of my hand motions, haptic controls engaging.

"-And, it really is a conundrum," I heard this new newscaster say. "These, these things- Hybrids- I mean, how many does the government have?"

"Oh boy, hybrids," Maria commentated, massaging her temple with a hand, now gazing out the window aimlessly, watching the houses go by. "Because we haven't heard enough about those yet."

"It's not the government," another person on the show chimed in, as I shot a glance towards the holographic heads-up display inside my car windshield showing this newsreel, taking a break from how I was resting my eyes while the autopilot did its thing. I took in his visage, some consultant calling in to the show, very much not a newsmember. "It's the private corporations, most prominently BioTek- they, that the government signed on to make them- the Hybrids." I noted to myself how this speaker spoke with too many awkward little pauses, chuckling, letting my mind flow to a relevant topic.

"You should hear Gabriel," I responded from the corner of my mouth in sarcasm. "He won't shut up about them. About how they made a bunch of fucked up, genetic experiments for like, no reason."

"-But *why*?" the other one on the show asked, their conversation apart from ours. "I mean, social experiments? You've got to be kidding me. These... things are designed to be cheaper workers, after all, after the closing of immigration in '41. They need to get their workers somewhere. Take what happened in White Horse for example- BioTek, or their parent company Elrond Industries, in this case, used them to work gold mines in the Yukon."

Maria sighed. "Gabriel?" She shook her head a little as she talked. "You know, he's a bad influence," She hissed softly, a tinge of worry in her voice.

"Yes, ElTek did that," One of the pundits on the broadcast said, their conversation continuing on unfazed. "but they did it primarily as a societal experiment. The gold was a secondary objective. They never needed them to mine, we have robots- drones, why would we need workers?" the other one said. "They just use robots, kill jobs and let the lower class descend further while they get richer from all the money they don't spend on real- human, workers. The hybrids are just their toys, and it just shows their selfishness. It's sickening."

"No Gabriel isn't," I responded. "I've known him for years. He's been my best friend since fourth grade."

"What was the number, how many of these things do they have worldwide? one-fifty million?" one of the newscasters spat.

"Yeah, and now he gets straight D's," Maria insisted. "You know he *failed* last year and didn't even care. All he cares about is guns and knives and that kind of edgy shit. I'm pretty sure he sells drugs, Noah."

"I believe the number is five hundred million. High estimates say a *billion*." the other newscaster responded, and his compatriot let out a worried whistle.

"Oh, he does not," I responded. "Look, I know Gabe. He's still the same, and even if he was, I'd be smarter than to listen to him. Yeah, he can be pretty... *Out there,* sometimes, with conspiracies and shit, but at least he's not as crazy as my dad and his castle in the woods."

"At first, they said they had five hundred thousand. Then they were telling us in December that they had just one million. What's next? What, do we count them in the global census? That puts earth at nearly 12 billion 'people', putting us well over what many theorists call the 'population collapse curve-"

"TV off," I finally groaned, somewhat impatiently, and the holographic screen blinked off, leaving us in silence.

Maria leaned back, the seat creaking ever so subtly. She held her head, massaging her temples. "Ugh... Why were you even watching the news?" She asked. "they always say good morning and they have to explain why it's not. It's always shitty."

"My dad always has the news on," I said.

"You need to get your own car."

"*You* need to get *your* own car."

"Ha." Maria paused. "Ugh. I've got a headache from finishing a report last night. More like, this morning," she said. "I'm running on like, two hours of sleep here."

"Take a nap," I said.

"the school is right there," She motioned down the road, towards the large, old brick-walled building. An eyesore amidst much more contemporary architecture.

"Well, we're gridlocked," I said, looking around. "We're this far away from the school, and everyone using autopilot we're not going anywhere. God," I crowed in exasperation. "Comp, date and time," I ordered the computer.

"The date is April 30, 2060, Noah," it told me. "Time is 7:49."

"I hope we're not gonna be late," I said. "Five minutes to go. Computer," I said again. "Have my coffee ready outside of the locker room."

"Mine too," Maria said.

"Of course," The computer chimed.

Within a couple seconds of pulling into the lot, The car found a suitable spot and parked itself. "Have a nice day," I quipped, and Maria let out a grunt of agreement. Or maybe a grunt of exasperated formality, and quickly left the vehicle and shambled off, as did I, right behind her. We walked solemnly to the coffee dispensary, a little machine in the center of the bike racks. Maria walked up and took her roast, before turning around to say goodbye again to me, such an occurrence being too commonplace to even be considered awkward; and I was already at the machine anyways, too busy to bid my farewell. Within a couple seconds, the dispenser produced my coffee, which I grabbed, seeing my account being charged in my hologlasses' heads-up display. I burnt my tongue, the coffee was still quite scalding. I thought they'd fix the dispensary bot by now, but I guess fixing the coffee dispensaries are low priority on the school's to-do list.

I arrived in the changing room and went to my locker, which popped open electronically as it sensed me approaching. I shoved my backpack and holos inside, pulling out my PE clothes. After putting them on, there was only a short walk to the weight room, my coffee still in my grip.

I stepped inside, to see everyone already getting started, the clink of weight sets and the beeps of various electronic fitness sensors clamoring out. I walked up to the coach, a short, stocky man with well-tanned skin and a cleanly shaven bald head and face, with a neck like a tree trunk and biceps just the same.

"Hey coach, I'm here," I said.

"Oh, just in time, Mr. Reed," He said, in the habit of calling people by the surname "mister", as he pressed some buttons on his tablet, marking me present. "Your group's waiting for you." he motioned over to the corner, where I saw two of my friends by one of the bench presses, with one of them lazily spotting and the other on the bench with an absurd amount of weight, the sensor console chirping out advice. "Oh, and try not to miss the track meet tomorrow, alright?"

"Yeah, yeah, I'll be there," I assured him. I walked on over, seeing Wilson on his hologlasses, making hand motions and controlling the haptic feedback as he was probably checking messages or playing a game or something, as subtly as he could.

"WILSON!" I heard Coach's voice boom out. Wilson's hologlasses lit up in red as they heard his name, an obvious hotword that would alert him if somebody around said it. Wilson stood up tall, surprised, looking past me, at coach. "No holos on in here. You can watch porn outside of class." the people around laughed, and I chuckled a little. Wilson whipped them off, stuffing them in his pocket, before flipping me off as he rolled his eyes.

"Bout time you showed up," Kyle said, on the bench, visibly straining as he pushed the barbell up and let it rest on the rack, with the computer chirping out "Weight secure. total repetitions: eight," as Kyle talked over it. "Wilson's a shitty spotter."

"Psht, whatever, Kyle," Wilson rolled his eyes. "I mean, come on. The computer will say something if I need to help." Kyle sat up and we slapped each other's hand nonchalantly.

"Where's Gabe?" I asked.

"Doin' cardio, with that vest of his on," Kyle said.

"Again?" I asked, more as a joking formality than any sort of genuine surprise. Kyle laughed a little.

"You know he's crazy," He mumbled quickly, wiping his brow with a towel and taking a gulp of energy water. "...Cardio kills your gains, dude. He's doin' that shit every day."

"Yeah, well, he doesn't have twig legs like you do," I mentioned, sitting down on a nearby rowing machine, putting my drink down and getting to work, the machine recognizing my presence and adjusting for it, going to my previous weight from yesterday. "How much can you squat? Two, three whole kilos? You max three point five, eh?" I quipped, straining a little as I worked the machine.

"Oh ho ho," Wilson remarked.

"Shut the fuck up Wilson, do some situps or somethin', li'l bitch, then talk shit."

Wilson 'tsk'ed. "Just sayin', dude," he said, going off to the abdominal machine, and manually putting it on the second-lowest setting, killing time as he pushed it, like he was pretending to do work.

"Really, you need to shut up about gains, it's not like that shit even matters," I went on.

"Sorry, are you a linebacker?" Kyle responded sarcastically, still panting off his previous workout.

"Are you still out of breath?" I shot back.

"Fuck you. Yesterday was leg day. And I ran yesterday," Kyle insisted.

"And you did one set of squats, man. One of these days you're gonna snap your legs off or your heart'll explode." He shook his head, and paused for a long time.

"You done yet?"

"Done telling you the truth?" I growled, in the middle of a row.

"No, dumbass, doing your rows. I need a spotter." I decided to quit, rolling my eyes, getting up as the machine beeped to bid me farewell, and I walked over to behind the barbell, ready to assist.

"Okay, up," I said.

"I don't need you to tell me my own shit," Kyle snarled with a tinge of viciousness, pushing up and lifting it from the rack, my hands hovering limply below the bar in case.

"Jeez, asshole, why do you need me then?" I barked. Kyle didn't respond, his brow furrowing and whole body quaking as he pushed hard, grunting. I leaned against the wall, holding my coffee.

As I lifted my drink to my lips, I saw Gabriel come through the open door leading outside, panting slightly and with energy to spare, evidenced by the bounce-like swagger in his step. He always walked like he was bigger than he was, with a sort of deadly rhythm to himself. He was short and somewhat wide, just over six foot and moved far heavier than he looked, with dirty blond hair cut short to his head (though he'd let it grow out for now) and perpetual stubble on his somewhat ugly, brutish face and under his wide jaw, with deep-set, dark green eyes that almost looked blue from a distance. He was built muscular, not nearly as much as Kyle but he seemed more streamlined, yet at the same time with a kind of soldier-like bulkiness in his arms, chest and thighs that was unlike Kyle's college-frat beefed look. "Sup, cocklords," he spat unceremoniously, hardly making eye contact, making a beeline to his water bottle in the corner.

"Stop any bullets today, dumbass?" Kyle grunted from under the barbell, noting Gabriel's coyote-brown colored plate carrier. I could see the goofy "WEIGHT VEST" velcro patches he had on its front and back, a little administrative touch he had to perform before Coach would let him do his thing.

"More than you ever will, dicklicker," Gabe spat from the corner of his lip with a smile, taking a swig as he intertwined his thumb into the shoulder strap of his heavy bulletproof vest. He turned, looking back over at me. "Coffee again, huh?" He said with an indignant smirk. "You want to get pumped, run a mile with this on, it'll get you going," He tapped his armored carapace, solid steel ringing out with knocking.

"No thanks, don't want to look like a terrorist,"

Gabriel scoffed. "What do you care if a bunch of retards think you're scary?"

"Well, I gotta live with these 'retards'," I shot back with a smile. Gabe looked at me for a couple of seconds with what I could describe as a skeptical smile on his face.

"Yeah, but just don't let 'em meet your dad," Gabe finally responded.

"I'm not my fuckin' dad," I growled back, leaning off.

"Hey, I'm just saying, no need to get all antsy about it," Gabe said in mock concern before he laughed. "You know your dad's got it right though," Gabe said. "The man's a one man army, and maybe you should-" sensing what was coming, I rolled my eyes and faked yawning before he could go on, and he rolled his eyes and grunted in amused indignance. "Alright, *sure*. But, just remember," he paused to point at my coffee. "Addictions'll kill you," He paused, to look around, catching Wilson's eye.

"What if I'm addicted to pussy?" Wilson said.

"Yeah, doubt it," Gabe said, tossing his water bottle.

"Wow, all this *hostility*," Wilson said with a smile and furrowed brow, jokingly.

"I've got Killers to do," Gabe said matter-of-factly, beginning.

"Don't wait for my approval," I said sarcastically as he squatted down, transitioning to a pushup, doing one, and then springing back up, beginning to count. Kyle finished, and he was shaking his head all the while.

"More cardio," He said in slight, playful disapproval quietly, to me. "There's somethin' fuckin' wrong with him."

"Kyle, you faggot," Gabriel grunted in the middle of one, hearing it. "Didn't you know women love a man with endurance? ...Ask your mom sometime, she'll agree I'm the best,"

"My mom lives in Cali, retard,"

"You're damn right she does, and she appreciates my *enduring* the long trip to get into her pants."

"You know my mom is like, twice your age, right retard?"

"Kyle... if it would piss you off, I'd fuck it. Because I love you *that* much."

"Would'ja fuck a hybrid?" Wilson chirped somewhat out-of-place, still sitting on the chair of the ab machine lazily.

"You kiddin' me?" Gabriel said with the raise of a brow, after a heavy pause. "You'd probably get furry herpes or something." He paused, standing in place and catching his breath.

"I dunno, man," Wilson said with a little laugh, raising his eyebrow, as if ogling an imaginary hybrid woman. Gabe paused.

"What are you, some kinda furfag?"

"What does that even mean?" Kyle asked. "You keep saying that shit."

"It means you're a furry, you furry."

"Yeah, what does that mean? You keep using that word." Gabriel said nothing, just looking at Kyle with an antagonistic smirk for a couple seconds, as if he was about to say something, but he never did. Kyle rolled his eyes. "Whatever, asshole,"

Gabriel did another set before springing up from his final rep, and breathed out a loud sigh, jumping up on his toes as he did it.

"Stop any bullets today, Noria?" Coach exclaimed.

"Ha ha ha, already heard it today, Coach," Gabe responded, and Coach smirked a little, turning to check in on other people. Gabriel reached to the clip on one of the shoulder pads, unhooking it, before undoing the velcro flap and letting the whole rig slide off of him. I simply stood there, leaning up against my machine, resting. He sighed, airing out his sweat-inundated tank top. "What, just standing around? Do some shit."

"Fuck off, Gabe," I said, before pausing. "besides, why are you even here?"

"Here?"

"Yeah, in this class."

"I gotta go to school. It's the law. Don't want to piss off the law now, do I?" He said, still grinning like an idiot.

"No, I mean, in this specific class. You don't have any sports to train for or anything."

"Yeah, and neither does Wilson, your point?" Gabriel said, and behind him, Wilson's holos lit up red, hearing his name. He whipped them off quickly, spurting "W-what?" almost guiltily, as if he'd been caught.

"Yeah, but he just sits around and doesn't do anything. You're actually trying."

"What? Can't a guy get physically fit if he wants to?" Gabriel quipped.

"Seriously?" I asked, brow raised.

"Yup," Gabriel said, sitting down on a quadricep machine. "Well, I guess it's useful for my job, too."

"Your job?" I asked. "You drive a delivery drone, don't you?"

"Well, being in shape never hurts, does it?" He said, straining the last word as he lifted his forelegs against the machine. I shook my head little, as he laughed at my exasperation.

## Chapter 2

"Now that we're all seated, class," My history teacher announced, as I sipped down the last of my still-warm coffee, "Let's talk about something that's been pretty relevant lately- the Doomsday Clock." She paused, to wave her hand at the haptic sensor to begin the presentation, revealing the image of an old-fashioned clock on her main board, holographic display glittering in the dark room. I took a glance downwards, seeing in my desk, the bright holoscreen showing the image duplicated. "Now, can anybody tell me what the doomsday clock is?" She paused, to glare intently into the corner with a smile at Gabriel, who sat there, disinterested and on his old-fashioned smartphone, flicking away. "Gabriel, since you're so invested in our current topic, how about you tell us?" She said with an accusatory tinge in her voice, as if to put the seemingly inattentive Gabriel on the spot.

"The Doomsday Clock, Ms. Haringer, is a metaphor for how close we are to the end of the world, midnight representing some kind of major irreversible disaster like a nuclear war," he mused dully, not even looking up for a second. Ms. Haringer paused, somewhat taken aback, before nodding, lips furling as if impressed.

"Very... good, Gabriel," She said, before addressing the rest of us. "As... As we interpret it, the Doomsday clock is a metaphor used as a way to describe how close we are to the end of civilization as we know it- Originally, by way of nuclear destruction. See, back in the twentieth century, we- America- were engaged in the cold war with the Russians, or Soviets, constantly edging at the idea of a... Like Gabriel said, a nuclear war pretty much ever since World War Two ended in 1946. Now, of course, it's taken on the broader term of an end to the world, an end to civilization as we know it in general. Now, the last time the Doomsday Clock has gone under a minute was as recent as last year- at fifty seconds to midnight, during the event I'm sure we've all been paying attention to, the White Horse Incident, the Hybrid scandal. Since the situation has been controlled as of late, the clock was pushed back to two minutes, however, just this morning, something very exciting took place- the United Nations has passed the motion that Hybrids are considered human beings in terms of rights and legalities, following the example of the Alaskan and Northwestern Canadian Integration Program. Even moreso, there's the fact that the perpetrators of the hybrid projects, mostly led under the quadrillion-dollar ElTek corporation are announcing, to the demand of the UN's Amnesty Peacekeeping charter, to declassify all projects and release all hybrids in current holding- which is, needless to say, somewhat jarring of a proposition. However, due to this and the controversy surrounding hybrids, the clock has been pushed forward to one minute to midnight. Honestly, I'm excited to see what the future brings," She said. "So perhaps every one of you will get to meet a hybrid. Who knows, we might even get exchange students."

"Better not be allergic," somebody snickered to a neighbor.

"Now," Ms. Haringer went on. "While we're still on the topic of the Doomsday clock, let's not get worried by this one minute to midnight. After all, we've been closer before, haven't we? Can somebody name a time when we got closer than 50 seconds?"

"How about 2045?" A girl piped up, and Ms. Haringer nodded her head, shrugging a little bit.

"of course," She said. "The so-called Standstill of 2045, has been the closest the world has come to nuclear destruction, closer even than the assassination of the Russian president during the Clinton presidency; and is, on record, as the closest moment. Now, to know this, we've got to go into the sciences- I'm sure we know some of the reasons as to why the Standstill happened, right?" The class was mostly silent, aside from a rather spindly looking boy chiming in, people all around silently groaning and rolling their eyes in exasperation as they heard his voice begin, some smiling to each other and motioning to him.

"Um, well," he began in a nasally voice, rattling off the facts like he'd rehearsed, if not for a slight stutter. "The Standstill of 2045 was primarily caused by a deceleration of technological progression. Before some time in the 2020s, technology was under the dynamic of increasing to double what it was every four years. However, as the development of electronic hardware was reaching a molecular scale, the progression began to slow dramatically. It was some time in 2040 when the effect on the stocks of electronics companies, unable to innovate any more, began to fall."

"That's right, Richard," The teacher proclaimed, eyeing the students who seemed to be more interested in poking fun at Richard's way of speaking than what he'd been saying. "However, that's not the whole story. As the stocks of tech companies fell dramatically and the stock market crashed, the inflation rates on currency all over the world skyrocketed- as well as the fact that, by then, we were already in a fuel, a population *and* a food crisis, not to mention the effects of drastic increases in global temperature and pollution. Then, in 2045, the president of the rogue nation North Korea died, kick-starting the Second Korean War. This moment in time is regarded as being three seconds to midnight, a tipping point so disastrous nobody expected the world to survive... But, as we know..." She paused, to motion around her, smiling and shrugging. "We found a way, didn't we?" She smiled amid meager chuckles. "It seemed like there was no hope, however, we found a way to pull through against all odds. China refused to back North Korea, who had, for the longest time, been completely unreasonable with them. The Southern Koreans took North Korea, and without a single nuclear weapon being detonated. Climate change as well, actually turned out to save us too: it turned inhospitable areas of frozen tundra into places where food could be grown, and the increased precipitation caused by a warmer earth provided lots of fresh water and even turned nearly seventy five percent of all deserts on earth into forests and jungles. And, the economic crisis, and even the pollution crisis was solved when ElTek purchased nearly all tech companies and forced tech prices to a record low, which managed to keep the tech industry from completely collapsing, simultaneously embarking on a philanthropy mission of a worldwide oceanic cleanup with new technologies."

"Yeah, and now they own us all, so don't go off sucking their dicks or anything," I heard a girl chime in, a girl with bright multicolored hair, like unicorn puke, as she leaned back in her chair. "they can do anything they want to us now. Just look at what they're doing with the hybrids."

"Eh, maybe you're right, Sam," the teacher responded. "Still beats living in a post-apocalyptic world though, right?" She smiled a little bit, and Sam sat back in her chair, in somewhat indignance. "Still... To think that every year a new model of electronic device would come out and something you bought two years before, being top of the line, slowly devolving into something archaic and inferior- can you imagine if you had to replace your hologlasses or tablets every few years? weird to think about, isn't it?" Nobody responded, save for the overly enthusiastic nods from Richard. "Now, as you know, most of this will be on the test next week..." She slowly drawled out, scanning the room, as her mouth moved as if preparing the next question for an unsuspecting student, searching for the perfect candidate. "Daniel, can you tell me one cause of the Standstill of 2045?" She barked out, looking out to the back of the class. I continued to lean against my desk, propping my head up on a fist, subconsciously awaiting Daniel's bored response to come from behind me. But, within a few seconds and a repetition of the question from the teacher, heads began to turn, as did mine. I saw, sitting a row and a column away from me the person in question, a young-faced teenager with dark skin and buzz-cut black hair busy with, quite to my surprise, a pad of paper and a mechanical pencil, the sound of it skritching away now that I focused on the noise, along with my classmates. His ears were plugged with the earpieces of his hologlasses, assumedly listening to music, and more than likely with his name notification function disabled. They looked old, anyways, so they could have just been malfunctioning- but beside that point, *he was writing on paper*. Or drawing, whatever. Why did he even have paper? Didn't he have a tablet? The school gives them away for free. from where I was sitting, it just looked like he was doodling or something. Why wasn't he just using the draw function in his holos?

"Ahem," Our teacher cleared her throat loudly, as students began to murmur. As she began to walk forward impatiently, only at that point did Daniel take notice of the still air of the classroom, and by the time he looked up, the teacher was towering above him. The color drained from his face in embarrassment and he dove to cover up his drawing. He also simultaneously whipped off his holos, gazing up at the teacher with a red face. She had opened her mouth to say something, but as she had approached him she caught a glimpse of what he'd been working on, and by her awkward silence, she seemed to have lost her breath for a moment. I, in curiosity, raised myself a little higher in my seat to try and sneak a look, but his arms covered most of it. "Daniel…" She murmured slowly.

"He's been drawing hybrid tits again, hasn't he?" a boy in the corner leaning off his chair said, smirking. This was met with low, growling chuckles emanating from the room, and Daniel's face got redder.

"Daniel, please, not in class," The teacher said, holding the bridge of her nose and closing her eyes. "You can… *Draw*, at home," She said, enunciating "draw" in a very specific sort of exasperation, one that didn't really want to acknowledge itself yet had to out of a cringing hope for salvaged dignity. He, like a bullet fired from a gun, whipped his hands away to slam shut his notebook and put his school tablet atop it, under the quiet laughs of his classmates. I didn't laugh. I think I felt pity, though I also think I felt disgust, admittedly. However, when he'd uncovered his notebook to close it, I caught a glimpse of what was on the paper, if only for an instant. I saw a dog like head on what must've been a humanlike body. It looked detailed and immaculate, something he'd really put his effort into. For that instant, I was given an eternity's worth of pause. I didn't really know what to feel besides a dull kind of deranged shock.

Like that the memory of what had happened faded back into class, the laughter dying like the wind and the bell soon coming, where I could shuffle to my feet and leave, like it'd never happened- until a couple rousing snickers as we all piled towards the door. I was already distracted by a message in my holos, something Wilson had found funny and sent to me- that I didn't notice as I bumped right into him, in that bustling chokehold of the doorway. Like he'd been attacked, the boy jolted past, not before his notebook slid from his grasp. I was struck dumb for a quarter second, and in that time, he was gone, and I stood there, over his fallen notebook laying on the ground. I wanted to call out, but it was like he'd practically disappeared.

The notebook had fallen to land adjacent to the walkway, hitting the trash can and flipping open as it did, the simple bound paper opening to a page that gave me even more pause, stopping like I'd taken a bug in the mouth while walking. There was a portrait of a strange, inhuman creature- a hybrid, I'd first assumed. Daniel was into that sort of stuff, wasn't he? I picked it up, getting a good, slow look, pulling my hologlasses up to rest them atop my head. A simple portrait of one of the weird lizard-y ones- was it a sketch of one that they interviewed on the news? It was black and white, pencil shaded, and I wouldn't have really been that perturbed by it until I saw the caption-

Lania Nove
5/21/2059

He'd drawn this thing, this character, this hybrid girl, before anybody even knew the hybrids existed.

"Huh. Looks like Danny's a future teller," Gabe's voice behind me chuckled morosely. I slowly closed it, as if released bit by bit from a daze. I looked at Gabe for a second, and he let out a chuckle before passing on. I put it into my bag, intending to give it back, proceeding to my next class, out into the halls where the thought would slowly simmer away.

### Chapter 3

I made my way over across the well-watered school courtyard lawn, walking past all those with their eyes blank, staring off into cyberspace. Still absorbed into my own media I took a seat at a table, where Gabriel sat in silence, observing those around him. Close by, I saw a few other friends, Wilson on his holos like usual, laughing occasionally and showing those around by tapping a few times to send what he was looking at to his friends' screens; Kyle and his girlfriend quietly on their phones, right next to each other but being completely silent, like neither one really knew the other was there.

I sat down across from Gabriel. He raised his sunglasses. I knew that they weren't holovisors or anything, because as he tipped them up away from his eyes, they didn't undim. They were just glasses, an old fashioned touch, he might even say with a smug chuckle. I sat there, pulling my backpack to the front to go for my lunch.

"Look at these people," I heard Gabriel say. I undimmed my glasses a little, looking over to him, despite how I was still distracting myself with my media.

"What?"

"I mean, look at them all."

"What about 'em?" I asked, taking my lunch out.

"All of them, waiting in line. So many. You know they're building a new window so they can serve food faster?" He said. "Now the school site allows you to make your order on your tablet, phone, hologlasses, holotacts, the works," He cleared his throat. "But even if they didn't get their food, they just stand there watching videos and playing games. They're complacent, but efficiently complacent. Why bother being efficient if you don't care? And just look at 'em, so many and yet they probably don't even know other people are around them. They bump into each other and don't even say sorry. Don't even fuckin' look up. And there's ten billion of them, and at least five billion are just like them, living the dream, a bunch of entitled little shits. Rushing around, getting their new auto piloting car to do things for them just so they can goof off."

"Yeah yeah they're all deer in the headlights, zombies and shit. Listen, you need to have some new material, instead of spouting the same things you always do," I remarked, yet before Gabriel could counter, I suddenly saw Kyle's visor flash for a second, and he looked up. It had flashed because the visor had heard a hotword- Kyle liked zombies.

"Hey," he said in a monotone, "Zombies. Hey Noah, isn't your dad ready for the zombies? With that fuckin' castle of his, up in the middle of nowhere?"

I looked over at him and cringed. I could feel a subtle exasperation exude from Gabriel as he slumped back with a shallow sigh, though his ever-present smirk taking advantage of my exasperation let him act unbothered. "Yeah, he's an apocalypse prepper and he's got a spot in a survival hideout," I said tiredly, and he gave out a shallow "ha."

"Dude, I'm like, totally going to your place when the zombies come," he said.

'Pfft, zombies," Gabriel said, rolling his eyes. "As if."

"Gabe, aren't you ready for the zombies too?" Kyle asked, and Gabriel gritted his teeth.

"Fuck zombies, man," He growled, "The notion of a zombie these days is fuckin' shameful, they used to be original and had a valid social commentary- but it's now lost on so many people that it's just used in movies and games to portray an apocalypse without any originality or creativity needed. You don't need undead to create an apocalypse, and it seems like an excuse nowadays, a lazy way to write a post apocalyptic world without putting any original thought-"

"Say, yo Noah," I heard Kyle continue, cutting Gabriel's rant off, who gritted his teeth in a quiet, playful anger, rolling his eyes and masking his perturbed nature with ever more smiling exasperation. "What *does* your dad even do?" He had asked this question before numerous times, but he always seemed to ask me again anyways. I thought he liked to talk crap about him to look better in front of his girlfriend or to stroke his ego. Or both.

"He... He works in nanotech," I answered, almost forgetting what my father actually does. I always thought of him as just "The Prepper". It was practically a job in itself.

"And he spends his time in the woods huntin' and fishin' and stuff?" He said. "What is he, rambo?" He said almost teasingly, turning is head to his girlfriend, the skinny stick that she was. She laughed at his joke, arching her head way too far back and laughing with a single "ha". "What, he ever in the military? What, he a navy seal?"

"Marine Recon," I corrected, taking a sip from a can of juice.

"Ah, so, yeah," He said, his smile shrinking a bit, his mocking falling short. "Well, I saw that pic of you on Facebook, with that big-ass gun," He continued. "Like, why does he even need that stuff?"

"I dunno, he thinks the world's gonna end or some shit," I shrugged. "He's got a castle up north he likes to go to dude, what do you expect?"

He did a laugh similar to that of his girlfriend's, before continuing. "What a pussy," He said. "Real men use their fists. I could kick his ass." I ought to have been offended, but I honestly thought the same- to me, despite his physique and snappy, "I'm always right" wit, my father was a crazy, pathetic old man.

Kyle continued eating and browsing his media feed, as if the conversation never happened.

I looked back up at Gabriel, who shook his head softly. "What," I proclaimed.

"Have you ever thought that your dad might have a bit of a point?" Gabriel said. "Just a tad?"

"What? Well, course I have," I said.

"So you're just complacent."

"I don't think there's anything to worry about."

"So you *are* complacent."

I scoffed, and was about to turn my hologlasses back on to the Internet, but I paused to watch Maria, who approached wordlessly before she slumped into the seat of the bench next to me.

"Hey, Noah," She said, sitting down beside me. "Sorry, the line was crazy." We leaned into each other's shoulder, going back to our media. Gabriel scoffed like it was funny.

"What?" I uttered, looking at him.

"So this is the extent of human interaction, huh?" He said like he was beginning to make a point, following what he'd started. I could see where this is going, and evidently so was Maria as she turned her head up at him.

"Just fuck off, Gabe," Maria snapped. Gabriel leaned back as if feigning some kind of dramatic satisfaction, closing his eyes and pursing his lips as he snapped his fingers.

"Oh, yeah, now I'm feelin' the love, keep it up."

"Go get a girlfriend, asshole," Maria snarled. Gabriel laughed again.

"You know I'm too misogynistic," Gabriel shot back, as I just sat there. "Hey buddy, you just gonna let your girl beat up on your best friend?" Gabriel was obviously having more than enough fun with Maria's ireful sass and she wasn't having it.

"Noah's all afraid of her," Wilson snarled to Gabe, who laughed and nodded back with a "Right?"

"What's your fucking problem, Noria?" Maria snarled quickly, jumping up.

"Oh, whipping out the last name like it means something, *Roach*?" Gabriel stood too, brow furrowed but his mouth curled up into a gaping, vicious smile of teeth. "Not my fault it's that time of the month, man." he laughed and I watched her fists curl.

"Hey, hey," I jutted in before things got too far, jumping up and coming between them. "Gabriel, chill."

"You best control your woman, Noah."

"*Cierra tu jodida boca,*" Maria was practically frothing.

"*¿Qué? ¿Le hice daño a su ego?*" Gabriel was snarling back. Maria approached.

"*¡Hablas tu lengua propia!*"

"*¡Obligame!*"

"GUYS!" I roared, and those two sets of insane eyes focused on me. "both of you sit down." I looked Gabriel in the eye, as if I'd spoken to him specifically. I saw his eyes flash for a second, like he wanted to go on, like he wanted to goad me on now, but my sternity must have gotten through because that compulsion of his faded in the next instant, as he reared back up, taking a step. Maria too, eyes still furious, took a tentative move back. Gabriel went to where he'd been sitting, slumping down. I watched him wait, waiting for Maria to sit too, and she did. I saw his eyes go to each one sitting there, person to person. Kyle, his girlfriend Holly, And Wilson with his dumb, entertained grin.

"I've got shit to do," Gabriel said, finally gathering up his bag and standing. He turned to face me. "hey, I need a ride, my ride here bailed. See you at three?" He motioned to me, slapping my shoulder with the knuckles of his open hand.

"Yeah, sure," I said. He grinned to me, as his eyes flashed to Maria.

"Sorry for spiking your blood pressure."

"just fuck off already." Gabriel grinned at this, before waltzing off, ever so casual. "You're giving him a ride?" Maria snarled to me as he left earshot.

"He's my friend, Maria. I'm not going to *choose* between the two of you."

"You best reign him in, then, or I will."

"hey, you didn't say anything when Gabe asked for a ride, only when he left," Wilson jutted in.

"mind your own fuckin' business, Wilson." Wilson shrugged, going back to his game.

I looked down at my can of juice, going to drink the rest, trying to ease my mind.

## Chapter 4

"Hey, thanks a lot," Gabriel said as He stooped close to my car, while we were parked, idling. I looked him over slowly, seeing his sweatshirt over him, zipped up. He also had his gym bag. "Hey, Maria. Sorry for earlier, right?" He gave a tentative smile, though he still seemed like he was in his edgy state of mind, only trying to get closer to pissing her off.

"Where are we going, Gabe?" I spat quickly to interrupt Maria before she got on his case. Gabriel pulled the backseat door open, sitting behind Maria and pulling his gym bag and his backpack in.

"There's a laundromat near my apartment place. I gotta wash some stuff."

"On a Thursday?" Maria was on his case immediately, and I suppressed a sigh.

"Hey, they're stinking the place up," He said back. "Can't a guy feel fresh on a friday?" She turned back to the front, and I moved forward, going to turn up the console.

"Hey there, guys and gals," The station DJ began. "We all know that tomorrow could get a bit crazy, with all the demonstrations planned. No matter what your politics are, we'd like to bid you a happy May Day, and we hope you'll all stay safe. So," The music began to cut in. "Freddie, take it away for all the revolutionaries out there! This is 98.7, The Twentieth Century's greatest music!"

"Oh, shit, is this Queen?" Gabriel said over the intro.

"Oh yeah, you think Queen is bad luck, sorry, I'll-" Gabe went to the console but Maria swatted at his hand.

"Hey, I like this song," Maria said, reigning in her sass.

"You know what?" Gabriel leaned back, sighing. "You need a little bad luck every now and then," He relaxed with a sigh. "Gotta have some bad luck if you want good, y'know?"

"Why is Queen bad luck again?" Maria let out, a tinge of condescension in her voice.

"Bad shit always goes down when I hear it. When mom died, we were driving home and this was on the radio. That's just one." Maria was silent: It was like she knew she'd hit a soft spot and would have apologized if it was anyone else. Anybody but him. Maybe that was because, to most people, Gabe didn't have a soft spot. "It's alright, I was like six. It was forever ago."

"That sucks," Maria finally said.

"Yeah, you know, you've lost people, right?" Gabriel got at. I watched his eyes in the rearview as I drove to Gabe's place.

"What, Noah tell you or something?" She uttered with a tinge of accusation in her voice, perturbed at his prodding.

"Eh, I kind of assumed," Gabe said. "You transfer here in freshman year, born in mexico, and ever since America closed the borders, the only way you could have gotten here is after the war in mexico, taken in legally as a war refugee. You must've been in Pheonix for a while before your dad got into the Solar Fields around here for work. Since, like, that shit happened like fourteen years ago, you must have been real young." He paused. "You know, you're always pissed. Kinda obvious that you're responding to trauma."

"I'm sorry, are you cross-examining me?" She barked back, trying to keep her cool.

"Hey, we're all armchair psychologists, aren't we?" Gabe was leaning back, staying casual. Maria sighed.

"Yeah," She answered finally, as if she was being diplomatic and looking for a bridge. "My brother was killed by a loyalist militia who thought he was *Un Zeta*." I was a little taken aback by her sudden willingness to open herself. I watched Gabriel's face, it stayed serious and unchanging. As if for effect, Maria turned around in her seat to look Gabriel in the face. "I watched him die." All this explained with this backdrop of music, which was a little jarring to say the least.

"That sucks." Gabriel was casual in his words, but his tone was as serious as can be.

"Yeah. It does." She turned back around slowly.

"So," Gabriel said, as if to change the topic, as the song was winding down with the slow, sweet vocalizations of Freddie Mercury. "Tomorrow's gonna be fun, huh? May Day. First of May. Day of the riots. Day of edgy jobless retards whining about corporations."

"Yup," I said. "That's what it's gonna be."

"Yeah, but what if it's not?" Gabe put forth.

"What would it be, Gabe?"

"You never know. What if that revolution they're always prattling on about actually comes? Blood running in the streets, some real biblical shit?"

"Yeah, well, it's not gonna."

"You sure?"

"Yeah, Gabe, I'm real fuckin' sure. It's always hyped up as some big thing but it's never a big thing. Every single time."

"They say that it keeps getting worse every year," Gabe put forth. "You know the purge movies? Purge 7 came out last year- and this like, the fourth time we remade that series," he laughed at that little detail. "But like, before you know it, May Day will be a day without laws. Shit going crazy. Last year it was something like nine quadrillion dollars worth of damage from the riots alone, up from six in 2058. And after what happened last november..." He paused.

"Oh what, are you saying the Hybrids are gonna join in too or something? All... two of the ones they let out yet?"

"*Two*? try five hundred thousand, with plans for a million distributed next year. Government's drawing straws to see which ones go to which cities, looking for vounteer households, like an exchange student thing but a little more *compulsory*. Shit, you know they have some real crazy ones? Centaurs and Minotaurs and dragons and all sorts of mythological shit. Shark ones, bug ones- You hear about the dinosaur ones? Like, fuckin' T-rex velociraptor freaks. Saurians, they call em. They're like nine feet tall on the *small* side. They got weird-ass centaur-y ones and ones with fucking spiders for a lower body. Would you let that into your house?" I was silent as Gabriel prattled on. "Anyways, what were we saying? Oh yeah. Like, it's not like the furries being revealed to the world, revealing that all the governments of the world were in cahoots over experimenting on 'human analogues' since the start of the fucking cold war is gonna make any of those fucking anarcho-commies any less ass-blasted."

"I thought they said that all the governments didn't know it was going on," I mused. "The governments privatized all the experiments after the end of the cold war."

"Yeah, sure. Like you're going to tell me that BioTek was going to, out of their own interests, just start mass-producing these fucking things because why not, and have been doing so since '89. Sociological experiments? Who is paying for these experiments? They said that each hybrid is supposed to have a good half billion worth of resources invested in them apiece. Do the fucking math, that's some bullshit."

"Then what's up with the lawsuit against BioTek?"

"The government is covering their ass. They figure if it wasn't them who made a half-billion fucking existential nightmare science experiments then people will chill."

"Let's be fair, nothing could make some people chill- like you," Maria interjected. Gabe chuckled a little, hitting the ground running with her snide comment.

"This way nothing ever takes me by surprise, *Roach*,"

"...Don't call me that."

"Look, Noah," Gabriel went back to me, as we pulled up to his apartment complex, a dingy place near the industrial sector. "If something is gonna go down, it's probably going to go down tomorrow. Hey, could you drive me to the laundromat that way?" He pointed down the street.

"Doesn't your apartment have a laundromat?"

"Yeah, but I like this one better. Take a left here." I eyed him as he leaned in.

"Seriously?"

"Yeah. They've got the better washers." I turned back, as Maria turned to look back at him now. "What?" He said. She turned back slowly, looking at me. I saw a look on her face, like she was concentrating and annoyed and perplexed all at once.

"Jeez, this is a shitty part of town," I said as we pulled up to the laundromat Gabriel supposedly liked so much. "You sure this is the right place?"

"Yup, thanks a bunch," Gabriel said, and as he was getting up and out, I realized how bulky he looked. He always did, but just a bit more right now. He leaned in to grab his stuff, and I saw, peeking out of the neck of his sweatshirt, a light brown cordura strap. "See you tomorrow, right?" He pointed and waved me off as he walked inside. I wanted to stay and watch him. I saw him go back, through the rows and rows of dingy old washing machines before disappearing into the back room, still carrying all his things. I set out, wheels slowly grinding against pavement.

"...He was wearing that vest of his," Maria said slowly. She'd noticed too.

"Yeah," I said.

"Noah... I don't trust him," She said. "Did you tell him that about me?"

"No, no I-" I began, as if I was covering my own back here to keep her from ragging on me. But the concerned look on her face rather than rage gave me pause. She wasn't suspicious of me. She was suspicious of Gabriel. There was no anger in her expression, only the faint musings of fear.

"Why would he be wearing that vest?" She said. "You don't machine-wash body armor, Noah."

"He... Maybe they've got dry cleaners there," I uttered half-mindedly as Maria sat back slowly, while we cruised, still listening to some tune from the 20th century. "I dunno, maybe he's gonna go work out too." Maria seemed very perturbed, as I hit the autopilot button, telling the car to go to the neighborhood where we lived. "You need a ride to karate tonight? Or- oh, sorry, that's tomorrow, right?" I said. She nodded.

"Y-yeah," She uttered.

"You uh... Getting your black belt?"

"Hope so."

"I remember when I got my karate black belt," I mumbled. "Before dad carted me off to Jiu Jitsu."

"Yeah."

"Then Aikido..."

"You've got your track thing tomorrow, right?" Maria said. "After school?"

"Yup, that's the one thing dad didn't force me to stop to do something else. Probably because there was no black belt for track-"

"No, I mean- Ugh. I was just saying I'll be there for you." She let out a forced chuckle, and I did too.

"Thanks," I muttered. "Your Karate is in the evening, right?"

"Seven to nine thirty," She answered.

"...Right." I paused, letting the awkward silence back in. "You gonna pick some other martial art up then? Like, did my dad convince your dad or something?"

"...Nah. I'm gonna stick with it." It was silent again, and it stayed silent, until we reached our respective abodes, bidding each other farewell.

Then I had to go home and deal with my dad.

**Chapter 5**

"Hey, son." I walked into the dining room, seeing my father standing there over a disassembled Armalite rifle, as he was swabbing down the bolt and bolt carrier of his personal AR-15.

"Hey dad," I said, going to the cupboard for a snack. "You gearing up for the gun range?" I asked.

"We just got back," he said slowly. "...You said you didn't want to come after school, so we just went while you were at school."

"Yeah, dad. It's a *thursday*." I turned, shutting the cupboard with a protein bar in my hands. I turned to face him, looking him all up and down as he cleaned his guns. He was a wide-set man, with shoulders like mountains and a stern, flat face, buzz-cut hair a golden blonde with light green eyes, he had the physique of an olympian despite the slow and careful way he moved, like a football lineman in a ballerina class.

"And, what's wrong with target practice on a thursday?" He said, going to his personal glock pistol, the small little one that he always carried on his person that had a little laser on it, as he worked the slide, seeing that it was well oiled, before loading it and putting it back into the concealed holster on his hip, whisking his shirt over it and it disappeared.

"You think something is going to happen tomorrow, don't you."

"Every year something happens on May Day."

"Yeah." I sighed, not wanting to have the conversation I'd already had. He picked up his larger, less-concealable glock pistol, a Model 34. I had one just like it. Everybody in the house did. He went to disassemble it, as I left upstairs, going to do my homework. Within an hour or so, there was knocking at my door.

"Come in," I said, sitting at my desk before my holographic display. The door creaked open, and in came my mother. She was the polar opposite of my father, slender with dark black hair and squinting asiatic eyes, dressed up in a simple blouse and jeans. "So how was the gun range?" I asked, practically spitting it out, like I was trying to steer the conversation.

"Me and your sister had fun," She said. I looked up at her.

"You took Rica to the gun range?" I practically spat. "She's twelve."

"Yeah, and she at least tries to humor her father," My mother said, her nerve showing through for a moment. I sighed harder to lean back in my seat.

"Yeah, I was all excited when I was twelve too. Doesn't matter, when she's in high school she'll be the class freak too. 'Oh, Noah, what'd your dad teach you to do this time, how to hide from the government or how to bomb an airport?" I snapped out. My mother sighed back.

"You know, you really shouldn't tell people- if you don't want people to know."

"Yeah? Really?" I said. "Why is that, huh? Because you know that it's creepy that I shouldn't have told anybody. Yeah, it kind of slips out when your dad's obsessed with the world ending." My mother sighed so hard we were practically in a contest over it.

"Your dad is just worried about your safety, that's all. He doesn't-"

"Oh, 'operational security'?" I snarled, meaner than I should have, but I was feeling nasty after all. "What are we, an army squad or a family? Come on." My mother sighed again.

"You know your father wants you to be safe, no matter what."

"I think I'd rather have been forced to wear a helmet in elementary school than this. No wonder you're homeschooling Rica."

"Please, Noah... Just consider your father this once. He's worried about tomorrow."

"He shouldn't be." My mother paused, to gather her thoughts, but I figured I wasn't done. "What, because of the hybrids makes this year worse? He wanted to move us all to that stupid castle back in November, mom."

"Well I think he has a point." I rolled my eyes, exasperation cutting through. I skipped sighing for once.

"I have a test to study for," I grumbled, and she left.

Dinnertime was in a couple hours, as mother had prepared a meal. I loathed going down to get it, sitting there with my family. My little sister sat across from me.

"I shot a real good score today," She spoke up, probably towards me. I tried to ignore her, but I knew I was the only one she could be addressing. "Dad says I'm good enough to compete."

"...Whatever."

"Why did you stop sport shooting?" She spoke up.

"It's boring."

"What's boring about shooting guns?" I dropped my sliverware to pause.

"Just eat your food." Rica shrugged.

"You know, Noah," My father's voice rang out. "Do you remember the standstill?"

"I was, like, three."

"Yes, Noah. You know why I do this?"

"Do what?" I uttered, though I knew exactly. He glared without anger at me.

"Prepare, Noah."

"For the apocalypse?"

"Sure, Noah. The apocalypse." He paused. I was unimpressed. "Noah, I want you to know something. It wasn't until I saw what was happening on the news when I knew I had to prepare. Prepare, because of my three year old son. I got a spot in that survival commune, I learned all these skills, I taught you all these skills."

"The world didn't end then and it didn't end in November, either."

"Yes, Noah, but it very well could have. I'd been in fights when I was in the military, during the Iranian Incursion before you were born. I've seen what people can become if you let them."

"Yeah, I get it," I grumbled in hopes of placating him.

"Noah," He said again. "I don't ever want to feel the fear I felt then ever again. Do you understand?"

"You know what, dad?" I barked suddenly. "I think you want it to happen." Silence washed over the room. "You want to be right."

"I think you're missing the point, Noah," He growled without rage. I was fed up with his smarter-than-thou attitude.

"No," I stood up, my chair screeching back on the hardwood floor. "I think you're making a point up. I'm done with this." I paced off to my room, their stares following my back as I left the dining room.

After all the homework and studying, I found the clock running down and I figured it was time for a shower. I went to the bathroom, stripping down and stepping into the little room, and as it felt my presence, the water shot on, up to temperature within half a second, and I stood there, recounting what was going on, getting my bearings. I triple-tapped the tiles, them brightening up as touchscreens immediately. "Welcome, Noah Reed," It said, and more things popped up. I quickly let my bladder go, and some more variables popped up- it was my statscreen, checking my health and wellness quickly.

"Noah, you have high blood pressure and an increased heart rate. You are suffering from elevated stress," The computer told me. "Will I notify your physician?"

"No thank you," I said quickly, scrubbing my hair with shampoo, and cleaning my body and face with a bar of soap.

"Well, please avoid getting in stressful situations to decrease your chances of heart problems in the future," The computer recommended, and I scoffed.

"Yeah. sure," I growled under my breath.

"You are clean," It said as it, actively scanning my body, determined my hygiene, the water turning off. I stood there in the little cubicle-like chamber for a second, before a great blast of dry heat cooked the water off of my skin immediately, leaving my skin only a tiny bit singed, giving me a little artificial tan.

I stepped out, grabbing my toothbrush and my toothpaste, putting some on the head, before running the device over my teeth, cleaning them to a sparkle instantly; only a few passes left my mouth fresh and clean. My mind was still elsewhere. What a silly old man. Why did I have to get him for a dad? I was full of loathing, all the way back to my room. I was done studying for my test, so I went to throw my tablet back into my bag- but it hit that notebook of Daniel's. I would have let it rest to just go mess around on my desktop, but that nagging curiosity I just couldn't leave alone.

I pulled it out, slapping it open. I saw the first few in this notebook, earlier drawings not quite as deftly done as some of the others, but there certainly was a- theme to it. Daniel drew a few humans here and there, but it seemed his forte was in these- these non-hybrids. pseudo-hybrids. Pre-hybrids? Or whatever Gabe called them when he was joking around. Furries. I just couldn't believe that somebody was so... obsessed with drawing them, especially before the White Horse incident. He seemed to like dragons most of all... in an interesting manner for sure, some pictures a little too risque for my tastes that I couldn't really look for long without my face forming into a sickly imaginative scowl. Even ones like from old fairy tales, on four legs with wings and all that, each one with emotive faces and eyes, like a person. Some happy, some lusty. It was like a freakshow right in front of my eyes, this spectacle of deviance before me. It boggled my mind, and the dates- some of them two years before the Incident, filling me with this dread-filled inquisition.

Having seen enough, I put it aside to go and watch some videos, maybe get my mind off of it, but the thought, the thoughts in my mind stayed, all the way to when I checked the clock, seeing it was time to sleep, and sleep met me through confused and sickly inspired machinations.

## Chapter 6

I awoke to the sound of my alarm, dragging myself awake. "May First, twenty-sixty. Six forty-five AM," My alarm console would chirp for me. "Noah, you have: One test and a track meet after school at three forty-five."

"Yeah, yeah." I stuffed my schoolbag, going for my things in a slumbered stupor, before I proceeded downstairs. I saw my father there at the table, fiddling with a hard body armor carapace, all set up with magazine pouches and a first-aid kit. I had one just like it, of course.

"Noah," He muttered. I scoffed, going to assemble a lunch, eating a fiber bar for my breakfast. I hoped that this would be the end of our conversation, though as I left the room, I heard behind me: "Noah, there's just one thing…" I paused in the doorway, preparing my sigh. "Your friend, Gabriel."

"Yeah?" I was a little taken aback. What did Gabriel factor into this?

"If anything happens, try and… Try and keep him with you, alright? He's a good kid. He's your best friend, after all. Ever since-"

"Third grade, Dad. I know. I will," I said, going to leave once again, but he spoke once again.

"Also, Noah…" He approached me. I saw him holding a pack of emergency food, the freeze-dried survival kind. I suppressed a sigh, looking him in the eyes, before I took it. I didn't want to start a scene now, and maybe I should placate him anyways.

"Thanks, dad," I said, putting it in my bag.

"Be safe today, son. I love you."

"Yeah," I muttered back. "See you after school."


I sat in the car in silence- I didn't want to listen to the radio or anything, I didn't even want to think about May Day and I know somebody would bring that stupidity up. I sat, waiting for Maria, and I watched her stream out her front door- I saw the way she walked, it was faster than usual. She got in hurriedly, and without a thing to say, she pointed to the central console. "Turn on the news," She ordered.

"What's-"

"Turn on the news, Noah. Right now." I activated the controls as we began to ride to school.

"-Arrests of May Day rioters are already-" She flipped through the channels, until it came to the local. I saw on the holographic screen, helicopter footage of a big, industrial building on fire.

"-Massive shootout last evening that killed thirty-seven people, Early estimates state twelve killed by gunshot and the remainder were killed in the fire of the building. Reports say that this was a meth lab, judging from the chemical composition of the burns and the explosive residues-"

"What, it's just some gang shooting, what are you-"

"Just wait for it, Noah," Maria barked. "Listen."

"-According to recovered CCTV footage, it appears that the perpetrator was a single gunman, shown here…" The display showed a man, standing with a short bullpup rifle with an octagonal suppressor protruding from the front of the gun, wearing a mask and a molle plate carrier. "The gunman acted alone and officials are stipulating that the motive was most certainly gang-related, as this drug lab our investigators have concluded had recently made an enemy of the Sinaloa Cartel's American Branch, who are the most likely perpetrators. As we know, during the Mexican Intervention in 2049, the Sinaloa cartel, now the single biggest drug trafficking organization in the world, was armed and supported by the united states during-"

"Look at that," Maria snapped, pausing the video and pointing to the blurry image of the perpetrator. "You know where this happened? Three blocks from where we dropped off Gabriel."

"What, are you saying my best friend killed thirty-seven people by himself?" I spat. I looked at his armor carrier. It looked *too* familiar.

"Noah, I know he's involved. You can't say you don't feel this too."

"The… Gabriel has blond hair," I said, pointing to the tufty hair poking out on his head behind that black mask. It was black as ink.

"I KNOW he's involved, Noah. Please. You need to stay away from him."

"You're being ridiculous," I said. She shook her head, before sitting back.

"Alright?" She snarled. "Fine. Fine. Get killed by that fucking *Siña* scumbag."

"Look, I know Gabe, alright? He didn't kill thirty-seven fucking people. How is that even possible?"

"Says he killed everyone on the first floor then burned it down," Maria snarled, motioning to the screen. "I KNOW Gabriel is involved somehow. I can feel it, Noah." I leaned back.

"Okay," I slapped the auto-driving steering wheel. "Let's say my best friend is some kind of superhuman who can kill twelve drug dealers in a row in, like, a minute. Okay. Sure. Yesterday he was wearing his vest because he was about to go on a killing spree, as the Cartel's personal weapon." I paused to glare at her. "Then why the fuck would he make it so obvious, making me drop him off right there and barely be hiding the fact that he's wearing armor?"

"Don't forget, he probably had that gun in that gym bag," She said, dead serious. I rolled my eyes. "Do you not think that this is all a little too coincidental, Noah?" She spat. I had nothing to say, leaning back. "Noah, you have to do something."

"…I'm not going to call the cops or anything, Maria."

"I *know* he's involved!" she reiterated.

"You don't even have any proof!"

"It's obvious, Noah! Look, that's his vest!" she viciously pointed at the screen, as if jabbing this pseudo-Gabriel on the holoscreen with a knife.

"We're here," I said as we pulled up. "Have a good day at school, Maria," I said as the car parked and I threw open my door.

"Stay away from him!" She cried. I just shook my head. I'd known him forever. He's not a fucking cartel hitman. It's impossible.

But it gnawed at me anyways, all through my putting my bag in my gym locker, changing into my workout gear, right to the point where I walked into the gym room.

I approached Kyle, who was doing bench presses, like always. I grunted at him in greeting and he grunted back. I felt so tired, leaning against the wall.

"...Where's Wilson?" I said, trying to take my mind off of Cartel Gabriel.

"Skipping, said he wanted to fuck shit up, probably at the protest downtown." I laughed with a single "Heh".

"Probably getting his ass beat."

"Heh. Yeah."

Silence again.

"I'm going out to the track, see what Gabriel is up to."

"See ya."

I walked through the door, towards that field. I walked, shambled even, like a zombie. There was no way. Thirty-seven people? My mouth was dry and full of cotton. I forgot to get coffee this morning, I remembered, and my head began to hurt. My feet dragged me across to the bleachers. I didn't see him yet. Was he not here? Was he dead? Could Maria be right?

"Sup, Noah," His voice called out, close to me.

I wheeled around seeing him sitting on one of the rows of bleachers, just behind me. Somehow I'd missed him. He was sipping out of his water bottle, that vest on his chest.

"H-hey, Gabe, y-you..." I saw his head. Buzz-cut. "You shaved your head."

"Yeah, I dunno about today," He said, getting up and waltzing down the steps, bouncing as he did. I saw the way he smiled, like he always did, how he moved. There was no way that you could kill thirty-seven people and walk like that, smile like that, like nothing happened. "Shaved heads are tactically superior to having a nice, grabbable head of hair. You should take after me," He tufted my somewhat long hair as he passed, and as I saw his back, it hit me.

The stubble of the hair of his head was black. He'd dyed it before he cut it.

It was a few moments of him smelling the air, looking up into the sky before he turned back to me. His smile was bigger than before. No, I thought. Impossible.

"What's up, hybrid got your tongue?" He laughed, before turning away. "It's okay. You should probably take a seat. It's a lot to take in." No way. No fucking way. "...oh, speak of the devil herself. Here comes your girl, Noah." I looked up at him, and it was barely a couple moments before I could discern her, walking swiftly towards the track, back hunched and teeth bared, gleaming in the morning sunlight. "My, she looks mad. Secret's out, I suppose."

"You... You're..."

"Yeah, Noah. That was me."

Maria was here, with murder in her eyes.


Maria's first strike was precise and quick, lunging from how she walked into a strong front jab. If I wasn't so out of it I would have been surprised; she didn't telegraph one bit- aside from the fact that she was frothing mad. But Gabriel- like he knew exactly what was going to happen a second before it did, casually brushed the strike away from his face, barely whisking a shaven hair upon his dyed black head. His smile did not change as she again swiped at him, and he just seemed to walk out of the way of every lashing of her balled hands.

Snarling and without words, in an almost animalistic rage, Maria's hand dug into her pocket, before her switchblade came out. It was a classy little automatic folding knife my father had gotten her about a year after we started dating, and I'd never imagined she'd be trying to kill my best friend with it.

It was like Gabriel didn't seem to mind, still slipping past the sliver of steel and wood with every strike, before he hit her right in the bottom of the solar plexus with a snap of a fist, taking her from her feet, with surprising power given how lightly he seemed to hit her, barely moving himself as he did, yet both her feet came off of the ground from such force that knocked the wind out of her instantaneously. She fell to the turf, coughing as the knife clattered.

"You know, I thought 50/50 odds that you would call the police instead of dealing with things yourself. Thanks, by the way. This is a whole lot less messy." With that, she screamed again, scrambling for the knife and going towards Gabriel in a stab. Gabriel was unshaken, taking a step to the side and whacking the side of her forearm with a knife-hand as easily as brushing her aside, and the knife spun from her grip and fell before me.

Maria was furious and grunted and snarled in spanish, words flowing from her mouth of the most vicious and vulgar-sounding gutterations, still striking out at Gabriel, who finally gave in and lunged, striking her once in the throat before grabbing her neck and throwing her to the ground.

"This is awfully embarrassing, you know. Too bad nobody else uses this field first period."

"Y-you..." She grunted, trying to breathe.

"GABRIEL." I barked out, behind him. Maria's knife was in my hand. I watched him look at it in my hand, Maria still on the ground. I watched him rise, as I pointed the knife at him, like a gun. "I want... Explain yourself." He chuckled again, and fear radiated through me. Who was this? Was this even my friend from all those years ago?

"First things first, Noah, do you-"

"EXPLAIN, Gabe." Gabriel paused.

"Didn't your dad tell you to be nice to me today?" He said, and he took a step forward, as I took one back.

"W-wh..."

"Noah, Noah. You don't think we're not still friends, do you?" His arms splayed akimbo, like reaching out for a hug where he stood. For the longest time, I couldn't find the words to say.

"...The Gabriel I know doesn't kill people."

"The Gabriel you know has been killing people for a while now," He responded in kind, and my face washed out. "What, you think I just picked this up last night as a hobby?" He laughed.

"W-wh... Why?" I saw Gabriel look down at his watch in nonchalance.

"Hell of a question to start with, huh? I'll go into detail later. Right now..." He took a glance at his watch, before he gazed up into the sky. "We've got a show to watch."

That was when it all went downhill.

## ACT II
## PARADIGM

### Chapter 7

Boom.

I winced, as Gabriel stood tall, unfazed. Like he expected the sudden shift in the wind, the commencement of chaotic sound. My eyes went up and I looked out to the distance, where the explosion had radiated from, seeing nothing. Before I knew it, the telephone lines on the street near the field popped and fizzled, transformers blowing. Cars crashing on the street, control lost.

"Gabriel, what did you do?!" Maria snarled, having regained her voice just barely.

"I just dropped the right hints, so you wouldn't be in the wrong place at the wrong time by getting you to come out here and fight, that's what," Gabriel said to the both of us without even looking, turning to walk back to the bleachers. I went to Maria, pulling her to her feet, but she simply pushed me off of her and paced past towards him herself, scooping her knife out of my hand, though she'd lost her appetite for violence, folding it discontentedly as she eyed around and subtly winced at cries of surprise and the spurts of light as the electronics in the control booth of the stadium exploded in sparks. "With you two in the same place this makes everything a lot simpler."

"What the fuck are you talking about?" I cried out. A car that had been making its way down the road beside the football field screeched it's tires, the car careening out-of-control into the curb and slamming into the telephone pole. I heard crashes in the distance, alarms going off, the far-off parking lot lit up with blares and sirens, like every car was going off, the fission cores of some of the newer models popping with bright little explosions, hydrogen cells lighting up and biodiesel tanks bursting. "Gabe, what the fuck is happening?!" I snapped, panic accumulating in my voice.

"You know what your dad thinks is always bound to happen?" He turned to me as he reached the side of the bleachers, near the door to the storage room that the bleachers made. "Well, it's happening."

"H-how do you know this?" I asked, doubting him. I heard, in the distance, helicopter rotors. I looked in that direction, expecting to see news choppers. They were dual-rotor craft, something that only the military could have.

"Let's say I got a tip. Let's stay out of sight, guys." I wanted to doubt him, to tell him he was wrong, but the drab-iron military VTOLs coming this way told a different story. Maria passed me, cursing to herself with wide eyes.

"What the fuck is the military doing here, Gabe?" Maria's voice was hard as a stone as the VTOLs roared overhead, soaring on past towards the center of the city, her rage quieted by a morose fascination and fearful curiosity. It was obvious Gabriel knew something, bidding us over to the side of the bleachers, where we could be underneath them.

"Good response time. They must've caught on to what was going to go down this morning too. Kinda sketchy, to be honest."

"Gabe, what's going on!?" I spat. His eye turned to me, that awful, smug grin still on his face.

"You know that one software update we all got about two weeks ago?" Gabriel smirked. "Well, me and the boys kind of noticed a little bug with a timer strapped to it was in that update. Somebody infected a whole lot of systems. Pretty much everything with ElTek stamped on the side."

"The boys?"

"My employers. You need me to spell everything out to you?"

"...He's..." Maria was silent, and I saw her eyes wide as she looked at her phone while the two of us bickered. It refused to power on. I went for my hologlasses. I was immediately met with a static screeching in the earpieces, and I ripped it off. I watched my hologlasses fizzle and pop, smoke coming from their circuits.

We were interrupted with a great ripping sound, something so close and distinct yet it drew our eyes up, through the slots of the bleachers we hid under. White-hot tracer rounds ripped through a VTOL up above us, one of the engines coming off and lighting up. I could hear screaming from the direction of the school, from those who had been watching, as that engine careened into the western wing of the school.

"Time to go," Gabriel said. "Before the rush begins, if you will."

"W-wait," I said. "I... I need my backpack." Gabriel's eyebrows raised. "I need my backpack, Gabe. It's got my... my first aid kit, and my stuff," Gabriel sighed.

"Well, fuck it," he groaned in a manner that wasn't entirely too worried. "If you must."

"R-really? Just like that?" I said. He nodded, concealing his usual smirk, though I could tell a laugh wanted to escape his lips.

"Yeah, lets go."

"Wait, what?" I said. I had so many questions. "Did... Did you make a deal with my dad or something?"

"Now you're catching on, Noah. Props." I think I would have been furious if not for what was happening all around us.

I made my way towards the gym area, dodging my way through screaming crowds of people rushing about, as the campus security officers who were now flustered out and about trying to do their best to direct people to the field, where the emergency evacuation protocols dictated we go. Nobody was interested in that, of course. I rushed up to my locker, trying to open it.

"Oh, shit Noah," Kyle was behind me. "What the fuck's going on?"

"Gabe says the world's ending," I muttered to him almost sarcastically, as others around me were rushing to their own respective lockers. I couldn't open mine, the biometrics were busted, probably by this virus or something.

"Hey, step aside," Gabe said, appearing next to me, practically making me jump, beginning to unzip his jacket, gym bag over his shoulder.

"What, you got a hacking-" I stopped dead as Gabriel produced a weapon, much like what I'd seen before. A short little bullpup with a big octagonal suppressor spanning half its length, an integrally suppressed assault rifle with a little solar powered dot sight and an illuminator and light on one of the rails on the side. I could hardly protest as it came out and with a rapid, thumping report of the suppressed, subsonic rounds into the lock, the locker swung open, shells clattering to the ground. Those around, already in turmoil, cried out and ducked away at the gunfire, despite how muffled it might have been from the can on the end.

"Get your shit, Noah," Gabe motioned with the smoking end of his gun.

"DROP THE GUN!" almost like I'd been expecting it, a security officer had emerged from the other door. I saw Gabe rear up, still facing away from the man who'd drawn a gun on his back, Gabriel emitting a tiny sigh. Gabriel, still sighing with a perturbed look on his face, raised his hands and let his rifle hang from it's sling- he was still wearing his sweatshirt and concealing his armor from the man behind him, though the gunfire was still loud enough to tip off the officer as to who exactly was the dangerous one. I gasped a little as the security officer approached, weapon quivering a bit. He was young and new, with slick black hair and a youthful face. "Dispatch, we're gonna- ugh!" the radio spewed bright sparks into his face, compromised from the hack evidently, and that was when Gabriel took the cue, spinning around.

In reaction, the cop's gun went off square into the ballistic plate of Gabriel's armor, who barely flinched, knocking it from the cop's hand with his right before striking him in the jaw with his left. Screams were quieter now that the nine millimeter round had went off in this enclosed space, deafeningly loud to all of us around, ringing ears.

"Jesus, Gabe!" I screamed as I came back to the present, ears ringing, seeing Gabriel's MDR right up against the underside of the neck of the unconscious cop on the ground, and I yanked the gun away by the sling. Gabriel grunted, a vicious look on his face as he redirected his attention to me. "Don't fuckin' kill him! What the fuck is wrong with you?!"

"We don't have time for this, Noah," he grunted, and now I felt fear, seeing his serious face for now, his eternal smile disappearing for an instant. I was more struck with fear now than when he admitted he was that man from the news. Fear like a dog you'd befriended growling at you for the first time, times a thousand. Like he sensed this, a smile grew. An evil smile, like all his other evil smiles, a smile of power and amusement. "Fair enough," Gabriel finally left his carbine to let it hang at his chest, soon walking over to that dropped gun of the cop's. He picked it up and shoved it in my hands, before turning back to the unconscious cop. He worked the straps of the unconscious cop's body armor vest off, as I watched in horror. He handed the carapace to me now, Maria standing in the doorway of the men's locker room.

"J-jesus, Gabe," She uttered.

"Yup," Gabe said as he was now undoing the utility gunbelt of the officer. "Put the body armor on, Noah. You ain't allowed to die today." I looked at him, before he reared up, poking me in the chest. "You're my objective, Noah. If I don't bring you in A-Grade condition back to your dad, my ass is out to dry. Get me?"

"What, I'm just a fucking objective to you?!"

"Yeah. and my best bud. Don't overthink things, that comes later." He stooped back down to finish pulling the gunbelt off of the officer, as I, figuring why not at this point, pulled that vest on, adjusting the straps.

"Jesus Christ, Noria!" Coach had emerged into the hallway, stopping dead as he saw Gabe in the process of robbing an unconscious police officer of his gear, Gabe standing up with the belt, before passing it to me.

"Don't want to hear it, coach," Gabe's weapon came up as he pointed it skyward with the stock resting on his hip, as if presenting it. Coach, seeing this, darted away, just as Kyle's girlfriend, Holly emerged from where Coach had run off to.

"Kyle! What's-" She began calling for Kyle, before also seeing Gabriel and me, strapped up. "J-jesus, Gabe!" She uttered, freezing in place and Gabe rolled his eyes before turning back, noticing that Kyle and another boy from weights class, one of Kyle's friends who I'd never really acquaintanced myself with, were cowering in the corner, terrified.

"You forget your school shooter jokes for once, bitch?" Gabriel snarked at her.

"Looks like we've got witnesses," Maria grumbled under her breath, practically rolling her eyes.

"Yeah, you don't say," I, before another explosion ripped through the air and we all winced, Holly falling to the ground with a yelp before scrambling over to Kyle.

"Gabe, what the fuck is going on?! You- Is he dead?!" Holly screeched about the cop. Gabe rolled his eyes.

"The world's ending. Me and Noah are leaving. I punched the cop in the face and borrowing his gear." He barked out rapidly, evidently out of patience.

"Really? For real?" Kyle stammered. "Shit, let's go then," He said, pulling himself and his comrades to their feet. Gabe sighed ever harder, so exasperated his shoulders probably would have popped right out of his back if not for the armor cuirass he wore.

"So, we taking these freeloaders?" Gabe sighed to me.

"W-what? Are you kidding me? We're not just gonna abandon them," I said. Gabe smirked with a "heh".

"Fair enough. Let's…"

"W-what the fuck?!" The security officer had evidently awoken. "You- You're-"

"I don't want to fuckin' hear it Johnny Law," Gabe pointed his weapon back at him and his eyes grew like saucers. "Get the fuck out of here, I swear to god." The officer scrambled to his feet.

"You're going to jail!" he practically screeched, proceeding to the exit.

"Really don't care about your opinion, dude." Gabe turned, walking swiftly for the exit, while Kyle, holly and that other boy proceeded behind us, me grabbing my bag.

"H-hey, I'm Antonio, uh, Anthony, by the-" The other kid began. He was a slender somewhat pale latin kid with slick inky hair and a clean-shaven face.

"Yeah, yeah, Tony. Sure. Don't lag behind and don't get in our way or I'll drop you like a bag of shit. Comprende?" Anthony was a little taken aback, but continued to follow, as we made our way through the school grounds, at a brisk, practically jogging pace through the bustling, screaming people. Seeing the two of us armed often got us a wide berth. "Military security drones are compromised," Gabriel explained, us seeing them flying overhead. A news chopper flew about, before tracers streaking from one of the robotic aircrafts lit it up with gunfire, as most of us gasped. "I'll bet your car doesn't work anymore too. We've gotta go by foot. Noah?" He said. "Gimme your gun." I pulled it out of the holster of the gunbelt I was wearing, looking down at it. Some police Glock 17, one of the brand new Gen Seven iterations. The red light of the biometrics was on, it obviously didn't recognize me, and the safety, one of the weird additions to the seventh generation of glock that I kinda didn't think so highly of, would not switch off. I handed it to him, as he went to activate his own hologlasses, focusing on the weapon.

"Hey, how come your holos work?"

"…This is a linux," Gabe said with a tap of his glasses. "…Third party is better anyways." He passed it back to me, and I held it. The green light was now on, and the safety actuated freely. "There you go. I just jailbroke your gun. Thank me later."

Downtown was a catastrophe. The more we moved, the worse it seemed to get. What had once been a demonstration had since evolved into a riot, people surging about. It was practically a brawl- We passed some streets upon which the cops were preserving a defensive position, retreating by foot. With their dead tech, they were obviously close to drastic measures. The barrels of police firearms stuck out from their testudo riot formations, and Gabriel was quick to hush us away from them, through the chaos of the riots.

An overturned police car sat in the middle of the street, seemingly abandoned by the cops. "Oh, shit," I heard Gabriel say.

"Jesus, how the fuck did this thing flip?" Kyle blurted out. "Musta been one of those military mechs, maybe somebody in power armor kicked it over." I looked to Gabriel, seeing a crazed look in his eyes like an opportunity was to be chanced before him.

"Hey, wha'dya wanna bet this's got free guns in it?" Gabriel immediately came up to the trunk, looking at the upside-down lock, though keeping his distance from the burning hydrogen cell, throwing that mask on- the mask that the killer, being him, from last night's news story had, obviously flameproof. He took a few swipes from his haptic hacking module, before the trunk beeped open and out tumbled a pair of rifle bags and a couple smaller range bags, thunking down heavily enough. "Ooh, nice. Hold onto this, would you?" Gabriel passed them off to Kyle, as I walked around the car, squinting.

"Oh, shit, somebody's in there," I said, pointing into the backseat. "Fuck, Gabe, come open the door!" Gabriel sighed, walking around.

"Well, there's gotta be more guns in the central console," He muttered, taking a few moments to go and open the actual driver-side door with his tech, before stooping in, smoke pouring out as coughing emitted from the backseat divider.

"Gh- Help! Get me out of here!" I heard a voice under the commotion, as Gabe went about getting the police shotgun locked into the center divide.

"Christ, Gabe!" I spat as I reached for the unlock so I could pull the backdoor open, and out poured none other than Wilson, coughing and sputtering.

"Oh, shit, what's up Wilson," Kyle laughed nervously, obviously trying to keep his cool with all this craziness going on, Wilson squeaking out like an inchworm, hands cuffed behind him. "You got arrested already dude? Bad-ass,"

"Get these fuckin' cuffs off me bro," Wilson was quick to blurt out. I went to fiddle with them as Gabe lusted over his spoils. "What, did school get cancelled?"

"Yeah, forever," Gabe said, coming up to Wilson and pushing me away a little to grab the handcuffs. "World's ending." With a beep the handcuffs came off, and he finally lifted his mask."

Before Wilson could even remark, canisters of smoke were produced, being thrown into the crowds. I looked, seeing the military security drones flying overhead, just before bullets ripped from them, blasting away at our surroundings, all of us ducking for cover, before the smoke grenades fell. But they weren't just smoke, and soon with how little I could breathe, I knew nothing else, I could think of nothing else but that I direly needed to move away from this place.

**Chapter 8**

---

"Alright, son," My dad was laughing a little as he spoke, all of us in good spirits. I looked up towards him, in the shadow of the big watchtower of the Citadel. I was standing there, so many years ago, my little body all wrapped up in a coat. A cold wind was blowing down the mountains, despite spring in full bloom all around me. My father's friends and others who lived or came here were all about; today was a training day. "You've never smelled pepper spray before, right?"

"What do you think, dad?" I laughed. He laughed too.

"You want to?" he asked, a little can of spray in his hands, before he sprayed it onto a piece of cardboard and presented it to me.

"Not so bad, huh?" he laughed. "Just like hot sauce."

"Yuck, it... it really burns," I grumbled, and he laughed a little.

"Doesn't it?" He said back. "Back when I was in the Marines part of our training was getting sprayed with this."

"Jeez, I guess I don't want to be a marine then," I said, and he laughed. This was all fun and games.

---

I was choking.

Stumbling through the chaos, I could hardly tell up from down. I couldn't open my eyes for very long before the mist forced them shut. I could hardly breathe, even through my shirt pulled over my mouth.

It was some old condemned office building, closed probably since the Standstill where I sought refuge, barging through the busted front door. I saw the initial reception area, passing beyond into the ancient cubicles, where I collapsed into. At least the crowd-control spray did wonders for my sinuses. Crying the salt out of my eyes, I heard a cry upstairs. Things being knocked around, shouting. At first I didn't pay it much heed, but then,

*Bang.*

It was a single gunshot followed shortly by the sound of broken glass, and more screaming. Flinching at this, in brief hesitation I got up, fidgeting with the vest Gabriel had stole for me, cinching it. Always wear armor high, up to the top of your sternal plate, I could remember. I was shaking a little as I drew the gun he'd stolen for me as well, that police glock with all the extra safeties. I checked the chamber, seeing that bullet in there, pulling out the magazine with its bulky extended baseplate to see 19 more, minus one from the shot taken at Gabriel. I looked at the biometric lock light on the side to check if Gabriel really had disabled it for me. It registered as ready-to-fire, the green light on.

I was shaking a little as I advanced up the stairs, getting a good grip on the pistol despite how I'd trembled. As I came from the stairwell, I could make out the voices a little better. I heard angry, disheveled shouts and the cries of a woman, pleading for mercy, and a man, in terror and rage, older sounding. Sweat began to bead down the corners of my face as I approached the office compartment on the far end of the building, past the strewn papers and dusty desks. I could make out a single, standing silhouette behind the opaque glass before me, and I paused as I gripped the door to the office. Gathering up my will, I burst in with a single, rapid motion, ready to fire, before my forward motion was stopped by what I saw, my brow furrowing and jaw going a tad slack as I took it in in what must have been only a handful of seconds.

Two... individuals were there, the easier one to describe being a disheveled-looking, older man. He was practically dressed in rags, hair and face dirty, one could practically smell him from just looking at him. He was obviously a homeless vagrant of some kind who barely had more fingers than teeth, and clutched in his dirty hands was an ugly, rusty handgun with a fat blocky slide, the cheap kind that were usually the least expensive gun whenever I went into a gunstore, easily had for about a thousand dollars or so. He had this crazy look in his bloodshot eyes, now that he was looking at me as I entered. But his gun, his gun was still pointed at the other, much harder-to-describe... person.

I'd seen hybrids on the news, reports from what happened in Whitehorse up in Canada last November, even a few interviews with ones released from harrowing conditions that the amnesty groups would document and hound with their cameras to drum up sympathy. I'd heard about how different and unique they could be, with strangely shaped bodies; the most boring of them were usually just a blend of human and some animal, while others were a menagerie of different things all blended together with human DNA to create something a little more interesting than walking, talking dogs or cats.

This one here must have been one of the latter, as it- or well, she, was sitting- laying? Cowering, definitely *cowering* In the corner, a pile of mismatched clothes covering her the best she could- But, what *was* she? I knew she was female, the breasts on her humanoid torso somewhat contoured through a sweatshirt she was wearing, and the voice of hers I heard earlier, and the way her face was shaped- though it was distinctly nonhuman, it seemed human enough that I could tell her sex easily from the rounded features, like looking at her strange muzzled face *reminded* me of a human female, if that makes any sense. She had two simple slits of nostrils for a nose, and face and jaw stretched out in an obviously inhuman snout, Her eyes were a brilliant mocha and more human than I'd ever imagined with rounded, small irises, big whites and an inflection and introspection to them that told you that this wasn't an animal, this was an intelligent, self-aware creature, a *person*: these eyes were the eyes of a human being and in the here and now they were full of fear and shock, the kind of fear and shock that made me pause, that same fear and shock spreading to me, though maybe for different reasons. It was a fearfulness that drew at my very soul in this moment, taking my breath from me for an instant and made my gun quiver.

Her arm was up in front of her face, covered in deep green skin. Her whole body was green except for brown accents nearly the same color as her mane of hair adorning her body. She had at least one pair of wings protruding from her back, somewhat batlike- she must've been one of the "dragon" ones I'd heard about. "Draconic", or something specific like that. Her nostrils flared as she breathed out slowly, I could see two long, white horns behind, gently curved twice in shape protruding from her head backwards; ears fluttering beneath her messy, hanging mane of hair atop her head in a way entirely inhuman: they looked more like cow's ears, being able to move this way and that, currently they were angled down and away fearfully like a dog after being struck, her head low in fear despite how she lay, her arms still up in defense, though now her eyes went to me, the new one here, laying there, panting, eyes pleading.

In the next second of my perturbed fascination, I saw how truly large she was. Despite how she was curled up and whimpering on the floor, her body seemed to keep going, and going, and going. Initially I thought that her legs were horribly malnourished or mutated or something, being strange and gangly with an opposable digit and garish long toes, like her feet were closer to being hands than feet or paws or whatever, but as the rear of her moved and shifted a little bit, I came to a wider realization. The best way to describe what she was is to think of a centaur- only instead of a human torso on a horse torso, it was a big, beastial quadrupedal dragon torso, beheaded then grafted onto a humanoid torso. Behind those two front legs with the hand-like feet, on that lower torso she had two more powerful rear legs, two more wings on her lower, secondary torso, and a thick, lizardlike tail, each and every one of her many limbs quivering in fear. Her lower torso body was roughly the size of a horse and the humanoid torso of hers was more like that of an abnormally large human woman, despite being somewhat concealed by the sweatshirt it looked like she'd stolen or something, the back ripped up so her upper pair of wings could come through.

"You a cop or what?!" The hobo was screeching to me in the very next instant. He must have been yelling at me for a little while, while I was lost gazing upon this hybrid... woman. I blinked.

"Wh..." I didn't know what to say. Her eyes were shining towards me, in horror, practically pleading for mercy, for help. She was full of fear, mouth slack, without the words to say, just like me. "Wuh... What's..." I didn't know where to begin.

"See, I found one of 'em!" The wind from the busted window was blowing in, and I could smell his stench. "Y'seen what they did up in Whitehorse?! It's happening again, this time here'n Vegas! International fuckin' incident! New World Order shit, tryin' to replace us!"

"H-hold on," I muttered. His whole head turned to me, eyes flashing in an enraged terror, his body moving back and forth, his fingers getting antsy. "We... Let's..." My gun was falling down inch by inch, as I wasn't so sure who was the real threat here.

"You fuckin' with me, man?!" The hobo said. "You ain't no fucking cop! You-" I saw his body turning, his gun following with him, to point at me. That enraged face. Violent. Ready to kill.

*Pop.*

I can't hardly remember the last time I'd fired a gun without wearing any hearing protection. Sure, the same gun had gone off when the cop confronted Gabriel, but this was much closer to me, and It was like I'd been slapped in both ears at the same time, the room and world growing quiet for a couple long instants.

He lay there on the ground where he'd crumpled, his high forehead spurting blood from a little hole my weapon had made. I breathed out in a gasp, lightness entering my head through my ringing ears. He pointed his gun at me and I acted like I'd been trained. I acted on instinct, and in a flash I'd killed him.

I looked back to the hybrid girl. She had ducked behind her outstretched arms and wings when the gun went off, letting out a yelp, head ducked off to the side like wincing in terror before it was her turn. With a creeping slowness, she came back out from behind her upheld hands of surrender. She breathed in and out slowly, both her conjoined torsos heaving, eyes drifting to the dead man on the ground before me as I stood tall, her arms slowly falling to grip herself in a sort of self-hug, gasping out, quivering.

"...Fuck," I gasped, my heart still racing and ears still screaming as I leaned back against the wall, taking a glance down at my smoking handgun. I looked back to her, as I felt my head. I figured I should say something in my dazed state. "You... You alright?" spilled from my mouth. It felt odd saying this, and it was like I'd rethought saying it halfway through my utterance, my "alright" falling apart as it spilled out of my mouth. She glanced away again, back at that dead man's head spilling blood, slower and slower with each passing moment.

"Y...Yeah." She nodded. Her voice was deep and full, given that centaurical hybrids like her had four lungs, but it was a distinctly female voice nonetheless. The voice of a young woman. She came to her feet slowly, all four of them, her wings all rustling uneasily as she did, eyes trailing to me as if reading me for a reaction, sometimes going down to look at my gun. I gulped, blood running cold for a second, my fingers pulsing on my weapon in low ready but doing my best to keep it non-threatening in my uneasy fear and awe, seeing her full physique. She must've stood more than seven feet tall. Maybe eight. I saw her eyes still going to my gun, probably noting how my hands were shaking. I made a move towards the door, and I saw her rear back a little with a turn of her head and downward fluttering of her ears, like she didn't want me to think she was a threat. Seeing her fear still lingering, I stopped to put my gun back into its holster ever so slowly, standing as I gazed at the blood pooling on the ground. I breathed out, leaning against the wall. That man's face, the rage in his eyes, just before he took my bullet. I closed my eyes and there it all was, like the flash of the gunshot captured it in my head. "...Y-you killed him," Her voice followed me and I opened my eyes. She'd begun to take a step toward me, but as I locked eyes with her she stopped her forward momentum, one of her forelegs with that weird little hand-like foot was still midair descending ever so slowly to the ground.

"Y...yeah. I did." I looked over at her clothes, the way she'd ripped the back of that sweatshirt open so her wings could poke through. It had some college logo on it, and I knew for sure that she'd probably picked it up somewhere.

"...You're... *not* a cop, are you?" The nervousness in her voice grew ever more.

"...How would you even know what a cop is?" I grumbled back, cocking my head a little, using the curiosity to distract myself from the dead hobo. From my murder. Her eyes shot to the ground, though her vision avoided that body, an arm coming up to grip her other arm's elbow, which hung limp, as she scratched at it within the sleeve of that sweatshirt.

"I... I dunno. W-why wouldn't I?" She uttered, though it felt like she was really asking herself, racking her brain. She looked back up at me, looking at that vest, seeing my clothes, my stolen gun with it's hacked biolock. I was still staring at her in awe, full of shock.

But as the hallway outside clattered out with noise, her head and muzzled face came up, body going stiff, her jaw still ajar yet gritted, those ears of hers shooting up towards the sky, like an inquisitive dog, eyes wide.

"Noah?!" Gabriel's voice radiated from back there. "Noah, you alive?! Talk to me, dude!"

"Yeah, Gabe, I'm good," I cried towards the door, biting down on my apprehension before I looked back over to her, and she looked frightened, looking to me with those big brown eyes. I didn't know what to say to her, I just motioned for her to stay back, and she walked over towards me to be behind me from the door, taking care not to step in what was left of the bloodied vagrant, picking a leg up while I took a deep and hesitant breath, working to calm myself as best I could.

"Heard a shot, you okay?!" He said, taking his time to make sure it was safe. He wasn't advancing.

"Yeah, Gabe. I... We're all good. Bad guy's dead." I looked out that doorway, seeing Gabriel advancing down the hallway, that compact rifle of his in low ready, that mask on his face. He proceeded briskly, yet carefully, making sure to look around each passed corner in high ready, before stopping in front of me, in the doorway, rearing up.

The first thing he noticed somehow was the man on the ground, for immediate confirmation. He took a cursory look to me before tilting his mask up to let it sit on his head. His eyes were flashing with crazy adrenaline, smiling away. But as he looked to me, he saw just what and who was behind me. For a second, that smile flickered, and the grip on his rifle quivered and his step faltered, though his weapon remained un-raised. A low, slow laugh, the scary kind of laugh radiated from him, while he took a step, brushing past me, looking up at... Her. "...Oh damn, you sure you shot the right one?" He joked. I heard the hybrid, centaurical dragon girl let out a tiny apprehensive gasp, barely out of my consciousness, backing up a little. Gabe let the rifle hang from the sling around him as he stooped down, picking up the pistol of the man I'd shot, sitting on the shores of the pool of blood there, about to get drenched if we left it there. He was staring at the hybrid all this time, not taking his eyes off her as his hands went about their task all on their own. I wondered for a brief moment why he didn't take more credence in questioning her, but it looked like he had his own... itinerary. "Hi-Point nine, classy, real fuckin James Bond if I ever saw one," He laughed a little at his joke, taking the magazine out before ejecting the round in the chamber, dumping it into his duffel bag, which was looking a lot fuller ever since we had been briefly separated. "Oh, shit Noah," He said, looking at the guy again as he whipped out a roll of duct tape. "I think I know this guy." He then slapped a piece of tape over the bleeding bullethole, going to check the hobo's pulse.

"You... what?" I uttered, hearing the others coming up the stairs in the distance, the hybrid girl uneasily teetering about behind me.

"Yeah, dude's name was Roy or some shit," Gabe said as he whipped off the vagrant's jacket. "Check this shit for stuff. He might have some more ammo for his gun," He threw it at me, the blood-sopped, stinking mass of clothes. I recoiled quite a bit, not eager to get any communicable diseases. The hybrid girl was quite curious at the ordeal, though her chest still heaved and sweat was still beading on her forehead as she brushed her mane-like hair from her eyes, uneasily watching the ordeal in a post-adrenal haze, like me. "See, Roy here was one of our lookouts, "freelanced", I think they like to say, like they actually matter. The homeless are good for that shit and cheap, too. Not that reliable though. This guy's grip on reality was less than solid, if I remember correctly. God damn, good fucking shooting; he's still got a pulse. You left his lizard brain intact, looks like." His eyes continued to wandered up at her and back down at his task as he toiled, fishing through his bag, the dragon-taur girl still not fully sure what to make of us humans at this point, watching Gabriel after stripping the man down some. "...No offense to any lizards," Gabriel uttered up to her as he slashed at the not-quite-yet-a-corpse's right shoulder with a knife, and the both of us in that corner together winced as we watched, too disturbed to ask just yet, Gabriel stabbing his knife into the chest cavity of the vagrant with an airy thunk to hold it in place, going back to finally fish out what he needed.

"Uh... I, I'm... not... uh, none taken," The dragontaur girl uttered at a loss for words, her fear overcome with macabre curiosity at Gabriel's grisly task.

"Ah ha, here we go," He whipped out a small, boxy machine. "Gift from your dad, Noah. Say he's crazy or not, the guy works wonders with microtech. Now, let us see here..." Gabriel went to strap it to his bare right shoulder, which zapped him and he grit his teeth. "Now, ain't this a lot of shit to take in? Born yesterday, watch a man die today. Welcome to earth," he laughed to the hybrid girl, whose eyes were still darting about, getting a hold of the situation, jaw still slack with a hand reaching up out of instinct from the gory goings-ons before her. Gabriel grunted, whipping it off and letting the little machine thunk to the ground as he pulled out a scalpel, rather more precise than his Ka-Bar. We collectively winced as he dug it into the flesh of his right deltoid with nary a pause. "Ah, so... that's a localized field generator. Blocks radio waves by... replaying signals back, makes them seem like they're still working when they're not," Gabriel snarled of the machine he'd used that was laying now in the pool of blood, before grunting and, with a couple more droplets of his own blood, dug out a tiny piece of electronics from his own flesh. A tiny transmitter with what looked like a tiny vial of liquid on it. "Here we go," He uttered in success, going to the homeless guy before sticking it into the wound he'd created. "Okay, let's wait a little bit. See, if I fucked with that without using the thingy your dad lent me," Gabriel motioned my dad's machine as he pulled his knife out of the chest of the hobo, taking a moment to wipe off the hobo blood using the pants of the very much irreversibly dying man. "It would have poisoned my ass, that tracker would be able to detect whether or not I'm fucking with it. This way it won't even know it switched bodies. Now that it's in this guy, let's see..." he looked down as he brushed the sleeve of his sweatshirt back to expose his watch, counting down as Maria finally approached behind us, to the entrance of the door.

"Gabe, where's-" she began, before Gabe, in complete nonchalance, pointed his MDR at the body, letting a burst of suppressed, subsonic ammo zip through the high chest, neck and low head of the corpse, effectively obliterating all structural integrity the low cranium once had, sending brains and spinal fluid flying everywhere, causing me to leap back a tad to avoid a good chunk headed towards my leg. Despite the silencer and the rounds he'd used, it still had bass loud enough to make the hybrid girl behind me scream out a little, me turning to see her cover her head again, Maria in the doorway stepping back too, now alerted to the large, green dragon girl in the corner and stopping dead.

"Whoa, holy shit!" Kyle screamed from down the hallway, only catching the tail-end of the bloody show. I heard his girlfriend scream a little as well upon seeing the desecrated cadaver.

"Noah's fine, he made a friend," Gabe told Maria as he motioned with his gun a little toward me and the draconic, my girlfriend finally emerging fully into the office. She saw me standing there, that hybrid girl practically leaning on my back with a hand tentatively reaching for my shoulder, almost subconciously of her, the both of us still rather shaken up, though I managed to fish a folding knife and a couple magazines for the homeless guy's gun out of his jacket during the fray, with them still clutched in my hands. "I just needed to clear my retirement with an old coworker," Gabriel grumbled with a smile, picking up all the shells, including the ones from both my gun and the single shot that the hobo had fired out the window, before I came into the picture. "Here, you hold onto this, keepsake from your cherry-popping," Gabriel tossed me the 9mm shell that wasn't the hobo's, which I scrambled to catch. The shell that sent the bullet that killed that guy- at least, the one I shot into him that got him started dying. "Let's go already."

"Oh- holy shit," Maria said, looking the hybrid girl all up and down, approaching slowly. The hybrid girl backed off a little, a little terrified of us humans at this point. "A h- G-gabe, who- what the fuck was that?!" She spat, motioning to the now very, very dead body, Maria not quite that sure who was the one worth paying attention to, the gory mess on the ground or the giant green girl-monster in the corner.

"Hey, don't look at me, Noah shot him first," Gabe said of the hobo, leaving the little office as Kyle looked on from the doorway, peeking in.

"Holy shit, dude!" He said at the corpse, laughing a little, girding nervousness and disturbedness with detached amusement. Even Wilson was somehow morosely amused, but Holly took one look before turning back, retching.

"Uugh... I'm gonna be sick," Holly groaned.

"*Fuck*, Gabe," Wilson hushed.

"Oh, shit, we got a fuckin hybrid in here," Kyle added as well, masking his tense feeling with a nervousness-masking laugh. The dragon-centaur girl looked down, a little bashful, feeling the judgemental stares. I backed closer to her, still overworked by this. I wanted to tell her not to sweat it or something, but Maria grabbed my arm and yanked me away before I could.

"That could have been you," She grumbled to me while motioning to the mess, hushed and still in shock. "I had a heart attack when I heard that gunshot. How could you run off on us?!" Her voice grew in viciousness, she was practically getting physical with me, shaking me. I shrugged, mouth still slack.

"I... hey, we all got separated in the riot," I said as she yanked me along towards the door, avoiding that homeless guy's body, the hybrid girl following behind like a lost puppy, meekly with her head low despite how she still towered to an almost comical degree. We'd only made it a few paces outside of the door before everybody really took a good notice of her, including some other faces of people who'd evidently followed Gabriel along. I recognized a few, there was a girl from our history class, I think her name was Samantha, she had some obviously over-dyed hair and a surplus of tacky apparel, both her and Holly's makeup were running from the gas that'd been unleashed, as well as Daniel from history class. It took me a second to really recognize him from under all the dirt and debris, but I knew that I knew him, he looked familiar. Gabriel, however, recognized him first.

"Oh, shit, you're that kid from history," Gabe said. "Ain't your name Danny or something?" The kid nodded quickly. "Yeah, you're the furfag who just had to finish his original character in class. Heh. You follow us all the way here like the rest of 'em?" The boy could hardly find the words to speak. Gabriel sighed, rolling his eyes. "So what, Noah, still want to have all these freaks mooching?" He cried to me. "I could make your problems go away real quick." I tensed up at this, and I could tell he was just trying to get a rise out of me with an edgy joke. At least, I hoped. I played it cool.

"No, Gabe- It's fine. He's fine."

"Really? This one looks about as much of a liability as sparklegirl," Gabriel motioned to Samantha, who seemed a bit taken aback by this. I just glared at him. "Okay, whatever. Fine. Moocher City. Let's get the fuck out of here."

"Can... Can I come?"

The room got quiet as we all turned to look back, at *her*. The dragon-centaur girl's question prompted an eerie quiet, with her standing still in the doorway of that abandoned office, away from the rest of us and looking on in worried prospect, everyone gazing around nervously. Even if I was in charge, she was looking right at Gabriel, who took a look at me as if to ask me, and I didn't shake my head, blinking back at him. He sighed, rolling his eyes back up to her.

"...You got something we can call you?" Gabriel inquired, not expecting an answer, speaking like a long sigh. Her face was blank, and it was her turn to blink at nothing. I saw her left hand crawl it's way up through the air, though it stopped just short of her right shoulder, like she was about to motion to the barcode she had, though her face morphed in embarrassment when she remembered she was wearing a sleeve over it, hand dropping. She made a cursory glance down, before furrowing her lips.

"I- I don't have a name."

"Wh- what, we're just gonna let the monster come along?" Maria said as the dragontaur girl looked off, a little dejected, scratching her right arm with her left hand.

"Those wings look useful to me. Who knows, we could use air support. So, you wanna *choose* a name, or...?" Gabriel turned his attention back to the dragon-centaur girl, and Maria backed off a little bit.

"I... I don't know."

"Green," Gabriel put forth, looking around to the rest of us with his proposition. "She's green, so she's Green. There, we know what to call her. Can we get on with it?"

"She needs a real n-" Daniel began, but I'd interrupted him in another instant, as I stood there, staring only at her, almost entranced by her alien figure.

"That sweatshirt's kinda small for you," I noted aloud, scanning her over. Given how self-concious she was, I could have found saying this to be a little rude, but didn't at the time, more overwhelmed by everything going on already.

"I..." She paused nervously, her eyes coming back to me, that trembling look that was attempting steadfastness. "I found it in here. I-in a closet."

"It's a Ralph Lauren," I uttered, remarking on the logo emblazoned beside her left breast. "...Lauren sounds good."

"You're naming her because of a sweatshirt she found?" Gabriel snarked.

"...I'm not gonna call her *Green*," I stated with offense on her behalf, turning to face him for a moment, before turning back. "What do you prefer? Green or Lauren?" I asked.

The hybrid girl really didn't know what to say, she just ended up nodding, before sort of doubling back realizing she wasn't asked a yes or no question, quickly uttering "I... Like Lauren," somewhat sheepishly before nodding again, ears no longer trembling down but poking out more assertively.

"Good enough," Gabriel was rolling his eyes. "Let's find a different place to hide."

"Look... *Hybrid*," Maria spat, turning on this newly-christened Lauren. The dragon-centaur girl was taken by surprise a little, backing off from being so close to me for once. "You lay your lizard hands on my boyfriend and I'll make a pair of boots out of your ass. You hear me?"

"...I- O-okay," She said with no malcontent in her heart and voice, eyes wide and frightened.

"Hey, Maria, lay off her," I said, pushing my overprotective girlfriend back a little with a hand up. "She's not gonna start anything."

"Hurry up, now. Let's go, you fuckin' children," Gabriel was quick down the stairs, as I, we, followed him. I tried to get out close to him, but Green, or Lauren, or whatever her name was now was sticking close to me again, though the other eyes all around eyed her, keeping their distance like she was some kind of vicious animal. Maria, though, was not so afraid- she was more concerned with keeping close to me, gripping my wrist as we walked, eyeing Lauren every few steps on the opposite side of me, Lauren looking somewhat happier yet not quite so, a sort of tentative, reserved happiness, the kind that one felt would be gone at any second.

We stood in the lobby of the building, looking out to the road. It was still full of smoke and dust, with a couple bodies here and there. The military security drones seemed to be away from the place for now, though it was morose enough of a situation that we hesitated.

"I like that building more," Gabriel pointed to the one across from the street. An explosion had shattered a lot of the windows on the first two floors, and it looked pretty impressive of a high-rise, much more modern than the one we were in now. "More structurally sound against fire."

"Why can't we just go to Noah's place?" Wilson demanded.

"You in a hurry to get shot? Too much shit going on, and it's a long way away. Tomorrow would be better. Right." Gabe took off his duffel bag, passing it to Lauren.

"Wh-" She began, gripping it, fumbling for a moment.

"Make yourself useful and carry that. You know what a rifle is?" Lauren nodded. "Give one to Noah," He ordered, and I came over to take one of the Armalites from the bag clutched in Lauren's hands. There were two, both of the ones he'd lifted out of that overturned police car, they were both 12" short-barreled M16 rifles, automatic because of the privilege that police officers got, though I rather loathed this barrel length. Ones this short were always so loud they'd hurt my ears even through earmuffs, which I definitely didn't have at the moment so I was against the proposition of setting one off. After extending the stock to the length I liked, I grabbed a magazine and loaded the weapon, though I did not charge it. I clicked it off safe though, to see the green light. All the biometrics had been hacked by Gabriel. "Right. Wilson," Gabriel ordered. "cross the street."

"Where's *my* gun?" Wilson spat.

"We can get to that later. Somebody starts shooting at you, duck so we don't hit you in the back. Now chop-chop." Wilson groaned, going to cross the street, in a light jog with his shirt pulled over his mouth, though most of the crowd-control gas had dispersed. "So how did it feel?" Gabriel asked me in a hushed tone while we stood shoulder-to-shoulder, watching Wilson dart between the abandoned cars.

"...What?"

"First kill," He said, finally looking at me, though he'd been scanning the road.

"How do you think?" I put back, a little tired of all the ups and downs today, though it wasn't even noon.

"That bad, huh?" Gabriel laughed, and Maria looked to me. "Don't worry. Gets easier. So," He spoke a little louder now. "Wilson's still alive so I think it's safe to cross. Me next. One at a time, guys, don't wait up, Noah you come last so we have somebody who can shoot half decently on each side. Greenie, you drop my shit and I'll kill you. ¿*Sabes?*" Lauren gulped and nodded wide-eyed, not really acclimated to Gabriel's razor's-edge humor yet. Gabriel then made his way across the street, in a little more hurried a pace than Wilson. somehow Gabriel was far, far more agile on his feet even with all that gear of his. Even with Wilson still relatively winded on the other side, Gabriel was still cool and collected.

"Don't worry, n-not all humans are like that," I heard Daniel finally speak up, however timidly, eyeing Lauren. Lauren nodded a little, a little "okay" crawling forth from her mouth, like she too was still overwhelmed from today and just wanted to be through with it all.

"Who's next?" Maria spoke, Gabe waving to us to send the next person over.

"I guess I'll go," The kid from the baseball team, Anthony offered, the fastest of the three as he sprinted, though again, he didn't have any armor to drag like Gabriel. I saw Lauren messing with Gabe's duffel bag a little, seeing if everything was closed. I saw how Maria was staring at her, like she was worried Lauren would steal something.

"Okay," Lauren cleared her throat, stepping up. I saw Daniel move a little, almost in reflex, but Lauren opened her wings, clutching the bag with her arms before leaping from a running start, wings throwing a blast of air in all of our faces with a voluminous POOM, gliding over the six lane main street, putting Anthony's speed to shame. It was quite impressive watching her fly, or glide as it were, even for so short a distance.

"Show off! Hah!" Gabe laughed as she landed gracefully on the other side.

"Cool," Samantha uttered.

The rest of us crossed eventually, though not without a few close calls, ducking around cars as the distant claxons of the military killdrones radiated down the street every now and then. "...So why again shouldn't we just head to my place?" I inquired as Gabriel walked first through this new lobby, us all following.

"Broad daylight with them bots and a group this big? I dunno about you, Noah, but I'm a tad averse to being shot at, despite it being in my job description," He said, heading for the stairs, talking and walking. "See, the bigger question is, how come y'all are following us? Fuck it, Daniel. You start. What's your deal? You aren't friends with us."

"I'm... Sam and I know each other," He said, and Sam nodded.

"Yeah, I-" Sam began, but was cut off.

"Hey, wait your turn now," He shot towards her, before turning back to Daniel. *"Really?"*

"I mean, yeah, we do have art class together," He put forth.

"He draw furries in art class too?" Gabe shot to Sam with a smirk before Daniel went on.

"...I... I saw, uh, Lauren flying. I followed her, to that building, then you guys showed up."

"Aww, you've got yourself a little fan, Greenie," Gabe smirked to the recently christened Lauren now. "Don't get too flattered. He probably wants to fuck you." Lauren reared back at this, eyes flashing to Daniel, who flew into a stammering fit.

"I- Ugh, I do n-not! He's lying!"

"Oh he'd be all over your ass like a green toaster strudel," Gabe laughed crassly, and I found Wilson laughing.

"What? That one was funny," He said to me as I eyed him.

"Don't be an ass, Gabe. We've all been through enough shit today," I snarled.

"Fair enough, moving on," He said, checking around the place, while I too was covering for him as we walked. "Hey, rawrgirl straight out of 2052. Why're you hanging with us?"

"I dunno, felt smart to follow the guy with a gun I vaguely know?" Samantha said back. He chuckled a smirk.

"Ain't you guys got families to run home to? Daniel?"

"...My parents are divorced," Daniel explained, and Gabe laughed.

"Furry in a one parent household, didn't see that coming," Gabe chuckled. "I suppose Sam's not any different?"

"Hey, I was planning on stickin' with you guys anyways, so you can skip me," Wilson uttered, smiling indignantly. "I mean, I planned on surviving with you guys when the world ends, before I got arrested."

"Kyle? Holly? You guys staying?" They nodded, Gabe looking to Anthony.

"Look, man," Anthony said. "I'm in concession with the 'guy with the gun who seems to know what he's doing' idea," He put forth.

"How about you, Green? Hybrids ain't got parents, do they?" Lauren's trotting slowed. "...You know what parents are, right?"

"Y-yeah," She said, awkwardly looking away, feeling uncomfortable, obviously. "I... I don't think I've got parents." Gabe laughed after a little pause.

"You don't think?"

"I dunno, okay? I don't. There?" She offered, though not without letting her frustration get to her. He scoffed.

"...So what else do you or don't you know? Anything weird you'd like to get off your chest?" Gabriel finally leaned against a cubicle, crossing his arms on his armor carrier, gun bobbing beneath his crossed arms.

She pointed out sideways to me, at my slung rifle. "I know how that- I know how to use a gun," She said. Eyes widened, and even Maria stepped away a little, standing to one side and putting her hand on her hip to glare at Gabriel as if to tell him not to do it, though Gabriel was beside himself with curiosity.

"Well?" Gabriel said, motioning to the duffel bag she had re-slung around her humanoid half. She reached in for the other police Armalite carbine. Maria stammered for a moment while Lauren looked at it for a few seconds, before, with one hand on the pistol grip, her free hand found the charging handle on the rear. She cocked it back, before realizing it should be loaded, going for a magazine. She pulled one out, inserting it in the right way and everything, tapping it on the bottom for good measure before racking the charging handle back all the way and sending it home free with a clack of brass upon steel, then even performing a press check, opening the chamber just enough to see the back end of the 5.56 cartridge, letting it fall forward before she pressed the forward assist for good measure, closing the dust cover again, flipping through the safe, semi and automatic modes of the police weapon, settling back on safe before she went to put the one-point sling over herself and get the stock at a comfortable length, which for her seemed to be all the way extended, and let it hang like a trophy.

"Hot damn, what're they teachin' you freaks in those hybrid factories?!" Gabriel was ecstatic in amusement, a moment away from clapping, Lauren now blushing subtly, happy enough to have approval, even a mild, abstract admiration. Maria was gobsmacked, glancing to me for a second as if to bolster her own objection, before spitting it forth.

"You think it's a good idea to let *it* have a gun?!"

"I dunno, Roach. You'd rather pass a babykiller-fifteen to *Daniel*? No offense," Gabriel laughed in his direction, evident that he wouldn't have cared if Daniel was offended anyways.

"None... Taken, not a gun person," He mumbled. Gabriel laughed again.

"Yeah, we'll see about that. What's your take, boss?" Gabriel turned to me, like he always did. Like I was the one in charge. As if.

"...I... I think it's fine," I said. "She... knows how to use it, it looks like."

"If she gets a gun, I'm getting a gun," Maria grumbled, going for the bag. I saw Lauren turn the bag away from her a little, Maria pausing, looking up at the 7-8 some foot tall dragon girl with cold rage boiling in her eyes like she'd jump up there and yank Lauren's tongue from her mouth. Lauren looked back at Gabriel, who shrugged, nodding to the big green walking armory, as she was at the time. I saw Lauren take off the bag, slowly holding it out to Maria, who snatched it like a dog snapping at a treat she'd been taunted with. Maria plopped it on the floor and went down to fish through the bag. She grumbled, grabbing the other police handgun that Gabriel probably found in that overturned car. Probably. She took the pistol as it hung in a gunbelt and holster, going to wrap the whole thing around her hips. I saw Lauren's green arm go up as if to offer assistance, her new rifle already slung around her, but Maria practically hissed at Lauren's attempt to help. Maria eventually cinched the belt up right before drawing the pistol and cocking it back. The round in the chamber flew out and she almost scrambled to catch it, Lauren obviously holding her tongue as Maria bent down to pick up the cartridge she'd inadvertently ejected, taking out the magazine and putting the gun back in the holster, clicking the bullet back into the magazine while she grumbled before slapping it back in the gun. Lauren just kind of stood there, looking off to the side all the while and scratching the corner of her muzzle, distracting herself. I saw the way she stood, one of her four feet tapping the ground a little sometimes. Gabriel shook his head in critique.

"Maria, she also needs spare ammo, Green only has one mag," Gabe commanded. "Give her another magazine."

"You want her to have MORE ammo?" Maria snarled.

"Uh, yeah," Gabe said. "Chop chop." Maria, with gritted teeth, reached into the bag after she was done fidgeting with her own gun, pulling out a spare STANAG magazine and passing it to Lauren. "Here you go, *lizard*," She said with only a tinge of nastiness, offering it to her. Lauren seemed flustered for a second, before reaching out and taking it, stuffing it into her sweatshirt pocket.

"I'm... I'm not a lizard," Lauren began, though Maria didn't seem to care, her scowl ever present.

"See? We can share. Good girls. Now if you would," Gabriel asked for his bag back and she obliged. Gabriel then pulled out the heavy police shotgun, the double barreled bullpup one and practically tossed it to Kyle.

"Aw, sweet, a KSG," Kyle remarked simply. "These are great shotguns."

"It's a DP-12, dumb ass, KSG only has one barrel," Gabriel snarled and Kyle scoffed.

"What about m-" Wilson began as Gabriel passed him the last gun- the homeless guy's Hi-Point. "Aw, are you fuckin serious?" He riffed. "How come Kyle gets that fuckin' cannon and I get stuck with this?! This thing looks like a Glock's retarded cousin!"

"Wilson, Kyle's gun is fifteen pounds. You'd tip over."

"...You shouldn't say retarded," Samantha said as she leaned against a cubicle. Wilson flipped her off with a scoffing snarl and she rolled her eyes.

Gabriel smugly watched, arms still crossed, as Wilson fumbled with the crudely oversized slide. "Hey, at least we've got a gun for you. You can thank Noah for *domeing* its original owner."

"Ugh, this was that hobo's gun?" Wilson nearly dropped it, going to hold it with two fingers as if it were diseased. "It's still sticky! I'm, I'mma go wash it off," He said, heading for the bathroom.

"...So why did we decide to be in this building instead?" Kyle was saying as he was taking a look around, going towards the side of the building towards the road, pretending to be all tactical with his gun, flailing it around every corner, holding his gun way too low but smashing his head practically sideways across the top of it trying to aim through the holographic sight. I figured I would have to go into instruction on how to actually hold and use a weapon for those of us who obviously had no clue. I looked over to Gabriel, and I could tell that he was thinking the same thing.

"Didn't really dig the other one, too furnished, too old. Felt like a fire could really fuck the place over, the hack's probably fucked with electric systems, a spark could fuck the place up at any time. This one is nice, made of steel and concrete. Windows are bigger, better visibility. So, we hunker down here until most of the bots and problems fuck off. We've got three days until people start getting hungry enough that the real shit starts, so as soon as things get quiet we should move out and move quick. Alright, so speaking of, we don't know when they'll shut the water off. Look for containers, plug the sinks of the bathrooms, fill up on water. I'm sure this place has a couple cafeterias. We've got a little work to do, so let's get to it."

### Chapter 9

After Wilson had returned with a somewhat cleaner gun and I used some duct-tape Gabriel had to couple my rifle magazines together in lieu of a loadbearing kit, as well as Lauren taping her spare magazine as well, we went about digging through cubicles on this second floor for a couple of hours. The place was abandoned in a hurry, it was almost eerie. With the wail of sirens and chaos in the distance, the claxon of security bots as well, here things were different, like we could kind of duck away from it all. Almost peaceful.

Wilson, Maria and I were walking through the cafeteria floor, after a few quick stops through the halls. Gabriel had gone over proper weapons technique with Kyle, who, despite his aloof nature, seemed to get the picture. I gave Wilson a few pointers, and now he seemed good to go, his gun tucked into the simple holster the hobo had on him that was now his, spare magazines all stuffed into pockets. We, with emptied backpacks (though since I had an armor plate in mine courtesy of my father, I'd given it to Maria to wear in lieu of armor since I had the police vest) went about, collecting containers and other interesting things and stuff.

"Think there might be any guns in the desks? Anybody crazy enough to bring their gun to work?" Wilson laughed nervously while we walked through the cafeteria of the 5th floor.

"You never know," Maria mumbled, while we were collecting things out of the dry storage, leaving the chilled goods for later.

"...You know..." Maria piped up, as we gathered. "I don't like any of this."

"What, that the world is ending?" I muttered back in a half-joke.

"...Dunno about that. I've been through worse," Maria grunted grimly. "I just don't know who I trust less, Gabe or the lizard." I suppressed a sigh.

"...You don't think Gabe's proven himself?" I put forth. "He seemed to be okay with... with killing that guy, who he said he worked with, to get away from Sinaloa," I said. "He removed his tracker and everything, said my dad gave him the machine to do it with. I mean, my dad trusts him. I'm assuming."

"That could be an act, you know."

"So he can do what, turn us in to the Cartel? Are we fugitives from them or something?"

"...Even if he really double crossed them," Maria stopped to rear up from searching a cabinet to look back at me, hands on her hips, thumbs dug into her gunbelt. "You know what that makes us? Accomplices. Now we're their enemies."

"...I thought you hated them anyways," I said. "They killed your brother."

"Yeah. In front of me, Noah." Maria added this as if to show how serious she really was. "I know how ruthless they are. If they know we're with him and they get the drop on us, we're all dead."

"Hey, look, I may be just third-wheelin' it here," Wilson finally put forth as he leaned against the stove, as he'd been behind the counter of the cafeteria now. "But I'm with Noah here. Gabriel blasted a dude for this, Maria- even if Noah, uh, blasted him first. He's on our side." Maria glared at him.

"Yeah. And now we're enemies of the cartel." Maria sighed. "Look, I know he's probably not with them anymore. It makes sense that he's using this, using you to... Retire. But if Siña finds us..." She said.

"...I'm sure Gabriel has thought this through," I mumbled, trying to wrestle with Gabe's ulterior motives in my head. He keeps deferring back to me, as if I'm in charge, even though it feels like he's in charge. It didn't sit right with me. *You are the objective*, Gabriel's words rang in my ears. *You staying alive is what matters.* Am I really still his friend, or am I a mission?

"I really hope you're right," Maria semi-scoffed. "Because if Gabriel's made us, he's a liability, Noah. You know this." I saw Maria's hand brisk past her pistol, almost motioning to it.

"You'll sell Gabriel out to the cartel that you hate so much?" I put forth. Maria's eyes narrowed and she looked away, sighing, as if thinking.

"I'd love to kill every last one of them, Noah. But you know that can't happen. If it comes down to us or him, we should be ready to make that choice."

"...I dunno," Wilson put forward. "So far Gabriel has been a lot of help, dude."

"...Yeah. He has." I half-expected Maria to tell Wilson to shut up, so when I heard her respond with this, dead serious as it was, I was taken aback. I saw steel in her eyes, a fiery will. She looked to me, capturing my gaze in that steel cage. "If I see Gabriel coming close to exposing us, either you deal with him or I will."

"...He won't expose us."

"You know you're betting your life on that. *Our* lives."

"...Jesus, Maria," Wilson scoffed, trying to play this off. Maria turned his head to look at him. "Okay, okay. I get it. Still, have a little faith in Gabe."

"I think I do," Maria asserted, throwing her chin out. "I trust him more than that... Thing."

"What, you think Lauren is gonna sell us out to the cartel too?"

"...I saw what happened up in Whitehorse. We all did. These... Hybrids don't sit well with me. I just know something doesn't add up about them."

"Yeah, well," I put forth. "She's been pretty useful so far."

"She's big. She'll eat a lot. She'll cut into our food a lot more than a normal person would." Maria paused. "That and she's not human. I don't think I can trust something that's not a human. How do you even know her brain works like ours? Or works right at all?" Maria says. "She says she's not sure if she has parents. She's not sure if she has a name. What if she's not sure about *not* turning us in to Sinaloa? Or exposing what happened here after all this blows over?" I sighed, my turn to look off into the distance and rack my brain. "Noah, Gabe beat a cop and stole like, six police guns. Do you have any idea how many felonies that is?! You're wearing a cop's stolen vest *right now*, Noah. And you shot a man with his gun."

"In self defense," I put forth.

"Yeah, and we stole *his* gun too- that thing probably has bodies on it already- then Gabe riddled his corpse with bullets with a machine gun. What are the crime scene investigators gonna think?"

"...Lauren was there when I shot him. He pointed his gun at me."

"You think that a judge is gonna take the word of one of those things?" Maria hissed. "What if she loses her mind and starts saying we took her hostage this whole time? Or if she just figures she can say that so she can't be held as an accomplice?"

"What if, what if?!" I spat back. "How about we focus on the right now, alright?" I growled, tired of being lectured to. "Right now, Gabriel is... helping me lead this group. He's kept us, kept us safe," I said, wishing I really believed what I said. Maria saw through this, poking me right in the chest of the police vest as if pointing at my very heart.

"Noah, it looks to me that Gabriel is keeping HIMSELF safe. You think Gabe gives a shit about, like, Wilson?!" She motioned with a wide sweep of her hand to Wilson, who had been watching this whole debacle.

"Hey, we've been friends since, like, sophomore year," Wilson put forth.

"Yeah, right. You're a bullet shield. You're a bullet shield *because* you trust him. Don't you see it?" Maria hissed to him.

"Right now Gabe hasn't used anybody as a bullet shield. Right now Gabe is on our side. And, and the hybrid hasn't gone crazy."

"And what if she does?! Gabriel handed her a fucking *machine gun*."

"If Gabriel was only looking after himself, why would Gabriel do that, then?!" I said. "If Gabriel, as selfish as you think he is, is okay with her, then I'm okay with her."

"You best make sure you've got her reigned in, Noah. Gabriel is bad enough. But I don't feel right around her. She's a fucking abomination, Noah. A science experiment gone wrong. Made for some mysterious reason they're not telling us. Sociological test subjects? *Human analogs*?" Maria scoffed. "They made half a billion *human analogs*, Noah. Billion with a *B*. Probably more since they're always saying they actually made more. There's something going on that they're not telling us. That and the fact that all the people in charge of it, everyone at the top of this shit, nobody can find any of them doesn't help their case. Something is *off* with this. All of this. First it was Whitehorse, now it's Vegas. Where is this gonna happen next? I just don't trust those things."

I remained silent. I didn't disagree. I just stared at her. "If she threatens our... Surviving, I'll deal with her. Same with Gabe."

"I just hope you're ready to." Maria turned, her bag full as she went to look out the window on the burning city, sighing.


Coming back down with our bags full was quiet and uneventful, the air was sufficiently thick enough with contemplation that not even Wilson's happy-go-lucky manner could crack through, and he kept his jokes to himself. We returned to the second story where we'd set up camp to see most everyone relaxing (as much as they could at a time like this) in the rec room. Anthony managed to get a television working, and most people were currently watching. Lauren was sitting on the floor with Samantha behind her on the couch, who had probably took the time to offer to wash Lauren's hair in a sink and was now humming quietly to herself as she braided away. Lauren locked eyes with me for a second and I saw her green skin blush behind an appreciative, yet tentative smile. She... looked nice. Human, even. Despite this, I felt Maria's air fill itself with unease as she walked in, seeing the weird centaur-dragon girl there.

"Yo, where's Gabe?" I piped up to break the awkward air, looking around, as footage of riots showed on that ancient-looking television that must have been from the turn of the century, buckets and containers of water and scavenged stuff laying all around in a semi-organized fashion.

"Gabriel's watching the road," Daniel said, looking up from a sketchbook, a much newer and less-used one than the one he had that other day, that was still at my house. Was he sketching Lauren or something? I felt bad for thinking that he was that creepy, also making a mental note to give him his other one back.

"Ooh, he's plotting," Wilson finally jeered at Maria, who elbowed him in the sternum hard and he stumbled back a little.

"As you can see, between the riots and the hacked drones..." Bursts of static and interference interrupted the broadcast. "We are in a state of emergen-"

"What, city news?" I asked.

"No," Holly said, practically cradling herself, Kyle all cuddled up close, Kyle's obscenely large shotgun leaning up against the couch. "This... this is Greater Angeles Bay."

"...Christ, it's all the way to the coast..." Maria said, going to lean against the wall, watching. Wilson was in the process of unloading his backpack, and I dropped mine, walking out.

Gabe was sitting a little ways away, before the big, shattered windows. Step after step, I approached, though when I was too far away for him to really hear me, he must have sensed me. "Yo, Noah," He said, throwing a hand up. I approached, circling around to look at him.

There he sat, in a widened shooting seat, forearms up against the inside of his thighs as he sat crisscrossed. I looked at his gun, realizing it looked different. The barrel was far, far longer and that big suppressor was gone, and instead of a little red-dot sight atop it there was a compact scope. I looked down to his duffel bag, seeing the old upper receiver of his bullpup assault rifle, the silenced one with the tiny reflex sight. "Pays to carry a conversion kit. 5.56, 19 inch barrel with a one in eight twist, one-to-six magnification illuminated scope with combat leads." He was still looking about with his gun, now a miniature sniper's rifle, scanning about as I stood somewhat behind him.

"That a tracking scope?" I muttered, as if to make small talk.

"Nah. Too finicky. Besides, in rolling combat you never end up using that faggot shit. You just put the blinky bit on the bad guy and pull the finger thingy till he falls down." Gabriel didn't bother laughing at his morose oversimplification, moving on quickly. "...So, the other kit is .300 Black, integrally suppressed. Good for bad-breath distance social work, not so much for field distance."

"...Is that a tiny suppressor on the end of your 5.56?" I asked, motioning to the barrel he currently had on his gun, though he didn't see my motions since I was behind him and stuff. I guess it was habit or instinct or something.

"Nah. Silencers mess with the harmonics too much for 200-plus yard shooting and I'm too lazy to load my own ammo. And I never saw the point in silencing a supersonic bullet like 5.56. Just a blast-forward brake, kinda like a silencer but no baffles and no endcap, throws the sound forward rather than muffle it. Easier on the ears, plus sort of throws off OpFor as to your position. More recoil though, but that's not a problem unless you're A little bitch." I stood in silence, taking in the sunset. "Penny for your thoughts?" I heard him utter.

"I... I dunno," I muttered. "About what?"

"Well, for starters, what's your take on Green?"

"...You worried about her too?"

Gabriel sighed, still looking down. "I'd like to think I can tell what kind of a person somebody is at a glance. Dunno about hybrids, but hey, they ain't robots. They're flesh and blood. See, I can trust an animal, animals got needs and shit. Green back there's an animal. She's gotta eat, gotta sleep, gotta feel safe and loved- appreciated. Right now I think I can put faith in that."

"Think so?" I mumbled, only mulling it over in cursory thought.

"Hierarchy of Needs, bro. Like I said, she's an animal, not a robot, and one based almost entirely off of human genes. And animals, especially human-y ones, need things. They need to feel like they belong. You see how she's trying to get along and stuff? Make *friends*?" He muttered, almost like it was an insult, yet just barely. It was kind of funny, and in retrospect I think it really was a joke.

"You don't think she's dangerous?"

"Oh, I hope she is, that's why I handed her an M16," Gabe said. "I figure if anything, us being her first and only real friends, she'll be ready to fuckin' kill for us if she needs to. Funny thing, loyalty. She ain't about to spoil what she knows is a good thing going. Not even those White Horse crazies can deny that. So what's your opinion?" He asked.

"I... I guess so," I said. He muttered a chuckle.

"Man of nuance, so it seems. You don't think she's unstable yourself, do you? Them acceleration chambers they grew 'em in coulda filled their brains with some Manchurian Candidate shit."

"Do I look like my dad?" I joked tiredly. Gabe chuckled morosely at this, however briefly.

"Jokes or no jokes, doesn't change the fact that she knows her guns almost as good as you or I."

"...She seems lucid enough," I uttered within a prolonged sigh. "But the guns are just one thing, after all. She seems pretty normal in everything else."

"Sure. But if somebody ever says the phrase 'would you kindly' while talking to her, you should keep your eyes out." I gazed at him for a second, as he looked back to me.

"Huh?" I asked in confusion, blinking.

"You know, don't you... never mind. I forgot you don't play the classics." I scoffed at this.

"...You and your stupid grandpa-games," I laughed as I leaned against a dividing beam of the window.

"Tellin' you man, you're missing out." He sighed back in a chuckle, eager enough to continue. "So then, second thing. The beau. How's Maria doing?" I sighed hard this time, looking up to the ceiling for a brief span, as if looking for guidance.

"She's doing fine. She's been through worse, you know this."

"She still mad at me for joining the guys that killed her brother?" I grunted, now glaring at him.

"...How *did* you join them?" I finally said, curious. He laughed once.

"Long story. I'll tell y'all later so I don't have to go through it one-by-one."

"...Good enough."

"So what's she think of me?"

"...She thinks you're a liability," I finally uttered after a long, tired pause. He clicked his tongue, though not quite in exasperation.

"Not bad, usin' that noggin of hers," Gabe said. "She's smart to not trust me."

"...Are you saying-"

"No, Noah," Gabe spat, cutting me off. "I'm not going to blow things. I promise you I'm twenty steps ahead of 'em, I've been working on this shit since I realized I was in too deep *years* ago. It's not your problem."

"...Can I believe that?"

"Shoot me and leave me in the middle of the street for 'em if you don't. I wouldn't blame you." There was a long silence, as I sighed. I really wanted to trust him. My best friend, who stuck up for me in grade school despite even the steepest odds and risk to himself. Bullies, no matter the number. No matter what he was always there for me. No matter what I just could not find anything in my mind to invalidate him, and I sighed again. As if sensing my thoughts, Gabriel spoke once more, knowing I'd decided to trust him. "You think this will all just blow over?"

"I... I don't know."

"Seems to me like you wouldn't want it to."

"Excuse me?"

"Well," Gabe groaned, shifting in his seat a little bit. "Forgive me for extrapolating, but you *did* blow a man's brains out. The dichotomy has shifted. If I were in your position-" Gabe's right hand slowly moved from the forend of the gun to the scope, clicking one of the knobs, messing with the magnification. "Childhood friend turns out to be a killer, take your first life, make friends with a *dragon*- you can't really go back to the old life now that so much has changed, it'd fuck you up. But despite all the weird shit, in the here and now everything's stable. Right now you know exactly where you stand, and exactly what needs to be done. No tests, no martial arts classes, no cops to arrest your ol' buddy for being a Siña piece of shit, no men-in-black types to come drag Green away kicking and screaming from her new friends, no judicial system judging you for the man you brained. Just survival. Simple." He finally took enough of a pause to look back up to me, as I leaned against a cubicle, arms crossed, contemplative scowl on my face. "If things went back to normal, everything would be a real hassle, now wouldn't it?" I didn't say much. I guess I agreed, even if I didn't want to. "Well, it's easy right now," Gabe said as he turned back, his voice turning morose. "But it's gonna get a lot harder soon."

The sickness in my gut told me he was right.

### Chapter 10

The rest of the short day wound down, a bit more scavenging, a bit more sitting around the TV and watching what was going on. A whole lot of nothing, really. Military drones and rioters were out in force, though usually not at the same time. Around here things were quiet enough, though. It was almost eerie. "Who do you think hacked us?" I'd mumble to Gabe.

"Dunno. Siña OpsCon didn't say much, mostly to be ready today."

"...Think it was the right wingers, or the left wingers?" I uttered morosely. Gabriel's smirk grew.

"Now that's a thought." He didn't seem to hold an opinion. Nobody at all had much to say, though we sat about. Some of us attempted to make some dinner using the appliances in the break room, until Gabriel took a break to give it his shot at this, turning out a pretty decent meal for all of us; though if anything, spirits still remained sullen and dour.

I was on watch for the first half of the night. It wasn't like I could sleep anyways, though most everybody else was in a similar, restless state. I guess it was easy enough, sitting out in that perch and watching the road below, wearing Gabriel's ballistic mask. It was pretty nice, though it interfaced mainly with his tac glasses, he set it up so I could wear it- it had a night vision ocular built in, to switch between infrared and thermal. He told me to post up behind a window and stick to IR, so if somebody else who had thermal vision couldn't see me behind the window. I was scanning, and nothing was happening now, everything was still. Gunshots would still crackle in the distance. My mind wandered as I scanned. My father really trusted Gabriel to keep me safe? I guess if Gabriel wants to come to the Citadel, that would be the right alibi. Did Gabriel tell my dad he was with the Cartel? If he didn't, why would my dad think he's capable of protecting me? And did Gabe tell him about the hack beforehand? Nothing made sense.

It must've been a couple hours before I heard a noise, behind me. I heard the door to the rec room crack slowly. I looked over my shoulder, seeing that big body of Lauren's creep out into the darkness in the pale green monochrome tinge of the NODs, as she shut the door behind her ever so slowly, with a click, having to step her big body out sideways in order to do so. I just watched her as she walked over, head swiveling to try and locate me, eyes shining in the infrared. I turned off the nightvision and pulled the mask off of my face, her body practically disappearing into the darkness as I did. In the dark, seeing her body slink inkily along in the faint blackness of night made my heart race- from the gleaming claws of her forelegs' hand-like mandibles to the horns that glittered all the way up above the rest of her powerful visage, I figured if I didn't know it was her I would have probably been terrified at this beast come to rip me to shreds. Still towering tall over where I was sitting, she came and sat (or lay, since she had four legs and her lower body laid down but her humanoid portion remained upright) down next to me, wearing a blanket around her upper body, draped about her nude body and over her folded upper pair of wings, it hanging down off of the side of her lower body as it drooped. "...See anybody?" She muttered groggily, trying to start up small talk.

"Not for a while." I sighed back in silence, though it was more of a sigh towards myself. I think she noticed anyways, and I looked to her again, slowly letting Gabriel's scoped rifle, which I had been using to scan the road, fall into my lap so we could talk. "...What's on your mind?" The phrase was practically as regular as breathing at this point. I couldn't help but feel condescending while uttering it just because of how much it had been repeated today, even if I knew it was sincere. I kinda wanted to get a better feel for her anyways, and make still the doubts Maria had placed in my head.

"Can't sleep. I…" She trailed off, pausing long to stare off into the ominous blackness of the world before us.

"...Bad dreams?" I put forth.

"Yeah," She sighed out with puffed cheeks, almost like she was embarrassed. I cheeked a smile with a subtle "humph" for her.

"...What about?"

"I… I can remember more about who I was- or who I was supposed to be. I… I think I was… I dunno. I feel like I remembered it, but I forgot as soon as I woke up." She paused for a long while. "...But that's kinda how I've been feeling ever since I… since they woke me up. Like I've just forgotten something. But it's getting better… I *think*." She paused again. "I- I'm sorry, I'm talking your ear off," She muttered.

"It's all right," I said. "You've got a lot on your mind." We didn't say much, sitting there, side-by-side. She was close to me, like she'd edged over. It was like she wanted to lean against me, to feel human contact- or personal contact or something of the sort. We just shared a contemplative glance before I opened my mouth again. "Lauren, can I ask you something?"

"Of course," She uttered, now taking a look out into that dark, dark night, an ear flicking in response to distant blasts and throwing a free strand of her brunette mane. I looked at her, really taking in details now. She had those brown marks across her body, and her fuzzy brown mane of hair ran all the way along her spine terminating at the very tip of her tail, though it began at her head as a scalp of hair, devolving to thick fur down her elongated spine.

"...Do you... What was it like back in there? In those hybrid making factories, where you came out of?"

Lauren was silent for a long while, her eyes shining in a quick second of remembrance and darting about, like she was pulling back old memories from the dark corners of her mind, memories she might have even thought she didn't have. "I... it's real fuzzy but I... I can remember a lot of different white rooms. They all look the same, but... but they're different... Hallways made of... Metal; it's always so cold. I can remember people in lab coats, pushing me around, and I'd just do whatever they told me to, kind of... Trapped inside myself. There were all these... Capsules, or chambers. Factory line is what I want to describe it as, but I don't really know what that is. Weird, huh?" She laughed just to laugh, a sad, desperate chuckle. I was still watching her as she spoke, taking in how she thought, how she moved when she articulated what was on her mind. "Like... They'd put me into chambers and, and the next thing I know it's like I'm waking up again. Every time I'm different, but I'm still the same- mostly. Bigger, older, bit by bit. They might pull me away to ask me a few questions but... but most of the time it's quick before they put me in again. And it's never the same people who put me in the chamber who take me out, and, and I know I go in there to sleep. I... I think they grew me. Every time I woke up I was different. Like not just physically, but... but as a person, too. Inside my head. I'd know things. I'd feel things." She finally looked over to me now, eyes shining in self-contemplative fear. "Then, the last time they did it... I woke up and there was nobody there. Just me. I, I walked out of my room, and all the other hybrids were there, waking up out of their... their *containers*, but no humans. That..." She was getting worked up. She looked like she was about to burst into tears.

"Hey," I went up next to her, inching close. I came to my knees, raising myself so I could get an arm around her as I held her, giving her that human contact she was looking for. "Stop. Don't tell me any more, alright? It's working you up."

"It... It is?" She said, sniffing in. She looked down at her hand, holding it up to her nose. "Oh... I, I guess, I guess you're right..." She stared blankly at her hand, before going up to wipe the tears and the rest away. "I'm... I'm kinda new to the 'having emotions' thing... I don't really know how to control how I'm feeling, it kinda just rushes through me..." She let out another sad chuckle.

"That's a human thing too, Lauren. Don't sweat it." She looked to me and I gave her a bolstering smile, which she reciprocated back. I patted her on her side (since I couldn't really reach up that high, and she had wings on her back anyways) and she seemed to appreciate it enough, snuggling up next to me.

"Thanks, Noah," She sighed, like a weight had been lifted off her. She leaned down beside me and I went back to sitting against the cubicle, before she lay her head on my lap, laying on her side as she gripped her blanket. "...Thanks for everything."

Through the dark hours we waited, sharing in each others' company. I noticed two things about her that I'd not first realized; firstly that she was very warm. She was definitely not cold blooded, and her skin didn't really feel like scales, or coarse at all. I always figured that these dragon hybrids were lizards, I guess they really weren't. They only resembled them, and even then, not by much. Secondly, her breaths came out in great big dozing, snoring sighs as she was asleep, four lungs emptying all at once through some interconnected tracheal system. This made me think, figuring I should ask Gabe or Daniel about more hybrid trivia sometime.

I looked to the watch my dad had gotten me as a birthday present, noting the tiny buzzing of the hourly alarm. 1 AM. Gabe's turn. I got up, shifting slowly, picking Lauren's head up out of my lap by a hand gripping a horn and the other hand beneath her muzzle and placing her head on the ground, though I guess I felt a little bad, seeing her dozing softly, though perturbed in her sleep now that her head was on hard ground rather than soft thigh, groaning and clawing at the ground a little with muttering. It was rather endearing to the point that I wanted to lay back down with her and keep her company, or at the very least go get her a pillow. I walked carefully and quietly around her big body, a wing splayed out to the side in the somewhat awkward sleeping position, with her muttering in her sleep, walking away to where everyone else was sleeping. I entered the rec room, full of snoring and whatnot, everybody sprawled into their own positions. Gabriel slept in the middle of the room, clutching his handgun holstered in a kydex sheath on his armored chest like the way Kyle was clutching Holly, a hand firmly on her ass. I chuckled in silence, going to tap Gabe on his shoulder with my shoe, but before I did. His eyes opened, focusing on me.

"Y-your watch," I muttered, quiet and a little taken by surprise by how he woke up to me as if on cue, as I un-slung his gun, pointing the buttstock towards him. He sat up with a grunt to take the gun, getting up, as I pulled off the mask. He mumbled something back at me in the affirmative as he took his mask, going to sling the rifle. But as he did, I grabbed one of the couch cushions and pushed it towards him, and he looked back at me, before his eyes searched the room in an instant.

"Green?" He hushed in a single word sentence, wearing that mask raised atop his head. I nodded and his smirk grew. He took it, laughing a little bit in seemingly drowsy silence, before going outside.

I laid down with Maria, sighing and grunting, almost exasperated. I looked at her on the floor, sprawled out. She muttered and turned her head in her sleep every now and then. I wanted to wake her up to tell her I was here, but I figured not to, laying alongside her, inches away at our very closest. It felt like forever I was laying there, staring at the ceiling, but it seemed like I just couldn't sleep. I figured it was the snoring in the room, so I got up, going outside. I slipped into a cubicle, where it was quiet. There was no more distant shooting or explosions now. I sat into a chair and let myself fall asleep.

At least, until a strange feeling disturbed me. Like a man possessed, I stood, peering towards that windowed wall towards the road, where I left Lauren and where Gabriel should be. I got up and walked over, seeing Lauren's big green body all curled around that pillow, her long body and tail snaking around to end with her head laying on the pillow in the center, where she dozed now, sighing breaths as carefree as she could be. Gabriel was nowhere to be seen. I saw a bunch of things, roughly organized on the ground. His duffel bag was gone, and all the spare 5.56-marked magazines were there, but the glint of a scope was what caught my eye most prominently. I, in intrigue, saw that he'd taken the 5.56 upper off of his weapon and laid it alongside the neat pile of magazines, and the silenced .300 Black upper was absent, all his 5.56 magazines and ammo here in the neat little pile. He'd changed his gun back? Why? Where was he? Was he in the bathroom? Why did he take his duffel bag?

Outside, I heard glass shatter.

I looked up with a start, to the road. I saw a car, an old biodiesel truck idling by the old building. I peered, looking closely. Nothing seemed to be moving, at least, until I saw the driver, distant as he was, covered in dark liquid. Blood. A shadow emerged from behind one of the abandoned cars, running right up to it, pausing before the door for a few quick seconds, pulling it open, the body tumbling out.

I gasped. I don't know why, but I felt compelled to investigate what Gabriel must be doing.

With my heart in my throat, I got up, pacing quickly and as quietly as I could, down the halls, down the stairs and to the road. I drew my pistol now, and felt naked as I'd pulled my armor off when I laid down to sleep with Maria. My feet pattering in the cold silence of the street, I drew up to that truck, pausing before the body outside the door with the bloody head, perforated by a single large, slow rifle bullet through glass.

I knew what was going on. I entered the building, checking corners slowly and making as little noise as possible, walking slow, one foot after another, listening with every hair on my neck on end until I was in the stairwell. I could hear voices, then the thudding sound of suppressed gunfire that made me wince and my heart race, strings of bursts of what I knew was Gabriel's MDR. Cold sweat beaded on my forehead as I listened to voices cry out, yells that I couldn't make out. Spanish, in pain.

I peeked out from the stairwell, gazing at a figure who stood above two more bodies, though one of them still moved, crying out in spanish. The one who was standing, Gabriel, stooped down ever so slowly. *"Es el mejor receibo, eh? Tres ameturs? No Aumentados como yo? Lintiernos, no Visionoche? No exoarmadura?"* Gabriel's tsk, like reprimanding a child, made my blood freeze. The man on the ground was quick to utter something in spanish, though Gabe drew his knife as quickly as it took for him to stop chuckling. *"Lo siento amigo,"* Gabriel mumbled, and with a flash of the blade, the still living Sinaloa body-man died gurgling. *So that's why we moved buildings, he needed to set a trap,* I thought in cold calculation. I was too tired to have really contemplated any further than that, before I felt I should slip away now, having seen more than enough. I slunk away, putting my gun away, the sick feeling of what Gabriel had done, what he does and did and is doing, all going through my mind. All the secrets he'd kept. I slunk past the dead Siña driver and through the road all the way back to the second floor of our building, and by the time I was back, standing over Lauren's dozing body once more with my wide eyes glittering in horror, the old building had begun to smoulder, its interior ablaze in a satanic glow. A figure walked alone across the road, back towards us. As the car began to burn just like the building, Gabriel's demonic silhouette was outlined in the blaze, his duffel bag full of loot as he walked back, head held high with his mask atop it, his face displaying a wrathful grin with eyes just as blazing as the building where he'd done his cruel deeds.

I just went to my cubicle again, hearing him come up the stairs and go into a bathroom, the water running. It was like a dream, I think I'd disassociated, it was all just one big dream. I figured I'd go back to sleep, hearing Gabriel washing the blood off the gear he'd looted off of his old dead comrades.

### Chapter 11

"See? Told you guys," Gabe said, as we watched the building smouldering down now, the sun rising in the distance. "Fire hazard. That coulda been our ass if we didn't move here."

"...What's with the new stuff?" Anthony asked, mulling over the three scuffed-up MDRs, like Gabriel's, but the 5.56 ones with the standard 16" carbine barrels rather than the 12" PDW barrels or the 19" rifle ones. There were also two old Beretta handguns, and what must've been the driver's 12" PDW-sized MDR, like Gabriel's shortened version but without the big suppressor. Gabriel was bidding people come and take them with a cursory safety lecture: "don't point it at shit you don't want to kill and keep your finger out of the trigger guard until you're ready to kill."

"Took a look around a little after the fire started," Gabriel's cover story began with everyone clamoring rather morosely over the loot, as Daniel was inspecting some of the new body armor, noticing spall marks and holes on the front of the nylon covers, a worried look on his face. They all looked worried, fearful of Gabriel. Nobody really seemed to fully believe his story, but nobody was about to question him. I sure as shit didn't want to bring up how exactly he went about acquiring the gear, more maybe because I knew what he was capable of. Even Maria's concerns boiled quietly in the corner. Gabriel saw this hesitance, and he was practically revelling in it. "Somebody had a little showdown a couple blocks down, a tracer round probably skipped through that buliding and started it all, if I had to guess. Surprised it didn't wake y'all up," Gabriel said while Daniel was placing the armor down gently and worriedly, like putting down broken china. "I had a look-see, managed to scavenge through what was left. Real bloodbath. Buncha pistols too, don't forget those," He ordered. Anthony and Wilson donned two of the armor vests while Kyle scoffed at the two slender boys, he himself not entirely ready to conceal his prized body under an armor carapace, easily letting Maria reach for the third.

"Ap, ap, Noah," He said, snapping to me. "Give your girl your vest. You're wearing this one."

"Wait, what?" I put forth, looking at one of the coyote-colored carriers. I could practically see the blood stains still on it. I wasn't about to put on a dead man's armor, I told myself.

"Yeah. This one's rifle-rated. Steel plates may suck, yeah, but it'll stop a whole lot more than the Dynamid soft vest you're wearing. Chop chop." I felt like I shouldn't make a scene, knowing that Gabriel murdered a man in cold blood for this "gift". I took mine off, handing it to Maria, who rolled her eyes as she strapped it on, picking up the final MDR and slinging it.

I looked at the carrier. It was one of those budget ones, not the best quality and certainly not as good quality as my personal one at home, but Gabriel had a point, this one offered rifle protection. "...You sure nobody shot it up?"

"I took a look at the plates. Rear one took a few bullets 'cuz the guy got shot from behind, nothing penetrated. It's steel, and the liner looks good. The shots that killed the guy hit him in the back of the neck and head. Was kind of a mess getting it off without ruining it." I couldn't help but let a chill wash over me when I heard Gabriel describe exactly how he killed that Siña cleaner, explaining it like he'd done an autopsy on somebody else's bloody work.

Like these cheap vests were, it was uncomfortable, fit for somebody somewhat smaller than I. Even after I adjusted the fit, it was still more than uncomfortable for the other, less physical reason, but I had to keep up the act. "...Side plates kinda digging into my ribs," I muttered while adjusting, trying to keep my mind off of it's original owner, looking at the rest of them. Anthony had acquainted himself with one of the M9 pistols that was strapped to his plate carrier, recognizing it almost instantly, though he showed less than stellar weapons handling technique, fumbling with the controls before Lauren came over and offered a hand to help with the weapon. He recoiled at first at her approach, though like everybody, he had softened up enough to her presence to pass it off. I saw in the fleeting moment Lauren's apprehension, a sort of subtle self-loathing, like slapping herself on the forehead for being an idiot for moving so suddenly, all within the way her eyes twinkled and an ear twitched.

"...Not gonna take a new pistol, Wilson?" Gabe chuckled as Wilson fiddled with the short PDW-MDR, the Hi-Point still in its cheap holster on his hip.

"I dunno, man. The block-glock's grown on me," He chuckled, while Lauren handled Anthony's scuffed-up surplus beretta deftly. I watched her perfectly perform a press check on the weapon, after cocking the hammer, before ending with a test of the decocker. She took the magazine out, looking at the slots on the back to see that the weapon was indeed topped off. Satisfied, she put the magazine back in with a healthy slap and put the weapon off safe, since the hammer was down anyways, and passed it back to Anthony, who took it wordlessly, before she drew her own pistol and repeated the procedure, inserting it back it into the kydex holster on the battle belt from one of the dead hitmen she now wore around her humanoid hip area, with plenty of spare magazine holders for it and her AR15 now too. I saw her adjust the belt in determined silence, since it was intended for human hips and not quite what she was equipped with physiologically, rotating around too much for her tastes, unable to really secure it without fasteners for body armor, which she couldn't wear as it would have just crushed her wings. She was fine with being naked to bullets for now, though she mentioned that with a bit of seamstressing she might be able to make leg or waist fasteners for it. It was kind of amusing and endearing, hearing her think up ways to customize her gear for her liking.

I checked our inventory, we had the two police rifles, the police shotgun, two more MDR carbines, one MDR PDW and Gabriel's own MDR rifle. Seven longarms between the ten of us, though Holly, Samantha and Daniel weren't keen on weapons anyway. Kind of lucky. We also had five extra sidearms, not counting Gabriel's Bren.

"...Are we moving out?" Wilson piped up, nothing that Gabriel was suiting up.

"I've got to check on a few things, to see it's safe. The drones seem to have fucked off and I want to know why. You guys should stay put." This was met with groans.

"...You fuckin' serious?" Kyle spat. "You expect us to hang around here for longer?"

"Safe thing to do."

"Gabe, there's like, nobody out there," I spoke up. Gabriel looked to me.

"Yeah. That's what's worrying me. No more drones, no more gunfire. I'm thinking FEMA's kicked in but I'm not sure. Looks to me like the National Guard's FUBAR, but the MilDrones being silent worries me."

"Shit," Anthony barked out as he was flipping through channels on the TV, having gone back to do so as soon as Gabriel had announced we were all staying put. "All the channels are dead. I'm... I'm with Gabriel on this one, guys. This is too weird."

"Yeah. This is all weird. But you know what's relatively safe and known-about? This building. We've got supplies and a defensible location. Unless the paradigm shifts again, we can stick around."

"...Maybe we should ditch the guns?" Daniel muttered, and Gabriel looked at him crossly.

"Oh, right. So we can just be waltzing down the street with our pet dragon-centaur pretending that we're incognito now that we're declawed. You think we can just stick a trench coat and a hat on her and she'll blend right in? She's a hair under eight foot with an ass the size of a Harley Davidson." Lauren shifted uncomfortably underneath Gabriel's backhanded judgement.

"I think you want us to have these guns in case the Cartel comes after you." The room fell silent for a tiny second, Gabriel swinging about to look at Maria, with a dead serious look in her eyes. Gabe took a moment to drum up a response, though as expertly as he had masked his apprehension, I could still feel it leak through.

"Okay, Maria." Gabe paused to sigh, looking down as a fist came up to his mouth, before exploding out in a brief hand gesture, like a man making a deal he didn't want to make. "Let's say that I fucked up. Left the wrong clue. Cartel's out in full force for me. Your deniability has already gone out the window. You can't expect them to play ball with somebody harboring a traitor, I.E. You. Let's say we don't have guns and the cartel comes knocking. You know what happens when the cartel wants you dead and you don't bother fighting back?" Gabriel took a step towards Maria. "I'm sure you remember, Maria."

There was a lengthy silence, before Maria conceded the point with a stark "Yeah. I know." Gabriel's smirk grew. It was a morose smirk. Violent. Maria's lip curled, and I saw her thumbing towards the safety selector of her new carbine in chilled anxious rage. I saw the hate in her eyes, the vindication. I knew what she was thinking. She wanted to get rid of Gabriel and the risk he brought, but she hated the Cartel enough to respect, even admire, his blatant disrespect for them. She still had a million questions, more than likely. And she certainly was lacking in trust. But she also realized how useful Gabriel was. Or, at least that was what I figured she thought, as she eased up on her gun, letting it hang from the sling.

"Jesus," Anthony remarked by the time Gabe pulled his empty duffel bag on and made his way to "check on" whatever he was going to check on, leaving us all there with nothing to do but ponder, taking his sweet time as he did. I didn't doubt Gabriel, unlike many others, and for all the knowledge my father had imparted on me, I believed him.

Mostly, I took my time resting from my restless sleep yesterday, though as I leaned against my backpack, watching the road. I saw how Lauren lay her lower body before one of the great shattered windows, her front foothands barely hanging off of the ledge and their toe-fingers flicking at the shards of glass, her cow-like ears whipping this way and that every now and then, listening, watching, waiting. She scratched at that dirty old sweatshirt she'd stole, fidgeting with her Armalite, less than content with the desolate post-chaos before her. I ought to have been as uncomfortable as her, yet I wasn't. Was it the training? The plan? Why wasn't I freaking out? Everyone else seemed just as jittery, save for Maria who stewed in her angst, watching the road too.

It was the deep afternoon by the time Gabriel came back, waltzing on up again. "Jesus, took you long enough," I uttered to him as the rest of us gathered around, seeing him there.

"Yeah, yeah. Let's go."

"...So all the drones really are dead?" I asked. Gabe nodded.

"Yup. Let's hit the road." He took a look around the room, as did I.

"...Really?"

"Yeah," He insisted, letting an air of defensiveness leak into his words. "Hey man, pretty sure about this. Trust me." I looked around again, seeing everyone suiting up. Guess they didn't need any more encouragement than that, and nobody's opinion seemed to have changed since yesterday. As far as I could tell, they were all stuck with me.

We moved slowly, almost sluggishly, emerging from the building as carefully as Gabriel intended for us to. At first, it was a little nerve-wracking, but as we moved under the cover of the burning sun of the deep afternoon, we seemed to loosen up. We moved down streets slowly, taking time in alleys and corners before moving at a brisk pace across open areas. Short-circuited drones sat here and there, like statues of death, immovable. Stains of blood and litter covered the streets, aside from the cars all littering the roadways.

"So who do you think is responsible?" I heard Anthony asking.

"Could be domestic. Could be some inter-governmental shit, World War Three." Gabriel's answer was already the same.

"...You got any predictions?" Anthony was asking again, scanning around with his MDR carbine trembling in his hastily-trained hands, fingers strumming the forend. Gabriel smirked.

"...I never trusted the fuckin' Chinese."

"But then why would the bots' rampage mode shut off like this?"

"Dunno. Guess they didn't want us to regain control of our drones, so they're all fried now."

"...Don't think it was Russians? They got mad pissed back in the '20s," Wilson put forth.

"Damn, you actually pay attention in history class?" Gabriel laughed back, and the conversation was abruptly skewered, as Lauren's wings rustled and she stammered a little bit, as we were leaving the business district and proceeding into a shopping center, dead and desolate.

"H-hey, uh," Lauren belted out quick as if to avoid being interrupted or spoken over, slowing her pace a little bit. I saw one of her rear wings reach out and poke Gabriel in the side with the thumb-like free digit of her wing, as he was closer to that limb than any of her other ones, not to mention the rifle in her hands at the moment. He, a little amused at her improvised use of the limb however subtle as it was, slowed as well with a toothy smirk towards her. "Can... Can we go in there?" She pointed to one of the clothing shops. Eyes followed to her, amid a few mindful grunts and chuckles. "I... I mean, if we're all going with Noah, we might as well get some stuff?" She gulped, unable to hide a bashful blush beneath green skin.

"...Yeah, we've all been wearing the same stuff for like, two days now," Holly piped up. Gabe looked about, before ending with me, prompting me to speak.

"Yeah, that's a good idea," I muttered, and we proceeded in a change of direction. Lauren's face grew into a withheld smile, blushing a little as we went.

"Wait, what about the security?" Maria uttered as we approached. "They've got cameras and stuff."

"Who's gonna arrest us, Maria?" Gabe spat amusedly. "You see any mall cops, you let me know."

"What about after all this is over, dumbass?" She snarled. "You think they'll just let us get away with this?" Gabe sighed.

"...Yeah, she's got a point," Wilson said. "I kinda want to avoid going to jail."

"Didn't you get arrested yesterday?" Kyle responded with snide, which was met with chuckles.

"Look, fine," Gabe muttered, as he approached the building. "Sit tight." I saw him enter, pulling on his mask, before disappearing from sight. Mere moments later, the lights flickered and he re-emerged from behind the wall. "C'mon, pussies. Security's dead."

We entered warily, though the easy-listening muzak of the store was a little calming. I watched Lauren scamper off the quickest to the women's department, and while others went about gathering clothes, I wandered about out of boredom, though I was a little intrigued with Lauren. I watched her go about to the women's underwear, selecting bra tops to hold up to herself, before deciding on a size. Given her extra large (by human standards, at least) frame, I wasn't surprised by her size choice. For her frame, she wasn't particularly well-endowed, she was just looking for something that would fit all the way around her chest and not bother her wings.

I went off to take a look anyways, watching Kyle collect muscle shirts a size too small for him, Samantha, girded in her strange ironies radiating towards the novelty men's shirts, ripping some of them in strategic points for extra irony or something before throwing them in her bag. I noted Lauren approaching from the side, shopping bag full of spoils, heading for the men's shirts as well. I saw her approach next to Kyle, who had now proceeded to the men's polos. As she began to collect a few, Kyle stopped to laugh in silence, only smirking in estranged amusement at her.

"W-what? They don't make women's shirts big enough for me," She reasoned, maybe a little embarassed. Kyle shrugged with a smile.

"It's just funny, that's all," He remarked, more cordial than I would have expected from him, as he went to take the size below what Lauren was grabbing.

"So, Green," The familiar vicious voice of Gabriel met us, and Lauren straightened up to look, most of us spread throughout the store eavesdropping despite some quiet, personal inter-conversations taking place. "they tell ya who's responsible for armageddon in those growin' chambers they pop you freaks out of?"

"I, uh…" She had little to say, awkwardly looking for a way out of the conversation other than simply stating she didn't know. Gabriel laughed before she could, knowing full well her apprehension, like she was ashamed of not knowing these things, yet knowing other things, but feeling like she should know more things than she did.

"…You know about countries?" He went on, feeling her apprehension. She paused up for a moment, though she soon continued slowly gathering garments, her wings ruffling a little bit.

"I, We're in… *the America*, right?" Gabe chuckled again, as did a few others, notably Kyle, and Lauren's ears drooped and her blush of embarrassment grew.

"Countries, not really; but how to run an AR-15, yes," Gabe chortled, mostly to himself. "Those Creators sure did have their priorities straight, huh?" He shot to me as Lauren shivered, holding her spoils close to herself, eyes darting about self-consciously. "…Don't sweat it, Green. I'm fuckin' with you." Gabe paused. "So, you got what you need?"

"I, uh…" Lauren shifted her bag a little bit, brushing up against her slung rifle. "Y-yeah. I think I got some good stuff. I… I'll need to fix them for my wings 'n stuff, but I… I think I can make do." Gabriel smirked.

"Well, we're burning moonlight. We ought to move."

We cleared out as the sun had just set, darkness falling over all. The streetlamps still worked, beaming light down eerily as we moved.

"…So…" Lauren talked soon enough again, though only to suppress her own jitters, as we passed a smouldering husk of a burned-out car. "Is… should it really be this quiet?"

"City's on lockdown. Martial law's been called," Gabe explained. "Guessing most people still think the bots are out and about."

"We haven't been seeing any cops, though," Maria mentioned back.

"Cops depended a lot on drones and a lot of tech that probably got destroyed. They're all really just hunkered in their stations, waiting for the national guard. My guess is they're fucked too."

"…This is real spooky," Anthony spoke up. "…No rioters or looters or anything?"

"Three day rule," I finally muttered as eyes and ears turned to me. "Basically, in any disaster it takes three days of starvation to get somebody worked up to the point where they get violent. If all the looters went home after the drones started shooting…"

"…They'll probably be home until tomorrow," Gabe finished.

A couple more blocks, a couple more minutes of silence, as we entered suburbia. "So…" Lauren uttered, head swiveling towards me. "Your… Your dad… You say we're going to meet him?"

"…Yup." Lauren's quiet was deafening. I saw her looking down, down to herself. Her body. She mussed with her gunbelt.

"What… What will he-" she began, stammering. She didn't quite know how to word her concerns, but I felt what she was edging towards. Her self-consciousness, the way she looked around, looking down at herself.

"He'll be good with you," I muttered. "My dad's…" I racked my brain, trying to reason a way that he'd accept her. "He's the kinda guy who's prepared for anything. If he thinks you can be useful, he'll… you know. I mean, like, really. Look, as long as I vouch for you he'll be alright. Okay?"

"Oh- Okay," Lauren stammered, though she kept looking at me with those big puppydog eyes of hers, mouth only a tiny bit slack. "Are… Are you sure?"

"Hey. Don't sweat it." I gave her a reassuring smile, trying to get her to smile back.

"Thanks, Noah, I…" She looked down, tilting her head as she looked to her front legs. "I really don't know what to say. You've been so nice to me, and I-"

"I'm just doing what I think is right, Lauren." I smiled again, and she smiled back full of warmth and belonging.

"…Fuckin' heartwarming," Gabriel smirked, as most of the rest of the group seemed rather amused, and I had to will myself to be steadfast here. I wasn't trying to seem corny or anything, and I think I meant what I said. Everybody mostly held their tongue, despite the charmed smiles. All the smiles except for Maria, whose visage simmered as she looked coldly ahead, her grip pulsing tightly around on the forend of her carbine.


There my cul-de-sac was.

My dad always talked about the virtues of a cul-de-sac in case of an event that might spell the end of peaceful society. "A cul-de-sac can be locked down and controlled much easier and safer as opposed to a through street, due to one exit and one entrance for vehicles," He used to say. I always questioned this, as I assumed his plan was to simply pack up and leave if this apocalypse ever came. "It's good to have back-ups," he always responded when I brought this up.

Almost immediately, I made note of the fact that all throughout my street, I was kicking my way through piles of fired cartridges, shells upon shells strewn along the ground. Not brass or steel cases, but plastic hulls. Upon hearing the tinkling sound beneath all our feet, Lauren froze. She quietly looked down with wide eyes, picking up a shell casing with her "fingers" of her frontal legs' foothands, raising it up and reaching down with her humanoid arm and taking the shell to bring it up to her face, looking at it like she had seen them before. I could already recognize them. "Drone ammo casings," I muttered of the rigid plastic hulls, before noting a couple burnt-out tankdrones lying in different parts of the street, shot to hell.

"Holy damn, your dad do this?" Kyle cawed, sticking his finger through a gigantic hole that had been bored through one of them, probably from my father's fifty-caliber anti-materiel rifle. Looking back, I guess it was funny, since he found a use for it after all. I always thought that gigantic sniper rifle of his was completely superfluous. Fun to shoot, though.

"Shit, where is he then? This whole place is dark," Wilson was saying as we looked upon my house. All the lights were out. I knew my dad said that keeping the lights off was a security thing. But he, or somebody should have been keeping watch and spotted us by now.

The front door was ajar at the end of the court, was my house. The façade was laid in rebar-filled cinderblock (my father's choice, of course), but the bricks were pockmarked with bulletholes. I saw a few charred blast marks about the walls, and almost every window was completely shot out. I looked to the side, the front door of my house was open, and a cold, icy feeling raced through my veins.

I began to run towards my house. "Oh, shit," I said over and over, fearing the worst.

I burst in the front door. Things were strewn about, trash covering the floor. I heard nothing but silence, as a great draft wafted through the place. "Oh, fuck," I said, taking a seat on the piano bench. My mother's family sword that usually hung there was gone from above the wall, pictures that hadn't been taken were skewed or had fallen to the floor after being rattled off from explosions. Bulletmarks pocked anywhere I looked. It was chilling.

Quietly, in determined shock, I began to search the building. The dining room table was overturned, a few bullets in various calibers strewn across the floor. Everything on the counter was overturned or broken, except the tupperware container with the lasagna from last night in it, resting there peacefully, almost comically. The pantry was open, and I saw that some food items were taken, but not much. Most of the cans were still there.

"Noah?" I heard Gabriel call out, as he entered the front door, kicking his way through the empty shell casings. I knew that my father wouldn't leave without picking up the shells- unless he was in a real hurry. Or dead. I actively prayed for the sooner of the two possibilities, as I looked about. The television-walls were relatively bullet-free, but I saw a piece of paper pinned up to the wall of the dining room written in pen, a message that made my heart rise.

*Noah,*
*I was going to wait for you, but the drones drove us off and the other Citadel members came by to pick us up. Your mother and sister are fine but I was hurt, but not bad. I know that Gabriel will make sure you make it, and I hope you are all right, as well as Maria. I offered to take the Delarochas with me to the Citadel, saying that Maria will probably be with you, but they refused saying that they'll rather wait for her. I left you your gear as well as the gear I bought for Maria that I planned to give her when she graduated, they're in the safe in the safe room, along with the keys to the Jeep. Bring as much of the leftover ammo as you can, and travel quick. Tell no one where you're going, and don't hesitate to defend yourself if you are attacked.*

*Stay safe and see you there. I love you, son.*


The last words stung like bullets. I'd hardly said hello or goodbye to my father when I left for school that morning. I growled to myself, thinking on it. I would have cried, if not for the fact that I couldn't really feel sad right now. "Tell no one where you are going." That's a laugh, too late now. Now I was carrying a team of teenage misfits, who were now gathered around me, waiting for information.

"I'm... Gonna go see if my folks are alright," Maria reasoned to me.

"Yeah. You should do that." Maria scuttled off with this, as everybody else stood there in the dining room with me. In a sort of abject silence, I turned away, walking slowly out of the room. I passed through all of them, walking with determination to the basement, down to the cold of the very corner of the cellar, stooping down to find the trapdoor to the chamber dug far below the foundation in there. I opened it, descending with nary a grunt down through the dark ladder well. Had I had my tactical holovisor, I might have been able to illuminate it with the infrared function, I thought, pondering the irony of it being down there with the rest of my gear. I descended about two floors worth of ladder, darker and darker, before my feet hit the cold, hard bedrock. I fished through the darkness for the lightbulb pull cord- an ancient little thing. My dad was old-school like that.

And with a click, there I was- the Spider Hole, the Bunker, The Quiet Room. I used to play here when I was little- it was my hideout, my temple, even if I grew to loathe what it represented as I grew older. It had a couple simple cots, and several blankets, some drinking water, and biohazard suits complete with filtration systems hanging in the closet, in case of nuclear warfare or something. I saw the big safe there- a secret, ominous thing, a black monolith that stood in the corner. There was usually gun parts all over the room- stuff that I myself would question the legality of, but they were mostly gone. I reached out for the old-fashioned crank knob there. I knew the code by heart, as the quietness of the room heard the faint clicking of the safe. A couple moments and thunk, it was open. Slowly, the creak of the safe rang out as it opened, illuminated by the light of the bulb, as I smiled a bit. Never had I ever been happier to see guns in my entire life. There it was, the Armalite rifle that was destined to be mine ever since dad picked it out for me. That vicious old thing had a 20 inch barrel, a select-fire binary trigger in there for more firepower, while skirting the law. It was adorned in beautiful walnut furniture, as if an exquisite dress- an old-school choice of furniture for a slightly less old-school weapon. It had a 2.5x combat scope atop it and a set of Tritium express secondary sights canted off to the side. My father often questioned my decision to make it look so old fashioned with the wood stock, but I think it looked a whole lot more pleasant than those aggressive black edges that other rifles had.

Hung in the next rack over was my helmet and armor plate carrier, the latest and greatest in armor plate technology, being able to deflect most full-powered armor-piercing rifle rounds, being a Level V Dynaceramid armor carapace with a force mitigation system built into the carrier, completely state of the art and a step away from being actual Exo Armor, my helmet a level III polydynamid with comms and enhanced tac goggles that came with both infrared and thermal strapped to its side rails and optic mount; my gear was lightweight enough for strenuous exercise and dissipated heat exceptionally, making wearing it in the heat of the desert bearable, and even worked to break up one's thermal profile. By all accounts, it was light-years ahead of Gabriel's simple Molle carrier, or the cheap one I currently donned, which I was in the process of doffing now, though I'm sure Gabriel's tac mask was probably comparable in terms of hardware. NOAH REED was embroidered on the front and back in patches along with my blood type and hanging on the lower chest was a six mag pouch full of 40 round STANAG magazines, as well as a two mag pouch for my sidearm's 20 round magazines next to it. I hoisted my good armor onto myself, feeling it there, rather comfortable considering the weight. After dropping my old weapon, I picked up the gun, slinging it over myself, it hanging limply over my back.

I also saw the keys to the jeep, as well as my tactical hologlasses- they were specially designed, able to deflect shrapnel, judge the distance to targets, identify armed people at 500 meters, pinpoint incoming gunfire, scan faces for signs of stress/lying, EMP-hardened, the whole works. They were only available to police and military, but my dad got his hands on some. He always does.

Lastly hanging there behind all that was my battle belt, holding more magazines, my ESEE Junglas knife on the left side in a wide kydex sheath: a little less for chopping people and a little more for chopping wood (but certainly could get the job done as it was the size of a small sword) another medical kit and holstered on the right side was a nine millimeter pistol, which I pulled out to inspect, seeing that blocky slide with the little red dot sight atop it. It was my fifth generation Glock 34, what I shot targets with generally. Little outdated, but fun. Putting it back, I unhinged that cop's utility belt to hook this one on. I looked to the gear dad had acquired for Maria, mostly more generic copies of what I had, an Armalite, some nice armor, a glock 17. I smiled to myself, figuring to give them to her later. I made another mental note: nine longarms, six pistols between all of us, and now plenty of ammo, noting the crates in the corner of the room that my dad left for us.

I climbed back up and made my way out of the basement, and those who were looking around were surprised at my emergence, if not startled by my now Operator-Tactical Super Ninja look. At any other time I would have felt self-conscious, but right now I felt the least worried since this all started. Kyle and Wilson had a quick moment to admire my new digs with a couple jokes and weird compliments, though most of the others were reading the note my dad left.

"Where is this place you're going?"

"What are you gonna do?"

"How'd your dad fight off the military drones?"

"I don't know," I answered all of them. Everyone had gathered to ask me questions, but I could answer none of them sufficiently enough. "Look- let's all discuss this tomorrow. I've got dad's jeep, so if you wanna come, you can. But if you decide to leave, you... You can still do that."

"Dude, you think my mom's got a plan for this shit?" Wilson laughed.

"Yeah, dude. We're all stuck with you," Anthony didn't laugh, his slight tinge of hopelessness shining through. After all, the way it was we had a society where parent and child were far apart- school raised you. Your friends raised you. As far as they were concerned, I was like an uncle or cousin to most of them.

I walked away quickly, heading for the front door, and then I heard Gabriel chuckle, as I passed him in the foyer. I didn't give him the satisfaction of whatever he was going to say, pulling the door open and proceeding down the street, to check on something.

### Chapter 12

Maria's house seemed like many of the other houses, quiet and closed with dim lights somewhere in with hushed voices and faces, nobody really making any noise. The electricity was still on, the streetlamps burning through the evening, as I walked full of gear, hair blowing in the stiff, lonely breeze.

I'd knocked on the door, and Mrs. Delarocha answered. She was a sweet lady, looking older than she was. She'd looked me up and down a couple times, eyes wide and full of fear. "Noah..." She said with a subtle accent, as if pondering on my name, eyes flashing. I nodded at her. "Maria... is in the dining room."

There wasn't much to say, under the burning light of their dining room lamp. A breeze wafted through the open screen door leading to the backyard, Mrs. Delarocha's flowers waving under the sunless periwinkle skies of twilight. Maria sat there at the table, across from her father- like his wife and his daughter, he was aged by sorrows far beyond his years, a solemn man always full of a quiet resolve, even reminding me of my father's similar utilitarian somberness. Maria looked down at the table on which her annexed weapon lay. Mr. Delarocha had taken a couple cursory glances at it, though now he stared right at his daughter, though his eyes shifted to me as I'd entered, glancing me over as well.

"...You really... seem to think this is happening, eh?" He mused over, voice growling, while he was leaning back in his seat. The silence hung like a weight, a pendulum that swung from person to person. With a creaking of his seat, he reached upon that weapon of Maria's on the table. "Yeah," He said. "I've seen this kind of gun, before." Maria nodded, though she was still looking down, as he flipped it over, looking about the old, cruel machine of metal within plastic. "I can remember everything about the day your brother died. Every last... detail." He flipped it over, staring at it in contemplation. "It's even the same color as the one that, that *Siña Loyalista* used. They say that the CIA sold these weapons to that cartel. Like they were their friends." A brief pause, like he was trying to find the words, if not the feeling within himself. "Had I known that America was responsible for the weapon that killed my son when I came to America, I would have kept moving, straight on to Canada." Another solemn silence, before after a long time, Mr. Delarocha addressed me, though he was still mulling over that MDR. "Your father has always been a friend to me, Mr. Reed. He's a good man." I nodded once, slowly, my arms crossed over my chest carrier. "He told me, in confidence, that there was a place he was going to. He told me that as a friend, asking us to come along."

"The Citadel, yeah."

"Yes." He paused, finally looking me in the eyes. "I don't know if he's right. That this really is it, that... the world, as we know it, is... *Changing*. I... I don't know what to believe. I guess the hybrids are proof to that, but I just don't know. What do you think, Noah?"

"...I don't know either."

"But you're going anyways?" His voice rang out.

"...Better safe than sorry," I muttered with as much conviction as I could muster alongside a nod. a smirk finally formed on his face, chuckling beneath his nod.

"...You really are your father's son," He muttered, nodding at me, as if remarking on all the gear I was sporting. Had anybody else said this at any time prior to a day ago, I think I would have been offended. I couldn't be now. Not with what was going on. It was kind of a compliment now. "My... My wife and I have discussed this already," He said. "We... We are done running, Mr. Reed."

"You're staying?" I uttered, a little confused.

"...Did you know I wasn't born in Mexico?" He uttered, after a long pause of delineation, moving past my objection. "I was... *am* Venezuelan, born in 2012. During the collapse there, when I was a young boy, I ran. I don't know what happened to my family. America may have closed the borders, but I made my way to Mexico. I never was a Mexican citizen, they could have killed me crossing that southern border, did you know that? It... It was during a monsoon. I had to crawl through a mile of mud at three in the morning just to make it to Mexico." He mulled over the rifle more. "You're the first person I've admitted this to, Mr. Reed." I could say nothing, just standing there to let this man speak his mind. "I found and wedded my wife, the mother of my son and daughter, in Mexico, but then... You know what happened." I nodded morosely. "By the grace of God we were able to make it to this country, Mr. Reed. Refugees of a neighboring war-torn country, we were some of the last allowed to emigrate." He looked back to me. "I'm done running, and my wife wants to be with me, Mr. Reed."

"W-what about Maria?" I uttered.

"...After what happened to her brother, I... I needed, I made a resolve, to keep her safe." He reached to a different object on the table, displaying his own pistol a simple, well-worn pistol, something he'd bought used in a pawn shop. He tilted the side of it up towards him, looking at the engraving in simple contemplation. "But I know your father. And I know what he taught you, Noah. You're a capable young man. Maybe... maybe even more capable than I." He paused to chuckle at nothing in particular, taking note of what I was wearing, probably. "If my daughter wants to go with you..." He mulled over it. "Then it is not my choice to make, but hers. I may be done running, but I cannot speak for Maria."

I looked to Maria, who was still looking into her hands, clasped together solemnly, almost like she was praying.

"...I need some time to think about this, Noah."


Back in my house, everybody else was gathered around the television wallscreen. "Yo, your dad's got the whole Protoblade series?" Anthony remarked. "This shit is like, vintage."

"My dad's always been big on this old japanese stuff," I answered in the affirmative, with everybody sitting back and watching it now, some expository bits happening in the movie now. "What, no news?" I turned to Gabe.

"Stations are all dead. If it's not dead, it's just emergency broadcast shit- creepy robot voice saying stay indoors, watch out for all the robots even though they all shut down yesterday, watch out for hybrids on the loose, yadda yadda. It was really scaring Green so we turned it off."

"...It was not!" Lauren protested as she sat there off to the side, before the fireplace of my house, a wing ruffling on her lower body as she eyed crossly over towards Gabe, who only smirked back. "It was just the alarm sound hurts my ears."

"...Are you making tea?" I muttered.

"Hey, be a shame to not use it, your mom had a nice collection she must've forgotten," Gabe said, snacking on an apple as he went about his brewing work. "Dang, these are some crisp suckers," he said of the apple in his opposing hand. "It's been what, two days?"

"From Maria's mom's apple tree."

"No shit? This ain't synthesized?" Gabe uttered, feigning astonishment. "Not bad. Speaking of, What's Maria doing over there anyhow?"

"...She doesn't know if she wants to come or not."

Gabe clicked his tongue. "She never struck me as indecisive."

"Her dad thinks he's making a statement, staying here. Not sure what Maria's thinking." I kind of half-expected Gabe to agree with me, as he sucked inward.

"Well, they're from a different kinda culture. Their families are more closely knit, like they actually give a shit about each other. I guess you can understand this since your dad's old-school, but the rest of us, eh. You know we're all from single- or no parent households," Gabe nodded at Lauren, who simply gulped and stared at the floor. "So it's not like she can just give her mom and pop up on a whim like everybody else. And if he didn't go when your dad offered him a ride, he ain't going," Gabriel sighed. I wanted to speak up, say "He might come with us," But I knew Maria's father well enough to know his resolve. Gabriel must have sensed this, his back stiffening up to look at me, going finally and decisively for the water boiler as it let out it's click. "Who wants chamomile?"

"I... I would," Lauren let out, raising her arm out of instinct as she called out.

"same," Kyle said. Wilson snickered.

"You drink tea, Kyle?" wilson guffawed.

"Fuck yeah, gotta stay hydrated, dude. Tea minimizes muscle atrophy."

"...Give me some too," I uttered ghostly, just sitting down at the dining room table and unslinging my AR15, placing it upon the table.

"Jeez, might need more than we got," He muttered, pouring the right amount into the tea steeper and turning to set the timer for ten minutes.

I mostly just sat there at the table, thinking. I felt the room around me, a sort of abstract feeling. Aside from the weight of armor and ammunition upon me, everything felt... The same, to be honest. Like nothing had gone wrong, *yet*. The 'yet' lingered. I knew something was wrong, undeniably. Something was so wrong with everything, at least when I thought about it all. But the more I thought, the more I found myself feeling like- everything would even at the very worst just be back to normal eventually. Gabe said that the robots were all dead, right? No, something wasn't right. Everything was... off.

"Don't you understand?" the shoddy dubbing on the telescreen uttered. "Hokuto-san, this is exactly what he wants." Swords flashed and clashed upon the screen.

"Don't give me that crap! I'm thinking clearly now, Soto! This is about more than that! This is about the world!"

"You're under his control!" More swipes of the brightly colored plasma swords onscreen.

"You know what's great about this?" Anthony jutted in, motioning forward to the movie. "The rain hits their swords and zaps off," He put forth. "It's all about those little details."

"...Where's Daniel?" I muttered to Gabriel, who was behind the counter across the room. Gabriel just motioned towards the other half of my house, the living room towards the foyer and entrance. I found him sitting alone in the quiet darkness of the living room, next to the big window of the front of the house. It was a strange, obscene place- riddled with bulletholes and shells, a bit of blood on the ground. The others avoided this room like wildfire- and, by spending a few minutes in here, I knew why. It was a statement to what we all were trying to ignore, the fact that things were changing for the worse; it made sense to ignore this room. But there Daniel was, sitting there, skritching away endlessly at his spare notebook, looking up every now and then, although I think he never saw me. He always seemed like that, omnipresent yet absent minded, observant yet oblivious.

"You didn't want to watch the movie?" I uttered.

"Seen it already," he said, looking up slowly. Despite his words, he seemed to be in a slightly better mood than usual from the weak smile on his face.

"What'cha drawing?" I asked, motioning to his spare notebook.

"This room," he said. "I mean, it looks kinda cool. With all the, you know," He motioned to the mess.

"Can I see?" I asked. He hesitated.

"I'm not too good with isometrics," He said quietly. "This is just practice."

"Can't be that bad," I said with a reassuring smile, motioning at his notebook. It was pretty basic, in black-and-white obviously, but he had just started on it so I couldn't blame him. "Better than I could do," I said, and he smiled shyly. I got up to go upstairs and get him his other notebook. The lights came on as I entered my room, automatically sensing me. I went to my holodesk, wanting to sit down and take a look on the net, but I was more preoccupied with the task at hand, picking up Daniel's notebook, exactly where I'd left it. I wonder if he'd be mad that I'd taken it? I mean, I picked it up to give back to him, right?

With it tucked in my hands, I heard a knocking at my door. A little startled, I reciprocated a "come in", gazing over.

The door creaked open, doorknob firmly grasped by a green hand. Lauren stooped down a little as she stuck her humanoid half through the door in a wave, as if to get confirmation to come in. "Hey, Lauren," I said as she walked through, though one of her horns clipped the top of the doorframe despite how she'd stooped.

"Ow- Hey, Noah," She said, coming in and having a look around. "H-hey, is this your room?"

"Yup." we shared a little awkward silence as she looked around, and I tucked the notebook under my forearm in my hand.

"...It's really nice. I totally wish I could, like, have had a room like this. With like, stuff. And furniture," one of her hands reached out to touch the corner of the desk. "I mean like, chairs, not really, since I come with my own," She let out a little awkward, hushed 'heh' with a backward swipe of an arm, motioning crudely. I found it endearing enough, smiling up at her.

"Uh, yeah. thanks," I uttered. She gave a little hesitant smile back. "You're not watching the movie?"

"...Oh, it made me a little squeamish," She muttered.

"Oh yeah, that must've been that part where a guy gets sliced in half," I muttered, a little amused. "I must've watched that when I was little and I got really grossed out."

"Heh, yeah," Lauren said, looking off into the corner, though her face was lowered, an arm raised to scratch the back of her head, where one of her two horns met her scalp, through her brunette mane of hair.

"...So what's up? Just looking around?" I asked cordially, leaning against my desk.

"I, uh... I was wondering if I can... Take a shower. In your bathroom. Or like- not in *your* bathroom, but, like, a bathroom here. Your house. I'm just... I dunno. I don't think I've ever, like, you know, had one, but I'm pretty sure I know how to *do* one. Right?" I couldn't help but smirk at how charming this simple request is.

"Yeah, sure," I said. "Just don't make a mess, okay?"

"I dunno, you seen what I'm working with?" She attempted a meager smile, motioning back to the rest of her body. "You see what they stuck me in? I'm a walking disaster with this many limbs. I always feel like I'm just gonna knock everything over." It was weird, like she was trying to drum up sympathy despite how she pretended to joke.

"It's okay. Can't possibly make too big a mess," I said, and she looked down, letting out a little chuckle that was sadder than it should have been, as she scratched an arm with the opposing one, staring down at her frontal foothands again.

"I'm... Can I ask you a question, Noah?" She uttered, and this should have really tipped me off to something, my smile disappearing into seriousness quickly. What was the issue? I really wasn't expecting what she was about to ask, and I'm not sure that was a good thing. "Uh... Look, I know some things, right? Like they put stuff in my brain. Like... I'm just wondering, that, uh..." She muttered to herself for a second or two, before those big brown eyes of hers came up to stare into me as she found the right words, the tips of her cheeks forming just the tiniest blush over what she figured to be a horribly phrased question, gasping outwardly as she spoke. "You and Maria, are like, girlfriend and boyfriend, right?" I slowly nodded, though something within me became perturbed at this topic and all its ramifications, especially seeing her blushing as subtly as she was, in her own awkward embarrassment at the time. But I almost felt a distinctly different feeling radiating from her.

"Yeah, we are," I answered in the affirmative. Lauren's eyes darted away from me then back to me in contemplation, her hands coming together, as if to fidget with one another, all her many wings ruffling.

"Like, this is a weird question, but like, when I hear those words, like I get an idea of, like, Kyle and Holly. But you two don't really... Act like girlfriend and boyfriend. Like, do I have the wrong definition of the word? Was I wrongly, uh, programmed or-"

"Me and Maria are... Yeah, we are, though," I uttered defensively. I didn't know what to say. I would have been insulted, matter of fact I kind of felt like I was at this point.

"Like... How?" She asked, and I sighed, leaning back and now racking my brain. We'd always had a... thing for each other, right? Go with that, I thought.

"Maria and I go way back, Lauren. We're... we... Ever since she moved in behind my house, we've always hung out and stuff. We just kinda- our love is more... laid back, you know?"

"Have you ever had sex?" practically spilled from her mouth, and had I been drinking anything, I would have undoubtedly spit it out. I blinked a little, as if doing a double take. "Oh, shit," Lauren gasped out as her hands came up to her muzzle, her green cheeks filled with much, much more red than before. "Oh, that's- God, that's a *really* personal question, isn't it?"

"Y...Yeah, Lauren, that's kind of... Y-you don't just ask..." It was like in a moment, as my brain swam through the masked judgement of Lauren, my own self-judgement bit down upon me and I was given pause, enough pause to need to justify myself. "Look, not all love needs to look like Kyle and Holly. They're... more physical."

"And... okay." I feel like Lauren wanted to prod further, ask why Maria and I weren't that physical, but her staunch embarrassment reined her in. "...S-sorry, Noah, I just- Ugh. I'm such an idiot," Lauren muttered with a hand on her forehead, one of her ears whipping a strand of hair away. "I'm... I'm gonna go take that shower and think about things, alright?"

"...Yeah. You do that," and with that she ducked away.

I walked back downstairs in a semi-daze, finding Daniel in his same spot, skritching away. I approached him, shaking Lauren's words from my head. I outstretched my arm, the notebook inches from his face. His eyes carried his head up, slowly, before they widened enough to the point of realization, and he practically snapped it away from me, though he paused as soon as it left my hand, looking down.

"You... you looked?" He asked, speaking as if a big sock was lumped in his throat, fingers strumming through pages.

"Yeah. I... I skimmed." His eyes, full of hesitant wariness, darted down. "...I think you're a... Good artist."

"Really think so?" he said tentatively, shifting uncomfortably in his seat. I don't think he believed me. "...Dunno if you're into my... my style."

"I swear," I said, with a laugh to ease tensions. He looked down. I sighed, as I heard him flipping through the notebook, semi-distressedly. His eyeballs shot up at me, as if looking for something to let him mistrust me. "Hey, you should be lucky that I snagged it, and not somebody else, like Kyle," I reasoned, and his pupils dilated in a sort of terrified realization, as he looked back up at me, still angry, but knowing I had a point.

"Thanks," he said coldly. I sighed again, looking over the room.

"Why all the notebooks? You've got a tablet," I asked, my curiosity getting the better of me.

"I like pencil. I feel it's more my style. I grew up with it, anyways."

"Really?" I asked.

"...My parents were drifters. Never had much money for buying electronics. I sketched in notebooks, they were cheap. As soon as I got enrolled around here for middle school, they gave me a tablet, but I still use this. I like it more." He looked up at me. As if on a dial, his hostility was gone. I turned to leave, back into the den with everybody else, but I felt a question linger, a misguided hope, perhaps? Something that I needed to hear.

"Hey, uh… Danny," I muttered. His head came up again, to look at me. "What do you think of Lauren?"

"She's… nice."

"Yeah?" I uttered. "…Nice?"

"Yeah, Noah. She's nice." My eyes flashed down to his notebook, as if to imply something. "Look, Noah. I'm not gonna… be *weird*, alright?" He muttered defensively and gripped his sketchbooks, before uttering "She's not even my type."

"W-what?"

"I just- she's not the kind of *person* that I'm into, Noah. She's- You don't have anything to worry about." I know what he meant by this, but I think I interpreted it wholly different than it was.

"…Don't have anything to worry about?" I asked, as if to confirm.

"Yeah, Noah. I'm not going to be weird, or creepy, or whatever. I won't make things awkward because I'm not into her."

Not into her? I didn't believe that. I wanted to call him out, but I found the words frozen in my chest. "Uh-okay," I uttered, drifting back into the den to watch the rest of the movie and take my mind off things. Off of everything, where things were simple.

But it gnawed at me that they weren't.

### Chapter 13

Waking up, things felt normal, if only for a couple quick seconds. In those quick, fleeting moments of oblivion between awakening and becoming conscious, where I could feel the world being as whole as it had ever been, until lucid memories flooded and the walls of my dreamlike, drowsy state fell one by one until I had to sit up.

I dragged myself out of bed, looking down at myself in nothing but my johns. I could appreciate my physique and toned body, maybe out of some vanity flexing for myself, knowing that my strength and fitness from years of track would come in handy with a smirk on my face. I turned to my ballistic cuirass hanging on the headboard of my bed by the shoulder strap, rifle leaned up nearby, my gunbelt on my desk. I dressed myself, mind swimming in recollection. I made a move towards my armor in contemplation before I decided to settle on just the belt for now.

I walked downstairs, seeing Maria in the living room. She'd gotten up early enough it seems, seeing most everybody else just waking up, if at that. She was enjoying, or at least trying to enjoy a cup of tea.

"…So what's your decision?" I muttered out, fishing through for some cereal, grabbing a bowl and a carton of synthmilk.

"…I'm still not really sure," She said to me, sitting there and staring at the wall.

"…How about your dad?"

"I think he's just really attached to that house." She sighed to lean back a little, her chair creaking a bit as she postulated. "I think it's the first real place that he's really felt safe in. He thinks that leaving would mean it isn't, and he doesn't want to have to run again." Maria sighed. "Well, it'll be good to have somebody staying here to watch our places, right?"

"Y-yeah." It was a while before I spoke again, just swimming through my thoughts. "Hey, uh," I muttered, sitting down as I poured my cereal and was some ways through breakfast. "So my dad got you some stuff. Gear." Maria's eyes followed me as I spoke, eating my cereal, and a smirk grew on her face, sort of like she'd expected this.

"Our parents always liked each other," She muttered with a laugh. "My dad never was big on guns, but your dad kinda convinced him. Kinda like how your dad would take the two of us shooting and got me into them. Funny right?" She smirked, almost just for herself. "So what, he got me my own gun?"

"It's… He got you an armor set, an AR15 and a Glock. They're down in the spiderhole. Safe should still be unlocked, I think." Maria nodded, though her eyes wandered.

"Yeah. Thanks." I seemed to sit there for a long time, the others rising up. As Maria made her way to the basement door, she pulled it open, surprised to see Lauren there, the basement being where Lauren settled down in for the night, with solitude from everybody else.

"Oh, hi Maria," She uttered, a little smile on her face, doing her best to be cheerful this morning.

"Hey," Maria grumbled halfheartedly, squeezing by her in the basement stairwell, despite how Lauren had stepped to the side a little. Lauren emerged from the basement, and I took a good look at her from where I sat.

"Thanks for letting me borrow your dad's shirts," She uttered of the black polo she was wearing, though it had been modified for her wings like all the rest of her shirts, of course. "Couldn't really fit into your… Your mom's stuff. Sorry about cutting them up, too."

"Don't worry. My dad would just appreciate that you found a use for it." I paused to let her look over her own tailor work. My father, who had always been a large man, seemed to wear a size under Lauren's, which was unfortunate for her, but it made me really realize and appreciate how big she was. It wasn't just her lower body that was big, she really earned her height. "…He's that kinda guy. The only disgrace is that which goes unused," I recited with waves of my spoon.

"Huh," Lauren muttered. "That's a… nice catchphrase."

"Yeah. He has a lot of those." I ate the last of my cereal, as Lauren stepped up from the passageway she stood in, brushing a strand of hair from where it hung on her horn and laying her lower body down upon the ground at the table, as if taking a seat beside me, coming to sitting height.

"So… The guy in that photo on the wall?" She motioned to the family photo that hung. "That's him?"

"Yup." Lauren crossed her arms on the table, to place her chin down upon her arms, eyes shining upwards in contemplation.

"…Nice family."

"Thanks."

Lauren giggled at our little awkward reparté, turning her head to look at me. "...I, uh, thanked you for saving my life, right?"

"Yeah, you did." She smiled a little more, looking off again.

"Well… Thanks again. It means a lot to me. Like, a lot lot. Since, you know. I'd be dead. And then I couldn't-"

"Oh damn, am I too late?" Gabriel burst in from the front door, interrupting Lauren's rambling, probably to her relief, as her face had been getting ever so slightly redder as she'd babbled. "Y'all having breakfast already? Ugh. I make some good-ass eggs," He stopped at the table, dropping his duffel bag, before going to wash his hands in the kitchen.

"Ooh! I want some!" Lauren perked right up, straightening up, her ears shooting up into the air.

"Gabriel, what the hell were *you* doing?" I uttered, getting up to pour my cereal milk down the drain, but stopping before it and figuring it'd be a waste, chugging it down instead.

"The usual, got more of my stuff; grabbed something we could use for the cop AR-15s," Gabriel uttered, reaching into his bag and pulling out a little cylinder-y object. "Yo Green, happy birthday, here's yours," He tossed it and Lauren fumbled in surprise, grasping the can before looking at it intently.

"Uh… Oh, birthday, that's a joke," She snapped back with her free hand, observing. "Oh, a silencer!" She remarked, and I coughed, gagging on the milk from my bowl, slamming my bowl down.

"Jesus Gabe!" I shot, wiping my face off before going over towards Lauren.

"I know, right? She knows what a suppressor is," Gabe remarked as I snatched it out of her green hands maybe only a tad too zealously.

"You know these are illegal?!" I shot, practically waving it back at him. I saw him eye me with growing antagonism, shifting his stance only a tad to let his weapon, which was converted back into an integrally suppressed carbine, shift about as if subtly displaying it.

"...You do remember you shot a hobo in the face with a hacked police handgun, right?" I sighed, looking at it, biting my lip. I looked back to Lauren, passing it to her and she took it, holding onto it like a little token of goodwill. "...Point is those shorty AR's are a bitch on the ears, even if she can spin hers around. Y'all want some eggs or not?"

"...Do you ever sleep?" I held the bridge of my nose, far past exasperation by this point as he went around to the kitchen, figuring out my stove before going to the fridge.

"Oh yeah, when I practice being dead. Loads of fun but gets old after an hour or two." I never really got Gabriel's humor, even now, a subtly flabbergasted look on my face. "Anyone else want some?" He held aloft the box of eggs.

"Shit, make me some too," Kyle said as he rose from where he slept on the couch, awoken from the ruckus. "Hold the yolk."

"How do you like yours, Green?" Gabriel asked, letting her answer by pausing hard, Lauren's face scrunching up a tad as she thought, tapping on her little gift.

"Uh… scrambled. Kinda raw… I think that's how I like 'em." Gabriel laughed back, not out of spite but rather simply to get her to loosen up, smiling back.

"Good choice. Comin' right up," Gabriel turned to toil at the task.

"...So you're being nice to Lauren now?" I murmured, approaching close as the rest of them spread out some.

"...I've always been chill with Green. She knows a gun from a stick on the ground, that puts her above Daniel, Samantha, and Holly as far as I'm concerned."

"Fuck you, dude, that's my girl you're dissing," Kyle grumbled, hearing-distance away with that stupid smile of his.

"Recoil would put her on her ass, Kyle. You need to feed her before she blows away on the breeze." I got up, leaving the others as they gathered around, waiting for Gabriel to make breakfast. I proceeded upstairs into the bathroom to freshen up, brushing my teeth. I looked around, noticing how clean the place was- Lauren really tidied the place up, the shower all clean and neat. I noticed another toothbrush there, recently unwrapped. It was one of those cheap ones that the dentist always gave you that I never used, since mine was electronic, but Lauren had apparently opened it up- especially since she'd left me a note on a little piece of paper, which I picked up to read.

*Hey Noah,*
*I borrowed one of the other toothbrushes that was just laying there in the packaging, some of your toothpaste, and some floss. I hope you don't mind! :)*
*-Lauren*

I let out a little "hm" as I noted this, brushing away. She had good handwriting, and she was evidently hygienic to a fault. Smiley face was charming, too. After finishing I picked up the little note, folding it up and shoving it in my pocket. It was charming enough to keep with me, and I should tell her it was alright. It also reminded me to bring all those complimentary dentist swag bags with us; my dad probably never threw them out for some similar reason. I walked downstairs after freshening up, Gabriel was serving breakfast, but I heard some commotion from my mother's office room. I peeked in, seeing Lauren there before the seamstress tools, quietly toiling away and refining her previous works, carefully cutting and measuring and sewing, apparently something else she just knew how to do. I saw the measurements she'd made, a little impressed by her resolve- I also noted she was wearing nothing but her underwear, one of those E-cup bra tops she'd salvaged. I kind of felt weird seeing her like that, the brastrap connecting above the top edge of her wings where they met her back, somewhat strung up on them. I quietly edged back out before she could notice I'd peeped on her.

I made my way back after some delineation into the garage. I was hoping the jeep was in good condition, despite the little battle in my front yard and some of the bulletholes in the garage door peeking light through. I saw the jeep as I advanced toward it, looking it over, it's hardened engine block, bulletproof doors and windows, raised suspension, biodiesel engine. EMP hardening, something I was thankful for, and was a stick shift, which I was a little less thankful for.

"So," Gabriel's voice followed me soon enough, causing me to straighten out with the realization I wasn't alone. "Why'd you mess up an AR with such shitty furniture?" Gabriel jabbed, critiquing my weapon.

"...What's wrong with wood?" I muttered.

"Shoot to many rounds and that sucker catches on fire."

"...I don't think I'll be shooting *that* many bullets."

You seem to certainly be carrying enough on the armor of yours. You've even got extra on your belt," He muttered with a smirk as he walked around me, looking my gear up and down. I went to sit in the jeep's cockpit, putting the ignition on to check the amount of fuel. It was full, and there was a full jerrycan of biodiesel strapped on the back.

"...I like wood," I uttered. "Why would you mess up a perfectly good gun with some ugly plastic?"

"You should get with the times, grandpa," Gabriel said. "Wood ain't practical."

"It looks nice. I like it."

"It adds weight."

"Oh? And the two flashlights on yours doesn't?"

"Just one of them is a flashlight. The other is an IR illuminator. It's useful."

"Yeah, if you need to tell a ghost story," I responded, beginning to smile. This felt actually kind of relieving- we were bantering to each other like in the good ol' days, and things felt normal, just for a second.

"Why the 20 incher?" He asked.

"Less blast, less recoil, makes the bullet go faster. Dad told me it was a good idea, anyways. Fifty-five grain rounds out of a 20 inch barrel will blow holes in cheap steel body armor. You know, like you're wearing," I smirked.

"Yeah, but have fun having *your* fancy armor stop more than a single digit's worth of shots."

"You get what you pay for, dude," I smirked. "...But the thing is, I think that if you're making a rifle, you should make a *rifle*. 20 inch barrel is a *rifle* barrel."

"Sure, it is, in *1960*," Gabe responded sarcastically, as I continued to check the jeep, walking about the outside of it. It was relatively bullet-free, thankfully, despite the garage door riddled with holes. Whatever bullets had struck it had bounced off of the ballistic carapace. "Don't you know munitions technology has gotten to the point where you don't need that much barrel?"

"This gun wasn't made to shoot match grade ten-bucks-a-shot stuff. This way any 5.56 I put through it is good."

"Fair enough, now what's with that fancy butter knife you got?" He asked of my hunting knife, on my battle belt.

"Why you hatin' on the Junglas?" I shot back. "Just because you can't afford one," I said, pointing to the black Ka-Bar Tanto strapped on his leg.

"Good on you for paying 1000 dollars for a piece of flat metal," He responded.

"Oh, what? You think that your Ka-Bar's better than a ESEE?"

"I got mine to chop people, not firewood," He responded.

I just chuckled. "This ain't Iwo Jima."

"Yeah, yeah. It's a *modernized* Ka-Bar. And this is more than enough." We didn't have that much to say as I leaned against the car, checking everything. Just banter. But I felt like I could darken the conversation a tad.

"So your gun," I began, my smile fading a bit. "CIA gave Sinaloa those, right?"

"Yup. Not my pistol though," He said, drawing his sidearm from the holster on his armor, displaying it. It looked much unlike anything else I'd ever seen. "Bren-10. Ten millimeter. Right load will punch through soft armor."

"...you got spare mags for it?" Gabe shrugged.

"I brought enough. I know your dad's not a fan of the ten so I have my own supply." I frowned to myself, wondering under what context Gabriel learned this about my father. "Anyways, was my grandpa's gun. This is a pretty rare gun, you know. Worth twenty thousand dollars, probs. I figure it's the one good thing I got out of my family." He paused to look at it, a morose smirk on his face.

"But your rifle was Sinaloa? It any good?"

Gabriel shoved his sidearm back into the kydex holster of his armor with a scrape of plastic. "Gets the work done. Not that bad, considering. Probably the best thing I got out of them before I skedaddled."

"Yeah, about that. How do you feel now that a massive crime organization, the biggest in the world, wants your head on a stake for fucking with them?"

"Hasty. We should leave soon," he shot back. I couldn't really disagree with that.

"We leave tomorrow. Maria needs time to decide."

"Yeah, sure. Just as long as you know what you're doing."

"I do, and we're not leaving until I say so." Upon saying this, I felt something inside me stir. I had the sinking feeling that this might be the last time I saw this old house. I really just figured that everything would go back to normal, but something sat wrong with me. I wanted to stay, to smell the familiar scent of my house one last time, which now smelled more like sulfur from all the gunpowder, to see the great plains of the desert and the shimmering solar fields in the distance, like I had all my life. I didn't want things to change, and I think Gabriel saw this.

"Sure, whatever," Gabriel said, seeing this sparkle in my eyes. "Just don't stay too long. We need to catch up with your dad."

We walked back inside, just at the same time that Lauren peeked out from the door, holding a plate and fork in her hands, her work finished, wearing it currently. "Thanks for the eggs, Gabe," She said to him. "Sorry I couldn't eat in the dining room, with the rest of 'em. I wanted to finish my shirts."

"I'm sure they don't mind." She slowly turned, trotting in place, like a fashion model mixed with a show pony.

"What do you think?" She asked of us, with a big smile, turning her upper body this way and that to display her modifications. "See my gunbelt too?" She picked up a frontal leg, displaying the straps around the pits of her forelegs. "I put straps on it around my legs so it stays in place. I- I set it up backwards, with the buckle in the back and having it below my upper wings, so that I can just put them on by stepping into them and pulling them up. I think next I'm gonna put bandoliers on the leg straps."

"Nice job," I remarked. "You... You've got a knack for seamstressing."

"You really think so?" She said, smiling with a sparkle in her eyes. I guess I found this charming enough to laugh a little, in an endearing manner. "I think it's fun, and I'd like to get good at it."

"Y-yeah! You, you should," I responded, doing my best to be supportive, and she beamed. "You know what," I put forth, stopping to address her more seriously now, to try and let her know I meant what I was saying. "You can bring the sewing stuff along to the Citadel. I think my dad would like it back anyways." Lauren practically squealed in adulation, and I beamed back, her enthusiasm contagious. With her happily trotting along alongside me, I turned, seeing Gabriel had already walked on ahead, as Lauren and I walked close to each other. She was humming, in a very, very good mood now that seemed impossible to sully.

We passed into the living room, with Lauren proceeding on to the kitchen to put her platter down before advancing ahead towards the backdoor. "I gotta go test how well this fits when I fly, I'll be right back," She said to me as she exited. I watched her proceed out there, before taking a couple rapid running steps to leap up and jump off the fence dividing the pool area from the garden of my backyard, a blast of air visibly kicked up as she darted upwards and out of sight.

"Man, it's freaky seeing something that big just start flying," Maria grunted behind me. I turned, seeing her geared out in a helmet and carapace with a 20" AR-15, like mine but minus the wood and other personal touches. I saw her adjusting her shoulder strap with a stern look, cinching it up just right. Maria Delarocha along with her blood type was emblazoned on the upper portion of her chest piece, and I wondered under what circumstances my father learned her blood type. She didn't seem to question it, though.

"How's it feel?" I asked.

"Not as comfy as the police vest, but a lot more protective." She breathed in and out to make sure she'd adjusted it with enough slack for a deep breath. "Dunno if it feels like I could take on the world. Sinaloa, maybe. Putting a few holes in their *sicarios* would do me some good, probably." She let out a little chuckle.

"You like the rifle?" I asked.

"Reminds me a lot less of when Martín died. Yeah." I didn't say anything towards this somber reminder. "I'm used to an AR-15 like yours, anyways," She said, recalling our sessions at the gun range back before all this, at the behest of my father. She pulled her helmet off, letting the multicam cranial carapace rest on the table, playing with the nightvision oculars a little, before her hand found her glock, again pretty much like mine, yet minus the wear of use; it looked brand-new. "Good thing your father was so paranoid, huh?" She said looking it over, operating the green laser/light module under the barrel to check it, before racking the slide open, inspecting the magazine chock full of 20 double-overpressured nine millimeter cartridges. "You know, though I've never been big on weapons... It's always felt damn good," She mused in contemplation, before letting the slide of her sidearm slam home. "...Being on the right side of a gun."

"Looks like Noah's dad really did rub off on you," Gabe spoke as he eavesdropped, the both of us looking over to him as he leaned on the countertop. A smirk formed on Maria's face.

"Yeah. I guess he did." She sighed again, leaning against the table, as Lauren landed in the backyard again, dust kicked up moments before she came into view, practically bouncing across the ground as she literally hit the ground running. I saw her smiling face shine over to us inside with her wings ruffling themselves into a folded position behind her, and she walked up to the back door and pulled it open, stooping down a little as she walked in. She was panting a little, barely winded, more exhilarated.

"Oh, hey Maria," She uttered. "Nice... Armor."

"Thanks." Maria's glock was shoved rather expediently back into it's kydex holster on her belt.

"You know what?" Lauren looked to me. "I should design armor for me, you know? That'd, that would be good," She said with cursory glances around the room as if to garner support for the idea, hooking her thumbs into her pistol belt to rest her arms.

"Hey, what's it like to fly?" Samantha was asking, as she was on the couch, enjoying her breakfast with an old japanese comic book, one of the vintage ones from my dad's collection. I was rather amused by her use out of it.

"Oh, it's great," Lauren gushed. "I- I could show you,"

"No thanks, it would freak me out," Sam said.

"It sounds like enough fun," I uttered, trying to keep the ball rolling. Lauren smiled to me.

"Oh, I-" Her eyes twitched off to the side, towards Maria. I could see Maria facing her, probably causing her verbal stumble. "I mean, I can show you if you want."

"You want to take my boyfriend up in the air, huh?" Maria's voice went from calm to razored indignance, hissing. Lauren stammered for real this time, like hitting a brick wall, a little shocked and scared at her tone. "...Fly around?"

"I, I mean... I- I don't *want* to, like, s-so much as..."

"As what, huh?" I heard a solemn rage building in the back of Maria's throat. I reached over to hold her shoulder.

"Hey, hey. It's okay, Maria. I don't feel like... flying."

"I swear to god, you so much as touch Noah..." Maria grunted to cut herself off, her finger raised like a dagger, Lauren practically backing off in her step, hands raised a little, eyes wide in concern.

"Jesus, what's wrong, Maria?" I uttered, somewhat concerned. Maria turned to me.

"I don't trust this lizard, Noah. You hear me?" Maria snapped at me. "I don't care if you do. I don't care if Gabe does."

"W-what did I ever do to you?" Lauren's voice rose. Her smile had since faded, eyes sparkling, face turned down in dejection.

"God, shut up, lizard bitch!"

"I'm... I'm not a lizard!" Lauren's resolve tightened with her fists, probably to keep herself from tears, her brow furrowing and her lips curling despite her frown. "You're crazy! I'm nothing but nice to you! Noah?! Gabe?! Are you gonna let her treat me like this?!"

"I'm sitting this one out dude," Gabe snarked, and before I could input, Maria roared into me.

"Noah, who's more important to you, huh?!" Maria was facing me still, as a hand shoved my shoulder. "Me, or that *thing?!*"

"Call me a *thing* again, you *bitch!*"

"Maria, just calm down, okay?" I spat.

"*Hija*. You're being irrational."

The room grew quiet from a voice that was aged beyond any adolescent here. As the silence fell, I could look around to see everybody had gathered to watch the fight, before this interruption. Eyes and heads turned now, to see, leading from the front door, Mr. Delarocha, bags of food that he'd brought for all of us, apparently, in his hands. Maria whirled around, seeing him standing there, sullen. He sighed, his feet carrying him morosely through the little crowd, between Maria and Lauren and to the table, where he lay the foodstuffs. Like he was now ready to address the giant green dragon in the room, his head turned to Lauren, giving her a thorough once-over before stepping back, so he could see the both of them, crossing his arms on his barrel chest. "A hybrid, huh?" He uttered, eyeing her with a steely vision. Lauren swallowed what was left of her raging nerves, to speak.

"Y...Yeah. I'm... I'm Lauren."

"That's a nice name. It's nice to meet you." He stuck out his hand, and she, trembling ever so slightly, took it, and he shook that big limp limb. Her hand was practically as big as his. With it still in his enlarged, work-worn paw, he turned to his daughter, who was now standing, practically at attention, brow still viciously daggered downward with a frown to match, despite how she looked at nothing but the floor now. His head swiveled back to Lauren one more time to speak. "I've never met a hybrid before, miss Lauren. You really are something special."

"I... I guess- Thank you, sir."

"Maria." He'd turned back, releasing Lauren's hand. "Perhaps if you have a problem with Lauren, you should discuss it with her like an adult."

"...You're right. I was being irrational. I don't have a problem with Lauren." Mr. Delarocha straightened up as he reared back, to sigh to himself.

"I came here to see if I could... trust these people with my daughter," He muttered like a statue, half to me, with his eyes scanning the room, holding each gaze for a brief moment before moving to the next pair of eyes, ending with and lingering upon Gabriel who leaned there, checking his nails feigning disinterest like he always did. "It seems like it's the other way around."

"I'm sorry, papa."

"I'm not the one you should be apologizing to." I saw his face, it was full of a controlled fire that, had he been looking at me, my gaze surely would have faltered.

Maria's head came up. I saw her swallow her resolve, looking to Lauren. "I'm sorry," She said with an iron face. "I've just got a lot on my mind right now." Lauren's head bobbed in a nod, and that was that.

### Chapter 14

"...Thanks for helping me load this stuff, Lauren," I uttered as the two of us positioned the water, our 88 gallon drum onto the back of the jeep after a heavy grunt and heave.

"No problem," She responded back. She seemed cheery, despite Maria's snapping at her. I looked her in the face, seeing that look of hers, that hesitance to give in to happiness out of fear of it vanishing. How she smirked rather than smile. Smiling for me when she saw me watching her, rather than smiling for herself. "I don't want to be a burden."

"You're not," I said, maybe just to get her more comfortable. Break that shell of hers. She looked down and away, scratching a little bit at her abdomen with a hand.

"A-anything else, Noah?" She put forth, looking back up to me.

"I think that's about all of it," I uttered, looking around. "Hey, uh… Look," I began. It must have been how she acted, how I felt sorry for her in a way. "Look, you… I'm sorry about Maria," I uttered. "I think she's kind of… Stressed out about all this. She… Doesn't really like to show it so much. She doesn't like asking for help, y'know." Lauren said nothing, looking up at me from how she bowed her head, despite her height. Kind of funny, like how she wished herself smaller, more petite. "Look, Lauren, I might be going out on a limb here but I want you to know that we… That *I'm* in this for you, Lauren. I'm not going to abandon you." I began with a far more neutral we, but I felt that putting my own stakes in this would make this more effective, so I corrected myself. To stake my claim here, to make her feel wanted once and for all.

"J-jeez Noah," She began, going to look away from me, scratching the back of her head, just below where one of her horns jutted out. "Y-you d-don't-" I reached in, grabbing her hanging hand and grasping it in mine.

"Don't play this off, Lauren," I declared, and her eyes came back to me, wide and practically flabbergasted. "Do you think that we would leave you? Abandon you, after all this?" I was very nearly impatient with her mental armor, the walls she'd put up. Maybe she'd been built with them. Preprogrammed to fear rejection, to resist softening up. Maybe it was just seeing this world for the first time, the horrible fear of loneliness that taught her to armor herself in such a short time, expecting that crushing lonliness again. "Lauren, I want you to know that no matter what anybody else says, I appreciate you as a *person* and as a friend. You're with us now. Alright?" I locked eyes with her, staring into her soul. She paused. I saw her eyes twinkling. Tearing up. Jaw going a little slack, lip trembling.

I came up and hugged her before the dam fell, and her eyes began to pour. It was a little awkward, how she was so much taller than I, but I knew in that moment that I had to do this, do this for her. Be there, be a comfort. "Hey. Hey. I'm here. It's alright."

"I… I just…" She was fighting back sobs. "I…"

"Shhh, hey. It's alright."

"…Why am I crying?" She uttered in a whisper, as her arms were down over my back, crossed so she could barely reach the small of my back. She stooped down a bit so I could hear. "I'm… Not sad…"

"You're just overwhelmed. That's all."

It was a lot of things. It must have been some blast of relief, some terrifying futures she'd been envisioning ever since I'd met her vanishing into thin air. All that horrible uncertainty, melted away. I knew I had to be resolved, for her. She didn't deserve to feel so afraid, I had the responsibility to do this and I did it willingly. I guess I mostly felt sorry for her, and that was where this all stemmed. She finally slid, falling to a laying position with her lower half, like a dog laying down, though her humanoid portion was upright as I held her, now shorter than me, almost like a child as she dampened my shirt with tears.

"…Man, f-fuck emotions," Lauren gasped out between sobs. I saw her smile return, gazing up to me. She looked like shit now, all her grace she'd maintained now torn asunder by a minute of tears, eyes red, nostrils running. She sniffed, rubbing her face with a sleeve, and I was so charmed I lent a corner of my shirt to wipe away a tear as she sniffed, staring up at me. There it was, her genuine smile. Overjoyed. Knowing she belonged, that fear buried. Maybe not buried deep, but buried nonetheless.

"They're a trip, aren't they?" I responded while wiping her face. She let out a breathless laugh, an ugly laugh, a laugh without makeup. A laugh to laugh back at, so I did. "...I'm here for you, Lauren. Don't forget that."

"...A-alright," she uttered, finally releasing me. I noticed for once, how while we embraced, her wings had slowly crept their way around me, in some sort of double-layered hug. It was charming more than anything, whimsical, straight out of a fantasy painting. I let her go as well, taking a step back, as she stared down at her forelegs, still laying there. I put a hand forward, a little knuckle of my index finger, going to raise the chin of her muzzle back up to me.

"...Don't you forget it," I said sternly, almost like an in-joke. She laughed another breathless laugh again, breaking eye contact again to gaze off to the side, before looking back at me with those big brown eyes of hers. God, how surprisingly charming she could be, even like this. A week ago I never would have seen myself comforting a hybrid like I would a human. Like I would a true friend. One hell of a human analog. "I'm gonna go and check on some stuff, alright?"

"I'm... I'm gonna stay here for a while," Lauren responded, tapping the ground a little bit with the claw of her foreleg. "Until my eyes aren't so washed out." I chuckled once.

"That's alright," I said, moving for the door. "Take your time, Lauren. Just remember, you're my friend. You... mean something to us. To me." It felt like the right thing to say.

I shut the door behind me to give her some privacy, going into the kitchen. Gabriel, Maria and her parents were there, preparing some food for the road. Endearing, practically. I was charmed with how Gabe was always wearing his body armor, no matter what. The apron over it just made it funnier.

"...Debo proclamar," Gabriel was belting off as I walked in, big smiles all around, save for Maria's reserved smirk. "Tamales son la comida Mexicana más portátil."

"Oh, Noah! I never knew your friend Gabriel speaks Spanish!" Mrs. Delarocha proclaimed, the four of them in the midst of making tamales with our oven, great billowing clouds of steam produced from opening the oven door.

"...Yeah, he's full of surprises," I muttered. Maria shrugged a little bit, still too on-edge to really let herself relax, helping from a distance, not laughing with the three of them there.

"Oh, look at the time," Mr. Delarocha proclaimed, dusting off his own apron. "The ones cooking in our oven must be done," He rushed up past me to exit, Mrs. Delarocha following in suit.

"Don't let those overcook, Señor Noria!" She shouted behind her, passing me.

"Yo se," Gabriel let out.

"...Maria's folks don't mind that you're Sinaloa?" I uttered after they'd left.

"Former, don't you forget;" Gabe responded quickly enough. "...It's a non-issue, so we haven't brought it up." I looked over to Maria, where she leaned against the counter, looking away for a moment before meeting my eyes, breathing in, her eyes shimmering, full of contemplation.

"You agree?" I said to Maria as I passed her to draw some water, taking a sip. Maria sighed.

"...Yeah. Doesn't matter. Noah..." She delineated, still staring into my eyes but tapping on the counter tile, as if she wasn't looking at me or currently in a conversation. "I'm going with you. I've made up my mind." I sighed, sucking in through my nose and furrowing my lips.

"Okay, yeah. Good." I nodded to myself. "Simplifies things." Maria sighed heavily again, looking away.

"...I don't want to leave my parents, but they're right. I'll... probably be safe with you. This is what I should do, anyways. I'm an adult, anyways. I can make my own choices."

"...You really could have chosen to stay with your parents," Gabe smirked. More of a joke, but Maria took this seriously enough, nodding to herself more than acknowledging the tone of what'd been said.

"I could. But I'm not going to." Maria adamantly said. "Besides," She was quick to brush off, getting up and pacing across the room, moving her body for the sake of movement itself, to help her process everything in her troubled mind. "It's not like we're leaving forever. Just until this all blows over, even if it takes a while."

"...Yeah. As long as you're sure."

"I am."

"...So what, we leaving now?" Gabriel said.

"First thing tomorrow morning," I said, beginning to hear yells and splashing outside. I could see through the kitchen window, shapes of people jumping through the air before tumbling into the waters of the pool. "...Hey, there's an idea," I smirked gently, motioning past. "Take our minds off things."

Proceeding outside, I noted Kyle and Wilson swimming already, Anthony off to the side dipping his legs in from where he sat on the edge, and Holly off in the shallow end watching, Sam kicking at the water on the steps. All of them wore some swimwear they'd lifted from that store. For the moments here I could really take my mind off things, just us friends having fun. I think I just spent a couple minutes watching, leaned up against the wall, disassociating. I could relax.

"...Hey!" Was cried out from above, and I craned my neck up towards the roof, where Lauren stood, the sun casting glorious rays away from her smiling face as she loosened up her wings there. "...You call those… cannonballs?!" She cried happily getting our attention, blasting off with a leap and ascending a fair bit, doing a loop-the-loop in the air to only shoot back down and crash spinning into the water, practically blasting Wilson onto the banks of the pool with a cry, Kyle bobbing amusedly as more than a couple gallons were lost over the edge of the pool. Lauren emerged out of the frothy bubbles, and now I could get a good look at her face. Relaxed, happy. A real first, there in nothing but her bra top, her usual upper garment shirked for makeshift swimwear. I saw her dive and flip about in the water like a fish, not really having that much space to swim around in though; using her wings like fins and zipping about, blasting out again and flipping over onto her back with her four legs sticking into the air with her arms behind her neck. I saw her look over to me and I must've had some dumb look on my face because she laughed immediately, a kind, comfortable, warm laugh. She shared but a moment staring back at me before Kyle splashed at her.

"Oh, you wanna play splash, huh?" Lauren flipped over to blast a tiny tidal wave towards him with a wing as everyone else joined in somewhat. "Ack! They're ganging up on me!" Lauren cried out to me, laughing still. "Noah! Back me up!"

"I- I'm not in my swim shorts!" I laughed back.

"Oh, you afraid to get wet, huh!?" I really should have seen this coming, as Lauren momentarily paused her defense to blast me with water with a wing, her usual mode of attack, and I jumped back, though she ended up getting my legs pretty good. I sighed, rolling my eyes and taking my gunbelt and shoes off, placing them aside. I ran up to the diving board as she cheered for her reinforcement.

"So you think that I'm gonna be on your side?!" I laughed and Lauren screamed in glee as I dove off, making sure to impact so that I'd splash right into her as she "stood" on the floor of the deep end with her rear legs. I barreled into her and she splashed back, though by the time everyone settled back down again, only me and Lauren were splashing at each other anymore, before even we wound down, just swimming about in the cool waters beside one another. She'd jostle me playfully, I never paid it much mind. I couldn't help but enjoy being around her, watching her be happy. I think she felt the same way, how happy she could be.

"Noah," Maria called from out the doorway, barely looking out at us in the pool. "We could use your help with the tamales." I guess that it wasn't quite the time to fully relax.

The day felt long, almost uncharacteristically so for such a fun, enjoyable time. Maybe it was that hanging feeling of discontent, of the truth that this world was changing irreversibly hanging over us all. Gabriel's past, hanging over us. Maria's world coming to a head, maybe even mine if it didn't feel like it. Everybody just hanging out before we got going tomorrow.

"...Gotta say," Wilson jeered as we all sat around my dad's backyard fire pit, intently roasting a marshmallow on a stick. "If this is the apocalypse, I think we'll do alright," He laughed, everyone else chuckling along in conversation this evening, watching the embers of the fire float lazily into the starry sky. I stood apart from them, watching the sky and sighing.

"Hey, Gabe," I called out as he was leaning up against a dark corner of the wall of my house, away from everyone. "...Seen Lauren around?" I asked. "I haven't seen her land yet."

"...You worried she might run off?" Gabriel asked, somewhat amused. Maybe at my worry.

"Something might have happened to her," I put forth. He shifted where he stood, scratching at his chin and neck a little.

"...She landed a while ago, said she was tired. Probably inside." I nodded a little, somewhat put at ease. With my nerves, as shaken as they'd been all day now cooler, I walked over to the pool, seeing Maria sitting by herself, legs dipped into the cool waters from where she sat on the edge.

"Hey," I greeted, still standing over her. I kind of wanted to pull my shoes and socks off to dip my legs as well, to sit there with her. I stood standing over her. "You still worried about leaving?"

"...Do I make it obvious?" Maria uttered, before erupting into a hasty sigh, kicking her legs a little, letting the still water ripple outwards, a shimmering moon bouncing in the waves.

"Obvious enough," I said, going to lean against the side of the house facing the pool, behind her. "I think it'll be fun. We've got a plan, supplies, training. All that stuff. If something bad happens we'll be good."

"...You say that, like I haven't already been telling *myself* that for the last twelve hours." it was my turn to chuckle and look down at my feet, kicking my toes here and there.

"Maybe I'm just trying to convince myself too."

"Yeah, that'd make sense," she added before another slow silence, a chuckle from some story Wilson was telling in the adjacent backyard. The chirping of crickets. No traffic noise, no passing cars. No planes overhead. Like outside of the bubble of my backyard the world just ceased to exist. Eerie, but ignorable. Only really got to you when you listened.

"H-hey, y'know," I said, something still biting at me a whole day later. "You know, we've... we've never fucked, have we?" I said. Her head turned a little, face in an apprehensive, yet warm smile.

"Yeah. must be our conservative upbringings." another silence. "Might as well. Apocalypse, y'know." She stood.

"O-oh, okay," I said. That easy? I guess I was a little shocked, at least on some level. "My... I think some survival kits in the basement have condoms in them. Dad always said they're really good survival tools, but..." I smiled back and she laughed, getting up out of the water.

"God, Noah. You're such a dork," A brightness suddenly seemed to come over her, like taking to heart this prospect of intimacy. She walked right up to me and kissed me on the lips, planting it hard before pulling back to look me in the eyes while her arms found their way around me. I saw her beautiful mocha-brown eyes, glittering toffee. "Yeah. You get those 'survival tools'."

"...Alright," I growled back, hiding my excitement by playing suave, which she totally saw right through, laughing in my face again. I grasped her hips and kissed her back, pushing her away from me and out of the kiss as we stood there.

"...I'll be in your room... Noah," She said with a flutter of the eyes.

Alright, alright *alright*. Going into the basement, towards the spiderhole. I popped open the hatch, looking down and seeing the light on. I heard scuttling, seeing a flash of green skin all the way down there.

"Lauren?" I cried out, close enough to a laugh, still riding the high I was on, utterly oblivious. "What are you doing down there all by yourself?" She didn't answer for a second, hearing her shambling down there, knocking something over.

"N-Noah! You're... You're not with the others?!" She cried. If I were in any other state of mind I could have heard a tinge of stress, of fear within her voice. Something subtle. Something *specific*.

"I oughta ask you the same thing," I cried back down, beginning to descend the ladder. Hearing me ambling down the rungs, I heard her stammer and scuttle about more. "What're you doing down there? We're... We're making s'mores, y'know. Y'know what those are? Melted marshmallows and chocolate on crackers. You'd really-" I descended the final steps, and turned around, and that was when it hit me that something really wasn't quite right.

There she lay in the far corner with her humanoid portion still sitting upright, my family's photo album clasped shut in her hands. Her hands that held it to her chest, her bare chest, covering it. Laying there, naked. Clothes on the floor.

"L-Lori, wh-" I think I wanted to try and play this off. Like some weird idiosyncrasy of hybrids like her, some brain thing. Like I had something better to be doing anyways. But even my idiotic, horny mind was brought back into reality by the sight of those clothes scattered on the ground. I'd thought they were hers, her projects maybe. But I could see they were actually my clothes, my dirty laundry. At that moment I didn't really know how to react, images and ideas and horrors floating through my head as it all dawned on me. Her big eyes gazing up to me, as she was laying there, sighing heavily with that photo album in her arms. "...What's going on?" was all I could say.

"I..." She hefted the book up. As she lifted it away from her chest I could see her nipples, like emeralds set in seas of jade, and that horrified, clear confusion flowed through me. "You...

Your..." Like she realised how this all looked, she covered her breasts with an arm, still holding the album in her other hand. Blushing hard, still panting. Sweat beading all over her skin. The entire room smelled... like her, in a way. A very, very horribly specific way. "Noah... I don't know what's happening to me," She said. Tears at the edges of her eyes, her voice hoarse in a whisper, not so she wouldn't be heard but so her voice wouldn't crack. "I... I can't take this feeling, Noah... I... Y-you said you'd help me through anything, right?" I didn't want to answer that. I didn't want to acknowledge what was unfolding before me, petrified in disbelief. "Noah... I... You're the only person that's... *been there* for me," Her tiny voice whimpered powerfully and my lip quivered, my head rolling back, looking down upon her. Laying there. In heat, ovulation. I was leaned back, like to escape. "I... I think I- I *need you to help me with these feelings, Noah.*"

No. no no no. My feet finally responded how my mind could not. Get out of there. I stepped back a single step and she sprang up, the photo album falling out of her hands to clatter on the ground. I saw pictures of me fly out, the strapping young man I must've been to her, pictures of me at sporting events, so proud of my own strength and form. God, she was massive. Now rather than a horrified disgust I felt true fear in this dim, tiny place, this huge creature who needed to crouch so as not to hit the ceiling lunging up at me, casting heavy shadow with the little light bulb behind her. Breasts released, her arms reaching out, clawing at me as she took step by wavering step. *"Noah, please."* She was begging, but the look in her eyes was that of a frenzied animal. A terrifying fear, not of me or anything around her, but of herself. The lust she was feeling, succumbing to. For the first time in her life experiencing her own sexuality, the whole ordeal hitting her like a ton of lead, helpless to contain it.

She was upon me, pressed up against that ladder. She was drooling down upon me, eyes entranced on me, wide as saucers. Those brown eyes. Mocha brown. Glittering toffee. Beautiful. Like she'd plucked Maria's right out of her skull, to use their magic upon me. Now I really could see they looked exactly the same, hauntingly so.

"Wh- b- Maria," I let out, watched by her dead stare, horrified at it. How it didn't blink, didn't shift away from me.

"Maria," She hushed. "You... You really love her." She said. A strange way of saying it, as she slunk back a little, receding from me. "You... you really love her?" her rationalization was now a question. *"Do you really love her, Noah?"* She asked, a growl encroaching on her words, teeth beginning to gnash. Her inquisition shone through and the animal was back, never having left. Her hands grasping my arms, feeling through me. Gripping me.

"Lauren... You're scaring me," I gulped. Trying to calm myself, to untangle the situation. To get a grip on things. I saw how she reacted, hands releasing me, hushing herself as she stood like a statue. Scaring you? She must have thought, horrified at how she let her base desires run rampant, for but a moment as her hormone-flooded mind, completely alien to the sensations of ovulation, returned in force. Reaching out, feeling me, groping me. *How dare you,* she uttered without saying a word. Growling like an animal. Pulling my clothes, feeling muscle, flesh. *I need contact, I need intimacy, I need love,* she frothed in perfect, wordless communication. *I don't understand why I feel like this, so powerfully, so suddenly,* the terrified animal in her eyes pleaded to me. *You're the only one I trust. The only one I'm willing to love.* Pleading for help, in some way, though the rest of her face was twisted into a perverse, drooling snarl, intent on taking that help she needed, that love she needed, that sexual release she didn't know she needed so desperately until right now. Taking it by force if she had to, gripping me and coming in for a kiss.

I couldn't help her, at least not in the way she must have wanted, at the time. The only thing I could do was drive my fist skyward into the soft of where her chin met her neck, clacking her jaws together and letting her ragdoll limply to the side, many limbs splaying about as I stood there over her laying on the ground, knocked down, stunned. Sobbing, sobbing up to me now in shame and pity. Like she knew she deserved that punch, she knew how disdainful she looked, how shamefully she pleaded up to me, grasping my leg. I kicked that groping hand away and without word went right back up that ladder, leaving her to cry there, regretting everything. Like fuck if I knew how to deal with any of this.

It was like a dream, like walking as a ghost, an out of body experience climbing the ladder back up to the basement, rung by rung, the sound resoundingly clanging in my head with Lauren's sobs receding in the background. What the fuck, what the fuck. I remembered the smell, the way she looked at me. Convinced I was her whole world. Was I? Fuck. Fuck, fuck *fuck*. What have I done, letting her come with us? What was I supposed to do? *What did I just do; what the fuck was I supposed to have done!?*

### Do you really love her?

That's what she asked me. I hadn't answered. I was lost in the situation, wasn't I? What kind of a ridiculous question is that; do I love my own girlfriend?! I couldn't get the image out of my head, how she... how much she wanted me. Nipples like emeralds. Blushing madly, sweating, trembling at the thought. I couldn't believe it all. I couldn't believe the thoughts I was responding with.

"Noah," Maria's voice shot through me as I stood in the doorway. Somehow in my stupor I'd made it all the way back upstairs, standing there like I was deranged, teleported there in an instant eternity of terrified confusion. I saw her sitting on my bed, in her underwear. Beautiful, I should have thought. She really was beautiful, sculpted and olympian. A hand came down on the spot beside her, like bidding me come on over, as I stood there like a fucking blood-soaked axe murderer, still mortified as I silhouetted the door. "...You got those condoms?"

"I..." I began. "...They... I couldn't find em." a pause, a pause enough for me to, for the first time, really measure the distance between the two of us. A cold pause, strange, like an awkward pause between strangers, not lovers.

"Oh." She didn't say much more for a long time. "...Well then."

I turned around, slowly. I felt dirty. Filthy. I didn't even do anything with Lauren, did I? Like it was already a distant memory. Becoming more and more repressed by the second. I turned my back on her, her beautiful self, sitting pretty there. "...I'm going to take a shower. By myself."

"-y-you don't want to... do it anyways?" She asked suddenly, with a creak of the bed as she shifted where she sat. I paused, nary a step away. A tinge of desperation? Just like Lauren. I must be going crazy. I couldn't help but think of Lauren, naked, ovulating, out of her mind in heat. How I could have given her what she wanted, right then and there. I could have gotten my rocks off with a fucking dragon-centaur. I should be disgusted at the thought. I was disgusted. Wasn't I?

**Wasn't I?!**

"...I dunno anymore," I uttered, not even looking back at her before proceeding into the bathroom, stripping down, and praying the water to wash my troubles, my shame away, ambling through my own mind, and my horror.

### Chapter 15

---

"Do you love me, Noah?"

Maria and I stood there, behind the bleachers. Nighttime. The football game roaring away above and beside us, the two of us standing there. High school freshmen. I must've been about fifteen. Felt like forever ago, even if it wasnt. She still had her accent, despite her momentous effort to hide it. It was charming, made me smile, that little piece of dysfunctionality she saw in herself.

"...I guess," I said. I saw her blush, chuckling plainly as she stared down at her hands, wavering herself from side to side. She was so pretty, wasn't she? Anybody else would be lucky to have her.

"God, you're such a dork," She said again. How she spoke back then, still with her accent. The accent she would work to eliminate, like the past she wanted to forget. She was happy. Taking my hands, pressing her face into mine. I stood there as we shared our first kiss. My very first kiss. I felt her happiness melt into it. I felt her happiness. I was... I was glad she, my girlfriend and my friend, was happy.

**But why wasn't I?**

---

Another morning, after a night of voidlike, dreamless sleep. Blinking at the ceiling in oblivion as I waltzed back into lucidity, remembering reality, as it were. God. What a shitshow.

Alone here I tried to fall back asleep, but I already knew I was just wasting my time laying here lazily. I couldn't escape reality again, no matter how much I wanted to. Maria, how I'd turned her down. Lauren, how I'd... also, turned her down. Ugh. I felt cold thinking about last night. Like I wanted to detach myself from these events, like a spectator and not a player. With that task impossible, I rose, bringing myself to my feet.

"...Lights on, turn on the news," I barked out. The console didn't recognize me. "Lights," I commanded again, pulling on some clothes. I finally walked over to the switch itself. Unresponsive; the power was finally out. Looks like this really was it.

The kitchen was somewhat lively, Gabriel cooking up pancakes on the gas stove. It ought to have been funny to me, but I was without humor, going to the fridge to get the milk. Warm, barely any left. I groaned a little as I went back, going to sit down next to Kyle who was helping himself to a hastily made protein shake.

"...Man, your dad has a fuckton of protein powder," He said as I grabbed the cereal, a bowl, a spoon.

"...It's weight efficient and lasts forever. Good for survival," I mumbled out, like on autopilot. Kyle snorted out a laugh.

"Heh. That's smart." I sat there before the bowl, my cereal, the milk. Just staring down, trying to disassociate. "So... You have some fun last night too?"

"W-what?" I spat, almost taken by surprise. Like Kyle found out about Lauren. Wait, where the fuck was Lauren anyways? Did she run off? Is she-

"Hell yeah," Kyle's voice sliced through my disassociation. "You got some ass from Maria, huh? Siiick. Me and Holly?" He went on. "Yeah. I scored too, bro. High five." I saw his hand up. I just stood back up, without my appetite, looking him in his dumb smiling face, hand still skyward.

"W-where's- You seen Maria?" I barked out, as if in a daze.

"I think she's in the shower, bro. Hogging all the hot water left." He scoffed playfully, hand slowly falling, playing off the fact that I left him hanging without skipping a beat.

"Lauren?"

"The dragon? Fuck if I know," Kyle snorted on. "What, you-"

"Garage, still loading stuff," Gabriel chimed in from a distance. I heard his voice like it came from within my head, like the world outside of me and Kyle there stopped existing. Everything too far away from me was just television static. "Said she wanted to think about things alone. Or something." My blood ran cold, but at least she was still with us. Wait, why did I care if she ran off? Wouldn't that solve this problem? I felt a sickness in my gut. Was I glad she was sticking with us? Sticking with me, after *that*?

"...Think about things?"

"I dunno, Green just said she doesn't want to be a burden. Maybe you haven't convinced her otherwise yet," Gabe said, turning on me, currently eating a pancake he'd made. One full of raspberries, he'd folded it in half and was eating it like a taco. Funny I guess. Everything was fuckin' funny. I saw Gabriel swallow his bite, eyeing me. That stupid perceptive gaze of his, stabbing through me. Like he knew. Like he knew everything and just didn't care, just noticed it all and chuckled to himself like he was watching a fucking sitcom. It made me feel a rage, a paranoia I didn't know why I had. Maybe I did know, the more I ruminated on it. I probably knew exactly why I was antsy, at least, here I was just looking for more excuses.

I ambled out. I had to... discuss, this? Of course I had to. It's the adult thing to do. Leader-like. What you have to do, need to do. Punching her in the face though? Ugh. I just wanted my mind to shut up, only making things worse with every thought. I stood there in the doorway, swinging it open, and there she was. Lauren was stand-sitting like she always did, her rear two legs sat firmly on the concrete while her anterior was upright, like how a dog would sit with its head still up, wings ruffling a little as she sat before the opened garage door, out into the pale blue sky and the miniature warzone of my front yard, how her hair would flutter in the breeze, wings fluttering like sails along with it. Sighing a breath, in and out. I saw her head turn finally, as she knew I was here, feeling my presence. She turned just enough so she could look to make sure that it was me there, the corner of her eye gazing back at me, before her head turned back to watching the street. A shiver, like a cringe washed over her while she turned back out to the open garage, the pale blue sky.

"Noah-"

"I'm sorry," I cut her off. Not to be rude or anything, I just had to be *heard*. I shut the door behind me with a resounding thud, still standing there on the topmost step into the house, leaning back into the door and crossing my arms, breathing in slow. Her rear legs pushed her completely standing as she slowly turned, strafing around sideways to me with her head turned to face me, mouth only a tad ajar. As she was still turning I spoke again. "...I'm sorry for hitting you."

"...I... I don't think you need to apologize," She hushed out guiltily. Like she'd thought this all over too. Of course she'd thought this over, she was still here. She wore those clothes she'd customized, her backwards battle belt with the webbing all strapped up with equipment, rifle hanging slung in front of her humanoid torso, Gabriel's little homemade silencer on the end of it. I stepped down the short stairs leading into the house after swallowing my hesitation, maybe so it didn't look like I was looking down on her. I felt like I owed her that. "I-"

"I forgive you, too." Interrupting her yet again she was shot silent, mouth slowly closing and eyes looking away. A hand, up until this point limp at her side, brushed past her gun on the way up to scratch at her neck, her jaw. Just about the place where I punched her. "Do you... Want to talk about it?"

A long sigh, looking back away. "...It was a one-time crazy thing, Noah, that's, that's all," she said, shamefully, subtly so, looking down to her outstretched palm of her hand, gripping it into a fist. "I just…"

"You're not… in *love* with me or anything?" I uttered. In any other context, this would be the funny part. Neither of us were even smiling.

"...I don't even think I know what that means," She uttered, as if in defeat, that arm going back down to slap at her sides. Her eyes shot up to me. "I just… I just know that I shouldn't have... been acting like that."

"...Do you think you're… Stable?" I asked, with some degree of hesitation. I saw her suck in, like gasping, biting her lip and staring back down. The question stung, and the longer the pause lasted, the more it went right back to me. "...Forget about that. You, uh… Yeah." Another long pause. Silence. Eerie silence, staring at each other. Ambling through our emotions.

"Yeah, I-"

"Yeah. sorry."

Just sharing an awkward moment, together here. Was this really making up? Progress? "Look, Lauren… I don't… dislike you. Okay? You're a… good person. I *like* you. Just... Just not…"

"...Not like that. Yeah, I know that." Back to feeling her own neck and jaw. Pretending to scratch rather than feel into the sore flesh, the bruise. "God, I'm such an idiot," She muttered. Maybe she really was saying this to herself, maybe she was trying to see how I'd respond.

"That's emotions for you. It… Happens."

"...Yeah. they're a trip." I watched her eyes sparkle as she spoke, those mocha brown orbs, glistening bright. Calm toffee. Caramel. I let a smile form on my face, as if to get her to reciprocate. She did her best to smile back, the ice between us melting slowly but surely.

"You're still coming with us?"

"Nowhere I'd rather be," She reasoned with a shrug, not entirely without humor, though her embarrassment lingered, an everlasting cringe that she fought through. I smirked out a silent chuckle, fighting through that cringe right there with her.

"Good," I said. "That's… Good." It was weird, how warm we could be. I expected this to be so painful, like pulling the world's most awkward band-aid. I couldn't help but lose myself in her charm, if only a little bit. She somehow made me feel so much more at-ease, getting it all out there. Solving this problem. I turned back around, to go back and make sure everyone else was ready to go.

"N-Noah, w-" I was holding onto the doorknob, the dawn sky behind me, behind her glowing silhouette as she stood, a hand reached out as if to reach all the way over and grab my shoulder. I looked back over my shoulder and her outstretched hand fell, inch by inch. "I… Nevermind. It's nothing."

"You sure?" I asked. I saw her face scrunch up and nostrils flare, sighing out as she stared down into the corner of the garage, tapping one of her forelegs on the ground, the hand-like talon on the end of it clacking its nails against the concrete floor. Bringing her eyes to it, picking that set of talons up off the ground to turn it around, looking into the palm of her weird not-quite-a-hand-yet-not-quite-a-foot. I read a sort of disappointed, cringing disgust on her face as she stared into it, asking herself what exactly she wanted to know, but couldn't bring herself to ask me as she balled it into a fist before placing it back down upon the concrete with a little thump.

"...Yeah," She grunted out a sigh, nostrils flaring again, still staring down at herself. "It's nothing. I'm fine." I stared into her for but another second, before retreating back inside.

The morning was almost over. It was time to get going.

## ACT III
## PILLARS OF SALT

### Chapter 16

Outside of the city and into the desert, I could finally remember how hot this place really was. The sun reigned supreme above all, uncontested by cloud or smoke. Behind us, the city glittered, and ahead of us lay the solar fields littering the craggy, rocky hills as we drove, weaving through the road full of abandoned cars. Above us a shadow was cast zipping along the ground some ways away from the rest of us, a product of Lauren soaring above. I watched the city behind us in the rearview mirror as the jeep ambled along, how from a distance it looked so… quaint, nestled there in the rocks. Almost forgettable. I could see the old casinos, long from relevant ever since the city became a hub for the energy sector. They stood like the sarcophagi of mausoleums, nothing more than a reminder now.

"Check in, check in Green," Gabriel uttered into the walkie-talkie he held grasped in a hand where he sat next to me. "What's the road look like?"

"Still… Pretty clear, I- I don't see any soldiers or anything," She uttered back, probably shielding the mouthpiece enough to speak, though the wind screeched in the radio. She sounded only a tad winded, breathing heavily where she soared, far faster than I could drive, circling us as she did. "Uh… Hey, question," She began, Gabriel perking up. "…Solar, right? The… shiny… stuff, we're... going towards?"

"Yeah. Solar fields. Vegas' runs the most of 'em in the country." Gabriel answered, sitting beside me, sat angled away from me with his rifle pointing at the low part of the door and shouldered, ready to be swung out should the need arise, slowly scanning as he did, though he was still on the radio as of now. Maria must've been right behind me, she'd yet to say anything to me today. Probably a little hurt from last night. I couldn't blame her, and let her watch out the window to the left just like Gabriel was, Anthony beside Maria, just like the other two of them with his own carbine resting on the doorframe, though he wasn't scanning as intently as the other two, rather like the rest of those sitting in the chuck of the jeep, daniel leaned up against the water barrel in the very back, doodling, everyone else up there next to him or in the divider beside Anthony and Maria. "…Told ya she'd be useful," Gabe smirked back to Maria, who I could assume was rolling her eyes, or pretending to ignore him, or both, while I simply kept driving on. It was quiet, but that wasn't necessarily surprising, since pretty much all the cars had been knocked out by the hack. I heard gunfire back behind me every now and then, and that put me ill-at-ease, especially with everything so calm here on the open road. "…You good, Noah?" I heard beside me.

"Yeah," I said, turning to Gabe. He smirked. I saw how he wore that mask like his tipped up on his head like a helmet sometimes, like he was now.

…"Goosebumps all over you." I swallowed my hesitation, looking back out to the road again.

"You know, I always thought the apocalypse would involve a lot more getting shot at," I said. "It's… quiet. Kinda creepy." Gabe chuckled again.

"You shouldn't miss getting shot at. Might be something wrong with you." I finally smirked back at his psychotically grinning face. "…Don't sweat it and don't jinx us."

Eventually we got off the freeway where it diverged, to take the off-road trail up through the solar arrays. "Y-you're not going to take the highway?" Lauren's voice crackled over the radio.

"Nah," I picked up the radio. "Better to stay off road. Who knows what's going on there. Look, we're gonna slow down a lot so come land and walk with us since we can't go that fast off-road and you're pretty fast."

"Uh… sure thing." Lauren sailed down and as she approached, dust kicked up as she alighted beside the jeep with a final beat of her wings sailing on down, the jeep now going quite a bit slower though as she trotted, still winding down. I slowed it to match her walking speed.

"Oh, now I can stretch," Wilson leapt down off of the back of the jeep, twisting in place a little. "Hey, how about we test fire our guns?"

"We're saving the ammo, Wilson," I muttered back. He rolled his eyes, while Lauren was off getting some water, Daniel passing her a filled canteen. I saw how she was sweating; it sure didn't look easy to fly.

"Oh, like this is an actual apocalypse," Wilson kicked a rock forcefully as he walked.

"Yeah, and like that's an actual illegal machine gun," Gabriel noted of the Shorty-MDR Wilson still had slung. Wilson seemed to be given pause, before rolling his eyes.

"…We have a plan for when somebody catches us with 'em?" I heard Holly speak up from where she sat, standing a little with her hands pulling her up by the roll cage, stretching now that we went slower.

"We won't. We don't have to get back on the roads until the pass at Shortstone, in Idaho," I uttered.

"…And then?" Daniel decided to chip in and ask, done sketching now that the road was bumpy, however slow as we went.

"We'll chuck 'em then if we need to. Besides, I'm sure that Noah's survival commune would be glad to take a couple automatic weapons off of us for the price of admission for y'all. Remember, it's just me, Noah and Maria who've got spots there, We've got to… make something work so they take us," Gabe was quick to say, glancing ever so subtly towards Lauren who paused panting to gulp and look down, kicking her worries away with a clump of dirt she flicked with her front talons.

"…Is this your way of saying you don't plan on ditching yours?" I uttered, maybe just to break the tension Gabriel had placed on Lauren. Gabriel clicked his tongue, smiling sweetly over to me with squinted eyes and an upturned chin.

"From my cold dead hands, Noah," He jested, while Lauren ambled closer to the door now, going to throw a hand on the rollcage above me as a way to lean.

"Phew… Just, uh… When you guys need me to check out something, o-or when you're ready to go faster again, just… Just let me know," Lauren uttered as she was catching her breath, now walking beside me, separated only by the driver side door as we on rolled ahead at this walking pace.

"…You… okay?" I asked, not completely without genuine concern.

"Yeah, it's just… y'know," She said, wings still fluttering as she folded them, nodding again as she panted, raising a sleeve to wipe her forehead and then going to check the rest of her gear, making sure her walkie talkie was secure in its pouch on her tactical webbing, checking her spare magazines and her slung rifle. "Tires me out. God, I'm hungry. Where's the protein bars?" She let the car pass forward a little to go behind and rifle through one of the backpacks for snacks. I saw Maria's face purse a little as Lauren did, probably concerned about our rations, inwardly-so.

"So, we're gonna cut through the solar fields. We'll be in them for about a day, I figure, since it goes on for quite a while through the plateau." I looked back over to Lauren after explaining everything to everyone else there.

"...The radio have anything on it when I was gone?" She asked, her words interrupting the drink she was having, going to drink more from the canteen.

"Nah. Just static and E-Broadcasts. We stopped trying a while ago." Lauren nodded back at the info, though she watched out in front of us as she walked, strumming her hands on her rifle after she stowed the canteen. "...You sure you're okay?" I noted of how flushed Lauren seemed. "We can stop and take a rest."

"I think she's fine," Maria dully noted, gazing into her from where she sat.

"...So, uhhh… Why's there so many?" Lauren began, perhaps mostly just to get the attention off of herself.

"Vegas provides most of the energy for the US," I said. "Well, it did. We used to burn, uh, coal but that all got sanctioned away. Some guy who was working for ElTek found out a way to make solar panels really efficient right in the nick of time in 2045 so that's where most of our energy comes from. Solar panels kinda used to suck," I reasoned, and her head nodded a little.

"...So, uh, when do we stop to eat?" Anthony was quick to ask as we drove, some ways down the road.

"We've got snacks in the bags. Help yourself," Gabriel was quick to snark.

"How are we supposed to eat anything on this bumpy-ass road?" Holly was quicker to shoot back.

"...We're stopping, Gabe," I said, slowing off on the throttle and pulling the brake.

"Not smart, in the solar fields," He said back, though not entirely so concerned for somebody apparently worried about an ambush.

"I thought you said that the solar fields would be good to hide us," I shot back, as people piled out and stood up to stretch.

"From aircraft and anybody outside of the fields, sure," He said, still scanning our right side as he slowly popped the door open, stepping off, by far the most attentive to his surroundings, with Lauren being the second most, still standing beside me but with her ears perked all the way up and eyes wide, somewhat concerned by Gabriel's own apprehension, still breathing heavily, though through her nostrils for now. "But a group of guys on foot in here could be problematic. Especially if there's a lot of them, or if they know what they're doing. Remember the three day rule?" Gabriel pontificated. "Must be some hungry people in the streets in Vegas about now. It's only begun to get grim, you know."

"Oh yeah, and they'll be after the… massive amount of food in the solar fields, right," I mused back humorously, interrupting myself momentarily with a grunt as I cinched my armor a little. It may have been marketed as "lightweight" but I wasn't feeling such a term to describe it right now.

"Or maybe in the synthetic meat factory next to it," Gabriel grunted back. "...Just be on your toes."

"...It's the apocalypse, Gabe. I am." He smirked, still scanning as I went around to the back, pulling my slung rifle so it hung behind me.

"You know what I'm gonna miss in the apocalypse, guys?" Wilson's shrill voice laughed out as he chewed on a protein bar. "This year's Call of Duty."

"...Wilson, Wilson," Gabriel 'tsk'ed, evidently listening as I was getting my own food. "You say that as if it's gonna be as good as *any* of the golden era ones."

"Pssht, you and your grandpa games," Wilson chuckled back.

"You know, two people telling me that doesn't make me any less correct," He said.

"...Call of Duty, that's the uh... shooty army video-game, right?" Lauren said, which was enough to create a momentary pause as nearly everyone looked at her.

"...How come hybrids know so much trivia again?" Wilson edged close to Gabe to say, who was still scanning, though he chuckled simultaneously.

"Guess whoever made 'em had a sense of humor," Gabe uttered, entertained enough at the very situation, though Lauren was blushing, somewhat embarrassed.

"Wait, no no no, let's see how deep this goes, huh?" Wilson turned back to being amused. "Who's right here, Lauren? Is Gabe right, are the old ones really better?"

"Uh- I mean, that's what... people say, isn't it?" Lauren put back. Gabe laughed out rather gleefully, considering how paranoidly he scanned the solar forest.

"Fuckin hybrid," Wilson shook his head madly as he turned back to the distance, chewing his food. Lauren's eyes wandered down again as she shrunk up on herself, arms crossing uncomfortably.

"...What I want to know is, what the fuck is the super bowl gonna look like with hybrids?" Kyle said. "Y'know, been thinking about that. Do we give 'em their own leagues?"

"Sounds interesting enough to actually watch, unlike actual sports," Samantha said, not eating but currently taking the time stopped to draw alongside Daniel, having stopped being jostled constantly by the bumpy road. I could see that there was a definite disparity in skill between them, Samantha just doing it for the sake of fitting in.

"I'm surprised that's not coming from Danny," Kyle crowed, laughing antagonistically. Daniel's hand slowed as he drawed, like distracted, though he did not look up, attempting to ignore it. "Something to get his rocks off to. Big muscley wolf dudes smashing into each other. Bet you like that, huh?"

"...Fuck you," Daniel muttered back, and if taken by his voice alone would sound like he was taking this in stride, though his hunched frame and meager line of eyesight spoke that he was still as meek and defensive as ever. Kyle laughed out again.

"Oh ho ho, the mouth on furry-boy," He guffawed. "Hey, why don't you say it again? I couldn't hear you so good. Really shouldn't talk to people with your back turned. I might get insulted."

"Kyle, you the bad guy from some stupid fuckin' high-school movie or something? Gettin' real cliche, dude," Anthony quipped soon.

"Oh, look at Tony with his movies," Kyle responded in kind. "And baseball. What sort of stupid fuckin' sport is that? Oh, you hit a ball with a stick. Big fuckin' whoop."

"Knock it off, Kyle, I'll make you walk home," I snarled, interrupting his bravado, figuring I ought to say something.

Kyle was out of quips, even his girlfriend was eyeing him sourly. Looking around, finally seeing even Lauren peeved by how much of a child he was making out to be, he got the picture that he wasn't heading the zeitgeist here. "...Yeah yeah," He played off without even blushing, though I could tell he was perturbed by how this went with only Wilson here to really back him up, and even Wilson wasn't having it, at least not as much as he usually did.

Everyone went back to eating, having their own subtle little conversations while I just ate, until suddenly Gabriel, scowled face only slightly more perturbed right now, walked beside me where I sat, munching away.

"Don't freak but we're being watched," He said, and my own chewing slowed. I raised my eyebrows while he leaned beside me, going and reaching in, putting his carbine down next to the water barrel as he reached for the food. I saw him drawing his pistol from the pistol holster slowly, only to perform a press check, seeing his gun good to go. "I'm thinking two guys. Maybe more, can't be sure. Both got rifles."

"A-are you serious?" I stammered, practically blurting, shifting in my seat.

"Shh," He stuck the wrapped protein bar he held in my face as if putting a finger to my lips. "Don't freak. Play it cool." I saw Gabe's eyes wander for a second, while my heart beat hard in my chest. "Hey there, Green. You eavesdropping?" I turned my head too, seeing Lauren's pale, concerned look and how she was now gripping her rifle, still chewing slowly, big brown eyes upturned. "Gonna need you to back us up too, anyways. Play it cool, cool..." She swallowed her bite and nodded, eyes darting. "One at one-o-clock, relative to the front of the jeep. One at three or four, looks like they're flanking, trying to get us at a crossfire. Don't get too freaked, if they were here to shoot us they'd have started already. Probably."

"W-why's that?" Lauren asked in a whisper, drawing a little close, foreleg quivering.

"...Getting too close. Look slowly when I tell you, one at a time. See the solar array about ten meters to the right-front corner of our jeep? Guy behind that one." I gulped too, putting my own protein bar down. Lauren looked slowly, trying not to make things obvious, before I did. I didn't see anybody.

"...You sure?"

"For that bogey, yeah. Positive that's where he's at. Waiting, getting their plan together, so we're gonna have to make the first move to force their hand. Here's the plan. I'mma act like I got to take a piss. I'm gonna go over there," He picked up a water bottle. "Figure if they're trying to rob us, a hostage for us will make things simpler. I'll pretend to piss, he'll jump out, point his gun at me. Expect to catch me with my dick in my hands, but he'll be my hostage instead with a couple quick moves and make this all a whole lot easier."

"...We're not gonna shoot?"

"Be nice to save the bullets. Plus a couple more guns that aren't soaked in blood and possibly full of bulletholes might be worth something down the line. Okay, Noah. I'mma start walking out. Stay close but not too close, keep it quiet. Just in case my plan goes sour I need a rifle backing me up. Put your fuckin' helmet on for once too. Green, you stay here and keep your eyes on that four-o-clock flanker. If he's stupid enough to shoot after I take his buddy as a prisoner he's probably not that great a shot nor is he gonna be that brave so if you don't want to murder the 'tard, just shoot over his head until he fucks off, make him nice and deaf, rattle his brains." Lauren nodded madly. "Keep it cool. Actor. You know what an actor is?"

"...In a movie?"

"Yeah. Be a fuckin action hero, Green. Green Steel. Cold as ice. Got it?" Lauren nodded again, more slowly this time. "Right-o. Lights, camera, action." Gabe began strolling out from where we stood near the rear left corner of the car that faced towards Vegas, and advanced around the front of the car to the opposite point, off towards where Gabriel's unsuspecting hostage-to-be apparently was. "Right, looks clear," Gabriel announced to everyone, while I was slinking towards the driver's seat of the jeep and my helmet laying there on the dash, slowly putting it on and trying to check my AR-15 as subtly as possible, turning the safety off. "I'm gonna go take a leak. Don't get in any gunfights without me."

"Thanks for letting us know, I'm sure you'll call when you need someone to shake your dick," Kyle rattled off.

"I wasn't, but I'm glad to have you on deck, I'm feeling the romance in the air already," Gabriel shot back, chuckling. I couldn't believe how he could be calmly quipping like that at a time like this. I got out of the driver's seat to stand there behind the engine block, my finger tapping the receiver of my weapon by the fire selector, doing my best to pretend not to be setting up our counter-ambush. I found myself blinking quite erratically, practically jittering as I breathed. I saw him with that water bottle, pretending to "pee" on the ground with it, his pistol in his other hand all this time. I couldn't even have time to gasp, seeing movement. Some subtle shift in the wind, the line of the column of the tower of the solar display morphing as they stepped forth. I could finally see a real distinction between the sands behind them as black steel came out, some armalite rifle, short like a 16" or 14" M4 barrel pointed straight up. They dashed out to lower the gun towards Gabriel but didn't expect a gun in their throat and a hand grabbing the barrel of the advancing rifle, keeping it held skyward. I swear that Gabriel rattled off some one liner, must have been something sparse like "Gotcha bitch!" or "Surprise!" but everything went down so quick I could hardly discern it. Screaming, yelling from that four o'clock position while Gabriel elbowed that figure in the face and wrenched that armalite away from the mysterious gunman and tossed it, pulling him back up to hold in a rear chokehold as his own hostage, wheeled around at the other gunman. The one at four o'clock had their weapon shouldered and was yelling out in a shrill voice, a woman, Gabe yelling back. Drop it, I'll kill him, et-cetera. Pow. Lauren's rifle went off, the roar of a 5.56 bullet screaming out of a shortened barrel hardly contained by the stubby suppressor Gabriel had made, still easily as loud as my own 20" AR sans ear protection. The girl Lauren had shot at, out of reflex, must have pulled her trigger, sand blasting up right between the legs of Gabriel's hostage, though it seemed to have gotten the point across as the gun tumbled out of her hands and she scrambled away. At this point everyone was up and alert with weapons drawn, me still pointing mine towards Gabriel and his catch, whipping back and forth between him and the one who'd fled. There were a couple seconds of silence as everyone got a grip on the situation.

"...Jesus christ! Gabe, that bitch almost shot you!" Kyle uttered shrilly, laying in the back of the jeep in a funky position with his ass in the air, having dove for cover.

"...Luck of the draw," Gabe uttered, like he ought to be smiling though he wasn't, still wrestling a little bit with his struggling victim.

"Nice shooting, Dragon; you missed," Wilson muttered to Lauren, mostly just to cool his own nerves, gun pointing around.

"I- It was a warning shot," She defensively hissed back.

"Sure it was."

"Hey, stop fuckin' around! They're still out there, get your eyes on," I ordered.

"Oh damn, another hybrid," Anthony proclaimed, and now that I stopped to really take a good look, walking up, it became apparent. Gabriel held in the crux of his arm, the head of a dog, though with big eyes with whites, the eyes of a human staring around, panicked but at this point just breathing, staring intensely towards us while Gabe lorded over him with his pistol, the dog-man's arms coming up to Gabe's neck-grasping choke and gripping out of reaction to being put in a headlock. In addition to his eyes, his head was big and domed too, full of a humanoid brain or something or other, though he still had a pointed muzzle and ears, flicking this way and that on the sides near the top of his head. He wore what I could only really describe as some sci-fi movie's bland work/utility clothes with a sort of quasi-denim overalls with suspenders and a striped shirt beneath it, his gear re-purposed as some sort of impromptu combat gear with magazine shelving where tools might once have been stored on his belt and chest rig, his brown-orange eyes only a little brighter in color than his orange fur with white and black streaks here and there, like a fox. Come to think of it, he was rather diminutive compared to Gabe. Granted, Gabe was a rather big guy, but the dog, or fox guy seemed like a child in his arms.

"...Let me guess, big misunderstanding? Sure you just wanted to be friends by jumping out and trying to shoot me, huh furfag?" Gabe asked, gun to the fox-man's head while he frothed in enraged panic for a couple seconds, fluffy orange tail whipping around behind him. "How many," Gabe snarled before the hybrid could utter a word, me coming up to secure our hybrid hostage's weapon. I took a moment to look at it, fourteen inch barrel, Colt proof marks, fire selector that had three positions, not two. This was an actual, genuine M4A1, all scuffed up. It looked like it saw every continent on the planet, practically a relic. I put it on safe and slung it around my back while going over for the weapon that the girl had dropped. She must've been a hybrid too.

"T-three," He grunted.

"Three; final answer?" I saw the fox person grit his teeth at Gabriel's persuasive tone.

"...Four. One kid."

"Call 'em out and make 'em toss their guns." More silence. "I said call 'em out here. You need a hole in your skull?" The fox man was gritting his teeth, but before he could even comply, while I stood there reaching for the girl's gun, I saw a creature step out at me from around the corner of the tower a ways away.

"H-hey, let's not- We were just, just-"

"DROP- DROP IT!" I roared, scrambling for my own rifle and jabbing it up towards him, and his own rifle spun out of his hands as his arms went up in the sky and his head bowed timidly.

"...Abel, you fokkin' knob-end," Gabriel's hostage was heard growling in a strangely distinct anglo accent, as I got a look at this big, chunky "Abel" before me, his arms stuck foolishly up in the sky, head in a shrug though trying not to look me in the eye. He looked less scared than ashamed, and as for species, he looked more like a german shepherd than a fox, and was kind of terrifying given that he had been trying to smile everything off and thought it was a good idea to be holding his rifle at the same time, bearing his teeth, not to mention he towered in excess of a foot above me even slumped sheepishly as he was. Beyond that, he seemed to be one like Lauren- a centaurical, which explained his height. He was wearing what looked like an undersized T-shirt, and over it some cheap, tactical chest rig like the kind sold at a sketchy surplus store for something cheap like less than two hundred dollars.

"I- We just, heh, look, we don't-" He was sputtering, gazing down the barrel of my rifle.

"STEP BACK FROM THE GUN AND GET ON THE GROUND!" I roared.

"O-okay," He complied meekly, trotting backwards with his arms still outstretched before laying his lower body down with his arms still raised, and I went, now holding my rifle by one hand, to scoop up both the girl hybrid's rifle and his under my arm. "W-where's the other one, the girl!?" I ordered, his ear flicking.

"S-sis? Reina?" He cried out behind him, turning his head.

"Okay, okay," The female voice that belonged to this "Reina" let out, hands pointing out from around the column I stood beside. I turned, seeing Gabriel advancing while the others held the fox one at multiple gunpoint, dragging him along as he let out aggravated proclamations saying he was complying, ever so passive aggressively so we could all have a "discussion."

"Where's the fourth?" Gabriel asked. The girl one that'd peeked out of cover bit her lip, going to look behind her.

"She's- Katt? You, uh... Honey, can you come out?" I saw another column further down, a little face peeking out as a hand pulled herself out a tiny bit. Given her name, it wasn't too surprising seeing the round-pointed ear of the little cat-like person, grey-blue fur on her face with cute, big eyes. "She's a kid, she doesn't have any guns," The german-shepherd girl, Abel's sister before me said. Unlike Abel or Lauren, Abel's sister Reina was a regular humanoid with two legs, standing only a hair less tall than I, wearing, like her brother, mismatched clothes. An army jacket several sizes too big and a cheapo tactical rig underneath it, wearing jeans that extended past her feet and were cinched way up by an overtightened belt, again, far too big. She had a mane of red hair flowing from her big head, the dog-taur guy having some shaggy hair about the top of his of the same color. Meanwhile, the younger iron-blue colored cat-girl peeking out concernedly from behind that pillar in the distance was a cobalt color with ice-white eyes, a little strand of braided blue hair falling down from her head from the angle where she leaned, from her own mane of hair. Those fearful eyes quivered towards me.

"...She doesn't have a gun, don't-"

"Yeah, irrelevant. You sure as hell aren't robbing us now."

"R-robbing us? You?" The big one, Abel yammered. "We- look, there's been a big misunderstanding, we-"

"Noah, those guns of theirs in condition zero or nah?" Gabe asked.

"...Pretty sure they were all ready to go," I said cooly. Gabe clicked his tongue.

"Ooh, circumstantial evidence, huh? Hell of a thing."

"No, really, we just... We were, uh, curious, since you uh... She's with you, which was... weird, we wanted to- y'know," Abel yammered. "Right, Archie? Reina?" The weird british fox-guy rolled his eyes at the centaurical Abel's goofy nature, hands still on his head while Abel glanced around at his two near compatriots.

"...God, just shut your fockin' gab, Abel,"

"W-what now?" The girl one, Reina asked.

"What now? We go our separate ways, and take your guns off you. Do you a favor before you shoot your eye out."

"Wh- We need those!" Reina proclaimed.

"Why's that? So you can rob the next group of retards? There are ten of us and there were three guns between you. You really know how to pick your battles, *mate*. We could have easily swiss-cheesed you."

"C-C'mon, what if we need to defend ourselves?" Abel asked.

"You know," Gabriel growled. "There's this term. Verbal judo. You gotta avoid *pissing people off*. You know we could just SHOOT you right now?!" Gabriel raised his voice, and that little girl burst out from cover, running up.

"NO!" She screeched, going out raising her little fists and running right up to Gabriel and punching him just under his armor vest in the gut from a running sprint. She bounced off Gabriel's abs like a brick wall, even though she aimed good enough, not breaking her fist on the hardened steel plate in his vest but what she'd probably assumed to be the soft of his gut and fell back over on the ground as he stood there, unmoved. He chuckled in surprised amusement as she got back up, leaping at his pistol arm. He held her aloft, hanging from his limb for a second, practically amused, before pulling her off by an arm. She screamed shrilly, while he put his pistol back in its holster.

"...Tenacious. Katt, huh?" He asked. The other three nodded simply. "Creative name. How come everybody else has real names and you phoned hers in?"

"...I named them. Kinda had to think 'em up on the fockin' spot y'know," Archie explained, calmly as he could.

"*Bloody roight that is, tea and crumpets*?" Gabriel smiled back antagonistically, still holding this twelve year old cat girl by the wrist as she flailed, trapped in his grip as if Gabriel were a statue struck out of marble. "Noah, any of those guns automatic?"

"Yeah his, the british one's was an M4. looks like military surplus." Gabriel clicked his tongue.

"The others?"

"A budget AR15 and a Kel-Tec bullpup. Semi auto only, civilian barrel lengths."

"...Whose guns are *those*?" Gabe asked.

"...Ours?"

"Oh, you buy those civvie pieces at a gun store? Noah, you think a hybrid could pass a background check? Guess there's no reason one couldn't, but why do I seriously doubt that's how you got them?" Archie grunted again.

"We got them out of the facility, where we came from." Gabriel bit his lip.

"...You... Think that's true, Gabe?" I asked.

"Read up on hybrids. Turns out a lot of these facilities were also used to store old military surplus, at least the shit they didn't sell to Sinaloa for a deep discount during the Intervention War. You probably didn't read about this, this was some classified stuff I came across. Personal to me and my... Line of work."

"Think he's telling the truth?" Maria asked.

"Could be. Doesn't explain the semi-autos."

"They... were in there." Archie was adamant. I saw the steel in his eyes. He may be on edge, but if he was lying he was a good liar.

"Could be true," Gabriel pontificated. "Heard that they've got some surplus police guns stored with them. Lot of cop agencies might opt for semi autos, unlike Las Vegas." Gabriel released Katt's wrist with a flick of his hand, sending her sprawling into the dust. I saw her clothes. She and Archie seemed to be the only ones wearing the right size of clothes. Even so, Katt's garb still seemed so much more... primitive.

"J-jerk!"

"Handful, huh?" Gabe proclaimed. "Okay, get the fuck out of our sight."

"Wh- What about our guns?" Archie blurted.

"You're British, aren't you? Aren't you supposed to be afraid of guns?"

"Look- firstly, I don't even know what you're on about. Just- We didn't steal them! What if somebody robs us?!"

"Then it'll be real fuckin' ironic. Write a book or something. Hey, speaking of, give us your ammo. Take your vests off."

"Jeez, Gabe," I put in. "You- This might be a bit harsh. We should let them keep one."

"Yeah, right. I wouldn't give these chucklefucks the Hi-Point."

"We could... Look, I don't feel right about leaving a little girl in the desert with nobody able to keep her safe," I found myself reasoning. "Even if she's a hybrid."

"...Yeah, actually, that's... kind of fucked up," Samantha put in her two cents.

"So what, you want to take the kitty-cat brat for safekeeping? To make you feel all warm and nice inside?" Gabriel glared back down at Katt, who went and glomped onto Reina's side, glaring at Gabriel with such fiery intensity that it was practically funny. "Looks like the furries are inseparable. Fuckin' disney movie shit, big eyes'n all." Gabe sighed. "But, it occurs to me that these fuckers with nothing to do now that we've taken their steel will probably end up following us, car or no. We can't exactly go that fast in the solar fields either. They're gonna be bugging us until we hit open trail again and I don't know if I can take being guilted for another day."

"So what, we take them? Are we running a fuckin' zoo?" Maria put forth.

"I guess we can call this the trust period. After we get out of the solar fields we'll give 'em their guns back if they behave."

"And they eat our food?" Maria said.

"We brought extra. We'll find some way to make 'em useful."

"Like what, push the fuckin' jeep?"

"There's an idea. Come up with a few more of those, why don't you?" Gabriel smirked and Maria scowled in return.

"Gabe," Maria was adamant. "They're Hybrids. You can't trus-"

"-Greenie girl, would you like to put your two cents in?" Gabriel interrupted quickly and Maria's mouth shut as her nostrils flared, Lauren trying to avoid being used as a bargaining piece in the argument. Fortunately for her, Gabriel's point made its mark.

"Wait- we, we never agreed to... go w-" Abel put forth, before Archie cut him off.

"Shut up Abel, we haven't any better ideas," Archie snarled. I smirked at his oddly out-of-place accent.

Looks like we were babysitting.

### Chapter 17

"So... What's the deal with your, uh... Hybrid?" I found the canid girl asking me, Reina, as she walked. She'd accepted some clothes more fitting for her that we had spare, same with the centaurical one, Abel. I drove the car at walking pace down that bumpy trail, eyeing her as she walked; to the left, Archie and Abel nearby, eyeing the conversation as they walked on our right flank, some more people wandering out in other directions.

"Lauren?" I put forth, of who was currently orbiting overhead, taking a quick scouting peek at Gabriel's behest, though she was drifting back down now. "Crazy hobo attacked her then me, I... stopped him. Guess she owes me or something." Reina's head bobbed a little, feeling the straps of her tank-top shirt. I saw that barcode of hers on her shoulder, like I'd seen before on Lauren. "...So what's with your accent, then, Archie?" I inquired with a turn of my head, redirecting my attention to the fox man on the other side.

"It's how I fockin' speak. I dunno 'bout any 'accent'."

"...British. That's what we call that, that kind of voice," I put forth. He nodded slowly, with that sour face of his scrunched up into a constant scowl.

"-Kinda more Irish if you ask me," Gabriel jutted in. "Cockney, maybe? Welsh? One of those fuckin' places."

"Whatever. Just some mental conditioning bullshit."

"...What?" I uttered, Lauren landing somewhere out front, re-adjusting where her rifle was slung, panting a little as the jeep slowly ambled towards her.

"You think I'm some sort of regular hybrid?" I saw him roll up his sleeve of that striped shirt of his. I saw his barcode- while it was like the others, it had a large letter E dominating the top of it. "I know what the fuck went on in that facility. Least I know now, for what it's worth. I'm an Engie. Engineer Hybrid. We kept that fockin' place running, thought it was some shite. A prison, living in some horrible world where your jobs are picked for you. That's what they brainwashed me to believe. One day all the shit goes wrong, containment breach, the scientists, you humans run for the hills and we're stuck there wondering what the fuck is going on. What the fuck an 'America' is. Now I know why you people made me, even if I don't know really *why*."

"Ah, taking your frustrations out on us passerby smooth-skins?" Gabriel chortled while Lauren tuned in on the conversation silently, walking by Gabriel in the shotgun seat with her ear angled out towards the other hybrids and Archie's conversation.

"Don't misinterpret me. Not like it was *your* fault, anyways. We're just trying to survive. It's either rob people out here or go back in. S'not pleasant in there, shit's *focked*. Yeah, eh dragon?" He paused to ask of Lauren, who rose her brow with puffed out cheeks as she exhaled, nodding with a subtle "yeah, it was pretty bad in there" following the pop of her lips, like the entire ordeal was highly exasperating. "...Just so you know I didn't ask for any of this *shite*."

"...Fair enough. What about their names?" I asked.

"Shepherd siblings are named after my brother and sister. The brother and sister that don't exist, that I was brainwashed to believe exist. Figured I'd-"

"Wait, siblings?"

"I mean, I figured as such," Archie said, brow raised. "They don't strike me as lovers. Both same genetic imprint to resemble something you'd call a German Shepherd, similar personalities to each other too. Reina Shepherd, Abel Shepherd. Keeps things simple."

"One of them's a centaur, though. Can't be related, can they?" I could hear Gabriel let out a little chuckle as I put this forth in curiosity.

"...Mate, you're really out of the loop about us, huh?" Archie's left eyebrow was practically leaving his head. "Same species. Same race, even. S'all phenotype. Like the color of your fuckin' eyes. Phenotype bull-shite genetic fuckery." Archie sighed. "...Guess I can't blame you. You didn't know about us anyways. Big secret 'n all that shite." Another small pause.

"What about... Katt?" I asked, seeing her walking out ahead, weaving through the solar towers, looking around for anything interesting. "She doesn't have a barcode."

"Yeah she does, you can see it with a blacklight. She's an experimental. Socio chamber subject."

"...Socio chamber subject?" Archie sighed heavily at my inquisition.

"Mate, you really gonna make me explain that nightmare shite? I do me best not to even think about it. Like what happened'a me but a million times worse." I just glared at him and he sighed harder, seeing me expect him to go on, as well as most everyone else in the car. "You really think her name is Katt? She can't stand her real name, trying to forget about where she came from. Imagine that, pinkskin."

"...What was her real name?" I asked.

"Susan Mulberry," Archie responded, ready to go on. "I may have been brainwashed to do work, but they were brainwashed so you humans could see what they'd do in certain situations. What do you think hybrids were made for? Just the fun of it? Sociological experiments, brov. She lived in this big underground dome they convinced her was the whole world. Experiment was some bullshit. Imagine you're living your life and one day you learn everything is wrong. You were tricked, you can remember your whole life but you were born last Thursday for the experiment of the week. Abel and Reina were lucky, they got born out of incubation chambers knowing nothing but how to speak, read, and barely conduct themselves in public." He scoffed, the shepherd siblings coughing plainly and trying to act unbothered by Archie's snap. "See, she's mad just like the way I am, learning your whole life was bullshit. Just a kid, that's all, dealing with it like a kid would. We had nothing to call her but what she was. A cat. Fockin' british shorthair lookin. So we call her Katt."

"Jesus," Anthony, who was listening as he walked behind the canid hybrids uttered.

"Jesus' right," Archie spat, before eyeing to Lauren walking in front of the car. "Reminds me, What was your deal, dragoness? You've got a barcode, no E, you don't act like a Socio. Guessin you a Tubie like the Shepherds?"

"Uh..."

"Accelerated growth chamber. Tube-born. Grown like a commodity, all you've ever known. Thas' you, innit?"

"...Yeah. You're... sounds about right. I wasn't in an experiment. I think." Lauren responded back with that heavy, exasperated sigh, put in discomfort by her very memories.

"You teach 'em to use those guns, or did they already know?" Gabriel asked Archie.

"They got the gist of it right quick, sure," Archie said. "Musta been some shite in the chambers."

"Did you come out knowing guns too?"

"I got a way with machines, mate. 'S in my blood, case you haven't noticed, program directive or some shite. I can figure out an M16."

"What about Katt?"

"You daft? I'm not giving a twelve-year-old a gun. Childhood's already been ruined a lot by account of it being a big lie. Figure she's got to enjoy what childhood she's got left."

"...So you just go robbing people in front of her, class act all right," Gabriel snarked back with that shit eating grin of his.

"...for what it's worth, we- we make her not watch," Abel chimed in, Archie rolling his eyes.

"But, do they know about call of duty?" Wilson asked with an engaged grin, walking to their left.

"Call of what?" Archie responded.

"Oh, that's the... army game, right?" Reina responded, and Archie faltered in his step a little bit, staring back at her in bafflement.

"...Yeah," Abel put in, a hand going up like he was pawing at an invisible answer. "V-video game with the soldiers."

"...I could have used some fockin' video games," Archie snarled, shrugging to himself with a disgusted look as they walked on.

It was probably the hybrids, but settling down to sleep for the evening felt a little more on-edge than back home. "Camping trip this ain't," was what Gabriel had to say on the subject. I tried to believe it didn't bother me, sleeping out here in this forest of steel in the desert. I was first watch tonight. I'd look at Gabriel in his sleep but it always looked like he was faking it. He didn't snore, he just sat there in the shotgun seat, not bothering with any sort of bedding just sitting there with his gun in his arms, motionless, dead still. Chest didn't even heave, unlike Lauren, the loudest snorer in the group, pawing at herself and mumbling in her dreams, cuddling with her rifle, ears flicking this way and that. Maria was just like Gabriel, except far less peaceful looking, with that mighty uncomfortable scowl on her face. I woke up Gabe, his eyes swiveling open just like he was never asleep in that creepy way of his. His watch. Time for me to sleep. I pulled off my helmet and vest and laid down with Maria.

Staring up at the stars again. Time to sleep, huh? Without city lights the stars screamed out light up there, a bright stripe across the top of the world. I fell asleep beside Maria with discontented thoughts about the size of the universe and how none of this shit mattered, in an altogether detached, amused fashion, like pondering this ironically, the thought roused in me from Archie and Katt's stories hours before.

I was awakened to the scent of sausages sizzling on the griddle, and the ear-piercing emergency broadcast klaxon screaming as Gabe had reached into the car console and turned the radio up all the way, onto whatever broadcast station there was.

"*Jesus*, Gabe," Lauren was grunting, grasping her ears. "Alright! We're awake!"

"Ugh, asshole," Kyle was snarling.

"Owe me some gratitude, fuckface," Gabriel was laughing to himself, tending to the meal he was making. "It's breakfast time."

"Wait, are you- oh, shit," Kyle uttered, smelling the bacon, eggs, and sausages on the little gas stove. "Aw, sweet!"

"...You're easily swayed," Maria grunted to Kyle, getting up to go to the radio, turn it down to an acceptable level and cycle through it. More E-Broadcasts, though now they had something different to say.

"STAND BY. MESSAGE FROM THE WHITE HOUSE AT 1200 HOURS," Followed the usual warning message.

"That's a lot of hours," Wilson said.

"That's noon," I grunted back, getting myself some food.

"...It was a joke," Wilson said after a little reflective pause, like it was obvious It wasn't really a joke but he had to lick his wounds somehow.

"Eat up and enjoy, this is the last of the non-preserved stuff until we can scrounge up some more," Gabriel said, before hefting his rifle, now back in that PDW configuration with the big suppressor and dot sight. "Though I managed to pop a jackrabbit, so that's today's mystery meat."

"Aw, we're letting the hybrids have some of the good stuff?" Kyle sneered.

"Kyle, if you take issue with my hospitality you're perfectly welcome to say so," Gabe said with that evil smile of his, like it was a threat, and though he glared at Gabe he hadn't much to say in response. "Probably at least another half day until we're out of the solar fields. They're behaving themselves, then we can ditch 'em…" Gabe looked around, seeing Katt and Samantha by the water, freshening their faces up with it. "...Unless any of you get attached."

"We don't have enough room on the jeep, though," Anthony reasoned.

"Yeah. So don't get attached."


A short drive through the morning, poking our way through those fields in boredom before noon rolled around. I drove, Wilson took shotgun while Gabriel was where Maria usually sat, in the seat behind me taking a rest with his seat lowered though he was still technically awake, eyes darting around and jutting in on conversations, next to him was Anthony, all the rest either sitting in the back or walking, Abel with Katt on his back riding close to me, Lauren landing a bit out in front after making her rounds, panting.

"It's noon," She uttered breathlessly, wings ruffling as she passed me to go for some water. "Aren't you going to-"

"Oh, yeah," I said, going for the radio. "Guys. Special message, everyone shut up." I turned on the full broadcast screen of the dashboard holographic, selecting through static to the news screen. Everyone was quiet, we were just in time as the usual emergency broadcast system had been replaced by the White House Seal and a dull flatline was playing.

There the president was, Henry Hernandez sitting in the oval office. I could read his composure, how he was all too obviously putting on a brave face despite the cold sweat beading on his head. "My fellow Americans," He spoke slowly, addressing us, as I turned it way up so all could hear. "Just a few days ago, a series of cyberattacks took down our infrastructures and the infrastructures of many hundreds of countries around the globe. Canada, Mexico, China, India, the European Confederacy and many more are all in a state of emergency, as are we. We have underestimated the seriousness of this problem we have encountered, and it has cost us dearly, and these new creatures, these new people, hybrids, are as much victims as you or me. I promise, my administration did all it could to try and ease the situation; it was the past administrations that allowed the political climate we find ourselves in to brew for so long. But, take our heartfelt apology, so that we might be able to make amends and fix that which others have broken, before it is too late. For those of you calling for war, I implore you... This is not the time... For rash decisions," He said with a pause, staring blankly at his podium for but a moment, while murmurs throughout my group were present as my brow furrowed sternly. "Please, as your president, I ask of you to not partake in any such violence, towards your brothers and sisters as civilized, rational, thinking beings, and as Americans. And the hybrids deserve no less: despite what they may look like, many of them think and feel just as you would. Show them the compassion you would show a fellow human, an American." Another pause, another insecure, worrisome pause. "We, as Americans, will get through this. As your president, I promise you this. All of you out there who might be in distress, stay strong, and those of you ready to destroy this great Union that has stood for nearly three hundred years, I implore you to reconsider, just so that we might be able to pull through this terrible series of events with no more unnecessary bloodshed." He looked up at the camera one last time. It was like he wanted to salute, his hand trembling on his desk though it never rose. I looked into his eyes and bumps formed on the back of my neck, for what he had to say next chilled me. Not what he said, but how he said it. "Long live the Republic, and *God* be with you all."

And with that, the broadcast was over. It eerily felt like a speech a captain would make right before going down with his ship.

"War?" Wilson asked, leaning in. "What the fuck is he talking about war?"

"...Maybe some assholes are getting it in their head to exterminate the hybrids. Wouldn't be surprised," Gabriel chuckled at the apprehension of the five hybrids among us.

"No, no, sounded different," Maria said. "You think we're blaming China for this or something?"

"...Well shit. Fuckin' wetback-in-chief could have extrapolated on what the fuck he meant," Gabe grunted, getting up a little. "Told y'all if it is, anyways. Never trusted the fuckin' Chinese."

"What's a predsy-dent?" I heard Katt ask Abel, scooting up on where she sat on his back close to him, as Abel's head turned, swiveling an ear towards her.

"It's the king of the humans," Abel murmured back, and Gabriel opened his mouth to correct this for but a moment, before he just laughed.

"He's not half off," He grunted to us, lowering his mask over his face again to cover his eyes and get more rest.

"I bet," Wilson said, turning to me, still with his right arm hanging out the window and pointing his finger up at me. "It might have been whoever was left of that cartel that tried to take over Mex-"

*Crack.*

### Chapter 18

"You know, son," I can remember my dad telling me, as I sat in the pit of the firing range. "When I was in the Marines, this is how they taught me to know if we were being shot at. Specifically, knowing the sound." The pit was a deep dugout, down on the firing lines of the shooting range of that survival commune, where we could safely operate the target mechanisms, raising targets to be shot at. "It's good to know the sound, good to know if you're being shot at. So you know what to do next, to take cover." I looked up at him. "Just to know the sound, of course. A bullet travels a lot faster than the speed of sound, at least out of a rifle. You're going to hear a snap, before you hear the gunshot. It might sound like two people are shooting at you, but it's just one. Okay, son?"

"...yeah," My little, prepubescent voice said back. "Makes sense." My dad smiled, raising his walkie talkie.

"Alright Chris, take a shot," He said to the other person on the line, somebody back in the shooting station of the range.

The crack whizzed by first, like a stick being snapped next to my ear, louder than I'd expected, then the boom of the gun echoing caught up to us, far less loud and pleasant.

"Huh," I let out a breathless, fascinated grunt, raising my eyebrows. Dad smiled back.

---

The hills echoed in a gunshot, the boom catching up with the bullwhip crack that pierced my ears. Here we were, finally on the edge of the solar fields. The highlands before us and to the right. And there Wilson was, hands around his neck. Blood bubbling out of his mouth with that look in his eyes, that deer-in-the-headlights look. That horror, that unimaginable horror. I wouldn't forget the look he gave me for the rest of my life.

*Crack, crack, crack.* Bullets pinged off of the carapace of the car, followed by echoing booms.

"CONTACT!" Gabriel screamed, piling out of his seat, bailing out with his duffel bag in his hands as he did. Screams from Holly and Samantha and Katt, Wilson tried to speak but nothing came out but gurgles. "GET OUT, SPREAD OUT! CONTACT RIGHT, ON THE RIDGE!" Gabriel was roaring. He immediately popped up and let out a string of automatic fire from his MDR, though it was still in the silenced, close-range configuration, firing to suppress. Wilson must have heard this, bailing out to the right unlike Anthony who began spraying bullets, much like Gabriel at the truck at the top of the ridge, from which silhouettes flashed about and muzzle pops screamed out from. Wilson fell to his knees as he tumbled out the door towards the hostiles, losing his balance and was unable to really catch himself with his left hand still wrapped around his throat. I saw in a flash the back of his neck, just off to the side of his spine where the bullet must've flew through. If I had the time to think on it, it must've blasted right through and barely grazed me. I was covered in the blood spray of his carotid, but of course I couldn't think on it, fishing for my rifle where it was stuck with my body armor. I tried to grab for all of my gear but more pops made me dive back out to the left with only my rifle. I felt naked, exposed. Wilson was out in front.

"We have to get Wilson!" I said.

"...Fucking shit," Gabriel was snarling to himself as he was taking the silenced upper receiver off his gun, to put the scoped rifle one on. I saw Abel run up to the car, popping up out of cover over the side of the jeep to fish for his gun, any gun. "Get down, you idiot!" Gabriel grunted. Another crack perforated Abel this time, I saw a hole open up in his back and he grunted like the wind had been knocked out of him and he fell over onto the ground, staring up into the sky with two rifles.

"Ow," He muttered out plainly, dazed and blinking with his eyes wide, gulping down, blood bubbling out of him. Gabriel sighed long and hard, like inconvenienced or exasperated, finally having assembled his rifle. He poked up for a second before bullets careened over our heads, Archie sprinting past to grab one of the rifles Abel had snagged.

"Noah, suppress him, I'll line up a shot with the sniper."

"Which one's the sniper?!" I spat out, not realising my own fearful voice crack. More snaps, Lauren ducked behind a tower shooting out from as much cover, though she yelped and pulled back, letting her gun hang from it's sling as she inspected the part of her upper wing closest to her torso, a little hole perforating it. I looked over, seeing Archie bleeding from the head already, grasping his ear and cursing.

"Jesus!" Lauren grunted.

"I'd say the one that can aim," Gabriel said. His nonchalance was eerie.

"We- We need to get Wilson!" Daniel said, the girls still screaming. More pops. Blood on the ground. We were hardly shooting back. Kyle was stooped over Holly on the ground. She wasn't moving, and he was petrified. Maria was running left, ducking this way and that around the towers, flanking them and drawing fire before she dove behind a rock, bullets kicking up all around that rock as she reloaded her Armalite, having fired till dry, evidently. Her face was wrapped into a mighty scowl, masking fear with an insulted rage. *How dare you,* her eyes spoke rage.

"We need to all shoot at once so Gabriel can get the sniper!" I yelled out, looking one by one at everyone still combat-effective, so to speak. Maria, on the far left, Lauren, close left. Archie and Reina on the close right. Anthony was rather unable to fight too, down in the bed of the jeep beside the seat where he'd been sitting, cowering behind the bulletproof door of the jeep and shooting his gun haphazardly through the rolled-down window and shrieking, reloading with shaking hands only to repeat his ineffective spraying as bullets bounced off of the car door loudly to make him scream and holler. "Alright, on three!" I ordered, before Daniel, probably in the hopes of saving Wilson, dashed out. "FUCK!" I screamed. Daniel pushing our hand as he ran out. "SHOOT! SHOOT!" By the time we started shooting I couldn't see him anymore. I couldn't see anything but the men we had to kill, so far away, a tunnel blocking out all else.

A cacophony of gunfire rose to follow Daniel, and sooner rather than later I was deaf. I thought I saw some of those silhouettes some hundred fifty meters away either duck away along the sand dunes or fall. I scanned, ears screaming. I saw one, getting up. He must think he could make a sprint to that rock before him, that we were out of ammo. I couldn't hear his gunfire as he shot while running, ears still ringing as he sprayed bullets haphazardly from his semi-automatic. I could feel them whizz around the air, see the muzzle pops, barely feeling the bass. Gabriel was reloading, I still had a handful of rounds. I didn't feel in danger, it practically looked like he was running away. I think I saw blood on him, peering at him through my 2.5x magnified optic. I sent a round that perforated him like a punch, body twisting as he dropped like he'd just lost his balance, like someone shoved him over, tripped him. I saw him getting up, slowly, flopping there. He was already bloody, knelt there trying to find his feet and get back up. His head rose to the sky, now crying out in pain. Another instant immortalized, seared into my mind, this man crying out to god there on his knees. I sent another bullet through him and he was done, rolling onto his back and laying still to clutch his rifle across his chest and die.

That was it.

---

I can remember taking a first aid course, at my father's behest of course. It was funny, those CPR dummies and messing around with the gauze, dressing a fake wound with a friend. Wilson was there, we partnered up most days for the practice stuff.

There was one day where we were shown images from autopsies and crime scenes, actual people, hurt and dead and dying, shown to us. Get us to take this seriously, maybe. I can remember brushing it all off. Just like with most things my dad involved me in, this was something else I'd never have to use, just another paranoid fantasy.

---

Screaming, screaming. Panicked whines that turned to yelps as my hearing returned to me, bit by tiny bit. I was still putting on my armor, my vest and helmet now that there was a lull in the fighting, but I sort of already knew it was over. Daniel had half crawled his way back to our side by the time we got up to get to him, Gabriel still covering the hill while those far less calm and collected had the unfortunate task of dragging Daniel back. There was a trail of blood in the sand following to the exact spot where Daniel had fell when he took a bullet.

"Noah- NOAH," Gabe bumped me. I had to read his mouth to really get what he was trying to tell me, my ears still screaming. "We're not out of it yet, keep your eyes open while we stabilize the wounded." He was handing me my reloaded rifle. I'd dropped it when I'd pulled my armor on. He reached out to slap that dumb look off my face again, with me taken by shock. I saw Kyle hulking over Holly on the ground. The top of Holly's skull was in bits. Her eyes were open but they didn't focus on anything, her skin was pale and growing paler by the second. Kyle's hands hovered over the wound, like to hold her brains in, indecisive whether or not to really touch her. He was whispering something. Trembling. I'd never seen somebody so big tremble like that before. Gabriel paused for a brief moment on his way to help out with Daniel, seeing Abel on the ground, holding a big square pad over his chest, stripped of his upper garment already. "Hold that wound shut, dogboy. Make sure the one on your back is on good too. We don't need your lung collapsing while we work on Daniel, even if you have three more. Got it?"

"...G-gotcha," He muttered, blood in his mouth, still staring up into the sky. Gabriel's eyes drifted to Kyle, figuring there was no point in telling Kyle to let her go, yet. There were more important things to be done, and he was still reeling.

"W-what about Wilson?!" I shouted to Gabriel, as Daniel screamed his lungs out getting lifted onto a tarp so we could work on his wound, Anthony cutting his shirt open with a knife, revealing a second, bloody belly button oozing blood and intestinal ichor as he writhed, those of us marginally functional trying to restrain his thrashing so he wouldn't hurt himself more, at Gabriel's demand.

"He's dead," Gabriel grunted back. He barely sounded disappointed, much less mournful. I paced to peek around the other side of the car, and instantly regretted it. There he was. A pile of blood and clothes. I stood there alone, gazing at the wreck of my friend. Head blown open by several bullets and jaw hanging slack, body dripping with holes, the soft armor of the police vest he wore useless against high-velocity rifle rounds. His PDW, that shorty MDR, or what was left of it was in his lap, perforated just like he was, plastic stock shattered into bits, barrel twisted and chewed by bullets, magazine having exploded, unfired rounds all over the ground mixing in with his blood. In his left hand, unlike his right that was barely hanging on by a thread after being shot up along with his primary weapon, was his secondary weapon. "...Died holding a fucking Hi-Point," Gabriel's black humor was not without its bitterness as he injected the current surgery patient, Daniel, with something out of his medical bag. Probably a painkiller.

"Oh my god! Oh my fucking god!" Daniel's voice was shrill. "I'm gonna die! I'm gonna fucking die!" He was thrashing as Gabriel did his best to tend to him, his limbs held down by Maria, Reina and Lauren, attempting to restrain him.

"Shut up Dan, you're gonna be fine. Most of your guts are on the right side of your skin. People've survived worse."

"F-FUCK YOU!" Daniel spat, calming down bit by bit as the opiates he was given began to take effect.

"...Anthony, you were trying to be a med student, right?" Anthony was helping, though he was obviously barely holding it together, chest heaving, cold sweat beading on pale skin, eyes with that crazed animal look.

"I-I'm an intern," He reasoned, as if he was trying to get out of doing anything. "I-"

"Good enough. We've gotta stitch him up, then it's the dog-taur's turn. Green," Gabriel ordered. Lauren's head shot over, her eyes wide in that same adrenal terror everyone was feeling. She'd been zoning out for the last while or so, just like me. At least she was lucid. And in one piece. "You good to fly?"

"I- My wing got shot," She reasoned. "W-wh-"

"It's just a little hole. Throw a band-aid on it. Can you secure the bad guys? We need to know if we're safe yet."

"...Something tells me they're dead," Archie grunted, tying his head up with gauze, from where his ear got an involuntary piercing.

"Damn, you can still hear?" Gabriel's humor was unstoppable, even if curbed by bitterness.

"I got... one left," He grunted.

"Noah, make yourself useful and secure their site while Lauren covers you from the air," Gabriel ordered over the moans and low shrieks of Daniel, slowly quieting as the drugs kicked in. "...Vehicle might still be good." It was all too much for me to watch, anyways.

I walked up through the open space. We were barely getting out of the solar fields, we walked right into an ambush. An ambush? Why? Who were these people? Some part of me expected this. The blood, the shooting. This is what the apocalypse is supposed to be, right? No. Why, then? Why?!

There my man, my mark, my latest nasty work was. Crumpled over on his back. He was staring up into the sky, unmoving, like a stone. I walked up on him with my gun pointing at him in case he suddenly came to life but he stayed, as I expected, motionless. Staring into the sun with the same look that Holly had back there. For a moment as I towered over him I wondered who he was, what his name was, what the fuck he was doing out here. He was a white guy, maybe slightly hispanic with black hair and dark eyes. His weapon lay clutched across his chest with his arms folded over it, an ancient looking, smoking surplus SKS rifle consisting of crummy wood and rusty, patinated steel, with a cheap dot sight atop its aftermarket gas tube. A bullet, probably one of mine had perforated its buttstock and it was spattered in blood but other than that it was fine. His old chinese surplus chest rig he wore was holed up with bullets and bloody just like he was. I took a long couple of seconds to pull his rifle off of him, peeling it from his limp arms to check the chamber. One round in the chamber, another in the magazine. I charged the bolt twice to unload it, the rounds falling into the dirt beside him, the gas assembly and chamber exuding smoke that disappeared in another moment. I was roused to peel the ammo rig off of him, his body flopping as I relieved him of his munitions, putting the ammo rig and his rifle a ways away. I didn't think that he was going to get up and start shooting again, a handful of oozing holes in his torso, holes that oozed slower and slower as the seconds passed. I took one final look in his eyes before stooping over to close them for him and wrapping his arms across his chest. It didn't make him look any more peaceful, nor did it make me feel any better, but it felt like the right thing to do. Respectful. There was more death ahead of me to attend to.

Wilson dead. Holly dead. Daniel dying. It was like wading through the waking afterthoughts of a nightmare, as I approached the truck there, thinking about everything and nothing all at once. I saw one man's head burst open laying beside the truck with the door open, blood and brains splattered into the cabin as he lay in front of his rifle, some old bolt-action with a scope that was shattered by a bullet. This must have been the sniper, shooting from the crux of his door as a support. I went along to the back of the truck, looking it all up and down all the while. Must have been an older ethanol one unlike mine, with minimal electronics to still be running after the hack. Bullets had pierced the whole thing and one of the tires had burst, being the old style that needed to be filled with air, unlike my jeep's skeletal wheels. There were holes all over the chassis. I wondered if it could even work now, walking around to the back. Another man lay in the bed, motionless, red-soaked as could be. Big and bald with a big bushy beard, clutching his bolt-action rifle. He'd probably bled to death laying there, his eyes were closed and there was a strange calmness on his face. I pried his rifle from his ironclad grip, another scoped bolt action, taking his revolver from its holster too, unloading them all.

I sat there on the edge of the truckbed for a minute, looking through the stuff, before I fell off of it and fell on all fours. This was all so horrible and it was all catching up with me now. I emptied my stomach on the ground, acid burning my throat and nasal passage. I couldn't even weep, I just channeled it into my vomit.

"you good?" Gabriel was there. Like a spectre, he was just there, having walked on up. Daniel was probably either dead or stable for him to be here now. I hadn't even heard him approach, but I guess that made sense given the state of my ears.

"...Looks like... three guys."

"If there were any more, looks like they've run off," His face was stern, staring about. "...Fuck." he came right up to where I knelt, grasping me by the body armor strap and wrenching me up suddenly, viciously, growling in my face. I was terrified in an instant as his eyes became daggers. "Never take this off out here again," He growled, referring to my armor. I nodded sharply, as he went about looking through their stuff. I saw Lauren taking off from where the guy I killed lay, holding his weapon and his ammo vest, to bring them over, the enemy vehicle secure. She landed before us, as Gabe dragged the body out of the bed of the truck with a grunt. "...Some white guy," He said, noting their complexion. I could see Maria walking up the ridge too now, towards us. Gabe looked around. He went to the ammo boxes in the bed, cracking one open to look inside as Lauren landed beside me with a final blast of her wings.

"I... I'm sorry, I should have been scouting, I would have seen these guys, I-I-"

"Green, you're alive. Take some credence in that first. Collect your thoughts. You feeling sorry for yourself isn't going to get us anywhere." Lauren shut her mouth, gritting her teeth for a second at Gabriel's rapid-fire reassurance concealed as forward-thinking. "...Besides. I was the one napping." It was like he actually felt bad but couldn't let himself show it, not really. How he grit his teeth, looking through their stuff.

Maria was back there towards the front of the truck, having walked out to us, looking the driver's seat sniper in the eye- at least, in the only one he had left. I was beginning to walk back, seeing her catch up next to me as I approached her, the two of us rather alone now, standing in what was the no man's land a mere five minutes before.

"...You remember what we said, Noah?" Maria was trying to stay calm, breathing heavy, a darkness, a wild animal in her eyes. Trying to think of the endgame, in her little way. But I saw the panic, I saw the rage. It practically took me by surprise.

"Wh-"

"Isn't it a little coincidental that trouble seems to follow us with Gabriel around, Noah?" She growled. I saw how she had her hand on her holstered pistol. She was trying to stay cool, act like she was just resting her hand, but I saw how she gripped the handle, how white her knuckles became. We walked there in quiet silence, Lauren back there with Gabe helping him take stock, and everyone else out in front of us.

"...You think those guys were... cartel?" I blurted back. I must admit that it wasn't beyond the realm of possibility.

"...Siña has a lot of money, Gabe. And white boys aren't exactly excluded from their ranks, I'm sure you know," Maria motioned her head over her shoulder, as if implying Gabriel, and even the three dead gunmen.

"You still don't have proof. They-"

"He's a risk, Noah. A risk Wilson and Holly dealt with their lives, and Daniel is dealing with right now." I bit my lip. I watched us approach, coming up to the jeep. Wilson's body laying some ways away, covered by the tarp. His equipment was on the ground next to where he was covered for now, shattered rifle, pistol, bloody ammo, shredded armor vest. All soaked in blood. Daniel was out of it for now, an IV strung up from the rafter of the jeep's rollcage, Abel laying on the ground and staring upwards with a blank, blinking expression now post-operation, the both of them stitched up good. Kyle was still motionless, but at least his position had changed, now with him sitting up against the wheel of the jeep and staring at Holly's body. Not draped in a tarp like Wilson's, but with her head covered by an old t-shirt. Suppose there was more left of her. Less of her that was blown to bits, unlike Wilson.

"Noah," Maria turned to me, that last time. Her pistol was in her hand, low. "Remember what we said. I'm going to have to deal with him if you don't." I saw her eyes. How serious she was. Hearts still pounding. I didn't know what to say. I was about to see my girlfriend kill my best friend. I saw that truck coasting down the hill with no engine. How it limped with that one busted wheel in the front, Lauren laying in the back as a counterweight, grabbed hold of the side of the truckbed and riding it down with him. She disembarked with a beat of her wings as Gabriel pulled the brakes.

"...Engine looks alright," He extrapolated. "We'll have to put the spare on if we want it to run good, but aside from that I think we can salvage this. Bulletholes and all," He said. People gathered round. Maria walked away from me, like she was to sulk in the shadows. Find the right place to line up a shot, shadowing Gabriel as he walked. "Hey, Archie. You good with machines?"

"...That *is* my fockin' job description," He responded, getting up from where he sat on the back of the jeep to head on over to the few short steps towards the truck, where Gabriel stood. "Lucky for you, they missed my brain," he tapped his ear, all clotted up with bandage, readjusting his M4 that he'd gotten back, slung around him.

"Huh, lucky, ain't it," Gabriel said, going on behind Archie for a second as Archie looked the cabin over. "You know what else is lucky?" He asked. "Now that we killed these guys, we get their stuff. They seemed to have an awful lot of 5.56, even though they didn't seem to be carrying any guns chambered in that round. A lot of loaded STANAG mags. AR magazines." Archie looked back slowly, as Maria came up behind Gabe. Her glock harshly quivering in her steady hands as she swallowed spittle. "Now why, Archie... Would a bunch of people hunting us incidentally have a bunch of ammunition and magazines to guns they don't have?"

Archie's pause was brief, but it was enough. A tinge of weakness, a crack for Gabriel to dive right into. His hands shot around Archie's throat, who gagged out loudly as Gabriel pressed him back, against the truck, Archie momentarily frozen in surprise and terror. "Awful lucky to have some bullet-shields to help you kill the pissed off *fucks* you stole your guns from, huh fox-boy?!" Gabriel roared, and Maria paused dead in her tracks, gun frozen. "You see that pile of guts over there under that tarp, Archie?! I knew that guy for four fucking years. He was a jackass but a good friend of mine, and now he's dead. I never had much respect for Kyle or his dumbfuck girl, but she's dead too and he might as well be at the moment. But in all this shooting you don't seem to have lost *anyone*. Awful lucky for your side, huh?!"

"A-Abel got shot too! I got shot!" He barely gagged out, pointing to his bandaged ear, like Gabriel had let off him for a second so he could speak, before he was hoisted higher and gagged out, his digitigrade feet leaving the ground, hoisted up into the air and kicking madly as Gabriel did his thing. I know Archie probably wasn't that heavy, but this was beyond impressive to the point of plain terrifying how Gabriel effortlessly could heft Archie about.

"NO!" Katt was screaming, going up to hit Gabriel in the side. Maria, still perplexed by the sheer plotline unfolding before her, couldn't help but want to see its end, in some bid for truth, if this gunfight really wasn't Gabriel's compatriots coming to collect his head. She holstered her gun slowly and subtly, as if she'd never drawn it.

"...Woulda saved me the trouble if they could shoot better," Gabriel growled, ignoring Katt's pitiful pleas. "You seen this truck before, Arch?" Gabriel nodded his head to the truck before us, his voice momentarily quieted, Katt now reduced to mindless bawling, falling down on the ground. Archie didn't respond, even if he was being gagged or not he was making no effort to answer. "ARCHIE, I DON'T APPRECIATE BEING *LIED* TO. AND I'M GOING TO START SQUEEZING THIS TINY NECK OF YOURS UNTIL SOMETHING POPS, UNLESS YOU TELL ME WHERE YOU GOT THOSE *FUCKING* GUNS FROM!!!" Gabriel was bellowing like a monster. I could see his eyes, the devil in them, face twisted beyond recognition. I'd never seen him this mad, it practically took my breath away, everyone around equally terrified. If I was in Archie's position I'd be wetting myself.

"P-put him down!" Reina was there. Her Kel-Tec pointed right at him. Guns came up, pointing back at her. Katt screamed, flailing over to her, gripping Reina's clothes and pulling herself up on her fellow hybrid to stare wide-eyed at the other guns pointed back at Reina, who she so dearly wanted to protect. Poor little Katt, not wanting to lose anything, lose anyone else. I saw the guns pointed at Reina, even Maria had drawn on her. Maria, defending Gabe's life now. What an odd twist. Lauren too, of course. "You on the human side or something?!" Reina shouted at Lauren. it was like Reina wanted to call Lauren a traitor but didn't feel that word was right.

"If you put it that way, yeah, I am!" Lauren uttered indignantly and Reina grit her teeth. I saw her gun quake, before it slowly went down a tad, but still stayed ready.

"...We stole the guns. Alright!?" Reina admitted, taking her right hand off the pistol grip and putting it in the air, a gesture of peace though it might as well be her swearing herself into court, and Archie responded to this by snarling to himself, as best he could with a half-crushed windpipe and practically disconnected cervical bones, still hovering midair thanks to Gabriel's ludicrous strength. Gabe's grip let up a little, but he still held Archie aloft, the tiptops of Archie's toes touching the ground again to give him breathing room.

"You did a half-job," Gabe growled of the pile of enemy guns Lauren had collected, bringing Archie close enough to snarl this in his face.

"...We only needed the guns for the... three of us. We felt bad, they told us they'd be defenseless with no guns," Archie hoarsely uttered.

"They guilted you. And here *we* are, Being guilted by you now. Where does the buck stop, Archie?" Another pause from Archie. Nothing to say. At least no way to say it, yet. "YOU PLANNING ON TAKING ADVANTAGE OF MY HOSPITALITY, ARCHIE?!" another low roar. Archie hoisted a little higher by his neck.

"W-we just want to survive out here!" He croaked.

"...You said you were lucky, and you are, you know that?" Gabriel said, putting Archie down on solid ground, slowly. "You're lucky you're a so-called engineer hybrid and that's why you're useful at the moment. The others you brought are stupid and harmless, but you?" Gabriel said. "You're the dangerous kind of stupid. Leave them with a grudge and the guns to still shoot you with. No wonder you make for such a shitty fucking highwayman. A thief with morals." Gabriel practically tossed Archie in the direction of the engine of the truck, him falling onto the ground and coughing, to feel his throat. Gabriel reached into the cabin to pull the lever to raise the hood, which popped open. "Take a fucking look. You're stuck with us until you fix this. I'm liable to make you come with us so you don't do any more retarded shit." Gabriel turned about, seeing Reina standing there, gun down. He approached, step by step with cold murder in his eyes and she froze, jaw going slack, eyes wide in terror as this... monster in human form approached. His left hand relieved her of her rifle and his right hand reared back to give her the backhand of her life in an instant, a brutal swipe across the cheek that everybody felt just by seeing and hearing it. Katt cried out at this brutality against her friend. "...Don't point a gun at somebody you're not going to shoot ever again, you stupid bitch. You hear?" He said, rattling her rifle, grabbing the magazine and ejecting it before pulling its charging handle back, seeing no round ejected. "...Not even fucking loaded. Don't bluff. This isn't a fucking game of cards out here. Next time'll get you killed." He tossed the rifle back into the jeep. "Go help Archie and don't fuck anything up."

"Asshole!" Katt ran up, kicking Gabe in the shin. Again, like she'd barely bumped into him. Gabriel only had to look at her once for the petite hybrid to freeze solid just as Reina had, some curse or utterance stuck in her throat like it grew arms and lodged itself there. That was all Gabriel had to say, until he moved around the jeep.

"Aw, shit."

There was a hole in the water barrel. "Shit," Gabe said again, approaching to stick his finger over the hole. The barrel was on the right side of the car, facing towards the people who were shooting at us. I bolted over. "Noah, hold the hole." I did so, more breathless as he was, as he got up to peel off the top of the big water drum. I saw the look on his face. That inconvenienced look, eyes narrowed. "...Yup." I peered up, seeing there the water all the way down to the level of the hole, a tiny, deformed bullet resting there at the very bottom. We barely had five gallons left, if at that.

"Wh- oh," Anthony said, seeing the wet ground all over.

"Poked a hole through the barrel. We've got a day's left at best."

"...You gonna blame us for that too?" Archie grunted, though not exactly without concern as he was looking over the engine.

"Must be that *luck* of yours," Gabriel's sardonic black humor was unstoppable. I looked some more, seeing the spare diesel tank also pierced. I reached in for the toolbag, throwing some duct tape over the holes.

"...Fuel's shot too. We're real low."

"Oh. Brilliant," Gabe sighed.

"We... We need to go back," Anthony was yelping. "We can't do this! We need to go back!"

"Go back to what?" Gabriel put forth. "Go back to what? Why don't you break your phone out, give 911 a ring?"

"...Jesus Christ, it's really happening," Samantha uttered, holding her head.

"Yeah, no shit." Gabriel spat. "Archie. Change of plans. We need water and fuel," He said, Archie slamming the hood shut, evidently done checking everything. "Where's this facility they made you freaks?"

"Wh- Excuse me?" Archie uttered, his free ear twitching.

"Y'know. Y'all keep talking about it. 'S got stuff in it. Where is it?" Archie was silent, leaning on the hood of the car.

"...North of here. Just over that ridge, 'bout ten miles on." Archie was unceremonious about it, going for the jack to replace that wheel. "You think you're gonna go trapseying through it? Isn't exactly a storage depot."

"Well, that is what the US government leased them as, so ElTek could have a good excuse to build 'em so big, or so I've been told," Gabriel extrapolated, crossing his arms. "And you're going to be our guide." Archie paused.

"...You're- You're out of your gourd," Archie uttered, Gabriel smiled. Gabriel was steering the conversation as always.

"Day's worth of water isn't worth much if we run out of fuel too. We're trying to avoid towns until we have to go through the pass at Shortstone."

"...Facility's a fuck of a lot more dangerous than any town!" Archie reasoned.

"Hence why we're bringing a guide."

"Sorry, didn't you say we can leave now?"

"You know, I wasn't being entirely facetious saying that you ought to be looked after," Gabe reasoned. "You know where we're going?" I opened my mouth, not really expecting what Gabe was about to say next, rather I was dreading it. "A survival commune. Nice place. Well defended, remote. Fucking fortress in the mountains near the canadian border."

"G-Gabriel!" I cried.

"You want to survive this bullshit, right?" Gabe reasoned to Archie, ignoring me.

"A- A place like that's gotta be humans-only," Archie yammered back.

"Maybe, maybe not. But we're bringing Green," Gabriel motioned to Lauren. "Besides, they might be able to use an Engie hybrid. They might like you."

"Gabe," I shot in before the conversation could continue, grabbing his arm and yanking him away. I saw his face, like I was now inconveniencing him, in the middle of something. "...can I talk to you a moment?" I coralled him away, so that the only one in hearing distance was Kyle sitting against that tire, though he was still motionless, staring blankly off. "What the fuck are you doing?"

"What, telling them where we're going, huh?" Gabe laughed a little, a cynical little laugh, amused like I was acting like a child. I guess it got to me a little. "I didn't think you wanted to ditch these guys, Noah. Did I guess wrong? Are you some coldhearted fuck only caring about your own ass?" Gabe laughed.

"Gabriel. The Citadel is a secret. We're bringing enough extras as it is."

"...Don't play the bitch here, Noah. You were always going to bring them along ever since you heard their little backstories. Look at yourself. This is practically a formality, you having to chew me out. You know it doesn't mean shit." He gave me that evil little shiteating grin all this time and I steamed. I steamed because he had a point.

"...What makes you think this is your place then, Gabe?" I snarled.

"As a member of this group, I made an executive decision. Filibustered. Can't be a mutiny if we're all in this together, huh?" Gabe shrugged and I clasped harder on his arms. "Don't sweat it. If you want to ditch 'em, we can still ditch 'em."

"We… We're not ditching anybody."

"So you admit there's no problem here and you're just making a scene because your dad taught you you're supposed to. Don't bring deadweights, huh?" Gabe closed in on me, his arms coming up to grasp my forearms, bringing his face close, with that fanged smile of his. "They're not deadweights if we can beat some use out of 'em. We need water. We need fuel. Archie is going to get us that and in return we're gonna string them along as backup in case we run through any more banditos. *Sabes?*" Gabe didn't need my answer. He read defeat in my eyes, shoving me off of him to turn and go back.

"Well, Archie?" Gabe shouted, as he was still changing the wheel; Reina, Anthony and Katt helping out beside him.

"...Fucking fine by me. Just more bullshit, huh?"

"That's right. Just more bullshit." Gabe turned back to me. "Speaking of, what's the word on the bodies?" He implored of me. "You wanna waste your time burying them?" I didn't answer for a while. I hadn't thought of this, even back at my house. I couldn't imagine a scenario where I'd be burying my friends.

"...We're not taking them with us. They're dead. No point now," I sighed. It was like I had to force myself to say it. I was so far past feeling that the words didn't even feel sad.

"Don't wanna leave them lying here? Makes no difference," Gabriel nodded his head to the side, deadly serious.

"Jesus, Gabe," I let out a violent sigh. I raised my hands to brush through my hair, seeing Kyle still staring blankly at the corpse of his girlfriend.

"We're burning daylight. What if those guys had friends?"

"Gabe, we can't just leave them lying around," I said, turning and going for one of the shovels strapped to the side of the jeep. "We're not going to."

"...We aren't doing it for the fucks who shot at us," Gabe reasoned, almost exasperated now. I went over to Kyle. I waved in front of his face, he was still out of it. Stroking his gun slowly. I reached out to take his shotgun from him, pulling the sling off him. He was like a doll, muttering, limp, ghost-faced.

"Come on," I whispered kindly in his ear, pulling him up and to his feet and motioning him to go sit on the bumper of the jeep, where he could stare somewhere else. "Who's gonna help me dig? I asked everyone, practically yelling. "After all, we're burning daylight," I glared back at Gabe, who shrugged, venom still in his eyes.

### Chapter 19

"...Anybody got anything to say?"

"I got nothing… Fuck."

"Kyle?"

"She..." Kyle was slow, still barely moving. How his lip trembled, eyes still quivering back and forth. "...She told me she'd marry me," Kyle's voice was hoarse. Tiny, far away. "She..." He couldn't even bring himself to say her name. That was all Kyle could muster, going to the jeep to collapse into a seat. "...Let's fucking go soon," He muttered.

Some funeral this was.

We had some ground to cover before dark. The facility was just over this hill before us, the highlands overlooking Vegas from the north. The city was distant, glittering, practically a speck. We in the jeep were out front, the truck was used as our medical vehicle, with Abel and Daniel transferred to them. Gabriel drove that one, Archie now sitting shotgun up front with me, our navigator.

"How are Daniel and Abel, Gabe?" I put into the walkie talkie.

"Stable as ever. Anthony just gave them their metabolic inducers. Should heal them up sooner rather than later."

"...guess you lifted those drugs from the cartel, right?"

"Guessed right." If I wasn't in such a dour mood, I would have chuckled.

"How's the sky, Lauren? See anyone?" I asked.

"Clear, so far. I'll... be coming back down soon." I could hear, seeing her circling above in the early twilight skies. I figured it would be dark soon. Be good to set up camp atop the plateau, where we could have a good vista. I felt my brain worm through these things, as a way to distract myself from all of what just happened. This, my working my way away from my own pain, spurred me to speak, if only to keep myself from thinking.

"...So what's the deal with this facility?" I asked to Archie, and I could see in the rearview that Reina too seemed discomforted by this topic by how she wiggled where she knelt in the very back of the jeep almost immediately, ears whipping more often than usual now and fixing her tail between her legs, trying to distract herself by watching out into the distance, yet also peering over her shoulder every now and then, uneasily tapping her trigger finger on the safety of her rifle. Archie too seemed incensed by the topic, shifting in his seat next to me a little. He'd been sharpening his knife for a little while, when the trail conditions permitted it and he wasn't being thrown about.

"...Noah, lemme ask you this first," He put forth after a pause. "Why do you think we escaped?"

"Escaped? If you put it that way I'm guessing it's bad, right...?"

"More than bad, mate. If I was just uncomfortable about getting lied to about my entire fockin' life, wouldn't push me out, not like this. Madhouse. Run by the crazies now."

"...But there is stuff in it, right?"

"Oh, no fockin' shite," Archie leaned back a little, putting the knife back in it's sheath on his molle utility webgear. "It's a self-contained system, requires no outside power, water or food," Archie said slowly. Despite how he held his composure, you could still see him quiver a little bit. "Aquaponic gardens, geo-domes... Geothermal power... A couple thousand stories straight into hell, one hundred thousand hybrids all fucked in the head- well, fucked *with*, brain experiments, that sort of thing," He looked to me now, checking over his gun. "...crammed in there like sardines. Deathtrap."

"You're pretty easily convinced to go into a deathtrap."

"*Back into* a deathtrap," Archie mulled over. "...I didn't see it getting any better by the time I left. Might be alright. Doubt it."

"So why did you stay in the first place? At- At first,"

"Gig was alright. We were in one of those buried geodomes. When security fell and the bullshit started I found my way to one of the domes. Guy, human there, the overseer- bit of an eccentric. Knew that getting out was more of a chore than it was worth so he asserted his dominance. Was alright but I never liked the guy."

"So this guy goes and plays king?"

"Nah, he ain't a despot. We just had a conflict of personality." I glared at Archie for a second, still perplexed. Archie's brow was raised at my own perplexion, as if I was prodding too much like an idiot. "...I think he's a prick, okay?"

"Gotcha," I said, turning back. "...But I'll get to meet this guy."

"Oh I think he'll introduce himself," Archie nodded facetiously.

"Did you piss him off?"

"Nah. He's the type that doesn't get pissed off. Would consider it a loss, that kinda guy." I rose an eyebrow slightly, staring back at Archie, bidding him to elaborate. "He'll just... you'll see." I sighed. I still didn't want to go back to my own thoughts, not yet.

"Anything else I need to know?"

"Just that you've probably never seen anything like it before. That Gabriel guy, though..." Archie rubbed his throat, an ear flicking. "...What can you tell me about *him*?"

"...You want to cover this one, Maria?" I said, seeing that it was her turn to be perturbed, sitting on the seat next to the motionless Kyle, Maria twitching immediately at the prospect, fiddling with her gun.

"You know what a Cartel is, Archie?" She began.

"...Some kind of criminal gang, right?"

"Well, Gabriel worked for the most powerful one on earth. He wanted out, you can't exactly put in a two-weeks notice."

"I can relate," Archie shot back with a tiny smirk, before realising only a little too late that the aire was far too foul still for jokes. "...Sorry. So...?"

"He's using this 'apocalypse' to quit. Escape in the confusion."

"...So what, he's some kind of gangster?"

"Somebody selling crack on the street corner is a 'gangster'. Gabriel is an *Ejecutor*. Means either 'executioner' or 'enforcer' but it doesn't matter. Both are a good word to describe one with."

"So he's an assassin?"

"Ex-*cuse* me?" The radio crackled, Gabriel's voice shooting through.

"J-Jesus! You listening this whole time?!" Archie spat, practically driven into a flashback at the sound of his voice.

"Hey, this is pretty interesting, I wouldn't want to miss it either," Lauren's somewhat amused voice came through too.

"*Ex-cuse me*, you twink *fuck*. Comparing me to one of those cowardly little shrimp-dicked faggots who stab people in the back and act all high and mighty because they get to go to high-profile parties and sip champagne while they do their mind-numbingly easy killings and cosplay being a high-class socialite while those of us with a *pair* have to trudge through miles of shit-inundated mud to blow compounds of un-affiliated drug labs full of armed-to-the-teeth crackheads to shreds with a combined arms assault outnumbered a hundred to one. The *Sicarios* are fucking faggots who shoot you in the back when you're unarmed, unarmored, asleep, unaware and alone. *Ejecutors* come for you when you're armed, armored, coked-up, on full-alert and you brought all of your friends with you ready to fucking fight. And we wipe the fucking *floor* with you. You send an assassin to kill the soft bitches who've never even been spanked and beg on their knees in their final moments. *Ejecutors* kill hard mother fuckers who need to be dragged to hell personally. I've never met a *Sicario* I couldn't kick the ass of with one hand and fist-fuck his significant other with my other simultaneously." My brow was raised. It seems that, while Gabe never really got angry, he grated against Archie's personality. Maybe this was the showman in him, driving home the fear. I thought for a moment that he was genuinely on-edge from all the death, but I seriously doubted that bothered him.

"Right, jeez, semantics, got it," Archie scratched at the collar of his shirt.

"That's *terminology*, engie-boy. You call me a pussy-bitch assassin ever again and I'll choke you straight, faggot. Same to the rest of you." Archie didn't have much to say now. "...So what else you wanna know?"

"...S-*seriously*?" Archie put back, practically in shock by Gabriel's shift.

"Yeah, sure. Kind of rude of you to not ask me first off, to be honest." All of Gabe's animosity was gone. Maybe he really was messing with Archie. Archie himself seemed to think so, stammering. I cracked a smile; I would have laughed if I didn't feel like shit.

"...You practice all that in the mirror?" I found crawling from my mouth. Some black humor yet unextinquished from my soul from this event, some last light I could hold onto in the form of a little roast.

"Fuck off. It's true. You'd know a Sicario if you met one. They *reek* because their head'sve been up their asses."

Another long spat of silence, wading through, before archie dreaded the silence enough to speak once more.

"Uh... Can I ask what makes these, uh... egg-heck-utors so special?"

"Need to work on your pronunciation, foxboy. It's just a whole lot of training. That and I'm not exactly the same human that crawled out of my mother's *hole*. Mother nature doesn't make *Ejecutores,* science does. I don't want to get into it."

"...You're not fucking with us still, right?" Maria asked, though it was almost like she'd rather ask more about his augmentations but didn't dare prod in that specific, touchy direction.

"Maria, remember how you saw me kill thirty something gang members on the news, right? Life's not an anime where some redhead bitch in a miniskirt armed with nothing but two pistols and some acrobatics can take on an army. Shit like that requires a little hard-wiring." There was another short silence now. I'm guessing Maria wanted to avoid the silence of her own thoughts as well, as she spoke again.

"When was this done?" She asked. It wasn't completely out of the realm of possibility, with what I'd seen, so I was already pretty sold.

"Noah, remember that summer camp I went to after the last year I was at middle school with you?" He said.

"That young?"

"They like 'em young. Get the genes while they're fresh."

Another silence, which Maria was eager to interrupt. "...The day this shit all started, how did you know I'd figure that was you on the news and come to fight you?"

"I banked on it. Figured I'd get you paranoid enough if you saw me wearing the vest the day before and acted just the right amount of sketch. I know you never trusted me, Maria."

"Fucking evil genius, huh?" Maria let out with a breathless laugh.

"Try to be," Gabe sang back.

Another pause, that we all loathed. "...You think you're going to miss anything about them? The cartel?" I don't know why she asked this, aside from just having something to talk about. Sounded kind of silly in retrospect, though maybe she asked this just for her own interrogation purposes. See how far she could really trust him, if he really betrayed the cartel she herself loathed so much.

"...My exosuit," Gabe reasoned. "Fucking custom made. I tried to requisition it from Siña Ops for that meth lab mission the night before all this shit went down, they never O.K.ed it, said it's too much of a hassle for escaping the cops if the mission went sideways. I'm pissed I couldn't get to bring that along on this apocalypse." We chuckled that chuckle, that sad, obligatory chuckle at this funny little detail, and before we knew it that fucking silence was back, that silence that rotted the air.

"...Ever wore power armor?" I asked.

"Yeah. Overhyped. It's too clumsy, the input lag sucks and you can't maneuver as good. I'll take exo armor with doubled plates any day. I prefer jump packs and agility mods, though. That's how you kill in style."

"What about that new stuff?" I asked. "The, uh… 'Sentinel' program?"

"Oh, the new models with predictive software in 'em?" Gabe said. "They're not exactly on the open market yet. Even so, I bet it's just a gimmick."

That was it, for the day, the silence returning and staying for good now. Time to be alone with our thoughts, as we rode along through the highlands. We settled down for the night after a while. Nobody said anything, like we'd run out of things to talk about by now. If we did talk it was that sort of ambulatory conversation, like what you'd discuss at a funeral. We made our bunks, Gabriel was on late watch, I asked Maria to cover my shift of watching. Didn't matter, we were all restless anyways. Didn't even make a campfire.

Sleep found me sooner than I'd expected.

## Chapter 20

It's quiet.

The Citadel has a big, central watchtower, towering like a skyscraper. Mostly steel and iron with a façade of concrete, to keep the old-style look. It's a big place, like an enclosed european town.

It's before dawn. I'm standing there on the very top of it, peering out from the crenelations. The height should take my breath away, but it doesn't. It's dark. It's later than late; it's early. I see Lauren, flying about in the skies. The world is so far away, I can see the curve. She's flying so high up, I don't want her to fall. The sun is rising. The sun is rising.

I'm stepping out there. Bringing myself up onto the balcony, reaching my hand out.

As I fall and the world tumbles out from underneath me and I awake, hitting the hard ground under my sleeping bag. I go to pull on and activate my hologlasses, to see what time it is. 04:29. I would have gone back to sleep, but that unease was still with me, and I was compelled to stand. I saw Maria where she slept like a stone beside where I'd been laying, Lauren curled into a ball on a blanket thrown over a big flat rock, everyone generally looking restless in their sleep. My hologlasses' medical functions pointed out their heartbeats, fast asleep. Of course. I saw that my glasses had selected, off in the distance, the city of Las Vegas. I could hardly see the great city in the darkness, but my hologlasses could, pointing it out to me. Tiny in the distance, a glittering jewel. Practically a speck from the highlands.

I saw my holos target several fast-moving vehicles zipping along a road, away from it. They identified them as government Humvees, the analyzation module of my hologlasses noting their speed in kilometers, 128. They were getting out, in a hurry. But why? I blinked. I took the glasses off, and I rubbed my eyes. My head hurt like a hangover I shouldn't even have. I wanted to turn away, to lie back down and go back to sleep, or at least go and put my armor back on if I stayed awake, but I could feel something. I could hear something. Something inside me telling me, don't you dare turn away, not even for a second. Don't even blink.

I see in the sky the early morning clouds, where the curvature of the Earth could allow the Sun's light to reach them before us down here on earth. But I saw one cloud, one irregular cloud, streaking through the sky from off to the right, brighter than the rest at its tip. A vapor trail. And It was headed straight for Las Vegas.

It only took me a second to figure out what it was, and as it did it struck my brain with terrified surprise. My eyes widened, as the missile flew over the city.

Light.

All the light of the sun itself, before my very eyes.

I could feel my retinas burn from having to adjust so quickly, and I was forced to shut my eyes for a couple shocking instants, which I slowly opened again as the blinding light dimmed, to reveal a massive, swelling mushroom cloud rising above a tremendous shockwave that radiated out in all directions, all in spine-tingling silence.

Even though the shockwave had yet to meet me, I swear in that moment my mind filled in the blanks and I could feel the Earth tremble ever so slightly beneath my feet, the little rocks dancing around my feet as the sonic pressure wave rippled over the desert in the distance in all directions from the thermonuclear detonation. I tried to proclaim, to yell out, to do something, but I was frozen in place, my entire body was under the spell. I couldn't even shut my eyes now. It was entrancing. All I could do was watch.

All I could do was watch the apocalypse.

The sonic wave hit me. The sand was kicked up in the wind, harsh and howling. It stung. I felt myself buffered, but I stood. My feet did not even shift. The noise of the explosion was tremendous. I could hear others screaming in surprise, waking up as the short sandstorm washed over us. I didn't so much as blink. The glowing mushroom cloud was all I could see in the distance, its spell cast upon me. The massive heat had turned the sand to obsidian glass, which flared red-hot, the glowing fallout raining down like a beautiful display of millions of red paper lanterns falling from the mushroom cloud, which hung enormous in the distance, rising above the sands, illuminated in radiant, red heat. Blood red.

The wind died down, and stayed still for a second, before it blew softly towards what was once the city I called home, my hair fluttering in the wind. It felt oddly calming, feeling this warm breeze, watching the pretty cloud, feeling the radiating, soothing heat. Like this was all still a dream.

When I was finally able to avert my gaze, I turned around, seeing everyone there. Everyone speechless, everyone watching. That look on their faces. How could this be possible? The only one without eyes blasted open in terror was Gabe, who stood leaning against the jeep. It was his watch, of course he was awake. He'd probably been standing there, watching me watch the apocalypse this whole time. In retrospect that little detail chilled my bones far more than the memory of that bomb would. I saw his eyes. That horrible, deadly shine in them, wide, face rigid, usual cold smile gone. This was his *shocked*. A sight to behold just as terrifying as the bomb, making the horror of the situation ever realer in my mind.

We could all watch and see it for a long time, until the glow faded away as the fallout cooled, leaving us in darkness once more, the image of the mushroom cloud ingrained in our minds, burned into our eyes.

Maria was the first to make a noise. Not to speak, but only to scream. How I saw her eyes wide, the ghost of her soul on display. How she fell to her knees as they gave out from beneath her, her hands reaching up to her face, out of reflex, staring out, petrified by the spell of the bomb. Mama, papa, she wanted to say, to bellow, how I read on her trembling lips. How everything was gone. How everyone was gone. How this truly was the end of everything she ever knew all over again.

She screamed, and screamed, and screamed, with tears running from bloodshot eyes down a pale, shuddering face and body until she could not scream any longer.

---

"Noah."

My dad stood there. Another one of his "serious" talks. "If something bad happens, so bad that we need to go to the citadel right away… I need you to understand that, you might not think it's that bad. That… you'll think everything will just go back to normal, and it might. Let me tell you about normalcy bias."

I think I must've been right around fourteen years old. Towards the tail end of me being into this "prepper" stuff. He probably knew this would be the last time I'd really listen to him.

"You need to really think critically about a situation, and about your own safety. People are known to go into denial when something horrible is happening, because they know what trouble they'd be in, how they'd be completely unprepared. For some, they'd rather die blissfully unaware than even make an attempt to survive." He was staring at his hands in his lap, feeling themselves over and over. "Most people, maybe even you, have a... preconception, of what they'd call an 'apocalypse'."

"Like zombies?" I asked. Father smiled plainly to himself.

"Yes, son. Like zombies. But it... *probably* won't be zombies. I'm trying to say that... don't try and think about what the 'apocalypse' will be like. Think about what the apocalypse won't be like. Don't wait for a sign to act. Wait for the signs of it not being an apocalypse to go away. Okay?" I nodded slowly. I supposed I got it. "Most people... would probably need to see something dramatic to understand that they are truly in danger. I've met a lot of people, and I can guarantee you that most people'd need to see it with their own two eyes, just to 'get' it. Like an atomic bomb going off."

An atomic bomb going off.

---

"Try it now." The truck's ignition coughed, Archie's voice nervous, shaking but doing his best to steel his resolve while Gabriel and him worked on the truck, seeing what electronics could be salvaged. I was sitting, motionless on the back bumper of the jeep, as the sun peeked over the eastern dunes. Was the city I grew up in truly gone? Even before I saw that huge, black, smoldering crater, way, way in the distance, so far it looked almost comically tiny, I knew I couldn't lie to myself. It was gone. It was all gone.

I didn't feel anything, not at the moment. If anything, I felt deep down, that I was waiting for something like this. An ultimate reason to leave. To never look back. To really "get" it.

And there it was. A city of 5 million people reduced to charred nothing by the sheer force of a megaton blast. More than a century of opulence and modern pleasures, functionally wiped from the face of the earth, the ground charred and the air poisoned for millennia to come.

I thought of my house. I remembered the bonfire, the calm, final night. My city, all the shops I liked and places I grew up in, the roads, the school, the old, glittering casinos- all of it unrecognizable, soaked in radiation. Barely a couple slumping landmarks left, burning away into the dawn. I felt puny. I felt weak. I felt sick to my stomach. Some others couldn't handle it either. They just stared at the crater in the middle, lost in it. It was all too much. Only Maria could not bear to look, still staring into the skies as she lay in rapture on her back, watching the wispy clouds float by. Lost in them.

I saw Katt, she approached me. Her eyes were wide and fearful. They looked larger than they were, with that eye color of hers a fiery orange. She looked out to the crater, then back at me, ever so slowly. "Is this really what you do?" she asked me, her voice quivering. "You humans really, have this... this power?"

"Yeah," I told her with a quiet nod. Not like I had any other way of putting it. Katt wandered away wordlessly, her jaw slack, unable to look back at it, trembling in horror at such unholy magic.

"West," I heard. Gabriel's voice, the truck idling in the distance of my mind while Archie worked on the rest of the diagnostics, Gabriel having taken a break to come up to me. I looked over my shoulder at him.

"Wh-"

"The missile came from the west." I was silent, turning slowly back at that crater and furling my lip in my jaw.

"...You saying we're at war with China or something?" My voice spiked with worry.

"I'm saying it came from the west." He sighed, way too calmly for somebody looking at a two-hours-fresh atomic crater. "After we get through this facility, we need to search for answers."

"...The facility..." I had to say, it slipped my mind. Huh. "...Maria." I turned, seeing her there, sitting up against the wheel. Unlike how Kyle had been she was... mostly lucid, her eyes coming back to me, dry of tears. "A-are you-" I felt compelled to hold her, to hug her and console her but I never did. I just stood there, separated by my own reserve, my own honoration. I didn't know how to put this. How to console her.

"...They probably didn't even feel a thing," She said, when she'd blinked and decided to look back at that crater again. "Just went to bed and... and..." I saw the dam breaking. I stepped forward. Compelled to. I fell to my knees and collapsed on her, throwing my arms around her. It was awkward, and in the end it didn't really feel right. I wished I had a better way of consoling her, but this was all I could do. She sat there, still petrified. Still staring. "I... I..." She knew what she wanted to say. That she didn't have anyone left. That there was only one way to go. That this was the real shit now. "...This... isn't going to just blow over, is it..."

Yeah.

### Chapter 21

"If you can still fight, you're in the front car. If you're feel like you can't pull through much more, you're in the truck."

That's all Gabriel had to say. I was feeling like shit too, so I let Gabriel drive the Jeep for a change, me in shotgun. Maria was still zoning out, but she was lucid enough to drive the truck. Archie and Reina sat in the backseats of the jeep, and Lauren did her thing as scout. Before long she flew down to stand- or lean or something, her hind legs planted in the chuck of the jeep behind the rear seats, her frontal legs and their hand-like talons holding onto the seats of Archie and Reina before her, her left hand, the 'true' hand of her upper half grasped onto the rollcage, her right hand hefting her rifle against her hip. Did the centaur types have hip bones, or something like them where their two... halves merged? I guess I really ought to have searched this up.

"There." It'd only been less than an hour or so of driving. Archie was pointing to what looked like some abandoned airplane hangar, out in the middle of nowhere.

"...Kind of a dump," Gabriel said disinterestedly.

"It's underground, this is just one of the entrances," Archie reasoned. I looked around, Seeing Reina getting uneasy again. Archie seemed uncomfortable too. Gabriel threw the brakes and we disembarked. I stood on the ground, looking back to the truck. Maria sat in it still, dead eyes staring at that building. I caught her gaze and she came out. Everyone who cared to gathered around.

"Alright. Me, Noah and Archie are going. Maria, you think you can be in charge until we get back?" Gabe ordered.

"...Yeah." I saw how she spoke. How she was still in so much pain. I read it in her eyes, how she was saying to herself that she's been through pain like this before. How she's not going to break down because she's stronger than that, no matter how much she wants, needs to. She knows she can't, not now. "...Just hurry the fuck up so we can get on with it."

"Keep a close watch on Daniel and Abel. Either one gets a fever, wet a cloth with some of the booze we found in the truck, not the water. Alcohol will evaporate faster anyways. Try not to drink all the water until we get back. Situation's gone from shitty to downright apocalyptic so everybody be on high alert. Lauren, don't fly around, just sit on top of the roof of this hangar here to keep an eye out. Matter of fact..." Gabe was pulling the upper receiver off his rifle, the long-barreled 5.56 one with the scope. "Anthony. C'mere." Anthony approached as Gabe put his disassembled gun into the jeep. "Lauren, give your M4 to Anthony, and take this gun." Gabriel disassembled Anthony's MDR carbine as well, going to put his long barrel with the scope on Anthony's rifle, passing the complete package to Lauren. "Now you've got a gun with a magnified optic. You're the lookout. Don't fuck with my scope, it's dead on at 200 meters. Since you're going to be in a position of elevation, it's probably going to shoot high like it's 300 so aim a little low, use the rangefinder and estimate the drop-off if you start getting sniped at from beyond that."

"Lauren?" Lauren uttered suddenly with her brow raised and her lips curled ever upwards in a hardly-restrained smile, holding her "new" MDR rifle.

"Uh... yeah? *Your name?*" Gabe grunted bluntly.

"You... you didn't call me 'Green' for once," Lauren let out a breathless laugh, almost blushing in how awkwardly she proclaimed this. Gabriel smirked.

"...Yeah, yeah. I promise I'm not getting too attached." Lauren tried to play this off like Gabe was, rolling her eyes, but by her blush she didn't seem too earnestly unbothered. Her eyes shifted to me for a second, and I finally realised how I was smiling like an idiot. She blushed more and furled her smile in her lips, like she was a little embarrassed. I think I just really loved to see her happy about something. How far she'd come. "Noah," Gabriel jostled me with an elbow as he finished assembling his MDR into the short, suppressed configuration, switching his 5.56 mags out for .300 Black ones. "...I don't think you want to lug a 20 inch around with a magnified optic inside a close-quarters environment. Switch your AR for an MDR, or the DP12. Anthony, take that silencer off the AR and give it to Archie. He probably isn't partial to losing the hearing in his other ear."

"W-what if I need to shoot it?" Anthony proclaimed, holding the cop AR with Gabe's homemade silencer on it.

"Don't miss and you'll get your killing over with quick."

While they went about tweaking things I was pulling my AR off of myself and lying it in the jeep's chuck, folding the sling over it. I picked up that big blocky shotgun, releasing the bolt to pull the pump back a bit so I could flip it over and check the chambers, the gun already topped off, before going to pull my AR15 magazine holders off of my armor's webbing, switching them out for the molle panels lined full of buckshot shells that was with the shotgun.

"Thanks," Archie let out as he screwed the silencer onto the threads of his rifle. "...I'd like an optic sight for it too, though."

"Tell you what. We survive this I'll buy you a fucking aimpoint with all the fixuns at the next gun store we come across." Archie scoffed out a laugh. "Noah, check your holos. Mine got fried from the EMP but yours probably still work since you have special ones. My mask's hardware seems functional too, thank the cartel for that." I pulled on my helmet, snapping the ear headsets down and turning them on, the silence of noise-reduction the ear-protectors produced made way for a clear sound picture of everyone around, boosting my hearing to boot. Every scuff of sand, every rustle, every wayward sigh was amplified.

"EMP didn't fry my comms, too. Gabe, try out the walkies."

"Testing, testing, Noah takes way too fucking long, over," I heard come through on the channel as he picked up the walkie talkie.

"Loud and clear."

"Damn, these are hardened too? Your dad gets you all the good stuff,"

"Nothing but the best," I muttered, putting on my hologlasses. The display greeted me, interfacing with comms. "Everyone link up."

"My utility earpiece and all my tech I had with me was the cheap shite. All of it got fried from the EMP. Remind me to grab some new gear," Archie reasoned, after testing his own comms system from his utility gear. He tossed the earpieces into the dust. "I'll just use the walkie talkie."

"Alright, my mask has comms, linked into the channel. If we're going underground this probably won't work unless we're close to each other. You want some body armor and a pistol, Archie?" Gabe put forth.

"Actually, yeah. That sounds good." Archie got one of the old cartel vests from Anthony that already had a horizontal holster on it, taking the old police glock to put in it so the both of us could share magazines. He pulled his utility webgear off to switch them, instantly huffing by the time he pulled it on and cinched it up to his size. "Jesus what is this made out of? Concrete?"

"Steel plate, nothing but the best," Gabe remarked. Archie let out a genuine, if breathless laugh, putting his knife sheath and magazine pouches on the vest's webbing. "...Word to the wise. Don't skip leg day."

"...Get focked," Archie hushed back. "Unlike you, I was genetically engineered to fix machines, not murder people."

"It's a developable skill, don't be a bitch. You ready, Noah?"

"...Yeah. I think so," I said. Gabe pulled his mask down from where it sat atop his head like a quasi-helmet and onto his face, the eyeslot lighting up once to signify its holographic display activating for him, as he plugged his earpieces in as well.

"...Let's go," I heard his voice changer let out, coming through on comms. "Alright. Guys, we'll be back in an hour. We-"

"Uh..." Archie suddenly put forth. Gabe stopped, head swiveling towards Archie. "...We're gonna need way more than an hour."

"...We'll be back. Don't go anywhere. Archie?" Gabe said. "Show the way."

We walked in that big building, towards what looked like a control panel in the middle of the concrete floor.

"Watch your step. It's a magnetic elevator." Archie rolled up his sleeve to display his engineer's barcode as he activated the scanner, going to get ahold of its controls. "...This isn't the only entrance. There are a lot of smaller ones all over the place." Archie's explanations went on and on, as I turned back. It felt strange. Like I might not see any of my friends ever again, preparing to descend into darkness. It was probably an irrational feeling, but I wanted to see these people who'd grown to depend on me one last time, even if it wasn't going to be the last time, I was telling myself. I looked at them watching us descend slowly, the freight elevator taking its time to accelerate. I caught Lauren's gaze, seeing her hand twitch, like she wanted to wave me goodbye. Instead we shared a warm smile. I looked through the crowd. Maria wasn't there, she was off to the side, alone with her horrible, horrible thoughts. I didn't want to disturb her.

Lauren, the tallest one there, was the last one I would see as we descended. That caring smile, traced with apprehension. With fear. The fear I wouldn't return. That fear of hers spurred fear in my own self, that maybe this wouldn't be easy; Lauren already had been in here once, and if she was afraid, if all the hybrids were, I ought to be too. But, as I saw that little tinge of fear in her eyes, I made a vow. No matter what I encountered down there, no matter what horrible things I would see, I would return no matter what. My friends are counting on us. **On me.**

A descent into blackness, that elevator speeding up. The sickness, the pit in my stomach opening up with it. I looked around. Archie was looking apprehensive and was shifting in his own skin uncomfortably, but he was by no means pissing himself. He was a lot more terrified when Gabriel was choking the life out of him, but that was understandable. I couldn't exactly read Gabriel's face with that mask of his on, but I gleaned enough from his body language, his casually rolling shoulders, slow breathing and slouched posture that the situation had yet to become a big deal for him. Knowing that he was with us calmed me down some; I was just hoping that *Ejecutors* really were all he cracked them up to be. I didn't doubt him though, for what it was worth.

"Alright. I think we're in the right block," Archie let out, slowing the elevator with his controls. I saw the doors all around. Big car-sized freight doors and smaller man-sized doors all around. "Okay. Right on ahead," He pointed to one of them, going up to activate the door. He revealed his barcode to the scanner.

"Verified, Technician B-729-H-12-C: Edmonton-Reginald, Archibald," The female voice of the computer said, Archie blushing at his own name. "You are… in seventeen different violations of code. Security has been alerted to your current position. Please remain where you are to incur no further penalt-"

"Get focked," Archie growled, prying the console open with his knife and cracking a wire. The door came to life, beginning to open. Gabriel's voice changer crackled, evidently him opening his mouth to speak, as the thing began to move. "-We're gonna make a quick detour. I need to get to my room to get some things." He interrupted Gabe before he could speak. "It's-"

"Edmonton-Reginald?" Gabriel chuckled.

"Look mate, I didn't fockin' pick it," he whined back, narrowing his eyes in snide. Me behind Archie, I stifle a chuckle. That chuckle however was short lived, as I hit the light on my shotgun to look. The hallways were lighted dimly by the emergency red lights, which didn't make me all that apprehensive, until I saw the bodies. I knew what I was looking at immediately, my senses helped to the conclusion with a thick, heady biological smell. One of death, of decay, of filth and disease and despair. I could smell the rusty smell of blood and the smell of bodily waste, both painted in dark mahogany browns about, that smell of rotting flesh. Flies buzzed here and there. The passageway's eerie red glow of the emergency lights didn't make things look better. I saw Archie gag a bit, pulling his shirt over his muzzle. Gabriel sniffed in through his mask.

"Welcome to my fockin' neighbourhood."

"Mm, charming."

"Jesus Christ," I added, retching.

"It's gotten a lot worse since I last been here," Archie noted, stepping out into the putrid stuff with a little squishing sound that sent a shiver up my spine. I saw the look on his face; he was glad that he had boots, some specially-made shoes for his digitigrade, wide paw-like feet. I did my best not to breathe through my nose, but the smell was so bad I could practically taste it anyways. "Come on, let's get through this and get over it. We're gonna grab my tech stuff and then go looking for the caches."

Walking through this otherworldly place, it was truly something else. Painted in shit and blood, I could hardly believe I was still on Earth, it was like a nightmarish dimension of its own. "Up here in these upper levels, it's probably not that bad," Archie extrapolated, stepping over some poor hybrid sans limbs and face, freshly chewed off by some primordial evil I'd yet to meet. As I stepped over another mutilated corpse so desecrated and decayed that I couldn't tell if it was human or hybrid, I doubted anywhere else could be worse than this. The flickering red emergency lights, that smell of death and the low, quiet, distant-sounding, constant woosh of the ventilation system and its respective cold air that blew like wind through the tunnels carrying the scent, only added to the creeping horror of this disgusting place. It was like I could hear sounds, voices on the hum of the place, probably just my imagination but it was beyond unnerving.

Many, many doors were open all around. They were cells, here in an engineer barracks block, one of many throughout the place apparently. The vast majority of them were open, and from within their dark recesses, I could hear voices, whispering. I could see eyes poke out of them. Hissing, growling. From subtle chuckling and hissing to maniacal, hyena-like laughter. Crying and cursing. My heads-up-display did well to point a lot of them out, detecting heartbeats and so on, but they couldn't hide the awfulness of the situation. I could feel my paranoia grow in the back of my head. My head swiveled about, the whispers seeming to stop as I looked in their direction, but resuming as soon as I turned away. "...These guys engineers like you too?"

"Probably not. Most of us scattered. You're looking at the vat-growns, what the shepherd siblings and your girl Green were. Busted out of containment before their 'programming' was complete, so they're not exactly playing with a full deck."

I looked ahead, trying to look somewhere other than in these dark rooms, these green slimy vaults where I thought that at any time some horrifying monstrosity would surge out to tear us limb from limb. There were so many doors, too many angles. We were armed to the teeth, but I couldn't help but feel like a bug about to be swatted by a cement mixer.

I saw, ahead of us, a couple hybrids sitting on the ground, practically emaciated, fur and bones. Flies buzzed above them, crawling into their big ears and upon their eyes, and they were covered in dried blood, smeared in shit. Some of their eyes were open, glassed over. I thought they were dead, until we approached into a range where my holos could scan them for life signs, detecting heartbeats, which made my skin crawl. But, just as that happened I watched them slowly rise like zombies, eyeballs circling in their heads to meet us. They stared at us. They stood at the walls like our prescences were magnetically opposed, like we forced them up against the walls simply by being there, but despite their fearful body movements their faces watched us without emotion or inflection, without even such subtleties as blinking, as we quietly passed them. I didn't take my eyes off of them for a second until they disappeared behind us, into the dim red darkness.

I felt a tiny urge of insanity in the back of my head from all of this, a voice that followed me that I was not entirely sure whether it was the hybrids' in the black cells or my own subconscious pitching in. Perhaps this was why they were all so mad in the head. Staying in this place in the shape it was now, even as briefly as I did made me feel as if I'd aged. Even stepping foot in here was bad for your health. The insanity was contagious.

Walking quickly now, we hurried along. It seemed like the tunnel was going on forever, as Archie took a right. We went down that corridor for a while, before taking another right. I turned around to check our six often, to see the hybrid heads that were peeking out at us duck back away. The whispers wouldn't go away, no matter how many times I looked or prayed for comforting silence; but I think that silence would have just made my anxiety worse.

"Ah, here's my Hab," Archie said quietly, and I let out a quiet sigh of relief. I lowered my weapon, though did not let it hang limp from my sling, my knuckles still white upon the weapon's grips. Archie opened the lock similarly to opening the door to this block, going to pry the console open with his knife to fiddle with the wires. Gabriel looked down the hall, I looked towards where we came from while he did his work. It beeped open and we stepped in. "...Lock is focked now so we can't close it but we won't be long. I just need some things."

"Homely," Gabe said, noting the rather spartan settings. Archie was pulling his drawers open, grabbing his utility bag and filling it up, notably with clothes. Plenty of drab colored stuff. I saw him get his tablet, checking that it worked for a second before stowing it. His personal hologlasses were next, I noted how the arms of it could reach over his ears while he wore them. He put them on, putting on their earpieces and going to sync it, motioning in front of his face with his hands to activate his haptic response to set up the radio.

"What channel are we on again?" Archie asked

"Twelve, right?" I said.

"I mean what megahertz. Mine has to be set up manually."

"Uh... 467.6625."

"This work?" He said, having input the data. I heard him in my earpiece.

"Sounds good, you got me?" I asked.

"Yup. How about you, Gabe?"

"Testing," Gabe said disinterestedly, looking about the room.

"Coming through clear."

**"How about me, darlings?"**

We all paused dead, hearing this mysterious fourth voice, a female. I read Archie's face, seeing him freeze up, before Gabe and I wheeled toward the door, and that was when the surreality really began. There was a person- no, just a head hanging upside-down, like a person standing on the ceiling outside the cell and peering in, her head gazing at us. In the instant that I saw her, and given her... position, upside down and all, I knew right away this wasn't a human I was looking at, though she had more human of a face than, say, Lauren with her nose-less, wide snout or Reina with her german shepherd-like muzzle complete with leather-skinned nose. It was a... human woman of sorts with short-cropped, wavy brunette hair atop (or below, since she was upside-down) a face mostly human, though I could only see the upper top half of her head I'd seen enough. I knew humans didn't have four eyes with massive irises that covered nearly the whole eye, or pointed elf-like ears. I also knew that humans didn't hang from the ceiling, but that was incidental at the moment. Gabriel and I raised our guns out of instinct and she retreated, leaving only her hands and the end of her hair draping down in a show of surrender.

"Now now, let's not be hasty, gentlemen," We heard both in front of us and in our headsets, as she'd stolen our comms channel. She had a distinctly anglo accent, sort of like Archie's but more refined, almost coy. Gabe turned while I still watched the door and the disembodied empty hands, back to Archie, who was looking more exasperated than concerned.

"Friend of yours?" Gabe asked, noting his exhausted nonchalance.

"-Gabriel, right?" The voice put forth, the hand on the left, her right hand pointed towards the right side of the room where Gabe was. "If you'd let me introduce myself, *Archie* wouldn't have to."

"She's a... Acquaintance isn't even the right word. I'd say nuisance but-"

"-but then I'd harass you for the rest of the week. That's how you'd put it, Archibald? Always the snide, passive-aggressive one. You could use to lighten up."

"What are you doing here, Selicia?" Archie asked quaintly, only showing that he was a tad perturbed. I saw her peek down again, first with two eyes, then with all four, then her entire head all the way to her neck and jaw. She had a seam where the cleft of her chin bisected and I could spot fangs in her mouth, her skin was dark, african, though I really doubted calling her 'african' would quite describe her... phylogeny. Her... 'human bits' were black. Nubian-ish. If she was a human, she'd be black, though she had straight hair that fell plainly. Indian, maybe? I was more confused than scared, or even startled at this point. Whatever she was was a bit beyond *race*.

"That's my line. You're the one that walked out." This 'Selicia' folded her arms on the top of the doorframe like she was leaning on it, still quite upside-down. When she opened her mouth to speak, I could truly... appreciate, how she had very, very fanged canine teeth in addition to the unhinging jaw that she popped in and out of place as she yawned. "...So, who are your new friends? I'm interested in this Gabriel person here, looking like Jason from Friday the Thirteenth and all," She said in reference to his mask. Gabriel chuckled, practically flattered.

"I- Who? Look," Archie went on. "I'm here to help these guys get supplies, they-"

"Ooh, *raiders* here to steal the wealth of this facility. Archie, you never struck me as dastardly, getting in with this sort of crowd. Mmm."

"Say what you want, but these guys aren't *insane*."

"Hm, hm." She extended her arm, pointing at me with a waving finger, spinning through the air like she was tracing my outline playfully, eyeing me with a cool, charming look in her many eyes. "Now, I'm curious about this one too. He looks like a downright boy scout. How come you're not as edgy or talkative as your masked accomplice?"

"Archie, do you want me to shoot this bitch or what?" Gabe uttered before I could respond. "We've got an itinerary to tend to."

"Ooh, you live up to your aesthetic, don't you, Mr. Voorhees? Voice changer is a *dashing* touch. Would you really shoot a *woman*?" Gabe raised his gun, and evidently this Selicia character wasn't beyond the prospect of Gabriel really being so villainous to do so, as she retreated seeing the end of Gabriel's silenced PDW.

"...I mean, you could. Probably the only way to keep her from pestering us," Archie reasoned, though not entirely seriously. "I mean, we might as well let her follow if not. She knows the place and the guy we're going to see, too."

"Yeah, given that I'm on your comms channel," She pointed out as her own radio cut in, still well out of sight. "Perhaps you could cut me in then, chaps?"

"...I don't think we can trust her," Gabe muttered.

"I suppose I shall keep my distance if you're going to be so distrustworthy," Selicia announced coyly though not entirely without animosity, as Gabe stepped up to peek out upwards.

"...*Shit*," Gabe said, not really concerned, but rather kind of impressed. "...fuckin' disappeared." I approached, looking up too. The ceiling was up about fifteen feet up and slick with no real handholds for her to have hung herself from, though there happened to be a ventilation grate just above Archie's door. It was big, about five-by-five feet. "Let me guess. You're in the vent."

"...No I'm not." Her voice rang through on comms.

"...We can hear your echo in the grate." There was no response.

"She's not going to get in our way. Probably. Let's press on," Archie said, emerging as well. "Alright, I've only got one spare locator. Who wants it?" Archie waved a drink coaster sized electronic chip, and I looked to Gabe.

"You can have it. Getting lost in here sounds like fun to me." I felt like Gabriel wasn't entirely joking here.

"...Not like we're gonna split up," I put forth, taking it.

"Alright. That locator has the map of the place on it. You should download it onto your holos as a backup," He said, as I hit the button, the holographic display of the locator itself lighting up in front of us. It was a 3D render of the entire facility, and my brow went up as I saw it all, given where our two blinking locators were. We were hardly halfway down even though it looked like we were a mile underground. I saw the twisting chasms, the big depot garages. Gabe rose his hand up to access its files on his own holographics, presumably downloading the map. I supposed a backup wouldn't hurt, doing so myself. "Oh, and a neat little hack I managed to do-" Archie reached for mine. He fiddled with the haptics for a little bit before bringing up a secondary option. "You can scan all wavelengths and see everybody with an active locator in the facility, like this. Everybody who's actually bound to adventure around in here probably already has one; the place is sort of already divided into territories run by different gangs so look out if there are too many." He turned this option on, going from our own private wavelength of just the two of us to the entire place, the massive spiraling grid lighting up like a christmas tree. Except, where we were, we saw from where we came in from our one specific elevator shaft, a peculiar amount of pings were headed our way, moving awfully fast towards us.

"Oh, shit," spilled from my mouth. "...That's not a glitch is it?"

"-Oh, by the way, I forgot to mention this since you were so hasty to chase me off," Selicia cracked in on the radio. "I happened to catch wind of a couple nasty sorts up to no good in the neighbourhood. I don't think they're pleased with you returning to what's now their territory, Archibald. I'd wager you tipped off one of their *watchdogs*, pardon the pun."

"Well shite, thanks for the fockin timely heads-up," Archie muttered, pulling his rifle to his front and checking the chamber quickly, trembling ever so slightly.

"Well, this is more my speed," Gabriel said, checking off his own weapon as I did so too. "Archie. What's the next step of your master plan?"

"...We're gonna go there," He activated the legend and pointed to a nearby security barracks on the 3D map. "Should have some stuff we could use."

"Let's move," I said. I could hear our pursuers down the hall from where we came. We shuffled down that hallway towards the security block. My heart was pounding and cold sweat beaded on my forehead. I covered the rear, looking behind. We seemed to be able to barely evade their sight at every turn. "Hey, uh, Selicia," I put in. "Can you tell us about these guys? They're right on our ass," I hurriedly skipped over puddles of biological hazards. No response.

"...She's probably... fucked off. Out of our... comms range," Archie said, huffing and puffing, a tad winded. I was winded too. It didn't even sound like Gabriel was breathing. Maybe his mask just didn't transmit the noise of him breathing. Actually a nice stealthy touch, thinking back on this.

"Well. isn't this perfect," I heard Gabe mutter.

"...Fffuck!" Archie let out. I turned around, seeing a pile of garbage there, almost high up to the ceiling. Some big pile of junk somebody put there, to slow anyone like us down.

"Fucking corralled us into a dead end," Gabriel remarked. He didn't sound winded in the least, and he was carrying the heaviest combat gear. "Smart fuckers. Looks like we're gonna have to fight after all. Sucks for them."

"Can you cool it with the fockin' jokes?!" Archie let out, as I tumbled onto the pile of metal and scrap.

"Shit, I think I can get through," I said, finding a narrow way in. "We can squeeze through." Gabriel let his weapon hang from his sling, grasping one of the big metal desks and picking it up like it was made out of wood, barely grunting as he let it slam down in the direction of our pursuers, who were growing louder as they approached. "...I think we can get through."

"Right behind you," Gabe said, going for his molle pouches on his vest. "You two go on ahead, I'll mop up the mooks. Real quick though, I could use your opinion. Think this calls for a frag claymore or a stunblast?" He said, walking out into the tunnel a ways rather briskly.

"...You have *mines*?" I huffed, still pulling myself through the gap, Archie right behind me.

"...You know what, stunblast would be more fun. I'll save the frags," He said, placing what looked like a yellow-striped claymore mine down, slightly camouflaging it with refuse. He then activated his holos, bringing up a haptic triggerswitch for his mine, by how he held an invisible detonator in his hand, as in if he brought his thumb down onto his clenched fist the bomb would go off.

"Shit, they're coming!" Archie let out. I turned back from where I was still stuck, seeing flashlights peering through the blackness, gruff voices throwing commands. "Hurry up, Noah!"

"...I don't think there's gonna be time for you, Archie. Get behind that other desk, we'll counter-ambush." Archie stammered for a quick second, practically hyperventilating. "Archie. Don't lose the plot now. Get into concealment or you're gonna get us both killed." Gabriel's voice was stern and fatherly. A bit of a tone shift, enough to engage Archie's brain to force him to comply, diving for cover.

I'd finally squeezed through into the dark black of the rest of the tunnel. The lights were out, me shining my light on my weapon about. Those shouts behind me. A sudden blast with light streaming through immediately preceded by bursts of gunfire. I felt bullets pierce through the barrier somewhat, ricocheting as I ducked to avoid any strays. Screams, enraged growls. More gunfire, until that petered out. Some pained yelps, and a couple shots in semi-automatic, coup-de-gras if I had to guess.

"Y-you guys alright?!" I let out in concern, going up to the trash to look through where I'd snuck through.

"Oh, they sound fine to me," I heard. Not on the radio, right next to my head. My eyes shot up and there she was, dangling down from the darkness. Selicia's four big green eyes with irises that were practically iridescent in this darkness staring into me, tantalizing. One of her arms crawling around my shoulder to hold me.

"Wh-" I began, but before I could even move away, her face darted forward and her mouth opened, those fangs piercing the soft of my neck. I seized up in terror for a moment, before the world faded with the sensation of my limp body being hoisted into the air to be dragged away.

**Chapter 22**

"Hey."

"unhh…"

"Heyyy… Wakie-wakie, boy scout."

"Ungh…" I groaned. I was awake, or something close enough to being awake. I opened my eyes, feeling the world cloaked in darkness. I could feel my limbs tingling, every limb held out. I tried to move, finding myself bound. I felt something pierce my arm, like a needle or syringe if I had to guess, and my heart rate instantly increased. "Ahhh… Just have to turn you up… before I can really turn you on." The voice was close, breath that was humid yet not all that warm puffing onto the site of injection, voice radiating from over there near my arm.

"W-wh-" I stammered, hyperventilating. I was incurred to panic, though I knew that it wouldn't do any good in this situation, my heart roaring away in my chest. I felt… Flesh pressed up against me, my body, strangely cool to the touch. She was touching me, embracing, groping, even. Was I naked? I was covered by something. Bound up like this. Her skin was lukewarm, not entirely cold but still caused goosebumps to rise.

With the dim light coming on as she activated the lights, I came face to face with her, this Selicia. Or… face-to-chest, more specifically. I looked up to her face, seeing her eyes, how she fluttered all of her many eyelids and smiled kindly, in coy fashion. Her upper lip curled ever so softly upwards, biting her lower lip. She was definitely making a move, if you could call it that.

"Uh, uh- Hey, w- wait," I stammered as she pressed a bare breast against my face. I grimaced and tried to look away, she forcing her chest upon me despite how I tried to avoid it.

"…don't be bashful," she spoke softly. "I won't bite… Again." sweat was pouring down my body and I was panting. "How about we get to know each other? It's not every day I get a man with… features like yours, down here. Oh, look at this body," A finger tracing the underline of my pectoral muscle. "No atrocious dog-snout or yucky hair that clumps in my mouth. A… Real boy. I'm wondering, what is the… *handle,* of the fine specimen before me?" That tracing finger of hers was getting lower and lower.

"N-Noah," I blurted, but before she could go on I continued. "I- I have a girlfriend," I uttered in a brief, instant wheeze, to blurt out anything to get her off me.

"Oh, and no wonder- she must be lucky with a… *catch* like you. But she's not here right now, now is she?" I was looking down, and my fear grew as I was able to see more of her, more of my own situation. Webs, sticky and fibrous twisting this way and that. I was suspended a good ten feet from the floor, tangled in the stuff. "…Down here," She said as I saw movement, movement I could hardly decipher. Her human body was already intimidatingly sizeable: if she was a regular human she'd be at least seven feet tall, amazonian in any sense of the word, but the rest of her body, It was like her human torso, her humanity… disappeared into into cold, black-scaled, rough edges. I saw the movements of the many, spindly legs precariously balancing themselves on her webbing, I saw that bulbous lower body of hers, hard and chitinous. From the… waist down she was a gigantic… Spider. My eyes were wide in terror, my whole body freezing up at this eldritch monster before me. Her hand softly brushed against my chin and pulled my face back up from where I'd been petrified by her inhuman lower body, to stare face to face and eye to eye, with the four of hers as she blinked slowly again, letting out a sultry, bashful chuckle.

"W-what are you?" I let out in a breathless gasp. I saw her retreat back a little, lowering her head to my belly, dancing her fingers along my abdominal muscles before she got to the only piece of clothing she left on me, maybe just to increase the dread of having it stripped off: my boxers, all tangled up in her web like the rest of me. She could see that I had a raging erection that I didn't even know I had until now.

"I'm a woman, Noah darling," She said, closing her face near my barely-covered genitals. She was still watching me down there, her top two eyes focused on my reaction. This must have been a lot of fun for her. I feel like Archie understated what kind of a *nuisance* she was.

I watched with horror as she reached one of her web feelers up, the two limbs sticking out in front of her legs that weren't for walking. One of them had a sheathed combat knife strapped to it, which she pulled out, and I gasped. She held it up to my member and smiled with her unsettlingly long tongue hanging out, watching me squirm. Any other time it would have practically retracted back inside me out of sheer fear, but she must have just injected me with something to keep it up. She slowly began to carve away the webbing around it with her blade, observing me intently all the while. The tiny part within me that wasn't absolutely petrified wanted to ask her to keep her eyes on what she was doing rather than watch my reaction.

*Shing.* She suddenly yanked the knife away and I practically yelped, my heart ready to jump through my chest. A wire beside her that she cut with a chop, and I screamed out, instantly flipped upside down, my spatial situation changed instantly to being hung upside-down by my ankles, now rather than spread out they were pressed together, and my arms, rather than become free were tied together at the wrists, myself all hung in a line perpendicular to the ground. She landed on the floor gracefully and cut the wire that held my hands toward the ground and I tried to reach around or something but she yanked that wire, holding me vertical, unable to curl up.

"...Don't worry about your girlfriend, Noah. We're gonna get real... close, you and I. Down here it's a whole new world. With pleasure you've never dreamed of. At least..." She cut a wire beside me, and I felt the mechanism she'd constructed slowly release me, and I began descending towards her, still bound, as she pulled me by my wrist-binds towards her. "...Pleasure for me." I began involuntarily drawing near to her, the pulley system she'd constructed now letting me descend towards her ever so gracefully as she slowly and deliberately licked her lips with a great helping of saliva, utilizing that unsettlingly long tongue of hers. I'd thought that I couldn't be more scared, but as she sheathed her knife to lift her hands to her jaw and with a couple audible pops, I saw it hang grotesquely open, her lower jaw split into two at the cleft and seemingly completely disconnected from her head with a couple more dislocations. "Ahhhh..." She let out with that monster-maw of hers. Easily big enough to fit my head inside. And my shoulders. And probably the rest of me.

"Oh- FUCK! OH FUCK FUCK!" I began to scream, trying to thrash as she reached up and gripped my wrists; I could not pull away. I saw her eyes narrow and her cheeks blush, letting out a sultry chuckle from that monster mouth of hers, putting my fists into her lukewarm throat. "N-NO! S-SELICIA!" I could smell her breath. At least she had a sense of oral hygiene, seeing her horrible gleaming fangs and smelling minty fresh. Just about the only silver lining on getting eaten alive, pulling my arms in, my head practically in her jaws, staring at her rows of teeth while she giggled and I hyperventilated, my vision about to vanish into warm, fleshy darkness.

*Thwhack.*

Before I'd known it, Selicia had collapsed down in on herself, my head and arms slipping out and barely missing her jagged fangs. As she'd released me when she lost consciousness, I instantly curled up on myself like a pulled spring, breathing so rapidly and heavily I was practically screaming with every breath out.

"...Fuckin' vore thot," Gabriel's voice grumbled while I was still curled up upon myself, shaking. Gabriel put his pistol back in its holster, from after he whacked her in the soft of the jaw with it, loooking up to me with his mask worn atop his head, off his face.

"F-FUUUCK!!! FUCK FUCK FUCK!" I was screaming, beside myself, hollering and quivering in revulsion for at least a good minute before being able to formulate my thoughts without thinking of the horror of being shoved inside her. "N-nice *fucking* timing, asshole!!!"

"Oh, you wanted me to have let her eat you?" Gabriel put forth, going to release the thread leveraging me from where it was caught under her body, unconscious on the ground, as I collapsed there beside her, quickly wriggling away from her in fear, still bound. "Talk more shit and I'll just leave you strung up, let her wake up and get back to it."

"...I told you she's bound to do some disturbin' shite," Archie proclaimed to Gabriel, stepping through wires as Gabe used that wire to release me and I hit the ground. Gabriel immediately laughed.

"Hah, you sure you weren't having fun there?" Gabriel chuckled as I covered my still raging erection, wriggling on the ground with my limbs still bound.

"S-she gave me something! Injected me! I swear!"

"Suure, buddy. Hey man, there are worse fetishes than vore… Not that many, but there are. No need to be ashamed." Gabriel laughed at my expense beneath his sarcasm. "...On the real though, sorry I didn't jump in sooner. Archie told me that when a hybrid that can eat people unhinges their jaw they expose a pressure point. Just tap that and they're out. Besides, she was looking right up at you, so I could sneak up from the front, and I couldn't exactly walk up behind her to knock her out with a sleeper hold. She's got too much… spider, in the way," Gabe kicked at one of her chitinous legs, letting it flop. "When she looked up to eat you she exposed a big ol' blind spot right in front of her."

"W-what would you have done if she fucking *swallowed me?!*" I belted, letting Gabriel cut my binds.

"I dunno, get her to barf you out? Besides, wouldn't be that big a deal, y'know." My eyes went up to him in scornful shock.

"Well, fuck you, dude! Try getting to the Citadel without me!" I yelped.

"Oh, shit, you don't know?" Gabe continued unabashed. "It's all in the hybrid documents. S'not lethal. Real fucking gross but it's not gonna get you digested. I thought your dad would have made you read the hybrid exposé," I was still beyond convinced, though my disgust was outweighing my lingering panic by now, my face contorted into a mighty scowl.

"Seriously mate," Archie interrupted my coming outburst as I stammered, speechless. "Some hybrids have got that ability 'n all, but it's… like, uh, not a real stomach, you get sent to, you can't get sent to the real stomach," I glared at him in incredulous disbelief. "...Look mate, I didn't design hybrids, but whoever did was some fucked cunt, alright? But at least they had the ethical foresight to not let them be able to digest people alive."

"Why even let them fucking… eat people in the first place?!" I bellowed.

"I dunno dude," Gabe put forth. "think about it. If you were going to make a bajillion furries with the sole intention of letting them run wild and fuck the world up, you'd be a fucked up dude into weird esoteric shit anyways. Throwing this in on top of it isn't that much of a stretch." I glared back at Gabe now. "Don't get me wrong, I bet it's some degenerate social conditioning N.W.O. bullshit just like the rest of this shit is. Look, think of it this way. Rather than just barely avoiding a slow painful death, you just barely avoided a... really niche form of sexual abuse. Just remember that and it'll wear a little less on your conscience."

"Don't have to take our word for it, brov. Once we get to that dome I can introduce you to some folks she's... 'eaten'," Archie threw up air-quotes, going to fish for my stuff, throwing me a towel to wipe myself down before throwing me my pants.

"Fine, I believe you," I shuddered, putting my clothes back on. "I think I'd rather forget about this for now."

"Oh yeah," Archie tossed me my locator. "Don't get fooled by the posh accent. She's notably daft. She basically just tossed this outside her door, didn't even turn it off. Must've been more focused on getting nasty."

"...Doesn't change the fact she built a fucking vore Rube-Goldberg machine," Gabriel twanged on one of the web strings still standing. "...Real idiot savant if I've ever seen one."

"Yeah. She's kind of an enigma. We think she was ordered by some high roller in their organization, made to order, custom personality settings."

"...As a sexual partner?" Gabriel asked.

"Most likely," Archie answered. Gabriel laughed, good and amused by now.

"See, Noah? People are *into* this fucking creepy shit. Just think there's a billionaire out there right now sittin' on his cot in a FEMA camp or something just fuckin livid that he never got sent his spider-waifu dominatrix to suck head. Literally." Gabe laughed again.

"I said, I really don't want to think about this shit."

"...You know, she probably ate you when she first knocked you out to carry you on the way here, just to keep you secure, probably spit you out and set all this up so she could really milk the experience out of you," Archie added while I was putting on my armor. "...S'sorta her M.O."

"*I SAID I DON'T WANT TO THINK ABOUT THIS.*" I almost felt compelled to sniff myself. Was that *me* smelling mint-flavored, the way her mouth smelled? Was it really all sweat covering me? Come to think about it, wasn't my hair a little damp when I'd woken up? Oh god, Archie was right, wasn't he? I practically had to hit myself in the face just to get the thought out of my mind. I looked back at Selicia on the ground, snoring by now, her jaw and tongue still all over the place. Gabe went to re-assemble her jaws, clicking all the joints back into place.

"Lookin' like a fuckin' necromorph," I heard him chuckle darkly as he corrected her face, before proceeding to have a look around. "Damn, she's got some good shit. Where the fuck did she find this?" Gabriel went for a leather shoulder holster hanging there, pulling out a massive silver revolver, gleaming in even this dim light. "Jesus, Is this a single-action army?" Gabriel laughed, looking the wheelgun over, flipping it in his hands to see each side. "...No, 'Ruger Super Blackhawk, Bisley Hunter'..." He read on the barrel. "And it's *engraved*. Whole thing's covered in flowers 'n thorn vines 'n shit; rosewood grips. This looks custom. You have got to be *fucking* with me."

"Unnhhhhh..." Selicia writhed on the ground. My eyes went wide and as she opened her eyes she was met with my two shotgun barrels staring right back at her.

"DON'T YOU FUCKING GET UP!" I screamed, and her eyes went wide, hands open in surrender; this time it was her that was frozen in terror. I saw her look around a little, seeing

Archie behind me, and Gabe off to the side messing with her things. Neither of them seemed quite as intense as I. "Fucking bitch! You- You..."

"Easy, Noe," Archie said, coming up to me. Selicia looked around again once I'd lowered my shotgun a little, sighing heavily.

"H-hey, my revolver!" she let out as Gabriel spun the cylinder, filling the room with delightful rapid clicking.

"It's a nice gun, I'll give you that," Gabriel remarked to her in surprising nonchalance as she watched with slightly grit teeth. "But the engraving gives you no tactical advantage whatsoever." Gabriel closed the loading gate of the revolver with an audible click that stopped the spin of the cylinder to create a resonating silence, to look up and glare into Selicia's eyes. "Unless you were planning to auction it off as a collector's item."

"...S-so this is the face of the... fabled masked m-" Selicia said, trying to save face by powering through with her usual shtick, play coy, but Gabriel put his hand up.

"You can drop the seductress act. You're *really* pushing it." Selicia was silenced under Gabriel's glare. That serious glare of his that made even my blood run cold. "Who gave you this gun? This ain't milsurp."

"...My husband," She said. "It was a gift. He's charming, witty, intelligent, handsome-"

"Yeah yeah, you can tell us about your mental conditioning later. Guy was probably a five foot two, one eighty pound skinny-fat pimple faced *dork* who got rich off cryptocoin. A fancy gun like this would be real useful for you to hold in his face while you tie him to his bed and fuck him with a strap on. You know how to use this pistol?"

"...Y-yeah," She said slowly.

"You're gonna have to do a better job of convincing me. Is that your final answer?"

"Yeah, I do," She said, a little more adamant.

"You ever shot it?" Selicia didn't respond now, biting her lip a little in frustration. She knew Gabriel could read her like an open book. This was probably the first time in her life where she actually felt intimidated, unable to use her only skill, her lewd charms.

"...I've never had to shoot anybody. I can usually evade people."

"But have you ever even test-fired it?" She was silent again. Gabriel sighed, putting the gun back in the shoulder holster and picking the whole holster rig up and throwing it over his armor. Given that it was sized for Selicia's amazonian frame, it fit rather loosely over Gabriel's heavily-armored barrel chest. I saw her get up, though I didn't scramble to shoot her as she approached Gabriel, an arm out, like a child ready to say "mine, mine, gimme back". Gabriel's eyes went back to her and she was struck dumb. A single gaze and she was paralyzed, hand falling back down. She towered above him, her breasts practically waving in his face but he was an immovable colossus, far larger than he really was.

Gabriel stepped around her as she hung there in her own shock, going to her open closet to get her a bra and a shirt. He picked out her most appropriately sporty underwear and tossed it over his shoulder to her as she watched, like she wanted to make some snide comment about him going through her underwear but seemed dumbstruck by his levels of boiling nonchalance, him getting a blouse as well, the plainest thing she owned and tossing it to her too. "You know why I know the man who you think you're destined for, this amazing husband you've never met, is trash?" Gabriel said. "He bought you too much terrible, useless shit to wear. Look at all this trashy stuff. You barely have any decent utility-wear." He scoffed, slamming the door with the beep of its lock, holding only her hologlasses, custom-made with four lenses rather than two, tossing them to her which she scrambled to catch.

"I-I-"

"Somebody like you needs to take a step back. Really evaluate your position, see what you can do to better yourself. You've been brainwashed to think you're a one-of-a-kind princess in a gilded castle tower waiting for prince charming but you're a made-to-order *whore* in a shit-smeared subterranean dungeon waiting for a loser with too much money and *way* too many fetishes. He's not coming, Selicia. You should count that as a blessing."

"Y-you're wrong," She said, clutching her glasses. Saying it like she didn't even believe it. Saying it because she had to, she was conditioned to. Gabriel glared back at her again, that piercing gaze like swords.

"...Put your clothes on. Come with us and show us you're worth trusting if you want this shiny ten-thousand-dollar paperweight you call a gun back. You know this guy in the sub-dome we're going to see? Archie tells me you've got history with him." Gabriel said. She nodded slowly, if not bashfully.

"W-wait, Gabe," I put forth. "We're- Are you-"

"She's not gonna do anything while I'm around, and this way she's not pestering us from a distance where I can't smack some sense into her," Gabriel growled plainly. I didn't want to believe him, I wanted to put up a fuss, but by how docile she was around Gabe's impenetrable aura, he really had a point.

"You... Would be okay with me coming?" She said. "I- I mean... I just want my gun back, after all," She was trying to play things off. Revert to her programming of being a femme fatale manipulator.

"I swear, if she tries anything else on m-"

"Get your brain out of the gutter, Noah," Gabriel barked and it was my turn to freeze. "At this point I'm liable to think you're projecting." He had a short chuckle at my expense with a smirk, punching me in the shoulder as he passed, heading for Archie and the door. I glared at Selicia, who stood there, dumbfounded at her lack of control over the situation, something very, very new to her. I had nothing to say to her, ducking out the door to follow. Just another freak joining the party, it seemed.

The three of us in front, Selicia trailing behind. I looked back every now and then to check our perimeter, seeing her sheepishly ducking about, her ego too bruised to really try and be witty or anything for now, though she caught my glances and sighed inwardly. I could tell she wanted to apologize or something. I don't think I would have believed her even if she did, figuring that if Gabriel wasn't here she'd be as grating as she could be.

"...What's up with all the pings in the security barracks?" Gabriel said.

"...I think it's fine," Archie said as we were turning the last corner until the straightaway right to said security barracks. "The security stations have a lot of spare locators in them."

"...Why would they be turned on, though?" Gabriel said. Archie shrugged, as he brought out his tablet, ready to hack open the door. Gabriel sighed. "At least try and see if it's already open f-" Gabriel reached out to the console and it beeped, the heavy door sliding up.

There they were. An awkward silence ensued as we came face to face with them. Mostly canids and felinids, sitting around in there. We were silent as we saw them, their blood-painted faces and clothing, their body armor appropriately modified to show their specific allegiances. The streaks of red blood in their fur radiating outwards from their faces. A human hand and forearm lay on the table, half eaten, probably from some scientist, a couple playing cards in the corner. We saw their mangy, bloody faces, lips ripped and scarred up.

"Oh, evening fellas," Gabriel said. The first to make a move were the card-players in the corner, going for their rifles. Gabriel shredded them with a burst from his MDR, as one of the closer ones leapt up. Gabriel drew his pistol with his off hand and fired, still stringing the rounds from his longarm across into a draconic hybrid in the corner, Gabriel's pistol going off simultaneously, boom, boom, boom. Gabriel was faster than every single one save for the canid furthest behind the table before them, the biggest one with the barrel chest ducking beneath as Gabriel emptied his pistol into the other two before him. As Gabriel's slide locked back, the big one leapt out. He was a centaurical upon finer inspection, bolting forward, ready to tackle Gabriel. Archie, who had ducked away as soon as the insanity began was cowering besides the door, me coming up to fire, but one of the hybrids that had been beside the door, rather than go for Gabriel saw me, bolting out. He was thin and lithe, dirty, with a sick look in his eyes. He knocked my gun away, grappling with it to take it from me but not initially realizing I was wearing a sling, said sling probably saving my life. He instead gripped into me, swiping at my face with his hands, dirty, vicious fingers digging for my eyes. I headbutted him with my helmet but he kept grabbing at me. My knife came out and I felt it slide into his meager guts. How he coughed and sputtered as I twisted and slashed to the side. His intestines spilled out of him as I watched, as he grasped with them, screaming and yelping sickly. I brought my shotgun back up and with a boom his head was decimated, showering Archie nearby with brains, who began coughing and screaming and sputtering in horrified disgust where he was cowering.

I looked up, seeing Gabriel tossed through the door, stumbling back. He was out of ammo in his rifle and his sidearm, this gigantic wolf-centaur man with his eyes aflame in rage, teeth gnashing, charging out.

Gabriel drew Selicia's weapon. Six shots rang out and six bloody holes opened up on the 'taur's humanoid upper body. Selicia behind me yelped at the noise of all the gunfire, Gabriel standing there having fanned the revolver. The 'taur still barreled into him and grasped at him, foaming at the mouth. I raised my shotgun, waiting for the 'taur guy to rear up so I could take a safe shot and fired the other barrel, blowing his jaw clean off and he fell atop Gabe, who rolled the big mass of fur and muscle off of himself.

"fucking goddamn," Gabriel said, getting up as I offered him a hand. Gabriel looked back to Selicia, who was still mortified at the goings-ons. Gabriel waved her revolver. "These aren't magnum rounds, these are fucking Specials. God, what a fucking princess you must be." Gabriel then turned to me as I huffed there, breathless. "...But you know these guns aren't supposed to let you fan them? You can't just hold down the trigger and slap the hammer back and shoot all six bullets like I just did. This is definitely custom. That's neat."

"...Is that what you want to focus on now?!" Archie yelped, still picking brains out of his fur.

"Well, I'm sorry, I was told the security barracks were empty," Gabriel put the revolver back into its holster, picking up his own pistol on the way in, reloading that.

"We..." One of the hybrids on the ground moaned.

"What? You alive, dickhead?" Gabriel walked over to the bloody mess, seeing the trail of blood smeared from where he crawled away from. Gabriel flipped the canid over with a foot, gun up and ready to shoot.

"Come and... Avenge..." He spoke into the hardlined locator. Gabriel saw where it was wired into the wall, like an old historical phone. Gabriel fired and his body spasmed once before laying limp on the floor.

"Oh, shit," Archie said, going for that console. "I… I think he just called for help,"

"Oh boy," Gabriel said, as Selicia peeked her head in.

"Is… is it safe?" She asked.

"It's actually the fuckin' opposite of safe," Gabriel chuckled grimly. "Get inside. We're gonna find our way through this. Archie," Gabe ordered while Selicia was getting through the door. "Check the map. What's the situation looking like?"

"Yeah, uh… Doesn't look good," Archie said, bringing it up as I was topping off my shotgun. I looked up, taking a quick peek. There were a whole lot of locator pings headed our way.

"Hey," Gabe said, flipping over another body that Gabriel had clipped in the back of the head with his pistol, off to the far left corner near the sealed weapons cabinets. "Shit, looks like one of your co-workers," He said, denoting the barcode with the E preceding it on this felinid. "This must be what he was working on. Archie, you think you can finish up what he was doing?" Gabe ordered, pointing to the security storage gate.

"I'm in the middle of something!" Archie said. I saw him fiddling with the controls. "I'm trying to reactivate the security protocols, close the doors- these guys must have fucked the whole system up even getting in here."

"We don't need that. Get over here."

"We just need-"

"Archie. If you would be so kind," Gabriel said, in that stern voice of his. Archie felt Gabriel's gaze on him, his own head raising to look back. Gabriel gave him a frigid smile. "Please. I'd like a new toy," He said. As Archie rolled his eyes, going for the simple lock activation of the door and proceeding over. Selicia, ever ready to do something rather than nothing, began taking the table and knocking it over, pushing it over before the door, throwing furniture towards it, her legs skittering about. "Selicia, if you really need something to do," Gabriel went on, noticing. I saw him take that holster rig for her gun off, motioning it to her. She advanced to take the shoulder holster, throwing it on over her blouse, looking more comfortable having her precious, shiny boat anchor of a weapon back. "…you reload that gun yourself with no hints and it's yours again." Gabriel went back to crossing his arms while Archie did his thing and I looked at the security feed and console, making no sense of it.

There they were, down that hallway. A million angry, glowing eyes, proceeding towards our door. Selicia was fumbling with her gun, it looked like she was merely imitating what she'd seen Gabriel do, slowly getting the hang of it, flicking the loading gate open. She pulled out one of the .44 rounds from the bandolier of the holster rig, finding that she needed to eject the old shell first, fiddling with it some more until she figured out the cylinder ramrod, knocking a single shell out to replace with a fresh .44 special round.

"Oh shit," I uttered, seeing them approach the door through the window. All of them painted up like the ones we'd killed so far. I saw the lankier ones go to drag that dead 'taur guy and the guy I'd killed out of the way. Somehow I doubted they were going to check for vitals.

Then, there was the big one. A wolf on two legs, his lips seemingly ripped off to reveal a jagged, ferocious grinning face, fangs. But below the neck he was nothing but steel and armor, his power armor he wore raising him a good head or two above his tallest lackeys.

"…There we go," Gabriel said just as I was about to alert everyone that we had serious company. I turned, seeing Gabriel pull out a massive hunk of iron, hardly a gun more than it was a block and a barrel. "Ma Deuce. *That's* what I'm talking about."

"Guys! We've got one of them in power armor!" I shouted, my heart racing. I saw Selicia seize up, still on her third shell reloaded, practically learning as she went.

"The bloke with no lips?" She noted. I nodded, motioning to the one-way window. I saw a shiftier one go and bring forward what he was carrying- a sizeable roundsaw, that nefarious power-armored wolf canid a little ways back from his entourage brimming with bloody satisfaction. They brought it up to the door and sparks began to fly, first outside, now in here.

"...Ain't no shit to the fifty," Gabriel chuckled, going for a belt of ammo.

"Y-you're not- It's huge," Archie said of Gabriel's new weapon. Gabriel was grinning wider than this new lipless nemesis of ours was.

"...Archie, buddy... Witness the power of *un ejecutor.*" Gabriel was charging the massive heavy machine gun as the roundsaw was progressing downward, while Selicia finally finished loading, and Archie and I began to prepare, going further back into the room and hunkering down, ready to fire. Just as the roundsaw nearly completed its journey through the lock, Gabriel picked that entire fucking autocannon up by its forward handle, the one not really meant for carrying it but simply to move it, for any other man but a superhuman *Ejecutor.* I saw his arm strain. How he grunted, grinning razors as the belt of ammo drooped onto the floor with a loud clatter.

*Thunk.* The door fell. Just barely from the mess that Selicia had made for a barricade, we could see them peeking through and begin to shove their way through the refuse, enough to see Gabriel standing there, a monolith of hate with hands full of steel, his wit not yet sapped from him as he sternly announced, "*Yiff in hell, furfags.*"

It was a roar unlike anything I'd heard, even down here. Selicia was the first to duck back and grab her elfish ears, teeth grit. Archie and his spare operator's comms didn't do that much to save his hearing either as he ducked back too. Even my ears were rattled beneath my state-of-the-art mufflers. But there Gabriel was, mask atop his head, ears wide in the breeze as far as I could tell, letting fire and hate rip from his new, mighty weapon. Shells and belt links rained to the ground, boom boom boom. The barrier Selicia had made was obliterated, steel and plastic shredded, even the door and wall facing outwards were no match. Blood, endless blood opened up before us. The first ones who'd been up against the barrier were reduced to mush in seconds. I saw an arm, severed by copper and lead and hate from this hundred-year-old automatic cannon fly through the air. Carnage down the hallway, each fifty BMG round chewing its way through what must have been twenty-some bodies. Gabriel was beyond fear, it didn't even seem like they were shooting back, any shooting they did was from reflex, trigger fingers tensing as brainstems were shredded by molten lead, spurring the body to twitch in final reflex from such doom unleashed before their carcasses. Gabriel was not merely firing, but walking forward as he did so, unabashed by recoil. Stepping over bodies upon bodies upon bodies. Bullets that tore his enemies limb from glorious limb. He stood in that doorway roaring away until his smoking weapon ran dry, and any left alive, much less in one piece, had already run off or hid. I saw Gabe standing there, triumphant, demonic, holding the world's most ridiculous magic wand spewing smoke. He looked back at me after gazing out into the killing field he'd created, the sopping wet piles of blood and guts and fur.

"So," Gabe uttered, breathless, with a look back at us. "Where's that fucker with the power armor again?"

*Clank. Clank. Clank.*

Gabriel had to crane his neck a little bit, seeing the captain waltz back out from the cell he'd ducked into to avoid the barrage. Though I probably should have just shot the big, ugly bastard, I was frozen. I felt from Gabriel's posture, from the very air itself, that I wanted, waited to see what would happen. Same with some of his other compatriots who had similarly ducked away, unarmed, rear-echelon "soldiers" of his, sneering distantly now, as if the shoe were on the other foot. Gabriel didn't seem bothered, at least from where I stood behind, noting only his posture. I'd love to have seen the look on his face, given what was about to happen.

"*Hel...Lo,*" The lipless canid snarled, tongue flapping in the breeze. I saw his power armor, exposing only his head, that awful, mangey, mangled looking head.

"That's you, huh? The boss?" Gabe hefted his machine gun in his arms. I saw the power-armored hybrid before us. How he had a massive sword hanging in a scabbard, how his forearms had large armor plates, like shields for him on the power armor he wore. This steel beast before us began to reach for his sword, as Gabriel spoke again. "Hey wait, don't helicopters eat their young?"

"...Huh?"

"Here, hold this, alright? Here you go," Gabe suddenly alley-ooped his machine gun to the power-armored enemy, how he went to fumble with the cannon as Gabriel's hand flashed up to his chest for his armor-mounted holster. *Pow*. His pistol went off and this shiver-inducing, terrifying metal-clad beast eight feet tall crashed down backwards, head opened up by a ten-millimeter copper pill, his cronies still standing behind him freezing up, Gabriel glaring at them once before they scampered away, practically yelping like the dogs they looked so much like.

I was beside myself, no real way to process what had just happened, as Gabriel turned back to me to take a look at us, to gauge audience reaction. That clever smirk of his, ready to make light of the situation.

"...No fucking helmet, can you believe that guy?" Gabriel laughed. "Fucking retard. Like, I get that he's a hybrid and all with a muzzle, can't exactly wear a normal human helmet, but like, fuck, man, weld some shit on there, make yourself one, goddamn," Gabriel sighed, exasperated.

"...Do helicopters... eat their young?" I put forth.

"It's a mental stop. See, he was expecting me to stand here, prepare to fight while he drew his sword- a fucking sword, man. Engraved display revolvers, where the fuck do you morons get all this shit?!" Gabriel bellowed back, presumably to Archie and Selicia, who were also beside themselves in shock, mouths agape. "...Anyways, he had a mental plan and I had to disrupt it before I could proceed with my real tactic- making sure he didn't cover his head. First thing, he probably realises that his head is his weak point. That's why he's got those big shield-y bracers of his on his forearms. If I just drew my gun he'd probably have covered his face. If I just tossed him the M2, he probably would have just let it bounce off of him. First I had to soften him up, sort of lighten his... *thinking* about me, then I..." Gabe paced over and reached down for the carry handle of his autocannon, slumped over the still body of our defeated adversary. "Made sure that he couldn't cover his head quickly, or draw his sword by tossing him a ninety-pound HMG that he was more receptive to catching. Like, damn. This is pretty elementary. What the fuck do you think I should have done? Bounced a bullet off the ceiling into his skull? This ain't no fuckin' Joss Whedon flick," Gabriel paced back towards me, as I stood there, blinking.

"...Power of an egg-hec-you-tore-ay, eh?" Archie muttered, As Gabe proceeded to pass him too, Gabe slapping him on the shoulder as he did, Archie practically taken off his feet by it.

"There you go. Getting closer on the pronunciation, keep it up." Selicia couldn't help but look away as Gabe gave her a glance, him smiling now, sighing gleefully as he landed his gun back down on the table, going for more ammo. Selicia was beside herself as well, before she blushed deeply, practically having to close her slackened jaw by force, swallowing down her terror, and her impressedness, as she holstered her finally fully loaded revolver, while he was reloading his new favorite weapon, going to throw more belts over his shoulders and picking up cans of ammo. "So where's this fucking guy?"

"Uh… About that," Archie said, still brushing off the current goings-ons as he did. "We're… right above him."

"No shit? Fucking great coincidence," Gabe said, ripping the charging handle back and leaning on that table, while Archie was walking back into the interior of the security station, awkwardly motioning to one of the elevators.

"…I, I mean I was g-gonna tell you, you just…" Archie yammered on, evident he didn't quite have any second part to his sentence. Gabe smirked.

"Hey, spidergirl. Be a dear and carry some more cans of ammo," He ordered, and she, just as breathless, complied with the order, while Archie motioned to the freight elevator that Gabriel and him piled into, soon followed by me and Selicia, carrying two more hundred round cans of fifty cal. It was a little cramped, of course, even if the elevator was gigantic. Selicia's amazonian humanoid belly was right in my face, her form towering above us, looking down at us in silence. I had to force myself not to think about how I almost ended up in there, even as she teetered back and forth and crowded up on me, as I turned all the way away, towards Archie there. The elevator began to move as Archie activated the console, and we began to descend, Gabriel with that autocannon over his shoulder smugly brushing the handle of his pistol off with his off-hand.

"…Having fun yet?" Gabe asked, looking to me. I grunted, the back of my helmet bumping into the bottom of one of Selicia's breasts and upper belly, me wincing and stepping away a little. I was still beside myself, Gabe chuckling. "…*I'm* having a lot of fun. Fuckin' adventure, dude." Archie was rolling his eyes, facing away from Gabe as he was still picking brains out of his fur.

Down we went.

### Chapter 23

I stepped forward a little in the elevator, up against the wall. We weren't just moving down, the elevator felt like it was getting whisked in different directions, side to side. It was dark, but I could just barely make out rapid movement, not unlike the elevator was actually see-through. I turned on the light of my shotgun, seeing that, yes, the walls were indeed glass. "Huh," I uttered. "Why would the walls be-"

Flash.

It was like I was blinded for a second, blinking there. I saw… buildings rushing about around us, springing up from the ground below. Was that… the sky above us? I looked around, seeing that it was like we were all inside an outdoor elevator connected to a skyscraper, which dominated the sky behind us. The sky, clouds floating above, the sun hanging there. It was like falling into a dream, how the world suddenly changed around me.

"…So this is the geodome, huh?" Gabriel was chuckling impressedly. I looked back, seeing the one wall that wasn't translucent behind me, the door wall. "…Are those flying cars?" Gabriel asked. I looked back out to this… "City", seeing aerial vehicles ambling about, adding to the surreality of this place. Truly another world.

"…Experimental tech. Macro-Quantum Levitation," Archie extrapolated.

"Yeah, I heard about it on the news," I responded. "Magnets using the earth's core to fly, huh?"

"-Earth's magnetic field to suspend vehicles in the air and propel them. Yeah," Archie corrected. Gabe laughed.

"...Looks like we're gonna get what we're looking for here," Gabe muttered contentedly.

The elevator stopped and the door opened, leading into the lobby of the place. Like a big hotel. We strolled out, still full of guns and at least two of us sopped in gore, being Gabriel, with that fifty cal slung over his shoulder. There was a receptionist there, all alone, one of the cat ones with a matte blue-grey fur color and rounded ears, a slim centaurical one sitting on her hind legs behind a big circular desk, mane of hair tied into a bun and wearing a headset and hologlasses, and a shimmering silver... I'd call it a pantsuit, but as she was a centaurical I suppose it was closer to being a bodysuit. I saw her see us and begin beaming in glee, and I almost felt self-conscious about all the weapons. "Hello," she greeted with a bright and happy smile, beaming as Gabriel walked right up to her desk, that chain of ammo swinging from his gun all the while, his eyebrow raised, mask still up above his head. I saw the bloody footprints he left while walking. "Welcome to Prosperia. You must have come from off-world, right?" She had that sort of voice, flowery yet dignified, genuinely putting on that sort of happy-to-see-you, professional front.

"Off... world?" Gabriel asked, Archie dodging a little as a tiny, circular robot was swiping across the ground behind us and darting around legs, cleaning up the floors to a sparkle once more.

"Well, welcome to Adondis VII, if you are new to the system. Prosperia is the capital of-"

"...A tall white fountain played," Archie suddenly blurted, interrupting the conversation. An awkward stillness presided over all, a momentary awkward stretch with this attendant staring at Archie with her brow raised.

"...Of," she continued, a little confused, as we all eyed Archie. "Of the current-"

"A TALL. WHITE. FOUNTAIN. PLAYED." Archie got closer, up in her face. She stopped again.

"...Sir, you're... making me uncomfortable," She looked down and away, scooting away a little. "...May I continue telling you about our city?" She continued unabashed.

"NO. Full stop. End program. Code KD6-3.7." Archie was practically pantomiming every syllable right in her face, her leaning way back practically to avoid spittle.

"...Would you like some help?" She asked this time. Archie brutally wrenched himself back, throwing his arms up for a moment as he gazed towards the sky.

"...Fucking unbelievable. He took out their deactivation hotwords."

"They're not exactly machines, Archie, you can't de-program hybrids like you can with computers," Selicia put forth. "See, she pauses every time you say it. It's still there but it keeps getting overridden."

"Shit, when'd you turn into the science chief, Legs?" Gabriel eyed Selicia with a brow raised. Selicia glared quickly back at him, evidently not amused by her new nickname.

"...Our population stands at a-" The attendant began anew.

"Overridden?" Archie blasted back to Selicia. "She's pausing because we're yelling in her face. She's got zero Manchurian Protocols left. She's basically a regular person at this point."

"...Isn't that the point of hybrids?" Gabe mused.

"...And our mayor, resides in the historic-"

"Hey. Hey," Archie began to snap in the attendant's face, interrupting her latest spiel. "Hey you. What's your name?"

"...Rebecca," She said slowly, going to motion to her nametag on her futuristic silver bodysuit. "...May I-"

"Oy, peep this bloke," Archie said, grasping Gabriel's forearm holding his M2 steady over his shoulder, Gabriel momentarily glaring over to Archie as a response for the sudden physical contact. "...What species is this guy?"

"S-species?" She uttered. I saw her face blank out, before she blinked a moment later. "Hello," She said, as if beginning anew. "Welcome, to Prosp-"

"...A fucking restart. See, they run into something they aren't allowed to process and they have to start over. They've got a few Manchurian protocols still fucking with them but the USEFUL ones happen to have been de-programmed."

"How about we just walk?" Gabe put forth. "It's not like she-"

"Oh, if you're in a hurry, you must want our tour guide instead!" Rebecca let out suddenly, Archie looking like he was ready to scream. "Oh, Lucille," She said into the PA. "We have visitors! Show them around!"

"FUCK! I just needed a bit to figure out a way to- RGH!" Archie let out as Gabe was pushing his way through the door, unbothered, while another door opened and out straddled a rather petite draconic hybrid, also wearing a futuristic dress with a miniskirt, her thick tail reaching out below it as she walked. She wore high heels, with feet like us humans, however she was barely as tall as my chin, hornless with a ponytail of hair. Unlike Lauren, her hair was relegated to her head alone, and her ears were less cow like as Lauren's were, and more fin-like, her snout having a ridge atop it. A more westernized dragon, I suppose you could say, her skin a bright cherry red contrasting the cobalt blue of her shimmering dress, carrying her tablet delicately in her hands, a pair of fancy, overfuturistically-dressed-up hologlasses on her face covering her glittering mint-green eyes.

"Hello, sirs and madam," This petite little dragoness beamed, waltzing up beside me with a warm smile while I followed Gabriel, Selicia behind me with Archie, ever exasperated, in tow. "...I think you'll enjoy our beautiful city as much as I do. It really is a wonderful place to live and visit."

Out on the... Streets, if you could call them that, the city was bustling. Cars zipping by overhead, the hybrids all wearing future-y getups like Lucille and Rebecca had been, I thought I saw a souped up prosthetic or two or a dozen. Really was like stumbling through a dream, how it was like the world around us changed. Fifteen minutes before we were surrounded by deranged, murderous hybrids, now we felt like we were a hundred years into the future. But there was that fakeness that presided over all. How nobody, none of these hybrid inhabitants really seemed to *notice* us. Forget that Gabriel and I were the only two humans in sight, but the fact that all four of us walked around covered in guns and blood was equally unnoticed.

"Yeah. Charming," Gabriel chatted back to her while the two conversed, Lucielle prattling on and on with Gabriel incredibly amused at the entire ordeal just as much as Archie was screaming internally at hearing Lucille's boilerplate explainer for the umpteenth time or so. "What's your favorite joint in this place, Lucy?"

"Oh, there's a fantastic nightclub and bar in the Ridley Gardens burrough. It's where I met my husband."

"Is he real?" Gabriel asked.

"Excuse me?" Lucille responded, barely pausing. Gabriel chuckled.

"...Damn, she's fast on the draw. You say they program these fuckers?" Gabe asked back to Archie.

"Everyone grown in accelerated growth chambers, for the lack of a better term, yeah, they're 'programmed'."

"Even you?" I asked, adding to the conversation as we walked, looking back at Archie. He grunted, nodding uncomfortably. "How come you're not like the ones here?"

"I wasn't a socio-chamber hybrid. We've got far less strict Manchurian Protocols."

"...Like what?"

"Like fock off."

"...I know his protocols," Selicia sang teasingly, stretching a little as she walked, gazing up into the sky. It really was just a sky like up on the surface, though it was a lot dimmer though it was still "daytime" with a blue sun in the sky, the sky's color a resounding purple, with a moon or planet complete with it's own ring hanging in the sky. I was enamored with the creativity of the place, pondering purpose as I walked.

"...Fock. Off," He enunciated.

"...Uh... So," Lucille tried to continue, desperately, even, Gabriel the most interested in the exposition of lore as he eyed her while we walked. "...We've got lots of-"

"...How about... Lauren? She's... Vat-grown, right? Does she have... Manchurian Protocols?" I asked alongside the babble of our tour guide.

"Well, 'Vat-growns' is a bit of a misnomer- you know that pretty much every hybrid around is vat-grown, right?" Archie put forth. I nodded. "Yeah, well we call ones like Lauren and Abel and Reina vat growns because that's all they've known. They aren't put in socio-experiments like Lucille here or Katt up top, or an Engineer Class made to keep the place running, like me. They were just works in progress when the shit popped off. As far as we know their kind didn't get any protocols but I bet there's probably something in there. They basically installed their personalities piece by piece, after all."

"...So if this... Breach didn't happen, would they have just been... Put in a socio-experiment eventually?"

"Fock if I know. Seems to me like the people in charge of this bullshit made way too many fucking vat-growns than they have geodomes to put them in; and they've got a fucking *ton* of geodomes. Shite's focked. I'd call it a conspiracy."

"...Theater, huh? What kind of movies you watch?" Gabriel asked, Lucille and him in a conversation at the moment. "Like, what's the last one you've seen?"

"Ooh, Mona Lisa Overdrive was great," She said. Gabriel smirked again.

"Damn, they got you living in the year 3000 but showing you movies from ages ago," Gabe said. "Did it bother you that everyone was a human in that movie?"

"A what?" she asked.

"You know. Like me," Gabe said, and Lucille stopped dead in her tracks, eyes unfocusing and as Selicia's belly bumped into the dragon girl, her wings fluttering as she "came back online".

"So what else would you like to know about?" she suddenly said, eyes brightening again for a moment before Selicia's hand landed heavily on her shoulder. I looked back, finally seeing that Selicia had taken her holster and blouse off and held them with her web feelers, and was in the middle of unhooking her bra with her other hand behind her back.

"...You know, I haven't... *met* you before," Selicia said and Lucy looked up and over her shoulder, rather concerned as Selicia tightened her grip. I watched with growing horror as Selicia licked her lips. "You seem like just my type, Lucy. Nice and... fun size. And, aside from humans I think I enjoy a good dragon the most. Well, Archie, you're tired of her blathering, aren't you? And Lucy... I'm sure your husband is the... sharing type," She said, as she reached her bra-unhooking hand up to her jaw, clicking it out. Lucille immediately figured out what was about to happen, trying to release herself in vain with terror in her eyes as Selicia's jaw swiftly came down over Lucille's head, her muffled screaming resounding as Selicia quickly advanced to the dragon girl's shoulders, her limbs flailing, wings flapping this way and that.

However, Selicia had not advanced any further than that as her eye rolled up to see Gabriel's ten millimeter in her face. She blinked once, slowly, Lucille's muffled yelps for help the only sound to this odd scene.

"...Selicia. Either you spit out my tour guide or I'll open some holes for her to crawl back out of."

"Oh, you can't be-" Archie began, but Gabriel glared at him as well, despite how his gun did not move.

"You're really going to watch her, *let* her do this? I thought you weren't into this, Archie."

"Ugh- 'Lucille' is going to be fine. She's just going to be a lot easier to ignore when she's inside her."

"Why do you say 'Lucille' like that? Like she isn't a person. What gives?"

"Didn't you mow down an army of hybrids and laugh about it five minutes ago?"

"They were trying to kill us. I like Lucy. She's got interesting shit to say."

"...Interesting for a mongoloid like you," Archie put forth, the trapped Lucille swinging her fist up at Selicia's face in futility, doing her pitiful best to free herself.

"...Selicia. Spit. Now, please." I saw her release Lucille's arms, the dragon girl sliding out and away, falling on the ground and gasping and coughing, scrambling away, panicked for a moment as Gabriel came before her, putting his machine gun on the ground to help her up. She shot a fearful gaze towards Selicia as Selicia rehinged her jaw, Selicia rolling her eyes as she redid her bra.

"...god, what do you have against me enjoying myself?" Selicia muttered. "I can understand Noah, but this is borderline irrational. She can still tell you all about her stupid fake city from inside my belly, anyways."

"I don't like having to decipher people's words while they're sobbing in terror like some faggot assassin. I like looking people in the eyes."

"T-thank you," She sobbed out, hanging onto Gabriel.

"Yeah. On your feet. You're fine, see? The rapey voraphile spider isn't gonna hurt you anymore. Now tell me about your socioeconomics, would you? Where are the slums of this place? You guys gotta have an underclass, that real cyber*punk* bite."

Sirens.

We all looked up, suddenly interrupted by plenty of those flying vehicles, but adorned with blue and red lights, strafing by as their exo-armored security descended from the sky on jump packs, little rocket engines on their calves and thighs, landing and seemingly surrounding us in an instant. I froze up, Archie froze up, even Selicia who was still putting her shirt on, by the time her head was through the collar she was frozen in terror too. The only one who didn't fail to act was Gabriel, instantly grappling Lucille to the front and putting his pistol to her jaw.

"BACK UP! BACK THE FUCK UP!" he was switched into gear in an instant, poor Lucille held in a rear choke by her own knight in shining armor. "Archie, I thought these guys aren't supposed to notice us," He growled.

"...You think I don't know that?!" Archie yelped, still in high ready, just like me.

"You think it has anything to do with their protocols being all fucky?!" Gabe shouted back. Lucille was sobbing. Selicia's hands were already in the air, web feelers also in the air for whatever reason.

"Oh, shit," Archie put forth. "Hey, uh... We gotta talk to Anon!" He shouted, loud and audibly. The armored hybrid cops were given pause- or at least more pause than they already had, looking to each other a little. "Archie and his friends need to talk to the mayor! Alright?!"

"Oh, shit, look who it is," A voice suddenly said. The police captain's holoprojector that he had on his bigger, bulkier suit of true power armor was active, displaying a screen. "Damn, Arch," The screen was blank, only showing the city seal of Prosperia. Funny that they had all these details about this fake city we were wandering about in. "Kinda left on short notice. Cold, aren't you?"

"What the fuck is with your security? We almost got in a firefight," Archie shouted, now letting his weapon hang from its sling.

"Oh, shit yeah. Damn, I can tell you all about it, actually. Funny story. Who's the one who's been manhandling Lucille?"

"...That one's called Selicia, I've been told you've already been acquainted," Gabriel responded nodding his head towards Selicia whose hands were slowly falling down though still in obvious surrender, meanwhile Gabriel's hostage was unconscious from shock, now practically carried in his arms. This faceless hologram let out a laugh, a genuine laugh, not something for the sake of theatrics.

"Ha! I like this dude. Yo, you can let Lucy go now. My guys won't shoot ya."

"...How about you order your goons to stand down first?" Gabriel said, not relinquishing his human- er, draconic shield.

"Ooh, smart fella," Anon crowed. "Safeties on, fellas. These aren't the usual banditos." The security lowered their weapons completely, and Gabriel slowly loosened his grip on Lucille, who had since fainted on the spot, letting her lay on the ground. "So," Anon began anew. "We oughta have a talk, since I figure that's what you're here for. My guys will bring you to my penthouse. Leave Lucille, my guys will tend to her. Ever ridden a flyin' fuckin car before? Shit's neato," Anon said as Gabriel picked his machine gun back up again.

"Holy shit dude," I muttered, pushing my weapon back, still in shock by how quickly all this was progressing. I looked back over at that hologram projection, the felinid police captain in his power armor still harshly unamused despite his superior holding his leash. We climbed in the big dispatch van, sitting with some of the stern officers as we rode. They almost seemed to ignore us as we sat there, it was enough to unnerve me. At least, more than I already was.

Gabriel, unstoppable as he was, was simply smiling at the prospect of quickening our little side-journey, having fun looking out the window as we rode, down upon the sprawling metropolis. He looked back to me, though he looked over to Archie, peeved as I was, and Selicia, a little less than enthusiastic but doing her best to encourage herself after avoiding another gunfight. "You good?" Gabe uttered as he caught my worried gaze.

"...Yeah. I think so," I said. I was still short of breath. Gabriel smirked.

"Having fun?"

"Well, my city is blown up, my dad abandoned me the one time I could actually use him, my girlfriend's parents and a couple of my friends are dead and world war three is probably raging and we're here fucking around in futureville. All things considered I'm having the time of my life," I muttered. Gabriel shrugged, presuming my exasperation with a chuckle.

A short flight over, we landed at one of the more impressive buildings, shorter yet stouter than many of the other reaching into what seemed to be the "Sky" of the place, probably so it could actually have a roof to land on unlike the massive, towering structure we had entered the place through looming heavy in the distance. I remembered that there was no way for the "sky" of this geodome to be that tall, figuring at some point that tower disappeared into the holographic projection of an alien sky. Our vehicle stopped at the edge of the mayor's tower outhang, opening up for us to pile out one by one, Selicia advancing primarily, followed by Archie, dropping the foot or so onto the floor of the rooftop, me piling out next to take a look back, seeing nothing but frigid mist drifting down from frost-caked spheres adorning the undercarriage of the police "van", almost like I expected strings or something, or at the very least giant fans or jets roaring away, hardly able to believe the simple hum of the misty quantum drives before me was all that was suspending the vehicle in space. Gabriel caught my smile, looking back at it, as the police captain from earlier came out as well, following us out in his power armor. "Shit, you believe this?" Gabriel laughed in glee at the sight, looking at the undercarriage as he craned down, seeing the quantum drives all misted up with frost.

"...Don't get too carried away," A voice called over from one of the poolside lounge couches as we were ogling the downright sublime technology. "Can't run off with one." Gabriel straightened back up, letting his machine gun slam onto the ground, crossing his arms over his armor looking towards the source of the voice. The place was laid back, more or less, a sound system a ways away blaring some music with heavy synth production, something out of a niche sci-fi movie sort of thing, a drink bar a ways away with a neon sign written in cursive on it. I saw the pool and some of the people lounging within, one being a long, slender female body cutting through its water as she swam. One of the snake hybrids, a serpentine if I wasn't mistaken, one of the female-only specieses, I could barely remember from what I'd seen on the news. I was confused at her phylogeny for a second, her upper body unremarkable from a human girl down to her pale skintone and the bikini top she wore, bright red hair on her head, however where her hips began she was all snake: a long, thick bright red tail instead of legs. I watched her flip over as she swam, cherry red eyes catching mine. She must've felt a little coy catching me gaping at her, as she smiled a little, revealing those same fangs like Selicia had, reaching a hand to adjust her bikini top. I nodded out of some detached form of acknowledgement, turning back to the figure sitting there on the pool lounger.

"...You this Anon guy?" Gabriel asked, standing there with a brow arched and a smile on his face. I looked to the man too, seeing a slightly older gentleman there wearing aviator sunglasses, an opened hawaiian shirt and a far too promiscuous pair of swimming briefs. He was rotund and hairy, hispanic or southeast asian if I had to guess from the color of his skin.

"...Wuss poppin'," He uttered, putting his drink down and crossing his arms behind his head, positioning his "package" a little as he rearranged his legs, making the situation a little more uncomfortable for me, though my compatriots were able to deal with this man's crassness in their own different ways. I took a moment to look around, first noting the hybrid beside him, another serpentine like the one in the water with a human face, her tail coiled on the ground before her lounger seat, though her skintone was a uniform powder white scale even over her human bits with bright pink irises amid black sclera, and an equally sultry nature to her. I turned about some, seeing other hybrids- all the ones that seemed to not be here for the titillation of the "mayor" were adorned on their barcodes with the E-preface like Archie, other engineer hybrids like him, or a couple humans too, probably scientists and technicians who took refuge here if I had to guess, though none quite as relaxed as Anon was. They all looked lithe or out of shape, not the soldierly type for sure, doing their best to relax though I took careful note of some here who made highly worried glances towards Selicia, who winked and licked her lips back to some of them. "About time X-Sec sent some of their guys here. Expected a few more, though two specialists I suppose will do the trick."

"Uh… X-Sec?" I put forth.

"Hey, roll with it," Anon muttered much more quietly now, eyeing about as he tipped his sunglasses lower at the other humans here, almost all eyes on us eagerly, not exactly eavesdropping but pretty damn close to it. "Here. Lemme get you boys a drink," He suddenly sprang up, gingerly touching the human-faced serpentine hybrid laying on the recliner beside where he had been laying on the shoulder, tracing across her back and other shoulder as she giggled sultrily, him walking around her. "C'mon." the four of us followed. I watched a thin caucasian human jump out of the way of the approaching Selicia, fear in his eyes as he scrambled ever so subtly towards the bathroom. Archie was rolling his eyes, and Selicia looked like if Gabriel wasn't here she'd be having a lot more fun. "So, Archie. You wouldn't be back for no reason, you never struck me as the indecisive type. Impulsive, maybe, but you stick to your guns." Anon hit the bar with his back, spinning around as he did to eye back at us out the top of his sunglasses. "Point I'm saying is I doubt you came back just to bring me these rough looking types. You want something, don't you- actually. No," He smiled, waggling his finger at Archie as the fox-like bartender with nonsense-less eyes behind him slid him another Martini. "You probably," He took a long, almost obnoxious sip. "Made friends with these folks and *they're* the ones who want something, eh?"

"...Let's start with one of these flying cars," Gabriel put forth before Archie could. Anon smiled back.

"That's unfortunate, friendo. Like I said. Merchandise stays here." Gabriel glared back, feeling the straps of his armor as he furled his lips, though as Gabriel antsily and subtly threatened with his armor, the police captain in his power armor coughed loudly, crossing his own arms across his armored frame as if to remind us to stay civil around the Mayor.

"How come?" Gabriel said, letting his ire burn through his tone, though held leashed of course.

"First off, gotta ask. Survey my fellow humans and all. What'd you think of the place? Fun, huh?" Anon twirled his finger towards the air like motioning to the whole place, while furling his lip right back at Gabriel, like he knew something Gabriel hadn't assumed yet. Gabriel barely nodded. "I was head designer for this place, and *am* current overseer. Head aesthetic and meta-immersion consultant. I was born in 2000. Zoomer son of a bitch if you ever knew one, but I always looked to the past, seeing how far we'd all come as a species and that was what informed my idea for the future, unlike you Generation-Standstill kiddos and your horrifying acceptance of the Technology Ceiling and the general stagnation of the human race. 2060 always struck me as the future, but here I am, and what do we have? You can wear your phone on your face now, I guess. Your kitchen appliances know your name, big whoop. Hardly haven't made a betterer computer since the forties. Fuck, we haven't even been back to the moon. Nearly a hundred years, that's some bullshit. Where's the neon? Where's the style, the feel? Where's the *flying cars,* eh?" Gabriel was a little bit more receptive to our host's spiel, though he was still a little incensed. I doubted Gabriel disagreed with the sentiment, with how enthralled he was with the place. "This place is an ElTek testing ground. To test these quantum levitation vehicles and a few other goodies, gauge population reaction and the applications the people would come up for it, using these hybrids. Not all these geodomes are *just* for social experiments. I mean, this one is, but specifically for testing products Elrond Industries plans, or *planned,* given the direness of the current geopolitical situation, on releasing to the public in a couple years. Vehicles, mostly, like I said. Lotta their tech gimmicks too. Too bad we haven't been able to make tech any better since the Standstill, so we just make 'em weirder and gimmickier, sell 'em here to the populace and see what sticks. Fucking insane and kind of overkill to do all this for what's basically just focus grouping, but it's a way to protect your ideas. I guess."

"...That's fascinating, but you haven't told us why you won't let us take a vehicle."

"Oh, you can take one. Go out on the street and rob some dog-faced freak of his ride, by all means go ahead. Piss off my police chief though but if you don't maim anybody I can get him to look the other way. But ol' Jim's irrelevant. This place was designed so that corporate espionage would be impossible. Can't get out the door with one." He took another pause to sip, to let Gabriel work through the logic.

"...So what, these things explode outside of here?"

"That would be too easy to foil; find the bomb and disable it. Nah. Try and fit one in the elevator. You remember how you got here, right? Multi-directional elevator, not entirely that big," He uttered, before motioning to that same massive tower stretching into "Space" above us. "This is isn't just a Geodome, this is a Superdome. Your average socio-chamber ain't really that big, maybe a mile or two in diameter. This one's basically an entire city. Not the entire city that the locals seem to think it is, we've got about… I want to say, fifty thousand hybrids here? Average geodome might have a tenth that. See, superdomes are so big that they need a strut to hold the roof up; that's the central tower you came down on. Locals think it's a space elevator, can't convince them otherwise. Not that I'd try and foil the aesthetic. Also can't cut open a door in the side, threatens the structural integrity. Perfect place to test your new fun stuff, gauge public reaction, employees can't get out the door with a prototype, especially in one piece. Place is 100% self-sufficient, ran on geothermals, aquaponic gardens, said flying magnet cars produced right here by the locals themselves. Cyberpunk paradise in a bubble, huh?"

"Wouldn't mind a vacation here, but it's a bit Disneyland for my tastes," Gabriel muttered, still mulling over the disappointment of not getting his hands on his own flying tank.

"...A real Hotel California," Anon muttered with a smile. "No place I'd rather be, though I kinda wish that they populated the city I painstakingly built with slightly realer personalities. Don't mind the furries, just wish they acted a little more *human*, y'know? I mean, I'm doing my best, trying to break into them a little. A couple hundred scientists and engies from the facility above are stuck here, they help out with management, though a lot of the aforementioned humans are just killing time dicking around in my city in bars and theaters 'n shit, probably a few brothels too knowing some of these fuckin' nerds. All of em just waiting for that "all clear" signal that's never coming. Most of them don't even know what's really happening up topside. Whole end of the world nonsense. I'm trying to keep that knowledge on the lowdown, can't have the ones still functional taking up binge drinking, figure I'll break it to them slowly. Might get some of them a little antsy even though we're mostly safe down here. Some of my vital workers might break down babbling about their poor family or some shit. I'd like to keep the social cohesion as long as possible. Hence, why I called you guys X-Sec."

"Yeah, about that," Gabe asked, now more than a little curious.

"See," He smacked his tongue as he racked his brain. "X-Sec is... *was*, Elrond Industries' secret corporate military. Designed to keep these places a secret, hunt down escaped hybrids and handle things if the... occupants decide to get a little out of hand. As of late I'm assuming they're a little stretched thin because of the whole worldwide facility breach nonsense, not to mention what I'm assuming is world war three starting up top, so as far as any other humans here are concerned, I'm gonna tell them you're here as two X-Sec specialists to help deal with my problem. It's a little detail. Avoid the breakdown, y'see?"

"...So what's this problem of yours?" Gabriel asked.

"I've got a little... Nemesis, so to say. Fucker's got a hateboner for me, keeps trying to get in here and be a cunt like a shitty cartoon villain. Given his sense of dramatics, the lowdown is he's been making operations down here hard. He'd love nothing more than to get in here and give me and the city I *built* a good dicking. Metaphorically, of course," He uttered with a wave of his drink after pounding his chest defensively, barely gagging a sip down before continuing his exposition. "Some half-baked hybrid but a real dickhead. Wants to grab all the tech in here and go on a crusade, killing all the humans on the surface with his army of hybrids. Impossible and retarded, sure, hence why he's some saturday-morning-cartoon-tier garbage vil- er, I guess that's a bit before your time, but you get what I'm sayin. He's a real fuckin' wackjob, wants total control of the facility before he can begin on his crusade of furfaggotry. Last I checked he was trying to fuck with our generators and stuff, or if not he was near one of the entrances to this place through a security depot. And since I can tell ol' Archibald is probably pissed about not being able to 'would you kindly' his way through my citizens, I'll explain that too." He took a sip, Archie and him sharing a glare. "Said fucker happens to have worked out the ManchPros of the citizens of my dear Prosperia, so, I disabled Manchurians for them because my *nemesis* was taking advantage of it. Storming in to wreak havoc, et cetera. Kinda running out of cops while I'm trying to raise an army to combat the guy, dire straits, you get the gist. Plenty of arms given the surplus depots but not enough soldierly types to wield it."

"...You didn't have much of a defense ready at the gates," Gabriel muttered.

"Yeah. I don't want skirmishes in the *foyer*. That tower gets damaged and the ceiling could collapse and everybody fucking dies and the coolest city on the planet gets buried, instead I try to ambush interlopers when they're far away from it. Like I got you guys. So..." Anon segued yet again. "Sound up to hunting this fucker down? I can't really spare the manpower at the moment. Er, furrypower. Whatever," Anon raised his drink to his police chief. I looked over to him and saw his ear flick, hybrid face still harshly unamused.

"Can we get a... physical description of the guy?" Gabriel uttered, swirling the straw of the drink he himself had ordered.

"Doesn't have lips, paints his guys in human blood, wears power armor, carries a sword. A fucking furry Skeletor. He *looks* like he needs his ass kicked."

"Shot him in the face," Gabriel said. At this revelation, Anon's eyes opened a little wider, forcing him to put down his drink.

"*Really?*"

"...Said it yourself. He looked like he needed his ass kicked."

"Well, shit. Nice job. And here I was with a big plan and everything." Anon caught Archie glaring at him, still waiting for his own explanation, though a little relieved that our sidetracking was moving at such a pace. "See, my plan had some ideas about you deposing him or something. You may actually have caused a little bit of a problem, honestly." Gabriel's brow raised, as did mine. "Now the... *tribes* he united are going to be in a fuckin' uproar. They might present a bigger issue than if you did it my way."

"I'm sorry, would you prefer him to be brought back to life?" Gabriel snarked.

"Look, man, I'm grateful. I'm just saying that now his lieutenants are going to be out for blood for his killers. I would prefer they all fought each other, but hey. Look. One of them might fill the power vacuum and my problem doesn't get solved. You guys should cause one last upset on your way out, but since you're here to go diving for supplies, I think that I have just the thing for you." Anon pulled out his own locator, opening the holographic map projection of the facility. "...You can take the multi-directional elevator to this surplus depot here-" He pointed to one of the many chambers snaking away from where the "sky elevator" of Prosperia diverted towards, one of the other many snaking tunnels leading back to the security waystation we came in through. "*Here* should be what you're looking for. Military rations, clean water tanks, some last gen military humvees. I think there's some power armor, too. I'll give you all activation codes for this one, but you gotta take this route back to the main elevator-" He then pointed to where the big tunnel leading away from it went through a far smaller, though still substantial geodome. "This was a military test ground here. The guy you offed used to run his operations here. City of Manbane he called it, just a bunch of awful slums. Zero fucking creativity. Military test geodomes are also known as darkdomes because they don't bother with putting a holographic sky and sun in, since it's bound to get shot up from the ordinance, so it's just got spotlights. Dive through there, take the roads through, only a mile or two, tiny fuckin' place. Stir the hornet's nest with some 40 Mike-Mike automatic grenade launcher surprise and Fast and Furious your way outta there. That should be enough to fuck up whoever's trying to usurp his throne. You be our stand-in for X-Sec and I'll give you full access to the whole depot there and some of the new armor; it's not like ElTek can sue anybody anymore for running off with a fancy new Sentinel program. Here- hang out in my penthouse, recharge a little here. Mi casa es su casa, amigos. Let my man Jimmy know you're ready to head out and you can vamos," Anon motioned back to the hybrid police captain, sourly watching the affair like he did. "Sound good?" Anon finished his proposition. Gabriel looked to me, smiling cooly. I sighed, almost hesitant.

"...A'ight."

### Chapter 24

A shower and some freshening up did some good for my soul, though I still felt the weight of the situation a bit too much. Some of Anon's servants were tasked with cleaning up our stuff, though I took my time going back out to the pool while Gabriel was having something to eat from the bartender, who'd fired up the grill special for us. It was only just before noon anyways, or something like that. In a borrowed pair of swim trunks I decided to take a swim, crashing in to gaze up at the dim violet alien sky of midday as I floated, that blue star in the distance. Really set the tone, even if I knew this was technically still earth we were on. Oddly calming.

"Hey," Gabriel said, sitting down near the pool and letting his legs drape into the water as he ate a taco above a paper plate to catch the fallen food. "You know. This place ain't that bad."

"It's a little fucky," I muttered back, just bobbing there. He nodded his head side to side, munching loudly before swallowing.

"Fake and all, yeah. Maybe after running this shit for Anon we could bring everyone down here, you know. Wait the bullshit out, then go to your dad's commune."

"I don't like this place," I put back, finally going to make myself vertical again rather than float on my back, treading water. "It's... I don't know. This is what the hybrids have been running from, isn't it?" I said. "Besides... I don't want to abandon my dad. He'll be worried."

"Yeah, yeah. Just so long as you've thought this through." He spoke with his mouth full. Always crass. "On that, this Wilson bullshit got me thinking," He said, and I sighed. Hard to even admit that I'd basically forgotten about it at that point. Too much to ponder in too little of a time. "We've got to train our friends so next time shit pops off it isn't so embarrassing. Three or four guys with shitty obsolete fucking guns and probably not that much training put four of us out of the fight, two permanently. That's not much of a win for us. Fuck, you see Anthony spraying bullets and screaming like a little girl? And he's one of the more level-headed of our group."

"Y-yeah. We should train them." I still hadn't much to say, staring back up at the starry sky. What was the lore for this place, anyhow? Orbiting a gas giant or something? Maybe I should have listened to Lucille. Fucking Anon thinking all this shit up. That reminded me, as I blinked to myself. "H-hey, yo, Anon guy," I yelled out, grappling the side of the pool towards where he sunbathed. "You know what's going on outside?"

"I know Vegas blew. All comms are down, nobody's telling *me* shit, buddy." He took a sip of his drink, almost a little perturbed himself, sitting there.

"...So, you aren't of those, uh... people who were in charge of what's going on with the hybrids that nobody can find?"

"Shit, do you see me running around in black robes, chanting to the dark gods in Latin?" Anon raised his sunglasses, his arm back around one of his serpentine entourage. "I mean, I only ever got *hints* that they existed until this shit even went down. I always thought this facility was the only one, turns out everyone else was told the same shit as me. The Creators, though; I always figured they'd send me an invitation one of these days but never got around to it. Fucking Creators, man. Real whackos."

"...Is that the name of their... organization?"

"Yeah. More like a cult, if you ask me. Probably wasn't the type. I was more of a general aesthetics guy. I never had any influence and I certainly couldn't give a fuck about ideology like some of the higher-ups I've talked to, them all just giving off really spooky Jim Jonesy vibes. I always thought that my bosses were too creepy but I enjoyed my fuckin' job, I was damn good at it. I never saw this apocalyptic shit coming." His compatriot beside him played with his chin a little with the tip of her finger, tailtip curling around one of his legs. "...But I'm not complaining, I get to enjoy the fruits of my labor, after all," He said to her giggling.

"Ugh," I muttered, leaning against the side of the pool where I floated, as I rested my eyes, laying my head against the side of the pool.

"You... feeling better, Noah love?" Selicia's weirdly quasi-british voice was behind me and I froze up again, only to become even more rigid as I felt her hands around the back of my neck. "Here... Before we head back out. Let me work out your kinks. Gosh, you're rather stiff..."

"Easy, Noah," Gabriel laughed a little as I was still shocked into a position of immobility, unable to even dart away at this point while her hands came over my neck and shoulders. "She's not gonna eat you again."

"Y-you sure?" I grunted while barely being able to hide a voice crack, as she, floating behind me presumably with her legs swimming her in the water kicked a little; I could feel her breath atop my head as she knurled my trapezius muscles and cervical joints with her knuckles, glaring at Gabriel.

"Of course," Gabriel said, standing up to leave as he licked his fingers clean of taco crumbs. "If she does I'll kill her." He didn't even laugh, smiling coldly at the amazonian spider-woman behind me, who "humph"ed, glaring back at him as he went away, presumably to get something else to eat or to get his stuff or something. Maybe just to edge me up, make sure I didn't start liking this place too much than to finish our mission here.

"...Noah," Selicia said in my ear, after half a minute or so. She was actually really, really good at this. I might even say that this was actually really relaxing if I ignored the fact that a monstrous woman-spider amalgamation that eats people for fun was the one administering this massage. I figured not to act bothered by it if I wanted to avoid her creepily sultry side. "You should tell me about your girlfriend."

"...You... *really* want to hear about that?" I muttered back, floating there with my arms crossed on the deck, my head leaning on my forearms. "It's- ah," I let out, as she dug a knuckle into a pressure point. "Oh- ooh," I uttered breathlessly. "You're- you're good at that. You do this often?"

"...not really, no- guess it's something they put in my brain," She said back, as if surprised at her own prowess. I let out a 'huh' of my own, arching my brow. "C'mon, love. Tell me about your boo."

"She's- Her name's Maria," I said. "...You want like, specifics or something? You want a physical description?"

"Well, what's *Maria* mean to you?" She asked. Going with the metaphysical, it seemed. I sighed.

"...We've... grown up together," I said. "She's really always been my- ooh- my other half," I said, feeling her working my muscles.

"I'd have guessed Gabriel is your other half, He's very possessive," Selicia let back playfully. "...Not like in a, uh, sexual way. I'm not saying you're gay... Unless you are, and- and that's not, not anything... bad," I turned a tad and looked back at her as she paused her massage, seeing her face twisted a little as if she'd said a bit too many foolish things and knew it. "...a- are y-"

"No, Selicia. Gabriel and I've just been friends forever."

"...Just like your beau, huh?" I glared at her, and her four eyes looked away a little, and I turned back to let the massage continue, as she worked her way down my spine and latissimus muscles. "So, uh... What's your favorite thing about her?" Selicia asked.

"She's..." I paused, racking my brain. I started to feel a little put-on-the-spot, and uncomfortable for it. "...You know, I really wasn't expecting this conversation."

"I- I mean, you don't *have* to answer," Selicia responded, in the way that made me think that me not responding was taking some sort of loss. I don't think Selicia framed it that way on purpose, it just sort of came out in her pre-programmed bitchiness, as she herself paused after saying it, as if condemning herself. "So if she loves you more than Gabriel does, how come she's not down here backing you up too?"

"...Her whole family just died. She needs a fuckin' minute," I muttered back, starting to get fed up. I ignored the fact that I still left her with the responsibility of being in charge of everyone. Maybe Lauren would have been a better choice. I sighed, softening my tone. "...I'm all she has left."

"I... hope you don't let her down, then," Selicia said again, that automatic bitchiness shining through again. Despite that, it felt like Selicia was being genuine saying this.

"...Yeah. I'm trying not to." Selicia finished up with my lumbar joints and the sides of my hips, advancing further for a moment, playing with my beltline before being brought away, knowing by now that she couldn't be lewd with Gabriel's demonic gaze following her from the barside. "...Thanks for the massage. I feel better." I got up and out of the pool. I didn't really feel better- I mean, I guess I did physically, my shoulders feeling a lot lighter, but the conversation just negated all the good the massage did. I guess I couldn't fault Selicia, she was *trying* to be less bitchy. I saw her go off to float around in the other end of the pool, causing one of the draconic engineer hybrids also in the pool to give her a wide berth of space, evidently somebody with history with her.

"Man, what did he do to Selicia? By this time she'd be groping somebody at the least, I haven't had to call security on her yet," Anon noted impressively from where he lay on the lounge chair, breaking up his romantic exchange with his current partner to remark on Selicia's stellar behavior.

"...Gabriel? He's a cartel assas... hitm... *enforcer*," I racked my brain as I stood there beside them, feeling like if I got it wrong he'd instantly know and look over at me too and freeze me solid with his gaze, standing all the way over there at the bar with Archie, also having cleaned himself up. "He's killed a lot of people. I think he's got augmentations. I'd be afraid of him too."

"...Augs, huh? Didn't think they could install the thot-exterminating gaze in a mortal man, or some shit like that. He takes a glance in her direction and she looks like she feels the shame she's never felt before in her life. Goddamn." Anon took his drink in his arm around his serpentine lover, taking a sip over her neck. "Cartel though, huh? He doesn't look too Mexican."

"...Kinda feels like that's why they hired him. Or chose him or whatever. Recruited. I dunno."

"How about you, Noah? What's your backstory?"

"I'm... unaffiliated." He chuckled.

"I coulda swore you were at least Army, if not some SOF. Your gear is snazzy."

"Dad was a prepper, an apocalypse survivor type. Bought my gear. Taught me how to shoot, how to fight."

"...How to kill?" Anon added, and I nodded back slowly, him taking another sip. "Well, it *is* a marketable skill. Kinda the first one ever. And probably the last, if this really is the end, y'know?" Anon smirked. It wasn't funny but I smirked back. I ended the conversation stiltedly by walking over to the bar at that point, still a little out of my own headspace at the moment, getting myself a cola and chugging the whole thing in one go.

"Not gonna have anything to eat?" Gabriel put forth as I slammed the empty can down. "Need fuel to survive, y'know."

"...I just wanna get the fuck out of this place." I looked to Archie, seeing him similarly cleaned up in a simple open shirt and fresh pair of band-aids for each side of his holed ear, enjoying the place even as unnerved as he seemed, downing a mimosa.

"...We heading out?" Selicia floated toward the bar-side of the pool. I stopped, seeing her crouched against the side of the wall. The mood went dead, all of us looking at her.

"...You mean back to your place?"

"I'd like to... come along." She looked away for a second, her gaze coming back to Gabriel as she brushed a strand of hair away from her face, clearing her throat ever so subtly. "...Anon said it'd be good for me. I need some exposure."

"Probably so you stop harassing his personnel," Gabriel mused cooly. Though Archie and I were visibly discomforted at the prospect, Gabriel seemed to actually be entertaining it.

"...It doesn't matter what he wants, I'm the one making this decision. I'd like to come with you and your group, Gabriel." Gabriel was spinning his drink a little, the way some liquor snob would stir their drink without touching it, more like he was just amused at the prospect.

"You don't even know where we're going," Gabriel put in before Archie or I could interject.

"Wait, you're not seriously-" Archie began.

"Dunno. Maybe Anon's right. She's got her skills, anyways. I'm sure she'd be useful, even with that museum piece of hers," Gabriel motioned with his drink to her holstered magnum on her pile of clothes off to the side, as she was currently in a swimsuit top as of now.

"Oh what, so we can have a masseuse on hand?"

"She can also create nanofiber with her body, which you'd know if you read the docs. But yeah, I nearly forgot about that whole massage thing. Gotta stay limber, you know. And if she starts any problems, we can just do her like Of Mice and Men." Selicia was less than apt to get the reference, though I glared back at Gabe while he took a sip, opening my mouth to speak.

"...I don't know if people will tolerate her."

"I'll make sure she stays tolerable. You think you can keep it together, Legs?" Gabe asked. She nodded, eyes bobbing in her head like Gabriel held her on a leash, her eyes holding a sort of reverence towards Gabriel.

"Jesus, what's Maria going to say?"

"You kidding me?" Gabe scoffed back at me. "Maria's probably going to be the most effective at keeping her in line." Gabriel nodded to me, while Selicia waited nearby, doing her best to seem aloof, less than invested in the conversation. Like she would come anyways, though she knew that if Gabriel didn't want her along, she certainly wasn't coming. "To be honest, I kinda agree with Anon here. She could use the fresh air. I'd like to see what becomes of her, without her destined, perfect prince charming she's programmed to fall for instantaneously. Kinda want to be there when it hits that she's just as alone as the rest of us poor, poor lonely souls. Y'know?" I sighed back, practically jumping off the barstool.

"Whatever. Let's fucking move."


Back in the flying police van after gearing back up, we waited as we flew through the air. I was still lost, staring out the window, seeing the great buildings pass, the aerial traffic zipping by. It was all like something out of a movie. Something beyond this world. Again, I knew that was the point, but now I guess I really started to appreciate it. I felt something new here, on my way to leave. A longing. It was kind of like Vegas, in its own way. It was not without its own specific beauty. I kind of wanted to stay longer, only here when I was leaving, cemented to our plan to leave. I wanted to see the nightlife, the different neighborhoods, the clubs and restaurants. I guess it couldn't be helped.

"...You know," I said slowly. "After all this- *if* all this blows over. We should come back to visit this place." Everyone was silent, contemplative.

"Yeah. I'd like that," Gabe mused back.

"It's... not that bad on the surface, right?" Selicia's voice pondered. I looked over to her slowly, where she crouched in the middle of the van.

"...It's pretty bad," I put back. She simply stared back out the window, four eyes blinking two at a time.

The central console was calling, Anon's city seal coming on. "Alright, folks. Downloaded the activation codes onto your gear. Arm up one of the humvees and have at it. Do a drive-by on their base on your way out and that's the last I'll ask for you."

"You really think a little shoot 'em up is gonna make a difference?" Gabriel mused back.

"Hey, couldn't hurt. I've got to have some time bought to raise my own army here. Don't exactly have the best choices among the populace. Supposed to represent the yuppy normie sales markets. I'm sure they've got a few hardasses though. Hopefully we can clean this whole place up. Y'all should come back and visit."

"Huh, we were just discussing that," Gabriel muttered back with a slight grin. "I'll take you up on that."

"Just don't get killed before you can witness Greater Prosperia. I'm boutta make what I always wanted to, make a real run of the place without the higher-ups shitting on my parade."

"Yeah. Sounds like a great time. Cyberpunk tomorrowland with furries." Gabe chuckled.

Back down at the central tower once more. Waltzing through the front door, taking a glance at the cat-centaur-y attendee from earlier, Rebecca, there at the front desk. "Welcome back, did you enjoy your visit to our city?" She asked.

"Yo, where's Lucille?" Gabe asked, M2 over his shoulder.

"She... Went home early. Wasn't feeling well," Rebecca said, while we went for one of the elevators, the one leading to the military depot. "W-wait! Could I ask you to fill out one of our questionnaires about what you thought about the city? We-"

"Busy day, 'Becca. Have a nice one. See you later, definitely do it then," Archie blurted in rapid succession as we piled into the elevator, and up we went. Another solemn silence, all of us crammed in there, one of Selicia's many spindly legs tapping against the ground restlessly. *Tap, tap tap.*

Archie was still incensed. "...Stop it." Selicia ceased for a little bit, until she tapped again, us still hurtling into the sky.

Disappearing into the black divide, the elevator skewed about as we were whisked along the route on the multi-directional lift. It was just as jarring as entering that place, if not worse. A couple long moments of being whisked this way and that, and we were there.

The garage.

To be honest, the depot would have been far closer to being a parking complex than a garage, if not an aircraft hangar. Coming up on the lift, we saw that the place was far from vacant, many of Anon's personnel littering the place, a forward operating base of his, full of various, colorful people toiling away on stuff, sparks flying in the distance, everyone looking uneasy and armed up, human security personnel, engineer hybrids, and "recruits" from

Prosperia all about, noticing us with a nod. it was all strangely uncanny. But, then again, this place was one of the more normal things I'd seen today.

"...This is one of the few ingress points to Prosperia that I've yet to fully seal off, aside from the security depot you came in through just in the nick of time after they killed my watchdogs," Anon's voice rang through comms as Gabriel and I led our way out of there. "Fuckers have been coming through other ones. This one's got high-end security that they've yet to crack, and pretty much the last of my guys on guard here to secure it. Big doors leading towards the darkdome probably got a few of 'em camping out behind, still trying to find a way to open up. I hope you don't mind me using your little escape as a means of first-striking them. Idea is you'll zip out, they'll send their warriors to chase you, I'll wait about ten minutes to send my guys will mop their base up while their fighting force is distracted by you. Divide and conquer."

"...So long as we don't get shot down in their darkdome," I put forth morosely.

"Yeah. Plan B is to rescue you guys if shit goes sideways. It'll be messy and I'll probably lose a lot more personnel that way, but I won't abandon y'all. At least not while you need me. Anyways, we've got plenty of Oshkosh JLTV's for ya," He explained, going up to one of the big beige vehicles, while I was looking at the few Rabbit and Gorilla-class combat walkers off in their own respective hangars in the corner, some of them being diagnostics-tested at this very moment, engies and human scientists relaying orders to test mechanisms, spooling up their 20mm gatling cannons and running diagnostics on targeting systems, also testing some of the noisy zipperbikes they had, big fans blasting air as they hovered around the place, buzzing as they ran diagnostics. I kinda wanted one if I didn't think that it was bound to get shot down going through the Darkdome, plus I hear they were energy hogs. Sure would have liked one of the new magnetic bikes I saw back down in Prosperia, though.

"Can we bring one of these?" I put forth about the mechas, more as a joke, looking at the weighty twenty-foot tall rotund bipedal behemoths and their autocannons and missile launchers.

"Too slow, finicky. We don't want to get bogged down. I bet Anon needs them for his little war anyways," Gabe said, going to stand before one of the JLTVs anon's guys were working on for us, engies filling up the internal water tank of the thing for us, as well as extra biodiesel for the humvee as well as my jeep, and some ethanol for the truck we'd commandeered. Gabriel whistled, seeing the armaments of the turret up top, still feeling his own M2 over his shoulder.

"God damn, double deuce on one side, flip the turret around and we got an auto grenade launcher," he walked around to the other side, seeing the shotgun seat. He hefted his own M2, slamming it down into the mount at the window, locking it into place. "There we go. Now we've got ourselves a killmobile."

"...Gonna want to drive around the left side of the darkdome so you can use the shotgun-seat gun more effectively," Anon put forth. "Their little 'city' is in the middle of the darkdome so you can't cut right across it. Don't expect you to, anyways. Oh, and while you're at it, Gabriel, go check with the armorer. I left you a gift."

"Oh?" He chuckled, going off in that direction. Archie was checking the JLTV himself and chatting with the other engies about specs and other assorted diagnostics for our presents. I went off to general supplies, finding myself a plethora of tactical hologlasses and hologoggles. I counted out in my head how many we needed, counting out me, Maria, Archie and Gabriel already having Smart HUD gear. We had Lauren, Anthony, Kyle... should I get some for even the people I don't expect to fight? I figure my dad would. One for Samantha, Daniel, and Katt, as well as the Shepherd siblings Abel and Reina. eight more I looked over to Selicia, seeing her quadruple holos on her face already, seeing her with a rather antsy Engie downloading what I presumed to be a Combat HUD onto her holos. I saw the JLTV, They'd removed the rear seating, so she could sit in the chuck of the vehicle behind the turret, she was awfully large so she was probably also planning out how she could fit.

"...Hey, Selicia, catch," I said, passing her an older M16A3 from the barracks that she reciprocated with a smile and a quip.

"Much obliged, darling, glad to know you're thinking of me," She winked. Apparently with Gabriel away for only a second it was apparent that her sultry side could bloom again. I felt that she'd be more of a problem than Gabe promised she'd be, though Archie, at the wheel already, checking diagnostics, rolled his eyes. I put the box of holos in the car, before looking up, for Gabe.

There he was, and I almost did a double take. A monster of metal ambling towards us, footsteps that shook the earth. There he was, seven feet tall with that mask atop his head, his face the only human thing left, everything else titanium and dynaceramid.

"Fuck, this Sentinel program ain't that gimmicky after all," he uttered. I saw him hefting supplies in his arms, another Prosperian draftee behind him, a felinetaur with his arms carrying another box. "I actually feel pretty limber. Hey Sel, c'mere." Selicia got up, and I saw that he was hefting his plate carrier in one of his hands. "Here, you need some body armor. Put my vest on, let out the cinch a little, you're probably a size above me. You can use my pistol holstered on it, but don't drop it and expect to live." She scrambled under its weight as he playfully tossed it upon her and she didn't expect it to be so heavy, having seen how nimble Gabriel could be wearing it.

"Where's the fun in this? I'll look all frumpy!" She mused of the armor.

"...Everybody looks stylish on their funeral, if you'd prefer," He grunted, and she furled her lip. She took off her own pistol rig to put the armor over her blouse.

"...Agh, it crushes my breasts," She whined.

"Let the shoulder straps out and cinch it more around the cummerbund." Gabriel slammed the box down, I saw more armalite rifles in it, mostly M16s, his follower in tow dropping a box full of helmets and body armor. Evidently Gabriel thought as well as I did, to gear everyone up appropriately. "...We should get you breast lipo while we're here. Jesus, how do you have a spine with those?" Gabriel laughed as she let out the top of the armor so much that it practically displayed her cleavage. "Always wear body armor high. It should come up to the top of your sternum."

"...I don't think I was designed for body armor," she put back.

"Yeah, well, we're not gonna be able to *cocksuck* our way through that darkdome. You best get ready to kill, or stay home." Gabriel looked to me now while Selicia complied. "Hey, check it out. Anon left me one. No helmet though, but I got Sentinel to interface with the HUD of my mask." He looked down at himself more. "Fuck, I feel like a fuckin' space marine. Time to crusade. Let's purge some heretics." he barely squeezed himself into the side door of the armored car while he laughed, popping up in the turret. "...A motherfuckin' double deuce and a forty mike-mike on the back, and if that don't work I can just punch 'em. This is gonna be fun. Archie, you driving?"

"Yeah, let's fockin' go," He said, having taken a helmet from the ones brought forth, Selicia throwing one on herself. Archie wore one of the high-cuts so his ears wouldn't be crushed, while Selicia was content with one with a face guard, also throwing on some pauldrons for her shoulders and forearm guards at Gabriel's behest, as she was the most exposed on the back there. I saw how her ears poked downward out from the ear cups, those long elf-like ears somewhat smushed up. She fiddled with the ballistic jaw-guard a little, so all four of her eyes could look out the plexiglas blast shield (that she was wearing her holos underneath anyways) while she picked up her new rifle and opened the underbarrel launcher, another engie bringing us some rocket tubes too, old surplus AT4s.

"Remember this about the launcher Selicia, don't have the back pointing inside the vehicle unless you want to roast us all. Pop out a little so the backblast doesn't kill us," Gabriel lowered his mask while I got in the shotgun seat of the vehicle, my heart beginning to race, bit by bit in aprehension. I saw the display HUD of the jeep light up, interfacing with Archie's own holographics as driver, while I fully activated the combat mode of mine, checking the window-gun before me, Gabriel's claimed fifty caliber.

"...Gotcha," Selicia went back on comms.

"We ready?" Archie asked. "Sound off."

"Good to go," Gabriel responded.

"I... I think I'm ready," Selicia said with apprehension, fiddling with her grenade launcher, loading the M16 with a forty round magazine and putting a grenade into the launcher with a thunk.

"...Let's do this," I said plainly, checking off the M2 before me, after checking out the rotary 40mm grenade launcher tucked in the shotgun seat for me to use. I loaded it with armor-liquidating rounds rather than high-frag, since I planned on using the machine gun for soft targets. Archie thumbs-upped to the guys at the garage station, who thumbs-upped back, while all personnel armed up around us.

The garage door blared, alarms going off. "All clear, doors opening. Please stand free, and mind the gap," The robotic female voice of the system blared on relay.

"Get ready! Tangoes on the other side are probably readying up! We clear the path for Alpha Group and head out in ten minutes!" The head security officer, a grizzled older human proclaimed.

"Guessin we're Alpha Group," Gabriel mused with a dark chuckle on comms. That door rose, and immediately we saw figures, hybrids prone and crawling under or shooting their guns under the doors, those blood-dyed hybrids chomping at the bit for a taste of combat. They were quickly mopped up by security around us, us sitting there plainly, saving our ammo while bullets pinged off the canopy of our vehicle, grenades going off here and there, each of us save for Gabriel wincing at it all. The doors opened enough for us to see them all, running in blasting their weapons off and getting chewed to bits by our side's guns quickly. Bodies fell, their forward camp set up in the tunnel revealed before us. One of the missiles from one of the activated mechs behind us streamed out, the blast easily clearing a path right through.

"That's our path. Let's go," Gabe said as Archie accelerated, the combat quickly slowing to a lull. It was like running over a hundred potholes, bumping over the bodies. I thought some of them were still alive, seeing them moving, groaning and screaming as the wheels crunched over them, the security forces behind us advancing out and executing survivors while we zipped into the blackness. It was unsettling and rose goosebumps on my neck, disappearing with that sad violence behind us, nothing but black cold tunnel before us, knowing what awaited us down that tunnel like breath caught in my throat, heart pounding. I looked to the HUD of the windshield, seeing the map of the place before us.

"We're basically going in blind," Archie grunted uneasily at the darkness. "Some of their guys were probably able to radio back to base before they died. I bet they heard the gunfire down the tunnel, too."

"Doesn't matter. We'll get through."

"...How are you sure?" Selicia's voice cut back, asking Gabe, while she crawled along the outside of the vehicle for now, a hand reaching out to hold onto Gabe's turret so she could watch where we were going rather than stare backwards into the eerie blackness, Gabe right beside her, double deuce at the ready.

"...If we don't, it won't be our problem anymore. But I ain't getting killed by no fuckin' furfags." Archie let out a breathless laugh at Gabe's cavalier behavior. I couldn't relate.

It was time for the real shitshow to begin.

**Chapter 25**

Light.

The darkness cut to bits in an instant. Massive spotlights shining down on us from above, Archie veering the steering wheel, cutting left. Was this an ambush? I saw great metal struts that Archie swerved within, Selicia climbing back into the relatively covered area of the rear of the vehicle. As we zipped underneath it, I could look back, seeing it sauntering as it turned around in the cold darkness. A large combat mech, easily a Gorilla class. Tracers lit up as bullets careened toward us, Archie veering again as Gabriel spun the turret back to begin firing the double-deuce, fifty caliber tracers zipping right back at our enemy.

"I think they were expecting more than just us!" Gabriel shouted. "At least we're taking them by surprise, more or less!"

"If they're gauging a counter-offensive already, does that mean-" I began. But as bullets now started coming from in front of us, my question was already answered. Archie threw on the high-beams, blinding those directly in front as the infantry line before us was advancing. "Watch out for ones with launchers!" I shouted before I began firing with my fifty, Archie veering again as a bright-tailed projectile lit up before us, Archie dodging this deftly, but hardly effortlessly, grunting as it veered past to explode somewhere else.

Gabriel was turning the turret around to fire on the left side while I chewed through targets on the right. I saw them dive for cover, those who didn't have their limbs and bodies macerated into red mush by my cannon fire. Screaming hybrids were tossed over the hood and across the windshield, one of them splitting their head on the glass, blood spraying up. Archie groaned violently, hitting the windshield wipers, while Gabriel was laughing a little. "Run, fuckers!" He was shouting, more of their lines up ahead that he fired into.

"Lock, lock-on! Everyone hold on!" Archie spouted as the HUD blinked. Another rocket flare in our rearview zipping up to meet us from the line we'd passed, the in-built countermeasures flaring up as Archie came up on the corner towards the entrance to the Darkdome, the bend in the tunnel to the place. Archie floored it while pulling the handbrake, wheels screaming and taking the corner at full speed, turning the wheel the wrong way after fishtailing it, drifting away from the blast that went off target to our right, Selicia screaming and holding on for dear life. Their vehicles were screaming around us, their guns clashing rounds all around us while Archie maneuvered, eyes wild, teeth bared. I saw a jeep heading straight towards us, intending to crash into our front-right side, towards me. I lit up the driver- and by extension, the entire occupancy of the car with a barrage of fire, my autocannon punching fist-sized holes in their laminated glass windshield and spraying red mist up from the seating area, letting it veer away, personnel replaced with gore. I never had any time to ruminate on the lives I'd so horribly ended before the next enemy came.

A screech, one of the hybrids clawing at my Browning. I was shocked, seeing a beak full of rage in my face, a knife slashing at me. I screamed, this winged, bird-like hybrid screaming wordlessly as I pulled back and away, taken by surprise. I drew my pistol and let round after round sink into him to no avail, feathers and blood flying before placing rounds into his head, brains depositing themselves all over myself and the inside of the car as he finally tumbled off, the rear right wheel of our vehicle crunching over his body like a speed bump. Selicia was lighting off grenades from her M16, sending their technicals sideways, she was aiming for their front wheels and undercages, trying to flip them with explosions. As she was reloading, one of the jeeps flanking that she was unable to get came up a little, the hybrid in the shotgun seat stringing off burst after uncontrolled burst with his machine gun, Selicia ducking for a moment before she got up a little bit more, revealing more of her body. I watched in a sort of peculiar awe as she, rather than finish reloading her launcher, curl the back end of her body to point forward beneath her and fire off a strand of her web from the orifice at the rearmost tip of her chitinous body, nailing their towing bar before looking over to a car still going the opposite way down towards the depot, shooting the other end of her stringy web onto said car heading the opposite direction to chain them together by her web, the first car suddenly being yanked upside-down in a front-flip, the opposite-heading passing car yanked in a barrel roll with the door attached to the web snapping off, red-dyed hybrids flying through the air screaming as both cars tumbled and crashed dramatically. Gabriel was laughing in glee, barely able to notice this as he was busy covering our rear-left side. I just wish I could have taken more than a single moment to marvel at her creative combat use of her peculiar ability.

"Gabriel, cover our front!" Archie cried, as another winged hybrid, a centaurical draconic now, brimming with muscles and bloody tomes of conquest, human fingers and ears worn on chains about him latched onto the hood, Archie drawing his pistol. "Off my fockin' bonnet!" Archie roared, letting rounds off as he stuck his gun out the window as I ran dry on my M2, drawing the entire bearing assembly the gun was on back into the window so I could put new ammo in from the safety of the cabin. The dragontaur dodged to the right towards me, though as Gabriel turned his turret around I saw the look in that big red bastard's eyes before he was shredded by Gabriel's weapons, upper body practically demolished before the lower half of him could fall over, once again painting Archie's windshield in ichor. "Fuck, FUCK!" Archie hit the wipers again. "CAN WE TRY NOT TO-"

"Keep your eyes on the road!" Gabriel roared over him. I saw him flipping the turret around, while the windshield cleared to show a massive barrier erected there, burning tires and all. Gabriel lit up the part right before us with the grenade launcher, blowing a good crater there where their wall had been and we were through in another moment, suspension screaming us over the divide as the tunnel ceiling disappeared into massive spotlights shining down from the heavens. The darkdome, a massive urban sprawl before us. It wasn't really an urban sprawl, per se, rather a facsimile of it. Walls of brick and concrete jutting out in peculiar angles, a massive training and testing ground meant to feel like a city, those massive lights blaring down from above in dramatic fashion. Tents and those sorts of fast-construction temporary buildings clustered closer to the core of the place as we quickly lost ourselves down one of the "streets" towards the left.

"Looks like we've lost our pursuers," Archie said.

"Check your weapons, top off," Gabriel ordered. I put a fresh magazine in my glock, looking around. I saw Selicia topping off her M16 similarly, checking the launcher. Gabriel was fiddling with his weapons, the ammo of the Double Deuce and the 40MM. Archie drove us a little slower down the winding streets, their "city" off to the far right, glowing up under the spotlights poorly simulating daytime.

"...Shit, this is fucking weird," I muttered. I saw their hybrids scattering in the nonexistent wind, dodging from our sight. Here they weren't murderers or monsters. Here they were scared, watching us. Some of their children came out to throw bits of concrete or metal as we passed, nobody bothering to shoot back. It really felt like we were riding through their living rooms like brash conquerors, unopposed now. "...Anon, you still listening?" I asked. "What will you do to these guys?"

"Yeah, you're still in range, I've got you on comms. I'll dispose of the broken ones and try to see who I can't convince to integrate into my side. I'd put the young ones in acceleration chambers to try and reprogram them. See if I can spit them out as useful adults if the fucking hack hadn't destroyed all the chambers' source codes. Figure it's something the Creators didn't want us to salvage or something. Gotta do everything the hard way now, try and get them working again." I was looking back from where we'd come from, seeing vehicles, having broken off from their counter-assault group, their lights shining as they were in pursuit of us interlopers again.

"Damn, these guys going after an obvious diversion," Gabriel laughed, bringing the turret around again. "Without central leadership they can't really keep all their troops in check and stick to a plan. Good for us."

"Good for us? That sounds even worse!" I uttered back, craning the machine gun's mount to angle it more backwards, readying myself up. But before our reinvigorated pursuers could return to us, a... I didn't quite know how to describe it, other than it was this massive scraping sound filling the air. Grinding metal on metal, an intense, sandpapery hum resounding from the center of that "city". It immediately reminded me of the pleasant electronic murmur of the quantum engines of the hovering vehicles in Prosperia, however distinctly more... broken. Like comparing a pleasantly-run, well-tuned engine's idle to one that obviously had more than a few nuts loose and was long overdue an oil change, that sound that grinds on your ears and you simply just *know* that something was wrong with it. A distinct, beige-khaki colored behemoth rising itself into the air.

"Looks like it got worse!" Archie uttered, that thing ambling about. Before our very eyes, this floating behemoth turning for a second in the distance, coming towards us. I saw it's flat angular body with a turret atop, a cannon protruding from it.

"A fucking flying tank?!" Gabriel cursed. "Anon you fucking liar! How'd that get out here, huh?!" Gabriel was busy flipping to the 40mm. "Sel, get the AT4s ready!"

"...I can hear that fucking thing screeching in your mouthpieces. You think that's one of *mine*?" Anon defended as this M1 Abrams lined with sparking wires, frost shuddering off of its own electromagnetic drives crackling with electricity faced us, rising above that city to amble towards us. It definitely looked jury-rigged. "They probably stole parts and got a stupid fucking idea of their own and made their engies slap something together. My advice is blow their bootlegged quantum drives off of it, ground it."

"Yeah, no shit!" Gabriel said, taking a hold-over on the tank, holding high as he strung out a burst of bright phosphor shells to test range. The tank's cannon went off and every sphincter in our vehicle collectively clenched as a white-hot shell careened in our direction, hurtling past us as it missed with a deafening scream and resounding, equally deafening boom, careening into one of those brick walls to our left and turning it into shrapnel-filled dust, the shell bouncing on past, explosions following it. Selicia yelped, lighting off her rocket launcher and missing wildly, letting it fly off into the oblivion of the darkdome and careening against the side of the dome's wall.

"Are you fucking serious, bitch?!" Gabriel screamed, Selicia already cringing as she tossed the empty tube out the side to go to another. "Keep your finger off the trigger until you have a shot lined up! You think this is a fucking video game and we've got infinite rockets?!"

"Save the fockin' monologue until we've got that thing!" Archie swore back as I was readying the rotary grenade launcher with armor-piercing rounds.

"Archie, go towards it! Take this street here!" Gabriel ordered. "Get me to an angle where we can blow out their hoverdrives!" Archie complied heavily, sighing like a scream of exasperation.

"It's funny how I agree with you for once!" Archie spouted, as the tank's co-axial machine gun began firing, though not quite accurately, while their main gun was still reloading. It looked like they wanted to cut us off like this road was the one we wanted to take, which evidently was our plan anyways. We had a good two hundred meters or so, Archie weaving through the jutting constructs, Gabriel and I firing away with our prospective grenade guns, trying to scrape rounds into the bottom of the armor or get the explosives to splash up into the electronics, though whoever was driving it must have been smarter than we thought, angling and making it difficult to target said electronics, however throwing off the gunner's next shot, another shell hurtling close by.

"Fuckers must know they've got a weak point!" Gabriel said, while the tank was lowering itself, maybe hoping to scrape the ground to bash into us and send us flying since their gunner wasn't worth much in a fight, apparently. "Selicia! You think you can jump onto them using your web when we pass!?"

"I... I think so!"

"Well, do that then! catch!" Gabriel tossed her one of his bombs, what looked like C4 or something with a sticky end. "If you can, throw it into their hatch!" She nodded back, hefting her M16 in one hand and the bomb in the other. We closed in on each other, the armor skirt of the hovertank scraping the ground hoping to catch us and toss us, however Archie was much better at maneuvering with our two ton vehicle than their sixty-something tank. Their hover-drives were not quite that graceful as it was straining to keep that behemoth airborne, Archie faking once to the left before veering right and getting right around them. Selicia, at Gabriel's behest, had crawled up to shoot her web onto the turret as we passed rapidly and let the momentum slingshot her forward, climbing onto it. Archie, now that we were behind our adversaries, hit the brakes, their vehicle still going. We screeched to a halt some fifty meters away while the tank still barreled on down the road. I saw her land and begin to make her way to the hatch, seeing it crack open as one of their personnel popped up with a pistol, though Selicia was much faster stringing a burst of fire from her M16 before throwing the satchel charge into the hatch with the dead hybrid, as she slammed the hatch shut with another web shot, yanking it as she jumped back a little, before turning around quickly.

"S-shouldn't I have a thing to press or-"

"Jump clear now, I'm setting it off!" Gabriel ordered, raising his armored hand up so it was in his holographic display, throwing the thumb of his power armor down, the haptic trigger detonating the plastic explosive. Selicia yelped as she threw herself off with the tank's turret bursting from the rest of the body of the tank, popping into the air as the ammunition and fuel flared up and the entire thing crashed, quantum drives failing with a spectacular shower of sparks and ice. The wreck grinded to a halt, closing off the way behind us, serving to cut us off from our other pursuers. Some of those behind us crashed into the destroyed tank's remains, vocal swearing loud enough to be heard over it.

"You had the trigger this whole time?!" Selicia ripped her helmet off to swear at Gabriel, all four eyes furious as she scampered on back.

"What? If you had the trigger and died, how would we have set the bomb off?!" Gabriel motioned to her with both arms in insolence. She pouted, furling her puffed lower lip up, until a gunshot from some concealed angle caused her to wince and duck, throwing her helmet back on as Archie hit the reverse, zipping back to let her jump into her old position and emptying the rest of her magazine at the hybrids crawling through the burning remains before switching out magazines.

"Shit, thanks for that. That seems like it would have been a problem, y'know. I owe ya," Anon crowed.

"That was my own personal C4, asshole," Gabriel snarled, stringing a burst of 50 cal over the heads of the growing crowd behind us, causing anyone trying to get a bead on us with a launcher to duck down.

"I'll write you an IOU. Y'all said you'll be back to see Greater Prosperia, after all," Anon paused. "Tell you what. I'll give you a hovertank built from the ground up. Set my engies on it." Gabriel grumbled, but conceded the gesture.

"...Let's get the fuck out of here in case their mech decides to come back for us."

"...We could try to use Selicia to web up the legs, drive around them like in Empire Strikes Back," I said.

"Psssht. Like you've seen the original," Gabriel grumbled back.

"...There was an original?" Selicia uttered. "I love that movie." Gabriel and I looked back to her again. "What? Hasn't everybody seen it?"

"...I could've used a fockin' movie," Archie grumbled, letting his ire burn through, though not before we were interrupted by their aerial fighters, winged hybrids zipping about and those dual-rotor zipperbikes buzzing this way and that, both harassing us with petty fire, some trying to get close with melee implements or explosives to throw. Selicia was the one to shoot most of the little ones down with her M16, Gabriel switching back to the fifty to blast down their bigger, less agile hovercycles, though Gabriel wasn't beyond shooting down centaurical ones, big as they were. One of the faster draconics swept low across the ground, coming in as Selicia ran dry on her current magazine, having to switch them out, instantly tacking her. He was yelping crazily and murderously, practically groping her as she screamed. Gabriel took notice of this, unable to really crane the turret down to get a good angle anyways, but before he could react any other way, Selicia reached for the front of her vest, Gabriel's vest, finding the chest holster with his own pistol in it. She pulled it back and loosed round after round into him before he toppled backwards, knife flying out of his hands as he tumbled back. Selicia continued to fire the pistol, but as Archie hit a bump of trash in the road, Selicia yelped and her hand slipped.

"STOP THE CAR!" Gabriel roared. If anybody else had screamed this, I doubt Archie would have listened, but hearing Gabriel's tone, unfazed at the prospect of shooting down a fucking flying tank now dead serious, even I hit an imaginary brake pedal while I was loading my rotary grenade launcher.

"What- what the fuck are you-" Archie began to protest as the engine idled after screeching to a halt, Gabriel was already dropping down from the turret, even as bullets rolled off of the vehicle all around us.

"Noah. You're on the turret." He came up next to me, unlocking my M2 from its mount since it was about the only weapon big enough for him to use well in his power armor. I, from that same sense of "Gabriel is being serious" fear, complied, crawling over while bullets still rang out over our canopy. I caught a glimpse of Selicia's eyes and face around them while crawling back in the car; despite her nubian complexion she was pale as death over dropping Gabriel's prized gun. I could only see her eyes, everything else concealed by her full helm, but they said enough. Gabriel didn't even need to chastise her, his spell over her already letting her know she fucked up.

"Is this really-" Archie began, before Gabriel interrupted him when he unleashed a string of fifty cal at a noisy zipperbike hovering midair, the hybrid sitting behind it's driver aiming what was probably an AT4 right at us. Gabriel practically blew the front rotor off of the thing with a few shots and they were downed, Gabriel repeating this with more of the flying hybrids approaching, bullets careening off of his armor in bright flashes of copper and lead bursting across his hardened steel and tytanaceramid body while he walked, belching death from the M2. I was on the turret, shooting at other aerial hybrids with Selicia who was working over her shame by shooting with me, for Gabriel's sake.

Out in the distance, towards which Gabriel walked, grumbling as he probably was at what must have been a minor inconvenience for him, there was a crowd amassing towards the core of the darkdome, out in the distance. Bursts of the double deuce I was operating always made them briefly reconsider advancing towards us, tracers flying over their heads. Briefly. They always seemed to form back up. There were silhouettes, shadows off to the sides in that fake city. They must have been trying to surround us.

"Is this really worth your focking gun?!" Archie yelped as he popped out the door to crouch there and provide some petty cover with his own rifle, though ducking back and grabbing his helmet, ears twitching whenever the crack of a rifle ripped towards us.

"You know what- That gun is?!" Gabriel roared, interrupting himself with the tympanic bursts of the fifty cal and grunts as bullets struck him. "That's a Bren Ten. You know how fucking rare those are?! Selicia should have dropped her own fucking obsolete piece of shit!" Gabriel roared. An especially suicidal hybrid charged Gabriel from the side, grenades in each hands, before any of us could shoot him. I winced as Gabriel turned around so violently, so quickly that, despite this hostile being too close for Gabe to shoot, Gabriel viciously brought the gun into the lower side of his head and it looked like this strike had disconnected the hybrid's brain stem from his spine. The hybrid toppled over, the grenades in his hands falling to the ground. Gabriel kicked them like tiny soccer balls towards the crowds flanking in the shadowy constructs, sending them reeling from the explosions. More approached him while he was doing this, and he brought the gun back around and ripped through them with no more than a couple well-placed rounds each. He filled the vehicles approaching with holes and corpses, until it looked like he was out of ammo. Rather than abandon what was obviously a fool's errand, he brought that gun up to grasp by the barrel and charged towards one that ran out with a submachine gun. The bullets from that MP5 bounced harmlessly off of Gabriel who held the heavy machine gun by its barrel like a club and bashed that insignificant felinid hostile downwards in the soft of his shoulder, who screamed as his collarbone and shoulder blade, as well as probably a whole lot more was shattered and he collapsed under it. Gabriel stepped over him to demolish the skull with another swing of his M2 like he was leisurely swinging a golf club, rending many of the approaching combatants shocked and terrified at this giant metal monstrosity with glowing red eyes and a gigantic weapon normally reserved for mounted emplacements that was far from useless even depleted of ammo, many of them letting out yelps from behind gritted teeth and retreating into the shadows and blind spots.

Gabriel made a quick motion that opened his power armor's arm to reveal his own hand so he could reach down for his pistol, picking the thing up rather gently, letting the magnetic clamps of his power armor hold the M2 on his back as he also reached for that MP5 and pulled the ammo bag off of the hybrid's miscellaneous bodily remains. "I'm gonna have to fucking buff this out. Look at that fucking scratch," He grumbled of his pistol in a sort of horrifying post-rage, Selicia still visibly shaken by the very idea of Gabriel being this angry so as to put everybody in jeopardy like this. "...Thought at least I got an MP5, too. These are pretty rare guns these days. Always kinda wanted one of my own." He began to walk back, letting us cover him, though none of the hybrids with melee implements dared to contest his hand-to-hand skill, even with the ninety pound machine gun he used as a warhammer magnetically secured to his back. "Start the fucking engine." He really sounded more perturbed than full of any sort of urgency, and at least that sort of calmed the rest of us down. Me, anyways, if only a tad. Most of the angry mob was just in terror of this gigantic metal warrior who could kill with such abandon. Maybe he just reminded them of their leader guy. There certainly was this sort of reverence at his level of savagery that I could feel in the air, how they held themselves back seeing what this Gabriel was capable of. It was good enough for me, anything that kept them from shooting at us more. Archie hit the reverse to back up and pick Gabriel up faster, swinging the vehicle to face the right side towards him, though Gabriel dropped his pistol and the other goodies he'd claimed in Selicia's fumbling arms with a stern glare that she practically withered beneath, going to deposit them in a secure place while he deposited the M2 back on the shotgun-seat window mount as I slid down to go back to the shotgun seat, him climbing back in through the side door and up into the turret. I groaned a little seeing the handles and receiver covered in ichor and brains, popping the glove compartment to get some wipes so I could clean the thing off before I bothered reloading it. Archie set off again, while that crowd was working it's steam back up again.

"S-sorr-"

"Save it." Selicia clamped her mouth shut, compelled to by Gabriel's mental hold over her. I focused my mind on reloading the M2 rather than feel the awkward aire. I kinda hoped we'd start getting shot at again soon, just to end this awkward silence.

Ahead was the tunnel, leading to the elevator towards the surface. "...Where we'd stepped off the big elevator coming in here was a little higher up than we are right now; the elevator is probably still there, we've gotta call it down here," Archie extrapolated as we drove, probably just to avoid the silence. I guess I was grateful, as we began to hurtle down the tunnel anew, lit by those dim red emergency lights. It was strange, all strange, how everything disappeared into silence.

"...Anon, you still with us?" Gabriel said into comms. No response. "...Looks like we're out of range. Shucks, wanted to say goodbye." We hurtled through the tunnel for a while, zipping around obstacles. I could see doorways, other twisting caverns and archways and pathways, Archie maneuvering down the correct path marked on the map, coming to the proper elevator gate, somewhat familiar. Archie sat in the car, bringing his hands off the wheel to activate the haptics of the holographic display, while the engine idled.

"Let me see if I can't open it from here," He said, followed by a moment of silence as we all checked our weapons, before he grunted. "Nope. Needs a physical input," Archie grunted, getting out.

"Noah, you're on turret again. Selicia, spread out to the right. Everyone, eyes up." Gabriel was all business, everyone tumbling out but me. I ambled back into the center of the car to pop up in the turret, scanning with the double deuce, as Gabriel was retrieving the window-mounted M2 once more. I sighed, almost wanting to remark on how he kept making me reload it for him to use as he stood there, Archie going into the security booth to open the doors, Selicia piling out towards the opposite side of the jeep that Gabriel was on, anxiously strumming the grenade launcher of a forend the older M16 had. I was staring out into the blackness of the tunnel we'd came from, the dim red lighting shoddy in places. I saw my tac glasses selecting targets in the blackness, pointing out humanoids beyond my meager field of vision skittering through the abyss, highlighted by luminescent rectangle brackets, red ones if the glasses thought they were armed.

"A-Archie, could you hurry it up?" I felt that anxiousness sneak back up on me. This was all too weird. All this fighting, now this silence. As the seconds progressed, my amplified hearing in my headset could make out explosions, gunfire in the distance. Anon's offensive must have begun.

Then, blip after blip began to appear. At first I thought it must have been just a group or two skittering past from those hallways off to the sides, but soon it was nothing but blips. A wall of targets, a disconcerting number of them red. I saw Gabriel tense up, aiming more definitively.

"...Somebody's out there," Selicia said back. I doubted she had her tactical functions fully activated, or whether or not she was even using them with four eyes and all, but I'd heard something about some hybrids being able to see well in the dark. I think she must have had a good sense for it all anyways.

"...More than just a somebody," Gabriel muttered back, and they stepped forth.

Dirty, cold, hungry. Shivering despite the stuffy hot air choking all with the sulfur of burnt gunpowder. Not many of them marked with the violent red warpaint, but a significant percentage nonetheless. There they all were, coming before us, purposeless, a legion of those damned to wander aimlessly through the tunnels of the facility. Many of them were from that violent place we'd left, but I felt a sort of... respect. Reverence, even. Gabriel took a step forward, metal sabaton thudding loudly, eyes glinting to him. I couldn't count all the hybrids, standing in darkness. Was this the mob that was pursuing us? I saw... women and children with them, gazing up to Gabriel. The sounds of battle echoing down the tunnel. Other arachnea like Selicia there, skin colors of tans and greys with hair short and long, more snake women too. Bug ones, bird ones, a plethora of hybrids as diverse as it gets.

I saw the red ones come forth to Gabriel. The marked ones, the warriors. Gabriel stared them down at the end of his M2, fearless, steadfast. In awe and fear, safe behind the twin-linked cannons and level five armor of the turret and canopy, I watched them in their sort of religious silence, bowing to him, presenting their weapons out in their arms, lowering their gaze. Every last warrior offering their weapons, averting their eyes.

"...What do they want?" I uttered.

"...A new leader," Gabriel put forth sternly, immovable from the ready position he was in, weapon rock steady, until he finally pulled his firing hand away from the rear trigger mechanism and let it hang by the carry handle. I watched his free hand come up to his mask, pulling it up atop his head with the powered hand. His gaze piercing out as they looked back up to him, entranced by the visage of their messiah that they lay their weapons down at the feet of. "You want a king or something?" Eyes hung on him. None of them said anything, even their bigger ones, obviously some of the old leader's lieutenants or something, here in awe of a new one. "I'm not a ruler. I killed your last one; what, is that how you choose who rules you? You think that I can make you strong or something?" The crescendo of war out in the distance did nothing to make the scene less tense. Some of their vehicles there, how they'd followed us, shadowing, afraid, cold, praying for a solution. "...Well, least you want to *choose* your leader. That's a start. Suppose it can't be helped." Gabriel sighed, despite my racing heart, Selicia's racing heart, even Archie crouching behind the console, still readying up the elevator, rifle poking up from behind the glass. "My name is Gabriel Noria. I made mistakes when I was a child and I'm an adult too early. I'm just a person. I'm tired too. I don't want any more shit. If you stood in my way, I killed you. That's how I do things. you all saw me do it. Wasn't personal. But I've killed your friends, I killed somebody you looked up to, worshiped even. If this is how you remember your leaders, by bowing down to whoever murdered them, you've got problems I can't possibly fix for you." The doors behind us began to open, Archie scrambling back to the humvee, Selicia too crawling into the back of it, gun still pointed towards the crowd.

"Gabe! Let's go! Platform's here!" Archie's voice called, but Gabriel wasn't quite near done with his audience.

"...But I can give you advice. If you want to think of me as king anyways, here's my command. Don't fight the man who comes, the man who sent me, who is fighting you now, back in the dome. Surrender to him, make him your leader, but don't make him your king. *Choose* to follow him. Choose whatever reason you want but don't see him like you saw the old leader, or like you see me now. He's not a savior or a warlord. Just a man, mortal, fallible, like me. But he can lead you, since that's what you want so much." Gabriel turned, hunching his M2 over his shoulder, letting the ammo chain spill out of the can and hang, as he walked alongside the humvee into the elevator platform, before turning back around to face his audience, on the edge of the elevator platform. "Or, you can fight, and you can die in a cave having never even seen the sky. It's up to you. Make whatever choice you want, and make your peace with it." Gabriel's eyes shone in the blackness, as we began to ascend as the elevator groaned to life to lift us, gazing down on his congregation on high, eyes shining up at him, their arms still holding their guns though they hung at their hips and bellies now, watching their king disappear with the gap, and we were gone, ascending. Gabriel sighed, placing the M2 back down on the ground to put the chain of ammo back into the ammunition box. We went up and away, alone again.

"...Jesus, had to do Anon a favor, didn't you?" Archie put back, killing the engine as he hopped out the door, Gabriel finishing up rearranging the ammo before picking the whole thing up and walking back over to the passenger door and slamming it back on the mount, locking it in place as I leaned against the turret's gun, still reeling from everything as Selicia sat there, taking her helmet off, reeling just like me. It was over.

"...Did *us* a favor. They were either going to crown me their stupid leader or shoot us. I picked the third option." Archie stared indignantly at Gabriel, who leaned against the hood of the car as Archie stood on the opposite side. "...I mean, I accepted the crown while not accepting it, that sort of thing. I talked our way out of there alive. Don't think I had enough ammo for all of 'em anyways." Archie blinked indignantly once more, like he hadn't considered the situation to its fullest, though he was still reeling. I was too busy sighing at the black, expansive ceiling to really notice, watching the tiny light above us grow as we approached the surface, the world above. "...Did them a favor too. Guess I felt bad for em, after stroking my ego and all. I gave them the best advice I could. I could give less of a shit if Anon is a dictator glassing their village and using us as bait to murder more of 'em more efficiently." Gabriel was sighing under his breath, Archie overtly sighing, as he turned away to lean against the vehicle, slipping down to hold his head.

"...Fock." It was all too much for him, anyways. For all of us. Here we were again, going to the surface, inch by inch. Bit by agonizing bit. Returning to the real world, away from our tiny little political war. It felt dirty. Anon didn't lie to us, but he *used* us, and we were... *fine* with it. Our own dirty little proxy war in a world far, far away. Something else to weigh on my shoulders. My body armor was light as a feather now.

And like that, bursting into the world of light, we were back from the abyss.

## Chapter 26

Coming out into the "real world" was disorientating, to say the very least. Where it felt like everything should make sense but within seconds it didn't, memories flooding back to me, like I became a different person up here, or maybe I was the different person down there. Everything just shifted, became hard to quantify. A little insanity hovered over me, staying with me from down there.

Boom, as the elevator's locks secured us in place. Everybody gathering around, eyes shining back at us, saviors, victors. "Hey!" Anthony was shouting, as everyone who was not in the close vicinity needed to be notified. "They're back!" I saw a flash of green zip down from the heavens off of the tall roof of the old hangar building, flapping her wings. Lauren circled back once to land before us, everyone else coming up to us at a somewhat hurried pace, Lauren letting out a breathless sort of sigh with that bright face of hers, ears high with a flushed smile.

"Y-you guys are back," She uttered rather quickly, like an unexpected surprise while I looked- no, stared at her, seeing her glad to see us. I felt the corner of my lip curling upwards, I wanted to smile, to be warmed by her warm presence but I was still full of ice.

"Nice car!" Anthony remarked in awe, everyone facing to the front of it.

"...That was fast, we expected you guys to be all day," Samantha remarked, tossing a strand of multicolored hair out of her face as she kicked off my own jeep, the vehicle still sitting where it'd been all this time. "It's not even noon." My eyebrow went up and that feeling increased. How I'd felt like I'd been down there for ages. Our own dirty little proxy war and it was barely lunchtime. Given that we went in sometime around 7 or 8 AM, I guess I couldn't be surprised.

"Y-you okay?" Lauren's voice met me like it was underwater. I hadn't even noticed her come up to me, it was like my world was falling apart right there. I was too busy being absorbed by everything just hitting me all over again. The nuke, the hybrids, the life I could never return to.

This ascent wasn't a return to the "real world" I'd constructed in my mind when I was down there. It was a return to an uncertain, anxious, uncomfortable reality.

"Y-yeah," I muttered.

"Wait, who's that?" I turned, seeing everyone take notice of the... "woman" on the back of the JLTV, Selicia. She was still wearing the helmet and was sitting with her lower body mostly concealed in the chuck of the vehicle, so she wasn't quite noteworthy until she stood up and skittered on out, pulling her helmet off, therefore revealing all of her aberrant features right then and there- though her four eyes were concealed by her quadruple-glasses, her dimming their brightness immediately. Just about everyone tense up at the sight of her, hands going to guns as she stepped forward, clearing her throat as she whipped her ponytail of hair, playing herself up.

"...Aren't you going to introduce me, Gabriel?" Selicia muttered, letting her british-esque ire shine through to show she was as unbothered as she could best be, unhooking the straps on Gabriel's vest and the pauldrons stuck onto it to pull the heavy thing off so she could be a little more casual.

"J-jesus!" People were exclaiming, even the other hybrids were more than unnerved at the sight. Anthony was pointing his carbine right at her as Selicia undid her hair, letting it drape.

"Whoa, *cool*," Samantha let out with a huff of estranged awe.

"...This is Selicia, an Arachnea hybrid," Gabe said. "She's harmless."

"Harmless? Don't think I'd bin myself like that," She let her british class fade in as much she could. "God, it's not nearly this bright down in Prosperia, do you people really live in this blinding sun?" Selicia continued, well and ready to complain, even as she dimmed them to take a good look around, Most everyone was still looking her over somewhat concernedly, but the power-armored Gabriel's nonchalance put almost everyone at ease, save for one last person still pointing his gun at her: Anthony, quivering there. I saw Selicia's smile grow, like she knew right away that Anthony either needed some additional charming, or was somebody that she roused a lasting response to, somebody she could sink her teeth into. I was just hoping it wouldn't be literal. "Hey, darling," She opened up, bright and happy with a hint of sultry as she took a couple slow, skittering steps, rearing herself up fully to cross her arms beneath her breasts, smirking on high at the perturbed Anthony. "Afraid of spiders, are we?"

"Jesus christ, are you fucking serious about this- her?!" Anthony belted to Gabriel. "...And are you in *power armor*?"

"Yeah, was a gift," Gabriel uttered, as he activated some haptic control and the entire back of the suit began to disengage, opening up and out, and out he climbed. I saw the plugsuit he was wearing, neural nodes at key points on the skintight suit. "...Chill out, Tony. The mission was a success." Anthony's attention lead him from the spider-girl to the mech suit, said suit now left standing there autonomously running diagnostics with the fingers articulating before the headless metal man announced "DIAGNOSTICS COMPLETE, AWAITING INSTRUCTIONS" and stood dormant, motionless there. Even without a head it was easily as tall as Gabriel. But in that span of time of Anthony watching the metal man go through it's motions, Selicia had strafed all the way around Anthony, who froze as the back of his head was pressed into her cleavage and her arms draped around his shoulders frighteningly quickly.

"Hey there, we were in the middle of a conversation, weren't we? Quite rude to ignore me. We could work on that... phobia, of yours," Anthony's head craned and eyes tremblingly went up to barely watch her lick her lips with that frighteningly long tongue of hers, the dislocatory joints of her jaw articulating with subtle pops and displaying her fangs all the while, enough to chill the blood of any man, much less some teenager who'd already been put on edge by watching his hometown get reduced to dust hours before.

"Selicia." Gabriel's voice was steel and she looked back over with her jaw coming back into place, seeing Gabriel there in that plugsuit as he went back to get his clothes in the JLTV, beginning to strip the plugsuit off. As he pulled the top of the jumper off, his thick musculature showed, as well as his tattoos. I hadn't really ever seen Gabriel shirtless, he always seemed to be wearing his gym clothes until he wasn't and I hadn't seen him swimming in at least half a decade, though I guess it made sense that he'd hide it. I saw words in Spanish, icons on his shoulders. Two crossed pistols below a skull with a dagger through the eye on his right shoulder, a machete dripping with blood above a skull on his left shoulder. On his left pectoral, tiny little stick figures, symbols of people, black silhouettes aligned in rows, some of them more fancily done. An official killcount perhaps, the fancy ones being high value or notable ones? There were far too many to count at a glance. He turned his back, and I saw the visage of a saint, distinctly latin-style, however instead of a person it was rather a black-robed skeleton with a silver crown with spikes like daggers atop his hooded head, his left hand clutching a black book bound in bloody flesh and his right hand up in a saintly salute, labeled below this devil's visage with SENOR MUERTE. It was missing the tilde on the N, which I thought was strange. I wasn't exactly the one to question it, as it made my skin crawl to see. Didn't change the fact that I was entranced nonetheless for the brief time it was uncovered, before Gabriel began to dress himself and it disappeared beneath fabric. "...It's been about a minute and you're already thotting it up. I'd advise you slow your roll if you want me to keep you along." Selicia, just as frozen as Anthony (who was practically smothered in breasts at this point) blinked blankly, before releasing Anthony, skittering back slowly.

"...Well, it's not like I'd like to *deceive* your.... compatriots of my nature," She put back, her sultriness in reserve for now, as much as she'd like to charm her way through Gabriel, though he looked over and gave her another icy glare that froze whatever lewdness was circulating within her at the time. Despite her glasses, I could practically see her eyes wide. She turned around, knocking Anthony on the shoulder softly. "...You alright? You're looking rather pale." He took a couple steps backwards.

"Uh..." He could barely look her in her dimmed eyes. Maybe it was the whole four-eyed spider lady thing, maybe it was the molasses-thick sexual tension. Maybe it was the sublime horror of both at once. "G-gabe, are you serious about her?!"

"...Your bashfulness is showing, Tony. She can smell it like blood to a shark."

"Ah, that's more like it, a proper compliment," Selicia's evil smile grew back again at this tiny stroking of her ego, licking her lips at Anthony, who was trying absolutely to avoid her gaze now.

"...So what'd you think of the place?" Lauren approached me, Gabriel still dressing himself, fixing up his armor again for himself, reloading his Bren and putting it back in the holster, Selicia going off to acquaint herself with the rest of the group, though her demonstration of character towards Anthony made everyone wary of her. I think that was her idea all along, get a baseline going, make sure nobody second guessed her, using her combination of attractive human bits and unnerving spider bits as the ultimate, horrifying juxtaposition. "N-Noah?" Lauren's voice came back to me. I was zoning out, again.

I didn't know what to say, for a couple seconds. I was still reeling. Everything coming up to me, the situation, the memories, everything. but I saw her kind eyes, her slight, reassuring smile. The kind of smile you make to get somebody else to smile. "...Kinda homely, nice place to get a timeshare, real buyers' market," I practically interrupted myself, my disassociation. My soul in its right place, here before a good friend, a trusted companion that I enjoyed being around. How she put me at ease, to crack a joke with. She let out a breathless laugh, letting her eyes wander for a moment before coming back to me.

"...I dunno. All the creepy flickering lights and men in suits really gives it a drawback to me." I chuckled back at her joke. Wasn't even a joke, really. I just wanted to laugh, to appreciate her, let her know. I was looking up into those big brown eyes as she smiled back. For a moment, I was almost whole again. Almost reinvigorated.

"Hey, Green. Gimme my upper reciever again," Gabriel strolled back out, kitted back up with his MDR in pieces again. Lauren let out an "oh" and strolled over there past me to comply, pulling the sling of her own MDR, which had Gabriel's barrel and scope that he wanted back, off of herself and leaving me there, surrounded by the group in awe over the JLTV and the goodies we'd got, or Selicia hanging around sizing up each individual. Though one of us was still leaning in the corner of the hangar cloaked in shade, unmoved from the moment we returned. Maria.

Maria's eyes met mine. Shining in the shadow, observing like she was miles away, engrossed in her disassociation like I was. Lauren and her calming aura was gone from me now and I was back in that haze. I saw Maria entombed in her own troubles and I felt a penetrating guilt. How I observed her pain, our pain. How things were strange, how we'd just lost such great pieces of ourselves.

She looked like she wanted to cry, but wasn't going to.


"Alright," Gabriel jumped up on the hood of the JLTV and called once we got all the vehicles together, crossing his arms. "We didn't exactly have our equipment one-to-one, so let's take note. As of now, we've got thirteen heads, so we got arms and armor for each one," Gabriel uttered loudly as everyone gathered around, Abel and Daniel sitting up in the truck, propped up despite their wounds to listen. "I know some of you don't have any interest in fighting and that's all right. Matter of fact, that's the right mindset. However like you've seen, we might not have a choice. We don't know what's going on in the world right now so it's best to go into this as ready as possible. Samantha, Daniel, even that little hybrid girl. You're all going to learn to pull your own weight."

"Y-you're going to give her a gun?" Reina, the bipedal shepherd sibling put forth, gripping Katt's shoulders as she stepped forth, ears twitching. "Archie, I thought you said-"

"Archie had the right mindset but made a miscalculation," Gabe reasoned, Archie standing nearby and obviously not the one in charge here, slumped up against the JLTV. "We can't have any dead weight." Gabe leapt back down, going to the chuck of the vehicle for the stuff. "So we had thirteen heads and ten rifles. I want us using as standardized a loadout as possible so the shotgun, and the SKS and bolt action rifles we lifted from those assholes I'm not counting. We're going to ditch them at some point. Everyone should be using rifles in five-five-six STANAG- that means the same magazines- and pistols in nine millimeter, so I've brought enough weapons. The exception being you..." Gabriel approached Katt who stood beside Reina, Reina almost reflexively hiding the girl but paralyzed by his presence as he approached the little girl, that MP5 he'd so bloodily claimed, clutched in his grip by its plastic forend with its built-in flashlight. He went forward as she quivered and he showed it to her. "You can't handle a rifle so here's a submachine gun. You're going to keep it in semi-auto so don't get too ahead of yourself. I'll teach you how to use it. Everyone else first. Noah, you..." It was evident that me helping would speed things along. I was still sitting there, blank-faced. No better than Archie who was sitting in the seat of the JLTV, well and dissociated at this point. I blinked again, getting up. Might as well power through.

"Yeah. Let's get to it."

Our first task was outfitting all the rifles with an optic, Gabriel having pilfered a quantity of last-gen Aimpoint Micros and some batteries or ACOGs with washed-out tritium. We drew a dot on the concrete of the hangar, laser-ranged about a hundred meters with Gabriel's scope and sat there, shot each gun, adjusting the sight to dial them in to the target, round after round, me and Gabriel there like an assembly line of accuracy, often ending each sighting-in with a "good enough" and passing the weapons back to their respective owners, or threw them in the back of the jeep if the current owner was a little less than stoked. "All right," Gabriel was saying. "Next up we all need to armor up. I've got a lot of plate carriers for all of you now, as well as helmets, the high-cut ones are for the Shepherd siblings and Archie, since they've got big ears, each one's got communications in it so that we can all stay in touch. All the armors are level three polydynamid, which means they're meant to stop regular rifle rounds but not armor piercing ones, luckily they're a lot lighter than most usual body armor so even newbies like y'all won't be too bothered by them. Cinch them up so you can feel that the top of the plate comes up to your sternal groove, and tighten the cummerbund- that's the side band- tighten it all the way while you're holding your deepest breath, so it's tight but won't restrict your breathing. If it's loose and your armor takes a round that entire plate is going to slap you and knock the wind out of you worse than if you're wearing it right. Green," Gabriel shifted, going to Lauren, standing there with her M4 after having re-affixed the silencer, with a brand-new optic up top, her feet trotting her a little closer as she paused in hesitation, watching everyone else going through the old army-surplus plate carriers and throwing them on. "Again, can't really get you armor but I got you some more webgear. I think it'll interface good with your battle belt. This one's a chest harness, but I guess if you're handy sometime you can sew a plate pocket into the rearside of it. Just try not to get shot in the back."

"Jeez, I mean, a single body armor plate really doesn't matter with a body like this," She said, flipping the cordura chest rig over some in her hands though still looking at Gabriel. It was more of a joke or anything, she still seemed grateful, but Gabriel took the opportunity to shine through businesslike as usual.

"Eh, tell that to the dogtaur," Gabriel nodded over to Abel, the centaurical canid one in the bed of the truck, still with patches over the hole in his chest and back looking at his new body armor where he lay. "...You saw him get holed. Could have been avoided, y'know. Just give it some thought."

"I'll put a plate in it," she said, maybe just to get Gabriel off her case. He smiled back plainly. "...It means a lot anyways." She scratched her head, looking around again, an ear flicking. She really was the least armored person here.

"...By the time you think you want armor, let me know. I've got a few ideas for headgear, too." Lauren smiled back a little less than enthusiastically, but she was obviously appreciating that he was considering her. She trotted back to put her new chest harness on over her blouse and the suspenders for her loadbearing belt, doing her best to fix it up so that it didn't interfere much with her wings, while working out a fastener for her battle belt to interface with the chest rig. "So," Gabe was saying to me while I was zoning out on Lauren toiling away at her craft. "Last thing. We need to teach these guys to shoot. We can go over comms etiquette, medical techniques and small squad tactics later, I'm thinking once we find a nice position to let everyone recharge at. For now we just need them to have the skill to make shots and it'll probably make a world of difference in our defensive ability."

"...Sounds good to me," I muttered back.

It wasn't much, other than a quick lecture on how the Armalite and MicroDynamic pattern rifles worked, Gabriel going over all the controls and quirks of the weapon. We took each one one-by-one and evaluated their shooting skill, first with a dry run and next having them take shots at the walls of the hangar as a sort of makeshift target practice, giving them pointers on stuff like handling flinching. Even the ones who weren't keen on it, like Sam and Daniel got the picture, though they still seemed rather uncomfortable about it. Gabriel remarked something along the lines of "gotta start somewhere". Finally, as Gabriel went off with Katt to instruct the felinid girl's operation of the MP5 he'd gotten her, I confronted Kyle, who had been gingerly inspecting a commandeered M16 for a while now. He stared down at it like an idol in his hands, a ghost in his eyes. He was stern, sterner than I'd ever seen him really be. Seeing him like this brought back the truth that ought to be fresh in my mind, that his girlfriend Holly and our friend Wilson were less than twenty four hours dead at this point. Something that should have stung me more than it should. Maybe it was the disassociation, a haze protecting me from horrible realities. I saw Kyle and remarked in my head that maybe this was a turning point for him. As sickening as the thought was maybe this would put things into perspective for him.

He mulled over his new weapon, cocking it and standing before the hangar wall, pocked with holes from everyone else's shooting practice. Before I could say anything, he was letting burst after burst loose, like taking on a little army all in his head, holes opening up in the rusted canopy of the place as he did so, sunshine streaked with dust wafting on through.

"...I think I got the hang of it," he practically whispered, his voice and mind a million miles away for all that mattered, gun hanging heavy and smoking in his grip. He looked me back in the eye as he reloaded, turning to waft away, face still ragged, ghostly, and I didn't think much of it, even as we all piled into the vehicles, getting started driving. In the rear, Anthony drove the truck, I was driving the Jeep and Gabriel was driving the JLTV out in front. Archie was still zoned out so he needed a bit of a break, sitting in one of the back seats of the jeep and staring off at the little wispy clouds. Maria sat next to me in shotgun, very much zoned out as well with nothing but sheer resolve driving her focus, knowing that she ought to lose herself in something productive for now, keeping watch. Kyle sat next to Archie, and seemed to be surprisingly engaged despite the recent trauma of the events, Lauren standing with her rear legs on the floor of the chuck of the jeep with her forelegs' talons grasping the rollcage, standing her up as she'd scouted out the area with a quick flight a few minutes before, slowly scanning from her turret-like position wearing one of the hologlasses Gabriel had gotten, everyone with similar sets of Tac-Holos. I looked ahead, seeing Selicia poking up in the back of the JLTV with Gabriel, smiling out, wearing her own glasses with the sunshade function still all the way maxed.

"One more thing," Gabriel explained, The turret of the JLTV rotating as the headless power armor suit manned it autonomously, a shoulder-mounted sensor popped up in lieu of an eye. "The Sentinel program of the power armor we got is also a general battlefield tactical AI and HUD augmentation. So Sentinel is downloaded to each of your holos and can give you general advice on stuff like rangefinding, probabilities, plans of action and combat leads for hitting a moving target. I think it's a gimmick but he could prove useful, if you're somehow separated from the rest of us and need a second opinion ask him."

"...Isn't the Sentinel program just to eliminate lag in power armor or something?" I asked.

"Yeah, originally. This is the new stuff. He's got lots of fancy tricks. Also, Anthony," Gabriel spoke back to Anthony who was driving the truck in the rear as we rambled down the dirt path. "remember, we're taking things slow. If I see something suspicious up ahead, we're gonna full stop and play things evasive. Lauren will go and check things out if it doesn't seem overtly dangerous. Remember to listen to whatever I say, Anthony," Gabriel said to him, as he was driving the rear vehicle. I doubted he would try anything stupid, since he was the makeshift medical vehicle in the very back with Daniel and Abel on makeshift bunks, Daniel's IV bag strung up from being tied to the roof of the cab with a little makeshift sunshade over it, Abel at this point stable enough to not need it so much as regular checking-up, with Sam in the back with them, and Reina and Katt sitting in the cab with Anthony.

"I- Okay. Gotcha." Anthony trailed off, enough to know that in seconds he had something else to remark on. "S-so why is *she* coming along again?" I heard Anthony ask through comms, bringing me back out of my disassociation.

"...You aren't talking about me, are you darling?" Selicia was quick on the response, tsking audibly. "You realise you can ask me, right?" A silence took over, Anthony's response frozen.

"Jesus christ Anthony," Gabe muttered to end this dreadful pause. "This isn't a good look for you."

"...I forgot her name," Anthony said and Gabe chuckled back, Selicia also chuckling, leaning up against the wall of the chuck of the JLTV, trailing a finger up along her temple as she probably stared back at Anthony through her impermeably dark goggles.

"...You sure you didn't just pretend to forget my name because you realised you were being legitimately rude just then?" Selicia prodded.

"Her name's Selicia, Anthony," Gabe said, basically just as soon as Selicia ended her last spiel, maybe so he could interject before things got worse, though playing it off in his sarcastic tone like he was just plain annoyed.

"Selicia," Anthony said. "Why'd you... want to come with us?"

"I wanted to see this world we supposedly all live in, darling. But it sounds like you don't trust me, but that's okay. I get the vibe I give off, really I do. Just try and take things in stride, alright hun?" She smirked.

Sensing Anthony's further questions, Gabriel was sure to speak. "...Also she can make nanofiber with her body and she's pretty utilitarian in a firefight. Plus she asked nicely to come. If you have a problem with her, you let me know."

"...Can we trust her?"

"I dunno, can we trust you?" Gabriel shot back. Anthony stammered for a second, before realising that his attachment to this group was about as reasoned as hers. "Keep it serious, the both of you now. Got it?"

Nobody had any objections for the rest of the way, and we were silent, slowly snaking our way through the rocky crags until we could find a place to settle in for the evening, in a highland above some tourist trap of an old ghost town.

### Chapter 27

It's morning again, after a sleep as dreamless as it was restless.

The first thing I see is the sun barely above the horizon shining light into my face, blazing along and crawling its way up into the sky. I'm laying on my back on the mat beside the lean-to we'd constructed aside the JLTV nestled in with the rocks, Maria next to me. I feel the stiff desert breeze blow through my hair, through the openings of the tarp tent we'd constructed.

I tried to sit up at first before finding myself stiffer than I would have liked, my back full of rocks. I'm sore all over- from my face to my ankles it hurts. Might have been the taxation of all the adrenaline running through my system from the day before. Honestly, in this pain, I'm amazed I could even fall asleep in the first place. I didn't even bother to take my armor off, maybe that was it, having spent half the night looking for bad guys in my thermal vision of my NODs while I was on watch. I sighed quietly as I lay there saggy-eyed, watching the floaters in my eyes. I could hear inside the JLTV, radio static interspersed with cuts, switching between channels. I finally willed myself to sit up, seeing Gabriel in there, as he sat in the shotgun seat before the radio of the vehicle itself, one of the mobile comms stations with wires laying all about.

"...Do you ever sleep, Gabe?" I put in, blinking to clear my vision.

"I'll catch up when I'm dead," he joked back, before turning the thing off.

"So, any news?" I asked as he cracked the door, coming around to the portable stove sitting there on the hood of the vehicle, quickly going for his knife to flip the last of the sausages.

"...Military chatter," He said. "Lot of it is couched in coded language. But it's mostly all English, except for a little splash of Spanish here and there, and I doubt the Mexicans are invading us. Bet you Civil War 2.0 is what's going down." He speared a finished sausage to bring it up and take a bite.

"...Don't think any of the Spanish stuff is guys looking for you?" I asked.

"Could be. But I'm not that much of a VIP and the Cartel has bigger assets to secure in a nuclear scenario, I should know since I know their protocols. *Ejecutor* or not I'm far enough down the chain of priorities that they've probably given up on me by now, might think I got dusted in Vegas when it blew. Maybe if Vegas had never been fried they'd be looking for me, but at the moment they're probably just as code-red as we are."

"...Any ideas on the nuke?"

"Well, I don't hear any chinese chatter so I think we can put them lower on the suspect list. Might be democrats launching a coup."

"...You really think a bunch of left-wing radicals would take over a missile silo or something and launch a nuke at Vegas? Pretty much the whole city votes blue," I uttered.

"Yeah, the politics are fucked and nothing makes sense. Can't say for sure, that's what bothers me about all this garbage," I pulled out my own knife to spear myself something to eat from his little cooking station. At least I was cognizant enough to be hungry. "Might be coup. The Cali governor was always a disgusting neomarx-y type, seems like his thing, even if I always thought he was all rhetoric. Never cared for politics but there are few people more disgusting than communists," Gabriel muttered. "Malignant as nazis but with an unwarranted self-righteousness with heads *firmly* up their own asses. I like to pretend I'm not a violent person but I enjoy killing those fuckers when I got the chance. We actually used to deal with a lot of commies in Mexico. Their gear is always shit; there's not much like holing a commie and watching him suffocate to death from a collapsing lung. Tampons are okay for bleeds- not good, *okay*- but they don't quite work as chest seals. Hell of a thing to find out during your last two minutes alive." Gabriel let out a laugh, he was probably joking, or something. Being edgy to grate my nerves, get me worked up, awake. "...After this is done I oughta start a PMC. Like the Grand Captain from Alloy Cog Hardened. Find some more of the cucks to fuck up." Gabriel chuckled in his dorky reference, and I just held my head.

"...Hasn't it been like, a week already?"

"...It's May sixth," Gabriel put back. I grunted, like it was an interesting factoid rather than a revelation that things were going sideways faster than I'd ever anticipated. I guess my dad was right about that three day rule, or something like that. "Guess the commies figured no sense in letting a good catastrophe go to waste."

"...Why would they start a civil war, though?" I mused. "Isn't the president a Democrat too?"

"Was, yeah. Last I checked most commies aren't fond of neoliberals, anyways. Like I said, shit's fucked and we're not going to get answers sitting on our asses." Gabriel brought up the holographic display of his own glasses, letting me see. "So we're overlooking Crystal Springs. I didn't see any big military activity there during my watch and I'm guessing you didn't either. Selicia was middle watch, I asked her before she went to sleep after she woke me up and she said she didn't see a thing."

"...Hm. Think we can have a little respite?"

"...Yeah, chill in the springs. Might as well check out the museums too. The hybrids might get a kick out of it," Gabriel mused playfully and I chuckled right back.

"Sounds fun." I looked back to the little camp stove, other people roused from sleep slowly, approaching the cooler on my jeep to get some food, seeing mostly MREs and preserved, dried food now, disappointment evident in their eyes, though Lauren was more than appreciative as best she could be, laying her lower body to gaze out at the desolate old place before us as she gnawed piece after piece of the carbohydrate block off, blowing an errant strand of hair out of her face as she did so, ever so charmingly. I saw everyone else rising, save for Selicia who was still dozing away in the JLTV, though as the sun peaked above the rocks she took a moment to pull her glasses back onto her eyes and blacken them all the way, going back to sleep.

I looked over to Maria, who was where I left her, staring up into the pale morning sky. It was so calm, I thought and she must have thought too, lost in the wisps of bright cloud somewhere far, far above us. It was too calm, too picturesque for the world to be ending. A sublime melancholy here, like she could ignore the nuke, the dead parents, the impending doom of it all. I speared the last sausage on the griddle, going back over to her and presenting it.

"...You... doing okay?" I asked. I came up close to her, sitting down where the outside of my thigh rubbed against her shoulder, as she reached up to take the handle of my knife.

"Yeah. I'll be fine." I saw her frizz her messy hair with her opposite hand as she still stared into the sky, eating the food. How she had that steadfast look in her eyes, being as unstoppable as she could be.

"You sure?" She looked over to me again as I said it, almost like I was interrupting her cloud-gazing, swallowing what she'd chewed. A flash of sadness in her eyes, before she sat up, hefting her rifle in her free hand.

"...Let's get to that spring already, I need a wash." She grunted throughout, as I still sat there, gazing up at her as she walked off to whip everybody else up.


We set out, rambling away down the road in our usual seats. I asked Archie to drive for once, I wasn't feeling well, taking the passenger seat of my jeep. We moved slow as we approached on high-alert, Lauren zipping back to land on the back of the jeep again after her all-clear. It was still quiet, all morning.

"...What's up with all this?" Archie was asking as we passed tents and trash tumbling along the ground, campfires deserted. A camping ghost town, left in a hurry.

"Campgrounds outside of the town. The town's a historical site, a relic from the old west that they fixed up recently to more closely resemble what it looked like two hundred years ago," I exposited.

"...campgrounds? I could have-"

"-Used a fucking vacation, we get it," Gabe shot back over radio at Archie, playful as ever. Lauren let out a chuckle above us. I saw Kyle turn in his seat behind me, looking a little antsy with the big green dragon-girl thing towering over him with herself braced on the rollcage as usual. I still noted him poking his M16 out the window a little too enthusiastically.

"Shit, where do you think they all went?" Sam gasped out as we passed vacant tent and cabins with their doors ajar.

"Hell of a way to end a vacation with a nuclear holocaust," Gabriel said again. "Keep your eyes out. I doubt an army is hiding in one of these trailers but I wouldn't put it past them." A few moments of eerie rumbling down the trail roads before we rolled to a stop nearest to one of the clearings, where the sign dictated a path towards the gently flowing creeks. "All right.

Freshen up if you have to but keep your wits about you and don't run off. Piss in the spring and we're going to leave you behind cuffed to a picnic table."

"It's so green here," Reina was saying as one of her ears flicked, getting out of the medical truck while Katt stayed in the cab, still worriedly looking about with those bright yellow eyes of hers.

"The water is a real neat shade of blue, I could see it from up where I was flying," Lauren said, leaping down off of the jeep as the suspension creaked in relief, a wingbeat sailing her a couple feet away towards the spring, as I too got up and out. It was a breath of respite to wash up in the springs, like letting out a sigh held in too long. Most of us changed into our swimwear rather quickly, leaving piles of body armor and rifles on the side, those of us who'd neglected to bring swimwear scrounged through the abandoned tents to find stuff, Reina borrowing an ill-fitting bikini that wasn't quite accommodating to her tail from one such tent, Lauren doing a bit of quick seamstressing so that Reina's tail could poke out the back of it.

I kicked off my boots to just drape my legs into the waters, figuring to keep watch despite my desire to relax, though Gabriel took a brief second to address the autonomous power armor occupying the turret. "Sentinel, receive instructions," He ordered the suit as it sat in the turret behind the double-deuce, already scanning the horizon. "Hold fire until actively engaged. Oh, and see the spider-looking one?" Gabriel pointed Selicia out, who paused as she was getting out of the JLTV, ready to seize the opportunity to unnerve some folks by showing some more of her skin as she tightened her bikini top. It still looked far too precariously small for what she was working with chest-wise, the strings of her bra held tight against flesh that bulged out around it. She stopped for a moment to look to Gabe and the autonomous robot suit with its pauldron-mounted sensor poking up in lieu of a helmet, hearing her likeness addressed. "If she starts eating anybody, shoot her. Just try not to hit the one she's eating, alright? Aim for her spider-bits."

"ORDERS ACKNOWLEDGED. LETHAL FORCE PARAMETERS SET, COMMENCING OVERWATCH."

"Heh, maybe that Sentinel program ain't so much of a gimmick after all, huh?" Gabriel laughed to me as he passed, elbowing me in the arm as he walked on to go and search through the campsite for anything useful.

"W-why am I the only one not allowed to eat people?!" Selicia stammered, though that implied that was something that was on her mind from the get-go anyways, everyone else also a little wide-eyed.

"...Because you're the only one who doesn't care about consent. Sentinel, receive new parameters."

"YES SIR. STANDING BY."

"See, only shoot her if it looks like she's forcing herself on somebody else, y'know? Like if it's obvious that only *one* of them is having a good time."

"ACKNOWLEDGED. VICTIM OF PROLONGED, CONSTRICTIVE PHYSICAL CONTACT MUST HAVE A HEARTBEAT OF PLUS-ONE-EIGHTY BPM AND DISPLAYING SIGNS OF DISTRESS BEFORE ENGAGEMENT." Gabriel laughed again as the group nervously teetered, though in some ways they all must have been relieved that Sentinel was here to keep the peace, though the fact that Selicia could eat people was apparently more than unnerving to the less knowledgeable.

"Hah, ain't that some shit? Talk about a whizbang doohickey right here," Gabriel laughed of the automaton before proceeding off.

"...*Eat people*?" Lauren's brow was arched and her lips curled with a mouth ajar, obviously in sheer reproach while she stood there already up to her lower belly in the spring pool. Selicia, lip snarling a little bit as she waded into the pool with her arms crossed, emoted enough that she was definitely peeved despite her eyes shrouded in blackness while she came up to Lauren in the pool. "J-jesus-"

"Oh you don't know?" She snarled. "...It's not like you can't do it yourself." Lauren's eyebrows went up further as her slack jaw bowed, practically falling over for a tiny instant before righting herself like a tiny nod as she blinked back at Selicia.

"Excuse m-" Selicia reached out in an instant and with a meaty pop dislocated Lauren's jaw. I didn't know what was going on at first and before I could even react, Sentinel's voice boomed out.

"NOTICE. PHYSICAL ASSAULT DETECTED." Selicia froze up again, people all around obviously more than a tad shaken up at the sudden blast of action, but frozen stiff by that electronic growl of a metal beast behind a twin-linked fifty-caliber autocannon.

"...She's fine, Sentinel, Don't shoot," Gabe called out in nonchalance far off and away, waving his hand in the air, seeming rather carefree given the situation, my own heart pounding.

"G-gaghk!" Lauren's hands went up to her mouth now hanging off to one side, hands up but not touching the dislocated joint in shock and pain. I could see her eyes watering, but she wasn't exactly screaming.

"Jeez, y-you've seriously never dislocated your jaw before? *ever*?" Selicia nervously laughed, as if it was no big deal, clicking her own jaw in and out of position, her weakly smiling face looking back at the singular raised eyesensor of the metal beast on that gun pointed straight for her. "J-just-" Selicia advanced again and Lauren backed off with a quick motion, evidently not really big on being touched further by somebody who'd just yanked half her mouth out of place, now disconnected from both her skull joint and the bisection of her lower jaw. "S-see, it hurts if you don't do it often, it's-"

"*Jesus,* Green," Gabe's laugh called out far and wide as he was rummaging through a tent. "Push it back into place already. It's like ripping off a band-aid. You stall, you freeze up, you make it worse." Lauren's hands gingerly went up to her jaw, an audible pop as in a moment she shoved upwards and was left there wheezing through gritted teeth and drool, tears ebbing at the corners of her eyes and a little snot dribbling out of one of her nostrils like she was just denied the mother of all sneezes, that kind of absolutely sublime meta-pain.

"...Wait, so I can eat people? That's what this is for?" Abel peaked out from the chuck of the truck, pointing to his jaw as he, without even using his hands, popped his jaw in and out of place. Come to think of it, he often did it as a fidget. The pop was barely audible for him. "Huh. Jeez, I... I don't want to hurt anybody..."

"...you can't, your real stomach is blocked off by a ring of bone and a blood vessel around your true esophagus, doesn't stretch like the storage one anyways; Creators must've not wanted hybrids to digest anybody, but still do that shit anyways, ethics or some shit," Gabriel was shouting back. "Don't any of you fucking people read the hybrid docs?!"

"...Yeah, that's true," Daniel coughed, raising a finger into the air. I watched Reina lift her hands to her own jaw and jimmy it around.

"What's up with mine?" She muttered in the slightest of frustration.

"...Normal bipedals can't, we're not big enough to anyways, we ain't got the... physiology, either," Archie sighed back.

"...So big hybrids can eat people?" Sam muttered, brow raised.

"Fucked up, ri-"

"...That's super hot," Sam noted, and a good portion of the group froze in place to slowly look over to her, with her staring out into the distance past everybody with a weird look of satisfaction on her face, biting her lower lip subtly. "W-what?" She asked as people were staring at her, Anthony beside her scooting a little away. Nobody could really comment on this aside from the gaping silence that formed in those quick moments, before the Selicia-Lauren situation developed further.

"You... Look, I'm, uh... Hey... Lizard, you alright?" Selicia was quivering nervously almost like she needed to offer Lauren an apology, forgetting her name, a couple of her legs twitching nervously as she edged closer to Lauren, who was bent all the way down like she'd just been wheezing, before she got up and wheeled an uppercut into Selicia's jaw. I saw how Selicia flopped backwards, shot up out of reflex in an attempt to dodge that was too little, too late, serving to basically flip her entire body about eight feet up into the air, somersaulting before she splashed back down on her back, very much dazed as Lauren leapt forward and ripped those glasses of hers off and tossed them to the shore. It was a quick few seconds of brutality before Lauren had Selicia by the armpits, wrenching her back up- but it wasn't enough to just pull her up out of the water, and Lauren was evidently feeling dramatic, rearing back on her rear legs to stand at what must have been twelve feet up in the air, her frontal legs practically cradling Selicia as her hands gripped Selicia's already large-frame like hoisting a child into the air. Selicia's jaw was dislocated at all three joints from the strike, looking quite silly squinting there with her mouth grotesquely hanging open while she was obviously concerned behind a deep, deep four-eyed squint, the tips of her legs barely dangling down into the surface of the water.

"Two things. Don't you ever fucking touch me, *or* call me a *lizard* again. Got it, *legs*?" Lauren gnashed her teeth in Selicia's face, Selicia's hands quiveringly raising up in a show of surrender, before Lauren, obviously the stronger of the two, shook Selicia back and forth in rage. I saw the fur that ran down Lauren's entire spine and tail was all on-end. "YOU FUCKING GOT IT?! SAY IT!"

"I-agh," Selicia's jaw was still all over the place, Lauren still glaring death into her. "Oghay," Selicia uttered before Lauren let her slide from her arms to fall back down and splash into the water. Lauren turned as she came back down to her regular eight foot height, looking back to the turret gunner watching the spectacle.

"Sentinel," She let out to the robot, raising a hand in a wave as she huffed, only a tad winded. "...We good?"

"LETHAL FORCE PARAMETERS HAVE NOT BEEN MET. OPERATIVE- 'GREEN, L.' CONFIRMED BLUEFORCE COMBATANT, FRIENDLY FIRE PARAMETERS CURRENTLY FULLY ACTIVE."

"B-blue force combatant?! What the fuck am I, then?!" Selicia yammered after she shoved her jaws back into place, going for her glasses at the shore again.

"...SUBJECT 'SELICIA' UNCONFIRMED CIVILIAN. FORMER GREEN CIVILIAN CLASSIFICATION CURRENTLY YELLOW, POSSIBLE INTERLOPER."

"You have me set as a *civilian*?!?" Selicia practically screeched towards the distant Gabe as soon as she pushed her jaw back into place, her strange quasi-anglo accent separating ci-vi-li-an into four syllables, screeching each one like its own word while she fished for her glasses, practically blind by how she padded around on the ground in her glasses' general vicinity.

"You're surprised?!" Gabriel laughed back. "Remember, you've yet to prove yourself, not a good look to physically assault our air support when she's trying to *relax*," Selicia looked back at Lauren, who was towering with her green face a surprising shade of red, Nostrils flaring, eyes spiteful with her arms crossed, musculature pulsing.

"Wait, that thing recognizes hybrids as… People?" Anthony put forth.

"AFFIRMATIVE. I HAVE ALL AVAILABLE DOSSIERS OF HYBRID SPECIES AND PHYLOGENY DOWNLOADED TO MY CURRENT MODEL FROM USER NORIA, G., ENABLING FULL COMBATANT IDENTIFICATION, VITAL ORGAN TARGETING AND LIFE SIGNS READINGS IN MY OPERATIONAL HEADS-UP-DISPLAY FOR MAXIMUM COMBAT EFFICIENCY AGAINST ALL POSSIBLE REDFORCE COMBATANTS."

"See, he's a better study than the rest of y'all, you guys need to snap to it," Gabriel reprimanded.

"Whatever, *barbarians*," Selicia muttered in between the new conversations, rolling her eyes so vividly that it was apparent beneath her muddy glasses. "I'm going back to sleep," Selicia let out trying to make it look like she wasn't admitting defeat, crawling back into the JLTV. Lauren humphed, heaving her chest a little as she waded back into deeper waters, downplaying her little victory, but not by much, as I could still see a spark of pride in her eyes as she finally could float around, her legs doggy-paddling her about in the deep as she sunk to her shoulders.

"…Fucking cunt," She was "humph"ing. I looked back around, seeing Anthony also similarly relieved that Selicia wouldn't be joining the swim, Kyle off to the side still brushing up his M16, sighing heavily as he gazed off, leaned there against a tree stump. I saw Abel, his arm elbow-deep down his own throat.

"Oh shit, I can feel my heart beating," He let out after pulling his arm back out with a quick gag, hand and forearm dripping. "Huh," He was about to put his hand back into his mouth and down his throat, to keep feeling around, before he noticed Sam staring at him with a dumb smile on her face. "W-what?"

"…You should probably stop, since you got shot and all," Daniel muttered before Sam could comment, Daniel having sat himself up bit by excruciating bit on the wall of the truckbed.

"Yo wait, how am I supposed to eat people if I've got a ribcage?" Abel asked.

"Your chest splays open. You have a two-piece sternum." I saw Abel look down as Daniel explained, though he tried to splay his chest back once before he was reminded of the lung wound that was hindering him as he let out an "ow".

"…Wanna try it out once you're healed?" I heard Sam's voice, feeling the uncomfortable air of everyone around her even at this distance.

"…Hybrids, huh?" I was jolted out of the charming wacky disassociation of watching the goings-ons in no particular order or focus as Maria slid down next to me, to drape her legs into the water too. It was almost shocking, how close she got in an instant. Rubbing up against my arm. A couple moments of intimacy that I don't think I'd ever experienced before, at least not from her, as she lay her head on my shoulder. "…All this…"

"You're… I thought you of all people would've shot Selicia by now," I muttered and she muttered out an equally dour chuckle.

"…It's more entertaining than I'd admit watching them fight. A dragon centaur just lifted a spider lady eight feet off the ground. Beats any *internovella* I've ever seen." It was my turn to chuckle as we sat there.

"Y-you're not worried she might eat you?" I put forth. Maria was silent, and though she was in her swimwear, a pair of men's swimming trunks though with a bikini top, her hand went to her pocket and out came her prized switchblade.

"Oh, I fucking dare her," She uttered as the blade snapped out, Maria lazily whisking it through the air a couple times before folding back in on itself. I chuckled back.

"...Heh. Yeah, fucking weird shit," I muttered back, nearly slipping back into my haze of disassociation, but Maria pulled be right back out as her head came down on the crux of my shoulder and neck atop the shoulder strap of my armor, an arm creeping around my side, having to dig into the soft of my armpit above the side plate of my body armor. It wasn't like I didn't expect her to need comforting, but there was something about this. How she came up close to me. I didn't know why at the time, but I felt this distance. Like it was… fake. Like she was reaching out for a substitute. Was she? Was it really her? I reached around her for a moment but my hand was lost, heavy, hovering there away from her. I had to force myself to hold her. How her teeth grit, beneath that calm, content composure I saw her cracks. Her real feelings. That dam she'd constructed to hold back the flow of tears, that incredible focus. Could I really help her? Could anybody?

I just looked back out to our friends enjoying themselves, the red-faced Lauren still somewhat unnerved as she now floated on her back in the deep of the stream, trying to take her mind off things with a good look at the sky, sparse clouds wafting past. I looked up too, to try and lose myself in the moment, loosen up. We were here to relax, after all.

Archie was getting out of the water, walking back to the vehicles, but Kyle stepped out in front of him, his chest puffed out, gilded in his combat armor. Archie stopped abruptly, before sidestepping. Kyle matched him, pretending not to notice from behind his deeply darkened hologlasses.

"What," He crowed in Archie's face, looking down on the smaller person beneath him, in nothing but his swim trunks. Archie, a little out of his element had the look on his face like "excuse me?" but didn't say anything, trying to pass again but this time Kyle stuck out his foot to trip Archie. "Watch your step," He snarled.

"Kyle, what the fuck are you doing?" I spat, breaking my embrace with Maria, who also looked over.

"What?!" Kyle roared defensively, hefting his rifle. I saw the look in his eyes, a mad dog. Something too furious. "You're gonna take this freak's side? You see what they do!"

"Toss off, cunt! What did I ever do to you?!" Archie spat as he brushed dirt off of his chest, sitting there. Kyle turned his head, his body still facing me, weapon quivering as his face grew in that insane, nervous look. I knew that this was serious in an instant, getting up.

"You- if it wasn't for you, Holly would still be alive!" He spat. I paused, a step away from him as I approached. His rifle barrel was inching up, up, up. I heard the tinge of sadness in his voice, quivering, wavering, subtly shrouded by a spiteful rage. It was that scary kind of sadness.

"You think that's my fault?! I didn't shoot-" His gun was up. I heard his safety disengage. The sadness that blinked into him was finally overtaken by rage.

"Shut... T-the fuck-" he began behind gritted teeth, before I was upon him. I pushed the gun away from Archie from where it was pointing out perpendicular to Kyle's center mass, his chest now facing me. Three rounds ripped from his gun, spitting up dirt and Archie winced in the other direction as the world grew quiet in my ears in response. The gun spun from Kyle's shaking grip; he was now grappling with me, rage in his eyes, teeth gnashing. He was always bigger than me, probably a good two hundred and fifty pounds at his six-foot-five as he momentarily snatched at my armor shoulder straps with both hands like a lapel grab, something I knew enough about. He was wearing his helmet and full body armor, but his neck was open. A swift spear-handed strike to the throat and his grip loosened for a moment before he could do anything else, though it by no means knocked him out, rather a momentary stun. Both my hands came up to split his grasp on me, throwing his arms off and I stepped quickly to his my left to retain his right wrist, with my right hand firmly securing his wrist and my left hand back at his throat, I did my best to try and get around him but he had more reach than I did and continued to face me directly, reversing my hasty arm lock to try and headbutt me. I ducked low and before he could bring the bridge of his helmet into my face like he'd wanted, I slammed the hard top of my skull into his relatively soft nose and he fell backwards, collapsing into the dirt for a moment. I scrambled over him, going back for his wrist as I flipped him to his back with his arm pinned, kneeling onto his arm gently yet securely as I undid his helmet with a quick snap. He tried to get up and I twisted his arm back against the crux of my knee and he screamed, though I could hear not much aside from the screeching of tinnitus in my ears.

"Stay down!" I was breathing heavily, in an instant it was over, thanks to a little Judo skill. I saw the blood dribbling out from his smashed nose.

"What in the fuck is this shit?!" Was the first thing I could hear as the ringing clear, Gabriel pacing forward. "I'm gone for a minute and two fights break out?! Are you going to act like fucking children all this time!?" Gabriel shoved me aside as he came upon Kyle, asserting his grip onto Kyle's trapped wrist. Gabriel was wrenching him up in an instant, Kyle protesting as Gabriel wordlessly ferried him off, and in an instant of my own disassociation beneath my ringing ears later, he was ziptied with his wrists around the bar of the rollcage of my jeep, almost everyone standing about, sighing heavily. Kyle sitting there on the back of the jeep, bound, starind down into the bed of the jeep.

"...Jesus," Lauren sighed. Even Selicia took note of the hectic goings-ons.

"What the fuck are you thinking?!" Gabriel was up in Kyle's face like a drill instructor, Kyle's eyes still avoiding him. "That's not a rhetorical question, asshole!" Gabriel slapped, then grabbed Kyle by the cheeks beneath his chin, wrenching his face up. Those panicked, wild eyes flashing back at Gabe.

"...I-I don't know." Gabriel released Kyle, like he was flicking feces off of his hand, whipping his whole arm with it and Kyle slumped back to sigh in shame, still bound.

"I WOULD LIKE TO PROVIDE MY ANALYSIS REPORT," Sentinel's voice chimed. Gabriel sighed, I sighed, we all sighed in our own little ways.

"...Go ahead." It was like Gabe felt like it couldn't hurt, might as well try and soften the happenings.

"SUBJECT: 'SELICIA'. HER ASSAULT WAS AGGRAVATED YET BRIEF BUT EMOTIONAL REACTION INDICATES A 72.5% CHANCE OF A LACK OF RECURRENCES IN THE FUTURE. SUBJECT: REYNOLDS, K. ASSAULT WITH A DEADLY WEAPON WITH INTENT TO MAIM OR KILL, 89% CHANCE OF PREMEDITATION. SIGNS INDICATE A BEHAVIORAL DISPOSITION TO VIOLENCE. RECURRENT BEHAVIOR HIGHLY LIKELY AT A 92.7% CHANCE OF RELAPSE. SEVERE WARNING OF JEOPARDIZATION OF UNIT COHESION. COURT MARTIAL SUGGESTED."

"...Well he's not telling us anything we don't know," Archie muttered. Kyle glared jaggedly towards Archie for a second, before realising that this must have reinforced Sentinel's prognosis, his animosity quickly returning to groveling in another instant.

Maria stepped up. She'd been silent, silent again. For a long time, until she stood before Kyle, getting up into the jeep. Leering down from where he sat bound. He looked up, seeing her fiery visage above. Her nostrils flaring, judgement, even so far as hate in her eyes.

"...Are you going to put us all in jeopardy?" Her voice was quiet and her eyes were deep behind a shadowed brow, vicious, jagged, as he gazed up at her. "...Vegas is gone. None of us can go home. There's one place for us to go and I won't let you *fuck* this up. You hear me?" She could have been roaring this for all the effect it was having, Kyle frozen as he gazed up. "We have *one* way to go." I noticed she was shaking as she spoke.

"M-Maria," I approached, jumping up there too. I reached out to gingerly grasp her shoulder, come close to her and give her human contact. I froze inches from her as she glared back at me, that intensity in her eyes momentarily cutting its way through me before her glare could soften. She sighed, going back as my arm fell.

"I HAVE A SCANNING REPORT." Sentinel's voice was loud and jagged, the solemn silence of the moment ever defiled whenever he spoke. "ADDITIONAL YELLOW TARGET IDENTIFIED, A.O. IS NO LONGER SECURED." We all froze up, instantly looking up.

A slightly distant, high-pitched "shit!" was let out, as a bush a good fifteen meters away across from the watering hole rattled and from behind it a… bright-colored figure, a blur whizzed into the air like the buzzing of a very, very large insect's wings flapping as it flew away. Before anyone could really react they were gone, Sentinel just following the sour-mouthed target with the turret's cannon as it sped away, buzzing through the air. Lauren barely had her wings unfolded before it disappeared, darting through the brush.

"Who- what the fuck was that?!"

"TARGET UNCONFIRMED. FLIGHT PATTERN AND PHYSICAL RESEMBLANCE SUGGESTS A SECTOID-CLASS HYBRID SPECIES. SPECULATION GIVES A 46% CHANCE OF A LEPIDAE HYBRID, 39% CHANCE OF A VESPID HYBRID, AND A 15% CHANCE OF A MANTID HYBRID.

"...A what now?"

"LEPIDAE: AN INTELLIGENT SPECIES OF INSECTOID HYBRID CONSISTING OF ROUGHLY 60% HUMAN GENOME, 30% MOTH INSECT AND 10% BUTTERFLY INSECT. A CENTAURICAL PHENOTYPE-ONLY HYBRID TYPICALLY CONSISTENT OF TWO PAIRS OF SMALL, FAST-BEATING WINGS, TWO PAIR OF LEGS AND A SINGLE PAIR OF ARMS, COVERED IN FUR WITH A THORAX-LIKE GROWTH FUNCTIONAL AS A TAIL. REVIEW OF SCANS GIVE A 87% CHANCE THAT SAID SUBJECT WAS UNARMED."

"...You think that was a scout?" I asked.

"You think the Chinese army would employ bug people?" Gabriel laughed back. "Now, the Californians, I could see that with their lip service to 'inclusiveness'. But I bet we just had a peeping tom. Lot of hybrids all over the place nowadays."

"We should probably move into town and check it out. That's where it went."

"...Well," Gabriel sighed, casually glancing back over to Kyle, who had yet to respond. "Not like we're accomplishing anything here. How do you think we should play this? Want to go in casual, without wearing body armor, put the JLTV in the back of the convoy?"

"Yeah. That's what I was thinking," I responded, and we were off.

**Chapter 28**

It used to be a ghost town, before it was renovated to more resemble what it might have looked like back in the day. A simple main street with an old courthouse, jailhouse and municipal building turned museum all in one, a general store (though renovated with a fuel pump) a couple period-correct houses down the side streets. It was all quiet, but we saw cars around, the place was definitely inhabited. It was a neat blend of old and modern, and we heavily suspected we weren't alone here.

"...Let's try the store first," I put forth, slowing the car. "Says it's open."

"Sentinel. Hold all fire. Visual scans only, report back through our holos if you see anybody. Let 'em shoot first. Greedo protocols."

"AFFIRMATIVE." Gabriel got out, wearing a T-shirt and shorts, disarmed save for his MDR slung around his back. I was dis-armored similarly, though going for one of the double-coupled magazines for my AR15 in case I needed a reload. Most everyone else went without weapons, some of us staying behind. Lauren accompanied us, though she still kept her pistol in its holster on her webgear. Gabriel, Maria, Archie, Lauren and I went in to the open shop, slowly stepping in and immediately greeted by a rather mundane looking variety shop, notably bearing a wrinkly, geriatric asian man sitting on a stool behind the counter with his arms crossed on his wide chest, a shotgun in the corner. As we looked around the place he hardly acknowledged us, it was like a painting's eerie eyes following you rather than an actual person, his eyelids the only thing moving as he gazed each of us down, barely breathing.

"Uh... Hello?" Gabriel asked, staring back.

"You. Dragon," He suddenly spat, like an animatronic coming to life. His scowl gazing into Lauren, who froze up a little. "You knock anything over with tail and wing, you buy. Be careful with big body or get out."

"Uh... Okay, s-sorry," Taken aback by his attitude, she sat her rear down, still standing at the same height though now she instantaneously seemed more cognizant of her many limbs, looking around as she stood in place, wings ruffling ever so carefully, tail twitching at the far end a little.

"You... You're not, uh, surprised to see hybrids or anything?" I asked slowly, my curiosity towards the man's steadfastness getting the best of me.

"I see dragon on news year ago. Surprise then, not now. same for one like him," He motioned with his eyes towards Archie, who was also looking about. "See more and more on the news ever since last year. Right now I see all kind of you everywhere. Less surprise. You have money to buy or just waste time?"

"You know what's going on right now, gramps?" Gabriel, who was the least startled by the shopkeeper's entire grumpy persona barked.

"Internet down. No phone no news. See hybrid like those two around. They come in store with no money to buy. I tell go away, have to chase off sometime with gun. They stupid, no listen. Brandon and Curtis and other people around say I need help them, like they say I need help tourist won't go home. Say world end, tourist go back to Vegas this morning only come back, say Vegas blow up. I no see atom bomb or missile, I no believe lie, they try trick me out of food. World not end if I still here; not care if you have dragon with gun and dog on two leg wear clothes. I say if world end, go bother Curtis who always think world end soon. I say one more time; no money, *no buy*. No credit card work either because network down. Cash only or get out."

"...Uh..." I began, just about to tell him about Vegas, but Gabriel cut me off.

"...You just have ethanol, or do you also have biodiesel? We've got enough fuel but we ought to top off before we head out."

"Yes. I have both fuel. Pump from old time when called gasoline, but is ethanol, also have biodiesel. You pay cash."

"...You take a trade?" Gabriel asked, leaning against a counter. The shopkeep paused, like the tough outer shell of his was already rocked.

"...What you have?" his mean demeanor was cracked, if only for a moment.

"We got a couple old rifles. Maybe you could-"

"Ahhh. You are mother fucker?" He reached over towards his gun, grasping the barrel and beating the stock on the ground once like a staff. "I follow law. Try to sell me gun no background check. You lucky I no get Brandon lock you up. You on thin ice. I make you leave store if not."

"I hate to break it to you gramps, but those tourists were right. Vegas is gone. We *saw* that nuke go off." Gabriel leaned on the counter. The old man scoffed, letting out a laugh as he sat there with his fingers twiddling on the gunsteel.

"You crazy. I think you-" Maria stepped forth, after pulling a bottle of coke out of one of the fridges.

"I'll buy this right now, sir. We'll see how much money we all have, I'll go around and ask." Maria pulled out a 10 from her wallet, and his persona, which had been hardening ever since we stepped in here was suddenly disarmed, his face brightening somewhat.

"Good. Nine dollar." He gave her the change, which she pocketed, before she pulled out the utility knife sheathed at her waist, using the bottle opener on the back end to pop it open and taking a swig, him smiling viciously at us.

"...You get resupplied lately?" Maria asked calmly between swigs, putting her knife away.

"Shipment late. Cell tower down so no fix. When cell back online I fine. Not stupid a-poc-a-lypse." He waved her inference away with a flick of his wrist.

"...When's the company coming here to fix it, then?"

"Brandon and Eduardo say things bad. Lot of cell towers down because hacker cause trouble. Not big problem. If company no come I get Edwardo do it or won't give him dirty Japanese comic he order and send to my store; he no have address, live out in desert and order through me. He already into hybrids before they on news, want fuck. He crazy mother fucker." Suddenly, the back door beside the shopkeeper swung open, and out stepped a quite peculiar and relevant individual, whose visage was more than familiar.

"Trùm! xuống đườ-" This… girl stopped short, freezing in place, wings ruffling. A moth-like hybrid, like Sentinel had hypothesized, covered in bright yellow fur wearing a set of loose-fitting overalls somewhat renovated for her odd body and a pair of goggles tipped up onto her forehead which fell down as her forehead feelers twitched, needing her to pull them off, and the entire back end of her denim overalls cut out to accommodate her secondary and tertiary torsos, her thorax-like tail twitching as her big buggy eyes with black sclera saw us all, her completely bisected jaw slack and the feelers on her forehead twitching, elf-like ears also twitching as her big buggy ice blue eyes gazed us all down, her arms, which had been outstretched for a moment as she burst through the door were now relegated at her sides, slowly curling towards each other as she stood there on three legs, one of her frontal legs still midair before slowly coming down to the ground with a pat.

"*Nó là gì?! ồn ào!*" The shopkeep began to yell back in the language the two of them shared, Vietnamese if I had to guess, The moth girl blushing deeply as she gulped, smoothing down her fuzzy yellow mane of hair with one of her chitchinous arms. I was looking her over slowly, intrigued with her physical body, how her body seemed to be sharing chitin shell exoskeleton and fleshy or furry skin, her front, chest and underbelly seeming to be soft flesh, the biceps of her arms also displayed flesh through her shell-like exterior, horn-like nubs around her twitching feelers on her head.

"...Is she with you?" Gabriel asked as soon as their back-and-forth cooled to a viable pause to interject.

"This Con-yay. She like other hybrid. Stupid and look like bug, but know more than just stupid English. She want to work for food and sleep in back, I say why not, but she can not fix cell tower. She always take break and no come back for long time. Stupid." This hybrid girl stood there, blushing somewhat, also somewhat flustered at our presence.

"Well jeez, I try my best," She muttered back, scratching her neck. She looked like standing upright she was a hair taller than me, but the way she held herself she seemed a lot smaller than she really was.

"Connie, huh?" Gabriel uttered, folding his arms. "You're the one who lit off on us when we were at the watering hole, eh?" She gazed back, still with her mouth pursed as her eyes darted, nodding briskly.

"...how do you know his language? You don't have an accent," Lauren asked, out of curiosity.

"I dunno. I just do. I heard him talk in it and I just... got it."

"See?" The shopkeep said again. "She stupid. Fly around and be lazy." Connie glared back at him in an instant, opening her mouth to speak back in Vietnamese, the two of them arguing for a moment.

"...You think *you* know any other languages?" Gabriel asked over his shoulder to Lauren, who was given pause, eyes going blank for a moment.

"I dunno," she uttered. "...Probably?"

"Look, how about we leave these two to it and go see if we can't get the money from everybody else," Maria proposed, walking past me and out into the open door, and as chitinous feet shuffled behind us, Connie calling out in a moment, we were already outside and upon this new scene, just as bizarre as the last, Connie just about to warn us about something.

It was... peculiar, but peculiar only *began* to describe it. A man stood in the middle of the road, already having been addressing the rest of us that were still with the vehicles. Sentinel's guns were bearing down on him, but he stood there, defiant, and... dressed up like a cowboy, long flowing coat with a shining star pinned to it, standing akimbo like a legendary gunfighter from ancient days. It was somehow one of the weirder things I'd seen, this man in full western garb standing there bow-legged with his fists at his hips, a well-twirled moustache on his face and a ten gallon hat on his head.

"Hey! You there! You the leaders of this rag-tag gang of *rustlers* Connie come'n tell me about?!" He bellowed at us, his shtick complete with a rustic accent as we came out, Connie blasting out behind and nearly grabbed me by the shoulder, pausing dead on the new scene unfolding. "Connie's been tellin me about some troublemakers come into town, shooting off their guns. Now as the law round here, I regret to inform you that you ladies and gentlemen need to mind yourselves!"

"...Who the fock is'is dafthouse?" Archie let out, though not entirely out of the hearing of this strange man.

"I," he was loud and clear, dramatically repeating himself. "Am Sherriff Brandon R. Hayes, as appointed by the Lincoln County of this good state of Nevada!" He polished the tin star on his lapel with the cuff of his jacket sleeve, Gabriel looking around a little, his face well displaying a joyous humor.

"Uh… Is this guy for real?" I asked back at Connie who was behind me, Connie nervously fiddling her fingers together as she glanced around.

"I SHALL HAVE YOU KNOW THAT I MAY BE ONE MAN," He was quick to bellow before Connie could explain herself. He brought out a tin can from his pocket, inexplicably carried around for some reason. He tossed it down the road, and it lay in the dirt for a moment. He reached down for his pistol, a period-fitting single-action revolver befitting of his character, however he brought up nothing but a finger and thumb, his hand in the shape of a gun and pointed it at the can. "BUT I AM ENDOWED WITH THE POWER OF-"

Zing, snap, boom. An echoing gunshot filling the entire town, a far-off sniper evidently as the can was tossed through the air with a plume of dust blowing up the sand, a gigantic hole ripped through it. Sheriff Brandon jumped some, before letting out a "Ver-DAMMIT Eduardo!" His hand shot back down to his jacket, breaking character to screech into a walkie-talkie. "Deputy, you were supposed to shoot when I say *bang*! Did you see me recoil this here finger gun?!" Silence, though the fact that he kept the accent was indubitably charming. "Eduardo, I swear to god I will de-deputize-"

"Agh- sorry," a female voice let through. "This- its M-Miia. Eddie said it was boring and stupid and he started walking down a while ago." Silence as we all watched this spectacle with reserved amusement and confusion, Brandon's face contorting in a mighty scowl as he was still working through a response. "...I hit the can, right?" Her voice was tiny and barely brimming with hope, yet creaking.

"Dammit Miia! You tell that boy… You tell him…" He was glaring at us as he spoke, evidently without a real way to keep the cowboy act up and say something that wasn't anachronistic, though at this point with an electronic device in his grasp the jig was up.

"*Jesus*, Mr. Hayes," A voice called, walking up the road behind the rambunctious Sheriff. A thin and lithe young hispanic man walked, garbed in multicam head to toe, save for his opened overshirt showing an obnoxiously colored japanese Idol-Girl shirt underneath, exasperated as could be, an incredibly fancy looking pistol with a bright cherry red grip in the holster on his hip. "...I don't have time for your stupid games. If they were here to shoot the place up they would have started already."

"Deputy! You-"

"Sorry about him, he takes his 'job' way too seriously," Eduardo muttered to us, going and passing all of us with hardly a notice, going for the shop. More strange silence as we collectively processed the goings-ons one bit at a time.

"...You really a sheriff?" Gabriel put forth as Brandon was evidently unable to salvage the act at this point, staring into the inside of his hat.

"I wasn't lyin'. I'm the law in this township."

"...He's a government official overseeing the historical museum," Eduardo sighed in the doorway, still entering the building. "He's only sherriff because he bugged the authorities enough to let him 'be' one. It doesn't mean anything."

"You shut your yap, boy!" Eduardo rolled his eyes, disappearing into the general store. Brandon rubbed his eyes. "Goddamn. I had that all planned out and he goes and ruins my moment. I was gonna say, I got the power of god, and finger-bang that tin can, and Eduardo was supposed to zing it with his fifty cal right then."

"I... I didn't h-hit it?" The voice on the other end of the walkie talkie, this Miia girl's voice was practically splitting in sadness, evidently listening. Brandon sighed again.

"No, you hit it... Good shot." Brandon was sighing as her mood changed in an instant, squealing.

"Really?! Eeee! I've never shot this far before. I'm gonna come get it for a trophy," Miia was evidently more than happy at this point.

"Sentinel, how far was that shot?" Sentinel was already aiming into the hills.

"I APPROXIMATE EIGHT HUNDRED AND SEVENTY-TWO METERS WITH ONE HUNDRED SEVENTY-NINE METERS ELEVATION. I APPROXIMATE 1.135 SECONDS OF BULLET TRAVEL FROM AN ESTIMATED FIFTY-BROWNING-MACHINE-GUN CARTRIDGE. SHALL I RETURN FIRE?" I saw in my hologlasses a little blip appear in my vision on the hills nearby, evidently a marker of Miia's position when she took the shot. I noticed a gleam there.

"Damn, She's either lucky or good, probably a little bit of both," Gabriel uttered.

"R-return fire?" Brandon uttered, finally worried for the first time.

"Stand down, she's not a problem," Gabriel ordered.

"AIR VEHICLE APPROACHING FROM SAME BEARING, BE ADVISED."

"Oh my GOD, old man!" came from inside the store. "Are you *fucking* with me now? You've had my new Jojo issue for a *week*?!" I turned, peeking inside.

"Fuck you pervert! Go fix cell tower! Cell company no come! Only then I give dirty magazine!"

"This one's not even a hentai! It's just a *manga*!" I could tell by his pronunciation that he was a... True *connoisseur* of Japanese culture.

"Jojo?" Gabriel scoffed, mostly to himself, though he eyed to Daniel in the car, who he figured was the most likely to get the reference. "Arraki's still alive, huh? Fucker's a goddamn vampire."

"I no care! All dirty japanese! Go fix tower!" Eduardo was sighing outrageously at the shopkeep's pigheadedness, pinching the bridge of his nose.

"...I already told you, there's nothing wrong with the tower! There's something going on that's keeping-"

"Blah blah, keeping what? World no end! I still here! You say you no have address living out in stupid bunker, you get me to receive your packages, I see them and it keep me up at night think how you look this garbage! Fuck you!" At this point, one of those flying bikes with the downward-facing turbines was approaching, buzzing incessantly and wavering this way and that as its pilot wrestled with the controls, finally plunking it down right before our JLTV. A girl had been driving it, human at the very first glance, but at first what I thought to be bags of things hanging off the side of the rotor-zipperbike, did I realise that this was a hybrid, one of the ones with a snake for a lower body with said lower body slung all about the vehicle, though her upper portion was that of a young woman, completely human-looking save for fanged teeth when she spoke, bright orange irises and scaled accents on the corners of her face, flowing red hair and most distinctively of her human half were her two long elf-like ears, red like the scales of her long tail under her miniskirt as she tumbled off, a gigantic rifle slung around her back.

"Wooh, jeez, they sure don't make these for my kind," She patted Eduardo's vehicle while we were all still reeling in this rapid-fire spectacle, dropping the rifle by its carry handle onto its bipod to sit there on the ground as she appreciated relieving herself of twenty pounds of weight with a sigh. She looked over to Sheriff Brandon, who nodded subtly as she slithered over to pick up the can she'd ripped in half from such a distance, squealing. "Look, Connie! Mr. Hayes! I really hit it!" She uttered breathlessly, the very end of her tail whipping around like a dog wagging its tail, practically swatting one of Lauren's legs, who stepped back some in surprise.

"Er... yeah. Nice shot." Brandon was still evidently a little shamed, having had his entire act turned on its head, though now that he stood before the one who messed it up he couldn't bring himself to tear down her adorable enthusiasm. Connie contented herself to congratulate the ecstatic Miia with a simple little chitinous thumbs up.

"*God*, you're so dense," Eduardo came back out to put his fists on his hips and sigh, rolling his eyes. For the first time did he really acknowledge us with a nod, our eyes shifting around from Brandon, Miia, Connie and him, the awkward silence so solemn you could practically hear us blinking.

"...Is that an FK BRNO?" Gabriel put forth, pointing to Eduardo's hip, breaking the silence.

"Yeah, actually, most people just think it's a CZ."

"...It basically is," Brandon let out and Eduardo gave him a glare.

"How do you like it? I hear the ammo's a bitch to find,"

"Yeah, it packs a punch though," He uttered. "Saw it in GasPunk and I wanted one ever since."

"Oh shit, GasPunk, that's a great anime," Gabriel smiled. "Last season felt tacked on, though. Didn't even have a villain after he got killed in season four."

"Yeah, you know, the studio probably just wanted to milk the franchise at that point and there was a lot of filler content in the manga they still hadn't explored."

"Of course, of course," Gabriel responded in kind.

"Ed! Check it out! I hit it!" Miia waved the can through the air.

"Nice shot Miia," Eduardo said, doing his best to smile back, Connie standing off to the side, still nervously looking around, feelers and wings twitching as Miia was still reveling in her accomplishment.

"So, uhh... You folks passing through or what?" Brandon asked slowly, polishing his tin star.

"Yeah." There weren't any crickets around, but my mind filled in the blanks.

"You guys... come in from Vegas?" Another round of sighs. Inconvenient realities.

"Yeah." I guess it went without saying that we looked the part- armed up, antsy and tired.

"You know what's going on?" Brandon asked, glancing over the radioactive question that was more than present in his mind. Yet another barrage of heavy sighs.

"Aside from the bomb, no." More silence, more imaginary crickets. Miia was now sheepishly grasping her trophy as she stood there, tugging at her blouse with a free hand, the scene having died out into melancholy utterances.

"What's up with your vehicle? And last I checked you couldn't exactly get power armor in the local surplus store."

"We went through an Elrond facility looking for supplies," Gabe said, figuring to go for the truth here, or at least most of it. "Guy there was rather generous."

"No shit?" Brandon chuckled, just for the sake of making noise as he walked up to it, looking the JLTV up and down, before noticing the bullet marks on the bullet-resistant carapace of my own jeep. He chuckled to himself wearily. "What's with you?" He asked to Kyle, who was zip-tied to the rollcage in the chuck of the jeep, staring over his shoulder in melancholy.

"He's on time-out. He's not taking everything so well with what's going on and flipped out," Gabriel reasoned before Kyle could speak for himself, though it didn't look like Kyle was going to start speaking anytime soon.

"Huh."

"You, uh…" Brandon went on. "So you don't have news."

"It sounds like if anybody should know, it should be Eduardo," Gabriel put forth looking over to him. His face washed out a little as he stood slumped against the wall. "On account of his bunker and all."

"Oh, for- god dammit old man," Eduardo muttered of the shopeep in the store. "Him and his big fucking mouth. I guess it doesn't matter now," He reasoned. "Look, I- I just-"

"You don't strike me as a apocalypse prepper," I put in as he stammered.

"I'm not. I got the place in an auction. I made a couple million during the Crypto resurgence in '57. I just prefer to be left alone so I can watch my anime and play my video games in peace. Still doesn't matter if I have to order by proxy through a nosy old man," Eduardo snarled.

"Jesus, you must have been fifteen by how you look," Gabe put in.

"Sixteen, actually." We were all blinking as we gazed at him. Even our hybrids who ought to have been out of the loop were similarly "getting" the oddity of the situation.

"…Can we see your place?"

"Wait, d-don't you guys want to see the museum? I swear it's just as hip," Brandon suddenly jutted in, for fear of being cut off, motioning to the historical building to his right.

"…The alien museum?" Lauren put forth, ears popping up eagerly. Brandon sighed.

"God dammit. Curtis and his stupid… ugh!" Brandon, despite being some-odd forty or fifty years old, stomped off into his museum down the road, slamming the door.

"…Well?" Gabriel turned back to Eduardo, who was also sighing.

We split up to check out the town and Edwardo's bunker, Gabe, Lauren, Archie and I leaving our rifles and going along into the bunker, the rest of us staying in town to relax, check out said museums, Maria sticking back to top off the fuel, get money out of everyone for fuel and some nicer things to eat than just protein powder and MREs. Eduardo's bunker was a peculiar, yet familiar place. My dad had a lot of friends who'd dug or otherwise inhabited their own bunkers. It was familiar like that, coming up to that heavy steel door after a short romp through a small cave beneath some unassuming big rock. Eduardo spoke a word or two into the PA system and the place opened ever so slowly, Eduardo and Miia walking and slithering on in.

"...That's a Hard Target Interdiction, huh?" Gabriel pointed out Eduardo's fifty caliber rifle, of which Miia had fired and was carrying.

"Yeah. Shoots like a dream. Ever since I saw it in-"

"-Boku no Ameratsu?"

"Nah, actually just Alloy Cog Hardened Six. you know, it's Silence's gun."

"Mm, woulda been my second guess," Gabriel put forth, Lauren tagging along behind me and Archie off to the side looking over the walls of the cave as we stood before the opening doors. "Just don't tell me Silence is your waifu."

"You fucking with me? The Captain is the best waifu in the series. Silence is a total pleb choice for casuals that only played the last game."

"Shit, man. You don't have half bad taste," Gabriel laughed, the two of them sharing a chuckle as the rest of us twiddled our thumbs. "...I've got an MDR by the same company. They make some nice guns."

"Shit, what's that again? Their automatic, right? That's what our special forces use or something, right?"

"Yeah, that's it. You dig DesertTech?" We steadily walked into the foyer of Ed's bunker, as he clapped, activating the lights. Tacky.

"I dunno. I only like buying guns I've seen."

"Heh, so you are a pleb, just perusing into guns and buying 'em if you see 'em in your chinese cartoons."

"...Uh... Anime's Japanese, right?" I put forth, the two of them pausing to antagonistically look back on me, like I was missing a joke or something. It was stupid and I shook it off.

"Woah, what's with this place?" Lauren was walking about the entrance hall and airlock, seeing the MOPP gear hanging up, armor carriers, a couple power armor suits autonomously standing in the corners near their working gear, currently deactivated. "...Oh wow, it's just like Sentinel," Lauren went up to one of them, dinking the helmet with a fingernail. Even without counting her horns, she was about half a head taller than the tallest armor in the room.

"Sentinel' is the name of the program in them to help them move. Every modern suit has them in some way or another," Ed explained slowly enough to Lauren, who nodded.

"...I wonder if somebody could make *me* some power armor," Lauren mused, her leg scuffing the ground. I looked up, seeing that there was a secondary exit, a ladder presumably reaching all the way up to the top of the hill.

"So some guy built this place back in '44 when it looked like the world was coming to an end back then. Decided that it wasn't, so he tried to cut his losses and I lucked out. Sucks for him, huh?" Ed laughed, entering into the living quarters, their little battlestations. People sat about, all humans save for one Draconic seated at the table, an engineer barcode obvious on his shoulder. Acoss from him was an obese African American man sitting at the table and on the couch a gruff and unassuming dirty white guy, a thin and tall neon-haired girl leaning her back against his side, everyone on their electronic devices, the pudgier black guy stil engrossed in his high-end VR headgear, the girl on her holos and tablet and the homely looking fellow on his laptop with the holographic display active.

"Jeez, way to welcome our guests," Miia muttered as she slithered through, going over into the armory room, the door open where I could see her hang the big rifle up onto the display wall. I could make out a reloading bench, a workbench, lathe and a mill, a 3D printer and all sorts of other goodies, guns, ammo and gun parts laying all about that room.

"Yeah yeah," The girl on the couch still enthralled by her VR holos and tablet raised an arm to wave Miia off.

"Hell of a squad, huh?" Ed was pacing about. "We're seeing what we can dig up from the network, a little datamining operation. Though we could get into shit for a little while, now the shit's basically down to LAN range after Vegas… y'know." While Eduardo was extrapolating, Lauren was ducking about, head bowed to avoid knocking her horns against the concrete ceiling, wings shifting self-consciously.

"…We ain't found shit," The average-looking guy said.

"So you don't know who blew up Vegas?" Gabe asked again.

"…I did some trajectory analysis," The rotund one uttered, apparently paying attention after all, like they all apparently were. "Whoever sent it was close. Might have been off the coast. Maybe even within the continent."

"…But you don't know who did it."

"a fuckin Alloy Cog, maybe. You never know if they made 'em in real life, government could have some nuclear-equipped mechs in operation." Gabe laughed back, amused enough.

"…Is… Was all this legal?" I'd poked my head into the armory, Miia still organizing the gear after somebody else had evidently moved a few of the guns in here, Grumbling as she finally left to slither past me. I turned to look back at Ed, Miia going for presumably her own room to put her shot-up can up as a trophy, clutched proudly in her hand all the while.

"…I took up gunsmithing as a way to generate side-revenue, that and selling my computational power to companies. And crypto mining."

"…Those AR15s in there look like their fire selector have an extra slot."

"Look, no shit I'm not squeaky clean but I keep my hands cleaner than you think, alright? Shit's fucked right now so I figure it'll be useful."

"Does Brandon know about this?"

"You kidding me?" He laughed breathlessly, his friends also temporarily bemused. "Every gun that Brandon has in that "police station" tacked onto the historical museum that isn't a cowboy era museum piece, are guns I made for him. Let's just say that some of his machine guns aren't exactly dealer post-samples." It was Gabriel's turn to laugh breathlessly, Lauren still standing about, twiddling her fingers, Ed waltzing over into the kitchen to grab a drink. Archie went over to see what Ed's friends were working on out of sheer curiosity, and I stole a glance as well. Most of them seemed to be just playing video games at the moment, save for the newest member, that draconic guy actually sifting through some files. Probably busywork. I laughed a little bit.

"...This can't be all of your facilities, huh?" I put forth.

"Oh, fuck no. We've got grow floors for oxygen and redundant food sourcing every other floor. Power comes from a geothermal deep-shaft, got a redundant bunkspace floor, another recreation floor, waterworks and aquaponics purification at the bottom. Guy who built the place was committed. Take a gander," He bid us towards what was evidently a stairwell, Gabe and I entering as Lauren stooped in, bonking her horns against the rim of the doorway as she did with a simple "ow", with me taking a second to look back and see she was alright, watching her give a tentative smile and thumbs up as she brushed a strand of hair out of her eye. We advanced down into the next floor, to enter rows upon rows of greenery stretching for quite a while. "It's a nice little operation. Used it to grow green before shit started popping off, think I'm going to go for more eat-able stuff since I can't exactly sell the weed right now," I was eyeing the large surplus of marijuana plants, the entire place lit up with simulated sunlight. Kind of similar to Anon's dome with a holographic sky projection, though not quite as fancy, how I could easily see the concrete ceiling behind the sunny hologram. "I've got a few protein synthesizers down below in aquaponics but I could use more. I didn't expect for all this shit to go down so I'll have to improvise a little. Slim eatings but it's better than nothing. Joey could use to lose some weight, after all." He chuckled to himself.

"You know what weed is, Green?" Gabe laughed. "Marijuana?"

"...It's like beer that you smoke, right?" Lauren responded.

"Heh, Miia said the same thing," Ed said. "...And a lot of the other hybrids."

"...fuckin' Creators."

"Bottom floor's got the geothermal probe extending way past it, also got our water. Even got a swimming pool. Heated using the excess energy of the geothermals, hell of a sauna. You wanna relax?"

"Honestly, sorta tired of the water," Lauren was the first to break the pause as she eyed about. By how she stood and teetered in place, I figured she was a little claustrophobic. "I could use some fresh air though."

"Oh, life support's regulated perfectly. Oxegenation, humidity, it's-"

"-I mean I want to go outside," Lauren uttered. Brandon stopped awkwardly, Gabriel laughing at the awkwardness.

"...Yeah. We've got that, I guess."

### Chapter 29

"Ahh. God, it's so much better to be out here. I can hardly stand small spaces," Lauren uttered, stretching her wings and arms as we came out into the open clearing, stamping her feet a little in the soil. "I don't see how you can stand being in a place like that. Or going into the facility like you did. I *hated* that place." She paused to shiver for a little bit as we stood there. "Did I mention that I really appreciate what you, Gabe and Archie did going in there? I mean I'm just saying that because I could never have gone back in there. God, what a fucking mess."

"I dunno, it's got some charm to it," I uttered as we started walking, just the two of us. "There was this big underground dome."

"That one with the spotlights and it's nothing but concrete? Brrr," She shivered yet again, crossing her arms over her chest and gripping her opposing biceps for dramatic effect. "There were so many *creeps* there. I never want to think about that place ever again."

"No, the other one," I put in, Lauren looking over to me quizzically all of a sudden.

"The one Katt was in? The forest one?"

"No, I didn't see that one. I mean the other one."

"...Really? There was a third?" She slowly enunciated as we walked through brush and scrub towards the northwest end of the town, the long way around as I grappled the sling of my rifle to amble down a big rock face without having it flop about, Lauren behind me.

"Yeah. Dunno if there are only three in that facility, but it... It has secret entrances but it's really big. It's this giant future city under a dome." I looked back at her as I hit dirt again, watching her there towering above me standing on the rock, biting her cheek with her molars with a furrowed brow, sort of a frustrated surprise, like being cheated readable on her muzzled face.

"...Nobody told me about a *city* in there," She muttered aloud as she slid down the rocks, wings keeping her stable as she bounced on down and we walked on through the shaded gulch.

"Yeah. Not really a city, just a testing ground for their new tech. It's actually bigger than the rest of the facility entirely. They uh, had a bunch of neat stuff in there, where they were testing their flying cars. The whole place is like something from a sci-fi movie, the guy who designed the place is basically running it now. Kind of a weirdo."

"...Okay, now you're just messing with me."

"No, really. Gabe, Archie, Selicia, they'll tell you all the same stuff. Ask them what color the sky was. It was fuckin' purple. Guy who made it calls the place Prosperia."

"Mm, I don't doubt you less with all of that super believable information. Sure." I rolled my eyes as we ambled along.

"Just ask any of them, alright? It was pretty cool. Almost made up for the rest of the place."

"Yeah, yeah." I watched her as we walked side by side, how she looked back over to me with that friendly smile of hers. She was having fun, wasn't she? Even if the facility was a bad memory to her she could still make light of it. It was something that glowed within her, how she could make the best of any situation, even a horrible memory. However, while I was lost in my mind over my admiration of her, she let out an "ow" as one of her horns clipped a tree branch when she'd turned her head down to watch her step over some rocks. "Fucking- Ugh!" she let out, that good mood of hers dashed a little bit as she paused in her tracks. I didn't think much of it at the time, stopping to look back, but she refused to move onward, going to lean on the trunk of that tree and look upwards at the branches, sighing.

"You alright?"

"...Oh, god dammit. I'm just... Ugh." She spat in the dirt behind me, wings ruffling. "Yeah. I'm fine... But..." I gazed into her as she formulated her words, those great big brown eyes coming back down to me finally like an admission of defeat. "That... Goddamn bitch. Does she really have to come along? The spider." I sighed through my nose. Back when I first heard about how Selicia was coming along, I figured my fellow humans would have the biggest problem with her, and I didn't even consider the hybrids of our group, especially not

Lauren. "I mean, I- I just don't- She…" Lauren trailed off, furling her lips and brow as she gazed into the horizon before sighing again, hair drooping down off her head as she worked through her self-frustration. "God, she's *infuriating*. Gabriel needs to put his foot down about her."

"Yeah, he does," I conceded. Lauren let out an uneasy laugh.

"Shit, it's obvious, isn't it? God." I finally noticed that, this entire time she'd been scratching her neck and jaw. I blinked for a moment, before her hand went back down, uneasily mussing with her other arm as her wings ruffled and we walked again.

"…Did what she say get to you?" I asked.

"W-what, did you- would you… If somebody came up to you and told you you were designed to eat people, how would you respond? *Fffuck*."

"You… You weren't designed to, you…"

"They did this shit to me. Made me this oversized freak with extra legs. It's like every day I feel more and more like a monster. God, I'm the biggest one in the group and I hate it. I feel like that's what everyone sees me as. Now I'm a huge monster that eats people. What's next? God fucking dammit. *Fucking* Creators." She fumbled with a little rock with her talon, looking down on it and her frontal legs in general as she did.

"…To be fair, she's a lot weirder than you are. Like, that's just my opinion but she's definitely more of a freak than you."

"It doesn't even bother her," Lauren sputtered, finally flicking that rock away with a snap of her talon-like toes. "God. She's such a tease." Another long pause. "I guess I'm kind of envious, y'know? How she can just be like that and *worry* less. I feel like all anybody sees of me is a monster with wings. Now I'm a monster with wings that eats people."

"…I don't think of you that way," I put back, putting on a defensive voice. More to make her really think about what she was saying. She furled her lip and brow, exhaling through flared nostrils.

"…Do you really?" She put forth, and now it was my turn to stop in my tracks, filled with indignation. "Like, deep down, do you-" She'd continued on and not really noticed my stopping. Maybe she was too lost in her own mind to really pay creedence to how I would respond. I had to interrupt her.

"I don't. Don't act like I do. If I thought you were a monster do you think I would have vouched for you? Really, you're just going to act like you don't give a shit about what I fronted for you?" I was still trying to keep smiling, but there really was something personal behind this. Something beyond just pissing in the wind. She stopped too, looking back. Sighing, the both of us just sighing. She wasn't hurt, more like she was trying to believe me. Not really believe what I'd just said but more that she was trying to believe the whole point of what I was saying. "You know I really hate it when you beat up on yourself." She turned back.

"We're back on the road. Getting close, aren't we?" The topic change was brutally jarring as she avoided my confrontation, but we needed to talk about something else anyways. Yet another sigh flew from her mouth like a shotgun blast nearly as violent as this shift-of-mind. "Look, that's got to be it." She was out in front anyways, going up onto the road to wave over to the museum. "Hey!! Is this the alien museum?!" She cried, as whoever was out there over near the door cried something back that neither of us could really hear. I took note of how fortified the entrance was, not really striking me until I approached behind the slowing Lauren, seeing the person there out in front jumping around and fiddling with a large contraption of tubes, suddenly pointed towards the both of us.

"Hold it right there!" He cried and we slowed to a stop.

"...I'm assuming you're Curtis?" Lauren uttered, closer than I.

"More of you alien bastards. Jesus, there's more of you every day."

"Ex- Excuse me?" Lauren's head cocked off just barely to the side, and her posture went from defensive to offensive, leaning forward a bit as if to ask for clarification as aggressively as possible, though her tone and conscious mind was yet to become offensive.

"Don't you play dumb, *alien*. You won't fool me," He pulled off his helmet for a second, showing the inside of it lined with shiny foil, before hurriedly sticking it back on. "You can't use your demon brainwave blast on me because I know what you are. We didn't make you. You really think *we* made you? Government is already full of you and you're gonna take over the planet. Over my dead body." By the arch of her brow far exceeding the disdainful curling of her lip, Lauren was obviously more perplexed than offended, stopped dead there as we stood there. I was probably more offended than she was, seeing as I had quite a eventful adventure in one of these places this man was claiming didn't exist, crouched there behind the sandbags with that ridiculous looking set of tubes and gauges formed into the shape of a gun pointing toward us.

"Uh… I'm, I… I'm not?" Lauren was beside herself in perplexion.

"See, that's exactly what they'd, what you'd say. *Alien.* Your kind may have fooled Ed, and fooled Brandon and even Mr. Truong, but I can see you for what you are. Ain't no brainwaves gonna get me, you big lizard. You think you're-"

"Ex-ex*cuse me*?" Lauren suddenly spouted, her threshhold having been crossed. "Did you just call me a *lizard*?! I'm warm-blooded! Do you *see* my *tits*?!" Lauren's indignance surprised this kook just barely more than it surprised me as she groped her own chest in rage. "You see this?!" She grabbed her fuzzy scalp with one hand and pointed with the other. "You see any fucking *iguanas* with this shit?! It's not a fucking wig! Are you *dense* or just an asshole?!"

Silence took over as Lauren steamed, This guy sitting there with his eyes wide, almost like he was presented with some stark counter-evidence. Of course I expected him to double down, crouched behind his little barrier, setting his weapon's stock against the sandbags and pulling off his helmet. He looked into the tinfoil lining inside, shuffling with it a bit, his eyes peeking back up at Lauren defensively who still had her arms crossed and one of her frontal legs trembling on the ground restlessly, the hand-like paw-talon limb gritting itself into the sand as she scowled mightily, flaring her nostrils with a horse-like snorting exhale and a furled lower lip. He finally put his helmet back on, gazing back up.

"...You, uh… You're a lot better at acting like an earthling than the rest of them, I'll give you that."

"Well, it's because I *am* an 'earthling', jackass. This is my planet too. I was born- or made, made here, whatever. You see me wearing a space suit? Does my gun look like it shoots lasers? I know one language and that's English." More silence. "...Probably," She whispered, more to me and kind of as a joke than to him, as he sat there in contemplation on how to justify his mindset.

"The aliens probably just sent you 'hybrids' down as sleeper agents. Something to change the uh… moral fiber of Earth to suit them. Or something. Just because they brainwashed you to forget everything and sent you down here doesn't mean you're native to Earth." Another pause, Lauren sighing. She looked over to me.

"You want to head back into town? Brandon's museum might be boring but at least I'm allowed to see it."

"W-wait, you're here to actually see the museum?" He suddenly interjected. "Actually- hey. Look, I- Maybe- yeah. I'm sorry about being so brash. You... I can give you a tour if you want." Lauren and I turned back to this guy slowly, still reeling in perplexion.

"...Wwhyyyy?" Lauren uttered, drawn-out in sheer skepticism, her eyes drawn like blades. He fiddled with his helmet.

"...Maybe if you see your history, the brainwashing might wear off. Maybe you'll remember your spaceship diagrams. If you suddenly remember how to build your F-t-L drives, That'd be worth it to me. But you gotta promise that if you suddenly remember everything you tell me. For science, of course. And you say I was right." Lauren sighed again.

"Fuck it. Okay. If I remember, I'll not only tell you about all of our wondrous alien technologies but I'll even tell you where I parked my flying saucer and give you the keys."

"Hey, if you're not gonna take this seriously you can go hang out with Brandon and listen to his delusional roleplaying. I mean it."

"I'm serious."

"You sure?"

"I swear by the dragon-centaur home planet of Kazerad Five." Lauren's face was steeled in exasperation putting her right hand up as if swearing herself into court despite her runaway rolling eyes.

"Whatever. But when you remember you also have to apologize for being such a jerk about it," He said, hefting back up the weird-looking tube assembly weapon and bidding us come inside.

Entering was interesting, to say the least. Kind of an old-fashioned place, like a big log cabin. It was one big room, little diorama displays of crashed flying saucers, ancient black and white and grainy color pictures of little gray men on operating tables and body bags.

"Now, most people think about New Mexico when you hear about aliens- that's the state to our southeast, you lost a saucer there about a century ago in 1947- that's Roswell. Ring any bells?"

"...I'll... I'll let you know," Lauren muttered back, still looking out to that particular diorama, the one closest to the door, the introduction to this place.

"So, yeah. You guys tend to like the entire American Southwest, not just New Mexico. Lots of lights out here. There's the Aztec extraterrestrial recovery in '49- *nineteen* forty-nine, that was also New Mexico but pretty much on the other side of the state. In 1950 there was a UFO flyby in Fort Worth, Texas to the east." Every new tidbit he pointed out he paused to look back at Lauren, who was still beyond stern, though I guess from how the very corner of her lip curled upwards that this was funny enough in its own little way. "...The Lubbock Lights in Texas, the Mariana UFO incident. Then there's the Robertson Panel incident, where a bunch of you slipped up your cloaking tech above our capitol and we even made a friggin' branch of the CIA about it."

"...What's this place?" Lauren had since moved over, pointing to a diorama of some air force base that was overwhelmingly primarily landing strips.

"South-southwest of here is Area 51. It's our biggest holding facility for you guys," He erroneously exposed. I could barely hold my tongue, figuring that Lauren already knew that was false and Curtis was beyond convincing. "They've got a real operation going. Reverse-engineering your tech. You heard about that new quantum levitation technology they're gonna start making flying cars with? We didn't design that. We took it off of your ships. It's like the B2 bomber and SR-71 Blackbird and the Helicopter and the atom bomb and plastic furniture for guns all over again. Same old shit."

"...So why'd it take you guys a hundred years?" Lauren put forth, intertwining her fingers into a big fist that she let hang below her hip area, cocking her head off to the side with those squinting, inquisitory eyes. Curtis' face went blank for a second.

"...We can't just unveil this tech all at once. The government's got to slowly put it out so as not to upset the status quo. Even you alien-human hybrids are old news, ever since the Nazis used alien tech to try to make a clone army to keep the war going, even invaded Britain."

"What if one of the other countries mass produces like, alien super laser guns and jet packs and takes your country over in an instant?" Lauren was apt to reply.

"You kidding me? The UN is more than just a formality. Everyone's all just shadow-sleeper states. You think that like, like the US and China are ruled by different people? Hah. You really are brainwashed. Your kind probably rules us all anyways. And if it's not you specifically, maybe you're just like, the combination of Earth genes with theirs so they can assimilate the Earth easier."

"...Sooo, you roll these crazy future inventions out slowly, but all the countries agree to do it together because we're all ruled by aliens, but the aliens didn't just come down and enslave us- sorry, *you*, with their already existing superior technology and instead slowly let you reverse-engineer it, which means that them taking earth over will now be more difficult now that earthlings have better tech that aliens gave them, but slowly." She paused to glare at him, knowing full well how ridiculously convoluted it all was.

"You're forgetting about the mental programming and mind-control being rolled out with the technology." Lauren sighed, masking the sigh good enough. Curtis really was on a roll, but I couldn't fault Lauren for giving it a shot.

"What's with your, uh... weapon?" I asked to break the tension, pointing over to that big assembly.

"Oh, that's my own design. This is my pneumatic toggle-action automatic," He went back over to pick the big ridiculous thing up. "This is better than any gun you can buy on the market. Fires a seventy caliber rifled-sabot projectile at eight hundred feet per second, accurate to three hundred yards. Zero chemical residue and super quiet- Eduardo and Brandon tell me that since it's an airgun it's okay to put a silencer on it. Aliens can't track my carbon footprint this way." I was prompted to smile at his quaint misuse of terminology.

"...You didn't just build this because you're legally not allowed to own firearms, right?" I said, trying to keep a straight face.

"...N-no... It's better than a gun. It runs off air. Air's free."

"*Okay.*" I was blushing as I beamed in amusement. I knew more than a few people who weren't allowed to own guns who turned to... alternative means of projectile acceleration. I didn't feel like pushing him since he technically was holding an automatic cannon, overly complex and hilariously gimmicky as it was.

"Got others like it. Spearguns and crossbows, mostly. I don't consider myself a scientist but I guess I fit the definition."

"Hm, yeah of course," I added, barely keeping a straight face.

"...So how come these guys all look like you?" Lauren was over near the "The Aliens Themselves" diorama, the little green and grey men. "I mean, I've got four legs, two arms, four wings, a tail, y'know. So if somebody mixes this DNA with yours they get me?" Lauren again was doing her best to humor the guy, pointing about at his diorama.

"Genetics is super intricate. You're what happens when, say, a carbon based life form and a silicon based life form mix. There are bound to be... mutations."

"I, uh, I might have been born a week ago and am *definitely* no scientist, but I'm like 90% sure that whatever you just said, you just made up."

"I did not! It's all high concept. I have almost a hundred-fifty IQ. Certified. I was tested as a child."

"...Okay, dude. Then what about the hybrids that look like dogs? You can't possibly say that I'm the same species as one of them."

"Probably not. You think the aliens just crossbred humans for their domination plans? Of course they'd diversify their genetics portfolio for maximum survivability in different tropic zones."

"I know one that's half human, half spider. Like pretty much like she was just stuck together. Grotesquely. You're going to say that's only half spider and half alien?"

"More likely that it's a third alien, a third spider and a third human, yeah."

"So she had three parents or something?"

"Look, I'm not 100% versed on alien biology. They could have three sexes. Besides, that's not exactly how genetics works."

"Okay, dude." Lauren turned back to me. "Yeah, this was kinda dumb. You wanna go?"

"Wait! Didn't you remember anything?" He suddenly blurted.

"...Not really man," She sighed heavily, biting her lip and shrugging. He looked over to the side antsily, with Lauren watching on expecting his disappointment in full.

"Okay. Alright. One more thing. I don't have this part of the museum public to just anyone because people might say I'm crazy. But if you remember..."

"*Okay*, dude. Sure. Shoot." Lauren shrugged again with wide eyes now, maybe a little more interested than she was before. Curtis walked over towards the direction he'd glanced in before in that second of doubt he had a moment earlier, over near his reception desk. With a very deliberate waving of his hands, almost a little dance of his fingers for the haptic sensor, a section of the rather less adorned parts behind his seat popped open like a door, and he bid us come.

"Sorry, the door really isn't for your kind," He noted to Lauren as she squeezed on through, the door rather smaller than most doors, and she already had problems with most doors anyways, serving to automatically exasperate her further, though as she looked up and around as I followed in behind her, our collective exasperation dissolved a little bit by an extended fascination, on top of the oddities we'd already experienced in the larger room behind us. "Welcome to the nerve center," He said. I noted the computers whirring away, the wires, but that was mundane compared to the new dioramas and maps around. "Not exactly as high-tech as Eduardo's, but I try to keep my methods old-fashioned. Can't hack into a string chart," He laughed nervously, waving past the big wall to the right, pictures and newspaper clippings and printed-out tidbits of interest all connected through trails of string held taut by thumbtacks. I noted one of the bigger centers of the threadmap being Elrond Industries, the holding company of ElTek and BioTek and obviously the progenitors of modern hybrid-kind. Threads connected Elrond to, quite expectantly, politicians and articles on buyouts, political donations and such, other holding companies, how Apple was bought by ElTek during the standstill, all the big government conspiracy tropes. But all the threads pointing down seemed to connect criminal organizations to Elrond. Vague references to the Chinese Triad, the Yakuza, the Russian Bratva, and of course Gabriel's ex employers, Sina. I saw shadowy images snapped at a distance of their higher-ups. 'Nevada/Idaho chapter leader, Mr. Rojo?' one of the captions read, a blurry image of a man in a suit with long frizzy red hair, his back turned to the PoV and head gazing to the side. Despite the low quality, I could see his protruding cheekbones casting shadow. It sent shivers down my spine.

"...Jaws can only crush if they come from both the bottom and the top," Lauren read aloud the big red marker-written header in fascination.

"...Yeah. It's kind of poetic. Kind of proud of that little… poeticism. See, I can prove- er, I've got good reason to suspect the Aliens have been using Elrond Industries as a front ever since their power grab at the end of the forties- nineteen forties. 'A supercompany to wage economic warfare against the commies' my ass. The aliens knew exactly how to play us, split us east and west just so they could lay the groundwork for those fuckers, same with how the USSR and us started making freaks to see if the Nazis were ever onto something. All just planned. Hybrids nowadays are just another step. Next there'll be aliens walking brazenly in the streets like conquerors without ever firing a shot."

"...Why does Elrond need to take over criminal organizations, though?" I jutted in.

"Think about it. Who's gonna mount an insurrection, who's going to spill the beans, who's going to breach containment? People who have no interest in what goes on in the daylight- those goings-ons being alien deception. Look at Zeta, back in the Intervention War. They tried to break free. Same with the old Triad before their leadership got couped. Siña are reliable, new Triad are reliable. CIA controlled? *Alien* controlled, more like. All coding. All obvious once you know what to look for."

"This doesn't prove anything about aliens though," Lauren muttered, waving to the string chart. Something within her, probably her miscellaneous knowledge made her realise this was a crazy person cliche. "...Just that Elrond is the one responsible."

"Yeah! Exactly! That's what they want you to think!" He pointed out, nodding profusely. Lauren could barely conceal her rolling eyes, turned away from the guy. I looked over to the other wall, seeing plenty of maps. The old standbys and cliches, the nuclear scenario maps, 100 warhead, 1,000 warhead and 10,000 warhead scenarios all lined up, Vegas already crossed off, along with a question mark on DC. Another map with military bases, Area 51 scrawled into it. But there was another map, just a regular map but with red push-pins scattered all about it.

"What's this one?" I asked, as the gimmick here wasn't quite as obvious.

"Oh, I've been looking around, seeing what people have to say. Sightings of cryptids- those're Aliens, 'hybrids', creatures-of-interest. Consolidating a lot of other stuff like suspicious government activity, vehicles disappearing down roads that lead nowhere, men-in-black types harassing civilians, tellin' them they ain't seen nothing and to go back to watching reality TV 'n stuff. I've got a pretty good idea where all the alien holding facilities could be, those're the push pins. There's a big one just south of here. All underground, disguised as an abandoned airway with a dilapidated hangar, y'know."

"*...You don't say,*" I uttered, hiding my sarcasm, nodding at him, Lauren nodding too, like the two of us were partaking in an inside joke.

"That's their way to hide 'em after they realised Area 51 gets too much attention. Just a little underground nowhere. Dilapidated buildings as an entrance- sometimes if they've got ones in cities they hide them in condemned buildings. Weirdoes and spooks disappearing inside 'em before emerging days later, like steppin' back out into the real world."

"Huh." Some silence as I looked over this map, seeing another one nearby Shortstone in Idaho. Probably were bound to be some hybrids there by the time we get there. I wondered if my dad saw any yet.

"...So... Miss Alien, what was your name again?"

"Lauren," She said, smacking her lips, looking back over to him and nodding, almost like she was looking at him like he was nuts.

"So, 'Lauren'... What now?"

"I, uh..." Lauren stopped. She ought to have expected this, really, and I guess she did by the way she sighed. "Can't say that I suddenly remember anything but guys in white suits in a laboratory. Like, I'm pretty sure that everyone in my 'child' memories was a human. I mean I didn't even have a childhood. I was grown in a lab and if it's not random information they pumped into my head it's the couple of times that they pulled me out, and I hardly remember that stuff. Like I was a littler version of myself for the very first times I can remember. They put me in growth chambers and like, every time they pulled me out for like, diagnostics or something and ask me a few vague questions, I was a little bigger and I knew more stuff than the last time I was 'awake'. It's all really fuzzy anyways, like a dream. I never really was *conscious* until about a week ago when I got out of the facility they were keeping me in. Even if I am an alien I was definitely grown here since my birth, and by humans."

"...you sure you saw *humans* wearing those white suits?"

"Yeah, man. Two eyes, cuppy ears, funny triangle nose, recessed muzzle, just like you. Sure as I can be." She let her arms slap at her sides. "Sorry, dude."

"Yeah, yeah." He sort of stood there, scratching himself. "Want a souvenir? Maybe if you keep it with you, you might remember something else." Lauren sighed, as he went over to the desk near the front door, pulling out a keychain. It had a little cast-iron rocket ship hanging from it, painted red and white. "Just when you remember, you have to-"

"Yeah, I'll come back. I promise." She took the little trinket with a halfhearted smile, going to clip it onto a molle loop of her battle belt. "...Thanks. You're... A pretty good human, Curt."

"You too. You're alright for an alien, yourself." Lauren smiled back, sticking her hand down towards him. He was apprehensive for a second before reaching up to take it, shaking on it. I guess it was better than sticking to animosity. Lauren turned back to me, seeing how I was beaming like an idiot and she smiled back with a tiny blush.

"...That was something," Lauren uttered as we left down the road towards the rest of the town. "Hey, uh. You, uh... Shit, this is a really weird question," She began, the tiniest blush in her cheeks as I stopped to watch her formulate her sentence. "You, uh... I dunno. Nevermind."

"No, what was it?" Lauren paused again, to stamp her feet a little there as she gazed up, like asking the heavenly powers for strength, a brief moment of feeling there was no good way to formulate what she had to say.

"You, you said you wanted- you'd want to try flying. With me. Remember?" It sort of slipped my mind, but I can remember saying something like that. And just like that, my heart beat a little harder in my chest.

"Yeah. I think so. You want to know if I meant it?" Lauren paused, as I presented her next question for her, with a tiny, wide-eyed nod. "Yeah."

"Y-you wanna fly back to town? I-it'll be quicker, and we might be able to, like, get a better view of-"

"You don't have to *convince* me, Lauren," I laughed a little. That blush of hers grew as she smiled with puffed cheeks and furled lips. I went up to her and she recoiled ever so subtly for a moment. "How are we gonna do this, like, uh-"

"Oh, shit. I forgot how freakishly tall I am," She did a little curtsey with her four legs as I ever so carefully stuck my leg over the shoulder of her lower body, where my legs could drape between where her humanoid wings stopped and her lower wings began. She hefted herself up, and to avoid slipping back I put my arms around the lower bit of her humanoid belly, my arms going under where her upper wings' membranes ended. I saw the muscles of her wings, first seeing the ones in front of me and then looking down to the ones bumping up against the bottom of my thighs, how those wing muscles were so tightly wound like bridge cables stretched too far. The rest of her body had a low amount of body fat overall but she was hardly sculpted with muscle, the apparent exception being her wings, jacked as all hell. I guess if you needed to lift a half ton off the ground it made sense for the body parts to be doing it to be incredibly powerful. "You're a little heavier than I thought you'd be," She huffed as she stood back up. "...You're an athlete so I guess. Got all that muscle in a... compact package."

"...You think you'll be able to take off?"

"Yeah, probably, I think I can use that dip over there past the road, sort of taking off from elevation, y'know?" She approached it, wings unruffling. "H-hold on, Noah. I don't want to drop you,"

"Yeah, me neither," I gripped my opposing wrist above her battle belt, locking myself around her as she pulled her hologoggles down over her eyes, and I guess I ought to as well, with the amount of wind that was about to be in my face.

A couple brief, hurried trots, and her rear wings opened. I felt the jolt, both the jolt of my heart skipping a beat and how gravity seemed to waver as the wind caught her sails, leaning her humanoid body forward and I leaned with her. She beat her frontal wings once, dipping her body upwards as she went forth down into the gulch. My heart crashed into my stomach as the wings behind me heaved. I could hear them tear through the air, a crescendo of power, and she banked, beating both pairs of wings one after the other. Boom, whoomph. Like the beating of a drum, this quick rhythm. We were getting higher and higher.

"You- you okay?" She panted. She must have been able to feel my tension, how I was frozen there. It was almost terrifying, this expression of her power over the wind, over gravity, so high up here. It was all melding together in my mind, until her words brought me forth out of my disassociation to realise *we were flying*. How my heart was released from anxiety, bit by bit, weaving between little puffy clouds so far away from the ground. This was something beyond just a gimmick, this was how she freed herself. How I found myself freer up here with her. How the earth was so far below, even if we weren't super high up it felt so much different than being down there. Like up here everything was simple, just a mess of streets and geography, a clear path north to safety could be easily mapped out. I found myself gradually sitting back up, my arms and body relaxing like a weight had been lifted off of me, my hands still grasping down at her humanoid hips and my legs clamped into her sides but aside from that I felt nothing but a deep serenity. My heart was still racing but it was no longer fear or anxiety, but pure elation.

"Yeah," I uttered breathlessly, gazing out to an endless horizon beneath an even bigger sky. How we sped along, bumped up with every wingbeat she repeated, just sailing, in a concert of the drums of her wings and her powerful breath after breath, accompanied only by the heaving of my own chest. "It's… Amazing."

"Yeah… Isn't it?" She uttered back, just as breathless. "Hey, trust me for a second, okay?" She blurted out in a huff and before I could even really process this, she dipped suddenly. She'd felt how I'd released up on her the minute before in my relaxation, and taking me by utter surprise here I almost nearly let out a scream as I felt how my hands, my legs slipped away from her. In a terrifying instant of slipping away from her, my lifeline, I watched her wings close and she rolled to face me as I fell, smiling back with big bright eyes to sort of persuade me that everything was all right, falling for a moment with me before shooting her wings back open and I landed, my face colliding with her humanoid belly as her arms and frontal talons closed around me gingerly, yet safely and securely. I gazed up to her, seeing her giggle a little bit from where I was smushed into the soft of her gut, still breathing heavy as we sailed downwards, not quite in a free fall but with such a leisurely fraction of gravity still impacting us, those wings able to slow us just enough for a comfortable falling speed. After a couple heart-pounding moments she finally spun back around, wings slamming back open and beating as she held me there beneath her, gaining more altitude, as I could practically kick the treetops with my dangling legs now that I turned around, with her carrying me beneath her. I was hollering at the time, out of reflex and fear, but as we zipped out and up my shouts and whoops became ones of thrilled elation. "See, now this- this is what it really feels like to fly!" She laughed out along with me. "Spread your arms, Noah! You're flying!" I was beyond words, laughing out. She gained more altitude to gingerly release me again and fall with me. It was only a couple seconds, like it was before, but it felt so much longer than that, adrenaline stretching this beautiful little moment out, but not nearly as long as I would have ever wanted. She turned her back to me as she came up beneath me, and I sat myself back down as she evened out, sailing out lazily and skimming the treetops as she stalled out, like pausing in midair, slowly winding back down as she finally alighted on the awning of the second story of the historical museum back in town.

"…That was *amazing*," I uttered, before getting off. I felt my legs shake like jelly there taking those first few steps, my heart still racing, practically collapsing back into her as an arm came around me to keep me from falling over. I looked up as I leaned into her, Lauren's bright smile so big that her teeth showed rather inadvertently, beaming in that I was happy there with her. She was panting, sweat beading across her skin. "God, and you can do that, like, anytime you want." I finally pushed myself off to stand on my own, jumping in place a little to get a feel for this more mundane dimension I usually lived in.

"Eh, until it… tires me out," She wheezed, coughing a little to clear her throat before resuming panting.

"I'm kind of jealous, Lauren."

"Yeah, well… Don't get too jealous. It comes with… Drawbacks." She motioned behind to the rest of herself, going for her canteen on her battle belt to take a swig, pouring some powdered electrolyte water into her canteen. It was at this point, now that we stood so close, that I could in this light just barely see what looked like trails of steam rising off of her wings. I looked closer.

"Hey- whoah," I touched one of her rear wings, feeling the muscle being super rigid, not to mention intensely hot, unhealthily so from any sort of glance. My hand went up to activate the haptic controls of my glasses for a second, and I turned on the medical function, seeing the scanner showing her hearts beating, one up in her humanoid chest and one far below in her posterior, bestial torso. I brought up the thermal display to read, grabbing at her big lower-body wing to focus on. One hundred and thirty nine degrees fahrenheit, fifty-nine degrees celsius. I looked up to her in concern as she pulled her own goggles off, scanning her head. She was about a hundred and three farenheit.

"W-what?"

"...Are you feeling okay?"

"Yeah, I just... I get a little flushed after I fly. Gimme a couple minutes and I'll be alright." She reached in a pouch, getting some more energy powder and ripped it open with her teeth, pouring more in her canteen. "...Gabe says that hybrid wings are... They have like, a super muscle or something; a fast-special-something muscle, I think he said, but I can't, I shouldn't use them for too long. Or to stop using them if I start to get tired. Says they can overheat if I don't stay... if I don't, uh... He said I needed this stuff," She shook the little empty packet in her hands before my concerned face, before stuffing it back in her aid pouch. "Light electros or whatever. My wings, uh, need a lot of them or something. He said it's all in the... docs. I should be okay after a little bit."

"I... you're sure?"

"Jeez Noah, I'm fine, if I'm dying you'll be the first one to know," She half-joked. I sternly looked down again, her wings ruffling a little before me. Just seeing steamed sweat rise off of them really put me ill at ease.

"Hey, let's *git* before we get spotted," Lauren huffed and bidding me come towards the balcony door, barely being able to see where we had parked the vehicles parked from around the corner of the roof, the balcony pointing out parallel to the road. "Don't want to get yelled at by your girl for *stealing you away*."

"Yeah, let's... Keep this between us," I uttered back at her joke as we went back in, towards the sound of talking in the big quasi-log cabin constructed there, set in the stone foundation. I could hear, somewhere down below us, a hushed conversation. I looked over to Lauren, her eyes widening some and showing a nervous, apprehensive grin, holding her finger up to the front of her muzzle as her ears twitched, and I nodded back. It sounded like a private conversation down there, something slow and serious, reverent even. Moving slowly across the creaking flooring, I guess it didn't matter as we heard shuffling.

"Yeah. I dunno. I just... Everything's so fucked right now." Was that Kyle's voice?

"Maybe you're right, Kyle. I mean, with the way things are right now, this might be what you need. I'm sure your friends don't dislike you, even if you did mess up like that. That's what stress does to people." Brandon? He was sounding especially lucid for once. Lauren and I, with Lauren using subtle little beats of her wings to lighten herself somewhat to make the floor creak less (with an exasperated roll of the eyes, silently complaining about her weight) proceeded down the stairs, going to the front door. I waved Lauren over, and I opened the door before shutting it. I heard their conversation stop.

"...Brandon?" I began, acting as if we'd just entered. "Hey, figured we might check out your museum before we-"

"Mr. Reed. Kyle would like to talk to you." Brandon came out, to wave me on over. I looked over to Lauren, who looked back at me.

"I'll... Be outside, then," She uttered, pointing to the door and taking her leave.

**Chapter 30**

I walked over to Brandon where he stood in the doorway of this little disguised portion of the wall, and there Kyle was, in the rear portion of the museum where the living quarters for Brandon were, his living room as it were, a rustic little joint, Kyle sitting there and staring down into a mug of hot chocolate.

"...Your friend Mr. Noria told him that he could walk around so long as I supervised him. Officer of the law and all, even if the law ain't worth bunk as of late," Brandon uttered sadly, tipping his hat back a little. "Heard what happened to his girl. It's unfortunate what you ran into outside Vegas- or where Vegas used to be. Hard to believe it myself, how something like that could be happening in the current day, y'know?"

"...I think he gets it," Kyle uttered over to Brandon, who looked down at his boots for a moment before nodding heartily.

"...I'll be in the other room so you two can talk." Brandon left, and silence took over. I sighed. I walked over to the chair slowly, slumping down into it. This was already uncomfortable, but I guess it was only leaderlike to discuss things.

"...That's some judo, right? What you used on me," Kyle uttered, still staring at the marshmallow dissolving in his drink, before I had a chance to formulate something to say, the after-effects of adrenaline from my previous activity mulling my mind.

"Some of it was. I couldn't put a name to it. It was a lot of things, stuff I learned from martial arts, just what I needed to do at the time."

"Huh, you ought to teach me one of these days," He uttered sadly, with a humphing smile.

"Sure, why not." Kyle was now battering the little sugary white island back and forth with his spoon. "...You okay?"

"I... I don't think so. I just-" Kyle sighed, that sigh you give when you just don't quite have the words yet. "Noah, I'd... I'd like to stay here." I'd be lying if I said this didn't take me by some shock, pausing there, my head nodding inadvertently as my eyes fluttered in surprise. "I'm just- I don't know if I can be around Archie. I... I don't think it's hybrids in specific. Or maybe it's you guys. But, like... I can't think about anything but her, Noah," his eyes finally came up to me. This big hunking wall of muscle gazing up at me in despair, in abject sorrow. "I see any of you and I see us, as a group, and I see Holly. Wilson too. I just..." He swallowed his sadness again, eyes falling back down to his hot chocolate that Brandon had made him. Nice guy, really. "I don't know. There are people here, and, and Brandon is... he's not *that* out there, and I heard about Ed and his bunker and how he's going to try and make sure we can survive everything, and the other lost campers who are out in the cottages and stuff. How they're gonna band together and we might be able to make a run of this place."

"...The survival retreat with my dad up in Idaho would be safer, though."

"I know. But it's still a long way to get there, and I don't know if I can keep it together. I... I feel like I need a... *vacation*. That sounds silly, right?" He chuckled another sad, desperate chuckle. "I guess I like this place, Noah. And I'll be able to... come to terms with myself, that's all. It's a new place, full of new people. I feel like if anywhere is the place to turn over a new leaf, it's here." I was watching him as he spoke. I'd never seen him so serious, it practically shocked me. "I guess when you get there you can... come back to get me when everything cools off or something? That's a lot to ask but you don't have to do it. Maybe just get in touch when the internet comes back or something. Heh, you could send... Lauren. Fly on out to say hi."

"Yeah, sounds about right," I chuckled back. "I... I think I'll miss having you along, Kyle."

"You too. But I need this. I... I need a minute, y'know?" He finally picked that mug up, taking a sip. I sighed again.

"Yeah. If you're sure."

Walking back out, seeing everyone's faces, eyes watching me, waiting for answers. Gabriel was there, leaned up against the wall of the general store. Some of the other refugees from the cottages were coming out to see us. I saw Sheriff Brandon there, hands at his hips. There were a few other hybrids like Connie, bug ones with fast little wings that hovered them in the air for short bits of time with chitin plates on parts of their bodies, a few other canid and felinid hybrids. Brandon stood there with Gabriel, leaning on the hood of the my jeep, A woman also dressed up in strange, period-centric clothes like Brandon, probably his wife if I had to guess, over near the open door of the JLTV talking to an enshadowed Selicia. I saw everyone else around, mostly just hanging about, bored with this place but anxious for the news.

"How's Kyle?" Gabriel asked sternly.

"He's staying. Says he needs some time on his own, with new people. Mr Hayes, sure you're good with watching him?" I asked to Brandon.

"Yeah. Nice enough kid. It's the least I can do. I took an oath, after all. Even if I am just a sheriff in technicality."

"A sheriff at the end of the world," Gabriel sighed in a sort of sad amusement. "Try to keep the rule of law going in your own way, huh?"

"It's the start of a new wild west. I'll do my best." I saw his sigh from a puffed-out chest, hands at his hips. "Ed has some power armor he says I can borrow. Hate to ditch my aesthetic like that but I guess the future has to come sometime."

"Hey, Brandon dearie. Come on over yonder and take a gander," Brandon's equally eccentric wife called out, waving him over. Gabriel took a look too, as Selicia got out there with her arms folded, many legs tapping a little as Brandon's wife held her revolver. "Maybe you'd be interested in a trade," She said. Brandon took the big gun.

"Ruger blackhawk. Engraved, too. Nice gun," He said, looking up at Selicia through the brim of his hat. "...But it's anachronistic. May look a little bit like a Single Action Army but there are specific differences. Won't fit in with the rest of the collection." He handed it back and she sighed a little, Squinting heavily as she stuck it back in her holster.

"Don't fret, darling. That's an excellent piece." Gabriel was off to the side, going for something in the jeep.

"Hey, Green," Gabe uttered and Lauren peeked up. Gabe walked over with some piece of gear in his hands. "Eduardo had a spare one of these lying around. It's a hydration bladder. See, since you need to keep your blood sugar up while flying and it's hard to drink out of your canteen midair, here you've got a tube to drink out of connected to this big pouch. You can either wear it by itself or strap it to the molle on your chest rig."

"Aw, thanks Gabe! That sounds great!" Lauren took it with beaming eyes and a big, bright smile, Cradling the big, molle-lined plastic pouch like a child. "This is perfect! Now I can fly longer!" She hugged it, as if she wanted to hug Gabe at the moment, though didn't since it was Gabe, after all.

"Just remember, if you start to feel sore or tired you should land right away. Electrolytes won't save you if your wings start to cook from the heat. Got it?" Lauren nodded profusely, that big happy smile all over her face.

Finally, Kyle was walking out behind us all, everyone turning. I guess the word got out fast, everyone somber, looking out to him as he strode. For a moment, I almost didn't recognize him- like he was a new man all of a sudden. He walked different, carried himself different. There was this bright spark in his eyes, his smile dull yet keeping itself up the best it could. It was the bravest I'd ever seen him.

"You'll be staying with us, then?" Brandon's wife uttered to Kyle as Brandon walked over to her, putting an arm around her hip.

"Yeah. I think so." Gabriel went around to the back of my jeep, pulling out Kyle's armor set, holding it out towards Kyle. "...Y-you sure?"

"Sheriff says he'll be keeping an eye on you, he'll be holding your rifle for now, says it's being around *us* that's gotten you so stressed anyway, probably give you it back sooner or later. Should be alright if you have your own tac gear when he deputizes you. It'll be collecting dust around us."

"...You might run into somebody you want to take along, again."

"Eh, we'll find something for them then. It's already sized for you, anyways." Kyle took one of those body armor straps, letting the heavy thing hang in his arms with the helmet in the other, tac goggles and nightvision and everything. "We gave those bolt actions and their ammo for Brandon and Ed, in exchange for some more fifty cal ammo," Gabriel turned to let me know, motioning over to Ed who sat on his rotorbike with Miia, hanging about as he did his best to be social. "Also let him download the new autonomous Sentinel program, just since he was kind enough to let us in on the little bit of intel he dug up."

"...I'll hold those guns in the station and label them as evidence, in the name of legalities, just to get Mr. Truong off the case," Brandon laughed a little nervous entertainer's laugh, though coming back down in a somber manner. "I took Gabe's statement. Sounds like you acted in self-defense doing what you did to their original owners. They shot first out of ambush, y'all were defending yourselves. Doubt you're going to get taken to court over it by their families with the way things look right now, and the jail's not exactly built for me to arrest the whole lot of you even if I wanted to, but hey. My word's on your side, from what it's worth. Call it a character assessment." He gave us a halfhearted smile.

"Oh, yeah. We gave you guys the coordinates of the hybrid facility to the south and all the entrance key activation codes, and how to get in touch with the guy in charge there. You ought to check the place out sometime Ed, probably when things even out. You'll dig that city inside it, Prosperia. Trust me. Shit's synthwave right down to the purple sky." Gabriel smiled while Lauren stood more upright, blinking a bit before rolling her eyes towards me as I nodded towards her with an enthusiastic smile of my own, having proved my point.

"...You know I'm a sucker for cyberpunk. I'll check it out." Eduardo gave a half-hearted smile back.

"Yeah! Sounds fun!" Miia beamed.

"Take Curtis along too. He'll probably enjoy the place for research purposes," Lauren chuckled with puffed cheeks, taking in a deep sigh of air behind her smile.

"You imagine the layers of tin foil he'll be wearing once he even agrees to go?" Brandon chuckled, adding in. "What a kook!"

"I... I'll probably miss you guys, y'know," Kyle said. "...But I'll make new friends. I'll be okay."

"I'll keep you in mind," I said back, and he have another smile. A fighter's smile, a smile for the sake of defeating despair at all cost. It really was like he was a different person, a new Kyle. It was a good look for him.

"...Remember, Gabriel," Eduardo called out. "I've been hearing the most chatter around Elko. if you want to figure out what's going on, that's the place to check out."

"...Yeah, I remember. Alright gang, let's move out."

We drove, setting out. Watching them wave to us behind us, ambling down that road. "Good luck, guys!" Miia slinked up like standing on that bike, Eduardo flying it off towards his bunker, everyone else waving too.

"Goodbye, Kyle! We won't forget you!" Lauren stood up on the back of the jeep again. I looked back on her, seeing her eyes a little wet. I guess mine were too, watching his arm fall down as his silhouette shrunk and shrunk, turning a corner to see him disappear, then coming up upon Curtis' museum. He waved tentatively at his battlements, giant airgun in hand, Lauren laughing a little as she waved. "Bye, Curtis!"

"Remember!" He shouted. "If you remember, you said you'd come right back and tell me all about it!"

"Yeah! The little green men!" Lauren laughed. "See you!"

Like that, we were gone from Crystal Springs, and onto the next leg of our journey. It wasn't like we were just out to survive, now. We were making our way towards mystery and intrigue and adventure, with such interesting places already behind us and nothing but the wide open world ahead of us, with our next stop in mind:

The city of Elko, where we'd find some answers.

### Chapter 31

Hours of driving, too many scarred rocks of the earth passing us as we proceeded north. More rocks. Back to that incessant hum of the engine, driving on out. Sentinel scanning out this way and that, Lauren making her sweep up above, like a four-winged green bat, practically microscopic at her altitude. She looked like a tiny little bird up there, and I knew how big she really was. She must've been a mile up, at least. God, that impressed me so much more now, after experiencing firsthand what exact sort of power she possessed in those wings of hers.

"Checking in, still clear all around," She was clearly panting through the radio. I could bring up the live feed of her hologoggles, able to see what she saw. I felt my jealousy spike again, since I knew a taste of what it was like to fly, but at the moment I was relegated to driving this boring grounded vehicle. I made a mental note to ask to fly again with her. "Holos are telling me... I'm at about two thousand meters. I'm gonna start gliding on down, should be back down in fifteen minutes or so, over."

"Copy."

"Hey, you ever get, like, short of breath up there?" I asked. "Like, the air gets thin the higher you get. You aren't worried about passing out or anything, right?"

"I've got four lungs for a reason. I'm pretty comfortable with the air up here," She responded. "If anything'll knock me out, it'll be a lack of blood sugar first."

"...Goddamn, it's in the docs, Noah. Get reading already," Gabriel's voice through the radio was lined with nonchalant exasperation, laid back as he drove the JLTV. We were going a good fifty miles an hour down the backroads, and there she was above us, keeping up with us well and good, even now as she lazily teetered about, her wings ceasing their flapping, gliding. "...The hybrids that can fly have a special kind of muscle for their wings. See, in the natural world, there are two kinds of muscle, fast twitch and slow twitch. There's also smooth muscle, but that doesn't matter for this. Fast twitch is more powerful but is meant to be used sparingly, slow twitch is less powerful but can sustain its usage. Hybrid wings use a hybridization of the two, no pun intended- a fast twitch muscle that can sustain itself like a slow twitch muscle, at the cost of a blood sugar intake so high that their metabolisms can't really keep up with it, aside from the electrolytes already in their bloodstream, not to mention a higher muscular operating temperature. Only problem is that if they run out of blood sugar they really can't metabolize body fat fast enough to keep those muscles operating, at least not at any sort of stable energy demand. So if she suddenly starts to feel more and more tired..." Gabriel made a tiny fart noise with his lips. "Splat. Here lies Green, she flew too high and God knocked her the fuck out for it like a modern Icarus. Not to mention that it might not even matter. If her body temperature runs too hot, her muscles cook inside her skin. Splat, same problem. That's why I tell her not to try to outdo herself. Least not until she's got some fuckin' jacked wings. I forgot my juice and HGH though, so she'll have to grow 'em natty."

"Jeez," I uttered back. "Y-you feel safe up there knowing all that?"

"I know what I'm capable of, I'm no superman," Lauren kidded, though not entirely putting me at ease. "Again, wait for me to get *SUPER MEGA FUCKIN' RRRIPPED* wings, I'll fly for days, youn't even know," She growled into the mic, mimicking a goofy professional wrestling voice or bodybuilder voice or something to that effect. "*No pain!? No gain!*" She laughed at her comical grunts and growls, being silly.

"...you ever see anyone pass out in the gym in the middle of their set before?" Gabriel laughed over to me. "See, Green crashing would be like that times a thousand. You'll see."

"Yeah, let's not, alright?"

"Easy now, at this rate you'll convince me to stay up here all day, above you *FOOOLISH MOORTALS*." Lauren laughed out an evil laugh like a supervillain, her dramatic persona switching by the second. I looked up, seeing her flight pattern grow more erratic and eccentric, kicking flips and twists and turns this way and that, like she was obviously having way too much fun. "I'm a *dragon*, after all. A legendary mythological creature. With a treasure trove. With GOLD! Also a centaur. But not really, since I'm like zero percent horse. centaur-*inspired*. Wait, genetics is weird. Am I a little bit horse? So that might be a twofer. Heh, what a funny word..."

"Is delusional blathering one of the symptoms of a winged hybrid about to waste 'emselves?" Archie asked in playful exasperation behind me in his seat, though I probably would have asked the same question genuinely, and nervously on that.

"Lauren, stop fooling around," I commanded.

"Yeah, you'll eat all our protein," Maria added next to me, also more amused than she'd like to admit.

"To be fair, with Kyle staying back we'll have a lot more to spare," Gabe reasoned.

"Hey, when society gets rebuilt, I want to make flying a sport. Because I'll be the best at it, and win all the gold medals and trophies. Y'know, so I can horde it. The gold. In my dragon horde." Lauren was giggling like a little girl, kicking this way and that, rolling and banking and flipping.

"Jesus, how do you keep from passing out from the G-forces?"

"Come on Noah, think," Gabe uttered, utterly exasperated. "You don't even need the docs for that one. What does she have two of?"

"Uh... Bodies?"

"Hearts, dumbass. Her upper one's dedicated for supplying blood to her brain. The creators went out of their way to simultaneously design as ridiculous and functional a creature as they could. Dragontaurs are hardly the weirdest. Not while the arachnid ones exist, at least."

"...You know it's hard to sleep while you're having your stupid little theatrics in our comms, correct?" Selicia's ire-infused voice broke up the amused conversation.

"Then mute us, bitch! Haha!" Lauren strung together some weird combination of a barrel roll and a loop-the-loop that made me feel sick by simply witnessing it. It was beyond me how she could pull such ridiculous stunts, and I was far past impressed by now.

"...You're lucky you're too fat to swallow. I ought to help myself to one of your friends instead. I'd even let you watch. Who exactly are you close to again?"

"Gabriel! And he carries a *lot* of knives!" Lauren sang.

"Never saw the insides of a spider before. Sounds fun," Gabriel snidely chipped in under his guffaws. "Let's set a date, Sellie. When are you free? Do you prefer serrated or plain blade?"

"NOTICE," Sentinel's voice jarringly came to life before Selicia could brush this off. "TARGETING PARAMETERS CONCERNING CIVILIAN 'SELICIA' STILL IN EFFECT. BE ADVISED." Selicia humphed, like she wanted to brush it off as "i was just joking" but hadn't the care to do so.

"Oh, shit, that reminds me," Gabriel uttered. "Jokes and getting a little too grabby-touchy aside, you've behaved yourself for most of today and I want to show my appreciation. Sentinel?"

"AWAITING INSTRUCTION."

"Set new parameters. Confirm Personnel 'Selicia' BluForOp. Reset friendly fire protocols.

"AFFIRMATIVE. REQUESTING FULL NAME OF NEW BLUEFORCE OPERATIVE FOR DATABASE."

"Selicia Recluse."

"AFFIRMATIVE. OPERATIVE-"

"Uh, *excuse* me," Selicia piped up. "What did you just *presume* my last name to be, Gabriel?"

"Recluse. Like, Brown Recluse. Your spider half is one. Looks like one, I mean."

"Okay, sure. But that's not my last name." A slow, awkward pause.

"...Okay?"

"Aren't you going to ask me what my own fucking name is?"

"She's thinking one up right now, give 'er time, give 'er time..." Lauren joked. I heard Selicia grunt a little.

"My name is Selicia Malligri, Sentinel."

"AFFIRMATIVE. OPERATIVE MALLIGRI, S. ADDED TO REGISTRY OF BLUEFORCE OPERATIVES. FRIENDLY FIRE PARAMETERS ACTIVE."

"*Malligri*?" Gabriel added back. "Well that's a new one. Not bad for thinking it up on the spot, I guess."

"I did not! You just... asked me what my last name was and it just came to me. I think I just realised it."

"...Fascinating. I still give it an 8/10 for effort."

"Jest all you want, but it's true," She humphed.

"...You gonna explain how or leave us on a cliffhanger?" Gabriel's voice was far more amused than impatient, but there was some impatience in there too for sure.

"...Might've had something to do wit'er *theoretical* husband," Archie remarked.

"Yes, yes it did. My *actual* husband." Another long pause full of shit-eating grins. "...I think." With that, Lauren appeared next to me, nearly taking me by surprise. She glided there next to where I was driving, skimming above the desert with little wingbeats, easily making pace with our driving speed, smiling over to me with a silly little wave.

"Sup," She blurted with a wink, before beating those wings of hers again and gliding over the top of my jeep, to ever so gracefully alight onto the back of the jeep in her usual spot, holding onto the rollcage as she did and having a breather, grabbing one of the protein bars out of the food storage, gazing out to the right as she got down to lay her lower bits down in the chuck of the jeep, content to take deep sighs and optimistically gaze about. Reina, who sat in the seat behind and to the right of me as I drove, shifted a little bit on her tail, ears whipping this way and that as she too gazed out to the right, Archie on her left fiddling with the optic on his armalite.

"...How about our rearguard? Yall've been staying quiet. You good, Tony?" Gabriel's voice carried to the back.

"If I have something to say, I'll say something," Anthony let up. "Everything's good here."

"...Yeah, we're good," Samantha said.

It wasn't until I heard their voices that I really realised the mood that had taken over, dominated even. It was all that sort of playfulness, the one you take up and put on when you know you need to. Odd to really quantify, it was just a response. While Lauren's playfulness emerged to take front stage, their hesitantly bright voices marred with doubt really encapsulated that things really weren't alright, even if they were alright at the moment. Lauren, Gabriel, everyone really was just tired, on our way to the next thing.

The next thing that, as twilight descended, lay sprawling out before us as we made our way into the highlands overlooking that fateful city: Elko.

There we stood on that ridge. The rest of us somewhere behind assembling the camp. The campfire shielded up by a quick cairn of rocks, whatever joy was within us this afternoon had since dwindled as we were back here in the face of black uncertainty.

"There's no way around the place. The highways are all clogged with abandoned vehicles," Gabriel pointed out, sitting there on the rock with his binoculars. I sighed as I took a seat, going to take them too. I looked out to the roads. I saw some burned out husks from when the hack destroyed some of the cars, but the smoke around the highways to the east and west had cleared. Coming up on the place, I don't think I saw any smoke rising from it either.

"What've you been hearing on the air?" I muttered.

"Not much. I don't like it."

"...Want me to fly over and take a look?" Lauren asked. I turned, seeing her standing there a little ways away.

"No. It doesn't look like there's anything going on in the heart of the city. Whole place is dead. No lights, Dead on thermals. We'd see something if there was something worth checking out." Lauren raked her lip with her teeth, nodding slowly, wings rustling, displaying her unease. "Get some rest. You too, Noah. It's been a long day."

"I've got something to do first," I uttered, Gabriel turning. He nodded me off, and I went back over to the fire.

Here around the fire, that somber human silence is all we had. Everyone was just about, entranced by the ghost of the city, waiting to get to sleep to get going. Everyone except for me, at least not yet.

It was something that my father said, stuck in my mind. How hair is a tactical liability, why soldiers always shaved their heads. I felt like I needed to do that one last thing to make the day more productive, another thing to do to keep from that hopelessness from taking over. I took the laser clippers in my hand, something Anon had thrown in for us, intended to be used for cutting stray fibers off of nylon or kevlar but it could, of course, be used for hair. I felt the hum in my hands, people looking up to me as I held it up to my head. Clump after clump of thick black hair fell off of my head. I can feel Maria staring at me distantly from across that fire, with that stare that you have when you want to say something but feel that you shouldn't, the kind of stare that spoke when you couldn't. She held her tongue for a while, until she finally spoke up when I was about half done.

"Noah..." she said quietly. "You..."

"It's hot out here, isn't it? Even with the sun down it's still hot." I said with a tiny smile, sensing her objection. her mouth closed, as she looked into me. "I know you like my hair, but I figure I'd be better without it."

"Here," she was suddenly beside me, like I'd blinked for far too long as she appeared over my shoulder, hands crawling down to take the razor from me gingerly. "...You're missing a few spots."

"Thanks." She buzzed away, despite her aching soul, her desperately quivering hands. Chopping clump after clump of charming hair that she loved to run her fingers through, cutting all of it away until it was all gone. A few moments and there I was, bald with nothing but black fuzz atop my head, as I felt it, grunting a little to myself as if to try and decide on whether or not I liked the feel. I didn't think I did.

I got up to walk back to our vehicles, seeing Sentinel quietly scanning left to right, left to right in that agonizing routine of his. The radio chatter is indistinct, it's all garbled military-esque orders and relays, there are no news stations broadcasting. "Troop movements are due soon. I'm estimating we've got less than a week, so we should move through quick," Gabriel extrapolated from all this raw data, doing his best to make sense of it. "Invading from the west. Other channels, I'm guessing the defenders are counter-mounting for this offensive, trying to get more reinforcements into the area from the east. Isn't sounding good for them, but if I had to guess we might have better luck going east than west."

"Can they tell we're listening?"

"Probably," Gabriel grunted, turning the knob, shutting it off. "Go to bed."


A chasm of blackness. Where the eyes pondered but did not decipher, could not.

Steel. Hard floor, hard walls, low ceiling. The grumble of the ventilation shaft.

I walk forward, down that black place. Through the pits of black horror. I'm walking faster now, faster. Faster. Running. Cold steel against my feet, my bare feet. Like I'm being chased, but I don't feel fear. I can fight, but I don't know how or where. I don't feel anything at all, other than the need to run. Where? Where. Where, where, where.

It's the facility, isn't it? I shouldn't be here. This place is for hybrids. I shouldn't be here. For scientists. I shouldn't be here. For soldiers. Shouldn't be here. They know I

Shouldn't be here. Where? Where. More blackness. Frigid, cold. Sterile. How the world ceased flowing, and how I stood, immovable. Consumed by steel and earth. Rigid. Cold. Alone.


I'm awake again, with a jolt, back into the real world, gasping a little before I realise that everything is still, quiet, dark. The moon beaming into my face.

I sat up ever so slowly, brushing Maria's arm off of me in the process from where she slept behind me, an arm over my body until now. The blanket had come off of us in the night, and I looked back down, seeing her body curl up a bit in response to losing my heat. I reached over to pull it back over her as I stood.

I walked over to take a leak, quietly scanning for Selicia, who must've been on watch now. I identified a mess of webs assembled into a hammock between two rocks where she perched with one of the longer-barreled armalites with a scope. I was a little charmed by her ingenuity, but as I heard a saw-like snore erupt from her, passing by enough to see her face lit in the moonlight, drooling all too charmingly with her mouth wide open and her four eyes sealed shut, legs dangling through the web. I smiled to myself, figuring Gabriel was due to give her a talking-to. I looked over to see Sentinel, ever vigilant with the turret swinging from one side to the other ever so slowly, scanning, scanning and scanning evermore.

I relieved myself off of one of the rocks, sniffling in as I found my throat dry as well, zipping back up to figure I'd go back and grab some water, but before that I reached into my pocket to retrieve my holos, flicking them on for a moment to see the time. A couple minutes to five. Hard to imagine forty-eight hours before I watched my city reduced to a crater. Here in my pretty-much-still-asleep mode I would have quantified this as funny, but I guess it stuck out that this was something I couldn't really put to rest. Early morning wake-ups would never be the same, I guess. I wasn't tired. Sleepy, sure, but a residual sleepiness, like waking up. My mind rushed it away while I stood, and I was left staring up into the sky. I sniffed deeply. Nothing. Everything smelled normal.

"Hey," I heard. It didn't scare me. It was like a voice in my own head, that subtle yet powerful voice full of forced calm that she had.

"You awake?" I muttered back. I heard the gear she wore shifting, the jittering of a rifle ever so subtly as it hung from its sling, the subtle pats of her four feet on craggy, sandy rock. "...You should get some rest, Lauren."

"Sleep doesn't agree with me," She uttered with a subtle little stretch, her four legs carrying her to me as her wings ruffled.

"You sound like Gabriel."

"You look like him," She was behind and to the side of me, towering there as I finally looked back. She must have been referring to my buzz cut, how her shoulders and the "hips" of her humanoid half moved, her arm closest to me twitching as if she wanted to reach out and run her fingers along my shaven head. I gazed into her and she was frozen a little. I must have looked like shit, my eyes bagged. No wonder I looked like Gabriel.

"...Is it the nightmares?"

"It's... a lot of things. But Gabriel says I, my kind, centaurical types need half an hour less sleep or something. We've got four lungs so we can refresh our bodies a little faster. I dunno. It's in those documents." She answered, scratching her neck again, an arm leaned on the stock of her rifle. I let out a contemplative, interested humph and we gazed out into that dark city before us. "Noah," She suddenly uttered, reigniting the conversation. "What's it like... For you? I-I mean," She went on before I could ask for her to clarify, sensing my confusion. "This is all I'm used to. This journey we're on. Your friends died, you... You saw your city, your home get... *destroyed*," She choked out, eyes glittering upon a jaw ever so slack. "I mean, I, I know all these things in my head. I know what a city is like and everything, but I've... I've never been connected to one, y'know? You... You have."

"Are you worried about how *I'm* doing?" I asked, as if on autopilot. I couldn't, for the life of me, find any definite feelings within myself at the question. Maybe it was the tiredness I was slogged down by, as I sighed there.

"N-no... Yes," She corrected herself. "I... Noah, that's a *big deal*," She hushed breathlessly with a nervous grin holding back her emotions. She wasn't feeling sad for me, she was feeling sad *for* me. On my behalf. The way her eyes sparkled, wet. "Everything going on is a big deal. I, I shouldn't know about things like what's 'normal' and what's not, but everything is telling me that this is all just so... fucked."

"...You're a good person, Lauren. You've got a lot of heart."

"Well, I do have a spare." I huffed out a chuckle and she grinned for the sake of grinning.

"Always fast on the draw, aren't you?" I shuffled my feet, my eyes down on them as I did, but not pausing for long before she could speak, so I could put her worries to rest. "I'm fine, Lauren. Doesn't matter what's happened. What matters is where we're going." She swallowed her apprehension yet again, her turn to gaze down at her foothands, her talons.

"...I guess. Yeah. That makes sense." She looked up to me again. "I'm glad I get to go on this journey with you."

"You too." Another shared smile. Somewhere between warmth and formality.

It'd be time to get up soon.

"Alright. I don't want any funny business," Gabriel was going as we prepared to take off. "We go in on full combat mode, slow-go, everybody have their eyes out. You see something, speak the fuck up. We take one bullet, see one corpse or so much as smell a trap, we stop and assess the situation. Everybody do exactly what I have to say. Top off with safeties on, don't get jittery. One negligent discharge and we could develop a completely avoidable and highly stressful situation; and stress is *not* good for the body. If we suddenly find ourselves in a full-on ambush and the option to turn around is long gone, we are going to blast right on through with the pedal to the metal with all guns opening up. Remember. If I say shoot. You all shoot. Doesn't matter if we hit, if we're in a real ambush, every shot going out is a shot more likely to make them duck away. We're not military, we're not here to kill so we're not looking to get into any extended engagements. We're going to make our way through along the eastern edge of the city and get into the rich neighborhood in the heights and commandeer a mansion where we can get a good vista of the city. Alright?" Most of us responded with nods, despite our wide eyes and trembling hands. "Abel, Daniel," Gabriel was addressing our wounded still in the truck. "You're both going to need to pull your weight. We need all the eyes we can get. Selicia, you be back with them as a true rear gunner. Take your smoke grenades, if we need to make a getaway you're going to use them. Lauren, don't get up on the rollcage like you usually do, stay down in the chuck of the jeep and watch the left side. Noah, drive the jeep, Maria, be in shotgun. Archie and reina, take the seats behind. Anthony, I've got Sentinel on the turret but I could use a door gunner up front with me. Sam, you think you're good driving the truck?"

"Yeah, I- uh, sure," She uttered.

"Good. Katt, it's up to you where you want to be. The truck will be the least likely to get shot up with it in the back, but it's got the least armor. Noah's jeep is in the middle with decent armor, but it's not great. The JLTV I'm driving can withstand grenades but it's the most likely to be shot at if we get in a fight. It's up to you where you want to be."

"Uh…" She uttered, hardly shivering, clutching that little MP5. The stock was extended to the very first position and it had that little red dot on it, but it still looked heavy in her arms. How she wore one of the small high cut helmets and minimalist 8x10 plate carriers, still a little big for her, her ears smashed out at the sides through the ear cuts, though she looked like she'd have her ears back in trepidation anyways, the way hybrids with ears tended to emote with them. "I'll… I'll be with you in the armored car."

"Hell of a choice. Let's get to it."


Driving on in, it was expectedly quiet. I was awash in hesitant fear, almost to the point of trembling. But I could feel a little bit better now, something put my mind at ease and I did not tremble or draw short breaths, and I couldn't put my finger on why I had such peace within me.

Junk littered the streets. It was quiet, so quiet, and I drove slowly, behind Gabriel. Our tac glasses were all on, scanning, pointing things out, but the world around us was silent, abandoned. Somewhere off I could smell smoke, the fire of burning tires, perhaps. A car every now and then lay abandoned. gunshots, sparse but troubling occasionally echoed through the skies. I heard a window somewhere shatter, somewhere close in these suburbs. I looked around, my jaw slack somewhat, the eyes of my compatriots filled with this same disturbed sparkle. Junk lay on lawns, cracked windows with the curtains all drawn surrounding us all, the occasional weary peek through those shades glaring across at us with eyes that told it all. Was this America? I felt like I was driving through a scene that I might have seen on a news site or in a war movie about some troubling crisis in a faraway land, or at the very least south of the border. And it was all so frightening, even the hybrids, Archie and Reina and Lauren all the way back there seemed awash with their own sorrows, gazing about in shock, our own fear radiating into them. And what we humans, who could lay waste to a city in the blink of an eye- what we were afraid of, the hybrids were more than wise to fear as well.

We drove along, avoiding the abandoned cars littered in the city streets, long burned out. But, we came to a bridge, finding it was completely blocked. The sight of the cars jamming the street made me jump a little, as we took a turn, to go around, proceeding to worm through the suburbs.

But even in there, our convoy halted, and with my heart in my throat, I looked up and ahead. We had stopped, seeing the road before us impassable, blocked by cars which had haphazardly been abandoned, it backing up quite a bit up the road.

"Shit," I said. I threw the car into park, standing up a little to look out for some way around. "See anything, Gabe?"

"No more than you can," Gabriel's voice called back. My heart beat in my throat. Something about this didn't sit right with me. I felt so paranoid, standing there and staring around. "Yo," Gabe spoke up after a little bit. "I think we can pass if we drive through those lawns," he said, pointing them out.

"Sounds good," I said.

"We're right behind you," Sam's voice met us.

Gabe backed up a little, before turning and driving off to the left, going through a driveway, a flower garden, a lawn, an ivy bush, and another lawn. I advanced right behind him, practically in his same tracks in the grass. The street we were going down was a long one ending at a T intersection, some long ways away.

I saw in one of the houses at the very end of the street, something move within a window. I looked at it once, and didn't give it too much attention- there were quite a few windows and my paranoia had my head on a swivel. I must've did a double take when it first became apparent that whoever was in there some plus-hundred meters away wasn't acting like any of the others ducking behind their shades. And that was when I saw a peculiar glint, before a bright flash of the dark room lighting up for an instant.

"G-GUN!" Gabriel's voice uttered and my heart stopped, just like everyone else in the car. Every last face washed out from color, from Maria's steely composition full of intensity to Lauren's subdued panic.

Crack, boom. Another thick, dry twig snapped beside my ears. We were all stopped. I looked back up after my head dived down a little out of instinct, despite the laminated armored windshield. I could hear Katt yelp out quickly all the way over in the JLTV.

"Who's hit?! Anyone hit?!" I screamed out.

"Headcount! Sound off!" Gabe cried.

"We're good!"

"I'm up!"

"Good!"

"All good! Nobody here's hit!" I looked around as this went down. Was he gone? I didn't see that shimmer any more.

"Sentinel! Where's he coming from?!" Gabe cried.

"REDFORCE UNCONFIRMED. A.O. IS UNSECURED. ADVISE SECURITY SWEEP."

"...Fucker's gone," Gabe said. "Sentinel. Send some rounds into that window just in case they're taking cover. Six round burst."

"AFFIRMATIVE." a rapid succession of fire ripped out of the double deuce for a split second, glass shattering, dust flying and rising from that window.

"Let's move! Hang a right here! Be on your guard!" Gabriel shouted, and floored it through the remaining front yards. It was nerve-wracking, of course, and it made my guts twist thinking that somebody could just shoot at you without warning and run off.

"Jesus, what the fuck do you think that was about?!" Anthony let out with a laugh as we made our way down the adjacent street, though I could tell he was less than calm despite playing things off.

"...Could be a scout. We might look like the wrong sort."

Despite my beating heart, feeling like every turn we took would be our last, we were finally in Elko Heights.

## Chapter 32

It felt like it took us the whole day to get through the town. It was a long way around, and many parts were blocked off and required us to find some way around them. It was all one big twisting maze, and was devoid of excitement. And that worried me. Even the brief battle with that sniper was less than exciting. Sure, it wasn't something I'd like to relive, but I don't know, I think I expected... More. More than just some guy taking a potshot at us. I saw the shadowy, sinewy figures darting out of windows, looking out fearfully every now and then. It felt like the facility; those tightly-packed corridors of Elko were maddeningly familiar. Both claustrophobic mazes of concrete, filled with whispers and gasps, strange noises and people, some fearful, some feared.

I was waiting for the riot, I was waiting for the chaos, that romanticized version of the apocalypse I'd always envisioned. But it seemed to have all grown quiet. The unfriendly people who were out watched from their sitting perch on porches with shotguns and rifles in their laps, their conversations pausing as we rolled by, eyeing us. Many windows were blacked out by trash bags, Trash lined the streets and the signs of looting were all about, but nothing really happened. every now and then the sporadic gunfire filling the skies would intensify, a scream or two in the distance and dogs barking and yelping, but it all felt strangely quiet and distant, despite it being right next to us for all we knew. And the proximity was frightening.

We took our time through the city, traveling around the suburban outskirts rather than passing through the center of the city; a lot of the gunfire came from there. I knew that our main objective was to stay alive, and to that wit, avoid trouble if at all possible.

An hour passed in an eternity of concrete and pavement. It's funny how long it takes to make one's way through a city as opposed to the open countryside. It didn't seem like we were going any slower; rather time was going faster, the synthetic maze of the urban and suburban sprawls forced time to flee faster than it would elsewhere, like a curse upon the land itself. It was messing with me. The sights and sounds and smells all around, everything was disorienting. troubling.

We made our way to the northern suburbs by circling around the eastern perimeter, and by the time we reached city limits the sun was falling. Part of me wanted to continue on past Elko, but another part made me mad with curiosity. We had mostly passed the city, and I had far more questions than when we entered, as if I expected answers in here, like a checkpoint full of talkative soldiers, people to talk to, anything. But no. Silence, silent eyes and pursed lips, and the occasional abandoned police roadblock was the best we got. We were never alone, and we were almost always watched, but it was still always silence. I hated silence. I could feel it in my group, as well. We all wanted to know. That's why we were going to stay here. That and it'd been a long time since any of us had slept in a real bed, might as well have been a lifetime.

There was an old mansion on top of a hill. My dad always said that these kinds of places would have been hit the hardest by looters. But, it was easily defensible from a tactical standpoint- atop a steep hill to fatigue any would-be looters, surrounded by tall fencing and then spanned by a coverless kill zone of a lawn on almost all sides. They were like fortresses, but their biggest and deadliest flaw was that they stood out, and nothing attracts attention quite so simply as standing out. You could easily defend a mansion for a day, a week, even upwards of a month with a small force armed with the most sparing of weapons, but your threats would be frequent if not constant, and you can only take so many shots from snipers until you run out of healthy and capable defenders; without reinforcements these places would be a logistical death trap. It would be a war of attrition, something that my dad was always prepared for, even if he put all the more creedence on other genres of survivalism aside from combat.

One of these mansions, after a good hour of surveillance, seemed deserted, already looted. We figured we had not only a large amount of people, and that we'd have already drawn quite enough attention to ourselves in this neighborhood, but that after all, we were only staying one night. and it's not like that trashed place would have anything that we didn't bring into it, so there wouldn't be much for anyone else to steal.

We rolled up on the gate, which stood wide open. It looked as if somebody had locked it the old-fashioned way with a chain after the electronics went down, but it had been smashed off of its hinges by being rammed by a vehicle. It saved us time, at least. The gardens and grasses still looked well-trimmed and only a little-under-watered. It made us realise how recently this all happened. "Even the stablest of societies is always nine meals from chaos," my dad's words rang in my head. That three-day rule. I couldn't believe that it would snap so quickly, that everything would crumble so fast. But I had training, I had something to fall back on and keep me from my shock, keep me on my toes. These other people, humans who'd lived all their lives sealed up in their respective bubbles, and hybrids, more or less the same, all they had to fall back on was me, Gabriel, and maybe Maria.

The mansion stood, full of smashed windows and torn drapes, walls pockmarked with more than a couple bulletholes. A fountain resided right in the middle of the grassy lawn, its water was no longer flowing but still relatively clear.

We drove right on up to the front steps, stopping before and looking at that ajar door. It was ominous, like the open gates of that big old facility façade, and made me hesitant for a second. I figured nothing in there could rival what we encountered in the facility. We got out with our guns ready, Sentinel watching over us, each of us quietly entering to check the place out. The doors had their biometric locks broken through, not so much by a hacking program like Gabriel's but rather crudely, specifically by a sabot slug from a twelve gauge. The air rustled coldly through trash scattered on the floor. The whole place was cold from the air, very cold. It must've been hot out, but the uncanny wind tunneling through sent chills up our spines.

We proceeded to the kitchen, Gabriel going right up to the broken open cupboards, seeing trash and some food thrown upon the floor, kicking through it. The fridge hung open, and it stunk. It didn't matter if it was open or not, the power was off and whatever was left had since spoiled. Anthony, bothered by it, closed it anyways to contain the smell. I walked up to the sink, pressing the lever but no water came out.

"Looks like water's out," I noted.

"Not that big a problem- look," Gabriel pointed out the back, and I saw a pool, full of sparkling clear blue water. There were specks of trash and ashes floating here and there, but I knew they could be fished out.

"Huh," I said.

"Thank god for the one percent, huh?" Gabe growled with a smile. We went out, and I stooped down. I took a sniff and a sip from my cupped hand.

"Chlorine," I said as I spit.

"Seriously? Sure, better than saltwater, but seriously? A rich fuck like this doesn't have fresh filtration? Your fuckin' dad had fresh filtration."

"Yeah, but my dad planned on drinking out of his pool when the world ended," I said.

"Exactly," Gabe sang with a smile. I hadn't noticed that I had just acted like I did before- with my dad as the crazy old man. Gabe smiled at me, and I grunted out a sigh, rolling my eyes.

I went back into the kitchen, Maria off clearing the upstairs of the place, others about, me going to lean quietly against the counter and watching everyone congregate outside around the pool, though they found more enrichment in enjoying the desert view than to go for a dip. I think we all figured that enough awkwardness seemed to happen around bodies of water, so nobody really looked like they wanted to take a swim. "Hey, we're still clearing this fuckin place, don't pull up a seat just yet," Gabriel uttered, and I sighed, figuring to follow, eventually leading us over to the basement staircase- a padlock on the latch. "Huh, weird," Gabe uttered. Even more perplexing was that it appears to have had it's internal lock already shot out, evident by the shrapnel holes and burn marks- but was now padlocked closed.

"Are we gonna-" Gabriel took the initiative, his weapon belching copper slugs into the lock until it fell shredded. Lauren, who'd since removed her comms earbuds, winced hard and jumped back, ears swept back against her head with her shoulders tensed and head bowed, teeth gritting. Gabriel stepped forward, weaponlight gleaming as he descended into the concrete passageway- it looked very dusty.

"...Shall we?" He chuckled back.

"...Y'think there was a reason w-why that was locked?" Lauren uttered.

"Probably. Let's find out."

"Oh- ugh," Lauren suddenly let out, hesitantly trailing behind at the top of the stairs. "You guys smell that?"

"Oh, ugh," I said. It was a strange smell, kind of nasty and unpleasant, and oddly familiar- not to mention quite heady and humid. But this whole day was rather familiar, so I passed it off as nothing, trying to keep my paranoia suppressed. Nonetheless, with Lauren still hanging by the top of the stairs, Gabriel walked on out, shining his light around. He shined it on the wall, seeing the bottles of wine stacked there.

"Oh, what do you know," he said, reaching out to pick up a bottle. "Napa Valley vintage," he said and nodded his head a little, humming to himself as he looked over the label. "2012. Shit, wasn't that like, the year of the end of the world? Mayans, right?" He scoffed out a laugh as Lauren was slowly ambling on down, ears low, neck craned and eyes wide. "...Leave it to prehistoric beanpickers to get things wrong. Heads up." A bottle alley-ooped towards Lauren, who scrambled for it behind a panicked grunting exclamation uttered from her grit teeth, bumping past me, the bottle jiggling in her arms, but it fell from her grasp onto the floor with a clank, the glass luckily not shattering.

"Jesus Gabe!" she reached out with her talon, picking it up and transferring it up to her hand like a one-woman fireman bucket brigade.

"Gotta be quicker than that," Gabe tsked.

"...Got too many limbs to take care of," She held it gingerly, like a child, Gabe smirking. Lauren was less than enthused.

"Fuck, Gabe," I uttered, still scanning around. The loud clattering of the wine resonated through the wine cellar. I saw the dark, damp hallways, and that smell persisted. "We've still got to clear this place! You smell that?"

"Yeah. smells like a dead body. Stay loose, man," Gabe uttered, bringing his gun up. "You too, Green," Lauren placed the bottle on the ground, rustling with her gear with her gun back up.

"God, I don't like this," Lauren uttered. "That smells really bad."

"...I've smelled worse. We've just gotta find who died here." Gabriel's light shined down to where I was standing, and that was when I realized that I was standing in a wet, red scraping trail. In a single blink after that horrible realization, something about this place felt so odd and familiar. It was dark and uncomfortable. I could remember the dim red lights of the facility, the steady woosh of ventilation. Here the air was still. Stagnant. Worse than that place, somehow, telling me to get out.

A slow advance down that dark tunnel, brightened up by our mounted flashlights. I looked over to Lauren sticking her comms earbuds back in, breathing heavy and slow, eyes flashing to me as I let out my breath, my own chest heaving. That narrow hallway. Rows of doors, many open, full of boxes and things, just stuff. The fact that the lights were off was the icing on the cake, though the blood still led down the hall.

Another door, hardly adjacent, down at the very end. It looked like a heavy metal door, where the smell is strongest. "Walk-in freezer, talk about the one percent," Gabe uttered with a smirk, reaching forth to peel the door open while I gazed through the crack with my rifle at the ready, watching the door open, Lauren behind and above both of us as well. Meat hanging from hooks, all well and spoiled by now. "Heh, get a load of that." I was peeking inside, slowly panning. It sure was messy in here, the pig carcasses hanging up on macabre hooks and everything, guts and ichor on the ground in corners. But something was off. Everything was… Re-organized. There were… marks on the meat hanging up, where the flies buzzed. And those piles of guts…

"...B-but what was the padlock on the door for?" Lauren's voice met me, as did the sight of what had to be a human skull, flayed of flesh, bloody and raw, only a single eyeball left in it. I gasped, seeing more evidence. Straps of clothing, hard objects. This used to be a person. Probably more than one.

"...Oh, fuck-" I began, but was cut off as Lauren screamed.

It was a flash, turning around. I saw her wings and limbs flail, as she retreated back into darkness. Like the shadows themselves came to life around her and drug her back. How her especially large frame was swallowed into shadow, her eyes flashing in terror, teeth gnashed. She had been the furthest back, Gabriel right ahead of her. A slimy tendril lashing out at him and he was knocked from his feet. I was turning around, my light shining forth. I heard something distinctly inhuman- and nothing like even any hybrid's scream, least of all Lauren. The shadows gained a silhouette, Lauren on the ground, lashed up by these black tendrils like rope that dug into her skin all across her body, blood forming.

Only in that brief moment of light before terror did I catch a glimpse of its face. It was a human face, twisted distinctly into something far more unnerving than a human. It was like a doll, hard, chitinous and shimmering, immovable save for great unblinking eyes full of pits for irises, and a jaw twisted into a mighty razor smile, the lower two mandibles articulating on their own as it screeched at the light, going to shield its face with more of its shadows. That damp, dank, awful smell, how the humidity was unbearable here.

Lauren was drawing her pistol as she flipped over. *Bang, bang, bang*, screaming from behind grit teeth, holding back terror with rage, firing up into the monster grappling her.

"FUCKING SHOOT IT!" Gabriel roared on the ground from where he'd been knocked, sending rounds from his rifle up into the creature, with me as well firing high to avoid hitting Lauren. The monster screeched again, face disappearing as it zipped down the hallway with inhuman speed, dragging Lauren along with it as she screamed.

"Lauren! LAUREN!" I screamed. No fear within me, the fear seeming to disappear with its horrible face. I had to move, Gabriel cursing on the ground. I saw his plate carrier, the cordura sliced diagonally, the holster for his pistol bearing a nasty gash all the way through the plastic. I was charging down the hallway. Heart racing. Lauren. Lauren. More gunfire.

I was so caught up in my chivalry that I had hardly the time to react as it had apparently re-decided upon its prey, apparently chucking Lauren down the hallway as she cried out and I heard bottles clatter, and those shadows before me seemed oddly dense and close as it turned to me, barreling forth. A million little razors. I was pulling my trigger but I was out of bullets. Only then did the fear return, as it showed me that doll face once more. A sick and twisted smile with eyes that paralyzed.

Like in slow motion, I felt a hand heavy on my shoulder. My gaze from this black death turned. Gabriel. Face shining, an ever so tiny smirk playing out on his face. A face just as terrifying as that doll head. Like in a millisecond I knew that this wasn't anything more than a simple challenge to him.

Gabriel's hand scraped past my battle belt, my Junglas knife borrowed in a flash of steel. The beast's many blades were fast, but Gabriel was far more purposeful and utterly more vengeful than petty slashes, his free arm coming up and out to take the cuts.

Another blood curdling screech, that inhuman-human scream. One of those black pits that this thing had for eyes was pierced, split wide with black blood and clear eye fluid spilling out. Gabriel's own knife came out now, reaching it up into where this thing's guts should be. In and out, in and out, in and out, like a sewing machine gone haywire he stabbed and lanced and thrusted. The creature took an inhuman leap back, perhaps to save itself from a monster more savage than it, however Gabriel found the initiative to draw his pistol. Ten rounds rang out in what felt like an instant. I'm sure every round connected, another screech, slash. The gun fell out of Gabriel's hand and his knife was the important weapon again. Gabriel was roaring. He drove the knife back into the mess of the abdomen, his sliced up free hand reaching for the blade within its face, those shadowy tentacles going wild. He ran past where Lauren lay, full of slashes and blood and shocked eyes, watching the battle behind her pistol with its slide locked back. Gabriel drove that creature right on up the stairs. It was screaming and screaming and screaming inhumanely, splitting our ears. If it could know fear, it certainly felt it then as it hissed upon the sensation of sunlight touching its mysterious flesh.

Gabriel and it were gone upstairs, more screams. I collapsed beside Lauren, pulling her to her feet. "W-we need to kill that f-fucking thing," She uttered, blinking with me, eyes wide, Like an automatic response, like she really wasn't there, out of shock. Despite how her protective earbuds were still in her cow-like ears, the way she watched me with that dull horrified blankness as I spoke to her told me she wasn't hearing me.

"C'mon, c'mon," I was uttering, beside myself, as we made our way upstairs, practically scrambling up as I helped her along. In the blink of an eye, we were up top again, following the trails of black blood with only slight specks of red, going down the hallway to emerge into the kitchen to see the back of Gabriel, who was enveloped in the blackness of the shadowy tentacles and surrounded by the screams of his enemy and the screams of everyone around shocked and horrified by the instantaneous fight. As they careened into the table and wall, black sludgy blood trickling everywhere, I saw how the pitch black vapor in the air hung, trailed through with long wisps of sunlight like black dust, like this creature steamed out in response to feeling the sun upon its body.

The sliding glass door leading to the back patio crashed as Gabriel steered that monster right out the back porch using those knife handles like joysticks. How he drove it towards the pool and shoved it, letting it fall in and flail around in there, the pool dyed black, that mist still rising, the humidity following. Gabriel stood there over where it thrashed and splashed, looking down upon his work with his chest heaving. That mass of tentacles there.

Lauren was beside him, hurriedly reloading her pistol. I too stepped forward on Gabriel's other side, unholstering mine, and we sent round after round into the black foamy water nearest to where the creature splashed, seeing it's horrible face every now and then as it screeched and bubbled. *Bang bang bang bang bang*, reloading to do it all over again, until it lay still, floating and bubbling and hissing.

Lauren was still shooting, frenzied as she sank magazine after magazine, teeth grit, eyes in a frenzy, until Gabriel, with a swipe, peeled her gun from her hands. Like in a trance, for but a moment her hands and fingers still mimicked the firing of a gun before she slumped down like a dog laying down, still with her upper body erect as she wheezed there, everyone else gathering around. I finally and slowly peeled off my own helmet, snapping the ear cups open as I did and let it bounce on the ground as I too collapsed into a seated position, as the black mist lifted around the pool, now rendered a pitch black bog.

"...Basement's clear now," Gabriel huffed out, looking down at his torn up forearm. Lauren wheezed out a laugh, and I fell back to lay on the pool deck and stare into the late afternoon sky.

### Chapter 33

I'm still shaking.

Sitting in one of the pool chairs on the deck in nothing but my tee and cargo shorts, I was looking up at the bright twilight sky bearing down on us all. That… thing was all stretched out on the patio deck, its bladelike tendrils and amorphous body visible now that the mist it generates had since dispersed after it had expired. I looked over to Lauren too, on the largest poolchair, practically a novelty but it seemed to barely be big enough for her body all laid out, with little bandages all across her body, her tail completely covered in gauze, evidently from where it'd slashed the most when the thing grabbed her and dragged her back. That thing had to have been incredibly strong from how it tossed her around effortlessly. Come to think of it, it took them a lot of work to move its massive body, not to mention how handling its sharp, barbed tentacles messed up a lot of gloves so we just used the pool equipment to shove it around once we fished it out. I saw a shaking glass of wine clutched in Lauren's hand. Wasn't she underage? Most hybrids were grown at an accelerated rate, weren't they? She was like two, wasn't she? How old was she supposed to be, like, genetically? She couldn't have been much older than me or Gabriel, something about her just told me innately she was a late teenager like the rest of us.

"...should Lauren be drinking if she took the heal meds?" I pondered worriedly towards Gabe.

"Best time to drink is when you're on heal drugs, metabolic inducers. She'll be sober faster." I wasn't quite sold, though I guess I rested easier given Gabriel's nonchalance to the situation. "...Romans invented wine as a water purification additive. Can't be that bad for you."

"That arm of yours going to be alright?" I asked now, Gabriel's left forearm entombed like a mummy, the rest of him full of bandages like Lauren was, though far more densely given how he'd stabbed the thing three-fourths to death, sitting there in nothing but his shorts, letting his tattoos gleam as his cuts all across his body had been bandaged. I was entranced with the tattoo on his right shoulder, like a pauldron. That screaming skull with a knife through the eye and coming out the other side, pistols crossed right beneath it.

"...I've had worse. Fucker put up a good fight. But damn, got me a nice hood ornament," Gabriel hefted up its severed head by its razor hair in his gloved right hand. I saw Sam, who was entranced by the thick black pool retch and look away when Gabriel hefted it up. "Shit, looks like those Creator fuckers crossbred Medusa and a Japanese demon. Well, I'll give 'em one for creativity," He uttered. The face was that shimmering hard plastic bone. Looked exactly like an Oni mask, with its one remaining unblinking eye sending shivers down my spine. It took me half an hour to get the rust off of my knife, evidently its blood was highly reactive. Gabriel put it down with a splat. "Heh, you need something to take the edge off, Greenie?" Gabriel laughed towards her as she tremblingly poured herself another glass.

"You think dragons live longer than humans?" I pondered aloud, sitting there. Maria was off to the side, gazing at the carcass in disdained curiosity, her rifle cradled with its stock beneath her armpit. "...Like they do in stories and stuff."

"...Not at this fuckin rate," Lauren burped, taking another hearty gulp. Gabriel let out a chuckle in response.

"It's in the docs, Noah. Hybrids all more or less have the same lifespans as humans. Sept for Euclid-class like our friend over there. They're bog-standard monsters." I finally sighed, deciding to reach for my hologlasses hung through a molle loop on my armor beside me. "Oh my fuck, are you actually going to look at it for once? Whaaaat?" I didn't indulge him with a response, half because my sense of humor had dulled after nearly having my throat sliced by that lovecraftian horror and half because my entire world was numb from said experience.

I looked through my tac glasses, flicking page by page through the exposé. I started with the table of contents, seeing the categories Sapient, Euclid and Benign. I could guess which categories Lauren and that thing fell into, though I guessed the monster category was more interesting at the moment.

"...Fucking biological cloaking abilities?" I muttered.

"...What, about Blackwalkers?" Gabriel chimed in, waving his pistol towards that carcass by the mansion. "Yeah. Crazy shit. Wish I could have gotten some interesting genetic mods like that, instead Sinaloa just gave me the most bog-standard augs." He rambled.

"...It releases a cloud of water vapor mixed with its own low-oxygenated blood when it breathes subcutaneously, however it can dry out easily and its sensitive eyes can be blinded by bright light so it stays in cool, damp and dark areas and sticks to its own territory, where its vapor is already present. Its vapor makes it almost invisible in dark areas and at nighttime, and hunts with its many tentacles tipped with knife-like protrusions and its barbed skin, killing its prey through a combination of strangulation and exsanguination." I shuddered, before looking up. "Why the fuck would somebody make this? Who thought this was a good idea?"

"...Why the ffffuck would somebody make a dragon-centaur? With *fat tits?*" Lauren slurred out. She was far too impatient for the glass, drinking straight from the bottle at this point. I reached over to disarm her of her drink before she got out of control, though I was still engrossed in the exposé.

"...Speculation, but I bet it's because they wanted to see if they *could* make a biological cloaking device, and decided to stick it on a horrible monster before they started sticking it in our slightly more expensive special forces guys. Or maybe that's just the result of human trials, you get turned into a lovecraftian shadow tentacle monster."

"...At least I'm not a tentacle monster..." Lauren uttered, after failing to get her drink back as I deftly dodged it away from her groping arms and frontal talons. Despite having twice the hands (or thumb-bearing appendages) as I did, she was far too out of it to effectively grapple.

"Heh, don't get too ahead of yourself, some people like that shit," Gabriel laughed, stretching out as he put his arms behind his head and sighed, cricking his back. "God damn, Green. You'd think with your weight you'd have a higher tolerance. Jesus, you didn't even finish the bottle,"

"...My weight... fuck you asshole, I can *fly*," She uttered, now licking her glass dropped in the grass for any residual alcohol. "...You don't think I'm... Fat, do you Noah?"

"No. Just drunk. Ugh, how many of these fucking things did they make?" I flicked through the digital catalogue of horrors.

"Too many. You think if you were going to end the world with furries and monsters, you'd stop at like, one or two different furries and monsters? C'mon. You've gotta think like a furfag mad scientist cult if you want to understand the Creators, Noah."

"...I don't have fur... D-don't call me a lizard, I'm not one either, I'm... I'm a hairless mammal. I'm... dragonses are the fuckin... Platypus of hybrids." Lauren blurted sloppily, bouncing a little where she lay on that long reclining pool chair made of bouncy bands stretched between the metal frame. "...Platypi." I was now back in the sentient hybrids section, browsing.

"...Wait, so there are fish people living in the Pacific Ocean in domes they made underwater?" I uttered. "...Jesus christ. That'd be neat if it wasn't insane."

"Told you, Noah. Gotta remember who we're dealing with. Fucking Creators, bro."

"...Selani, though aesthetically modeled after great white and tiger sharks, are based almost entirely on a hybridization of dolphin and human genes. They have no gills and are mammalian. As noted, there are no true water-breathing hybrids, the Walen, based off of blue and killer-whale genes are similar despite their macrospecies subcategorization, as well as the Serenae, a sister species of the monofem class species Serpentine resembling the mythic mermaid, and the Anuraea, while based off of frog genes and being exothermal, are not true amphibians, as they breathe air their entire lives," I read verbatim, pausing. "So it says the Creators sort of let the selani set up an empire in the Pacific as one of these socio experiments? ...Where did they get the funding for this shit?"

"Government grant, post cold war surplus, buyouts... You know everyone figured Elrond Industries was doing shady shit while they ran the world, but this sort of... jumps the shark, doesn't it?" I took a moment to glare at Gabriel, who smirked behind his sunglasses and gazed into the sky at his little pun.

"I guess you could say... They were having a whale of a time?" Lauren blurted again, eyeing over. I was half tempted to just get up and walk back inside from the pun overdose.

"I'd like to fight one." Gabe said, not skipping a beat and interrupting my thought to find a way to exit this pun-filled conversation.

"Huh?"

"You know, a Walen, the whale guys?" He grunted. "Can't be that tough. It said that they're not too comfortable being out of the water, seeing as they weigh a shitton. Ought to slow them a bit. And besides, everybody's got a jugular,"

"They'd fucking eat you."

"Why the fuck would they eat me? Even if they were capable of digesting a person, which they happen not to be, my knife would give me free reign on all of their squishy important bits. Hybrids eating people was for some psyops societal degeneration master plan shit, not killing; they'd have to pick up a gun or a knife or a baseball bat or ball up their hands into fists like any other shmuck."

"...There's more to life than fighting," I scoffed, after taking in this information I had skimmed over, not really wanting to dwell on the whole maneating aspect of certain large hybrids, seeing Selicia entering hearing range as she walked about the place. "So, did you or didn't you memorize the book on Hybrids?" I asked, only semi-mockingly.

"Fuck off. Read or don't read." Gabriel was now fiddling with his pistol. "...Fucking hentai monster scratched my gun. Look at that shit," he raised the pistol, showing where the tentacle of the creature had sliced through his holster and into his gun, a nasty scratch in the metal of the slide.

"...It's just a gun," I muttered, and Gabriel tilted his glasses with the tip of his pistol.

"You fucking with me? This is a Bren Ten. A piece of fucking history. This gun is worth more than your whole kit."

"Why don't you sell it, then? Buy a different one." I asked. Gabriel paused, almost taken aback.

"...I shoot well with it. It feels good in the hand. I can't stand plastic guns and it's hard to find a ten millimeter these days that isn't."

"Don't you own an MDR?" I muttered, smiling.

"...plastic *pistols*. Rifles are different."

"Whatever, prima donna."

"Would you like me to sit the next monster fight out? By all means, shishkebab yourself one next time. I'll be glad to rate your performance." I sat back again, crossing my arms behind my head to just sunbathe. I guess it was just the afterburn of the adrenaline. I was still trembling ever so slightly, seeing it charging at me back in that basement every time I closed my eyes- but it was easier to put to rest seeing Gabriel towering over its dismembered head.

I'd fallen asleep with a short nap there, only to wake when the sun was disappearing beneath the horizon. Gabriel was gone, Lauren was passed out in that chair with her tongue hanging out of her gaping mouth, another bottle clutched in her hand. Everyone was over towards the grill of the back patio; though we didn't have much, Gabriel was over there grilling up some squirrels somebody had chanced to hunt on the grill. Was Gabriel grilling up pieces of the Blackwalker, too? I saw its dead body laying all the way over, looking rather shriveled now that it had dried out some more. Selicia was standing before it, having taken her custom holos off to inspect it, as the periwinkle skies of twilight hurt her eyes far less than the usual full brunt of the daytime. She didn't seem too impressed at its vicious, spiny body, kicking it with one of her many legs.

I got up, ambling on over towards them. This reminded me of being back home, the calm before the storm, when we were all just hanging out and relaxing, grilling up some food, laughing and playing. Nobody was laughing or playing, everyone looked anxious, and we sure as shit weren't swimming in the inky pool. We were afraid, unsure. It was still and quiet, even if Gabriel's usual bright, cheery personality hung over all. Maria as indomitable as usual.

"...You're gonna let Lauren drink *all* the booze?" I muttered, noting more empty bottles.

"Hey man, I'm cooking with it. Besides, everybody else ought to stay sober, despite the hardcore party mood going on, and at this rate she'll drink up the whole house' worth," Gabriel waved in the air with his tongs sarcastically, bandaged hand still hanging all wrapped up. "We'll take some with us, but right now the only one allowed to be on break is Lauren. Her rear wings got cut up a little so I don't want her flying until they've healed some, and that's what she's mainly good for, air support. Figure if she's too drunk to stand she won't try and fly, anyways."

"...Well, stop enabling her now. I don't want a drunk dragon stumbling around with a machine gun if shit suddenly goes haywire. And get her to take enough FastHeal so she can fly again soon, hangover or not. You too with your hand."

"Yeah, yeah. *Yo se*. She'll probably be good by the time we reach Idaho. Speaking of, Abel, the dog-taur guy's hole has sealed over and it looks like he'll be good within the week. Speaking of shit going haywire," Gabriel reached over to the portable radio nearby to where he grilled. "...You should get a kick out of this. Take a listen," He threw it on. A legible broadcast for once.

"...Of the United States Constitution and the true will of the Founding Fathers. We will bring these collectivist criminals, the so-called People's Democracy of California, and its monstrous despot to justice. We of the New American Alliance will see fit that the reprehensible annihilation of Vegas and Juneau is avenged, and put an end to this so called Operation Sledgehammer. We of the New American Alliance are well trained, well armed and more than ready to defend our homeland, the true heartland of the United States of America. You are playing on our turf and every man defending his home is far better armed and disciplined than you of the so-called Californian People's Army. You claim an army of ten million strong? We see ten million corpses condemned to die for a despot and an ideology that cares little for the puny individual beneath their jackboot. We shall engage you with weapons you illegally and unconstitutionally sought to rend from our hands on a federal level that you yourself completely relinquished through foolish laws of your own, and you will meet your end for it. You claim to field hybrid specialists of considerable ability and claim virtue over us for this shallow minstrel show of inclusivity, but this is by no means unique to you. We have patriotic men and women of all shape and species who have taken up oath and arms to defend the rightful law of this land, and you will be expelled like the true animals you are." Gabriel looked over to me, as a computerized voice uttered "Set to repeat. Standby." over some almost corny patriotic tune. I could practically envision the waving american flag with it playing.

"Wanna hear the Blue's propaganda broadcast?" Gabe smirked, completely enthralled, as if he were witnessing an especially sublime performance art piece and not literal propaganda, speaking on as the message began to repeat from the top, that dead serious gruff man's voice comically overshadowed by Gabriel's amused cheer. "It's more about how the red states are dickheads for blowing up DC and LA, how Repubs' are a bunch of retarded hicks who think that a couple AR15s are going to make a difference, and how their army of ten million is going to stomp the fuck out of the right wingers, who happen to be a little spread out fighting the Eastern Seaboard Alliance and the Allied Great Lakes States too, who are on side blue. I just picked the red broadcast to listen to because I think it's funnier. Got the whole 1776 vibe to it I'm diggin. Blue's is practically Soviet style, though. Pretty avant-garde stuff, 'specially when you play 'em off each other."

"Yeah, I think I get it," I uttered only a little concernedly, Gabriel shutting it off, him being the only one smiling there, everyone else all the more uncomfortable hearing it again. "Shit, you said they blew up DC and LA?"

"Juneau too. If I had to guess, Arizona was a little slow on the draw and they needed to buy time against the blue invasion. They probably struck Greater Angeles right after Vegas went up. DC is a bit obvious, we've got- we *had* a blue president. Juneau was since Alaska threw themselves into the fray right quick, were about to try and invade on land through Canada,

Washington and Oregon happen to have allied with Cali at the moment but don't seem too keen on the conflict. Cali just did what they had to do to slow down an Alaskan invasion, which at this point seems like a no-show."

"Why Vegas though? Pretty much the whole city votes Democrat."

"That's a little unclear, though I'm guessing the Reds were in a better position to take the city. Kind of a chokepoint, it's got the Hoover dam and everything." I sighed inwardly. "From context I'm assuming other nukes were used, but those four are the big name ones. Not really that much nuking now it seems, since it looks like everybody has their anti-ballistic missile systems up and under complete control, after seizing all the silos. They got the nuking in while the nuking was good, looks like."

"...Sounds like there's no going back now."

"Really does."

"You think that guy today was a scout?" I asked. "Which side you think he was on?"

"Dunno. Might be some trigger happy yahoo. I'd be on edge too. Matter of fact, I am," He uttered, taking a swig of wine from the bottle in his hand before splashing some on the meat on the grill. "Hoo, damn," He blurted. "Don't think the Creators made these guys for the taste, I can't seem to get these misty bastards seared right," Gabriel uttered with a jarring change of subject, stabbing himself a piece of the blackwalker tentacle, which coughed black vapor as it trailed towards me and I recoiled. "You up for hentai monster calamari?" He raised the skewered bit to my face and I put my hand up, shaking my head. He shrugged. "Eh. What it really needs is a bit more seasoning. I'll make you tasty, you fucking son of a bitch," Gabriel fished for the spice rack he'd brought out of the pantry, throwing some on as the fire flared. "You gotta cook on low, sear to finish. Easy peasy, always is,"

"...Why don't you just try frying it?" Selicia's voice wafted over, peering in. "There's oil for that in this house, it would be-"

"Bitch, you fucking mention frying one more fucking time," Gabriel, still at work and glaring down onto the grill pointed his finger back at her and she was silent. "I swear to fuck. I'm not a fucking culinary kindergardener and if that shit slips your whore mouth one more fucking time I'll fucking eat *you*." Gabriel was too busy at work to notice her recoil, thrashing like a madman, an auteur pianist before his piano, making music with his whole body, an otherworldly display of fire and smell before him.

"...He keeps trying to cook that... thing right," Anthony muttered to me, edging past. "It's scaring me, dude. He makes me eat it and I tell him it's okay, it's edible, but he won't stop," He whimpered in my ear.

"...I think I'll have the squirrel," I muttered back, looking around, ready to leave Gabriel to his Herculean task.

There was Maria, standing before the pool, facing the city before us, to the west. Watching the Sun sink behind the Sierra Nevada mountains.

"It's pretty, isn't it," She uttered.

"You don't usually call things pretty."

"Yeah, well I need a better outlook on things. At least I'm going to, anyways."

"Hm."

She stood there, hair all lit up in the blaze of the evening. God, wasn't she pretty? I suppose she was. "...Looks like the world is on fire," She said, a chuckle escaping her lips, the first smile crossing them in god knows how long. "We're here just watching it burn."

"I'll skip on burning it myself. Looks like they're doing a good job of it themselves."

"Yup." She finally looked back to me. "Life's short, huh?" She uttered. "Nothing good ever lasts. America didn't even make it to its tricentennial." She smiled again, but it disappeared bit by bit as she turned back over to the sunset, as the Sun vanished bit by agonizing bit, almost as if it would never rise again in this dramatic moment. "I ought to be happy, y'know. America killed my brother. The CIA, I mean. Learned all about it, bit by bit. One cartel tries overthrowing Mexico, the CIA gives guns to the other cartel, one of those guns puts a bullet through Martín's head." She sighed. I couldn't see her face, but I saw her chest heave, ever so slowly. "Mom and Dad knew about it too. At least I figure. I never understood why we didn't just go straight on to Canada. They didn't kill my brother." Her voice waned, like it was about to break. "...I'm holding it together," She said, like responding to a thought I didn't even have, let alone say. I took a step, reaching finally for her hand.

"Let's..." She turned back to me. I saw that wet sparkle in her eyes, how she was trying, fighting to smile. "Let's make it through this together, okay?" I uttered. I don't know why, or at least I didn't then, but this felt weak to me. Saying this to her face, something within me stung. Like I said the wrong thing. I saw how her eyes sparkled, how she could see this too. She heard it in my voice. But she smiled anyways, turning to take both my hands.

"Let's start tonight."

### Chapter 34

Lauren was there, laying before me. God, I could just get lost in those eyes. Her flowing hair. It used to put me ill at ease, seeing her strange, monstrous elements flow into her humanity, but now it was more akin to poetry. Something exciting and exotic. Here in the quiet of the morning.

*Boom. Boom.*

*Boom, boom.* My eyes shot open, and Lauren was gone. Maria's eyes shot open, her face in mine. *Boom.* A loud, low sound somewhere, far off. always in twos, one loud one distant, a shot and an impact, though not in that order.

"What the fuck," came muttered from my lips as I sat up in bed, squinting. I suddenly leapt from bed, stark raving naked, and I ran to the window of the master bedroom, where we'd slept.

I ran out onto the balcony. I looked out to the city below us, and I saw rising smoke. Helicopters and drones buzzed the sky, as glowing tracers ripped from their turrets. Far off artillery was firing, and much closer, it hit home; two booms.

"Fucking shit's going down?!" I said, turning to Maria, who sat up in bed, also naked. I saw her going for her underwear, before Gabe barged in. Any other woman would shriek, but Maria's pistol came up towards the door, as I turned around, covering my genitals.

"Nice. Time to go." Maria sighed at Gabriel's intrusion, though not entirely without apprehension given the situation, tossing the pistol onto the bed as she covered her chest, getting up and throwing her armor on, skipping a bra, settling for her sports panties alone beneath her loadbearing kit and helmet. I too ran over for my boxers, going for my clothes. "We gotta fucking go now!" Gabriel bellowed, and I figured that very liberal business casual would work for this, skipping clothes for body armor instead.

I ran downstairs, in nothing but boxers and my pate carrier, slinging my rifle. People were beginning to get up, and I saw Gabriel peeking by the door on his knees, watching the road out the front door through the scope on his rifle.

"Are we under attack?!" Anthony blurted.

"No, it's a parade with fireworks," Gabe uttered with snide, before turning to me in my half-nudity and laughing. He was one of the few fully clothed and armored, despite one of his hands bound up entirely. Everyone else was hurrying around, both trying to get dressed. It was an understatement to say panic was in the air, and every concussive explosion of artillery made everyone jump. The shells were getting closer. The next shell shook the entire mansion, the chandelier swinging. Gabe cursed, and I saw, outside, a plume of dirt thrown about as a crater opened itself up in the lawn.

At first, I figured this was a fluke. They couldn't be shelling *us*, right? then the second one fell, demolishing the fountain out front in a brilliant shower of water and porcelain, pebbles zipping through the windows like bullets.

"Agh!" I heard a scream from behind, and I watched as Lauren herself oh-so gracefully tumbled down the stairs, right towards me as a flying half ton of green flesh. I took a bounding leap to the side, just as she planted right on the bottom of the stairs. "Owww..." She groaned, and I paused to help her up. I noticed that she too was in similar straits to Maria, in nothing but her combat gear and bra. I saw Gabe laugh a little but, but as another explosion hit, he bit down on his teeth, as Selicia, who emerged from the darkness of the basement screamed out, covering her head in an instant, squinting about at the panic. The whole place shook.

"You good?!" I shouted to Lauren, as I helped her up, pausing to cinch her chest carrier right, as the magazine shelving was practically diagonal.

"...So much for no hangover," She muttered in a deep squint of her own, messy hair falling all over the place as she held her evidently throbbing head and Gabe tsked.

"That's not the booze, that's the artillery." He seemed to be having too good of a time. I reached for my comms.

"Sentinel! Why didn't you warn us!?"

"NO REDFORCE COMBATANTS HAVE ENTERED MY ACTIVE ENGAGEMENT RANGE. HOWEVER, WE SEEM TO BE TAKING HEAVY MORTAR FIRE."

"My bad, I forgot to reset him," Gabe was still too entertained than any sane person should be right now. "Sentinel. Estimate hostile headcount within one kilometer."

"ESTIMATE OF TEN THOUSAND NON-BLUEFORCE PERSONNEL IN ONE THOUSAND METER PERIMETER. ESTIMATING BETWEEN NINE HUNDRED AND FOUR THOUSAND ACTIVE REDFORCE PERSONNEL CONVERGING TOWARDS OUR CURRENT LOCATION. RECOMMEND EVASIVE ACTION." The number certainly didn't help me feel any better.

"Fire for effect, Sentinel. Return fire when engaged. *Guys,*" Gabriel roared, as Sentinel began stringing off bursts on the double deuce outside. "Headcount! We're leaving!" Everyone was assembling, trembling as they did, and I made sure to check that everyone was here.

"Everybody's here!"

"We sure? We're not gonna make a second trip!" The shelling appeared to slow. "Alright! Everybody knows who's doing what? Archie, Noah, you drive! Maria, you get up with me and be on the passenger side gun! I've already got the quickest route out of the city in mind, you follow me! Don't lag behind!" We ran out into the courtyard, to pile into the vehicles. "I want everyone firing!" The artillery was slowing. I felt the ground attack was soon to commence.

The house was on an elevated position, and we could see a mob down below us, swarming. Like a rising wave, they came. We could practically see the anger in their eyes as they flooded those streets. A good 100 degrees of our vision before us produced a hundred heads, and a hundred more behind them. The din and clamor of the guns in the distance soon became the background to many, many voices, all roaring, their gleaming knives and clubs and miscellaneous weaponry raised in the air in full charge. This wasn't an army. It was more akin to a riot.

"Oh, fuck," Anthony hushed beside me. Gabriel was charging the vehicle straight towards them. It was practically sickening, Sentinel's guns ripping through them. I could see red where they dispersed, some falling to never get up again.

"Californians," Gabe cracked as he sailed into the human wave. Many ducked out of the way but a fair couple found themselves caught in the grill of the JLTV, the macabre head of the Blackwalker stuck onto the hood as a bloody ornament of war being the last thing some of them would see, the dusty colored military vehicle painted in splotches of blood as heads were cracked against the hood and windshield. Bullets whizzed past our heads, any of these blue-clad 'soldiers' with guns were firing, rather ineffectually without any sort of true marksmanship, but it wasn't quite beyond unnerving zipping through the crowd . I could see their eyes, bloodshot. They'd more than likely given them a drug or something to rile them up, they practically looked like an army of the furious dead for a split second, my head turning to see one shaking his weapon at me, mouth wide and agape. This was no soldier, this was some noodle-armed kid with a blue bandanna and a kitchen knife high out of his mind. Ten million poor bastards just like this one behind him. "I fucking hate Californians," Gabriel was muttering, still as dourly amused as ever, our guns returning fire on anybody that stepped forward with a firearm.

Under the roar of the double deuce we fought. We fired from every window, if only to get our all-encompassing enemy to duck away, and it was deafening, confusing, horrifying. "How are we gonna do this?!" I shouted up to Gabriel between Sentinel's reload.

"Two rights and a left! We're almost through!" He uttered, though one right later and Gabriel screeched to a stop.

"HALT!" He shouted. "Shit, we're blocked off!" The road was completely covered in trashed cars. This wasn't like before, this looked fresh.

"We're a sitting duck here!" Archie uttered. Selicia was on the back of the truck, firing her M16 burst after burst from the hip, horror in her eyes. The crowd hung back.

"Jesus, they're everywhere!" She was screaming, in the middle of a reload.

"I should go see what's going on!" Lauren cried to me, moving as if she were to jump off and fly.

"Don't!" I cried, waving her down. "You'll just get shot down!" The crowd was getting gutsier. Not many of them were shooting, and more worriedly, Sentinel wasn't firing back, even at the ones who were. They stood there, edging towards us, murder in their eyes. "Gabriel?!" I shouted, my voice barely cracking. I saw some of them producing molotov cocktails.

"Sentinel! Open fire, all targets!"

"TARGETING SENSORS DAMAGED. AUTOMATIC ENGAGEMENT PROTOCOLS COMPROMISED." I saw that power armor in the turret. The pauldron-mounted sensor was sparking.

"Sentinel's camera took some shrapnel! Noah!" I saw Gabriel get out of the jeep, his MDR belching rounds from the hip, as he was down a hand. He caught one of the ones trying to light a molotov, who burst into flames, the crowd scattering and receding. "Get up here, Noah!" Anthony, you drive the jeep!"

"What are you saying?!" I shouted. Gabriel drew his pistol after his rifle ran dry, shooting a rifle-wielding Blue atop a building.

"Get in the fucking robot, Noah!" Gabriel pulled the door open.

"Wh- don't I need that plugsuit?!"

"There's no time for that! You'll have to put up with the lag. We need you to move the cars with it. You're the only one I authorized to use it aside from myself and my hand's fucked up. CMON! Sentinel, open up!" He bellowed. Sentinel was moving away from the turret, down and exiting out of the door, popping open in the back for me. I could hardly believe the plan, but I figured it was better than none.

I pulled my armor off for a brief second, popping myself up into the frame. I felt how the haptics sealed to my hands and feet, how it closed around me. My headset interfaced with the Sentinel program within the second. More bullets ricocheted around us. I could have sworn one of them hit me, bouncing harmlessly off my armor.

Maria was up on the big gun now, firing off 40mm rounds one at a time from the reverse weapon of the JLTV. Selicia was also firing to suppress, but the more time went on the more Californian gunmen arrived. I took a moment to get a feel for the thing, before I began to walk around the JLTV. I felt the immense strength I had now, a sort of weightless feeling, yet ever so clumsy, stomping around on those raised boots. I saw one of the vans off to the side of the wall, where there looked to be no cars behind it or anything, and if I moved it, we could squeeze through. I bent down to work it over, feeling my extended arms and my metal fingers, fully under my control despite being inches away from my real ones, to tip it up onto its side and roll it out of the way.

"Get ready to move! We're almost through!" Gabriel remarked of my progress, before that car fell over, rolling, and I was met with a dozen screaming blues charging forth at me.

I reacted, seeing a machete coming towards me. Before it could land, I brushed him aside entirely; lacking a plugsuit I couldn't really do any precise movements so I did what I could, brushing him aside with a backhanded swoosh. I felt his ribs snapping, his spine bending, his lung bursting as the back of my titanium knuckles impacted the flesh above his raised right arm, poised to strike. He rolled and whined out a groan with his machete flying out of his hand, the next coming forth. I simply dove my other hand at him in some sort of primitive, childlike punch given the lack of coordination. I felt his sternum crunch and his face wash out from color as he coughed blood, the wind to end all winds knocked out of him, falling to die of a crushed heart more than likely. More and more swarming me, blades careening off of my arms as I held them up to protect my head. I groped out to find one of their necks, feeling it snap effortlessly in my monstrous metal hand. One of them had a pistol, firing as I protected my face with my arms, the rounds hitting me like hailstones, the HUD sparkling up as I saw the diagnostics in my plain helmet register the hits on my forearms. With my hands up I kicked him in the gut, feeling his spine and hips splinter. It was inhuman how I fought, how I brushed these men, hardly adults aside. Blood spraying as I dove my limbs at them. By the time Gabriel drove by, blaring the horn, I could hardly hear him tell me to grab the fifty out of the passenger side of the JLTV and get up onto the medical truck's bed. I was entranced by death, by carnage before my eyes, but I shook it away as Gabriel's voice returned and I took up that great autocannon. I saw Maria looking down on me from the turret as she was reloading. She paused for a moment as she saw me, painted red, though as the convoy ambled forward and Selicia popped the truckbed open for me, I saw their faces, full of terror and the rage of combat.

I got up there with my weapon and rained fire at the technicals that had finally caught up with us from behind, trucks and cars filled to the brim with angry blue gunmen. The first car was a minivan, guns poking out of every window, the two in the front with eyes of rage and terror as I turned the fifty on them. What madness, what horror as the blood and pieces flew as that was minivan filled with the jellified remains of those men. The crowd was throwing molotovs from the side, and the haphazard coordination the suit had without the plugsuit interface seemed not to matter as it was harder to miss than it was to hit. I saw arms, legs fly, chewed off by .50 BMG rounds. I was out of control, empty shells pooling at my feet as death roared. Bullets would strike me like flies colliding with my chest. It was like I wasn't even there anymore.

"We're home free. Nice job, guys," Gabriel uttered. War raged behind where we drove, in front of me as I stood and watched us drive off, facing towards the city we were leaving. I could see the fires inside the city, feel the explosions. Gunfire, the sound of roaring crowds. A furious city in flames.

"Oh, shit," Gabriel uttered, bringing me back into the present. We could see in the open scrubland sprawling out ahead of us, an entirely new bunch of people, red being their color of choice rather than blue, armbands here and there amid a sea of camouflage gear, the American flag being the next most common patch of ID on them. "Looks like this must be the NAA." They looked at us for a good, long time as we passed slowly. I could see war machines, from mere technicals and zipperbikes to a sparse handful of military-grade mechs in the fields meandering towards the city. And they, despite being far, far more thinly-spread than the Californians, were much more heavily armed individually. The Californians had only a dozen rifles between every hundred fighters, here every man certainly had a rifle of some sort and was dressed in some sort of tactical fashion. Body armor, comms, webgear, LBE, the works. Every last one had plenty of ammo per head given the lack of limp pouches and presence of fully stocked bandoliers, some even had a spare shotgun, bolt action or .22 slung over their backs, all the things the Californians viciously lacked.

"...I think they think we're Repubs too, given the blood," Gabriel muttered, and the hairs rose on the back of my neck as I noticed how my armor was sopped in red. "Don't make any fast moves, guys. If you've got red stuff, best to get it out. Don't make it look too obvious now." They hardly looked like stupid hicks, but they sure looked mean. "Smile and wave, boys," Gabe said. "Smile and wave."

"These guys really think we're one of them?" I asked Gabe back in my comms, standing there to look pretty for the glaring eyes behind semi-automatic carbines.

"It doesn't matter. Let's just get the fuck out of here."

It was a while before I could get out of that suit and bring myself to vomit. This was a war, and it already felt like hell.

## ACT IV
## BAPTISM

### Chapter 35

"Hey."

Like a fly buzzing in my ear as I sat there in my disassociation.

"...Noah. You good?"

"Yeah, I'm fine, fuck off," I muttered all at once. Staring up at the sky. Sun was set to go down now. I saw Lauren finally sail around back, passing overhead to spiral down.

I sat up, seeing the landscape. The dense brush had gradually changed as we had since crossed the state line into Idaho, high desert morphing into sparse forestry. We were going north and it was getting colder and wetter.

We sat somewhere north of Boise, here in a quiet moment in some dark forest campground, away from the chaos for a couple precious moments. the original plan was to go around the west of Boise, but this war made things complicated, and we'd passed it on the east, before the mountain range would corridor us towards Montana and Canada. Boise was captured as a Republican stronghold, or so the broadcasts claimed. I can remember the image of Boise in flames to our left as we zipped on by, slipping past the rear lines of this chaotic war. The assault from the western states was relentless, that city hanging ghostlike behind us, as if a distant memory already in my mind, yet another target of the Pacific Alliance's Operation Sledgehammer, if only a secondary one. I was surprised in the retrospect that it didn't have that big of an impact on me, given how brutal my morning was. I could practically still taste the blood in my mouth, despite how I'd washed my face in the first stream we passed.

"God, I've never seen so much green," Lauren uttered breathlessly, wings ruffling after landing. Gabriel smirked from where he stood, like a joke had caught itself in his throat. "The forest is beautiful. It looks like it goes on forever."

"Yeah. Just about does." Gabriel smirked back, less willing to take a swipe at her than usual. I bet he was going to remark on his nickname/assigned last name for her. I guess I ought to have registered this polite change but it was beyond me. "...I never asked you," He suddenly tapped my shoulders with his knuckles. "What'd you think about power armor?"

"I killed the fucking shit out of those people." I coughed, Gabriel looked down.

"Only good commie's a dead commie, right?" He muttered.

"...Sure. Whatever." Gabriel sat on one of the park benches nearest to where I had been laying, in the backseat of my jeep. "...You know, I don't think we'll be able to go around Shortstone. Mountains to the east, a fucking war to the west." Gabriel sighed heavy at my nonchalant dourness.

"Was kind of hoping we'd avoid the place. I've got associates there, since it's become bigger than the state capital, lots of business to be done there. Sure is these days now that Boise's on fire. They catch on that I'm still alive, we'll have a fuckin' problem."

"...Then we won't spend long there."

"Hm, that's the thing," Gabriel uttered. "This is going to be a sensitive operation, moving through Shortstone. I feel like we're gonna need a lot more than a couple red armbands to get through undetected." I sighed.

"Maybe. We'll see," I muttered, going back to lay back again and stare up at the stars just beginning to emerge into the twilight. Lauren had been standing awkwardly there, a witness to our conversation, thumbs twiddling together. I saw how she trembled, fighting back hopeless worry with a sense of awe at how the world could be, looking around. She couldn't get enough of the trees, it seemed. "...You think the whole world was desert?"

"Huh?"

"You seem pretty engrossed," I uttered to her. "The forest. You act like you've never seen it before."

"I haven't, though," she uttered, before furling her lips, stomping one of her legs a little. "I mean, I always had the idea, but I didn't know what it really looked like, until I saw it all." I smiled and she smiled weakly back. I'd have loved to see it from the air too, with her. I could tell that she'd love to show me just as much. I guess in my dissociation all I could do was bathe in the secondhand euphoria.

I was quiet and still, staring there. The smoke from Boise rising in the distance, on this ridge where we stayed. There was a lot of verticality on the way up to Shortstone, that city that wasn't yet in sight. It was so uneasy, the thought of being here, of what we were about to do. I could see Daniel off before the fire, drawing in his sketchbook. I was glad he was up and about, though I saw the ghost in his eyes, the terror. Selicia had climbed one of the redwoods, off up somewhere gazing into the distance, being more useful than usual, though really she was simply constructing another one of her hammocks to lounge in, well in sight for the rest of us, that show-offy nature of hers on display. After sharing her presence with me for long enough, Lauren ambled off herself, to go by the streamside where Anthony was fishing to spite his jitters. Abel was nearby, also healed well, attempting to climb a tree as well, inspired by Selicia. I chuckled, less than focused. He sure looked funny, with all those limbs digging into that redwood, ears and tail whipping ineffectually with a determined look on his face. What a silly creature of a person. I could almost find myself smiling watching him, Selicia somewhere above similarly amused by his antics.

"...How do you think Kyle is doing?" I asked Gabriel with a turn of my head and eyes, who furled his lips.

"If they know what's good for them, everyone in Crystal Springs ought to be in that bunker that nerd owns." I furled my own lip now.

"Maybe we should have stayed there to wait this shit out."

"Probably, maybe, maybe not. Little late now."

"Yup." Maria was somewhere off, as Gabriel ambled off on his own now. I saw her approaching, wearing clothes for now. She stopped by, but it felt weirdly cold as she laid her hand on my shoulder.

"You good?"

"Yeah."

"Last night was... fun."

"Yeah."

A weak smile to be shared. I still felt the world between us. Her smile, forced. Her rigid hand retreating after a while, as the breath in my lungs could escape now. She was still looking toward me, swallowing her apprehension.

The night was lonely and practically sleepless, before we could set out once more. A quiet hour of slinking through the woods and we emerged onto a long, open vantage point before that city, Shortstone. Biggest city in Idaho, stretching out in the little valley beside the impassable mountains and the smoke to the west.

"Something about this isn't right," Gabe said. He watched the city through the looking glass atop his rifle, scanning back and forth slowly as we waited sickly with our hearts in our guts. "It looks kinda empty on the outskirts… But…" He said. "For all the people that are passing through, I'm not seeing many people going out. Comms aren't giving us anything aside from propaganda, either."

"It's gotta be just today," I said. "It's a fluke."

"I'm with Gabe on this one," Archie said. "I may not have the best grasp on human cities but there is definitely something going on here."

"Want me to go look?" I heard a voice from behind me say. I turned around, seeing Lauren standing there, wings rustling on her back in anticipation.

"It's a risk, but I think we'll have to take it," Gabe said. "the one thing you can really depend on is intel, which we seem to lack."

"She shouldn't go alone, though," I uttered, looking back to her as her ears perked up. "I'm going with." The group became silent, and Gabriel's face formed a smile.

"Christ, Noah," I heard Gabe say with a bit of a laugh.

"A-are you serious?" Maria uttered.

"What?" I said, as Lauren nodded profusely, glad to fly with me again, curtseying down a little as I approached, masking my anticipation. With a silent grunt, I hoisted myself onto the part of her back closest to her humanoid portion, where the gap between her front and rear wings were the greatest. My usual position, as she stood back up, taking a single look over her shoulder as she checked her gear.

"D-don't you dare drop my boyfriend!" Maria growled.

"Gabe, Archie, guys, stay in touch over comms, alright?" I asked them and tapped the earcup of my helmet. Lauren seemed rather shocked by my idea, along with everyone else, but within seconds, she was beaming.

"Alright," Lauren "tsk"ed, as if she were about to show off, and her wings ruffled a little and she stretched them out. She must've been smiling like crazy. "Hold on, okay?" My heart began to pound and I began to sweat when I realised what I just roped myself into, as she walked up to that steep ledge.

"Don't fall off, Noah," Daniel muttered with a little smile.

"I got him, I got him!" Lauren assured them.

"I'm… I'm good," I said to them, before leaning in. "Try not to do so many tricks this time, huh?" I whispered.

"Oh, now you're asking too much," She joked quietly back. I laughed, then I groaned in worry. "Wait- what's the plan here?"

"You're gonna look for reds. Specifically try to map out where they're garrisoned," Gabriel ordered. "I've got the city map here, just tell me the street names."

"...What if we happen to get shot down?" Lauren went on.

"Heh. We'll try to get to you if you tell us the street name. Don't expect a hot extraction, though. I doubt the dozen of us can take on the Republican army, even for a short smash-and-grab. Oh, speaking of," Gabriel tossed us articles of red cloth. "Tie onto your right bicep. That's what they're doing, I think. If you have to bluff, tell 'em you're from Wyoming. Last I heard they're having a rough patch with intel, operating around here on a whim."

"What if we get surrounded by Democrats?"

"Not likely, but..." He pulled out two blue ones. "Here. Stow 'em. If you get captured just tell them half the truth- *that's* the disguise. As far as they should care you're reds. But how about don't get shot down."

"Right," I uttered, tying mine over the arm, Lauren doing the same. I checked my rifle and cinched up my armor, Lauren checking her gear, checking her hydration pouch too.

"Nice knowing you, mate!" I heard Archie cry out, as Lauren edged back, ready to charge.

"Here we go!" She yelped in reserved glee, before leaping off of and falling down the chasm, with me stuck on like a mollusk on a speedboat. I had to bite my tongue to keep from letting out a cry of exhilaration of my own, the terror from last time gone as I was more than ready for this again. Though, it still felt like my heart fell into my stomach with a splash as I felt gravity loosen its grip on me, and I tightened my grip on Lauren.

*Poom.* She opened her wings, and I felt all my blood drain from my head with a sickening, downward jolt- but in the course of a second, the velocity transformed from vertical to horizontal, and with blinding speed we rocketed along. My breath flew out of my mouth. We were flying once more.

Lauren's spine streamlined into one line, both torsos parallel, wings alternating as they beat, great blasts of air propelling us forward and upward. I had to lean in, my chest against her lower humanoid back to hold on. I was surprised how low she flew. she skimmed above most treetops, although she darted between the taller ones. Her wingspan was by no means compact, needing to be big enough to lift her off of the ground and then some; I was worried she would clip them and it would all be over. But she seemed to instinctually sense exactly how much space she took up, she flew according to that, dipping and tilting with every turn around every tree. At first, I tried to keep myself upright, but I quickly caught onto how I needed to lean with her to make a smoother flight. Not having stirrups, however, made those leans seem like that much more dangerous.

She flew low, every beat was voluminous, carrying massive pressure (enough to lift her half-ton body, me, and then probably a whole lot more without much difficulty), but she beat them between trees, making those low "*pomph*" sounds that shook the trees she passed. We were going fast.

"Having fun?" She blurted with a smile, back to me, tipping her head to eye at me.

"Eyes- Keep your eyes on the- road!" I cried out, as she dodged a tree blindly, as if she knew it was there.

"Loosen *up*, Noe! We're not getting shot at yet!" she said with a laugh as she looked back forward, beating her wings and tilting forward a bit, accelerating instantly. Truth was, I was having fun, and I think she knew it, laughing for the both of us.

She blazed along, now hovering talon-distance from the deserted highway below us, close enough that if she wanted to she could probably swing out a talon or hand and grab a sideview mirror from one of those abandoned cars lying dead on the side of the road, all four of her wings angled like a flying V and simply gliding off of her own velocity. Her speed was like a blur. I'd seen her flying on many occasions, and only now could I appreciate her speed, almost like I'd forgotten what it was like since last time. When I watched her, she seemed to zip across the sky so fast she looked like a tiny bird or something, but even knowing how big and heavy she was in reality, I really couldn't appreciate the sheer speed, the power she seemed to possess until I was flying with her. It was like magic. Of course, I figured I slowed her down a bit- but keeping in mind she was carrying me while attaining such speeds only made me more impressed.

She, with her speed draining, suddenly pulled up, and just as she began to stall, her horizontal velocity nearly zero, she latched onto a redwood, and I grunted, trying to hold on.

"Ah…" she panted. "How… How was that?"

"I don't care what we have to barter, we're getting you a saddle," I said, kind of exhausted myself. "Hanging on like this is nerve-wracking."

"What… don't even buy me a drink, before you get into that… Kinky shit?" She laughed between breaths, going for her hydration tube. I coughed out a laugh.

"Piss around all you want, but, I need, I need stirrups-"

"Are you… out of breath?" She interrupted with a huff, laughing back now. I rolled my eyes. "You want to flap your arms, fly on ahead? be my guest," she muttered amusedly at my breathlessness. "…Real-talk, You wanna do this more often?"

"What gave it away?" She smirked at my humor.

"…The saddle's a good idea, then. I don't want you to slip off; I can feel you holding on for dear life right now," she said, and I think I blushed a little. "I care for you… you guys." A pause hung off her statement, something awkward and little.

"Look, Lauren…" I said, before adding a pause of my own. a hand went up to the haptic controls and I muted my comms for a moment. Lauren saw me wave to her, and she took her own hologlasses off, which shut off as soon as they were unable to sense her retinas, looking at me concernedly in apprehension of what we had to say. I didn't want Gabriel or Maria to be listening, I wanted a truly private heart-to-heart. "I got to ask, do you still… you know, have feelings for me?" I don't know quite why I asked it, especially here. I guess it was riding on my mind for some time now. Lauren looked back away from where she'd been gazing at me with a single eye over her shoulder, but I could practically see the pained look on her muzzled dragon face as she focused on something in the distance, looking away from me. I felt her body tense, her steaming wings rustle uneasily.

"W-what do you mean, Noah?" She asked. I knew that she knew exactly what I meant. "I- I like you as a friend," She said, before I could even clarify. "I- I mean, I wasn't thinking, back when I… You know. I was being stupid. It's in the past." Hearing those words should have put me at ease, but they didn't. I could remember that kiss, more passion than Maria had ever put into any one of hers, of ours. I remembered the way Lauren's hands gripped my hips, then my arms, her wings wrapped around me, hugging me, enclosing me, tight up there next to her, her bending down to kiss me and holding me up under her against her breasts. I felt small, I felt weak and helpless beside her half-ton, meter-and-a-half tall frame, a creature that could eat me up; but at the same time, I felt as if I was the one thing she needed. Not wanted, but needed; and it was as if I could simply tap her and she would fall to bits.

Her words, somehow, felt like a lie. I don't know if she was lying or not. Either option wouldn't have surprised me. But in that moment, I treated them as a lie, if only to myself.

Then, it was her turn to put me in that uncomfortable spot. "Well… Did you ever, you know, feel that way back?" she asked, and my blood ran cold. "I mean, I don't care- I shouldn't really, but…" She paused. I jumped to answer.

"I don't know." Her eye came back to me, looking back over.

"What, are… Are you saying you did?"

"I'm saying I don't know, okay?! I don't! I…" I stopped. I cleared my throat. "Let's just go check the place out, all right?" I said.

she was still staring at me quietly, as if she needed to look me in the eye, those big brown eyes half glaring at me. I shifted, and after a somber forever, she turned back around, putting her hologlasses back on.

"You good? Audio cut out for a second there," Gabe's voice met my ears as we took back off.

"Yeah, I-" My mouth was dry. "Everything is fine." I didn't know. I was lost in thought I leaned into her as we began sailing forth once more. I didn't know. She wasn't human; she had four legs, green skin and flew through the air, how could we ever even think about being together, regardless of Maria and I? I didn't know.

That didn't stop it from bugging me.


We sailed through the southern suburbs quietly, on the way to the urban sector. They were nearly deserted, with burnt out cars blocking most roads. In truth, it seemed to have created a maze, only specific roads were passable and it was all so labyrinthian, thought out, unlike the random downed traffic of Elko. I knew something was at work here, but I didn't know what.

The closer we got to the heart of the city, the denser it became. The skyline was pockmarked with massive buildings stretching nearly a kilometer into the air, tall apartment buildings and several story flats were the norm, skirting the skyscrapers.

Lauren took to running across the rooftops and leaping from building to building, a flap of the wings sailing us from one high point to the next. It was somewhat more covert, and probably efficient too- not nearly as much fun, but hey. There would be a time for that, I figured. We watched the commotion in the streets below. We saw traffic edging it's way through the town, up to a little checkpoint at the center of the city. The whole northwest half of Shortstone seemed to be cordoned off, downed cars making many places impassable. But we couldn't get all that good of a overall look, as we didn't want to fly up too high on the first run. Maybe on the way back we'd get more altitude.

We saw people, quietly crowded around old metal barrels spouting fire, warming their hands. We saw a checkpoint up ahead, as an entrance to this main, safe part of the city, full of soldiers and people, all quietly soaking in their own somberness, like the walking dead risen from their graves. It had barely been more than week, but the smiles and optimism were gone from their faces.

As Lauren leapt from one building to the next to get a closer look, I zoomed in on my glasses. I saw them checking each car before letting them into the big FEMA camps in the main city. The sports stadiums all looked clogged up with cars, full of people, dirty and miserable.

"Looks like they're checking 'em," Lauren said, as I watched to see she wasn't kidding. "What's going on here, Noah?" she asked.

"Don't know," I said. "You getting this, Gabe?"

"He's taking a piss," Archie's voice muttered in my ear. Archie watched through my own camera, seeing my zoom-in. We watched as a truck pulled up to the main checkpoint, the back covered over by blankets. Men with weapons, all wearing bits and pieces of what I could describe as republican uniform walked out, many of them armed with nothing more than machetes. We watched as they looked under the blankets, to find a couple of rifles and shotguns. Quickly they began to yell out, and we watched as they drug a man from the driver's side, a pistol to his head, and, standing there with that gun to his throat, they "talked". He looked back, to see his weapons being taken from the cars. The man looked pissed and disappointed, but there wasn't much he could do with a gun in his face.

"They're taking the guns," Lauren said with a little gasp.

"Shit, they are," I said with a hushed groan. "What the fuck are the Republicans doing taking guns? Sort of doesn't seem like their thing,"

"They aren't getting mine, that's for sure," Lauren said, feeling the stock of her armalite. I silently chuckled, pulling my own rifle off of my back. The sling was bugging me, as I took the whole thing off. It'd loosened a little on the flight over.

"You've been listening to Gabriel too much."

"You think they're just posing as Republicans?" Lauren turned to look at me over her shoulder. "Would explain the comms silence. They-"

A snap. That old, terrifying snap.

It echoed throughout the skies, as loud to me as if it'd been snapped right next to my ears. A supersonic fragment of copper and lead breaking the sound barrier, cleaving it's way through sky and fleshy bone. It was the sound of a sniper's shot, a great rifle somewhere distant dialed in on Lauren's skull. Like a snapshot, I saw one of her horns explode in fragments. How she winced and was suddenly out of it. Before I had time to even panic, I found myself lying on my back, bucked off of Lauren, and she lay on the ground, moaning and grabbing at her head, flopping about on the ground.

Blood.

I saw blood.

"Oh," I uttered, before it really hit me. All I could do was groan and look around. "Laur- Lauren!"

Lauren called out my name, her voice sickly, like it croaked and crawled up and out her very throat. "Noah, Noah," she said, her mind dipped forcibly in and out of consciousness by adrenaline and terror, trying to look around. I saw she was about to get up, but I scooted over and grabbed her, throwing myself over her to force her down. immediately as I touched her she began to flail, her wings hitting me. They certainly weren't weak, those great, muscle-strapped limbs smashing into me.

"Lauren! I'm here! I'm here!" I shouted into her very ear. The world seemed to cease to exist right there, I could comprehend nothing but the two of us and this third actor, this sniper. She tried to get up in panic, and I grabbed her closer to the ground and myself. "Stay down!" I said, and another snap cracked over us, the fizzing "*weeew*" sound as a round ricocheted off of the old stairwell roof entrance behind us, hitting the concrete and spewing chunks. I saw Lauren's left horn, cleaved in half over in one part of the roof and a bloody, pulpy stump left on the back of her head, her hair running with the blood.

It was only now, in the echoing of that second shot, I could hear, down in the streets, shouting, legs pumping and beating against the concrete. I heard them in the building below, tromping up the stairs. My rifle.

Where was my rifle?

"Oh, shit," I said, looking around for my gun, leaving Lauren to writhe on the ground and groan. Lauren cried out again and again, she was facing away from me but I could see blood on her hands, every time she lifted them to her head. all I could focus on was my gun, my gun, laying there, clattered over to the side. But I took a single, crawling step, and down he descended.

Another hybrid, a dragon crashed into me, kicking me as he impacted. I only saw him for a split second as he careened out of the blue- he was a deep red hue with yellow accents, and four horns on the back and top of his head. His ears fin-like, unlike Lauren's cow-like ones. I coughed, as he looked down to me in scorn, brushing his mismatched camouflage uniform off, wearing multicam pants and a realtree jacket, holes cut in them for his wings and tail. He looked down upon me with a vicious, angular face, he was tall and lithe. He saw me going for my pistol, kicking me in the face and throwing me onto my back, stepping onto my wrist before stooping down and prying the pistol from my hands. My voice was hoarse from how he'd knocked the wind out of me, my armor plate not saving me from his body slam. "Lauren, Lauren", I was trying to wheeze just as she got up to see me. She drew her pistol, stumbling, to point it at him, but he'd already furiously hoisted me up to hold my gun to the back of my neck. right under my helmet. At this point, I could finally hear Gabriel shouting once or twice through comms, but he probably figured it was no use now. The dragon who held me at gunpoint waved at Lauren with my pistol, to drop her gun. I could feel Lauren's utter hesitation, past her panic and terror. This wasn't a facility psycho- this was her kinsman, a fellow dragon, nearly whole, healthy and sane.

I wanted to tell her to shoot him, but I found myself unable to articulate this. I looked up slowly into the red dragon's eyes. His lips were tightened and pursed, like giving judgement from upon high. His free hand groped at my red armband, ripping it off in disgust. His flaming yellow eyes hidden partially behind droopy dark red eyelids darted from me, to Lauren, back to me. I could hear the footsteps down below. They would be here soon. Lauren had tears welled in her eyes. Tears of pain, tears of fear. With them, her pistol dropped from her hands with a clatter, the rest of the militia down below stomping up the stairs. As her pistol fell, so too did my heart. Like a betrayal that couldn't be helped.

"Lauren," her name escaped my lips, almost all on their own. She certainly didn't hear me, slumped there in defeat. It was too late for anything. I met the face of the first outraged man. He was a little pudgy. Kind of funny watching this soft looking man charging at me. A stunstick was shoved into the gap of my armor plates, and amid that instant of pain, my vision was out.

---

"Alright, son, are you sure?" I heard my dad say, all of us gathered there at the banks of the great big lake. I could even see the reflection of the tall tower of the Citadel in the glassy water, its form wavering and rippling as the cool breeze coming off the snow-capped mountain created shimmers in that water.

"Y-yeah," I said, somewhat giddy. "You said it's important to know what it feels like in case it happens to me in the apocalypse, right?"

"...Well, maybe," Dad said.

"Sure you want to let me taze your son on his birthday?" I heard one of dad's prepping compatriots say, standing there next to him, holding that little black and yellow gadget. "Hell of a thirteenth birthday present."

"I can handle it, dad." I saw a glint of apprehension in my father's eyes. "C'mon."

"Alright, but no crying, right?" I saw my dad smile a little at this. I laughed. It was funny. Stupid, but funny.

"Alright, do it."

*Thwack.*

---

### Chapter 36

Splash.

A torrent of cold. Doused in water, laughter erupting from a world unseen as I opened my eyes.

"Wake up, you piece of shit. There you are. Morning, sleeping beauty," A gruff voice met me, as I came back to Earth. Held there by two of them. I coughed, looking up. Some nondescript cell. The two men holding me up dropped me there, and I tried to get up, but the big hispanic one in front kicked me over. "Take a seat." I looked around- that same dragon from before who'd taken me by surprise atop that building was one of the men who had been holding me up by my arm. He had my rifle slung across his back, my pistol in the holster of my battlebelt that he happened to be wearing as well. I saw their red armbands, and his lack of them. Given how he was bright cherry red, I suppose they figured he didn't need one. The two humans, the ringleader and the other mook smiled and guffawed. Oh, shit. I could smell it, this place smelled like blood and burnt gunpowder, that sulfur scent. The police station, more than likely, repurposed as a tiny little gulag.

"L-Lauren," I muttered, still in shock. "Where's-"

"Don't worry. we're treating your little girlfriend good. Doctor, butler, masseuse- whole nine yards. Only the best for our honored guests," He guffawed and my blood ran cold. I watched the two humans laugh darkly as the dragon who'd been responsible for me was still staring into me with those dead yellow eyes. Trying to get up again in my stupor, I was kicked harder this time, right in the chest. "Don't fuck around, idiot. We've got our eye on you, you little spy. We're dialed in on you like our guy was dialed in on your partner."

"I'm... We're not spies, we're on your side," I coughed. "W-Wyoming-"

"...tell it to the captain, you sneaky fuckin' blue. He's always down for a good stageplay. You'd better have your lines down pat, he hates ad libbing as much as he loves to sniff it out. Real *critical* guy." They were retreating now, the cell door slamming, standing there at the bars laughing as they locked the cell. I got up, taking steps. This was a mistake. Don't kill her. Don't kill us. I didn't know what to say, and they just left me there, their evil gazes left hanging in my mind.

I didn't know whether or not Lauren was even alive anymore, shambling down to sit on the cell bed, creaking. I rubbed my eyes, beginning to shiver, before pain hit me as I realised that my nose was broken at some point, out of alignment and throbbing. I held my nose for a moment before righting the cartilage with a wheezing grunt of pain as my body trembled and I grit my teeth. Slowly now, I took my sopping wet shirt off, laying it on the unoccupied top bunk to let it hang and dry, getting up to pace. To work myself up, warm my body up.

"Hey... You really a red?" I heard. I looked up, seeing a man in the cell across from me. He was mangy and old, he looked like he was homeless, at least before all this, thin as a rail, teeth missing and yellow.

"Y-yeah. Wyoming scout division. We're cut off, I got sent here to-"

"Ha! They'll never believe you," this less than polite fellow interrupted my cover story, chattering feverishly. "They're gonna *kill* you two. It doesn't matter what you say. You might as well admit and get a quick death. You hear what they were saying?" He laughed some more, perversely this time. I think he was touching himself with the hand that wasn't gripping the bars. "There's no fuckin' doctor. They're raping her. Your little green girlfriend- little, ha! You're a freak, man! Fucking around with those *freaks* like that!" he was beside himself, spitting and whooping. I wanted to tell him off, but the thought put me beside myself. I was breathing heavier now, chiding myself in my mind for not fighting back or something, disarming one of them and shooting them all to make my escape like in some action movie, or like I'd simulated a million times before in countless martial arts dojos. I slid down against the wall, trembling in rage. God, where was Gabriel when I needed him? To barge through the wall in power armor with machine guns blazing. I thought it was coming any second, at first. Praying. But I realised more and more that I'd have to save myself. We'd have to save *our*selves; I thought of Lauren, and my terror, my apprehension, my dread returned. What were they doing to her? This helplessness, this dread. I couldn't think of anything else but her. I had to protect her, but I didn't even know where she was. If she was even alive.

I made up my mind. Stick to the story. She's probably still alive. I could envision what she'd do, her quick wit. That's what she'd be doing, talking her way out of here. I had to trust that she'd be working just as hard as I was to get out of this deathtrap, the only way she could.

But I couldn't shake the thought of her in mortal danger, I practically forgot that we were in that same situation as I was fixated on the thought of never seeing her again, as much as I willed myself to trust in her abilities. They were using this place as a holding cell? I was hearing gunfire outside. Nobody was saying anything here, how rowdy I'd envisioned a jail cell was quite contrary to what was going on in the here and now. This horror, this fear in the air. They were using this place to hold people- until they executed them. Firing squads outside. We were going to end up dead if we stuck around. We'd have to rescue ourselves, and we couldn't let that fear get to us. I had to stay calm, stick to the story, trust Lauren.

I knew I couldn't fight my way out of here. I was out of it when they dragged us, dragged me in here. I don't know the layout of the place, I don't know how many guys they've got here, I don't know where in the city we are. I bit my lip, cursing my circumstance. We'd have to talk our way out of here alive. I took a moment to pray for Lauren's wit, if not for her safety. I was still shaking. Those bastards. I was going to kill every last one of them if they laid a finger on her.

They let me stew for what must have been an hour, before that same one as before approached me again. He was alone, this time, that sad-eyed draconic. "...Reed, N.," He addressed me by my name as it had been written on a patch on my body armor, going to unlock the door, pulling up a chair so he could sit before me in the doorway, as I sat on my bunk, arching my own eyebrow at how he regarded me, all by his lonesome. I looked him in the face, seeing how he looked like I was a chore. I saw how he wore my rifle, my battle belt. He was wearing my pistol and my knife way too far back. I ought to have been insulted, seeing him brazenly address me like this, engrossed into his wrist-mounted holographics, haptically selecting the record audio function. "...Boss wants your individual statement. Start with who you're with, please."

"The N-double-A, Wyoming Scout and Sabotage Corps. You want me to say it slowly this time?" I feigned nonchalant impatience, to try and convince him that this was a mistake. I was hinging my life on it, after all; that hobo in the cell over began to cackle.

"Good one! Bahaha!"

"Ignore him. Can you give me your unit number and the name of your captain?"

Shit. I sure as fuck hadn't planned on this. In retrospect, maybe I ought to, but there was no sense in overthinking this. I could use this to gather some intel too, couldn't I? "...Fuck, man. They keep moving us around. A flight and recon specialist, Silent Wings, no motors or anything, y'know," He didn't seem very impressed, his face never changing. "One day we're in the 101st, the next day they're shoehorning us into the 82nd. It's some bullshit. I won't even lie, I completely forget my current unit's number and our top guy. Leader of our entire division, though- M or N-something. Younger guy, but a real hardass. Shit, he's got a latino last name but he's white- I mean he's a little mexican, a quarter mexican if I had to guess, but passing as white, y'know?" I just hoped that if Gabriel came to save us he was being as obvious as I took him to be, and didn't pretend to be a four star general. *If* he came to save us, of course. I figured luck got me this far. "I only met him a couple times. My partner should, she usually has a good memory. She could tell you more."

"Huh. That's what she said about you," He muttered with his brow arched, and I felt my heart colliding against my ribcage. "With her head injury and all, she's having a hard time stringing a sentence together." Good, she was feigning memory loss. That freed me up a lot. At least I was hoping she was *feigning* memory loss. "Mr. Reed, what was your unit's mission here?"

"Well, shit man, I'd ask you the same thing, but I look around and I get the gist of it," I uttered. "What's with the radio silence? Our guys can't hail you. Outskirts of the city are deserted, sketchy activity going on, no shit they sent us to check things out before walking into what could be a fucking ambush."

"Hm. Smart. Instead it's just you two who get ambushed. Any reason why you were still flying your colors if you thought this was a blue zone?" He questioned. "...Especially given how you had blue colors on you that you weren't wearing. Let me guess, as a backup, right?"

"Yeah," I nodded my head about. "We never thought this was a blue zone but it never hurts to be sure, that's why we had to check it out. Fuck, man, it was a toss up between blue or red and I'd rather not wear the colors of soy-drinking scumbags who've been shooting my buddies unless I absolutely have to." I smiled on the inside, this was literally the truth, more or less. "Now lemme ask you this," I uttered as he opened his muzzle, which shut with an outward snort from his nostrils as I'd cut him off. "We were flying our colors. What's the big deal trying to shoot my partner in the fucking head?"

"...Unregistered flying hybrid," He explained with a sigh. "You Wyoming guys have it easy in the heartland. Here near the front lines we have to wear these IR strobes," He turned a little bit, wagging his tail. There was a little device seemingly embedded in the very tip of his tail. "Shit, sucks if you didn't know that. Your partner doesn't even have one. We'll be sure to get her one right away if you guys are operating in here. We're opening up our comms next week, so we'll be able to slip you out sooner rather than later once we get your boss on the line, but as of now, you'll have to stay put. Our boss' orders."

"Well shit, you're delaying the good news and your own backup if you wait that long. What if the Californians step forward with their Operation Sledgehammer? You ought to set us free ASAP if you want reinforcements." Figured I might as well be cheeky if I wanted to really sell this, and get out sooner rather than later. Name-dropping couldn't hurt, too.

"...Californians aren't what we're worried about up here. Oregon and Washington are our problem, but they're not as mobilized as the Californians, they aren't quite as warlike, given that they're not quite as hard blue as Cali. We're expecting their full mobilization in a month or two." I bit my tongue at getting that detail wrong, but rolled on through. So well so far. Good to get the info.

"That guy's not a red! That's a blue if I ever saw one! Lookit'em, rippin his shirt off like a god-damned metrosexual!" The dragon before me squinted a little, wincing at the bellowing. He put his finger up.

"Well, Mr. Reed. We're done for now." The draconic got up to leave. "Stay put. We'll be back in a little if we have any questions."

"Hey, what about my partner?" I asked.

"We've just got to make sure your stories match up. With her head injury that's not that simple but, if it's worth anything, I believe you. Just stay put for now."

"Hey, aren't you going to lock his cell? HEY!" The other prisoner shouted as he began to leave.

"That's none of your concern. You'd better watch your tone with the commander visiting."

"Pssht, I'm as clean as they come. I'm not scared of him." The draconic paused, as if to remark on this, but just shook his words away and went to walk away, leaving me with that cell door wide open. I didn't quite know what to do, but at this point I really didn't feel like pushing my luck and if I ventured far that cellmate would definitely make quite the racket. I lay back down on the bunk, worriedly looking up to the ajar cell door. God, it was torture seeing that open cell. Eventually I sort of expected that dragon guy to come back, but I guess he was done with me.

More hours passed by as I stared into the ceiling, listening to the periodic "FIRE" and clap of rifles from the firing squad outside practically bi-hourly. God, I wanted to get up and walk around, even just to get a lay of the place and find Lauren. I figured hey, they were already inclined to believe me, I ought to at least look around the place, right? The only thing that held me back, aside from that noisy busybody across from me was that I really had to sell this act. He told me to stay put, so I did. God, it almost made me feel like I was being messed with. Probably was. I really wasn't scared anymore, just confused, and anxious.

"Hey!" The other guy was yelling again. "Hey, guards! You gonna just leave this prisoner's cell o-" His voice stopped dead as the footsteps drew closer. While he'd been doing this to practically every passing guard, this was different, how his words petered out, how his voice turned to a dull squeak, and how the stomps of footsteps were... clackier. Finer shoes than those of a fighting man were walking their way down the aisle, accompanied by another pair of jackboots, not quite as distinct.

I was brought forth out of my dissociation for the umpteenth time, sitting up slowly at the sheer deafening silence after the bootfalls stopped to see two men standing there and facing away, towards that cell across from me and its inhabitant with his eyes wide as saucers, body rigid and twitching. I could see only the backs of two men, one big and wide, another lithe and tall- *too* tall. Inhumanly so. That voice- it was different. It wasn't gruff and showmanlike, or weird and bored. It was calm, but radiated, filled the whole hall. It was what compelled me to wake, to sit up as he spoke to fill that silence, goosebumps growing.

"Well? Would you like to finish that thought?" The lithe one barely moved as he spoke, despite how his voice filled this world up, his hands cradled within each other behind his back, slightly wrinkled pale skin and close-cut nails only accentuating how his flesh looked as if it held back turned wire, hands like mechanical visegrips, or perhaps the talons of a hawk, despite the obvious human species of this man. "...Captain, what is this one's story?"

"I... He's some vagrant, social parasite. Says he'll fight for food but he got in an altercation at recruitment," This massive, muscle-bound man explained. How he trembled as he spoke was remarkable. I was finding myself sitting more and more at attention, but gazing into that tall one, absorbing each of his mesmerizing details. He wore what must have been an expensive Italian three-piece-suit, the way it sucked itself to his frame, the pinstripes racing up and down the steep and angled ridges of his lanky, rigid body, but how the one contrast of his viciously sharp attire being a frizzy head of greasy red hair topping his frame off, almost unnatural in its bright color and unkempt nature.

"You are rather old for a soldier. Are you a veteran? Iran? Mexico, perhaps?" The way his voice inflected upon the final statement, almost a small piece of irony lodging itself in there.

"I... I..." I could only see his face, his expression, how he was frozen there. It was uncanny, like this man had fallen under a spell. But if I could dial in on his eyes, their wide, shimmering orbs, it was like I fell under that same spell. He was in the grasp of a great beast, a mouse to a hawk.

"Well?" The taller one whose voice sent my spine shivering uttered, his patience wearing thin and in it making me anxious. Like I was watching a car crash about to happen. "On your feet. Captain, open his cell."

"Yes sir." The wide one did as he was told, moving over there as the commander's hands disappeared from me, clasping themselves in front of him with a great clap. "*On your feet. Show me, soldier.*" The vagrant stood but could do not much more. His cell door was open, and this... Man strode forth. "*Defend yourself.*"

"I-" It was a moment, a single, brief flash and there he was. Finally relaxed, hanging limp from a knife embedded through his cranium, spanning just beneath the jaw diagonally through to the top of the opposite side of his head. A long, slender bowie knife holding him there as his eyes twitched and his breath gurgled, slowly drawn back out to let his lifeless body slump to the ground, the hardy captain coughing and averting his gaze beneath his short army cap as if unnerved. I saw that flow of blood, how the man fell sliding against the wall of his cell like a doll dropped, the back of his head smearing onto the concrete wall before he toppled over with a splat. And somehow, seeing how that guy's head practically came apart when it hit the ground was only the second most unnerving thing in the room.

"Useless," The commander sighed sadly. Like an inconvenience, not necessarily disgust as he cleaned his knife simply with a kerchief from his pocket. "My fellow compatriot, you would do well to recognize the inherent difference between cannon fodder and soldiers in your recruitment. This man would have been a liability, an asset to the enemy. Consider this favor free of charge, a *lesson* to be learned." The way he spoke already chilled my blood, but then his head turned ever so slightly as if to look at his underling but finding me instead, and that was when I finally saw his bright brown eye, gazing back at me. All at once every hair on my body rose as if this was no man staring back at me, but a hawk, a beast of prey wearing the eyes, the face, the skin of a human. The impartial hate in his bagged eyes, endless and foreboding; the sheer paleness of his skin. I'd seen many hybrids. No matter how strange they could be, every last one of them was more human than this thing standing here. I'd only seen a gaze this frigid from Gabriel at his most serious, but even that paled in comparison, as he raked the blade of his knife with the edge of a fingernail, playing with his great talon. "...Why is this prisoner's cell open?"

"I... Uh, this is, uh," The other one stammered at the question, turning. As the thin man's gaze turned back to him, I felt a weight lifted off my chest, and I saw this powerful captain brimming with muscles falter yet again, like stumbling in place from sheer intimidation, the weight of the evil gaze now back upon him. "...The guy from- Says he's from Wyoming. Flew in on a dragon-type."

"...The centaurical with her horn shot off? Hm." He turned his eyes back down to his blade and his follower breathed easier, as I was praying that he wouldn't turn and face me again, sitting up more. Like I was compelled to stand at attention, despite my cavalier behavior so far. I wanted to sit, to lay down, to be less in his vision, but there I was, frozen in place as he spun fully to face me and I could take in his horrible visage.

A face in the guise of a human, carved out of pewter and marble, clean shaven, the finest attention to detail for certain. The lines of the flesh of his face raced along his skull, cutting close at every turn and twist with his recessed cheeks and their mountainous bones, his dagger nose and sharp jaw. But his eyes- those sunken pits a million miles away. Like the sight of God, ripping into me as they widened, as if seeing, perceiving something they hadn't before. I felt sick. No, not the sight of God, but something unholy. A demon standing before me, towering. He must have been almost seven feet tall for all I could tell, opening the right side of his coat to place his knife back into its sheath in his shoulder holster rig, wiping his bony hands together and mussing a little with the blood red cuff of his shirt, the same blood red shirt revealed in the interior of his jacket and at his neckline, a tie black as night, and another icon of red on his chest, an even bloodier handkerchief folded into a triangle poking up from his breast pocket, soaked in the blood of that corpse behind him. But none of that mattered as his mouth opened, eyes floating right where they stayed in that apparition of frigid hate before me.

"...I feel like I know you from somewhere," He uttered, finishing his readjustment of his cuff with a single, sharp ruffle that made me flinch. The inquisition of his voice, playful almost like he was amused, roused the fear that I ought to have been feeling: the fear that had missed me in my shock and my daze, the fear my character that I'd been playing had lacked, it was all here. It was before me, telling me to run. Get out. You're going to die. Every cell in my body screaming to run, paralyzed by fear, as he stood in the open gate of my cell. His weapon was away but that danger remained in his hateful eyes. An animal here to hunt me, to rend blood and guts and bone. "Do you- Ha, what am I saying," He responded to himself, as my blood curdled watching him smile, his visage producing a smirk. "*Did* you have family in Vegas? It's almost like I know your face from there."

"Y-yessir." It escaped me in a whisper. I couldn't even think up a lie or an excuse, the truth ready to pour out. He could have asked me if I was from Vegas and I would have given that same answer. Asked me if I wasn't who I said I was, lying to avoid the firing squad. No lie could escape my lips under his haunting gaze. His smirk stayed, like this animal knew it had its hooks in me.

"You almost remind me of somebody. A... friend, of one of my... *sons.*" A pause to let me sweat, horror ever growing, realization creeping, while his eyes scanned me up and down. I'd removed my shirt all that time ago because it was wet and cold and I finally felt naked here. Naked as a baby. I could have been fully clothed but it would have made no difference, this creature of a man that could perceive all. "...And my, what a specimen. Practically olympian," He remarked of my body, which had began curling in on itself in terror ever so slowly, like a dream where one finally realises they are naked. "Anybody can slay a dragon, but it takes a certain breed of man to ride one into battle," He noted with brightly inspired eyes. A compliment from the devil that I found myself nodding to, my body moving on its own accord beneath this crushing power. "Perhaps if your... situation persists, you could find yourself persuaded to join my outfit. No more uncertainty, switching to this unit, that unit." He spoke slowly with a radiating eloquence, but I could taste just the smallest hint of an accent. There was no way this guy was *Mexican*, was he? If he was even human. "Matter of fact..." He reached into his jacket. I felt my bones crawl upon seeing his pistol, holstered under his left armpit there. It was a brief moment, but I know for sure I saw the butt of a shimmeringly polished 1911, the grips carved ivory, engravings all across the handle, its backstrap and the bottom of the flush-fit magazine. Skulls in joyous laughter. He produced a single white card with a scrape of paper against cloth from within the inner coat pocket beside his glittering silver sidearm. In a glance I could see one word written- **ROJO**, with a phone number beneath it, and above the number the insignia of a black skull with a dagger through the eye and pistols crossed at its chin. Gabriel's tattoo burning itself into my mind. I looked upon it for a moment, like he was pointing his great knife at me. I wanted to recede from it, this unholy token.

Then suddenly he flicked it up between his fingers to look at it, his gaze lowering to it, that smirk growing. Self amusement a step from embarrassment on display. It was haunting to watch this creature before me displaying that level of humanity. "How silly of me. I'd forgotten that the phone lines are down. This is useless," He stowed his business card back into his inner jacket pocket once more and my breath escaped me, but as he watched me there, his hand stayed within his jacket. A cigarette case was produced in the card's stead, from some different pocket. The mirror sheen lined with more of those laughing skulls, clicking open to see the old-fashioned cigarettes and matches lining the inside of the case. "You seem to have let my *lesson* get the better of your nerves. This place is... corrosive, after all. Care for a smoke?" I paused in my fear, long enough for him to rattle it softly before me. Every move he made through space was deliberate, terrifying, powerful. Not the power of body, but a sort of magic in his vicious fingers, like a million guns pointed at you. That bony hand of his in my face. "Please. Help yourself."

"I don't smoke," finally fought its way out of my throat, a dying croak as I swallowed. A battle against the devil. Another smirk, a curl of his eyebrow.

"Oh? Trying to stay... Healthy, perhaps?" To stay alive, more like. Something deep within me told me that taking any gift from him would have constituted a deal for my very soul. "...That's certainly respectable, for a man as athletic as you." He paused again, flicking the cigarette holder closed with a resounding snap that nearly made me jump. "Once you've been cleared of this place, ask for **Red**, if you and your partner wish to take me up on my offer. We take care of our own. But I'll be going now. I've got places to be, dragonrider. I do hope we meet again." Like that he stepped back. Once he turned to walk away, slinking through space as if he was never there and leaving the other man in his stead, I felt that weight lifted from my chest and that I could breathe again, but in his absence, watching that other man leave with a grimace towards me, I felt an unbearable claustrophobia, alone again. He knew who I was. He knew where I was from, he knew I was lying, it was a game to him, I was convinced beyond rationality. I had to get out of here, Lauren was in danger. I was in danger. All he had to do was turn around and decide to ask me directly and I would be helpless but to tell the truth.

I was trembling. My hand went up to my face, feeling wetness falling down my cheeks. I was sobbing uncontrollably, in utter silence. I'd never felt so alone. So claustrophobic, smothered by the concrete, the blood trail before me from some lackey having to drag that poor bastard's body away like a path to salvation. The door is open, I can just walk out, I should just walk out- I need to get out of here. I *need to get out.*

I had to talk myself out of it. To stick to the plan. So what if some creepy guy was in charge here? It's not like he has magic powers, right? He's just *some guy.*

I'd close my eyes in a blink and see him staring at me. Reading me. I can't think, I can't breathe. I sat myself down on the bed again. They brought me food, which was okay for being tasteless protein paste, obviously synthesized out of the worst materials, until they came for me as the world grew dark, the sun ready to set.

"Reed," It was some guy. Another nobody henchman. "We're moving you from this bloc. Come with me." He didn't handcuff me or anything, let me pick my still damp shirt back up to drape over my forearm and made me walk out in front of him with his police submachine gun cradled beneath an arm in nonchalance behind me, telling me where to go. I wanted to ask questions, but it was all beside me by now. I just wanted to know what they'd decide for me.

Lauren.

There she was, in that cell. How she'd laid down on a mat on the ground, her now shorter horn tightly wrapped at its new tip with gauze, neck entombed in a concussion brace. She really did look like shit, laying there, dozing quietly. I was shoved in there, and as I turned, I saw him slam the gate shut and leave us. I didn't know why I was suddenly moved in there with her, or what they were planning, but seeing her breathe and her eyes opening filled me with relief.

"Noah," She uttered, as I fell to my knees before her on the edge of her mat, throwing my shirt aside in an instant without a moment's thought.

"Are you okay? Don't- don't move," I uttered as she sat up.

"Noah, you're-" She was about to proclaim how I was okay, but I was moved to embrace her. I hugged her as she lay there with her body up, and her own arms came around me in response, albeit slowly.

"I'm so glad you're okay," I uttered. My eyes were still wet, I was almost embarrassed. I felt how her arms came around me, feeling along my back, as if verifying that it really was me. Her wings were in the way, I hugged her by crossing my arms up behind her neck a little, my arms beneath hers like that, her wings coming around me, enclosing me. I edged back, to look her in the eyes, in here within her wings. I wanted to speak, to ask her a million questions. To see if she was alright. But here, her hand came up to her face, index finger before her pursed lips, telling me to be quiet. She then tapped her neck brace with a nail before holding up her open hand with her index finger and thumb in a circle. She was okay, faking or overemphasizing the concussion if I had to guess, and I nodded. Next she flicked her ear, before pointing to her eye, then right upwards. We were being watched and listened to. I nodded, and she winked at me with a grateful smile, making my heart ease up a little. God bless her. Indomitable to the very end.

"...I knew we should've volunteered for the Minnesota invasion instead," She muttered slowly, her wings folding again as we finished our "hug" as she held her head, me sitting back on my feet in my kneeling position before her. I chuckled back, and she smiled weakly.

"Hows- How's your head?" I went along with the act.

"Shitty," She groaned back, acting right along. "...Why are you shirtless?"

"It got wet. It was cold." She smirked.

"...Reminds me that I'm almost a little frustrated that you've got a girlfriend," She joked with a cough, risque as it was to the point of sort of making me a little uncomfortable. I remembered our conversation this morning, able to qualify this as more of a joke than being her earnest thoughts, before she brought me out of my mental stutter by poking me in the front of the armpit and side of the pectoral where I finally noticed the big red welt there. "Heh, you got tazed in the titty."

I chuckled at the silliness. I felt so much better, so much more in the moment here with her. This cold cell, this horrible situation, all of it seemed to melt around her. Even if we were pretending to be people we weren't. But that danger stayed, residual. I was still uncomfortable. "...Did... Did some guy in red talk to you?" I huffed finally.

"Uh... yeah?" She looked at me playfully, like I was crazy since everyone here was wearing red, and one look at her told me she lacked the icy fear that had run through my veins. I didn't want to speak of him anymore, so I didn't prod further, assuming that, given her reaction, she definitely hadn't seen *that man*. I shook my head a little.

"N-nevermind. You think they're gonna let us out?"

"I can hardly balance on my own four feet," She wobbled a little, even mostly on the ground as she was. All part of the act, I assumed. "There's no way I'm flying out of here, that's for sure."

"...I'm sure that they'll send somebody for us. We sent a lot of intel back, they know this is friendly territory. At least, maybe until they saw us get shot at in our videofeed."

"Gabe'll be pissed," She chuckled back, and though I tried to keep things light, I knew that man I'd seen would not leave my mind. A skull with a knife through the eye above two crossed pistols. His insignia, Gabriel's haunting tattoo. "All's I'm sayin is they better open up comms if they don't want an unfriendly-friendly fire incident when he rolls in for us."

"Yeah." I was still out of the conversation, but that was the end of it.

Lauren laid back down once more against the wall of the cell, and I got up to go over to the bunk. I was a little cold, shivering as the sun had set. She'd rolled to her side and curled up some, her elongated body bent into a subtle U on the mat they'd been gracious enough to bring her. "Hey, can I get a blanket?" I uttered to a passing guard.

"...You've already got one. Why don't you share?" He sniveled vindictively. Certainly one of the less nice employees of the republican militia, a canid, big with puffy fur poking out of his red shirt and ancient-looking surplus body armor. He looked like the bastard child of an Akita and a Samoyed that got punched really hard in the nose, upturned and snarling a smile. "...We're all out anyways. Consider yourself lucky," He smiled like he was bullshitting me, waltzing away with a smirk.

"...Yeah, that guy's a bit of a prick," Lauren noted. Still laying down, she grasped the edge of the blanket over her with her frontal talon to raise it in the air, offering the blanket to me. "Here. I'm... I'm not cold." I took it for a moment, watching her smile meekly to me, before I whipped it open over her, letting it drift down again as she watched me, surprised. I went to go right into the apex of the curve of her body and sit up against her big lower belly, the edge of the blanket over my shoulders, draping all along the length of her body. She smiled, hiding her blushing, as I looked to my left to see her humanoid half.

"...Your belly's warm," I leaned back into it.

"...Thanks?" She uttered, laying her head again, at ease with me in the very crux of the curve of her long body, curving herself back so that she could easily see me, there leaned against the very middle of her. "...as long as it's not soft. Gotta stay strong, y'know." I chuckled silently, leaning back.

"...You really shouldn't sweat it. You're probably stronger than Gabriel."

"Probably, gigantic monster and all. I still wouldn't want to fight him, he'd probably kick my half-ton ass," She was more than willing to chuckle her fears away. "...That's not the point, though. If I was too fat I couldn't fly. God, that'd be torture."

"Almost as bad as not having wings? Oh yeah, sucks to be us," One of her frontal legs shoved me a little.

"Really does. Flying's kinda the one thing I like about myself." A short little silence presided between us in the following moment, as she lay there chewing her cheek and feeling her own words over. I covered a sigh.

"...you dog yourself too much. I think you're really pretty, actually." Another silence, and it was my turn to chew my cheek, furl my lips and raise my brows having let that escape from my mouth. She wasn't just pretty, she was *really* pretty. Why did I say it like that? I turned finally, seeing her look back up at me, eyes telling me she was far from bashful or playful, with her lip curled, sort of confused, almost disgusted.

"H-how?" I sighed again, forcing a weak smile for her sake. She certainly put a skeptical front forward, with her mouth ajar and brow furrowed, ears slicked back. She wasn't smiling yet, but I saw the tiniest blush in the corners of her cheeks.

"...I always thought your ears are cute. They always tell me what mood you're in." Almost immediately, that blush grew. I could have told her any little detail about her that charmed me, and she probably would have blushed anyways, fighting back that smile. I saw her ears flick once. "See? You're bashful. And now you're just trying to hide it."

"...You humans and your stupid cuppy ears," She pouted back, though not entirely without playfulness.

"Yeah, they're stupid, aren't they?" I uttered back. "You know what else I like?" I really didn't know why I was continuing on this tangent. Maybe just to kill the time, but somehow this felt obligatory. She always had a hard time with her body, and I did think she was more aesthetically pleasing than she ever thought of herself. Maybe it was a side effect of her seeing a lot more human faces than any of her own kind. I don't know if I could imagine myself in her position. "I like your muzzle. Its cute when your nostrils do the thing."

"Ugh, really?" She choked out a fake little laugh. "I can't stand this fucking thing. It's always sticking out there, in the way."

"...at least you don't have a nose that sticks out," I uttered, pointing to my own face, reminding myself how it'd been broken once earlier today. "Those are stupid."

"I must be the first and only person you've met with a face like this; fucking nostril holes," She uttered, pointing to her own visage.

"Yeah," I sighed outwardly, to show her I was being earnest. "I guess I didn't realise how stupid human faces look until I saw you." She laughed a little, like she didn't believe me but was too charmed to admit it.

"Wow. If I didn't know any better, I'd say you're flirting," she joked, letting her voice grow gradually more playful. My brow went up as I looked away now, breathing outwardly.

"Heh heh. I guess I'm being corny," I uttered. "I just…"

"...You're not being corny, you just…" she let the sentence trail off just like I let mine, as we just sat and laid there, communing in the comforting presence of one another. "...I disagree with you. I don't think humans look stupid. I actually think your noses are cute."

"...Damn, now I know what it feels like, I... really don't have a response for that," I sighed outwardly after a long pause, and she finally let her laughter escape her in response. It was music to my ears, like what I was trying to get all along.

"Take it with some grace, guy," She smoothly chuckled out, face beaming, knocking me in the ribs with the knuckles of one of her foreleg's handpaws. "Agree and say thanks. Do better than clumsy old me. C'mon."

"Oh, c'mon yourself; *clumsy* my ass. You're always knocking yourself down a peg. This is why you have issues."

"I appreciate the sentiment, Noah, but I got ten limbs. Eleven if you count the tail. You know how many times I trip over myself or knock something over on a daily basis?" She hushed with squinted eyes.

"Hey, if you were clumsy, how would you do all those tricks when you fly?"

"I dunno, it's kind of an improvisational midair seizure more than anything. Luck and aerodynamics just keep me from crashing," She joked, deadpan serious as it was. I couldn't help but chortle.

"Maybe you just don't have your land legs. You're a creature of the air."

"Oh, you said it buddy. I'm a *creature* all right."

"...You want me to get up and take the blanket?" I shot back, grinning, also playfully. "Look here, missy. Lauren is one of my very best friends and I won't just let you talk shit behind her back, you bully."

"It's hard not to, since y'know my back is all over the place. My spine just keeps going, and going, and..." She watched me glare at her, her lips pursing as I raised my brow to her, putting on a condescending face. "...Sorry. I guess I'm on a roll." I guess it stopped there, we really didn't have anything else to say. As a minute passed, I realised that I kinda missed talking. I guess I was just pushing the conversation along when it was going. "...You know," Lauren began anew. I looked her in the eye, figuring that she probably thought just the same. "Today could have gone a lot worse."

"Yeah."

"I'm glad that you're here with me, Noah."

"You're a hell of a person to spend the apocalypse with, yourself." She smiled.

"Always got to be the gentleman, huh?" She yawned. "...Better cool it. Sooner or later the act is gonna get old."

"...Yeah. Better save it for the firing squad." Another laugh, a more desperate one, just barely creaking with fear coming from the both of us. I guess it had to come back to the reality of our situation.

That was enough to tide us over until sleep met us.

### Chapter 37

Back in the blackness again. Floating, waiting, *being*.

Nowhere to hide.

That **red** eye is back. The fires of hell, in the cold distance of space, light years away but looming, massive. No cover, no stretch of space to save me.

But there is love behind me. Acceptance, a force just as great to my back. Something to fall back into. Do I have to be afraid? I guess I don't. There's not much that I, that we can't do.

But she's going away. What? Was it something I did? Don't leave me here. Please don't leave me.

    I'm so alone.

"Hey."

My eyes opened. Gazing into that ceiling, the cold concrete of the jail. Oh, right. We're still here. Memories dashing away that tiny amnesia of waking up, leaving me blinking. I felt my body, how I lay flat on my back on the mat, hands crossed over my bare chest, covered only by that itchy wool blanket that had been draped over me graciously.

Lauren was standing there, step by step she shadowed me until she hovered right above me, towering in all her glory. She had a brick-shaped object in her hand, pointed down to me, the other one with her own in it, her face with that sort of concerned, hesitantly pleased look in her face, still wearing her neck brace above her simple brown T-shirt. She wagged my protein block once, and I reached up for it.

"...You were sleeping. I didn't want to wake you," She explained, munching along on the other side of her cheek.

"Until you did," I grunted back.

"You make weird noises in your sleep, Noah." I finally began to sit up, brushing the blanket off and taking that little carbo brick packaged in paper wrap. I took a sniff.

"...Only the finest ingredients," Lauren spoke for me as she watched my face wring itself in disgust. "The trick is to not breathe when you're chewing." I chuckled again, digging into it. It was brittle and turned to powder in my mouth. I made said mistake of breathing and it instantly got into my sinuses.

"Agh, god," I choked. "I need some fuckin' water."

"...You've got a glass over by the door." I got up to get it there by the cell door, going back to sit on the bunk. We ate in solemn silence, before she was done, far before me.

"Here," I shoved my protein block towards her, and her hand went up a little.

"I'm... Not hungry."

"Neither am I," I uttered, shaking it again. "C'mon. You're a lot bigger than I am. You need more fuel to burn." She was silent, looking down once sheepishly before taking it. Guess she was hungry after all.

"Alright, you two. Boss wants to see you," One of the guards uttered, finally approaching our cell and rapping his nightstick on it the bars. For a moment, my blood ran cold. But as I looked over, seeing Lauren give me a sheepish smile, the kind of smile you give to get someone else to smile, and I felt a little better. Couldn't have been that red guy, could it? Down the halls, seeing guards here and there. Icons of red, angry, tired eyes everywhere.

An interrogation cell. Just like in TV and movies. We were herded in there, guards there in each corner, armed with submachine guns. It was dark and dim, a table, two chairs before us, and across the table was that hulking monstrosity of a man, the guy who'd been bossed around by **Red** yesterday, the commander of the garrison here, the other half of Lauren's blasted off horn in his hands that he fiddled with amusedly, marrow still damp on the inside. I felt a little relieved. Of course it wouldn't have been that creepy guy, why was I even worried?

"...You serious with this?" Lauren's mouth was open first, pointing down to the two chairs as she stepped forward, before motioning to the rest of her behind herself, wings ruffling. "You really think this through?" She pushed it aside ever so slowly, gazing into the commander sitting there with his fingers crossed over that long slender piece of her skull, as I took my own chair.

"You're feeling better, aren't you? One hell of a *concussion*." Lauren grunted, laying down to sitting-height next to me and crossing her arms.

"I got a good night's sleep." The commander took a moment to flip her horn over a couple times, grinning. He was a stubby, ugly person for sure. He wasn't short but he looked like it at a glance by how wide he was.

"So, uh... What's the deal?" I finally uttered. "Can we go now?"

"My, my. What a question." Another chuckle. I grunted silently, that obviously didn't answer anything. "I'm a little curious, my Wyomingian friends. How come you were in the area?" We paused, a little taken aback.

"...Didn't I tell the guy who came to question me?" I put forth.

"I must have missed the memo," He lied. "Take it from the top one more time. I insist." His grin betrayed his feelings.

"Radio silence, We don't know what's going on, we're here to see what's going on," Lauren uttered, before motioning to that horn of hers in his thick mitts. "Then you blew a piece of my head off."

"Yeah. Hell of a warning shot, eh lizard?" Lauren's ire was put forth for a second, lip curling and teeth gnashing. My eyebrows went up. Definitely not her favorite word, as he dropped it onto the table and slid it over to her. "Here. Perhaps you'll be wanting this back. So, you two get sent here by Wyoming's forward scouting attachment, correct?"

"Uh... Yeah."

"That's odd, given how on encrypted channels to your higher ups we've already established that Shortstone is republican territory and our reinforcements from Wyoming aren't due for another week." I paused again, my heart skipping a beat, Lauren's knuckles whitening over her horn for a moment. This certainly wasn't going well.

"Well," Lauren hissed after swallowing her rage, her grimace warped into a sort of sardonic smile. "You know how the chain of command is. I'm not even sure our captain really even listens to the general. He's a little unhinged."

"Sounds like an interesting guy, this captain of yours. A real character. He doesn't like the general, huh? I never did like Matheson myself. Always a bit of a dork, huh?" Oh yeah, Scott Matheson. The governor of Wyoming. He's got to be in charge now, right?

"Yeah. Gotta agree myself," I uttered, leaning back a little. His smile grew as his eyes squinted.

"Great thing he's dead, huh?"

"He's dead? Damn, when did that happen?"

"May second. The current general of Wyoming did it." My eyes went up. "But let me guess. Your 'chain of command' didn't pass this info down to you, huh?"

"Shit man, it's news to me," I tried to laugh it off, looking around. The guards weren't having it.

"When did you first join up?"

"...May second," I uttered. Another smile.

"Huh. Funny how Wyoming didn't declare independence until the third, merged with Montana on the fourth, and declared war until the fifth. You want to rephrase that too?"

"Uh-" I put forth. "Join up really wasn't the right word for it. See, it's kind of more like a bunch of, uh-"

"You can cut the shit now, Mr. Reed. *If* that's your name," He growled, and I gulped. I was already sweating like a pig. "But look. I like your gumption. And my boss happens to like your guts too. An honest-to-god dragonfucker sitting here, before me. Fearless enough to scream his way through the sky and try and lie his way out of a firing squad. And let's not forget you," He turned to Lauren. "Noah's right. You really are down on yourself too much," Again she grit her teeth at the insolence of this man, how he was trying to get a rise out of her anyways by showing that he had been watching us last night, even if we already knew he did. "But what could really raise your spirits might be a change of company. After all, you're being switched from unit to unit all the time," He gave a shit-eating grin and my skin crawled. "My boss, the commander of Shortstone Civil Defense here wants you two. And not as janitors, like maybe I'd hire you chucklefucks, or medieval-style jesters with the shenanigans you pull. But I could give less of a shit. You're audacious enough to the point where you amuse me, and yesterday I set a little trap. Left your doors open, had one of the guards talking to you carry an empty pistol way back on his gear and act slow, see if you'd attempt an escape, and you stayed put. I think you'd like to be a republican guardsman, but would rather play pretend jumping over rooftops than come up and enlist and put your asses on the line. So," He paused again, to lean back. "Here's the deal. *I'm* not going to shoot you because you behaved yourselves and my boss likes you. You can wait around until the rest of Wyoming gets here, and they can decide what to do with you, seeing as you'd been impersonating their personnel. I'll be nice, tell them you've played nice as a treat. Or, I can ring up **Red** anyways, and your asses will officially belong to him. Oh, and what he'll do to them," He chuckled darkly. "Or, maybe I'm wrong. Maybe your superior officer will roll into town and come calling, huh?" He couldn't stop chuckling, as we sat there, stewing. We really were fucked now. We'd have to formulate our own escape now. "Is your commander that 'Gabriel' guy you two mentioned last night?" I paused to open my mouth, but he wasn't quite done, interrupting me again. "You can save it. I've had enough with you two. Guards, bring them-"

"Sir!" A man barged through the door, like a messenger from heaven itself, the timing could not possibly have been better. He was panicked, breathing heavily. "We- there's a guy here! Soldiers from Wyoming!" He uttered. Like that my brow raised, my heart, already thumping, going crazy at this. Uh oh.

"Well, well. Isn't that a coincidence? Here early, huh, looks like this'll go a lot faster," He chuckled over to us. "Bring them. **Red** can wait. We'll see about this." The two of us were hoisted up by the arms, two guards going over to Lauren, obviously uncomfortable at her size as she towered over most of us, still jostling us along as that commander waltzed out in front, practically dancing, smug, but with an edge of apprehension. Like we could be right. But how could we be right? We were lying our asses off.

"What is your major malfunction, soldier?!" a bellowing voice. Was that…? No.

        No way.

We turned a corner and there he was. Gabriel-Fucking-Noria standing there, a golem of tytanaceramid, power armor gleaming red, pauldrons painted with rank stripes. An honest to god cowboy hat on his head, aviators on his face, not to mention the lit cigar chomped in his mouth covered in an unfailing smile despite his rage. He was practically unrecognizable. "Boy, you get that goddamn gun out of my face or we're about to have a friendly fire incident. Who's fucking side are you on, you incontinent imbecile?!" The voice he was putting on only added to the layers of his persona he was playing, some deep west cowboy type. Clint Eastwood with a chainsaw, John Wayne on juice, staring down one of the guards there with his rifle pointed towards him. On all sides of him were my, *our* friends. Even Maria there, kitted out with similar dark glasses on. I could barely see her shift as she saw me, but I knew she was more than glad to see me, but there was an act to be sold. Selicia on the other side of Gabriel with another big smirk and her arms crossed around her armor above the stock of her rifle, Reina there serious just like Maria. I almost lost myself in elation upon seeing the four of them, but I knew they were playing a character just like I, just like we were supposed to be. Lauren's ears were up and she was fighting back her smile. "You," Gabriel turned to the leader here. "You better talk some smarts into your boy before me or my beautiful entourage places his firearm inside of his bodily cavity by force."

"Stand down, stand down," He uttered, stepping forth. "Now who the fuck are you?" Gabriel sucked on that cigar some more, puffing out of the corner of his mouth like he actually was a smoker, without a single cough or choke. I don't think I'd ever seen him smoke.

"I was about to ask the same question to you, meathead. You better have a good fucking excuse for holding my- and WHAT the fuck is that?!" With the cigar stuck between his metal fingers, he pointed it like a bloody saber towards Lauren's head. "Have you and your men lost your fucking minds?! We were flying the fucking colors! WHAT THE FUCK IS YOUR MALFUNCTION?!" I really couldn't tell if Gabriel was playing his character now. It felt a lot more earnest than before as his rage boiled upon seeing Lauren in a concussion brace. "You im-bee-cilic sons of *whores!* Do you have any idea the judgement I would be endowing upon you if my operator was KIA?!"

"Well, she's alive, *captain*," The boss snarled back, crossing his arms as he stood there. "You best watch your tone. You're speaking to a colonel."

"Oh, a colonel? Kernel popcorn, jiffy pop?! I don't know if you've caught on, *colonel*," Gabriel, absolutely unstoppable, flicked his burnt-down stogie from his metal fingers and it bounced off of the colonel's body armor with a flash of embers as my jaw (and Lauren's) dropped at his sheer audacity, him standing there, practically glowing, commanding the conversation and the room like the very man to end all men himself. "You *may* outrank me, but in technicality only. Specialist Malligri."

"Yes, sir," Selicia uttered, standing there like a real special forces hardass on all of her many legs, with her head shawled in the red sweatshirt she donned beneath her plate carrier, eyes cloaked in blackness from behind her many glasses.

"This man orders you to shoot me. I order you to shoot this man. Who are you shooting?"

"That man, sir."

"You're goddamn motherfucking skippy. Colonel, we may be on the same side, my boss and your boss may be working for the same goal and we may fly the same colors, but you hold no jurisdiction over me or my men. I couldn't give less of a shit if you were the five-star general of the Idaho NAA itself unless *my* boss tells me to give a shit. Is-that-fucking-clear, *Colonel?*"

"...Can I know who I'm speaking to now?" The colonel was trying to play this off, but it was obvious he was failing.

"Captain Gabriel Noriega of the Wyoming Raiders Second Division. We're as special as special gets. You should know, given how I'm sure your mother used to call you special on a daily fucking basis by how long it's taking you to get this basic fucking information, *Colonel*. You aren't even supposed to know we're here but your dumb ass almost peeled my Sergeant Major's cap off. That fine dray-conic specimen you've been man-handling is worth every idiot with no trigger discipline in this room that happens to be in your employ, unlike *mine*. Can you even *spell* professionalism, Kernel Jiffy Pop?!"

"Who's your superior, Captain Noriega? I don't think he'd appreciate how you conduct yourself."

"I get my orders from Benjamin F. Garrison, President of the Independent Republic of Wyoming and Montana and General of their Armed Forces himself. And I don't think he'd appreciate how you use his special dispatch for target practice. You think I'm mad? Wait until you talk to my boss. I'm as well mannered as a fucking *Ja-pa-nese* schoolgirl compared to the storm you're about to have to answer to, *maggot*. And you best believe I can speak upon his behalf like I speak for the very voice of *god*. And the voice of god is telling me that you best re-lieve my men of your grubby hands before the discussion gets *physical*." Gabriel had walked up to him, towering above the once massive colonel in his cherry red power armor. It was clear that things weren't going the Colonel's way, as he furled his lip, biting down. He looked back to us, fuming quietly, though now he looked more like a crying child how he smushed his face up madly behind a steaming blush. Didn't help him that he was bald as a baby, of course. Lauren was enveloped in schadenfreude watching him squirm, barely able to keep from beaming and contenting herself to clutch her lips with her teeth.

"You've got some nerve, Noriega," the Colonel snarled, up in Gabriel's chest as he gazed down, barely even cranking his head down to look at the Colonel. "Talking to me like that in front of my men."

"With all due re-spect. I'd speak the same if you were in front of your mother, every woman that ever felt sexually attracted to you, and every last one of your punk-ass children. Did I mention that I don't like you, I don't respect you, and I highly doubt anybody willingly spends time with you who don't see you as nothin' but an opportunity for a promotion?" Gabriel dropped insults like bombs. I was more surprised how Selicia, Maria and Reina kept a straight face, Lauren coming apart at the seams. Then again we were all focused on how if Gabriel so much as stuttered this was all going to go up in smoke and this would quickly become a hot extraction rather than the farce it currently was, wildly entertaining or not. "...The general himself is going to *re-quest* to have you demoted to a fucking milk-man by the end of the week. At this point you're lucky to avoid the firing squad if you don't give me my, and his, personnel back right fucking quick. *Colonel.*" Another pause as they stood eye to eye- well, chin to forehead.

"...Take em," The colonel snarled. If I didn't know better it looked like he was trying his damndest not to tear up, face scrunched up into a mighty scowl. We were pushed forward, and my legs practically turned to jelly, Lauren catching me a little. Gabriel's head turned to me, like on a swivel. I could see myself in the reflection of his aviators. He smirked ever so subtly at me, but the Colonel wasn't done. "...You better pray I get fired, you fucking weasel. I'll show you real friendly fire. I'd kill you personally, *Captain*. And slow."

Gabriel finally turned his head down as his antagonistic smile vanished, metal hand coming to the frame of his glasses. "Excuse me colonel, I do regret to inform you that I in fact have a slight cognitive deficit in the venue of determining humor," Gabriel paused to take his aviators off to unsheath that frigid glare. The Colonel's face shuddered, his knees shook for but a moment. Just like yesterday when Red gazed into him. The eyes of the devil. I felt secondhand terror upon seeing them, the Colonel straightening out, sweat beading on his head. Gabriel was ice cold, not even breaking a sweat. He was in his element, betting absolutely everything on a single stare. "...So you had better inform me that was just a *joke*."

"It... It was," He grunted as he squirmed, as if losing control of his own words for a moment in a way that was quite familiar to what I'd experienced, and Gabriel's aviators and smile came back on, and like that this man was released from Gabriel's grip, left panting there.

"Good. Don't fuck around, Colonel. Remember now, your men are like your kids. If you don't discipline them, someone else will." Gabriel's power armored arm came around me as I approached, like a ghost, drifting towards him. Like a father, patting me on the back. Holy shit. Holy fucking shit. We're actually *walking* out of here. Lauren looked the same as I did, eyes wide, jaw shut only because she forced it to not be slack, but she had this sparkle in her face. I could bet she was half tempted to turn around, wink and stick her tongue out at the colonel with a "nyeah-nyeah" as we left. What a fucking show, walking out the door as the reds outside stopped, Standing at attention seeing Gabriel's stripes, Gabriel saluting back with that crazy grin and shimmering aviators. I could hardly believe it, seeing the JLTV and my Jeep idling there. Almost everyone was there. Sunglasses on every last one, each vehicle soaked in red. The dead Blackwalker head skewered onto the front end of the JLTV, something that the nearby soldiers were evidently impressed by.

A minute or two of blinking later, as we set off down the road. Gabriel sitting up on the turret, more like a throne than a tactical position at this point. I was back to sitting there in the backseat of my thinly-disguised jeep, where Maria just couldn't hold it in anymore. She latched onto me and I froze. Gripping me. She didn't laugh, she didn't cry, she didn't even smile. Just shivering there with me. My hands came around her ever so slowly, around her shell of body armor. She felt so far away as she gripped me.

But holy shit. We'd made it. Lauren was sitting back there, gazing at her horn in her hands. She looked up to me, smiling, pulling her neck brace off and waving her hair off, straightening it all out. She laughed for a second, before suddenly convulsing, going for the edge of the jeep with a wet, splashing "bleahhhh" as she emptied her stomach. A moment of silence as she spat and spat. I took a water bottle up from one of the bags, passing it back as she rinsed her mouth out.

"...Shit, I was seeing my life flashing in front of my eyes," She gagged, spitting repeatedly. "Imagine all your brain's got to work with is two weeks of being alive, if that. I just kept getting replays of my most embarrassing moments. *Fuck.*" She held her head again with the hand that had her horn in it, the other one clutching her water bottle.

"...They took our gear," I uttered out, sitting there.

"Shit man, they nearly took our lives," Lauren uttered back, rinsing her mouth some more.

"My dad gave me that gun." Lauren was silent now, of course, still sloshing the water in her mouth.

"We'll get it back later," Maria reasoned while Lauren spit.

"...Hey Gabe, does... Will my horn grow back?" Lauren was gazing at her horn as she spoke into comms.

"...Yeah. Probably take a year or two. Expose says it grows like body hair, out to a certain length. Might be a little stubby for a while." Lauren was back staring at it, before she was staring at her hand, concentrating. This all felt like a dream, this little unbelievable prison break. Seeing people in the streets all around, stopping to watch our little convoy pass. Red. They feared the color on us, shivering, stopping to watch us pass. If any of them waved, it was more akin to a salute. We saw other republicans, too. There were a lot of houses with big X's crossed over their front doors, trash strewn on lawns and streets. We passed some republicans with a truck full of stuff there, like movers loading the contents of the house out as people lined up on the lawn on their knees with their hands behind their heads, republicans with guns watching them. "...Smile and nod," Gabriel was waving as some republicans spotted his rank and insignia and saluted. Gabriel was obviously enjoying himself on some level, but I was nothing but unnerved. This was America, now. Thieves on behalf of their partisan colors rooting through houses as the occupants could do nothing but wait for an uncertain future. "Republicans have taken to looting unoccupied houses. But if they can find somebody who can't prove they live there, they see fit to take what they please. If they weren't a registered voter or registered for the wrong side... Use your imagination." It was like a movie. Some horrible collapsing dystopia. "Look. An X on the front door means it's been looted already. A single slash means that they found something worth coming back to, an embedded safe or a reinforced room, something they need to come back with a roundsaw or something to crack it."

"...You did your research," I muttered.

"Had to. I couldn't just brainlessly charge in to rescue you, I'd end up getting everybody killed. Besides. Better to save the ammo." I sighed, staring out the window more. It was entrancing, the hopelessness, the dystopia around us as we drove. "...Slinked around, got a few names I could drop. Just the right amount of information to bullshit my way in. Pretending to be authority has its perks, most grunts won't try and get on your bad side. And pretending to speak for an authority above you has more perks. Nobody wants to piss off the guy who will have a much bigger guy also pissed off on his behalf. That colonel… pfft. Now that guy had me worried. Wasn't really used to having people tell him what to do. Power armor really helped sell my shtick, though, since I'm sure that fatass thinks he's physically imposing. Fuckin poetry in motion if I do say so myself," He aped his cowboy bit with those final words, a short guffaw following it. I wanted to bring up Red, but felt that this wasn't the place for that.

"Uh…" Lauren began. I turned back to her behind me. With her left hand with the horn in it, she held up her right hand. "…I must be going crazy, but," She began to move her hand. I didn't realize it for a moment, before she seemingly spelled out letter by letter her name in sign language. She gazed up at me for a moment, as I was perplexed for another moment. Her ears sunk and face drooped a little bit, almost embarrassed. "…Jeez. that's... never mind. I- I just-"

"Your name?" I uttered, raising my eyebrow. Her eyes widened, before her ears shot up again and her mouth began smiling once more.

"Wait, is this- real?" She passed me her horn to free up her other hand, and began doing more. My sign language was rusty, but my smile grew as hers did and she began making more motions.

"Yeah, I can understand you," I spoke in response to her signed question. "My sign language is a bit rusty since I took the class in sophomore year." Her jaw opened and her eyes sparkled, hands coming up to her cheeks.

"Oh my gosh I know SIGN LANGUAGE?!" She practically squealed. "Gabriel! I-I know sign language!"

"…Ought to get shot in the head more often," He remarked back as she was too psyched to even hear it, practically about to leap up for joy.

"I knew I had something else in this stupid brain of mine! I, I was trying to talk to you quietly the other night so they wouldn't hear," she was exclaiming to me, beaming, magic in her eyes. "And I was making those hand motions- that wasn't sign language, that was just like, 'what sort of things can I do to make you understand me without talking,' and I was like, 'wait would he get that' because I like knew- I knew that stuff but I didn't know if you'd know that stuff! I just had to try and communicate with my hands in a way that you could understand and BAM! I realised I had this whole language in my head I wasn't sure I could even use! I suddenly knew that I know sign language!" She was beside herself in celebration. "Noah! You-" She stopped, throwing up her hands and beginning to speak with them, biting her lip in a massive smile with her ears whipping as she signed away, getting probably a sentence or two in about how I ought to practice with her (I guess) before I put up a hand.

"Whoa, whoa, I said I was rusty, remember?!" I laughed back. "You probably know a lot more of it than I do."

"I- I probably do!" She said, still smiling, until her smile shrinked, her doubtful side finally deciding to speak for her now. "Y'know, that's kind of creepy," She muttered, scratching her side as her brow furrowed. "Why did they put *sign language,* of all things, in my brain?"

"…Hey, there might be some deaf people around. You think there are any French people around?" Selicia barged in on comms. "Fucking French. Who am I gonna speak French to?"

"You know French?... Actually, I feel like that fits you," Gabriel snarked.

"…I wonder what I know," Reina chipped in, on the seat in front of me, scratching her furry chin as I watched her brow furrow in the rearview mirror.

I guess that this giddiness, this celebratory attitude in the air was more due to our impossible rescue rather than any other thing. Perhaps even our way of overlooking the dystopia unfolding around us. The surreality of it all sort of got to me, as I just sat there, my mind consumed by that demonic man yesterday and the evil surrounding us, just contenting myself to feeling Lauren's horn in my hands.

## Chapter 38

The convoy, directed by Gabriel of course, turned into a cul-de-sac in the rather nice northeastern suburb part of town. The quietest place of the city from what I could tell, maybe a little classier, with big two story houses everywhere. We stopped in front of one that had yet to be exed out. Probably easier to squat in this way, as squatting in an exed out house was probably going to draw attention.

"Ah, welcome to our new home," Gabriel said as he burst through the front door into the foyer, beginning the dismount protocols to get out of his armor, standing there in his plugsuit as he used Sentinel as a hat rack, putting the cowboy hat with his aviators on the brim of the hat atop Sentinel's frame. "On a cul-de-sac so it's more defensible, not much through traffic. Five bedroom, three bath, chlorinated pool in the back. Game room in the basement. could be worse," he said. It was certainly smaller than the mansion. A step down? Yeah. More covert? Definitely. "Less people around this area too," He said. "The food distribution and Redboy command centers are farther away, the closest one is at a school nearby," he explained. "a mile and a half or so to the south, and it's the only one for about 10 miles. Fewer people round here, less patrols." It certainly was homely, considering how many of us were to fit in here. I knew that our group, as it stood, would be somewhat cramped together in this place.

"What, we staying?" I put forth, my nervousness growing.

"Roads north are all cordoned off. Side roads too, and the forest is too dense for vehicles. We're going to have to figure something out. For the time being, I'm saying we need to stay put and keep out of sight. As soon as the Wyoming reinforcements link up here and make it obvious that we weren't with them, they're going to start looking for us. But what we should be really worried about is the offensive coming, and we do *not* want to get stuck in that crossfire. I give us at least a month to find a workaround. We'll have to do some more intel gathering before we can move."

"Gabe, can I talk to you for a sec?" I uttered a little bit more subtly, going forth to grab him by his arm.

"...Can I get changed first? This thing chafes," He muttered of his neural suit. I grit my teeth behind pursed lips, nodding a little. I didn't like sitting on this information.

"...I'll be outside," I muttered, going for the door again. I could use some fresh air, after all. A change of clothes and a shower too, but that could wait. Was the water working here? I hoped so.

I walked outside, seeing the garage off beyond the front door, the garage door open and Archie parking the JLTV inside, cursing under his breath in concentrated rage. I looked into the garage, seeing the previous owners used the garage more for junk storage than for vehicle storage.

"God, You'd think these cunts never heard of an attic," Archie snarled. "Garages are for *automobiles*."

"...Can't say I disagree." I saw my Jeep still parked out there in the driveway, the truck on the street. It looked like some of us were moving the junk out of the garage so that my jeep could park in there too, Anthony over there ferrying boxes.

"Oh hey Noah, you survived," Anthony proclaimed, rather nonchalant. I think he noticed his own accidental nonchalance, looking away as a sort of weird self-reflection on what he'd said before looking back to me. "Uh… How was jail?"

"Eh."

"Yeah, so… Good to see you." He walked away with the box he was carrying. Man, that guy was out of his element.

"They torture you?" I practically jumped, wheeling around to see Selicia there, eyeing me behind her dimmed hologlasses.

"Not physically." She smirked, towering there over me as I took steps back as she skittered around me, watching Archie now swearing profusely now that he'd parked so close to the wall that he couldn't open his door, or any door really with all that junk there, eventually crawling out of the turret that just barely scraped the ceiling.

"Mmm. Mental torture. That's the best kind." She stuck her pointy tongue out just a tad.

"...You're really committed to the edgy seductress act, aren't you?" I uttered with a raised brow and an indolent smirk. Maybe it was just Lauren rubbing off on me, trying to keep things jovial with a rapid-ready response. Maybe it was Gabriel's fearless counter-edge. Sure didn't feel like my own words, in retrospect.

"What can I say? It's how I get my kinks- I mean... my kicks." Anthony turned the corner again with Selicia still facing me, absorbed in her own joke. I watched as he froze and backed away behind the corner once seeing Selicia's back there, eyeing down upon me. I could practically read his thoughts upon his face, something to the tune of "Welp, I can always get back to cleaning the garage later" as he disappeared back into cover as silently as possible. I huffed out a short "huh" of a laugh. She looked to her right, where Anthony had once been, before looking back to me. "...That Gabriel though," She practically purred, a hand coming up to her lip. "Man. That felt good just watching him rip into that ugly knucklehead. Gabe doesn't have a girlfriend, does he?"

"I… Kinda doubt he'd interested in you," I uttered, getting what she was hinting at.

"That doesn't answer my *question*, though. What are his preferences? He's not gay, is he?"

"He's-" I stopped dead, petering off. What exactly was Gabriel? He hasn't had a girlfriend since… ever. Or a boyfriend, or… anybody, so I really was at a loss for words. "You know, maybe if you're curious, you ought to ask him," I said. I figured feigning playful banter was the best way to sneak out of this conversation.

"Hm. Sure. Well then," She saluted as she walked away. "I'll be in the basement taking my noon nap if you need me." I sighed with exasperation upon seeing her gone. She wasn't that unnerving anymore, I guess exasperation was just a response to her being around, as I walked over to Archie there shoving the boxes out of the way, while I walked over. He was unloading the passenger window M2 which had been removed to fit the vehicle into the garage, the gun in one of the back seats of the JLTV, underneath the turret, dragging it out and slamming it down on one of the boxes.

"God, how the fock does Gabriel lift this bloody thing," He huffed. "It's not even loaded. God, ANTHONY," Archie hollered, and he peeked out from around the corner.

"...Is she gone?"

"You're supposed to be cleaning the garage out, you cunt. We leave you here to do that and this is as far as you get?"

"I- I did! See? The humvee fits now!"

"Barely! Are you really *that* bothered by Selicia?"

"She- she's always bothering me," Anthony came up to me now, trying to get me to take a side here. "She keeps coming onto me and it's freaking me out, man. Which I would kind of be alright with it if she didn't want to EAT ME."

"...She doesn't want to eat you, dude," I uttered, trying to be the diplomatic leader type I certainly could hardly pull off. Saying this and knowing perfectly well the kink that spider-girl-thing had, I really felt like I was lying to him, but at least lying diplomatically, grunting to myself. "She just uses innuendo and stupid things like that because you get bashful and she just wants to get a rise out of you."

"She cornered me in the attic and swallowed my arm!" He shrieked, pointing to his left shoulder. "Up to here! She was staring at me and giggling with my fucking shoulder in her mouth and my hand in her stomach! I could see my hand pressing against the inside of her skin, man! You know how *fucked* that is?!"

"...You know it's not a real stomach, right?" Archie uttered with his brow raised like Anthony was making a big commotion. "Her human-half belly is empty. It's a storage thingy. Like a kangaroo pouch. She's lit'rally just fucking with you."

"Fuck. That. Shit, man. I don't care what it is, it's *disturbing*. Kangaroos don't run up on people and start shoving them in their pouches."

"...Might be kangaroo hybrids, some might be into that," Archie muttered, still not taking Anthony seriously.

"Look, Anthony," I muttered. "I'll talk to her. Okay? She's edgy but she's not going to hurt you. Gabriel would tear her in half and she knows it. In the meantime, *you* need to ease up."

"What, Selicia is still buggin?" Gabriel's voice shot out as he stood in the doorway to the garage, clothed in his casual shirt and shorts now, letting out a chuckle. I turned to see him step down into the mess of the garage, boxes everywhere. "Tony, it's how you act. She gets off on people being uncomfortable."

"And that's my problem how?"

"Listen. We'll have a talking-to. Just try and relax, okay?" I was standing before where Archie leaned against the stacks upon stacks of boxes, ears flicking. I finally looked down at the M2, before noticing something on it, on the very top, the flat plate of the loading gate atop the receiver, something I somehow had overlooked until now. I saw, etched into the metal, a series of years and words, scratched in with a knife. Each one looked like a different handwriting, some sloppier, some nicer. Incheon, 1959. Saigon, '69. Grenada, 83. Kuwait, 91. Baghdad, 2003. Bagram, '22. Tehran, '35. Tijuana, '51. And finally, the latest and most recent addition: VIVA LAS VEGAS! 2060. I looked up, seeing Gabriel there having watched me, a cold, meta-sarcastic smirk on his face.

"I couldn't resist adding to the list," He uttered. "Figure I ought to have thrown Elko on there too. Maybe after all of this we can scratch Elko, this shithole, and the Citadel on as well."

"Hell of a life to live," I muttered of the well-worn steel monstrosity. "Imagine the lives this thing has taken."

"Browning M2, baby. King of the battlefield from world-war-one till the end of time." I smirked a little, Archie and Anthony still reeling in their exasperation. "Anthony, shouldn't you be cleaning out the garage?" Gabe put forth, Anthony rolling his eyes again.

"Yeah, Gabe," He uttered, going back to the boxes, Archie going to try and crack the door of the JLTV open to get his headset from the seat. "...Jeez, what is in these things? This is pretty heavy," He uttered. "Magazines?" he read on the side. "Hey, I think I found some gun stuff," He uttered of a new box, the two of us waltzing over as he popped it open. They weren't the magazines we were expecting, seeing stacks upon stacks of flat, softcover books. "What the hell are these?"

"Those are paper magazines," Gabriel muttered of Anthony's ignorance. "Used to be a thing before the internet really sunk them. Kinda stuck around for a while, though." I reached for one, flipping it open. May 2023.

"...Fuckin' ancient," I muttered, putting it back down.

"Take the boxes like this and put them in front of the windows of the living room. They'll be good for bulletproofing some gun ports," Gabriel ordered, Anthony nodding. "Now what was that you wanted to mention to me?" I took Gabriel by the arm, leading him into the front yard, so nobody else could hear. This was rather confidential, and he read this on my face, serious all of a sudden. I'd been this serious on the ride back, it fresh on my mind, but it was ever present now, and his own darkening expression mirrored mine before either of us spoke.

"...I think I found that associate of yours you mentioned the other day," I uttered. Gabriel's seriousness did not falter, and I swear the shadows in his eyes grew, lips pursing. "...Some guy... The commander of Shortstone visited the precinct yesterday, and he talked to me. He- Do you know anybody called **Red**?"

Like that, his eyes and face glazed over for but a second, shimmering there suspended in space. A deep sigh rushed into his chest, to escape moments later.

"What'd he look like?"

"Shit, man... Ginger. Tall as fuck. Made me asthmatic when he looked at me, scary as all fuck." I didn't need to say any more, Gabe's face reading my shivering said it all.

"Yeah. I figured as such." Still gazing off into the distance, towards the garage where Anthony and Archie toiled, but past them, through them. "He probably knows I'm here, after all this." I couldn't get that man's face out of my head. God, one hell of a boss.

"Shit, man," I uttered, the breath leaving my chest at the prospect of that man coming back for us. For me. "God, I'm so-"

"Don't apologize, it's not your fault. We did what we had to do and busted you out without losing anybody. Even if we went in guns blazing and pulled it off flawlessly we'd have brought way too much attention to ourselves." Gabe was silent again as we stood there in the driveway. "Shortstone is a big city. I know Red, he'll think he's got bigger fish to fry but that doesn't mean we can slack off. We should lay low but intel is the top priority. We need to-"

"Hey!" We practically jumped, or at least I did, this discussion having put me on edge. We glanced over to our right, up the street. A man had been approaching us, an older gentleman with quite the look in his eyes. "That's it! You think you're some real army, huh?!" He hollered, as we stood there.

"Uh, can we help you?" Gabriel uttered.

"What the hell do you think you're doing in this house?" The older man snarled as soon as he saw my face.

"Do you own this house, sir?" I asked. I wasn't trying to be rude, as I legitimately wanted to know, but I think he took it that way anyways.

"You goddamn squatters," He grumbled. "How dare you take Frank's house."

"...Who?"

"My neighbor. He told me to look after his house after he left for Texas when this started going down, and I see you thugs *destroying* it. I don't care if you're with your stupid little army. You think you're the real Americans, huh? Real fucking patriots." He scoffed, hands stuck into his belt loop as we witnessed him revel in his outrage, Archie peeking from around the corner with Anthony watching on, a box in his hands. "Real Americans don't steal other Americans' things like thieves. Do any of you even know what the third amendment is?"

"Uh… That's the one about not letting soldiers into your home, right?"

"That's *correct*." He crossed his arms, charged with indignation as the two of us stood there, a good seven feet between us and this man. I took Gabe's arm, and the both of us turned away to talk.

"...What are we doing about this guy?" I asked, now whispering.

"I'm guessing you don't want to shoot him," Gabe put back, also whispering. I sighed.

"No shit." We turned back briefly, him still standing there. "Listen, sir," I put in. "We're… We need a safehouse in this area. But we'll take as good care of it as we can, okay?" I uttered. He didn't seem impressed, but then again, he sort of knew there wasn't much he could do. He had a set of balls, for sure, walking up to us like this. I wouldn't have chanced it if I was in his situation, that's for sure.

"Whatever. You best watch yourself." There really wasn't much else he could say, storming off.

"Well that could've gone worse, right?" Gabriel uttered, and I sighed again, watching him go.

"He could complain to the authorities if we don't keep up the act."

"So we play nice," Gabriel uttered, though it didn't take him long to sigh like I was in worried exasperation. "Or we could tell him who we really are."

"What? Why?" I uttered back.

"He's going to work it out sooner or later. We're not exactly going to have patrols or turn the place into a fortress. He did admit to us he's going to keep an eye on us, and he could blow us the instant he works it out."

"...Look, whatever we do," I muttered. "I need a change of clothes. And a shower, to be honest. Let's decide later, okay?" I turned back to the house to go through the front door. I re-entered our new little forward operating base. "Water works, right?" I muttered.

"Yeah. Ready to go," Gabe responded, walking alongside me. "Reds are keeping the main on. It's alright." I passed Anthony stacking the boxes full of dense magazines near the windows, going for the living quarters with the television to see a couple people watching the screen. Electricity and local network was working too, so it seemed. There was only one channel available apparently, and it was the local access broadcasting, playing the New Republican Alliance "news", which was almost exactly as propaganda-filled as I'd expect.

"Why are you watching this junk?" Gabriel followed in, Sam on the couch with the remote control in her hands, Abel off to the side watching as well.

"Because it's the closest thing to news and the internet is still pretty much down?" Samantha said. "Fuckin' Repub scum. If it wasn't for what I saw at Elko I'd join the Democrats."

"Yeah, fuckin' assholes," Abel said, laying on the ground next to her. She quietly scratched him behind the ears, fuzzing his messy hair too. He smiled, letting out a little "Mmm", enjoying the attention.

"Are you conditioning Abel to be a greenie pinko like you, Sam?" Gabriel said with a laugh. Sam shot a look at him. "I'm sure the readers of your social justice blog will be proud of your subliminal, hypnotic enslavement of a fellow sapient being," Gabriel scoffed with a smile.

"Fuck off." Gabriel was gone, to attend to other things as he laughed his way away. I was going to go for the shower, but I just walked into the backyard. It was almost beautiful, in this secluded neighborhood, evergreen trees shrouding the view of the mountains to the east, the mist shrouding the mountains.

I saw the pool over there, going over to maybe freshen up as I felt that a shower felt weird at this point in the day. I already saw Lauren all spread out in the deep end, floating there peacefully and staring up into the sky motionlessly, still in the shirt she'd been wearing in jail. One of my dad's old polos. I just nearly smirked. I almost was worried she'd drowned or something before I saw her blinking, still gazing up into the clouds. Maybe she didn't notice me, zoning out like she did, maybe me being here was besides the point. I pulled my shoes off to dip my toes in, regretting it almost immediately.

"Yeesh," I uttered. I finally saw Lauren's eye looking over to me. "How can you stand this water?"

"...I got used to the cold after a while," She sighed out. "It's cold up here in Idaho. It's so much different, but... This house is a lot like yours." She motioned to the house with a submerged splashing hand and I smirked, able to find this interesting in the abstract, distracting myself from how my actual house was a crater now, digging into my cargo pocket and pulling her horn back out.

"You want this?" She took a quick glance, another sigh escaping her.

"Nah. I'll grow a new one."

"...Ought to grind it up and snort it for good luck," I joked, looking down to it. She snorted back a laugh.

"I thought you were Japanese, not Chinese." I smiled plainly, still looking the thing over, mostly glossing over how Lauren had the knowledge of the cultural intricacies between the Chinese and Japanese, thinking of it more as funny than any sort of genuine oddity. I guess she was nothing but oddities, so it was easy to overlook as I analyzed her horn. A doubly bent spike of hard bone a good nine inches long, at least the half in my hand. I guess if we had to have gotten ourselves out of the jail, it would have made an exceptional weapon with a little filing of the tip.

"...If I was Chinese I'd snort it to get lower cholesterol and a bigger dick," I proposed and Lauren laughed again.

"Sounds like a plan in that case," She muttered.

"...I'll keep it around," I finally put forth. "Just in case."

"If it'll make you happy," she put back as I was walking away. Only when I reached the back door again did I question her wording. Make me happy? That was a funny way of putting it. I could practically envision her slapping her forehead in cringe as she realised what she'd said. I guess the thought itself was charming enough.

Given how frigid the pool was, I figured I could use the warmth so I found a shower in the downstairs bathroom, stripping down. I turned on the water, relieved to see that not only the power was on, but the water was too. Sure, Gabriel told me it was, but seeing it for myself was what really sold it for me.

It was a simple shower, no UI interface or health scanners or anything of the sort, something truly old-school but it was more than enough. The first hot shower in what must have felt like a lifetime, standing there to let it all wash over me. I got some of the weird old-people shampoo that was in the shower supplies hanger to clean my hair, only to remember rather foolishly that I'd shaved it all off earlier this week. Also felt a lifetime ago. I felt the stubble on my face, too. I must have looked different as compared to when all this started. Like this whole ordeal was changing me.

Using that shampoo, I sudsed up, eliminating the grimy feeling a scrub at a time. But as I cleaned, I looked over to Lauren's horn, that I'd stuck in the shower supplies hanger. For some reason, I'd dragged it all the way on in here, and there I was, holding it again. Why did I pick it up? I guess to clean the shot-up end up, scrubbing a little bit at the dried crusty marrow. I ought to polish it up, I thought. A nice keepsake, or something. I guess the thought put me at ease, so I put it back down, making a mental note.

**Chapter 39**

---

"Noah," My father began, yet again. I must have been young, but not all that young. "There may come a time where you have to choose between safety and comfort. Clothes, body soap- all of these things take up precious space and can and will slow you down. Sure, you can talk and plan and ponder about minimizing your unnecessaries, but in the end a lack of them may drive you crazy." He paused, looking down at the bag I'd packed for the trip to the Citadel one day when I was younger. "You need a balance- something realistic. You can get by wearing the same underwear over and over for a month, but you'll feel uncomfortable, and sticky and nasty. And if you need to ever fight for your life, hunt or even do simple gathering, you will need to be as comfortable as possible, because these situations are going to be about as uncomfortable as they get."

"I get it," I said. "It's like you say, 'plan for the worst, hope for the best'?" I asked in my creaking little prepubescent voice. He smiled.

"More or less- but you need to find balance. That's all life is really about, too. Balance."

Balance.

"People are irrational," Dad went on. "You see this?" He said, holding a single bar of soap. "This- this kind of thing," he showed other things. Toothpaste. a hairbrush. deodorant. "You grow up using these things, you never notice them- they become a part of you. And then when they're gone, they drive you crazy. In these situations, earthquakes and floods and hurricanes, these little post-apocalypses in history, you'd find people killing over them- not because they needed it, but because they *thought,* they *felt* they needed it. They'd been so used to it for so long that it becomes a part of them they never ponder- it makes them human. And they want to feel human, to have that dignity of being clean, to wear clean clothes and smell nice. When you stink and you're dirty and your clothes are disgusting beyond all belief, when you haven't washed in a month you'll want to kill over that feeling too." He paused, hefting up his hunting rifle, an AR10 with a scope on top. "There is no question, this will be the most expensive thing you will have with you," He said, removing the magazine to look upon the cartridges, before putting it back in with a slap that echoed out as we sat there in our house at the citadel, a nice little place. "But these things- these small things so many people forget about, they will be similarly valuable, in their own ways. Do you understand?"

"Yes sir."

---

"...We sure we want to do this?" I uttered, walking back out into the den of the place to see Gabriel pulling food out of the pantry where we'd restocked the standing food with our own, grabbing only the good rations. Nice stuff that wasn't just muscle powder or protein synthesate.

"We'll get more. The gift helps sell us as friends, after all." The instincts imbued in me from my father told me that this was not a good idea in the least, that we ought to always horde food and supplies. I tugged at my new clean clothes, seeing Maria over there too, Standing there in her casual clothes- as if everything that wasn't bulletproof wasn't just casual clothes now, her wearing short shorts, a snug yet ample blouse and her hair tied back, only her gunbelt on its suspenders as her sole tactical kit.

I could hardly get in her head as she stood there. She looked indignant, I supposed, gazing off like she was avoiding my gaze. She was glad I was back, right? She looked uncomfortable, uncomfortable in her own skin. Was she uncomfortable with this plan of telling our new neighbors the truth? She didn't seem like it, willing to pitch in. When I finally caught her gaze, she could only offer back a weak smile. Like there were tears in her dry eyes, standing apart from me, that constant chasm between the two of us.

"So how are we going to play this?" I asked, the bags quickly close to filled with our peace offering.

"No playing. We're here to be friends," Gabe said. He smirked but he really wasn't joking.

"Is this kind of friendliness something you picked up on the job?" I asked again, full of jokes despite my own aching heart.

"I consider my neighborly nature extra-employatory resumé padding," Gabe joked in his ever forward manner. I was practically prompted to roll my eyes.

"...So what," I sighed on. "We give him food if he promises to keep his mouth shut?"

"Oh, no," Gabe responded quickly, waving me off like I was missing something obvious. "That's a deal. We want this to be a gift, gifts are nicer. If we act like this is a deal we're making he's going to be suspect off the bat. Angels give gifts, devils make deals. I may be anti-religious but the trope is culturally pervasive."

"He's right. This is our best chance to earn some trust," Maria put back. More and more I was inclined to agree.

"So when do we say hi to 'em?" Lauren suddenly entered the room, her nails clicking on the floor the only thing preceding her entry. I was more surprised that somebody as massive as her could sneak around than how she'd taken us by surprise. Gabe was looking up, brows arched and mouth furled with that look that said he was about to explain something else that didn't need explaining, something a little bit more painful this time.

"...Sorry Green," Gabriel began with that little smile. I could tell it didn't bother Gabriel that much, he was just being polite for once, pretending to tiptoe around this issue as he leaned against the wall beside the pantry door to look at Lauren, me practically between the two of them. I looked over, seeing Lauren's hair dressed up under a towel in a bun, her horns captured inside them, wearing a fresh blouse and bra. "Hybrids are kind of a… sensitive issue. We want to make a good impression on the old fogies. You might be a bit too new-wave for 'em."

"We've got hybrids in our group, though," She put forth, slapping her hands at her sides, masking her offense with a raised brow and ever so slightly curled lip. "If anything, we should be honest. They might respect that." Gabriel was still having that uncomfortable face, Lauren crossing her arms.

"I, uh, don't mean to knock your self-esteem down a peg, Greenie," Gabriel uttered. His diplomacy was something to see, a peculiar oddity as I knew he could tear into anyone's soul with impunity, much less Lauren with her own rampant insecurities. I guess he was just taking this serious despite his rapid-fire attitude. "But I'd see bringing a eight foot tall, half ton ten-limbed dragon to a first meeting is less of a diplomatic move and more of an intimidation tactic."

"Intimidation?" She practically spat. "I'm-" she paused, stamping one of her front talons a little, before reserving herself to tap the talon's nail on the tile floor quickly as she rose an arm from where her arms were crossed at her low chest, to poke at her mouth in ponderation. "So who are you bringing?"

"Not me; fuckin' pensioner can rot for all I care, I helped him up when he tripped the other day and he made like he was gonna shot me," Archie responded, finally having kicked back on the sofa to watch the "news". Reina too seemed less than sold on the plan, sitting by the fire in the corner still in full combat gear, an ear flicking from under that high-cut helmet. Guess she liked the feel of an armored shell.

"So who else? Selicia?" Lauren scoffed. "You think I'm the edgy scary one? She'd offer to suck that old guy's dick if you took your eyes off her," She spat.

"I can *hear* you, and also: ew," came from the ajar basement door beside Lauren, down into the creepy darkness below. Lauren donkey-kicked the door shut without even a look back.

"Abel," Gabriel said, as of the big lunk on the carpet before the TV, Sam rubbing his belly. He looked up from where he lay in such a silly fashion.

"Him?" Lauren was indignant. "I'd hardly want him to be our ambassador for all hybrids. No offense," She motioned over with a little wave.

"It's okay, I really don't want that responsibility either," He put forth, Sam looking up in offense, about to get offended for his behalf before he spoke. "Hey, get a little more on the side, right? I got an itch there," He spoke to Sam and she obliged. Lauren was glaring at Gabe, nostrils flared, absolutely steadfast.

"You know, I think Lauren's our best bet," I put forth. "Aside from the whole… Big dragon thing, she's really well spoken. I think she might be the best *because* she's big and scary," Gabriel, Maria and even Lauren herself obviously wanted me to explain how I came to this surprising conclusion. "I think once he realises that Lauren, an eight-foot-tall, ten-limbed dragon like you said, is just as much of a person as any human, he'll be a lot more sold on hybrids in general. And I think she's the most personable, relatable hybrid here. No offense," I mentioned to Archie, Reina and Abel.

"Whatever. Good fucking luck," Archie spat.

"You sure you won't fuck this up?" Maria asked. "You knock over a priceless vase with one of your wings or back your ass into an armoire and this all goes up in smoke."

"Hey, it's been a while since I got shot in the head. I'm cognizant of my bodily garbage," Lauren smiled back, smiling and joking to get a smile back. Maria was beyond amusement at the moment.

"Welp, freshen up. No guns, no armor, no weapons, no gear, look presentable. We do this at dinnertime."

Hell of a plan.


I walked down the sidewalk, unarmed and unarmored, Maria by my side, Gabe in front, and Lauren behind with the backpack of gifts cradled in her arms like an infant of good-tidings. She had her hair in a simple braided bun, her shot-up horn now filed a bit to get the rough edges off, no longer gory or bleeding. On that short walk next door, I took a single glance, seeing her reciprocate a brave smile back. Lauren Green, the Indomitable.

Gabe came up to the door. "Everybody smile, look presentable," Gabe offered in finality. Lauren nodded profusely, quietly coming behind me and holding her gifts at her upper belly, slinking down some and putting on a bright, happy smile (without baring her teeth, of course), trying to not look as tall and monstrous as usual. For enhanced lack of contrast, Maria and I stood up as tall and presentable as we could (even though the two of us were still quite a bit shorter than Lauren), Gabriel ringing the doorbell.

I waited for a couple seconds, expecting that grumpy old man to return with a gun and tell us to get the fuck off his property. But, to my surprise, the door cracked open without a word before it, and standing there was a bright-cheeked, cheerful older woman. And she was positively delighted to see us, or at the very least was putting up this personable and welcoming front in fear that we might be republicans here to judge them harshly, despite none of us wearing any piece of red. It was practically shocking, taking the words right out of my mouth how positively ecstatic this kind old lady was.

"Oh, hello! You must be the new soldiers using Frank's house," She said. She offered Gabriel her hand, Gabriel not missing a beat and reciprocating that friendly grin as he took her hand. "I don't know what my dear husband has been telling you, but I think you all seem like awfully decent people and I'm sure you'll take plenty good care of Frank's house, now won't you?"

"That's the plan," Gabriel uttered, and she laughed again. That sort of fake laugh to let you know she wasn't afraid or frustrated, like I'd heard it a million times before.

"Oh, good, good. Frank always loved that house. I'm sure Steven was a little jealous of it, he always loved that big basement of Frank's, and the pool out back. Back when our kids lived here they swam in it all the time with Frank's kids."

"Nica? Who's that at the door?" I heard the old man's gravelly voice in the background. I saw, from the den emerge that old man, with a mossberg in his hands. He racked the pump. "It's those god-damn role-players, aren't they?"

"Steven! For God sakes, put the gun down, don't make a scene!" she said, as if merely embarrassed at her husband's reckless brandishing of a deadly weapon, all four of us there slowly turning our palms outward in a subtle surrender pose, Lauren hefting the bag with one hand and freeing her right hand as well, shrinking a little with her ears drooping. "These people seem all right, don't they? Why don't we introduce ourselves? My name's Nica Pendrew, and this is Steven. We're married."

"We're pleased to make your acquaintance," Gabriel began, not even the tiniest bit flustered. I guess he figured he had an in with this Nica character as opposed to her stalwart husband. "I'm Gabriel. This is my childhood friend since elementary school, Noah, his highschool sweetheart Maria, and our new friend." Lauren nodded and let out a tiny "Hi, I'm Lauren" with a calm, toothless smile.

"A fucking hybrid, huh?!" Steven uttered. "You think you can really be *friends* with one of those things?!" Lauren was well and good keeping her mouth shut and letting the ever-competent Gabriel take the reigns, though I could see her ego bruise from this. She was prepared for this outcome, of course, taking it in stride and barely flinching.

"Matter of fact we have. As of May first, twenty-sixty. She's quite the seamstress, in fact." Lauren did certainly appreciate Gabriel's ego boost, even if performatory, blushing behind puffed cheeks of a now suppressed grin.

"Steven! Put the gun down! You want to make the news?!" Steven stood there for a moment, before grumblingly slamming it down on the table to cross his arms and stand there, glaring at us. Nica finally turned back to see Lauren, who now jittered a bit, feeling this analytical judgement beginning, clutching the pack. "My, what a beautiful creature," She said, somewhat awed, or at least being polite. Steven rolled his eyes. "You look so strong, so voluptuous- Look at your wings! Can you fly, Miss Lauren?"

"Yes," She said. "Yes ma'am, I can."

"Oh, drop the 'ma'am', I'm not some kind of snob," she said with a little comfortable laugh, Steven rolling his eyes. "well, Steve's got his opinions, but I'm sure you're not some kind of delinquent, young lady!"

"Thank you!" Lauren offered back as happily as she could muster.

"And what's that you've got there?" Lauren stepped forward, passing the bag to Gabe.

"We don't want to make the wrong impression. We'd like to share some of our food with you."

"*What?!*" Nica cried. "Why would you be the ones giving us gifts?! why, I ought to feel ashamed! We should be giving you a housewarming gift, not you giving us one! Now we're just being rude, Steven!" She hissed to her husband, who rolled his eyes yet again. "Come in, come in! Don't just stand around!" She said, opening the door wide. "Come in, come in! Make yourself at home!"

We walked in, with Steven standing there with his finger tapping the stock of his shotgun on the table, 'tsk'ing. He whistled for the dog, and in came an old german shepherd. As soon as the dog came out, he took one look at Lauren before going for Steven, cowering there. I almost felt bad, seeing Lauren's ears droop again, nerves wracked in her self-consciousness as she stepped gingerly about their foyer, again making sure not to bump into anything.

"Well, we were just making dinner," Nica said as we followed them through into the kitchen. I could smell it- meat was quietly simmering in a pan on the old electric stove. We walked over, as I watched Lauren edge carefully by the slow, lumbering beast who laid down on the carpet to watch us distantly, Steven standing over the old dog. Gabriel and I slowly sat in chairs around the table, and Lauren lay her lower body beside me in lieu of a chair, Maria on my opposite side. "Ah, meat's so hard to come by recently with everything going on, you know," She said. "good thing we've got plenty." I noticed, sitting in the corner just barely out of sight was a large, leather saddle for a horse.

"Nice saddle," I said, pointing to it, as Ms. Pendrew served me some meat, which I began to cut into, putting some in my mouth and chewing. It tasted like a mixture of venison and beef- but it wasn't ground, it was fibrous like a steak. "You use it much? Ride horses?"

"Used to," Steven growled as he took a slow seat at the head of the table. "More when our kids lived here, before they grew up and moved away. We used to ride horses all the time. We even owned one."

"Oh?" I said, chewing and swallowing, Lauren doing the same. "What happened to it? I'm sure you must-"

Suddenly, the man reached down, pulling out his pistol from his belt and letting it plunk on the table with a razor sigh, as if it was causing him discomfort, lodged in the crux of his belt. "We shot him," He said. silence filled the room. "So we could eat." I stopped chewing, looking down at the plate. My appetite was diminished, as my utensils fell to the plate with a clatter.

"Mm, this is pretty good," Gabriel said, ravenously smacking his lips. "It's a little gluey if you ask me."

"Welp, I'm… I ate earlier," Lauren uttered, refusing a serving. Maria didn't seem to mind, like Gabe, eating.

"Oh, but I made a fantastic pie for dessert too," She said.

"Nica," Mr. Pendrew said. "That pie is for us."

'Oh, but we'd be oh-so rude to not share."

"Well, I'd feel rude to overstay our welcome," I said.

"Then you can leave," Mr. Pendrew growled.

"*Steven*," Nica practically growled. Another roll of the eyes.

"Look, Mr. Pendrew…" I slowly began, eyeing over to Gabe. He looked up at me. "We're uh… We would like to discuss something with you."

"Yeah, first thing," Gabe interjected. "What's your opinion on this war going on?"

His silverware clattered to the plate, as he swallowed what he was chewing and sat up to intertwine his fingers and glare at us, at me. "If I don't give an opinion you like, are you going to have me dragged outside and shot?" He spat. Cheeky for an old man. I was almost impressed by his sheer gumption.

"I guess that we ought to couch this, that this is between us, one man to another," Gabriel uttered, still eating, seeming unbothered, as he prepared to drop the shocking truth, my own heart falling into my stomach as I realised the turn this conversation was to take. "But you seem to be under the impression that we're some of those republican paramilitaries."

"You're not?" He uttered, predicting the flow of the conversation perfectly, right down the road Gabe was leading him. "What are you then, mercenaries?"

"Yeah. Let's go with that for now," He uttered. "Would you like to know my politics, Mr. Pendrew?"

"You seem ready to monologue. Sure. Why not."

"Fuck this war. Fuck the left, fuck the right. It's all bullshit, bullshit that's been a long time coming because bullshit salesmen sold bullshit to the public for decades, maybe a century. Say what you want about the Creators or whoever you think ended the world, but at the end of the day, they couldn't have done this without us Americans being complicit in it. Everyone fighting right now is *choosing* to fight. I say fuck reactionary politics, fuck american pride, fuck the media. All anybody ever cared about was winning the argument, being correct and getting pats on the back from people they'd hardly consider friends; not making this country a better place or helping people, and this is what it all leads to. A war fueled by indignance and moronic, practically religious conviction. The other side is evil, my side is good and just. It is moral and right to kill my enemy, if you are not with me you are against me and I will take pride in your death. Fuck all of it."

"...But you're a mercenary."

"I never said I was, *you* did. You wanted a quick answer, I gave you one. Sure, you could say we are mercenaries. Self-employed, to be precise. I'm not blue, I'm not red, I'm not a revolutionary or a conservative. The pay I'm after is getting out alive." Gabriel paused to let it all sink in. "We're passing through, to the north. We needed a way to slip past the republicans, red paint, a couple good names to drop and a couple more red bandanas happened to do the trick. We're not here to turn your buddy's house into a fortress, matter of fact, we like the place and want to keep it as nice as possible to keep the republicans off our case. We're here to lay low, and I just wanted to get all pretenses out of the way, because I don't respect liars, or the omission of truth, and I'm sure you don't either." For the first time, I saw that old man smile.

"You've got balls for a freak-show ringleader," Steven uttered, his eyes drifting towards Lauren who was still being silently polite, eyeing about the table. "You know what? You might not be an asshole. But let's move on, let me answer you, about my politics. I've voted red all my life and it's been a long time since I was this disappointed with the party. These 'republicans' are a disgrace, a bunch of god-damned shameless communists pretending to crusade for conservatism. Look at my guns," he said, motioning to his pistol and shotgun. "To them, having two guns consists of an 'arsenal' and you're 'hoarding vital supplies'. That's enough to warrant a summary execution, or immediate drafting into the front lines. Same thing, really. Hell, even if you have one gun they'll take it anyways if they don't like your attitude. They're spreading the wealth- to themselves. And if you're not willing to bend over and let them violate you they'll think you're 'resisting' and beat the everloving shit out of you, if not just put one in your head and leave you for the birds. Do you know how many guns I have?" He snarled. "Quite a few more than these. and these days guns and bullets are just about the only thing that's worth their weight in goddamn gold- after all, that's why they want them all. They want the wealth so they can keep on fighting this stupid war and boxing us in their 'new american empire' like zoo animals. See, you happen to have me at an impasse. If I rat you folks out, the Republicans will start snooping around. And I don't look like the innocent little star servant of their new glorious People's Republic. I'm old. They don't like the old, think that we don't have any use for them. I'm just getting by here, trying to stay out of it, just like you. And I can see they won't like that." He paused, as if to take a breath. "I just want to survive, like you and your colorful little group of freaks and geeks. And I don't want you to bring attention to *me*, either. Can we both agree to keep a low profile, Mr. Gabriel?"

"Absolutely," Gabriel answered with a shit-eating grin. "...That's what we came here for." Mr. Pendrew squinted at the rest of us, judging our seriousness.

"Good." And he went back to eating.

"Hey, uh," Lauren spoke up soon enough, Mrs. Pendrew glancing up with an unstoppable smile of her own. "So, you... Don't have a horse anymore, right?" She motioned over to the saddle in the corner. I smirked in response.

### Chapter 40

The evening with the Pendrews was a success, as far as we were concerned. We returned feeling somewhat better, Lauren clutching her new gift, that saddle, the happiest one of us as she cradled her newest project- it wasn't exactly fit for her, as her wings would doubtlessly be a little in the way of the drop-down portion of it, but I could tell she was already thinking up a workaround.

The first night in Frank's house, I slept a dreamless, uninterrupted sleep. I awoke to a rooster crowing in the distance, smiling a little at the cliché as I lay there. I got up to look out, I saw the sky was pale and nearly cloudless, the moon still out, sun shining as it peaked over the mountains to the east. Maria dozed calmly in the bed, still very asleep. I wanted to activate the telewall out of instinct, but I knew it would be nothing but Repub propaganda on the very limited network and I didn't feel like waking her, though I did ponder how long I'd been away from home, how long it'd been since life was normal. May the first. what day even was it?

"Computer," I coughed out. "Date please. Quietly."

"May tenth, 2060."

"Fuck…" I muttered. It felt like so much longer. Staying in Vegas, traveling, Elko… I sighed. What a journey, for us to end up here, so close to our destination, stopped dead by the blockade. For a second, my brain scrambled to find something to think about, some problem, some solution, some *thing*… But I had nothing. I just spaced out, before dressing up and getting up. I pulled on one of the other gunbelt harnesses, grimacing a little seeing that pistol there that certainly wasn't my glock. I didn't have a problem with berettas, they just seemed awfully old-fashioned and heavy, given it was made out of steel rather than modern plastic. I sort of smirked thinking about how someone like Mr. Pendrew would think the opposite.

I walked past the upstairs bathroom. I heard the water shut off, before hearing the quick poof of the superhot particles drying the inhabitant in an instant. I guess at least one of the showers here was high-tech, the one downstairs apparently an afterthought, yet to be upgraded. The door opened, and out hobbled Archie in nothing but his boxers; his fur was a lighter, cleaner shade of pale orange looking funny, his fur all standing up with static. "Oh, morning Noah," he said quickly as he smoothed his fur down. I walked forward, looking in the rooms. They were simple guest rooms, uninhabited for years. In the first one with the door slightly ajar, where I guessed Archie had come from, Daniel quietly slept on one of the single beds, another unoccupied single on the other side of the room where Archie had been sleeping. Abel was in a weird pose on the ground, his rear body curled up but his upper humanoid part sprawled out. I witnessed as he arose from sleep, his whole body straightening out and stretching as he yawned.

In the room next door was the girls' room apparently, with Reina sleeping next to Katt, and Sam trailing off of the same cramped-up bed. Sam had taken after mine and Gabriel's tactical advice and shaved off her already short hair last night, it didn't particularly surprise me. Lauren curled into a ball on the ground around her new prize, that saddle she'd been messing with, snoring rather lightly.

Downstairs, I found Anthony leaned up against the windowsill towards the front with his rifle in his lap, snoring, in the little pillbox of heavy boxes full of junk. I went towards the kitchen, finally finding Gabriel at the kitchen table. His pistol was disassembled in front of him, and he sat with a clean rag and a bottle of solvent quietly wiping the carbon from any part he figured needed it. His carbine sat, suppressor gleaming, ready for use. "Sun Tzu once said," He began mirthfully, slipping the barrel back into the slide and noticing how I noticed two of his guns left at the ready and presumably loaded, "Never clean all of your guns at once." Upon the punchline, he slipped the slide back onto his handgun, racking it back and forth, before manually decocking the hammer.

"Do you ever sleep?" I asked, the same old question. He smiled at the formality.

"When I'm dead, probably. Maybe," Gabe said smilingly.

"What's the itinerary?" I muttered, rubbing my eyes.

"Finish up on the garage and the rest of the house. I'll go digging for intel tonight, see if I can't find an edge on the situation. Recon, y'know. But after that, we've got to train." I let out a breathless 'huh', weird how I guess we ought to play things slow and careful now. "As for the short term…" He said. "The Pendrews keep some chickens in their backyard. They probably woke you up. How do you like your eggs?"

"…I'll just have a carbo block, thanks," I muttered back, not wanting to bother him.

"Mm, suit yourself," He uttered, as the doubled clattering of claws announced a large, green creature trouncing her way on down the stairs, Lauren emerging into the dining room as she rose her arms to yawn and stretch, doing her best not to smack the ceiling. She had her saddle plopped between her rear wings, having it more forward on the shoulders of her frontal legs.

"Hey, Noah, Gabe," She yawned. "I think the saddle is almost fully set up for me, I just needed to get it more forward. How's it look?" She spun around a little, trotting in place like a show pony.

"Leather's a bit risqué for everyday wear," Gabe joked, going to start up the stovetop. Lauren playfully rolled her eyes back.

"I like it," I put forward, smiling as warm as I could.

"Mm, kinky; now ask him if he wants to go for a *ride*," Gabriel was busy cracking eggs open into the pan. Lauren's playful exasperation knew no bounds.

"It's not finished yet. I'm gonna put the saddlebags beneath my wings, have one be a rifle scabbard. Also gotta make sure it doesn't shift in-flight. Then, I'll need somebody to test it with," She rose her eyebrows at me and I reciprocated a hearty grin, feeling my heart flutter. I was more than ready to hit the skies again. Gabriel had a quaint little chuckle, rolling his eyes.

Breakfast was quaint, everyone coming forth to enjoy a decent meal, one of us turning on the TV in the background for some ambient noise. Again, it was the closest thing to news, though you'd have to unpack the information from beneath layers upon layers of propaganda. Selicia was somehow upstairs during the night, taken to the attic, the highest floor of the house with a little window overlooking the street, where she'd taken up her guard post for the latter half of the night. Daniel was up and about once more as well, in much better shape. He wasn't taking the metabolic inducers anymore, so I guessed he was mostly healed. I'd also noticed that Gabriel's hand, though scarred up, was mostly good. He healed pretty fast, even while on quick-heal meds.

"Damn, I didn't know eggs could be, like, good," Anthony put forth. "Usually if I tried to scramble 'em they'd just end up all mushy."

"You probably had synthesized eggs. Helps to use the organic stuff,"

All of a sudden, there was a knocking at the door, and up I rose. It didn't set me on edge like it ought to have in retrospect, I guess I was still reeling from the way the world was changing. I did peek out the peephole before just opening it, seeing Mrs. Pendrew there, heading the two of them rather brightly with her husband in tow, glancing around in grumbling exasperation. I opened the door for them, a couple of us coming up behind me to see as well.

"Good morning!" Nica cheerfully greeted.

"Morning," I said groggily, at the door, before clearing my throat, figuring I should wake myself up a bit, be more presentable. I looked at them. They were both dressed rather nicely. Mr.

Pendrew, of course, was not nearly as cheerful looking. "What's the occasion?" I asked slowly.

"We're going to church," She said. "and it would be rude of us not to invite you along. Do any of you want to come?" She asked. I looked back in, seeing others curiously wondering what they wanted. Gabriel, who'd peeked out, visibly scoffed.

It was a quiet drive, about a mile or two to the church. It was down the road to the north past the very city limits, at the end of the blocked-off road to the north. I sat in the bed of Mr. Pendrew's truck with Anthony, Lauren and Maria, while Katt sat up front on Mrs. Pendrew's lap, the kindly old lady taking a liking to the plucky preteen hybrid.

"You aren't making trouble in that house, are you?" Steven grumbled with his usual accusatory tone.

"That's the plan," I uttered through the open rear window of the truck's cab.

"Be sure to stay dry tonight, with the storm rolling in," Mrs. Pendrew uttered, ever the caring foil to Steven's hardheadedness.

"So what's church like?" I heard Katt ask, through the little separating window behind the cabin. She was sitting on Mrs. Pendrew's lap looking at Gabriel's mask, trying to decide what she should do next. She was a slow and meticulous worker for her age, it seemed- maybe she just wanted it to be special. Gabriel, strangely, put up with her borrowing of it, but he didn't want to come along, for obvious reasons.

"Wonderful," Ms. Pendrew said, full of pep. "At church, you hear about God, and Jesus, and how much he loves you."

"Jesus?" Katt said. "Who's that?" Ms. Pendrew smiled cheerfully.

"You'll see, dear."

The old church sat atop a hill. It seemed to be bustling with refugees, and only then did I figure this might be awkward given the amount of red soldiers about, though I guess the fact that we were in a different precinct set my mind at ease. I bet Lauren and I didn't exactly have our faces pinned up in every garrison point as a Person of Interest just yet. Tents, mats and sleeping bags were everywhere, and the smell of filth-encrusted humanity was all around. People were silent, without much to say here either, sitting under the guns of the "protective" republican troops.

On the other side of the hill facing the northwest, a graveyard sat, silent and quiet as the refugee camp, but without the government eyes keeping watch. It's inhabitants certainly weren't going anywhere, even the newer, crude graves more than probably republican troops killed in early offensives against the democrats to the west, those like them all barely a week old, and instead of headstones there were simple wooden crosses. And the mere sight of how many they were- this graveyard must've been at least a hundred years old back before Shortstone was a real city, but the fresh, hasty graves outnumbered the older, more proper ones with actual headstones. people stood, knelt and sat before many of the new graves, quietly looking into the dirt, many draped in black. The majority were human, but the mourners were not without hybrid representation. It all seemed strangely communal, such different looking people standing together, weeping together, even if many refused to so much as acknowledge the ones standing next to them. a man or woman with spite for hybrid kind might've been using one of their shoulders to cry on.

A long soup line stretched out, tailing from the tables at which young women with old, tired eyes ladled out food for the hungry, from vast pots that they reached far inside to reach the contents, a little bit further and further each time. Republican militiamen stood watching the ordeal, involving themselves in the process as they pleased, making sure nobody was given too much or making trouble.

Again, seeing Republicans here made me a little nervous. I don't know, it felt uncanny after being in the jail and being interrogated to see them again, out en-force. Sure, they were all over the city, but here it felt like they were genuinely in charge, even though they only claimed to be overseers.

Inside the main building of the church, a stink radiated above everything. A human stink, that of unwashed clothes and skin and old sweat and dried blood. The stink that you'd be able to pinpoint in a heartbeat. People, dirty and downtrodden sat around in the pews. Some were dressed in black, and most were gazing up to the cross, some with arms spread and palms outstretched. Many sat and knelt before the steps up to the cross itself, gazing upwards into the glass panes letting down colored light from above, giving their penances in their own individual ways. some wailed and cried, others remained silent and motionless, some sat in little circles and hummed sad tunes and hymns solemnly, nodding and bobbing and crying out, like speaking in tongues. Upon closing in towards the cross, I couldn't help but hear from the corner of my ear the voice of Maria, whispering something in Latin. I turned to see her crossing herself, looking at her feet the entire time, before looking up to the cross once at the end and nodding, kissing her thumb knuckles subtly.

Mrs. Pendrew giggled. "Maria, this is a Protestant church," She quipped, with a smile.

"Nica, let the girl give her respects," Mr. Pendrew replied. "This is no time for petty differences."

"I'm just saying, it's kind of funny," she reasoned, holding onto her sense of humor despite the darkness of the situation. Mr. Pendrew sighed in a slight tinge of exasperation. The Pendrews, arm-in-arm, walked on ahead, with us following quietly in attendance. They led us to the front, sliding into some pews. We all took a seat, although Lauren had to sit in the aisles, as pews weren't exactly designed with their physiology in mind.

The pastor was a tall, spry man, with a shaved head and face of black stubble, walking slowly up the center aisle towards the little stage to reach the podium. "Welcome, children of god," he greeted, pausing. "These days are dark ones. The days of brother turning against brother, and the light of peace going out across the globe. We forget this, we forget that we are all children of god, and we are all brothers and sisters in Christ." He paused, to look down and consolidate his thoughts. "I see a lot of hybrids here today," He said, and I looked over, seeing Lauren suck inwardly a little, as if self-conscious, the pastor staring down the crowd from up on high. "Yes, the hybrids. Sinful, broken, imperfect. As we humans are. And who are we, us mere, sinful, broken humans, to say that hybrids are not also our brothers and our sisters?" he finally said, and Lauren's gaze went back up again. "Jesus shared his table with tax collectors, murderers and con men, pimps and prostitutes. He gave his company to the leper and the Gentile. Jesus, the spitting image of perfected humanity, found the most undesirable and estranged among us, and gave his wisdom, support and attention to them as if they were his own brother. And yet some of us, flawed as can be, see ourselves as being superior to others over looks; over some strange, fascinating shape of body or state of mind, despite every last one of us sharing the souls of God's light. Human or hybrid. Democrat or Republican. We cloud ourselves with hatred and lose sight of God, as we stare down the sights of a gun towards our own brothers." He paused again, to lean in. "I cannot claim to know the will of God, but His Word is clear- Treat your neighbor as you would treat yourself. Christ tells us our neighbors are those whom we share the world with. We cannot claim to represent the will of God while we blow our neighbors away with guns, with bombs and rockets; not over food, over land, even over money- but simply by having a different opinion?

Picking these arbitrary, redundant sides, red or blue?" He paused again, standing back again, looking through the crowd, his gaze seeming to connect with every last eye, even mine. "These are dark times, and the world is changing. Perhaps we even live in the end times. We are all scared, we are all confused, hungry and tired; you are, and I am. but with the light of God, we may light our paths towards the end of these dark times, so we may see the break of dawn, the light of peace and happiness again, hand in hand with our new brothers and sisters. Only through trust in God and love for our neighbors can we hope for a better tomorrow."

The sermon was a short one, much shorter than I'd expected. Maybe the pastor didn't have that much to say; perhaps he was just repeating himself at this point. He looked and seemed frustrated, almost angry somewhat. I figured the former. Like a funeral procession, we filed out of our seats, standing slowly to amble on outside. I supposed that before all this, the Pendrews would meet with the other churchgoers in the community hall, to talk and laugh with mugs of warm coffee in their hands, but the hall was filled with cots for refugees now. And besides, by how the Pendrews didn't stray far from us, I figured most of their church friends had already left the town, or worse.

In silence, I went to sit down on one of the benches outside, sighing heavily as I took in the scenery, all these dirty, downtrodden people, people I could never hope to help. I wondered why all of this was happening; a useless thought, not even comforting. The Creators? Political clashes a long time coming? It didn't matter now. I looked over to the rest, who stood around outside, somber as always. A stuffy, hot wind blew past and Katt walked up to me, sitting down next to me and shuddering a little, her tail sticking out behind her on the bench curling around the wrist of her arm she leaned back on, kicking her legs a little and furling her lips as she gazed up into the sky. I realised I'd never really talked to her, as I looked over at her as she watched the clouds passing, closing her eyes to sniff in. I figured that I should do the leaderlike thing and get to know her.

"Katt," I began slowly, and her bright eyes opened again to look over to me. "What was it like?"

"Huh?" she asked, seeming more bored than anything else. It seemed to be her way of conveying moroseness.

"You were in one of those... simulations, right?"

"...D-don't call it that."

"Alright," I conceeded. She took a long, silent time to sigh.

"It... I don't really know how to explain it. It's not fake- it didn't feel that way. I guess that was the point." She paused. "My dad was a... blacksmith. He was happy. The way we lived- we thought we were all we were. I mean, us. Feline-ids, or whatever you call us. It was also... It was like it was a long time ago, you know? Like we were from the past, but we weren't- God, what the fuck were they trying to prove, doing this to us?" She growled, at her former captors. "Were we being tested or something?"

"Probably," I said. She sighed.

"I had parents, in this village. It was just us, and we were happy. But one day, it changed."

"Did the... what happened, did... *it*, the experiment end when the... world ended?" I asked, not quite knowing what to call it.

"I... I don't think so," She said. "No. When everything got bad, I know it was on purpose now, part of the game they were playing with us. At least now I do. It- Bandits attacked our... our village one day. I watched my mom get killed in front of me…" She paused, gulping. "Then, for a long time, we were running. I couldn't have imagined it was fake or whatever. One day though, something definitely changed. The… The sun didn't rise one day and there were no stars above us. It was just night for… forever. Everything stopped, what was happening sort of… kept going but not. So I kept walking, until I found a door out, got into that metal place and met Archie and his friends." She sighed. "I guess I was upset at first. I felt like I'd been… lied to. After a while though, it felt like nothing I did really mattered, or at least that's what I learned from it. none of that shit mattered. It was all bullshit. everything was set up." She paused, looking me in the eye. I was kind of impressed at how eloquent she could be, somewhat taken by surprise. "You know, even *your* world feels set up. Maybe not in the same way, but from what I've seen- it feels like somebody wanted this to happen. Your world to fall apart, like mine. Somebody *caused* this. all… All this pain." She sighed one final time, long and hard. "I… I kinda just accepted it, you know… None of it matters, we're all being played. I don't care if there's an afterlife, either. I don't think I'd want an afterlife, if there wasn't a god. That'd mean that at least we can finally get away from a… a mega-maniac, watching our every move, causing us pain… It means we'd finally get to see the end of it and just be left alone."

"Kind of weird to think this at a church," I noted.

"Yeah, I don't know why I came," Katt said. "I guess I needed… vindy-cation." Her vocabulary made me smile.

"For a preteen, you seem pretty well-spoken, Katt."

"I guess," She said, kicking her feet some more. "Noah, uh… Look," She went on, coughing. "Call me Susan, okay?"

"…I thought you didn't like your name."

"I don't. But it's not going to solve anything acting like I can just run away from my memories. I… I want to be better than that."

"That's noble of you," I said. "…Susan." She sighed, looking down at her swinging legs, letting them slowly stop swinging, just letting the momentum die out, before she hopped off.

"Thanks, Noah," She fluffed out her blouse a little with her hands, going over to where Mr. and Mrs. Pendrew were chatting with the pastor, walking with a little pep in her step, tail whipping energetically.

As I watched her go, I saw it was just in time to see a red-skinned dragon man, wings drooping just like his eyes and dressed in a chest rig and the uniform of a Republican officer, pile out of red-painted trucks with his men and approach the pastor, flanked on both sides, and followed by a multitude of machete and pistol-wielding Republicans, while he was armed with none other than my AR-15, that very same rifle-length Armalite with a wooden stock set. I knew it was him, the one who'd tackled me, right down to those lifeless, tallow-yellow eyes of his.

"G-good morning, gentlemen-" The pastor began, but the red dragon wasn't much for small talk.

"You know why we're here, sir. We've come to collect our share for the troops," he said in a rather formal tone, looking down and to the side a little bit, with a sigh on his lips, his troops walking past him towards the foyer of the church to the community hall where the kitchens were, making food to serve the refugees. As I looked away and covered my face with a scratching hand to disguise myself they stormed right past, Katt- or Susan, now stepping out of the way so she wouldn't be shoved out of the way by the imposing men. All business at the moment, scowls on their faces, pushing past the door.

"You know, Michael, there is no need for weapons in this place. We are happy to comply with you and the authorities," The pastor said, putting on his best smile.

"Sorry, Davis, but you know Republican policy. We need to be ready to fight at any time." The pastor looked down somberly, as the men began carting out scores upon scores of the canned foods that had been donated to the church, loading them into the vehicles they had arrived in.

"H-hey, you can't take all that!" one of the church council members stepped forward in protest, who was met by Republicans reaching for their weapons. The red dragon who had my gun, Michael, raised his hand to hold his men back.

"Sorry, Adams. We've got a war to fight. I hope you can understand." Adams slowly stepped back, swallowing his pride despite his ego, seeing all the weapons nearly pointed at him.

They finished taking food soon thereafter, piling into their cars, leaving Michael standing there with the pastor. "See you next week, Pastor," Michael said, beginning to walk away. It felt like a threat, and I furrowed my brow, a little pissed on behalf of the church.

"Stay safe," The pastor responded, if only a bit weakly. Michael got back into the truck, and they drove away.

"...Fucking vultures," Mr. Pendrew noted, his hand on his side, where I could see the bump of his 1911 pistol in a concealed holster in his beltline, as he took his hand away from his jacket.

"Now, now Steven... We will make do. God will provide." Mr. Pendrew growled upon this. "Have faith, brother."

"Faith is hard to have when God's shitting fire and brimstone down on us," Steven growled again.

"Steven... This is not the end. When He decides when the end of days shall come, we will all be sure of it. Until then, we owe it to each other to live righteously."

Steven rolled his eyes, coming up to the rest of us. "Come on, gang. Let's go."

I left with him, sharing his disgust.


We returned to see the garage fully cleaned out, Most everyone pitching in with Gabriel there overseeing. "How was the fairytale house?" He muttered amusedly as we were walking on up while the Pendrews parked their vehicle.

"Fuck off Gabe," Maria passed all of us to head for the house, Lauren standing there beside me, the Pendrews going on in their house, and Susan ambling about in the street walking back to us, hands in the pockets of her sweatshirt with the hood up, tail drooping but not so entirely that she seemed depressed or anything.

"It was... Gave me a lot to think about," Lauren put forth.

"Yeah, well. Don't be so open minded that your brain falls out," Gabriel chortled.

"...Opinionated as usual, Gabriel," I muttered, slowly taking my time to look at the progress made. Seemed like we'd be able to park the jeep inside by tonight. It was a two car garage, and a pretty big one at that, so we'd leave the truck out front. Guess it doesn't matter that much, it was pretty low-profile, minus the bulletholes. Everyone was working, Even Selicia was pitching in, somehow roused from her crypt to actually be a productive member of society. Anthony skittered on inside before she took notice, per usual- she wasn't all that productive, after all, sighing heavily and taking her sweet time moving the lightest of boxes. "You gonna start giving sermons of your own about how great atheism is?"

"If you insist. Green, you want a fun fact? You know why they sing songs in church? Specifically, at the *beginning* before the pastor shoves his namby-pamby bullshit down your throat?" He gnashed with an evil little smile. "Singing stimulates the emotional centers of your brain and slows down your critical reactions. Opens you right up to be preached to. *Literally.* And aren't you agnostic, Noah?" He shot back at me, speaking quickly and loudly to keep from being interrupted.

"Yeah, but I'm polite." Gabriel rolled his eyes.

"Waste of your fuckin' time."

"I don't think it's a waste of time," Lauren put forth, our eyes turning to her, more or less realising she was still here. She gulped down at Gabriel's stare, eyes dancing off to the side for but a moment before returning. "The church we went to was *helping* people. They had a camp for refugees." Gabriel rolled his eyes again. "Are you really gonna say that's not a good thing?"

"Look, *Green*," Gabriel began, a condescending tinge beginning to rear its ugly head. "You're not even two weeks old. You haven't seen much. Maybe now they're putting on a little minstrel show of compassion, but throughout history the only thing religion has been good for is holding back the progress of mankind and killing each other."

"So?" Lauren scoffed back, her indignance coming out in response, arms crossing over her shirt and legs stamping a little bit in place. "Who cares what happened a hundred years ago? Right now they're *helping* people." Gabriel laughed in response, which only steamed Lauren further, seeing him brush her off in sheer condescension.

"...Fail to learn from history and you're doomed to repeat it," He crowed. Lauren's nostrils flared.

"It looks to me like they did learn from history. That's why they're helping people." Gabriel's neverending smirk even managed to give me a bit of secondhand rage, Lauren was a step away from being beside herself, gritting her teeth.

"You'll see. Couple centuries of these new dark ages we're being plunged into with this little apocalypse and religion will do what it does best and fuck up any attempt to restart civilization."

"Oh? You can tell the future now?" At this point, I stepped in, landing a hand on Lauren's side as her wings fluttered a little, obviously getting physically worked up. Though I'm sure that Lauren's pragmatic, diplomatic side knew that placing hands on Gabriel was certainly not to end well for her, and I was just as certain that Gabriel was certainly in no danger, I still felt like I ought to intervene.

"C'mon, you're not going to win this," I muttered to her.

"Yeah, because I'm right." Gabriel was relentless.

"Yeah, because you're a fucking mental gymnast," Lauren snarled, practically shaking.

"Ooh, digging the fancy buzzword. Did *god* teach you that or did *science* get it programmed into your *man-made* brain?" I had to practically shove Lauren the other way to take us both inside, as Gabriel was getting testier.

"...What is Gabe's problem?!" Lauren instantly steamed to me as the front door slammed shut behind us, pretty much as soon as it latched shut she was off, pacing out in the wide living room beside the entry space, wings kicking as she trotted.

"Religion is sort of his... Topic of interest. He's always sort of been like that."

"He used to be a lot worse about it," Maria's voice traveled on in from the dining room, where I heard her getting something to eat for lunch.

"Just... Don't bring it up around him or you'll get his lectures."

"Don't try to argue either. He'll just lead you in circles," Maria also added. Lauren sighed slowly, her pacing coming to an end.

"...You want to have some lunch?" I offered.

"I'm going to work on my saddle," She paced off past me, leaving me there to reel in the moment.

I guess lunch for myself wouldn't be half bad.

### Chapter 41

I helped with the clean-up, and by late afternoon when we'd finished, I then relegated myself to taking stock. I just couldn't sit idly by, there was just something innate about the situation that I just had to keep busy. This all felt unnatural, anyways. Making our little home base, stopping in any place but the Citadel. I tried to relax after cleaning out the garage, but it was beyond me, so there I was, seeing what goods we had.

At some point in the evening where I was walking around the perimeter of the house, outside near the shed and watching the dark clouds in the distance of the horizon I was suddenly accosted by a serious-faced Lauren who grabbed out at my arm as soon as I'd turned the corner. "Good, you're here. C'mon. Time to test it out," She suddenly said before I could so much as respond. She released my wrist, to turn around a bit to show it. "How's it look?" I took a moment, watching her with that look on her face, scrunched-up determination as she steadily stamped in place. I saw the stirrups, the fasteners reaching down around her secondary torso and a newer one around her humanoid torso, added-on, where it sat the seat of the saddle as far forward as possible.

"...Are you still mad?" I uttered, and she sighed with a quick burst of her nostrils, stamping her legs a bit more.

"It doesn't matter. Get on."

"Hey, whoa, okay," I uttered, trying to keep things light. "You think that you ought to fly angry?" She'd picked up a bottle of water turned a color of blue by some electrolyte packet.

"I'm not angry." I stood there to raise my eyebrows, leaning back. She sighed again, finally cracking a smile, putting that bottle down. "I'm more mad they took my hydration pouch," She grimaced.

"Gabe'll get you a new one."

"Yeah, he said he would." Another silence. "...Well?" She stamped a foreleg yet again, how she stood a little diagonal to me, doing a subtle little curtsey and nodding her head back. I couldn't help but smile back.

"Shouldn't we be telling somebody that we're leaving?" I took steps toward her, going to unfurl that stirrup and pull myself up, stepping in.

"It's fine, we'll only be gone a minute," Lauren muttered. Upon sitting down with a grunt from the both of us and threading my other shoe into the other stirrup, I could immediately discern a difference. Comfortable, sure. Secure, I guess. "We ready?" Lauren uttered, going out into the widest part of the backyard, wings unfurling.

"W-what about the infrared tags for your tail?"

"They won't shoot me this time. We'll fly *away* from the city. Now, you ready?"

"As I'll ever be," I let out in a hesitant sigh and like that there was nothing more that needed to be said. She bounded forward, leaping up with a short burst to the fence, gaining the real height to flap her wings with the next pounce into the skies, dodging past the evergreens before us.

That quick and we were flying, sure- but now it was more than that. This wasn't back when we were scouting the town: this now was pure, unfettered flight for its own sake, just like that first time back in Crystal Springs.

I sat back as Lauren was gone into the hills and highlands, and I with her. It was… far less exhilarating than usual, somehow. I couldn't be getting used to it, could I? The wind screamed in my face and stung my lips despite my nonchalance, my peacefulness upon being back up here, back where the world didn't matter. It was hot and humid, but with the wind flowing through me it felt colder. Refreshing. We weren't all that high up yet, though I could look down and see mountains and trees pass like in some video game on my old holo-console or something like that, but here you'd know it was real by how gravity tugged at you and pulled you horrifyingly back down, how the world was vibrant and whirled around you. I could look to the horizon and see for miles, see the mountains, the valleys, the hills. And the sea of clouds above us.

Lauren broke into the cloud layer, zipping through the mist, wet and stinging, leaving dew on our skins. A few moments and then I could look up and see a pale blue sky, and in the distance, a valley of beautiful clouds as the setting sun painted them in dazzling orange and pink. It was all so pretty, I could hardly feel anything but a deep, deep belonging here. Though in that looming eastern distance, great ominous clouds were rolling in. These mighty gray behemoths dwarfed us tiny mortal creatures, and they moved like giants, lumbering towards Shortstone. Lightning cracked in the distance, and we could see rain falling from them, in what looked like waves of distant mist surging from them at a slant.

For a while, Lauren was content with sailing by the edge of the storm, the floor before the mighty cliff towering over us. Neither one of us spoke, we just shared in the moment here in the crux between storm and calm. The howling of wind, the hiss of the mists, the distant grumble of lightning, the beating of wings. All of it was entrancing. I sort of wanted to speak up, remind Lauren that we should keep track of our bearing so we could make our way back, as the ground was obscured by clouds. But I felt that discontent within Lauren, that desire to excel. Something with how she so stiffly remained silent, how tensely she flew. She hadn't thrown a single trick or laughed or even so much as chuckled this entire time. I kind of missed her barrel rolls and loop-the-loops, especially now that I could properly enjoy them with the new security of the saddle. I was nearly to the point of suggesting it as she was now content to coast, stall, coast and stall and peter this way and that, maybe as some way to test the saddle, before she finally veered off before I could drudge up the will to say anything, beating her wings harder this time, rolling right to spin about away from the storm, then sharply turning back to it. Beating her wings harder, harder, harder. She was grunting, huffing, if not growling. Some beast within her spurring her onward.

"Lauren?" I asked. She sensed what I was about to say.

"I'm gonna... scale that cliff," she put forth, panting. "Looks like a challenge!"

"D-don't forget, you can't overheat your wings," Her whole body heaved as she worked her four massive sails, one pair after the other, sort of rocking me in the middle back and forth.

"I... Had two bottles of electro-aide before we left, we're good," I was looking right and left. That wasn't the mist of the clouds rising off of her pulsing wing muscles, by any means.

"That doesn't matter if you overwork yourself! Your muscles will heat up!" I put forth. She scoffed out a laugh, and I was worriedly lowering myself to her, clutching on as if it would make this any safer. Now I felt that exhilaration, that fear. But it wasn't fun like before. This was getting concerning.

"Almost... There," She said, after an agonizingly long minute, us now dipping into the wall of the storm on our way to the ceiling of it. The air felt a little thinner now, black darkness abounding around us. She was breathing harder. Her wingbeats became less uniform, less rhythmic.

"Lauren, you're not looking so well," I said. I looked down. Lightning was striking below us.

"I've... Got it," she said. She dipped from side to side.

"Lauren," I groaned. Her form deteriorated. "What's happening, Lauren?!"

"Fuck it... I..." she said, and with that, *poof.* We emerged into the sunlight, into a moment beneath periwinkle skies, blinding heights, my breathing heavy and head light. I knew if it wasn't for adrenaline, there was no way I could be conscious up here. That adrenaline of the incredible danger we suddenly found ourselves in. I heard her gasp, and like that I looked to the side, seeing her wings folding and wavering, not spreading out properly, practically bellowing steam.

And, like that, she sailed on for a quiet moment, here at the top of the world, but she lacked the strength to take in her accomplishment. And so, we fell.

It was so strange, as if she'd slipped off of a ledge. in the course of a second, we were no longer going up, but down. Her left wings spread out, but her right wings could not spread out as far for some reason, and she rolled.

I fell up off of her. well, it was a lot more like she fell out from under me. I tried to grab onto the knob of the saddle, her shirt, some leather fitting, anything, but it happened so fast. I felt my feet slip through the stirrups, and my heart flew into my stomach. This wasn't her playing, to turn around and catch me. This was beyond her control and that was where the horror began.

Before I could even think, I struck out a hand and grabbed direly at the only thing in reach- her remaining long, double-curved horn. Her head turned erratically as I had yanked her horn, and with it, her whole body followed, her head was like a rudder, and whatever control she had was lost in an instant.

Lauren was screaming. her hand went up and grabbed my wrist. I let go for a second, as if I expected her to hold on, but I slipped from her hand and fell below her. Her wings were still flailing through the air, and I had far less air resistance than she. "N-Noah!" she screamed, clawing down at me as I fell away from her. The last thing I could see before I fell into the storm clouds was her big, brown eyes sparkling in terror.

"Lauren!" I screamed up out of it, swallowed by the giant. The water stunned me with stinging rage, soaked me to the bitter bone.

I'd been skydiving once or twice. I remembered the basics. Spread my arms and legs out. Air resistance. I didn't have a parachute, and I certainly didn't have wings, but I just had to stall, to get back with Lauren and figure out how to save us.

I rocketed forward, towards where the sky was open and stormless. I screamed all the while to let her hear me, and I soon emerged from the great gray beast. I was now unsettlingly close to the main cloud layer, and I knew the ground wasn't far below it. I flipped onto my back, to see Lauren still screaming up above me, fifty, twenty-five meters.

"Noah!" She cried, seeing me. I could see the terror in her eyes.

---

"Noah, this feeling you get when you are nearing doom," He said. "It is far more dangerous than what might really be threatening you. This feeling will sabotage you, it will corrode your will to live if you don't know how to funnel it, to channel it. It's not inherently bad," He said. He'd get up, quietly circling the campfire. "Your elevated heartbeat, your twitching muscles, your heavy breathing. It's all designed to get you ready to fight. But, if you cannot control your arms and your breath, you will not be able to shoot your gun straight, or reload. Your punches will be sloppy and predictable, your tactics will decay. You will want to run, this is what this feeling is meant to prepare you for.

"But sometimes you cannot run. And I'm not talking your pride is at stake. I mean your back is against the wall. This is a moment where you will need precision, you will need your wits and your fine motor skills. they will try to run from you, even if you cannot run yourself. How do you do this? How do you make your hands precise and your movements swift?

"My son, this is the one thing that cannot be taught through words or even through physical training. but it is the most powerful weapon in your arsenal. It is a weapon. It is a weapon that will bring strength up from your soul that you never thought possible, it will bring you courage in the darkest of times. It will bring you up from the realm of dead men waiting to die.

"It is your willpower."

---

I'd felt my willpower before. When the bullets were flying over my head, I had that will to shoot to kill. When we found ourselves digging through Lovecraftian hell in that facility, every step I took depended upon my will to keep things together. When Elko erupted into madness, I had the will to keep myself going, to keep panic from my mind's doorstep, to keep on thinking. And when we were locked in the jail with only our words to fall back on, willpower bought us more than enough time.

I could feel my will in other places, sure. On the sparring mats where I'd spent so many weekends and evenings of my childhood, out in the forest when I had to slide a blade into the belly of a still warm deer carcass and remove the entrails, in those places I could feel it. But it was different then. It wasn't my life at stake. My reputation, my stomach, maybe. But the chips were far from all in.

But here, here up above the Earth and powerless now, was where I felt my will more than ever before. I looked into Lauren's eyes, and in an instant, I heard my father's words. They flashed in and out of my mind's ear in the blink of an eye, and there, I felt my will like my beating heart. It was instinct back then in the gunfights, raw and emotional but will nonetheless. But here, here in front of me up above it all, it was poetic. I could feel it. See it. Taste it.

I had a plan. the only problem was Lauren didn't. Panic was taking her over, body and spirit, infecting her soul like death's hand. And we would both be dead if she couldn't regain her will.

She slammed into me, grabbing onto me. She was in tears, babbling. I grabbed her by the head, and, with our noses inches from each other, I stared her right in the eyes. Her incomprehensible babbling slowed as I stared at her. I knew that words could only make this worse, until she could regain the spirit to listen to me. I channeled my calm through my eyes, my gaze, looking her in the eye, and that terror was slowly peeled back.

I hugged her quickly. with my mouth by her ear, I spoke.

"Lauren?" I said, softly but sternly. She babbled and wailed. "Lauren," I said more sternly. "Lauren, look at me. We need to work together, alright?"

"I'm sorry!" she coughed out, hoarse in breath.

"Lauren, you need to pull through here. We need to get your wings open."

"They're broken!" she cried.

"No, they're not. They've stalled." At least, that was the only way I could put it. "Can you move them?"

"No!" She said.

"Yes, yes you can! Look! You are right now! They're just a bit sore, that's all." With haste I pulled myself onto her back. My hands and arms were trembling. I looked down and my will faltered. We were seconds from impacting the lower cloud layer.

as quickly as I could, I unfastened the saddle. "Take it with your talons!" I ordered, and she pulled it down towards her front legs, holding it with the frontal handpaws. Her wings stretched out as best she could, but they looked rigid and could not stretch out fully, still sizzling, bubbling. I felt the wind resistance they made, shuddering like a rickety old biplane, and gravity returned slowly, as I tapped the major muscles on them with my thumbs, a simple massage, somewhat painful by how she cried out and twitched upon each one. They were stiff as a board, and hot as all hell, slick with rain and her sweat, practically boiling.

We broke into the clouds. Lauren cried out.

"Looking better!" I cried out to her. I did my best to massage the muscles and joints of her two major wings. "When we get close to landing, you throw your saddle towards the ground!" I ordered. It was basic physics. Couldn't hurt, could it?

When we broke the clouds, there below us that forest waited. It was close. Closer than I thought. I could spot a lake in the distance. "Aim for the lake!" The thunder of the outraged storm behind us cracked in the distance. I heard Lauren let out a whimper-like cry in fear. "You're doing great!" I shouted. I did not let my voice falter. If Lauren gave up, doubted my encouragement, we would be doomed.

We sped in a decline. Lauren's wings were stiff, but spread. They shook terribly. "You're doing it!" I shouted. I didn't know if we would survive this. But I believed. My willpower to believe emanated into her. I needed her to believe, and the only way I could do that is if I stuck by my own words. I believed. I believed. She's fine.

"I don't think we can make the water!"

"Yes we can, Lauren! Don't give up!"

"Noah," She said. I heard her voice crack. "If we don't make this, I want to tell you-"

"We're gonna be fine, Lauren!" I said. "I know you can do this!" I said. My voice was followed by thunder. I could practically see the terrified, unsure look on Lauren's face, pointing on ahead. "This isn't the first time you've flown! and It won't be the last! I promise!"

I felt a change.

Lauren roared in pain. Not any human, sapient scream, something far more primeval and primordial, something full of indiscriminate rage and hate and… Power. This was like the roar of a lion. The battle cry of a billion warriors throughout history. Her wings extended past where they'd been jammed and she evened out. Boom. She threw the saddle, and, like a shot, she, we were horizontal once more, if only for a couple decisive moments. Thunder cracked. blinding speed, as I bailed off of her, kicking her up in the process so she would be able to fall slower without my weight, turning and looking each other in the eye one last time, spreading my arms and legs and gazing back at her, her eyes wide as she looked down upon me in as I impacted the water first.

Splash.

Like that, the world was still once more. There underwater, I floated in place. That dead calm of mine, somehow roused up as I floated there, looking over as her body crashed and foamed in the waves, impacting there, floating there. My body still felt the sensation of flying forward, my head spun, but the stillness of the deep was comforting, to say the least. I floated there quaintly for a few seconds before I felt the need to breathe and I made myself swim on up, to reunite with Lauren, on the other side.

We survived.

I saw her body floating there, her eyes wide. She was belly up, her wings spread out but still seized up and twitching and foaming underwater, and her mouth was a little bit slack as she stared at the sky. Was she in shock? "Lauren," I let out, still reeling in my own shock, swimming up to her. I grasped at her arm, going to ever so slowly swim the both of us over to the shore, feeling the earth finally, mud beneath my feet there as she came back on, blinking steadily.

"N-Noah-"

"C'mon, let's get to shore," I said. I was still on autopilot, I really couldn't process the situation. Our brush with death and subsequent triumph over it. But as she yanked back, getting me to stop, like she'd screamed through grit teeth. She hadn't screamed, she was dead silent, but it was like it shot through me, all of this everything. She spun me back and her arms came over me, gripping me, nails digging into my back, tightly clasping me.

Here in that eerie silence, we remained motionless in this embrace until the waters calmed to a glassy sheen, the steam, the mist falling off of her wings and quietly pooling around us, spreading out across the surface around us. Must have been minutes before she sobbed once, still biting down on her horror, on her regret, on the aftershock of her adrenaline.

"Hey, Lauren, hey," I was whispering up to her. She'd stooped down some, our heads on each other's shoulders. "It's-" She sobbed again, her tears beginning to flow. "Hey, we're okay."

"You- w-we almost…" She sobbed again, gripping me harder. I heard the pitter patter of the rain catching up with us. The storm finally above us in this deluge. Standing up to our stomachs in frigid water, cold, and alone together.

"We didn't. We won, Lauren." her seized up wings were quivering, still steaming. She tried to laugh, sobbing it out. I didn't really know why I phrased it that way, saying that we'd won. I guess it was just all that could come to mind. We beat this trial, we cheated death.

"...We won?" She began, stammering. I could tell she found the phrasing weird too, taking a moment to almost compose herself, to try and pull herself out of the shock with a comeback. "D-do I get a trophy?"

"Yeah. A nice big one," I was whispering, the two of us standing there and soaked. We eased up on each other, leaning back to look each other in the eyes. I saw her sparkling brown eyes, her tears had stopped and were now indistinguishable from the rain that fell from the beast above. She was smiling, in that post-adrenal euphoria. I was smiling back too, the both of us just grinning like idiots.

"L-let's get out of here," Lauren finally said, looking about, going to walk on past me, finally releasing my shoulders and neck where she'd been resting her arms, her eyes dashing about as she walked to shore beneath the pounding rain.

"Yeah," I responded, following. "Which way did we come from?"

"Uh..." I gazed at her, her face blanking out, eyes widening for but a moment. She looked back at me, now with a rather embarrassed, meager blushing smile that you couldn't help but be charmed by. "S-south?"

### Chapter 42

"See, I always figured hybrids with wings would come with a keen sense of direction," I found myself muttering semi-sarcastically as we walked around the perimeter of the lake towards what I figured to be the south side of it.

"Look Noah, I see it, I fly to it. That's my sense of direction." She ambled past one of the branches carefully that was low enough to smack her in the face, though far too high up to be a problem for me. It was her usual height-based quirk, grumbling with her arm up to brush past the twigs in her face. "...I mean, we might. I sure as hell don't. I'm a bargain-bin dragon they assembled out of spare parts, you know. Like, they accidentally tacked on way too much... everything."

"Buy one get half for free," I put back, figuring not to try and be too serious and tell her to stop being so down on herself like usual. She was joking, so I figured I'd joke too.

"Yeah, I'm on clearance."

"I'd buy you," I put back, before a slight awkward silence took over for but a half-moment as I processed what I'd said. "...You're a quality deal," I added to soften the blow.

"Mm, now this..." She ducked under another branch, grunting. "...Conversational train of thought is getting *weird*."

I sighed, the two of us stopping as I looked back up to the storm raging above, feeling the wind. "Okay, we go that way," I motioned into the forest, away from the lake. "The storm came from the west, so the wind is blowing eastward. We walk this way and we should get within spitting distance of Shortstone."

"You *think*?" She commented. "I can't believe you of all people, mister super survival man, forgot your compass."

"I'm sorry, I was told that we'd just be testing a saddle, not my navigation skills," Lauren snorted out her nostrils a little. "Speaking of, we need to find that saddle. Pendrews might get mad if we completely ditched it on its first new use."

"Yeah, not to mention I'll be *sad*," Lauren huffed sort of semi-sarcastically.

"...Always a salient point," I muttered, keeping things light, looking back to the water. "I think we crashed... from that direction," I used my hand like a little aeroplane to envision our angle of impact again, facing back towards the lake. "From the southwest. So we should move southwest first, then move south. As long as we can see the mountains to the east we should then be able to follow the range south. I mean, we can't because it's raining, but we can use them to judge if we're going the right way, if we hug the mountains, find ourselves on a slope."

"S-sure," Lauren said. I looked back, almost like she was somewhat impressed by this line of thought. She certainly wasn't kidding about the shoddiness of her own navigation skills, apparently. This stuff was pretty basic to me. "So," she began as we made our way towards what we presumed to be the saddle's ground zero, me drawing my pistol so I could use the light mounted on its underlug to look up into the trees for a big mass of leather, if it was hanging. I regretted that this wasn't my own battle belt, my own gear confiscated. I knew I had a compass on that gear, but not on this loaner harness I was sporting. I made a mental note to make sure everyone had a little compass on their gear at some point. "...You thinking we should watch out for patrols?"

"Gabriel said this place was a no-man's land, right?" I put back, still searching, looking for broken branches, evidence of a crash, shining the gun about. "It's just that the roads are blocked off."

"...Why don't you think they're occupying the forest then?" Lauren asked, increasingly uneased, shaking her bent-up wings a little, seeing if she could move them, rather unsuccessfully. She just let them droop as we walked, figuring they'd be good... Eventually. They had stopped steaming by now, which was good for sure. We still weren't flying out of here.

"Not enough manpower is what I'd guess," I said. "Place is pretty big anyways. You really think they'd have a soldier behind every tree or something?"

"Hm, yeah I guess that makes sense," She was still tentatively looking around, and not necessarily for her saddle. "...You don't think they're... scared of this place, or something?"

"Really think that if the Democrats were launching their invasion, we'd have seen it by now," I put back. Thunder was cracking in the distance.

"...What if it's not the Democrats?" I sighed a little, not really following along in her worry, looking up at a plethora of freshly snapped branches.

"Here we go," I said while inadvertently interrupting her train of thought (though maybe because I didn't have anything to reply), going on over to see an especially large blobby object hanging from some pine branch, sagging the whole thing. "Shit, that's kind of far up," I said, identifying her saddle. "You think you can reach it?" She approached the trunk, rearing back on her rear legs and walking herself up with her frontal ones, fishing for it with her arms. "Don't fall over,"

"I'm not *that* clumsy," she uttered, finally freeing it, going to bring herself back down on all four legs. I smiled, some little quip about how she didn't self-deprecate for once came in and out of my head but I let the thought pass me on, too exasperated to say it. "Shit, we kinda fucked it up..." She was tumbling it over in her arms concernedly.

"Better it than us. We'll fix it," I said, taking it from her as she presented her side to me, so I could put it over her again and strap it down, despite its damage. "It doesn't look that bad, just some of your modifications need some more TLC. Oh, and the stirrup's kind of fucked," I noted, of how the leather was nearly disconnected on one of them, going to fold the stirrups all up on themselves with the tie-down, get them out of the way. I figured we'd patch the busted one up. "Now let's just get back to base," I uttered.

A couple minutes of walking through the forest really made me cognizant of how I was soaked to the bone. Lauren probably wasn't cold yet, given how her temperature was up from using her wings to their very limit. Nonetheless, she'd probably start feeling the cold eventually, the world dark now. I'd since holstered my pistol, letting my eyes adjust without the light.

"You good?" I asked back, leading the way, hearing her feet crunching through the marshy mud, brushing past moss upon the ground, a wing scraping past a tree. All four of her wings were still somewhat open, sort of stuck in that half-cocked position that by no means looked natural or comfortable, drooping down a little though thankfully not dragging on the ground, just barely. I could hear the rain pattering on her wings like tarps. "Your wings," I clarified, before she could respond back to ask what exactly I was talking about, feeling that awkward pause as her mind felt things over.

"...I can't really feel them," She muttered. Maybe in disappointment. Some sad, frustrated emotion, beyond the realm of solid, tangible thought. Like it hadn't really registered yet, or she was suppressing her true feelings, consciously or subconsciously. "I… I hope they'll be alright." That worry in her voice told me everything, she was just keeping it together with a helping of cognitive dissonance.

"I hope so too. You feeling tired or anything?" I asked now, turning my head back a little as I passed the broken trunk of a tree I walked around.

"No, why?"

"Your wings use a lot of energy. You sure you're not tired?"

"I… I mean, I guess. I think I just pushed the muscles too hard and they quit on me," She glanced back at her seized muscles with only a tinge of worry.

"...Sure," I said back, us continuing on.

"Are *you* cold?" She asked next.

"Well, I'm soaked, it's raining, I barely have an idea on how to get home, need I go on?" I uttered.

"Heh, just let me know if you get hypothermia," She uttered with a smile. "I could eat you to keep you warm."

"...Let's skip the part where you'd definitely get lost without me leading you," I began, grunting back with a smile. "But, uh, *ew*? You sure Selicia isn't rubbing off on you?"

"...Okay, first, fuck you," She shot back, also trying to keep things light, "Secondly, if you freeze to death I'm definitely going to be in a rough spot, not counting the fact that *you'd be dead* and Maria would kill me next."

"I'm fine. You'll be the first to know if I'm not, you *walking sleeping bag*." I was looking back at her, as she flipped me off, rolling her eyes. "...Jesus, fucking Creators. I thought that shit bothers you."

"I mean, it's not like it doesn't," She ambled around a bend of trees, as we came to a little slope that I began to slide down on my side, trying to slow myself on the way down. I was wet and muddy anyways, a little more mud couldn't hurt. "...But Gabe told me some people are into it and that's got me *fucked* up."

"Well, you've met Selicia," I uttered as I stood back up, shaking some of the mud off.

"No, I mean there are people, humans, into *getting* eaten." I stopped for a moment, blinking, looking back up to her on the top of that little ridge with my lip curled a bit upwards.

"He's bullshitting you," I put back with a shake of my head, as she went to slide down, trying to use her wings to slow her for a moment before realising she'd forgotten they were temporarily inoperable. I almost just let her go on, until my horrified disgust got the better of me. "...S-seriously? That's not- how- that wasn't even possible until hybrids got invented, what-"

"I dunno, he started talking about people on the internet. I... Really didn't want to press him." I turned about, raising my eyebrows like I'd taken a whiff of something rancid. Lauren seemed to share my sentiment.

"...I can kind of get how... Ones like Selicia are about it, being the eat-er, sure, but like, people into *being* eaten?" I put out. "No fucking way."

"Don't you remember Sam?"

"S- Sam was joking!" I blurted. "I mean, I hope! Hoped! What the fuck, are you saying she's serious?!"

"Look, if I'm bullshitting you, Gabriel was bullshitting me," She said back. "He said so. Something about the internet and it doing bad things to society. I mean, where do you think the Creators got the idea for it?"

"I'm... I-ugh... Y'know, I could have gone my whole life without thinking about *any* of this; thanks a bunch," I put back facetiously, still reeling as she slid her way to me.

"Sorry for making you dwell on it by right of me *existing*," Lauren shot back with a huff, rolling her eyes with a sardonic little smile. "If I had any say in it I think I'd have opted out of it, personally. I must have missed the questionnaire when they were passing it out."

"I was 'thanking' the Creators," I said. "Though they could be right about one thing. Maybe we needed an apocalypse after all, fall of Rome sorta deal. See, there was a society a long time ago-"

"They fell apart because their society stopped working, right?" Lauren postulated. I nodded, looking back.

"...Yeah," I said. "That's what they say. Degeneracy, they called it."

"...Yeah. Everybody was gross and stuff. I, uh, think I got basic Earth history in my brain." Lauren's sigh was breathless, following in step. But like that, like we were so occupied in our little reparté, it was a sudden shift, to hear the crack of a rifle. Despite the pouring of the rain and the distant thunder, this was a lot more specific. My hand went up, Lauren's feet still stomping towards me before her head presumably went up to see me rigid, staring off into the night.

"...Gunfire," I said. I could tell by the pause that Lauren wanted to object, say it was just the lightning or something to that effect, but her soon to be words were interrupted by rapid fire. It was close, closer than comfortable. I could hear bullets snapping by us, Lauren letting out a short holler that she suppressed as she dove by where I was, behind a tree. We got down slowly, laying in a gulch full of water and mud. We could see the flashes in the distance, in the dark.

"...This isn't good," Lauren took the words right out of my mouth. Every hair on my neck was on end. I could hear orders shouted, relayed. Not in a calm manner, rather panicked. My heart was beating its way out of my chest as I looked to Lauren, seeing the feeling reciprocated. "I can't see anybody. Do we move?"

"Hold on," I ordered. There was no gunfire. Something was coming.

From the black darkness here in the post-twilight, I could hear the soft crunch of great footpaws finding their way through the underbrush, barely audible under the pitter-patter of rain. Step after step from the blackness, at first I didn't see exactly how much of it there was from the movement, the inky figure sounding so much smaller than it was, by no means louder than Lauren's footfalls yet the creature it propelled was so much bigger than even her. Black fur and a voice, a voice as it breathed and barked and... spoke. Not anything legible, like someone calling out in a foreign language you'd never heard before, but within that, or above it, below it- like the guttural pre-words were being spoken over by true animalistic grunts and growls, a beast, snorting as it breathed, fiery eyes glaring through the darkness and cutting through the world the only thing I could make of what I was seeing.

A couple heavy moments behind nothing but that pistol, the two of us dead still, and it moved on, leaving us in the silence, alone, for those long minutes until we found the courage to finally move on.

### Chapter 43

It was sometime around nine we passed the church, sneaking our way past the barriers erected across and around the road. It was a lot less intimidating to cross back into city limits than I'd thought, at least compared to what we'd seen back there.

"God, I can't wait to get something to eat," Lauren noted.

"I just want dry underwear," I muttered back. She humphed in a sort of physically uncomfortable, relatable amusement, going to look back at her wings again while we walked, those limbs of hers still all funky and mangled-looking, seized up in weird angles. A few more minutes and we found our way to friendly territory, without seeing a single Republican patrol. I guess they had better things to do this time of night. Practically felt like there wasn't even a war going on.

"Finally, our street," Lauren moaned. She picked up the pace a little, and I walked up, slamming my fist on the door.

The door creaked open, and Gabe was there, fully geared up. I paused for a second seeing him like he was ready to head out, armed up but with his big overcoat covering everything. He looked like a small tent from behind, the way how if he turned to see you your heart would stop upon realising this was more than just a man in a poncho, but a killer loaded for bear.

"What the fuck?" Gabe uttered, taken aback, before he began to laugh, throwing his hood off and dropping his mask on the shoe cabinet within the foyer space. We could see through into the kitchen, catching a glimpse of others in the kitchen around their gear, looking through. "H- holy fuck, you guys look like shit," he said. "I mean, it's better than the alternative," He remarked in his usual pleasantly surprised tone, though it was obvious that he was minutes away from going out looking for us.

I took off my shirt and my shoes and socks. "This place better have a working dryer, because it might not let up for a while," I growled, but as I looked up, I saw Maria there. She was kitted out just like Gabriel was, all of her recon loadout beneath the overcoat she'd gotten, and there beneath the deep hood it looked like her eyes were miles away. Her nostrils were flared as she stood there, apart from me.

Maria's usual calm was compromised in a second, if not a moment. She was stomping up to me, in my face. I shrunk back, colliding with Lauren's belly, Lauren too edging back as Maria hovered inches from me as she screeched. "Do you have any idea how worried we were? I was?!" she wailed. "First the jail, now this shit?! You- You fucking lizard *bitch*!" Maria flew at Lauren like a pit bull frothing at the mouth, ripping me out of the way and off to the side. She leapt to punch Lauren right in the throat in a brutal lunge, and grabbed her head by the base of her horns, wrestling her down to her level as Lauren began to yelp, which quickly turned to a fighting snarl. She headbutted Maria right in the chest, and using the massive amount of leverage her weight and four legs enabled her with, she drove Maria backward, driving herself forward before being veered into a table. Maria coughed, the wind knocked from her, wrestling herself out and grabbing Lauren in a guillotine headlock. Lauren, still down there, reached up to claw at Maria's face, and they both growled and screamed. Lauren yanked Maria's hair and head, and with my girlfriend screaming, yanked her to the ground.

"Holy shit," I said, and at this point, I really noticed how nobody was stopping this. it all happened so fast.

"Girls- *Girls!*" I suddenly heard an indignant screech. Lauren looked out of the corner of her eye to see the woman from next door standing in the very end of the hallway towards the dining room disturbed upon the ordeal.

With an awkward cough, the two relinquished their hands on one another, Lauren straightening back out. "Girls! Shame on you! Maybe Steven was right!"

"But Miss P-" Maria blurted.

"No butts, Miss Rocha," the older woman growled sternly. "You apologize. For god's sakes, shame on you."

"Y-you can't be-" Maria was steaming for once. I was still standing there, mostly overwhelmed by the turn of events. "...Well, not like you respect my boyfriend enough not to fly off with him!" Maria hissed.

"I didn't do anything with Noah! We were just testing my-"

"*GIRLS!!!*" Mrs. Pendrew's voice boomed like the thunder outside. "Ap-o-lo-gize!"

Lauren's nostrils flared as she stood there, crossing her arms, still sopping wet and more than exasperated at this delay of getting herself dry. "I'm sorry," Maria finally admitted.

"For *whaat*?" Mrs. Pendrew was incredulous.

"I'm sorry for attacking you," Maria said.

"...and?" Lauren demanded in indignation, arms stacked atop each other.

"...And what?" Maria quite nearly rolled her eyes.

"Maria," Ms. Pendrew hissed.

"...For calling you a lizard." Lauren huffed out her nostrils in indignation.

"There you go. Now shake hands," She said.

After a pause, they shook hands, staring each other in the eyes sternly. "Smile." They bared their fangs. "...Like you mean it." They tightened up their cheeks and perked their eyes. "There you go. You'd better not act like this out and about with the militia on your tails." They stood there for a second, Maria gazing back to me. She still trembled, like she had something to say, but bit it down. She'd spent her words, her emotions on Lauren. Maria knew that the Maria she was trying to be didn't let emotions get the most of her. But here she was, nonetheless. "Noah," Mrs. Pendrew spoke for Maria, spoke those very words she herself was currently choking on. "...You really shouldn't run off like that without telling anybody. Either of you. Everyone was worried about you two, especially-" Mrs. Pendrew paused, as Maria embraced me. There we were, separated by the armor she wore.

"Don't..." She choked out. She wasn't sobbing, but it was like she was sick, trying to cough up phlegm. Like it was a hassle, not that she was overcome by grief. "...I'm not gonna lose you too." She'd whispered it in my ear, only I could have heard it.

Lauren passed us by to go and change, and then I too retreated to the master bedroom where we'd made our personal space, me and Maria. Maria stripping her armor off there, with me undressing to go into the shower. I wasn't dirty, but I could use the warmth.

I'd emerged minutes later, passing Maria staring up into the ceiling of the master bedroom on the bed, coming back downstairs as the storm raged outside. Mrs. Pendrew was still there, Lauren was there too, switched into clean clothes and all dried up.

"...Evening," I muttered to Mrs. Pendrew, who was busy massaging Lauren's wing muscles as she sat on the carpet beside her, Lauren restlessly laying there on all fours with a burger in her hands, a plate laying on the ground before her between her two forelegs, munching away. "...Man, we missed burger night, looks like."

"We made you one too," Mrs. Pendrew noted, pointing over her shoulder, kneading away at Lauren, Lauren looking like she was making an attempt to slip into relaxation but obviously a little uncomfortable at the tough kneading she was being put through; the old lady was certainly spry despite her age, her wiry hands like the grips of a machine. I saw a hamburger sitting on another plate on the table, sitting there plainly, with the leftover condiments waiting to be assembled. "...Your friend Gabriel is quite the cook. He managed to make horse meat more palatable." I took my seat before the burger, going to assemble the toppings and take a bite. It was a big step up from what we'd sampled yesterday.

"Yeah, he's full of surprises," I muttered back with my mouth full, scanning the room for the man himself. Gabriel wasn't present, probably taking his gear off or whatnot, but Abel, Reina, Sam and Archie were there, watching the local propaganda, more than likely to try to get some information out of the situation. Maybe they were watching for the faces of Lauren and I on the most-wanted list, but I'm sure they'd be telling me if they'd seen it thus far, so I wasn't worried. "...Where's your husband?"

"He's at home. He's not too keen on you all yet, but he's bound to come around, you'll see." I smiled a little, letting out a little humph. "...But you could say I'm over here, because as a veterinarian, I'd been fascinated by these hybrids ever since I'd heard about them. I couldn't resist an opportunity to examine their physiology," She said. "Did you know that the larger ones like the centauricals seem to have a series of... pseudo stomachs that fight overheating by running air through them? An interesting solution to the square-cube law."

"Y-yeah, more or less," I said, smirking. She was a lot more scientific than I'd initially given her credit for. "...I mean, that's in interesting... use. Organ, for an organ." I was still chewing awkwardly, going to swallow. This train of conversation brought me to realise that I'd seen neither Anthony or Selicia, somewhat worrying me. "...Have you seen Selicia? She's... The spider one. Arachnea, I think."

"Oh, yeah. She's quite the specimen. Last I checked she was in the room she claimed for herself, in the basement. I think my husband likes her the least."

"Heh, join the club," Lauren spouted, almost done with her burger. She looked like she could use another two or five of them, sitting there, but too polite to really object, though not quite polite enough to avoid a joke at Selicia's expense.

"So doc," I began, taking another bite. What's the prognosis?"

"Lauren's wings have seized up. Pretty self explanatory."

"Yeah, almost killed us," She said breathlessly, between bites. Nica Pendrew felt them over slowly, feeling those rock-hard muscles.

"They're incredibly hot, even now," She said, scanning their temperature with her own medical hologlasses. "Acute lactic muscle fatigue. You were out flying when it happened, of course. That must have been dangerous. I'm glad you two are all right."

"...Mostly all right," Lauren added.

"Have you been flying recently? do you fly often?"

"I try to," she said.

"Well, this is about the most serious athletic cramp I've ever seen."

"Will I be able to fly again?" Lauren said, having finished eating, more than concerned, ears hanging cocked back.

"Probably," Mrs. Pendrew said. "You're just a bit sore- and you mentioned you *are* unusually hungry," she noted. "This must indicate a spike in the metabolic process- a large caloric usage. Your wings," she said, beginning to diagnose. "Must run at a rate far higher than any other muscle in your body. When used, they also operate at such intensity their endothermal heat spikes incredibly. you're reading forty-two celsius on your wing and back muscles, although you're cooling off. You must've gotten to fifty, maybe fifty-five or even sixty when they seized."

"Yeah. I pushed myself too hard," Lauren muttered. "I don't think I ran out of electrolytes, I just pushed my wings until they cooked off." another little pause, a dreaded question hanging. "So I can still fly?"

"Certainly, in a week, probably less," She said. Lauren's face drooped a little.

"It uses more calories so you ought to do a whole lot less of it now that we don't need the air support, Green," Gabriel growled, entering the room like a spectre, practically making me jump as he appeared from the other room, back in his casual attire. I was constantly surprised at how he could just appear like that, despite how he was well over two hundred pounds in weight. "All this food won't last forever. I don't want *any*body to exert themselves, wings or not."

"Yeah, yeah," Lauren didn't seem that receptive to Gabriel's order, and it didn't seem like that much of a problem to him anyways.

"You know," Mrs. Pendrew butted back in. "My husband is also a veterinarian. It's how we met. He doesn't like hybrids, though," She extrapolated to me. "Something about God and the natural order, how he thinks that everything going wrong right now is God's wrath- I think a part of him blames hybrids for all this. But he's smarter than that. I think he's just worried about our kids," She paused, and I caught a glimpse of Gabriel off to the side, ever amused at the mention of religion, though a little charmed at her quaint grandmotherly nature. "I am too, but I believe they'll be all right. I hope and I pray, at least. We both pray for them every day. I think Steven also blames himself for this, that the kids moved away from Shortstone because of him, he's like that. You'll... grow on him, eventually." I looked at her. It seemed to me like she was the opposite of how she described her husband, like she was just a lonely old lady who wanted new children to look after. When she saw us, she'd jumped at the opportunity. Even Gabriel wasn't complaining. I guess he liked the old man's gumption.

I was tired. I went upstairs, into the master bedroom. I saw Maria sitting in a bathrobe, and it almost looked like she'd been there this whole time. "...You enjoying the hot water after a week?" I muttered, passing her to go and take a piss.

"I- Noah," she stammered, gazing into me as I stopped dead about to turn the corner to the master bath. I felt her eyes on her, feeling just like the sigh about to escape my lungs. "N-Noah," she trailed off. A little laugh, like she was embarrassed, a laugh to hide harsher feelings. I turned to see her, I staring at her for a few seconds, blinking.

"What?"

"I… You know I don't wash with hot water, right?"

"O-oh? Oh yeah," I said, trailing off. That sounded familiar. I almost wanted to ask her why she was making a big deal out of this, but I knew that asking that would be a poor move, so I spent my time racking my brain.

"Do you remember why?" she asked, with only the subtlest accusatory tinge in her voice. She fought it back with a smile, with a playful front she could barely keep up. Like keeping tears back.

"You- you do it, use cold water for… your brother, to remember him," I said, it coming to me just in the nick of time. "Like a thing to make you remember. Going without something." I didn't want it to seem like I'd forgotten, but I feel like she saw right through me. I felt her frustration, seeing her nostrils flare but she smiled a little. Fighting her true feelings. She must've been doing it for me, looking back on it all. She got up, walked over to me and placed a hand upon my shoulder, and her body up against my arm. She was naked under the towel.

"We should get married," she told me. "Here. In the city. We can have that pastor do it."

"W-what?" I blurted out as she switched the flow of the conversation up on me in an instant, her hands coming upon my hips, pulling me close. "Even with all this going on? You serious?"

"Why not?" She uttered. "If the world's coming to an end, why not?"

"It's… Don't you think we should do this at the Citadel?"

"No better time than now, no better place than here," She put back, rattling the words off quick with her eyes squinting into me. Like she was looking for something under a thin veneer of playfulness. "C'mon. Carpe Diem."

"I… I really don't think this is the time for this," I said.

"Then when is, Noah?" Her cover of a mirthful back and forth was gone, if only for a second where her frustration shone through.

"At the Citadel!" I put back. "Look, when we get there… I promise. Alright?" I said.

"What if that's-" She interrupted herself with a vicious sigh. "You're being ridiculous."

"I don't feel comfortable, okay?" I said. "I don't want to…" I stopped myself. I don't want to do anything I'd regret, the words were ready to roll off my tongue. Regret? Was I going to regret this? Why was I going to say that?

"You don't want to marry me?" She shot.

"N-no, that's not-"

"Why not? What are you afraid of?!" She put forth. "Noah, we had *sex*. We... We could have a kid together. And don't give me that shit about raising it in this world. We've... gotta re-populate the world somehow," She let out in a breathless laugh, a joke in lieu of an excuse as she began to massage my shoulders. Trying to work humor back into this, but I was gone already. This wasn't funny. I really ought to have been questioning why she was bringing this up, but I was lost in my own world. Swimming through my own emotions. I saw her, envisioning her with my eyes closed. God, she was pretty. Brave, courageous, strong, refined, well-spoken. Any man would be lucky to have her. But why was I... Why do I feel so alone with her here with me?

"...I need some time to think." With that, I vacated the room, leaving her. I knew I wasn't sleeping with her tonight, by any means. I'd probably be on watch, then sleep on a couch somewhere. And that was what I ended up doing, staring into a ceiling for an hour just mulling things over until I slipped into unconsciousness.

### Chapter 44

Darkness.

The howling of creatures, far off and near alike, a cacophony of demonic wails and bellows and roars and howls, and the rustle of leaves and branches and twigs.

"Noah!" I heard Anthony bark towards me. I barely twitched. "Noah, what do we do?!" He cried. I turned, ever so slowly, seeing through the darkness my friends, all of us, standing there, broken, bleeding, bruised, eyes wide and faces bloody with terror. breaths puffed out in front of faces, a chill taking over all. Every last one was hurt.

"We..." I uttered slowly. I could hear the beasts coming, coming for us all.

We were doomed.

"Noah?" Lauren stood there, limping a little bit in place, a wing twisted sickly. Gabriel was strapped to her back. He couldn't walk, he'd lost so much blood he was barely even awake. His valued opinion was unable to be given at the moment, and I saw nothing but sheer terror in Lauren's eyes, yet with it, a sick anticipation.

My left hand released the foregrip of my rifle. It drooped to the side, hanging from my right by the pistol grip, the flash hider digging into the soft soil, standing there, until my right hand released. That wood-stocked AR15 clattered to the mud. My eyes were wide and I could barely breathe. I saw the moonlit, shining eyes of all of these dear friends, waiting on me. Waiting for me. I wanted Gabriel to help me, to say something, but he was a stone.

I could hear them, drawing closer in the distance.

My hand slowly rose to my plate carrier. From between the molle loops I slowly drew out my road flare. I gazed down at it, feeling it's rough plastic and worn paper labeling. Dad always told me to keep one on my chest rig. A desperate smirk reached the corner of my mouth.

"Noah?" Lauren asked again. I I looked up at her. I looked up at all of them.

"The safe house is close," I whispered. "You know where." I gripped the flare with both hands. "I'll keep them distracted. You make a break for it. Okay?"

"Noah, wait," Lauren said. I looked into her eyes, sparkling with fear, her jaw slack with terror. I didn't let her continue.

"No," I said. "We're all dead otherwise. I can still run, so I… I can get them far enough away. You get to the safe house. You need to go. You need to make it." I knew time was a pressing issue. I gazed up at Lauren. She closed her mouth, swallowing her fear, looking at me. Her eyes were welling up. "Lauren, I…" I paused. "I just want to say that I… even back since Vegas, I've… I've always…"

I paused again.

Maria was behind me, staring at me. "Always what," she said, not even moving her lips. The way her eyes fluttered, her cheeks clenched and forehead furrowed.

I turned away, taking one last look, the image of an expectant Maria stuck in my mind, before I cracked open that flare and was blinded, seeing the numerous faces of my friends for but one more instant, before I took a few steps backward and they disapparated into darkness.

There I was, in the clearing of the forest. I raised that flare up above my head, and, with one foot in front of the other, I began to run.

*Paft, paft*. My boots hitting the dirt. The creatures howling. Roaring and hissing, gnashing amongst themselves. my free hand reached up to the shoulder clip of my armor. I clicked it open, before I reached down to the cummerbund flap. I ripped at it, and like that, the big, heavy cuirass fell to the dirt leaving me in my undershirt. I ran, I ran with all that was within me, before the shadows surged inward to consume the light.

I awoke with a start to the sight of a plaster ceiling, rubbing my eyes. Fucking nightmare, I could practically still feel the claws. Morning light was streaming in through the window of the front room of the house where I'd been the night before, someone else's loaned M16 clutched in my crossed arms upon my chest like the remains of a knight buried with his sword. I felt like shit; my sleep was useless. I didn't like this place, trapped here behind a pane of glass.

I got up slowly, sitting to look around again and smack my lips. I heard snoring, and I could see in front of me a big webby hammock hanging from the ceiling of the spacious front room and foyer, Selicia hanging within it with her threads anchored on several points to different angles of the ceiling and holding the main body of her hammock to the tri-corner. I even saw she made a bit of a hanger for her armor and rifle, like little chandeliers. Her four eyes followed me as I walked out, the rest of her body so still, and even snoring a little as if asleep, it fooled me into thinking she was still asleep- like it was something that her kind just did, sleeping with their eyes open.

"Morning, Noah," she came to life jarringly enough to the point where I jumped a little, her many legs sprawled on her hammock, wearing only a loose white sleeping shirt, pressed up against that array of webs she'd made. I could see her pronounced nipples through the shirt and was immediately perturbed by her reservations against wearing a bra and her devotion to lewdity. Though Anthony was right, if she wasn't a spider, she'd be incredibly attractive. It definitely just made her all the more uncanny. "Man, you look like shit," She scoffed with a smile while I heard Gabriel's unintelligible voice wafting from the dining room and den, past the arch of the stairway behind me in quiet conversation, rubbing my eyes. "Sleeping down here and all. Maria not letting you nookie?" I blinked at her, still half asleep. "You know, I wouldn't leave you blue-balled. Why don't you experiment a little? A new experience never hurt anybody. I'll be gentle, I promise."

"Don't be gross, Sel…" I growled, getting up to stretch a little.

"Fraid'a spiders, baby?" I didn't respond, and she laughed to herself, albeit groggily, as she was half asleep herself. Or something. Maybe she was acting. I couldn't exactly work her out. "Don't worry, I'm not a black widow or anything. I'm brown recluse, I think. I wouldn't eat you *right* after sex... Unless you insist on skipping to that part," She proceeded to pat her amazonian humanoid belly with a couple ample slaps, ringing like a drum. "...That's my *favorite* part." At least she helped me wake up faster by scaring me to prompt me to escape, though I doubted that was her motivation.

"...I've been awake for less than a minute and already you've made me think about that fucking sick shit again. Thanks a lot."

"A-ny-time," Selicia grinned evilly, her fangs barely poking out of the lips of her toothless grin. God, the corners of her lips extended into her cheeks when she smiled like that. I could see the hinging mandible bisecting the cleft of her chin popping in and out a little to aggravate me further.

"...Don't you have the basement all to yourself?" I inquisited. "You know, you put your webs everywhere and Mr. Pendrew is bound to shoot you."

"This is my watchout perch," She reasoned. "I can see more out the window hung up here. I should make a little ladder for you, so other people can use it. It's rather advantageous," She let her weird quasi-british charm soak into her words again, and I felt my exasperation grow.

"No thanks, I prefer not to be in a BDSM harness when I'm shooting," I quipped back. "Besides, you have no cover."

"Not a problem. With these eyes, I'll see anybody else first," She motioned to her own face, eyes still squinting away, yet to put her holos back on. Hanging there she was in a blind spot to the rays of sunlight coming in from outside, so I guess it made sense. I finally turned to walk into the kitchen. "Don't forget, handsome. My offer still stands, think about iiiiiit," She sang as I made my way into the other room, my skin crawling and shoulders rolling in exasperation.

"Hey Noah," Lauren was sitting her rear down in the den with the TV on before her, turning to see me over her shoulder. She was working her wings about, still stiff as boards, though she could move them now, which was good. "...Gabriel tell you about what he's thinking?"

"...Never does," I muttered back, turning my head to see him in the kitchen, wrapping up these little ration things he was making. Looked like hardtack. At least he was making good use of the reserves of cooking products the previous owners left behind.

"We need to train everyone," Gabriel explained. "The situation might get hairy again. You know I don't want a repeat of the desert."

"You already taught us how to shoot," Sam snarled back. I'd practically not noticed her sitting in the recliner.

"Yeah, Gabe," Lauren smiled back more playfully, though she grunted, working out a kink in one of the muscles of her big rear wings, unable to really extend or retract it more than a few inches either way.

"...Yeah, but there's more to fighting than shooting. You know, Mrs. Pendrew told you to go easy on your wings for the next week," Gabriel remarked, and Lauren froze for a moment.

"I want to go for my morning flight; not flying for too long makes me anxious," She whined, her spirits dampened a little. I watched her ears droop and couldn't help but be charmed, like usual, even if I was being charmed by her distress. "God, how am I going to survive a whole week like this?! I'm going crazy!" Well, at least she was peppy, if anything. Taking her plight with a little showmanshippy flare, sort of post-ironically complaining or something.

"...See, we need to occupy their minds anyways for the time being, avoid cabin fever," Gabriel said to me as an aside, inching closer as he did. "I figure going over medical and individual tactics will tide them over."

"Okay, I'm sold," I put back. "I guess we just get everyone together, right? Let's do it," I said.

"Yeah, but your girl absconded a while ago, went with Mrs. Pendrew to help out at the fairytale house," Gabriel noted. I processed the information, blanking for a second.

"...Maria knows a lot about most of this stuff. She'd be fine with this." This was the turn for Gabriel to pause, looking over to me in a sort of pumped-up disbelief, him too having fun. Maybe it was the atmosphere of the room, Lauren and Gabriel's playfulness complimenting each other. Then again, I was yet to feel it, though I'm sure it was more that I was still reeling from an interaction with Selicia.

"You seem concerned for her well being, huh?" Gabriel uttered facetiously, smirking.

"She's her own woman. If she wants to go help the refugees at the church she has every right to."

"...You guys fought last night, didn't you."

"They diiid," Selicia sang in the middle of her yawn as she entered the room, before I could respond.

"We... did not. We're just..." I scanned the room, maybe out of instinct. I lingered on Lauren's inquisitive face, only a hint of worry in her eyes, most of it simple concern. "I think this is getting to her. She acts like she's handled this kind of a situation before, and... and she has, of course, but I think she... I think her family... really got to her," I said. It wasn't half off from the truth, though I felt a little bad saying it. God, what a way to go. It's like I'd forgotten until now, repressed. I blinked my disassociation away.

"Sure, but why would that make her mad at you?"

"She's not mad at me."

"She seemed mad." Selicia's commentary was relentless as she plopped down before the table to await whatever Gabriel was cooking up, and I sighed.

"Look, I don't wanna talk about it, okay?" I barked. "We'll wait 'till she gets back. You happy now?"

"Jeez, Noah," Lauren began at my short outburst, and I glared at her, before softening my mood. God, I really was upset, wasn't I? This was all stupid. Lauren coughed a little bit, as I threw open the back door to go and get some fresh air or something.

"You know, you'd feel better if you had breakf-" Gabriel's voice carried to me before I slammed the door behind me.

I saw Anthony, Reina and Archie hanging out by the pool, Anthony boredly walking on a little wall on the far side of the pool separating the water from the flower garden where Reina was looking at the flowers, Archie dipping his feet into the water and kicking them back and forth. I plopped down on the little stone waterfall with where Anthony was strolling back and forth and Archie was sitting, sighing loudly.

"You, uh... Are you and Maria alright?" Anthony asked.

"...Go feed yourself to the spider, Tony," I snapped and Anthony's (and everybody's) brow raised at my snap.

"That bad, huh," Reina muttered to Anthony as an aside as if I wasn't going to hear. I rolled my eyes to go and find somewhere to keep myself busy until Maria got back.

More inventory. Enough to drive me crazy. It was only a little while until the Pendrews and Maria got back, looking none the worse for wear than usual, me in the garage there looking through the vehicles.

Maria walked in through that open garage door, took a quick look at me with the Pendrews trailing off to go to their house. She passed me briskly, having only looked at me once to go inside.

At least it told me she was still upset.

### Chapter 45

"So, you know how to shoot a gun," Gabriel began, everyone gathered around. "I've seen you all handle a gun, and you know the basics. Point the loud end at the bad guy and pull the finger thingy. I'd even say some of you are decent shots." He paused, to look around. I stood near him, leaning against a wall behind him, as we all stood there in the living room of Frank's house. "Now, thanks to my tireless efforts, most all seem to have a decent long gun at your disposal, at the moment."

"Uh, Gabe dearie," Selicia spoke up, one hand rising up from how her arms were crossed. "We all know how to shoot."

"Combat is a little more nuanced than just 'shooting'. This isn't a leisurely day at your local gun range."

"C'mon, Gabriel, we've all been shot at before," Reina said, motioning with her own Armalite a little as she stood there. I saw Selicia shift a little bit as she stood, looking away from Gabe.

"We've lost people, haven't we?" He put forth. "Of course; and any number above zero is unacceptable, isn't it?" He stopped, to gauge the response. "Look around. Do you think anyone here is expendable? I mean, *I* could answer this question like a cold-hearted fuck, but are *you* really going to accept any more losses?" Everyone warily seemed to agree, after a moment of thought, despite the strained relations to some. "So, I'd like to start out with a little quiz, since you think you already know everything. Will somebody tell me what priority number one is, in a firefight?" He smirked, waiting for the 'obvious' answer to come from his audience.

"Kill the enemy?" Anthony proposed amid the awkward silence of hesitant, wandering stares. Gabriel's smirk reached ear-to-ear.

"Noah, what's the right answer?" He turned towards me.

"...Don't get killed," I sighed loudly, Maria beside me, the two of us watching as Gabe led the little lesson. Gabriel let out his breath with a wincing "ooh" for dramatic flare.

"Daddy taught you well, huh?" He said, turning back to his captive audience. "Don't, get, shot. Rule numero uno. Rule number two- don't *do* shit that gets you or your buddies shot. Number three, cover supersedes returning fire. Run away from the bullets, don't stand there and get shot. If there is no conceivable cover to be had, then and only then you start shooting while out in the open. Point four, body armor doesn't make you invincible, it simply raises your odds, so you better get your ass to cover. And finally, shooting back accurately is always a better solution to spraying bullets, especially when since we're working with barebones logistics and zero backup. If shit goes wrong, every round we shoot has to count." He paused again, to gauge reaction. "Of course, there are more rules, more sets of rules, and certain exceptions to said rules. There's a lot of number one rules, but that's my top five for you. The basics. Now, once more, tell me. Somebody is trying to kill you. What's the first thing you do?"

"...Shoot him?" Anthony offered. Gabriel rolled his eyes, turning to me.

"This is gonna take a while," He moaned.

"Fine, run away?" Anthony corrected.

"Run to cover," Gabriel corrected as Anthony scoffed.

"What's the difference?"

"... A long while," Gabriel muttered to himself, like he was pretending to utter this as an aside, despite how he clearly intended everyone to hear his exasperation. "Run away means you *don't* kill this motherfucker who wants you and your friends dead, which could bite you in the ass down the road. This is in direct violation of rule two, so yes, you need to shoot him, but first you run your ass to cover so you can shoot back without getting shot in the process." He turned again. "Now: bushes, wood fencing, not cover. Drywall, doors, tables, windows, not cover. your average car door- not cover. Brick walls, big trees, rocks, an *entire* car- those, *can* be cover. Bullets can still get through them though, so use discretion. If it looks and feels heavy, solid and thick, then it's probably a better bullet trap than your ass. This is lesson one. Now, what's priority number one?"

"Don't get shot," most of them seemed to mumble together, still hesitantly eyeing about. Gabriel gripped his eyes and mouth shut, smiling and nodding with his whole body, almost sarcastically in the fact that he had to stress this point so much to get it through their heads.

"And how do we accomplish this?"

"Get to cover?" Gabriel snapped emphatically at this answer.

"Get your fat asses to cover, and get them there fuckin' snappy. Once you're in a place where it's hard to get shot from, you shoot that faggot right in the middle. 'Course, shooting a living, breathing human being- or hybrid, isn't the same as punching a hole in paper. This brings us to lesson two: Killing. First things first, another question. Would you consider the human being fragile?" Again, a long, uncomfortable pause. "C'mon here, it's just opinions. no wrong answers. Rei?" he called on Reina, seeing her preemptively moving her hand forward a little, lips shadowing a possible answer.

"...Yes?" The shepherd sister answered.

"Hm. Wrong."

"But you just said-"

"It's possible to have a wrong opinion. Reina, what if I told you the average human creature only needed thirty percent of their intestines to survive?" Reina gazed around uncomfortably. "Ancient man wasn't the top of the food chain because he was a mamby-pamby that died because some sabertooth tiger chewed on him a little. Our tolerance to pain is among the highest of all fauna. We have among the most hyperactive scar tissue in the animal kingdom and survive from seemingly deadly blows with relative ease. You know what a broken leg is for your average animal? A death sentence. You know what it is for a human? A nostalgic childhood memory. We heal in weeks what would take an animal months, if not years to recover from. You know what species is second to the human in its ability to keep pace with us? Dogs. And dogs cry out like little babies if you step on their foot. We even mastered cosmetic surgery aeons before the invention of anesthetics. We've performed emergency medical procedures on ourselves with nothing more than scraps while lesser creatures would succumb to lesser wounds and die crying in a pool of their own blood. Now all you hybrids should stop and appreciate for a second that the greatest species on planet earth made you in their image. Out of our own flesh and blood, y'know, that sort of pseudo-religious philosophy shit if you're into it."

"Okay, Gabe, now that you're done jerking off your species," Archie spoke up. "How's about you get back to your little lesson?"

"My point, *Mister Edmonton-Reginald*, is humanity's your ancestor too," Gabriel said as Archie scowled while Gabriel smiled at his use of Archie's ridiculous surname. "Matter of fact, lemme extrapolate on that for a moment. You know, Green," Gabriel redirected his attention to her and she eyed around rather nervously as his hawkish focus fell on her. "Green the dragon. Dragons, a staple of mythology. Usually either ageless demigods of profound magical power or the utmost apex of the natural food chain, sometimes a combination of both. Such a mainstay of human mythos that spans race and culture that we, humanity, decided to make *you* first a century ago," He chuckled. "But here you are and you don't even breathe fire. Doubt to fuck you're immortal either. Some magical supreme life form you turned out to be. You kind of just look like a dragon and that's it. I'm sure you'd agree we ended up making you far more mundane than your namesake, right?"

"I... I guess," Lauren extrapolated.

"Would you consider yourself mundane?"

"Y-yeah?" It was less like she was thinking through her answer and more like she was trying to follow the flow of Gabriel's conversation, Gabriel having led her into something like a little trap for whatever point he was building on.

"Also false." Lauren blinked a couple times, perhaps trying to suppress a blush as she must have felt a little silly thinking her answer through. "If there were a such thing as a soul, *you'd* have one. You all do. The result of three and a half billion years of evolution churned out humanity, and the result of 200 or so more years of the industrial era, here you stand as our latest, possibly ultimate accomplishment. Successor, offshoot, spinoff, who knows. But every vaguely abstract concept that codifies humanity applies to all of you test-tube chimera freaks and that's fucking *amazing*. I don't know what the creators' plan is and I don't know where *my* species will end up, but I know as long as any of us are around, human, hybrid... Humanity will still exist as a concept, the soul, abstract concept or not will still exist; *humanity* will still rule over the earth." Utter silence took over as Gabriel extrapolated on this strange, though profound tangent. "Greenie girl, you're real fuckin' special. And the retarded faggy-ass concept of what a dragon was before you came along can never hope to stand up to you. Because you're *real*. You're real and you've got *humanity*, human or not. Humanity is your great, profound power and you'd better pin it to your chest like a fucking badge of honor. Anyways,"

It was like the wind shifting as the other shoe dropped, Gabriel clapping once almost to signify his getting back on topic and everyone jumping a little, not even letting his words set in, sort of just marinating in our subconscious while he lectured on. In retrospect, it was very *him*. "I guess my point is, humanity and 'the soul' isn't exclusive to us. Never expect your enemy to be worse at failing to die than you are. No matter how stupid, how ill-trained and inequipped he is, he's still a living, thinking person, human or not, with hopes and dreams, and therefore he probably doesn't want to die just as much as you do. You're damn right he's gonna be running and ducking and weaving and taking cover and *shooting to fucking kill* just like you are. Rule number one of *killing*- when it's life or death, there's no such thing as an *un*fair fight. all bets are off. You aim right in his middle. Not for his head, not even for his heart- you aim right at the bottom of his solar plexus, so if you're even five inches off the mark, you still get your message across. And if, by chance, you don't see the entirety of this man's body, you still aim for the biggest part of him. If it's just his head poking out, you don't aim up for the brain, no, you aim right in the middle of what you can surmise is there. Aim for the center. Rule two- death is never pretty, never dignified, and never, ever, EVER as quick as you think. When you shoot a man, all you do is cause a tiny piece of metal to enter and possibly exit his body in the blink of an eye. Guns are not magical death sticks, us mortals tend to cling hopelessly to life like the stubborn bastards we are. Daniel, what happens when you get shot in the heart?" He asked suddenly, putting a new face on the spot.

"...You die?"

"Maybe. Maybe not, probably..." Gabe said to the incredulous stares of the room. "Let me tell you guys a story. A long time ago around the turn of the millenia in a little town called Skokie, Illinois, a man trying to kill a cop had to be shot 17 times before he gave up. Again, not die, but to simply stop trying to kill that piggie. Among his wounds, he had a bullet through each lung and his heart and three through his head. It took that man somewhere around 11 hours to die on the operating table, and he nearly took the cop who did it with him. No drugs, no cover, no body armor. Just rage, hate, pretty decent physical conditioning and the human fucking spirit. Again, kind of a superpower. The thing to take away from this is that the heart is not the magical capsule of the soul, it's just a muscle with the very specific job of pumping blood to all your limbs and organs and shit. you will not keel over dead once your heart is wounded. Instead, you messily bleed all over the place, scream and cry a little, maybe pass out from lack of blood and die after you've lost enough of it. Nevertheless, if some street gang foot soldier who can't be called a professional gunfighter in any sense of the word can chew up seven-fucking-teen forty-five hollow points like candy, then I'm more than certain at the very least one of the fourlegs here could pose a challenge," Gabe paused to motion to Lauren and Abel, maybe Selicia with a little antecedent wave. "People don't like to die. People tend to try and resist it. In fact, trying to kill somebody might make them just want to kill *you* even more. It's a tragic cycle, really. A cycle that should end with you, my dear friends, putting fresh holes in Mr. Bad Guy's torso until he stops trying to get back up, which may take longer than you'd think from watching movies and playing all those video games.

"Finally, rule three, in this specific set of rules. More like a reminder than a rule, and kind of a no-brainer, but still something that gets neglected to be mentioned an awful lot- once the two-way gun range opens, the fun factor drops to zero and the suck factor increases exponentially. You need to remember that this isn't going to be easy. unless you're really good and really crazy, it probably isn't going to be fun either. You should never yearn for battle. It's going to suck. Your friends may probably die. You may die. And you will probably have to kill a lot of people. I'm sure we all know this after what happened in the desert, but I just want to make this clear. that was only three or four guys with shitty antique guns. Here we've got a whole army wyling for some shit to kill. In this environment, if shit goes south and we have to blast our ways out of here, you are probably all going to have to kill a lot, and I mean *a lot*, of people to get out alive. There is going to be screaming, there is going to be guts, there are going to be missing limbs and pieces of shrapnel embedded in your skin and face and you will see lots and lots of blood, even your own. You are going to be covered in dirt, mud, dust and sweat, you will simultaneously be sweating your ass off and be ice-cold, your legs and arms will go numb and your hands will turn to flippers and your fingers will cease to work individually. Your head will pound with the biggest migraine you've ever had, you won't be able to hold your gun steady, you'll get shit in your eyes and you won't be able to see, your ears will ring to the point where you won't even be able to hear your friends screaming for their fucking lives right in your ears; you'll probably cry, wet or shit yourself, and scream out for mama, especially if you end up with bits and puddles of yourself on the floor. And you will see things you'll *never* forget. What I'm trying to get across is that there is going to be an inevitable suck factor. We should try to minimize that factor by knowing what to do in these stressful situations. Having a plan, being able to operate your weapon, having enough ammo for your weapon so you aren't having a panic attack every time you hear click instead of bang."

"Now, incidentally, each one of you has two medical kits, one on the back of your armor for a buddy, one on the front for you. Now, contrary to what war movies might teach you where only one or two guys is a doctor, everybody needs to be able to serve as a medic in small squad, zero-reinforcement tactics, like how they teach spec ops guys. I doubt you'll all get to Navy SEAL-levels of skills, but we'll get fucking close. Those guys are pussies, anyways. So for today, we'll start with teaching each of you how to save people, before we get into how to really kill people."

First things first, remember that body armor does not make you invincible. Most of you have a level three polydynamid cuirass, pauldrons and helmet. Some of you even have a face guard, forearm guards or an abdominal armor extension. This means that your torso, shoulders and head should be impervious to non-armor piercing rifle rounds even at close ranges. However, never underestimate the prevalence of armor-piercing rounds. If somebody thinks he's a big shit he'll probably have some. Not to mention, even with all this armor, the vast majority of your bodies are not covered. Armor is mainly supposed to protect your vitals against firearms, blunt force impacts and shrapnel. But like I said, don't get to thinking just because you've got fancy armor that you can take on the world. Human, hybrid, every last one of you here that walks on two legs is only four pints of blood away from death at any given moment. You bigger freaks, I'd estimate ten pints. But don't get jealous of all that extra body, guys. Just means there's more there to shoot. Now, let's talk medicine."

The rest of the day was limited to teaching each person the basics of combat first aid. We teached how to apply an autocast- which was basically a rolled up piece of plastic that became a splint for arm or leg breaks. Chest seals were simple enough, just an airtight band-aid to keep someone's lung from collapsing from a chest wound. Gabriel had acquired localized anesthesia drugs in case of a blown-off finger or survivable gunshot wound in the heat of battle where nobody could afford to not still fight. For more severe blood loss he had plasma autoinjectors: These little intravenous drip machines that you could strap onto yourself if you lost a lot of blood and needed to keep your blood pressure up. The average serum for one included differing amounts of epinephrine percentages based upon the seriousness of previous blood loss, letting one stay conscious to continue fighting even after losing a large amount of blood, interfacing with the medical functions of each person's hologlasses. Syringes of fastclot were also administered- if you had been shot through an artery, you could inject the wound with the synthetic clotting agent then bandage over it to stop the bleed. We even went into tourniquetting as a low-tech last-ditch maneuver, but not without Gabriel morosely reminding us that a tourniquet solving an arterial bleed would be ultimately followed by amputation. We practiced firemans' carries and using the drag handle on our cuirasses, and did a quick reminder of CPR. We even went over using defibrillator pads, all stuff that Gabriel had dragged out of the military depot in the facility. For other methods of revival, we had smelling salts and general epinephrine.

"What about morphine?" Daniel asked as we were going over the drugs.

"The way we're going to have to fight, with no backup or exfiltration by helicopter or anything, morphine would be a post-combat drug. If you need morphine, that'll mean you're out of the fight for good. During combat, if somebody needs something to deal with pain, you'll take ibuprofen, localized anesthesia or epinephrine. That's not to say we won't have morphine, it's just that when it's time for morphine we'll be in a far less stressful situation. It'll be easier to administer and you won't have to fall back on training, since you'll have the time to just read it out of a book. Speaking of, all of you are going to study these principles. There *will* be a quiz tomorrow," Gabe said, passing out old combat medical field guides, much to the groaning of the group. "Hey, hey, passing or failing *this* quiz won't be the difference between your dad beating you or not, it'll be the difference between living a long, happy life in a stupid giant castle in north Idaho or dying miserably in a puddle of your own entrails after crying your eyes dry and shitting your pants. This little paper booklet right here is more meaningful than every last textbook you've ever loaded onto your glasses put together. And I've got plenty more of these lessons, and everyone here is going to be an A student if it's the death of me. You should be able to recite the lessons in this shit in your sleep. Physiology will be your bitch and pain will be a welcomed friend. You're gonna break every bone in your legs and still walk it off. Got it, chumps?" everyone nodded, feeling just a little bit more motivated. "Alright. Class dismissed. Read up."

After that point, we relegated ourselves to tending after the little things. Mrs. Pendrew came over to hand out with Sam, Reina and even Selicia to tend the garden in the back to pass the time. She was more than glad to help us plant some fruit and vegetable seeds. Lauren was off in her makeshift workshop in the big shed, working on her saddle as a way to wait out her wings healing. Anthony and Abel were constructing and test shooting slingshots with which to hunt small game with. If somebody was idle, Gabriel seemed to have a suggestion for them- though he ended up, with Maria and I in the basement, playing pool on the big pool table, after this long day. Despite Selicia's webs sprawling ominously from the basement bedroom nearby the rec room, it was pretty nice. The clink of the billiard balls, the telescreen in the corner playing- surprise surprise- more of the local propaganda.

"Sure you don't want to play?" Gabriel offered with a raised voice into Selica's room, the guest room of the basement, black and ominous. I was a little scared to even peek inside, as if she set up a snare trap for nefarious, perverted purposes.

"I'm sorry, didn't you tell us to study, dearie?" Her voice wafted out in airy nonchalance.

"I mean, you don't have to study *right now*."

"Gabe, she said she doesn't want to play. And she's studying for your quiz. Let's count our blessings." Gabriel rolled his eyes as Maria rattled off. We continued going around, just playing for points in silence. We really didn't have anything to say, which I suppose was a good thing. It was quiet, it was simple. I didn't know to bring anything up with Maria or anything, though she was getting along with Gabriel well enough. I guess that was satisfying. But I still felt distant from her, like she was still mad. *Should I ask her? Ask her what? I don't know. If she meant what she said last night. What kind of a question is that? I-* "Your turn, Noah," She was saying to me. I couldn't read her face; ever really, here especially. Like she just wanted to play a stupid game and forget everything.

I circled the billiard table with my stick in hand, seeing into Selicia's room in the background, her head sticking out from the top of the doorway just barely, the top two of her eyes only. Hanging from the ceiling again, like she was bound to do. I humphed, charmed. "Thought you were studying," I put forth, hitting the white ball, bouncing into the number fourteen, narrowly missing the hole to bounce off again, 'tsk'ing mindlessly.

"Nice miss," She put forth and I rolled my eyes.

"...You digging the material?" Gabriel asked, not even looking up as he walked around to take his turn.

"I like the diagrams. Gets into the messy details."

"You know, Gabe, I appreciate the sentiment, teaching everyone medical stuff," Maria let out. "But I don't think I'd feel comfortable with her performing surgery. On anybody." It was Selicia's turn to glare back with her four eyes.

"...Yeah, well, we work with what we get. Like you said, I'll be grateful she's willing to study," Gabriel smirked, Maria rolling her own eyes again, her rolling eyes finally ending on me. I stood there a little awkwardly, letting her gaze slowly push into me, the way we both shared a sigh, Gabriel's turn on the pool table. I smiled back, guessing that Maria was… a little less upset now. I knew she was at the very least feeling better. We didn't need to talk, at least not yet. That would come later. But now, we could enjoy ourselves.

"Hey, Sel," Lauren's voice wafted down the stairs, where she stood at the doorframe of the outdoor cellar entrance, saddle in her arms. "I need your special skill."

"Who needs to be eaten? You know I couldn't fit you in if I tried, hate to burst your bubble," Selicia grinned antagonistically.

"Don't be fucking gross. I need your web."

"Oh, yes. Our grounded air support's pet project," Selicia proclaimed in her usual ironically full-of-herself attitude, finally having taken a look at Lauren, jumping down from her perch and straddling on out of the guestroom she occupied. At least she was wearing a bra for once, oddly modest for her usual demeanor, pulling her holos on and standing in the outdoor-leading stairwell as Lauren took steps down, about halfway to watch me take my billiard shot. "I must say, the color of your saddle could do a lot more to compliment your natural tones, you know. Your two colors are brown and green anyways. Bo-ring," Selicia was strumming the side of her face with her spindly fingers as Lauren's ears drooped a little, not really expecting the confrontation.

"Natural camouflage. Can't do much better," Gabriel chimed in.

"...I'm not thinking anything too garish- Perhaps magenta rather than the mahogany hue it already is."

"...Does that really matter? It works for what I want it to do, dying it is a lot of unnecessary work," Lauren put forth somewhat confrontationally.

"Oh, if it works why are you coming to me for help?" Lauren's lips pursed and her brow lowered, grunting out as Selicia sang in her self-righteousness.

"Selicia. Go help the air support. Don't be difficult without a good fucking reason to be, alright?" Gabriel muttered unamused, his turn to hit the ball. When Gabriel phrased it like this, Selicia found it hard to have it within herself to continue to banter. I suppose he really did know how to run her.

"...Fine. I call next game," She put in, going to leave.

"I thought you didn't want to play," Maria added as she took her turn.

"Yeah, well... I do." With that, she absconded in her usual calmly-flustered manner, following Lauren on out to work with her project.

"...At least the two of them are artsy-craftsy," Gabriel muttered.

"Lauren's the better of the two. More practical." I was surprised to hear Maria putting this forth.

"Oh yeah. Not nearly as obnoxious, huh?"

"She's..." Maria sighed heavily, rearing back to lean on the wall. "I don't think I mind Lauren anymore. I think I *get* her more than anybody else here. God, it would suck to come into a world like this like she did, wouldn't it?" She paused to feel over her own hands, like reading her life over again. "What if I never could have gotten out of Mexico, back in the war? That's what it must be like, to her. All her life is this kind of... subsistence, this whole post-apocalyptic surviving- But she's pulling through, doing her best to help. She's got hope. And that gives *me* hope, you know?" It may have been Maria's turn, but she was beside herself for the moment, sighing, feeling the pool cue in her hands like the emotions she mulled over in her mind. "I've lost hope before. When I watched Martín die, I could say I lost hope. But Lauren's at rock bottom, but she still has hope. And that gives me hope." Maria sighed. "She has no family. No one to fall back on. She started with nothing. Absolutely nothing, and...

She's come a long way." Maria's voice cracked. I saw a sparkling wetness in her eyes, but she wasn't quite moved enough to cry. "But now she's got us- imagine all the other hybrids, all alone out there." She paused, letting that sink in. This little monologue she was giving, feeling through her own thoughts. "I renounced God the day Martín died, but I think I've decided to believe again, because I pray for those hybrids- and everyone else. There's nothing else to do for them but pray." She sighed, looking up at me, Gabriel smirking amusedly. Like he was listening to a small child rambling.

"...Fair enough," He uttered, the two of us looking back at him. We knew his opinion on the subject, there was nothing really to say. He was just laughing in his own mind, ever so elevated above Maria's quaint, old-fashioned beliefs.

"Don't get me wrong," She went on all of a sudden, like she was ready to cut him off before he could let his usual atheist edge shine through. "I don't appreciate when she drops you out of the sky," She said over to me.

"Me neither. She's working on that." a quaint little humph of a chuckle. I came a little closer, maybe to hold her hand or do one of those stupid things couples would do, feeling the vibe of the room.

"Hey, uh…" She responded to me, though she quickly ducked away to finally take her turn on the pool table. "You know, I'm still pissed at you," she hit the ball almost antagonistically. I stared at her back as she turned around to gaze at me.

"Yeah," I sighed. She gave me a weird little meager smile. Kind of like she wanted to say it wasn't a big deal, she understood, even if she had the desire and the right to be livid. "...How pissed?"

"Pissed enough." She sighed again. It felt like a formality at this point, this strange exasperation. I knew it was the atmosphere, the situation, this whole stressful world we now inhabited- Lauren's world, I'm sure Maria would say.

"You know… Maybe it's not a bad idea," I put forth, and for a second there, Maria's face flushed out, like she was taken by surprise. Like a little ecstatic beam in her eyes for but a second. Then in the reeling silence of the response, I'd wondered a little why I'd said it. I suppose I said it to help make her feel better- but it felt like a little white lie. As the tension grew, it felt more and more beyond that. Nobody was playing the game anymore, Maria just staring at me.

"N-Noah,"

"I mean, if… you know," I stammered. I let a meager smile towards her, and my façade was cracking. It was like she knew, that sparkle deep in her eyes turned to that saddened doubt while her face as a whole was brightening, switching palettes. I tried to smile until I caught Gabriel's gaze. This wasn't his usual playful devil-may-care attitude. He was gazing in a judgement of sorts, something that told me that he was looking into my soul here, finding my intentions wanting. What he must have been thinking, to tell me. Advise me as a friend, with Maria looking and ready too.

It was all beyond definition, and the feeling would not subside for the rest of the evening.

### Chapter 46

Another eternal night falling through blackness. Here I was, alone. There was nobody. I could look out, feel that demonic gaze from those nights ago- but it was different this time. Not an adversary, but one of critique. Its gaze was far more acute, far more penetrating. This was far worse than the first one so many nights ago, that old dream. But where the togetherness, the acceptance was once behind me, I instead felt a longing, a desire I could not satiate. There was something about that aura that could not tide me over. My anxiety was all that I could feel, that calm bright brown behind me unable to help me.

Another stupid dream and shitty night, I was thinking to myself as I sat up in bed that next morning. I looked over my shoulder, Maria still there. She'd been facing me in her sleep, hands trailing out. My hand slowly crawled over to hers for a moment, before I retracted it without ever touching her. I'll let her sleep.

Waking myself up to walk downstairs, I saw Gabriel in the den, standing there with Abel armored up and pointing his weapon across the room. Everyone else was there in the den geared-up with empty weapons and magazines for this little exercise, Daniel and Selicia and Samantha and Reina and so on, watching the little one-on-one lesson going down. Sentinel stood in the center of the dining room adjacent from the den, the whole table moved over a little. The red paint was all but removed by now, I noticed.

"Alright, you've got time because you scanned and there are no threats. You just spent a lot of bullets, but you think you might be close to being out and me or Noah tells you to top off before the next wave comes. how do you reload?" Gabriel presented. Abel rose his left hand up as he pressed the magazine release with his right index, dropping the magazine into his hand. He lowered the ejected magazine to his drop pouch, hanging from the side of his animalistic chest and humanoid hip on his battle belt, a copy of Lauren's rig. He then reached for a fresh magazine from his chest rig, inserting it in the weapon. Gabriel watched intently as Abel inserted the magazine, smacking it on the bottom for good measure, before turning the rifle to inspect the chamber with a press check, as if a bullet was in the chamber. "That's right," Gabriel said, as he reached in to yank the charging handle back. Since the magazine was empty, per this weird little training exercise, the bolt remained locked back. "Alright, same deal, but with you knowing you've run out." Abel again took the magazine out of his Armalite to place in his dump pouch, before reaching for a fresh one. "Look up, head up, you're scanning for threats while you load," Gabriel instructed. Abel's eyes shot up, an ear twitching, taking the magazine and putting it in the well. "Alright…" Abel then turned the gun. "You visually inspect that the bolt is locked back, so you…" Abel smacked the bolt release button with the flat of his palm on the other side, and the bolt slammed home. "Fan-fucking-tastic. Good boy, Abel," Gabriel reached into his pocket, pulling out a lollipop and sticking it in Abel's face, who dropped his rifle to let it hang from the sling and proceeded to grasp on it, eyes wide and smiling like an idiot, big tail swooshing back and forth behind him. Abel, enthralled by the candy he'd received, began to lick it, as Gabriel reached up to scratch one of Abel's ears, sticking out from the ear cut of his helmet.

"Jesus, Gabe," I scoffed.

"What? Positive reinforcement, Pavlovian shit, helps train the caveman brain," Gabe said.

"You don't have to treat him like he's a dog."

"C'mon, he's gotta be like, three fourths dog, you know," Gabe said. "Besides, shit's working."

"Dude, he's standing right there," I sighed in exasperation, before directing my words to the german shepherd-y centaurical himself. "Don't you mind being treated like an animal?"

"I like treats and scratches dude, don't judge me," Abel explained simply, hardly defensively. Gabriel shrugged with a smug face and shrewd smile. I rolled my eyes, walking over to get myself something to eat out of the pantry. I opened it, seeing the food we had. We had enough for a while but that didn't stop me from feeling worried.

"Alright, one more time before we switch to someone else to practice with," Gabe said, snatching the lollipop from Abel's muzzle, while I was still taking in how much food we had, like I was counting without numbers. I heard the mechanisms of the gun clicking and shifting.

"Watch it! Threat threat threat!" Gabe called, and I turned my head to watch the spectacle. I saw Abel, in response to this, let his rifle fall to sag in his sling; he reached for his sidearm, drawing it. "Suppress, suppress, suppress! Get to cover!" Abel clicked the trigger over and over, the pistol held in his right hand, using his imagination for the most part as he sprayed imaginary bullets at what I assumed the mock enemy to be, Sentinel standing there in the dining room table, Abel pantomiming with his empty pistol. He squat down somewhat on his legs, moving towards the reclining chair of the den, getting it between him and his adversary. "He's still out there! You're in cover, but he's coming for you! A pistol ain't shit but a noisemaker; get your real gun loaded!" Abel, with hands shaking ever so slightly, reholstered his sidearm with a scrape of kydex, his left hand still clutching a rifle magazine. He went to grip his rifle's pistol grip with his right hand, fumbling a bit as he reached for it as it hung from his sling. "Bang bang, he's shooting at you, dumb fuck! He's gonna kill your friends and skullfuck 'em! You're headed for a mass fucking grave if you don't start shooting back!" Gabriel goaded as he bent over to get up in Abel's face, trying to throw off his focus, smacking him on the back of the helmet. "Kill him, motherfucker!" Abel finally loaded his rifle, slamming his bolt home. He pointed that rifle right back at Sentinel, and the hammer fell with a click.

"Good hustle, you just saved yourself from a machete in the face," Gabriel congratulated, and Abel's teeth clinked against the lollipop as Gabe shoved it back in his mouth. "Take a break; Sam, you're up next," Gabe said as he reached down to scratch the underside of Abel's chin, Abel laying there beside that couch, as Gabe started walking towards me. "I'm gonna make an operator out of dogboy yet, eh?"

"Sure hope so," I said.

"Noticed most of the hybrids got a bit of a killer instinct to them," Gabe said as he sat down in the chair on the end of the dining room table with a sigh, patting Sentinel as he passed the armor suit. "Must be the animal in 'em. Still, I can't complain. Gives me something to work with." At that point, Lauren entered the room from the back. She was whipping her wings about a little, looking ever more mobile yet obviously stunted in their own degrees. At least they seemed uniformly misshapen now, one side not sticking awkwardly away unlike the other.

I saw her saddle, looking sturdier than it had after we'd tossed it. She had a rifle bag underneath a wing, extending backwards. She'd fixed up one of the spare battle belts like her old one, the way she liked it to sit on her humanoid hips/frontal legs' shoulders, interfacing it with the wrap-around strap of the saddle to keep the saddle closer to the front to clear her rear wings. It didn't exactly match color-wise, but it was that sort of practical-tactical that was charismatic enough, which she was steadily claiming as her aesthetic, even if unintentionally.

"Did he do as good as me?" Lauren asked, and I noticed a mug of coffee in her hand, taking a sip.

"Just about," Gabriel said. After everyone was assembled with the least amount of haste as I downed a carbo block for breakfast, Gabriel and I had a short oral quiz with everyone. Most things were pretty basic, and aside from the squeamishness of imagining dealing with wounds, everyone seemed to have an idea of what to do for each hypothetical injury. Gabriel went through his depictions in sickening detail, as he was trying to make people uncomfortable with his macabre depictions. "When we hunt something like a deer out in the woods, we'll have a short anatomy lesson," Gabe paused, to feel the exasperation rise from his audience. "Squeamishness is your enemy. Squeamishness is the difference between saving your friends life and letting them bleed to death. By being squeamish, you are stabbing the rest of us in the back. Now, turn to the person next to you…" Gabriel paused to let each person shuffle where they sat, stood and leaned, looking over to their compatriots. "Now, repeat after me… I promise…"

"I promise," they began, somewhat unenthusiastically, barely hiding their exasperation. Gabriel rolled his eyes, pausing, and they turned their heads to look at him.

"C'mon, guys. Like you fuckin' mean it. Now, I *promise*..." they began anew, turning back to their neighbors. "I, will not let you die without a fight."

"I will not let you die without a fight," they said, somewhat slowly.

"If your guts are on the ground, I will scoop them up and put them back in you."

Some of them only mumbled this, past exasperation at this point and taken aback by this sudden, vivid detail. Gabe sighed. "*Again*," he snarled, and they finally all said it, voices finally piercing that threshold Gabe so desired. "...I," he said again, beginning to pace forward, to make sure they were all making eye contact and were otherwise sincere. "Will bend your legs back into place and bandage the stump of your former arm," they said it slowly. "I will not let you die, and I expect the same from you."

"I will not let you die, and I expect the same from you."

"Alright, alright. Gucci. That's the combat medic version of the Hippocratic Oath. Know it and live it, folks. Every last one of you is a combat doctor. Even you, Katt," Gabriel said, and the cat girl nodded, swallowing her fear. Sam next to her pushed her shoulder a bit with her fist in encouragement, and she smiled, courage bolstering her. "So congrats," Gabriel began anew, turning away from the crowd. "You've all conquered lesson one- how to deal with getting shot. Lesson two, however, is a bit more multi-faceted- how to not *get* shot. So, let's start with hardware- you've all gotten acquainted with your new guns, right?" nods and "yeah"s rose from the audience. "As many of you have probably noticed, each of your longarms comes with a specific attachment- a light. If you've played around with them, which I have no doubt many of you have, you might also notice that the light does not stay on once you press it like most flashlights, instead it is only on as long as you are pressing it. Maria, can you tell me why?"

Maria spoke first. "Because we're not supposed to keep the light on."

"Yes, Maria, that's right; but can you tell me why we shouldn't?"

"Because if we do, the enemy might spot us."

"Fan-fucking-tastic, Delarocha. I don't suppose you learned that back in Mexico, did ya? Running away from *Los Renegadas,* armed with nothing but *un lintierno,* eh?" Gabe crowed, as Maria's scowl grew. "See, fun fact, I learned that in Mexico too. Thing is, I kinda had a gun attached to my flashlight."

"Gabe, can you cut the whole being-a-cunt thing and get back to the lesson?" I reprimanded, behind him.

"Alright, alright," He laughed, as Maria seemed a little less peeved, leaning back into the wall on the opposite side of Gabriel to me, arms gripping each other tensely.

"...What about this other one?" Abel asked, turning his rifle over in his hands. There was a second flashlight on the other side, a little boxy module. "What's that do?"

"Good question. That's your infrared illuminator." Abel pressed the pressure pad switch a couple times.

"...It's not very good at illuminating," he noted with a mumble, nothing happening.

"It interfaces with the nightvision module you've all got that you can stick on your tac holos," Gabriel explained. "See, nightvision isn't a magic reveal-all. Nightvision without an illum is like a gun without bullets."

"Oh damn, you blokes can't see this?" Selicia noted, pulling up her M16 and clicking her illuminator a couple times, raising her darkened holos onto the top of her head to peer with her eyes. "Heh. I come with my own nightvision," She chuckled as she looked in a darker corner, activating the infrared a few times, evidently. "Hey, it's got a laser too. Neat. You guys really can't see that spectrum of light, huh?" She was practically gloating.

"Course, we have some exceptions, like the special snowflake of the group," Gabriel pointed out in response to the spider girl's proud assertion. "See, her glasses are customr, so I got the tactical and medical functions downloaded onto it but the nightvision attachments wouldn't have worked with them. I figured she could see good enough at night so I guess we've lucked out." Selicia smirked, evidently enamored with herself.

"Uh…" Sam now said. "So we've all got nightvision. What's the point of a stupid flashlight?"

"Mm. Good question." Gabe began to pace again, whipping his finger in the air as if to facilitate salient thought in the usual introspective way. "There's a couple uses for a flashlight. You could lose your NODs and bam, you're blind. Lot of guys I worked with didn't have a visible light on their rifles and said the same thing, saying they'd switch to their pistols that had lights on them if their NV went down. I just find that fucking stupid. Again, pistol's a noisemaker. Rifle's what's good at killing. Anyways, let's talk a little more about visible light etiquette," Gabe re-segued. "You turn the flashlight on only when you need to take a look at something. Rest of the time, you get your finger off that switch, use your technological nightvision, or your natural nightvision if you find yourself NOD-less, just let your eyes adjust. You press the light at the wrong time and you might just get you and everyone near you killed. This goes for infrared, too. We may have an advantage in equipment over 90% of the fuckers out there but that remaining 10% are going to be some special ops wannabes, this means enemy nightvision too. If we end up getting in a scrap with other professionals, or even some freaks along the lines of Selicia here with *special eyes* you can be sure as shit they'll see the infrared flashlights just as well as visible light ones. Got it?"

"Sure."

"Now, let's move on to comms," Gabe continued, motioning to the headsets and radios everyone had. "Arguably the most important aspect of working as a team, communications really help out with Rule 2… helping to not get you or your friends shot. Good use of comms means knowing the relative positions of friends and foes. Shit use of comms means shooting your friends and mistakenly thinking *bad* guys *aren't*. Now, comms are simple, yet can be used against you, just like your gun lights or infras, if somebody intercepts them. We've got a basic scrambler relay- this big radio machine not only acts as a hub for comms, but it automatically switches our channel about every thirty seconds. A little difficult, but not impossible to intercept by any ne'er-do-wells we might face. Now, If an enemy intercepts your comms, they can pretty much track your movement- this is why you should only use comms sparingly and talk to those around you by way of voice. On comms, we won't be using terms like 'safehouse' or enemy headquarters. Instead, we use codenames like site A and B. If we go on an actual operation, we need to know beforehand what each codename will be. Now, this culdesac, should we ever need to communicate this, will be Foxtrot Site. Foxtrot, like F, for the guy who used to own this house, Frank. Hostiles will be under the Codename Golf-Bravos. You need help remembering this, just think like the old Republican presidents George Bush, and how they're Republicans, like who we'll probably end up fighting here. Republicans, George Bush, GB, Golf Bravo. Even if they turn out to be blues, still call 'em GB's, that'll be the catch-all term for enemy. Now, friendlies. What are we going to call ourselves? I was thinking Wolverines, but, you know, that last remake they made kinda fuckin' sucked."

"...I thought that was a sequel," I heard Anthony say, thinking aloud. Everyone was silent for a second, some turning towards him. "Wait, you're talking about the one that came out last year, right?"

"Shit, they made a sequel to the 2057 one too?" Gabriel sighed. "Why the fuck would they make a sequel to that garbage? It was a direct-to-StreamFlix film too, wasn't it? Fuckin' hell,"

"Independents?" Sam put forth. "...Or whatever the military term for I is? That makes sense,"

"You know what?" Gabe began. "I think you've got something there. All in favor of calling friendlies Indigoes?" Almost every hand raised. "Then it's settled. Now, those are the basics. If we need to make more, we will. Now, onto the simplest part of not shooting your friends- Identification. Now, with each of your armor, I have included three bandannas. One red, one blue, and one green. Now, our default color will be green- just tie the bandanna to one of your shoulder pauldrons, preferably the one that's not gonna get in the way of shouldering your weapon, so if you're right handed, that's the left shoulder plate. Now, I included the red and blue just in case we need a quick disguise to slip past Republicans or Democrats without bloodshed. Don't expect the disguise to hold up under scrutiny though, it's so if we find ourselves trapped between Democrats and Republicans, we might be able to slip by one of them if we're able to get in a blind spot. If we're completely surrounded, we'll be kind of fucked so we'll have to make our own exit. With bullets. Hence all the fucking guns. So, questions?" Nobody said anything. "Well then, class adjourned. Practice with your gear, tomorrow we'll be going over something else."

Gabriel and I paced outside while everyone shuffled about to go around and do as they'd been told. Their enthusiasm was still somewhat dim, but at least they seemed receptive. It was probably still the desert shootout fresh in people's minds, or the close call in Elko.

"...So what else is on the curriculum?" I asked.

"Hand to hand tomorrow. Think that's gonna be fun, though a lot of it's gonna be prototypical since a two-legged takedown on one of the 'taurs or Selicia might be... interesting. I think most things are applicable, pressure points 'n shit."

"...You have a martial arts background?" I asked with a smirk, almost implying my relative advantage in this field.

"A little. We got bits and pieces in Siña Ops. This is more your thing, I was gonna ask you your take on the prospect anyways. My extent of martial arts is knifing and disarming."

"...You took on Maria pretty good," I noted of what had happened on May first.

"She was emotionally compromised. Brown belt or not that sort of thing makes you shaky. Imprecise."

"Yeah, and you're never emotionally compromised," I added back, still grinning.

"Cut that part right out of my brain, y'know," He smirked back, like he was implying it was funny even though he really didn't think so. "Aside from that, still gonna intersperse some one-on-one weapons training periodically, couple medical pop quizzes. Think later we could take half the group into the woods for some small squad tactics, one half at a time. Dry run of course, don't want us spraying bullets we ought to be saving and getting the attention of the locals doing so."

"Uh... I mentioned. "We might want to bring *some* ammo. Lauren and I ran into- well, we didn't shoot, uh, it was sort of a-" Gabriel was hanging onto each word, brow furrowed, interested of course, but rather upset that I hadn't mentioned this earlier. "I think we've got more than just Republicans to worry about."

"...You serious?" Gabriel came closer, as if anyone else was listening. "Like what, monsters?"

"Yeah." Gabriel nodded with a breathless laugh, with this new information in his mind.

"Though," He went on. "I think you need some practice yourself, y'know."

"...With what?" Gabriel turned on his comms and promptly answered my question.

"Hey Sentinel. Let's go outside."

"AFFIRMATIVE." I turned over, seeing Sentinel approach the back door, going to slide the glass door open with a big metal hand. It was rather endearing, watching this half ton killing machine gingerly making his way outside as we followed. "AWAITING INSTRUCTIONS."

"Here," Gabriel reached into the admin bag of the power armor, whipping out the plugsuit. He kept it with the armor at all times, it seemed. Convenient. "Go change." I did so, going around the corner where there was nobody, near the shed where Lauren's did her projects. I took all my clothes and the battle belt off, pulling on the jumper.

"It's not very tight," I uttered as I came back out. "Is it sized for you?"

"Flip the switch the wristwatch-looking thing," Gabriel said. I did so, and it was skintight in a moment, as if it were sized snugly to me. It sort of felt good as it sucked itself up to me. "Alright. You're gonna want to come up behind the armor and tell it to open."

"Uh... Open, Sentinel," I ordered, and like that the back swung open, the back of the hamstrings of the legs opening as well, the sabatons widening. The arms sort of swung inward as well, the back opening straight up and swiveling. I let out a little "Huh", it really was that easy.

"See, it recognizes you immediately as an authorized user. You don't have to use exact words, just as long as you tell Sentinel you want to wear him he'll open up for you."

"Man, put it like that and it's kind of gay," I muttered with a smirk.

"It's only gay if you think about it. It's a fucking robot, it doesn't have genitals."

"I CAN SWITCH TO A FEMALE VOICE IF YOU PREFER, MR. REED," Sentinel said. "I HAVE MANY VOICES TO CHOOSE FROM. CURRENT SETTING IS PROCESSED MALE, INTENDED FOR MAXIMUM INTIMIDATION."

"It doesn't matter," I sighed in exasperation. "Alright, what's the best way to get in... it?"

"Put your legs in first, then stick your head through the neck hole and your arms in as well. You've got to kind of arch your back but as you straighten up it'll automatically tell you're in and close up." I did so, feeling the hermetic seal as the thing ratcheted shut. For a moment it was like I was feeling like I was going to be crushed, claustrophobia taking over, but as the suit's pressure seal regulated and the footholds adjusted for my height and build, the hand controls doing similarly to account for my slightly longer arms as compared to Gabriel, I instantly felt so much better and lighter. This was far different from wearing it sans plugsuit, this felt effortless to move and control. I felt how much taller I was with the raised legs, how before back in Elko it was like I was walking in ridiculous high heels, now it really was like I was seven feet tall.

"...Feels good," I said, looking over the carapace of my arms. I jumped up and down in place for a moment, rocking up and down on the feet. I took a short walk around the yard as Gabriel yapped on.

"So the onboard systems and the microreactor are on the back. This is an enemy-forward sort of deal- the Mark Seven is a Hoplite-Class armor. Mass production. They had these during the Mexican Intervention War and all. Hoplite-Class armor is the... lightest of power armors, if you can call it light. The next step up from Exo-Armor. Level four extremities, your arms, legs and helmet- if we had one- can withstand armor piercing rifle rounds, level five cuirass, your torso can withstand fifty caliber BMG fire. Argonaut-Class would be a step up, level six torso and level five extremities. Anything bigger than a Argonaut would be a rabbit-class Mech. Lastly there's Orpheus class, or HellWalker. Name's sort of self-explanatory. Think a HazMat suit on juice, though your average power armor, like what you're wearing now, should give you some protection against radiation and biohazards, it'd certainly be a step up from a MOPP suit, however it'd be not be that great without a helmet, so don't go exploring any nuclear craters. Now," Gabriel mentioned. "Hoplite-Class is more versatile, or so I've been told, because your hands, or the hands of the suit that your hands within the arms control can still be used for smallarms. Here, stick your thumb and pinky out from a fist like a surfer dude and shake it up and down a little." I did so, and all of a sudden the hand deactivated and swiveled back on the inside of the arm, the armor ratcheting back a little and there my own hand in the glove of the plugsuit was. "See, you can technically use anything, but an M16 is going to be real clumsy with the real power armor hand. The hands are more intended for the OICWs they developed or for other assorted heavy weapons, or for just punching the shit out of people. For now, all we have that's really usable in design for the power armor hands is the M2 machine gun that's usually on the passenger seat of the JLTV."

"Can't use those AT4's we hoarded?" I asked. Gabriel clicked his tongue.

"You can, just dunno if we want our bullet-sponge to be carrying heavy explosives, y'know," Gabriel pointed out, and my eyebrows went up, nodding my head from side to side a little with a "huh".

"Oh, neat," We suddenly heard as the backdoor opened, seeing Lauren strolling on out. She had one of the vests in her arms, evidently not hers as Daniel trailed behind, sulking as usual. He was certainly looking better. "Practicing with Sentinel?"

"That's the idea," I said, as I then did that same motion with the thumb and pinky to close up the hand, the hand of the suit reactivated once more. "...Oh," Lauren said, looking. "...I don't get it. You make the motion for phone to activate the suit's hand, what's the connection?"

"Dunno. Probably just something that you're not likely to do on accident," I said, Lauren nodding dully with big eyes, that "I guess so" look. "What's up with you?"

Daniel opened his mouth to speak, but Lauren spoke first, explaining as she hefted the dynamid armor. "Danny needs his armor cinched up," She explained. "I'm gonna see what I can't do with my stuff."

"Neat, have fun with that," I smirked and they proceeded onward to the shed. "What else?" I turned back to Gabe. He had Maria's tac helm in his hand, the one that was most like mine, souped up to all hell. He stuck it on my head, snapped the comms cups onto my ears. the armor connected with the HUD of the tac glasses, and I could see the display.

"Check out the display. It shows the current synchronization percentile. Should be in the upper nineties at the moment, basically as to how well the armor is interfacing with the plugsuit, and therefore you. Now look at the little man, the little suit of armor there in the corner. That's how well the armor is holding up. It'll give you readings as to structural integrity, hermetic sealing, busted servos or joints, the works. It already is detecting that you just have a standard helmet and no gas mask to boot, not a fully-integrated power armor helmet, so your estimated healthy radiation-resistance counter should be reading pretty low. Again, this isn't an Orpheus-class, but typically most any power armor is pretty decent for CBRN protection. Just try and stay out of places where the radiation happens to be boiling puddles of water right in front of you, power-helmet or not. Come back with a HellWalker if that's your fancy."

"Gotcha. Anything else?"

"Just familiarize yourself to the motions a little bit more, see what the readouts tell you when you're doing stuff. Go move those boxes with the junk next to the porch around."

"What, give me a multi-million dollar wearable death robot and you have me do menial labor?" I laughed, going over anyways.

"Yeah. Builds character." I noticed just how effortless it still was- there was raw feedback of course, a sort of tingling downward sensation but the suit was doing more than most of the work.

"Okay," I was soon to say. "I think I get it."

"...if you think so. That's all for today," Gabe said.

"Alright, open, let me out," I ordered and sentinel compiled as I felt the back come open and I slipped out. Now in that skintight jumper, I went back around to where I'd left my clothes piled, hearing the two of them working there. I sighed a little, figuring they were busy enough on the workbench fiddling with the armor carrier, Daniel standing there uncomfortably as Lauren was yammering on in her own little diagnosis of the armor. But her eyes wandered to me, seeing me standing there, and her words trailed to a stop, looking at me with my clothes under my arm, in that suit. I think I saw the slightest flushing of red on her cheeks within a second as she cleared her throat. Daniel was there, staring at me too behind those worrisome eyes, arms limp at his sides. "Y... You think you know what you're doing?" I asked. It was weird, like I was compelled to fill the silence, the void that hung between us, Daniel between us awkwardly.

"...Yeah?" Daniel was the first to talk. Maybe he was just acting clueless, since there was a definite vibe going on, Lauren's eyes wandering up and down my body though she fought to look me in the eye. I guess I found it funnier than I'd want to admit, to try and break away from this haunting awkwardness. I chuckled a little, hefting my clothes under my arm.

"Yeah, h-have fun," I uttered and made my exit, eyes raising. Have fun? What a stupid thing to say. I saw Gabriel there, leaning on Sentinel and smirking self-indulgently. I felt his judgement again, and I just avoided his gaze to make my way inside and change.

### Chapter 47

It hadn't even been a week, but this sedentarism was something else. Again, we had to be moving forward, shouldn't we? But here I was, hanging out, pretending to relax with everyone. Play a couple board games, shoot some pool, help the Pendrews with chores to be neighborly, do some gardening, go swimming. They used some of the confectionery to make cookies for everyone, maybe just to raise some spirits, but it didn't help that feeling in me. Beyond that, I could tell that it wasn't just me who was anxious, it really lingered in the air. It seemed like the Pendrews were the real calm ones; *we* were so far from home, so out of our element. As for the hybrids, our unease fell upon them anyways. I guess it was more the situation than any sort of homesickness on their part.

The day passed. I had another dream in the night, something I'd forgotten by the time I woke up, sitting up and looking to Maria next to me. She was still asleep. I sat there for a couple seconds, taking in the light streaming through as the Sun peaked up along the horizon. Must've been barely morning. I leaned in, as if to kiss Maria upon the cheek gently, but never did, just sighing and going on down.

I walked downstairs unceremoniously, to find Lauren sitting there with Gabriel.

"Hey Noah," She said. She was wearing a grey hoodie, her battle belt with it's harness under her sweatshirt and her saddle sat on her back, her stirrups were rolled up on the saddle's sides, ready to be deployed should they need be- after all, she seemed to regard the saddle as clothing first, utility second.

"You're… You guys're up early," I finally responded, blinking and wiping sleep from my eyes.

"I've seen deer in the forest," Lauren said, her wings, just barely still stiff quivering behind her. "And Gabriel said we ought to try hunting. Monsters or not."

"Couldn't hurt our food supply," He said. He was looking at the guts of the SKS we'd lifted from our first shootout. It felt so long ago, seeing it. Like a relic from forever ago, just like it was an antique in its own sense.

"So why are we up so early?" I said.

"To hunt; the real question is, why are *you* up so early?" Gabriel asked. I blinked. I guess that sounded fun. "…Besides, I was thinking we could use this to do a little refresher in small-squad tactics with Maria, you and I. I figured you'd be down. Go see if she's up." I nodded slowly, going back upstairs.

Entering the master bedroom again, I tried to turn on the lights, but I let out a "huh" as I saw the electricity was out right now. That was a little concerning, but I guess it was to be expected with everything going on right now. Maria was now somewhat awake, her eyes following me from where she lay. "Hey… Maria," I said.

"Hm?" She asked, sensing a question.

"We're gonna go hunting," I said. Even as it rolled off the tongue it felt silly. Like, of course we'd hunt, my father always said that I'd have to provide in this way, but saying it now felt surreal, like a post-apocalyptic fantasy.

"Who's going?" She asked. "Gabriel?" she didn't sit up or look at me, as if she wanted to stay in bed.

"Yeah," I said. "And Lauren." She shifted, groaning, as she got up, smacking her lips and smoothing down her hair.

"Let's get to it, then," She got up to dress herself.

We took the truck and hit the road sometime before eight. "Just the four of us, huh?" Gabe said. He drove. Lauren sat shotgun, sitting down where the seat had been but was now removed. Maria and I sat in the back. "This is good, you know? less people to deal with, to mess up a shot, you know," He said, bumbling along the road. "Although technically you could hunt by just getting a fuckin' mob to comb the forest and chase the deer to the point of exhaustion, like our ancestors did; fuckin' stab a wooly mammoth to death with a rock, y'know?" Gabriel smiled.

"Huh," Lauren said, one of her hands up hanging off of the little interior handle of the cab just above the window.

"Any rules against it?" I asked, scanning slow and trying to look unremarkable whilst doing so. Not that it mattered, we didn't see any Republican troops. "Hunting?"

"Well, you know, no guns allowed unless you're the Repubs, or else you're a hoarder and therefore a traitor, so be quiet?" He said.

"I really haven't been seeing many people out there when I'd flown over it," Lauren responded.

"Well, I do," Gabe said. "You're not looking hard enough, from way up there. Spending all that time flying and you'll get all distant with everyone." Lauren looked at Gabriel sternly. He didn't even have to turn his head to know she was glaring at him.

"You're just jealous," she said, ruffling her prized wings, even if they were still rather inoperable.

"Honestly, what would you do if you couldn't fly?" Gabriel mulled over, not so much out of inquisition but rather to just get to her. "You'd be stuck on the ground, with the rest of us to rot in the mud."

"That's what being a… a superior life form is all about," Lauren asserted, as she smirked indignantly and raised her chin at Gabriel, trying to one-up him at his own game.

"Cute, getting in touch with your inner Nazi. Don't forget that if it wasn't for humans you wouldn't be here."

"Hey look, alls I'm sayin' is that a weird cabal of humans figured humanity needed a mark two and created *your successor*," Lauren squinted at Gabe with a smile, waving at herself as she puffed her chest.

"*Ach javhol, einer kameraden*," Gabriel threw up a mocking roman salute as he spat german gibberish. I was guessing Spanish was his only other language. "...Just don't start reciting the dragon version of The Fourteen Words or I'll make you walk home." Gabe shot back along. I guess he was just enjoying himself at this point. I was glad that Lauren played into it, rather than try to self-deprecate like usual.


We drove up into those hills to the east as we really couldn't go north due to the roadblocks, parking in some old camping spot, which wasn't hard seeing as Shortstone was home to a lot of campgrounds before it grew into an actual city of its own, getting out. The morning was damp with dew and mists wafting across the land. It was quiet, and the heat of the Sun had begun to bring the water in the ground to rise and evaporate into mists, as if the very earth was on fire, some places thick enough so that you could hardly see through the haze. I guess it was pretty, really drove an atmosphere.

Lauren picked up her own Armalite, stowing it in the rifle bag extending under her wing on her saddle. Gabriel's MDR was assembled into rifle configuration, Maria had her personal 20 inch AR like mine, and I had that SKS. "Let's split into pairs. C'mon Green, you're with me. Lemme see how *Das Ubermensch* hunts," He mocked playfully as she smirked back at him with a winky squint.


It seemed a lot more simple than it was, hunting. You'd always see deer just meandering about in the outer suburbs. It even seemed like nature was more than happy to reclaim what it could, now with humanity so wrapped up in choking itself. But here, our game seemed to evade us.

Maria and I walked alone. Every now and then we'd hear a little whistle in the distance, and I'd whistle back. I whistled, and Gabriel whistled in response, our low-tech comms solution, even if we had radios we figured to practice the Native Method. Maria walked next to me, out of arm's reach, but I could see steel and venom in her eyes. She'd never been on a hunt before, but she was no stranger to adversity, nor was she to her weapon. She clutched that rifle like her lifeline, eyes scanning back and forth, back and forth, lost in the hunt.

However for me, I seemed to be everywhere but in the moment, lost in thought rather than the goal here. I thought too much, wondering about what we were doing here, pondering how I felt about it. We'd stopped moving forward like we hit a brick wall. I wondered what dad was doing right about now. If he was worried about me. But all the while I was brought into the present by noticing things, little things. I noticed how the wind gradually affected the trees as it blew, one tree moving, then the next as the breeze reached it. I noticed how loud my footsteps were. I noticed how Maria walked with one foot before the other, stepping gently with the pad of her foot before planting the whole thing. A silent walk, rather moreso than mine. A tiptoeing walk she'd performed before.

We walked. It was quiet. But, as we walked, we came upon a stream, winding its way down the slope. It was quaint enough to look upon, Lauren and Gabe well before us further up it, Lauren herself quietly walking up to her ankles in the water, with her gun slung as she gazed around, wings ruffling and smiling as she felt the water rush through her toes and talon-fingers, spinning a little bit as she trot in place. She'd turned to face me and suddenly saw me, eyes widening and mouth opening in surprise, before smiling, pink rushing into her cheeks for a moment before she coughed, caught in her silly little moment there.

"God, I'm hungry," Maria uttered as we'd come to a stop, and at that point I realised how hungry I was too- I hadn't eaten breakfast. I looked over to Maria, staring off into the distance with her gun in her arms, leg up on a rock.

"Megabar?" Gabe said suddenly, appearing off to the side, shoving an energy bar in my face. I took it awkwardly. "Welp, deer weren't biting today," He sighed, hands on his hips. I nodded a little, taking a bite as Gabriel gave Maria one of the energy bars.

"Well, this was a waste of time," I said with a full mouth.

"Maybe stalking isn't our thing. We're too loud. Better to stakeout next time."


We drove back. Nothing had happened. Honestly, I wasn't that disappointed; I was still groggy from the lack of sleep. I looked at Lauren, and as we drove, I zoned out on her head- She'd rearranged her hair yet again, this time into a thick single braid that hung from between her two horns, the rest of the hair of her spine left alone for now, but there were a couple braids down the nape of her neck, disappearing into her sweatshirt. I wondered if she'd eventually have the entirety of her spinal fur braided. That would be kind of charming.

We returned, surprised enough to see in front of the Pendrews' house in their front yard was Mrs. Pendrew herself, accompanied by none other than Selicia, her spindly legs folded compactly beneath her the way she "sat" as the two of them toiled in the garden over the flowers, Selicia in a big spring hat that enveloped her upper body in shadow, despite the heavily overcast nature of today and that hat, she still wore her glasses dimmed, though we could see her eyes behind them for once.

"...Now would you look at that," Gabriel uttered what we were all thinking. "Is the resident prima donna being helpful for once?"

"Mr. Noria, you joke too much," Mrs. Pendrew in all her flowery grace responded with a sardonic smirk. "See, that always irks me. I was sort of a recluse myself growing up, when I'd come down and hear people remark things like 'oh, look who decided to be social', it never really made me want to be social. Quite the opposite, in fact. Maybe if you like this behavior you ought to try and reward it rather than make snide comments."

"She's in a good mood too, Selicia must *actually* be helping," Lauren muttered from the corner of her mouth just for the four of us.

"...You get anything out there?" Mrs. Pendrew went on to ask.

"N-no," I stammered, going on. "...You're not... Off put by the whole spider thing?" I asked. As far as I knew this was the first time Selicia was social with either of the Pendrews. "No offense, Selicia."

"...I'm used to it," She muttered though not entirely without ire, squinting a little behind a sarcastic smile.

"I actually think she's very pretty, not in spite of her spider-ness, but accentuated because of it. My husband has his reservations, but you know him," She sang. I did take notice of how he was on the front porch with his M1A rifle in his lap, scowling away in his eternal exasperation. It made me smirk.

"Mrs. Pendrew actually judges people on things other than how they look," Selicia humphed.

"...If that's true, she doesn't judge on personality either," Lauren was full of jokes evidently, muttering again to those of us around as we were parking the vehicle.

"Just tending the flowers?" Maria put forth plainly, maybe trying to change the discussion as it was rather razor's-edge.

"Oh, and planting some tomatoes too. If this is an apocalypse we might start acting like it," She sang with a laugh. "Always good to have more food."

"...You ought to plant those in the backyard," Gabriel growled. "It might attract attention."

"The backyard's already full, we can't plant anything else there without making it too dense. Fruits and vegetables need room to grow."

"Then pull up your backyard lawn. You're not getting any use out of the grass." Pendrew just beamed at this, like it was so incredibly charming and quaint of a suggestion, though Gabriel was now dead serious and certainly showing it.

"...Ever the pragmatic one right down to the expense of aesthetics, is he not?" Selicia rolled all four of her eyes.

"You have to appreciate it though," Mrs. Pendrew put forth. "He does think on his feet. What exactly did you do before all this, Mr. Noria?"

Gabriel smirked. "Military."

"Well, obviously," She smirked. "What branch?" Her eyes narrowed as her smile remained the same.

"...Army CAG, CIA auxiliary," Gabriel was quick with a plausible lie that may or may not have been rehearsed while Maria and I awkwardly stood there looking about with our eyes wide.

"Oh, Delta? You're awfully young for special forces," Mrs. Pendrew was squinting through that amused smile now, like she wanted to press him on this. I could see Mr. Pendrew ever so subtly lean in, more curious than he would admit.

"Let's just say I had a head start. You seem to know a lot, yourself."

"Steven was a Ranger, back in the day before his knee problems got him discharged. I've spent a lot of time around his kind. It rubs off."

"Fair enough."

"...Might explain why she's so comfortable around a half-spider monster, got them killer instincts," Lauren muttered again, ever so sarcastic.

"...You're one to talk," Maria snarled back. Lauren quickly threw up a couple signs, something my marginal understanding in sign language interpreted along the lines of "whatever, cunt".

"Well, uh, have fun," Gabriel was responding as he walked away back into the house, almost trying to escape before he was further questioned, Mrs. Pendrew coyly eyeing him.

"Hey, uh," Lauren approached Mrs. Pendrew as Maria was back at the car unloading the rifles before going inside. "My wings are feeling a lot better. Could you… give me your opinion on them? If I can fly soon?"

"...Okay, open them all the way," Mrs. Pendrew sat up to watch and Lauren complied, going as far as she could. She still seemed sore, but it was definitely an improvement. "Close again," and she complied, still unable to close them fully, but getting quite close. "You look good. Tomorrow after a warm-up you should be pretty close to normal. You should be able to fly if you're not carrying anything by tonight, though, so long as you take it easy and don't-"

"You really think so?" Lauren, keeping her giddiness down ever so barely though still interrupting Mrs. Pendrew, eyes sparkling. She definitely wanted to fly as soon as possible.

"Remember, Lauren. Safety first," Mrs. Pendrew ordered. "Promise me you won't push it again. And especially not with Noah with you," She ordered.

"Y-yes. Of course," Lauren said, hiding her smile until she turned around, looking back at me, now grinning again. I couldn't help but grin back as she gave me double thumbs-ups.

"Don't get too ahead of yourself," I uttered with an earnest smile as we walked back inside. "You break 'em again, they might fall off." Like that, her smile dimmed a little bit, but she was still trying to play things happy and smile her way forward, grinning without teeth now, though I could tell at the very least she took the concern seriously.


Within half an hour Gabriel had assembled everyone again, and the next lesson had begun. "Alright, folks," Gabriel began, as everyone listened. "We've gone over how not to get killed. Now, we're gonna go over how to kill. Again, most of you know your way around shooters, thanks to our tireless effort. While this is alright, there are fundamentals, things that supercede weapon or person. One of these fundamentals, is that you really don't know how to take a man down until you can do it with a knife-" he motioned to the tanto knife hanging off of his side. "Or your bare hands. Now," He began to pace again. "Knife fights are probably the most rare occurrences on a modern battlefield. If you find yourself with nothing but a knife bearing down on somebody with a gun, chances are you either are about to make a big mistake or you already have. However, as knives were humanity's first invention, logic dictates that it was probably first for a damn good reason. Knives are immensely useful if somebody is grabbing at your gun and they're just too close to shoot. A couple hard pokes and the vast majority of people will get the picture and back the fuck up to a range where you can blast 'em. Of course, if you end up having to stab somebody to *death*, you're probably going to need some serious counseling." There was another awkward pause, as Gabriel cleared his mind and his throat to extrapolate, whilst letting the silence paint the right picture in his audience's heads, letting us use our imagination to paint a better picture than he ever could. A tactical, tactful pause. "So, in training you to fight, we will work our way back up to guns. Again, most of you know how to shoot, and some of you know how to fight with a gun. But for now we'll talk about the art of the open hand."

Throughout the early noon, Gabriel, Maria and I instructed everyone on techniques to defend oneself with bare hands. Teaching 'taurs and 'taur-centric techniques was a little bit trickier, but it seemed like a lot of the fundamentals held over, though Abel must have been Gabe's guinea pig lately, and he demonstrated techniques he'd devised here.

"Now, 'taurs may look intimidating, as most of them are a lot bigger than you," Gabe said. "However, in hand-to-hand combat, they have a fatal shortcoming- they are junk at strafing and turning, since they've got more legs and more body to deal with. If you act quickly enough, you can easily get around one, to a position like here-" he demonstrated by getting to the side of Lauren's humanoid hip, right next to her frontal legs and rather diagonally. "Then, simply get down, reach out and grab both frontal legs, and pull them together towards your body while extending your legs and leaning forward, shifting their balance point-" he did so, quickly toppling Lauren upon the carpet with a sizeable thump as they collapsed upon the ground, Gabe atop the side of her humanoid torso. "Now you've got a couple seconds to get to the head." he faked a couple strikes to Lauren's jaw and temple, Lauren laying there in exasperation. "A few quick jabs and your four-legged bad guy'll go right to sleep. In particular, that jaw hinge is surprisingly tender and a bit more sensitive than the rest of us non-degenerate types who can't dislocate our mouths and eat people for fun. If you can surprise 'em with a straight jab to that little joint bisecting the cleft of their jaw-" Gabriel motioned with a thumb to the cleft of his own chin for demonstration purposes, before pointing to Lauren's on the ground, "That's a real good stunner. That is, if you can reach it."

"...Even if I never use it?" Lauren questioned. In response to this, Gabe quickly grabbed her jaw, and with a squeeze of his fingers and a quick twist, the left side of her jaw popped out of place.

"Still there, ain't it?" Gabe said, and she, somewhat flustered and embarrassed, popped the side of her jaw back in with a pained growl.

"Don't *do* that, that hurts!" she cried.

"Pfft, amateur..." Selicia audibly berated under her breath, and Lauren shot her a cross look. "Besides, Gabe. What if we come across an Arachnae like me? I mean, I wouldn't go down so easy."

"Sure you would," Gabe said. "Just gotta grab half of your legs. For Lauren it was two, for you it'd be four."

"Oh yeah?" She said, raising her arms. "Try me." As soon as she said this, Gabriel got up slowly, chuckling and shaking his head. He approached her slowly, almost cautiously. She folded her arms over her chest, smirking indignantly. Gabriel slowly circled her at a distance, as she turned, still facing him, following his movements. "See? I'm not like other 'taurs. I can turn better than most *humans*." She herself skittered from side to side on those eight spindly legs of hers, before spinning three-sixty quicker than I'd seen either of the centauricals trot in place all the way around.

"Tough talk from somebody not wearing shoes," Gabe reprimanded with a grin, and her brow furrowed, almost a little confused, yet amused.

"W-what?!" she laughed, before Gabe's foot encountered the end of one of her legs, pinning the little foot-esque chitin joint to the floor for a split second as she'd been momentarily distracted by Gabriel's strange comment. Her whole body yanked as she tried unsuccessfully to move away, as he then, immediately following her resulting momentary mental slip, fell forward, grasping the two frontal-most legs on that side, his arms advancing quickly to grab the other two frontal ones on the opposing side. Selicia's heart dropped and the smile disappeared from her face, replaced by wide-eyed, stunned terror, as Gabriel's arms shimmied down a joint, before yanking in. Her four most frontal legs were now in the air and nearly horizontal in Gabe's arms, and he extended his legs, lifting her body up on her back legs, her balance falling as Gabriel twisted her spider thorax out of sheer leverage, and she fell just as readily as Lauren did- if not more, so much so that she rolled upon her back, and Gabriel climbed atop her humanoid chest within a quarter of a second, a hand around her throat and a fist reared back. That fist sailed towards her face, before slowing and gently tapping the little indentation bisecting the cleft of her chin.

Selicia just stared up at the man mounting her chest for a couple awkward, embarrassed seconds, blushing hard. Gabriel smiled razors.

"Y-you gonna buy me a drink sometime?" She tried to joke, unsuccessfully hiding her flusteredness. Gabriel leaned in, kissing close, for an awkwardly long time.

"Don't flatter yourself," Gabe uttered in an almost whisper, plenty audible here. He then leapt up off of her, and she lay there, blushing and rather angrily embarrassed, before rolling back over to come to all eight of her feet. "Remember the term 'center of gravity' kids. Feel where it is in yourself and you should be able to guess where the other guys' is." He sprung off. "Most 'taurs are taller than you, this also means that most 'taurs have a higher center of gravity than you. Use it."

"W-what about us? What are we supposed to do?" Abel asked.

"Well, if somebody comes at you with a low grab like that, just remember to get low. It's harder to get to you if we have to bend down more. Aside from that, use your weight." Abel seemed flustered, if not a little confounded. "Look, just try and spread your legs, get down and use all the torque you've got to force them away. Do some old-fashioned body slams. Maybe surprise 'em with those frontal legs of yours with a couple good slashes, since you've got claws on your front feet-hands." Abel nodded, looking at his own handpaws, and Gabriel went on. "Now, pain is an excellent distraction; dislocating a joint with a well-placed strike is often a lot easier than breaking a bone, and almost just as effective. Now, the wings of dragons are quite tough- however, as dragons can use their wings to defend and feint and strike with them, this puts them in your reach often. And, as when they do, they are often at a prime angle for break strikes, at a direct 90 degrees to the articulation range of the joint. Now, for the rest of us, there are still moves you can do. You stamp down on the inside of somebody's high ankle, and he'll probably feel it when his foot starts flopping around."

"Now, the knife," He went on. "There are a lot of techniques you can do with knives- how to use a knife so that if someone grabs your wrist when you're holding one, you can slip out and cut them in the same motion. There's biomechanical cutting, slicing at tendons and muscles. There's a thick layer of bullshit covering the so-called 'art' of knife fighting on all angles. However, when we get down to it, there's one real technique that works from all levels of training, from DEVGRU to a scared prostitute in an alleyway- we call that the sewing machine technique. Relatively simple-" Gabriel drew his knife and thrust it towards an imaginary assailant. "Step one, insert knife in bad guy," he then pulled his knife back. "Step two, pull knife out of bad guy," He then shoved the knife through the air once again. "Step three, re-insert knife in bad guy," He pulled the knife back again. "Repeat at a fast pace until desired effects are achieved. Desired effects range from bad guy backing away, screaming, seeing internal organs fall out, most notably intestines, kidneys, stomachs, eyeballs, brains, livers, et-cetera; bad guy falling over and ceasing movement, the list goes on. Use your imagination. The sewing machine technique, despite its name, happens to be probably the oldest technique in so-called schools of knife fighting. The Ancient Greeks had their Lakonia, a stubby little sword with a fat, wide, short blade that was apt at doing a lot of internal damage in thrusting. The Romans expanded on this with the Gladius, a bit skinnier but a lot longer than the Greek sword, with more reach and a better chance of running your enemy through. A single stab wound from a short, thin knife like a switchblade or your average pocket knife typically isn't going to do much unless the guy you're stabbing is a walking fucking vagina of a human being. Unless you have a blade long enough to run somebody through or one wide enough that the resulting wound displaces a lot of organs, you're going to need to repeat this procedure a lot. Even if you do have a blade that fills those categories, you'll probably need to repeat yourself anyways. And I don't seem to recall giving many of you gladiuses. Or gladii, whatever the plural for that shit is. So work on repetition."

Everyone had a knife, if not on their armor then attached to a belt or a bandolier. Even Susan had a vicious trench knife attached to her mini plate carrier, the sheath jutting high up above her shoulder next to her chin, the grip's jagged guard poking its way towards her chin and down towards those arrays of submachine gun magazines. Gabe paused to pose once more, demonstrating the simple idea, holding his blade. "Remember, good grip, secure stance- repeated back and forth motion. Be vicious, get angry, drive yourself into a frenzy. Don't bother with anything fancy, you're all a bit too thick for that shit, especially in the heat of battle where all that fancy bullshit just becomes background noise in your head. Just stick to poking really hard. Follow this up with shooting or more stabbing. Just make sure at the end of the day they stop being a threat, one way or the other. Sure, if the other guy has a knife, you're probably going to get poked. You're probably going to get cut. It's gonna hurt, you're gonna see your own blood. But as long as you win that poking contest, you can live long enough to get to lick your wounds and whimper about the pain. That's what this is all about anyways, prolonging our misery. Got it?" Nods and "yeah"s permeated the atmosphere.

"Alright, class adjourned. You are all now knife fighting experts. We'll have a few more one on one lessons for stuff like wrist locks and how to disarm your opponent for the rest of the week before we start to work on working as a fireteam."

### Chapter 48

The day rolled on, to a point where the Sun came low to the horizon. Night was coming soon, and I sat near a window with an AR-15 in my lap, that same unease biting at me.

I felt antsy. Even if we were laying low and all and technically supposed to be taking things relatively easy, train the group while we wait out the siege, I still felt like there was something that needed doing, even if considered how hunting this morning would normally have made me quite exhausted. I still felt restless.

I found Gabriel in the garage, occupying himself with examining the guns for the umpteenth time. The old stereo system nearby was plugged into his MP3 player, and music was blaring. It was some rap track, something I don't think I'd ever heard before. It must've been a song from the turn of the century; Gabe liked that old stuff.

"Gabe," I blurted.

"Hm?" he didn't look up at me, he was busy inspecting another Armalite's chamber.

"Gabe?" I repeated, more impatiently this time, letting the AR in my hands clatter against the wall as I leaned it there haphazardly. He looked up at me finally, seeing me standing there like a zombie. I paused for a second. "What the fuck are we doing here?"

He didn't say anything at first. He looked back down at the gun. "Road's closed," he offered, going for a nearby cup now, taking a swig of water.

"That's bullshit," I said. "We should be thinking up a way around that blockade."

"Yeah. We should. But you know how it is. We shouldn't rush things, that's how mistakes happen."

"...The Citadel is so close," I sighed. "We should be there by now."

"You worried about your family?"

"I'm worried about them worried about me." Gabriel furled his lip a little bit. "And I'm worried about your boss."

"...I understand the apprehension, but I know the guy's modus operandi by heart. I'm on top of it." I wished I could believe it. By the way he was glaring darkly at me with a confident smile, he wished I believed him too.

"I... I'm gonna map out the blockade tomorrow."

"I'd go by foot. Vehicle might need to be ditched if you need to dodge a patrol. Be a shame to lose a survival automobile like that."

"I'm... I'm not gonna take a car," I responded, and he paused disassembling the AR to look at me.

"Oh, you're taking Green for a spin again? She's barely got her wings back," he noted.

"You know Lauren. She doesn't let things stop her that easy, especially when it comes to flying." Gabriel smirked.

"...Just so long as it doesn't end up like it did last time," Gabriel chuckled, back to work. "...She's outside getting them working again. You'll see her." I smirked again, wondering just what she was doing. I could already picture her eccentric acrobatics and it forced a real smile out of me.

I briskly walked outside into the front drive in this late orange afternoon, Sun hanging low in the distance. I could see the shadow cast long of the building and I turned, looking up at Lauren, sitting there at the very top of the roof above the attic window, sitting like a sphinx with her front talons barely drooping over the edge. Her arms were crossed and her wings were stretching, taking in the evening sun. Her eyes were closed, and she looked like she was meditating. For a second, I was taken aback by the sight. The world's most beautiful gargoyle basking in the world there in her sports shirt and braided ponytail. I laughed to imagine Gabriel's reaction.

For a while, I didn't say anything, just taking her in. She breathed slowly, the wind fluttering past. Her hair and wings waved, her sleeveless T-shirt lapping against her green side. Steam rose off of her wings in the hot Sun.

After a long while her eyes opened, cutting through the clear fog of this hot, humid day to see me standing down in the middle of the street staring up at her perched there, wings slowly closing more from where they'd been completely outstretched.

"Noah," she let out quietly in a gasp, as if surprised, though we'd been sharing a stare for so long. She got up, standing tall before me in the sun. The wind blew by harder, her sails waved, and those mocha brown, more-than-human eyes gazed into me. She smiled a little bit, before leaping off and gliding down, landing a few feet in front of me. It was the most graceful thing I'd ever seen, striking me as if this were a dream, watching the vapors trail off of the points of her wings, tracing her flight down. She walked up to me, and straining my neck to look up at her I could appreciate how much bigger she was than me. I wanted to remark on how she looked up there, but I didn't want to look like some kind of awkward idiot and I felt like it's what I'd look like if I did. I held my tongue, but as if she sensed what I was thinking, she spoke. "I was praying," she said slowly, explaining herself. She scratched her neck. "I just... I was thinking about God, you know? I felt thankful that my wings are starting to work again and I needed to thank somebody... Yeah, that kind of sounds dumb," She blushed a little.

"N-no, you love flying more than anything, it's not dumb," I said, nodding my head slowly. I must've sounded a little less than sure of myself. She must have taken this as a lack of enthusiasm on my part.

"...I dunno, Noah, I just..." she said, looking away and continuing to awkwardly scratch herself, as if embarrassed. I think she blushed a little bit.

"Wanna go flying?" It spilled out of my mouth and filled the air like it didn't belong there, an almost random interjection that I forced out. She paused, looking back at me. She smiled. I think she appreciated my awkward interruption, she wanted a topic change. "T-tomorrow. We coul- need to check out the blockade and take pictures."

"Sure," She uttered enthusiastically. "...Check out what Mr. Pendrew had," She motioned to her new hydration bladder strapped between the crux of her upper wings. "He fished this out of his old army stuff. Said I could have it," she beamed plainly, expositioning a little awkwardly. "...Just like my last one." In the moment I was too starstruck to really notice how goofy the subject change was.

"He's actually kind of nice, isn't he?" I didn't exactly know why I said this, he was pretty confrontational for all the times I'd interacted with him. But I guess the thought of him giving what I'd assume he'd think of as one of the most monstrous hybrids in our group a gift sort of persuaded me that he was a nice guy in actuality. It made sense in the abstract, after all.

"He said that at least I'd get a use out of it. I think he's just being nice because of his wife." I laughed aloud, and she chuckled along with my laughing, grinning happily with us together. "So what's up? You came out here just to let me know we've got a 'mission' tomorrow?" She bumped my arm a little with her knuckles, still smiling away with me.

"Yeah, pretty much," I teetered my head from side to side a little.

"Want to critique my form or something?" She offered, wings fluttering, done steaming. "I mean, I'd offer you a ride, but Mrs. Pendrew said, y'know," She teetered from side to side, rolling her eyes charmingly, like implying Mrs. Pendrew's implications were ill-placed, though deep down we both knew the old lady had a point.

"Yeah, sure," I said, and watched as Lauren rose her hand and sign "one moment please" with a little wink, before turning to advance to the house. I was a little perplexed watching her scaling the front overhang of the garage, going to climb up to the very roof by using the drainpipes, her long body pretty apt for climbing, making it look pretty effortless. "What, you need to take off from elevation or something?"

Still climbing but almost up there, Lauren snapped her fingers over her shoulder and pointed at me. "We have a winner, that's exactly right," She uttered and I chuckled, still standing there in the middle of the street lost in my awe. She let out a huff as she stood back up there, back where she started. "Gravity can eat my big green ass! You can't keep me down!" She laughed out and I laughed out with her as she barreled off with her wings spread, swooping low, one of her forelegs smacking me plainly in the head as I stood there and she rocketed off, swooping back up to the roof of the opposing house and turning about, raising her arms in victory while I laughed, sipping on her electrolytes before taking off once more, jumping from rooftop to rooftop, trotting along effortlessly before diving off the Pendrews' with a twist, barrel-rolling for a moment as I gasped, almost letting my worry get the better of me before she took off towards me in a green flash and this time I ducked down and laughed as she swiped to smack me with a foreleg again, turning around to watch her stall out and let out a little silent "Dammit!" as she shook her fist, having barely missed me. We were laughing and laughing. That feeling from earlier was gone. It didn't matter that the world was ending, it didn't matter that we had places to be. What mattered was this deep, deep peace I felt when I was with her.

"Noah." It felt like waking up from a dream, being forced to come back to everyone else. There I was, sitting at the kitchen table. Dinnertime. Squirrel, pigeon and rat stew with the usual Gabriel flair. I suppose it tasted pretty good considering the content. "Could you pass the salt?" Maria was asking me as I sat there. I'd been reliving Lauren's flight in my head for a while now. Where was she now? Oh yeah, eating her soup on the roof, doing her gargoyle thing. I should go out and watch her again after dinner. She's probably gotten her wings working a lot better by n

"Noah." A voice cutting through my wandering mind. "You want me to pass the salt for you?" Gabriel was there, sitting and eating beside me on the opposite side of Maria to me, still in his ridiculous apron. I blinked, grabbing it and putting it on Maria's side. Another flash of disassociation, dinner was done, there we were sitting on the couch watching one of the movies left from Frank. Some movie from a hundred years ago or something. Maria was on my side, leaning her head on mine and staring ahead. Where was Lauren? We all were here, even Selicia was there. She was trying to be more social, good for her. Anthony, sitting on the floor, was so engrossed in the movie he hadn't even realised he'd been leaning into the arachnea girl's belly for at least the last half hour, and she looked pretty content to be his headrest. Archie was laying in front, hands intertwined at his chest and leaning on Abel's bestial, secondary belly, Sam leaning her head on his humanoid one as well like he was some sort of ground couch, Abel looking from this angle like he was asleep, practically snoring. I could see everyone here, but Lauren. Was she still out flying? I felt uncomfortable here, shifting a little, Maria's skull knocking against mine and she straightened out from the little wake-up, leaning back. I wanted to get up and leave, so I did, muttering something about the bathroom, stepping over Abel and circling past Anthony and Selicia, Anthony becoming cognizant of me just as he realised that Selicia's arm was draped around his chest and his eyes instantly widened and he froze up. I'm sure if I stuck around for another minute I'd watch cold sweat bead on his forehead, his predicament as humorous as always, but in this state, this constant dissociation into the coming flight tomorrow, I could hardly take notice of it in anything but a passing emotion.

It was only when I arrived in the bathroom when I really questioned my state. Why exactly did I want to fly so much? I really did like spending time around Lauren. I… I think I might...

A knock at the door.

"Noah," Maria said as I stood there, practically clueless. Had I disassociated again? How long was I aimlessly standing here? "Noah," She said again. Not impatiently, but almost sweetly, like pleading. I opened the door, seeing her there, looking up at me with big eyes. "You… Okay?"

"…I'm just…" I began. Hell of a question. "Are you… I'm just kind of weirded out by this situation, y'know?" I said with a scoffing, forced laugh and she stood there without reciprocating one of her own. Like she expected me to go on even though that could have meant literally anything. "It's just this waiting game, okay?" I blurted. "I know that we can't just go, and I know we should train everybody, and we are, and that's good, but…" Suddenly her hands crawled around my hips as we stood in that doorway. Gazing into me, with those orbs. What calm mocha brown. I felt my breath in my chest, frozen solid, her cold hands practically digging into me.

"…That's good," She teetered her head from side to side. "I dunno. Gabriel's been pretty smart about everything lately. He seems like he's got this under control. But it's good that you want to keep moving forward." My brow furrowed. It wasn't like I already knew this.

"I'm tired," I suddenly uttered, moving away from her. I just wanted the next day to come. To see the blockade, right? That's why I was so eager to move forward in time?

"It's barely nine," Maria uttered.

"I'm going to bed."

I lay there, still lost in my own mind. God, this wasn't pleasant. I just wanted to get out there. I wanted to go. I wanted to

A blink and Maria was here again. I looked at the clock, an hour had passed. There she sat beside me on the bed, the lights on. She leaned in to kiss me, on the lips. Her lips were cold and I wanted to move away, still paralyzed by my staring at the ceiling by the time she finished, reared up over me.

I sat up, compelled to, as if by the kiss. I looked in Maria's eyes, and I couldn't help but think of Lauren, for just a second. A smile came across my face and I came in close to kiss her. Her hand went up and placed a finger upon my lips and she glared at me with an icy smile.

"I'm still pissed at you," she hissed, turning away. I stared at her back as she turned around, waggling her rear end a little as she undressed. She wasn't wearing her usual sport panties, these were black lace. She undressed, before turning around, still with an angry little smirk on her face. "What do you want, Noah?" She said, rather playfully, though not without a showy anger.

"What do you have?" I asked. A joke seemed appropriate. She kept on smirking, crawling onto the bed as I laid back down there, watching, waiting.

"Good question," She came in for another slow kiss. I did my best to reciprocate. "But you know what I want?"

"Is this about the marriage thing?" She rolled her eyes, coming to lay down beside me, intertwining her fingers on her chest and staring up at the ceiling just like I was.

"I wish *I* could fly sometimes," Maria sighed. "I'd fly you all the way to the Citadel." I smirked along.

"You should go flying with Lauren if you really want to- we've, she got a saddle," I said. Maria rolled her eyes.

"...D-do you like her?" She asked, more tired than accusing. She couldn't bring herself to accuse me of anything. Not here. Not yet.

"As a person, yeah," I uttered awkwardly.

"Really now?" her brow raised.

"No, I don't have feelings for her," I clarified. The truth as far as I was willing to think about it.

"You don't like her and that weird-ass body of hers? You think her ass is better than mine? You like a big ass?" She said, giggling a little. That giggle felt a little forced and my mind flashed for a moment that this conversation implied more than it was.

"I'm not into her!" I said. We were both smiling, but at the same time I knew we were having a very, very serious conversation. "I love your silky black hair, and your little sharp smile- and your eyes are so dark, but radiant-" I paused, for a second. "And that fire you breathe takes my breath away," I jested. She smiled.

"I've always liked dragons," She began anew, after a soft pause. "What if *you* were a dragon?"

"You mean, like Lauren?"

"I mean like the real ones, the ones that are huge and breathe fire and eat people," She said.

"Well they're not the real ones any more, are they? The real ones are like Lauren."

"You never know, maybe they made some like that." Maria chuckled. "Yeah. Maybe one might come and show Lauren who's boss," She laughed a little and I laughed along with her.
  "...Yeah. I think I'd like to be one like that, personally." I looked over to Maria upon her saying this, my brow raising. I saw her face sort of scrunch up as it escaped her mouth. Did she mean to say that? Was it a slip or something? I couldn't tell.

"Seriously?"

"Always been told I have a fiery personality," She uttered, still looking away. "It'd be... fun."

"Huh."

"...But *you* don't, Noah?"

"I dunno, I'm fine with being human."

"You like flying with Lauren, don't you? Enough to do it twice." Three times, I almost corrected.

"Yeah, but..." I didn't have much to say, my mind lingering on my silenced correction, like something that was about to be implied. "This is a weird conversation."

"...Yeah."


I felt her body, those supple hips and her slender, yet powerful muscles bound like wire upon her arms, letting one of my fingers trace down the side of her thigh. I sighed. She slowly kissed me on the cheek, rearing back a little and gazing into me for a couple of seconds. I followed her prompt to curl my arm around her and knelt up, taking my shorts off as she lay there winking up to me, doing her best to smile for me, a hand coming around my head to pull me in close again. Another kiss and we'd begin. Consummate the marriage we were soon to have, she must have thought.


There I was, standing alone in the middle of a bustling venue, surrounded by moving, writhing bodies, everyone busy on their way to the various attractions around us. The sounds of glee, the scent of sweet fried foods, and the iridescent glow of lights surrounding us led me to realise we stood in a theme park of sorts, packed to the brim, and with twilight upon us. Off in the distance, the lights glimmered on the ocean's surface, dancing this way and that as the waves caressed them.

**We**. I felt the presence of another, not a stranger but an... accomplice. Trusted friend, more than that. **She** followed along with me, talking and laughing and simply existing with me.

Who is she?

She felt very familiar, standing there with me. I knew who she was. I just didn't know, **who** she was. My mind swam. The people around us whisked by in a flash, as I lost myself in the singularity of her eyes.

Human. Yeah, she was a human, but why was that standing out to me? It's not like I'd ever known anything else than humans. Human. No alternative. I could lose myself in her eyes. I was used to humans. She was beautiful, and I wanted to embrace her, to kiss her, to proclaim my love, but there was something. Something in the air, something about her very aura. Something was strange. Something was off.

I've never seen this girl, this woman before, yet I have.

We entered a church. A pastor was reading wedding rites, and I stood there in my tuxedo, with her, my bride, opposite me. I felt glee. Happiness. Finally getting what I'd been missing for so long. but something was biting at me. She was beautiful but I'd never seen her before. I loved her like no other and I knew her close, but I'd never seen her before. She looked alien. Inhuman. But how was that possible? Was somebody lying to me? Was she? Was I?

"And you, Noah Reed," The pastor began. "Do you pledge to cherish and love… all of your days, 'till death do you part?" Like a piece had been cut right out of his voice where she'd supposed to have been. Haze standing next to me. The love of my life made of television static.

I said nothing. I stared at her. She was ecstatic, I saw it in her brown eyes, in the waving of her long brown hair beneath her wedding shawl, an ear to ear smile on her radiant face. She awaited my words. She looked like she'd never been happier. and I knew I ought to have been happy here with her, and I was. Wasn't I?

I didn't say anything. Like a zombie, I stepped away. "Mr. Reed?" The pastor asked, as the smile disappeared from this strange, inhuman human face. I stumbled down the aisle, looking about at the faces gawking at me. Masks, caricatures. People I knew but didn't know. Twisting plastic and wood and metal masks, grinding themselves up.

"Look at you, with that thing," I heard the voice of my father echo in a whisper. I turned to face a silent mask, sitting in the front row. His head swiveled to look at me. None of these masks were happy. None of these plastic faces smiled.

"N-Noah?!" She cried. **Lauren** cried. She wasn't beautiful here. I didn't look back at her in her terrible, ugly, *wrong* form. I wept because I couldn't see anything but a façade standing there. I shielded my tearful face and made a break for the exit.

I stumbled for the doorway and light hit my eyes.

### Chapter 49

The morning came and Maria was draped across my bare chest. I was still gazing up into the ceiling, blinking, as she too was writhing forth from slumber, still less than conscious. I suppose I was too. For a moment I wanted to peel her off, leave her to let her sleep, but she gripped around me reminding me she was awake. She brought her face up to mine in silence, as if expecting a kiss, and in my stupor I never gave one. She leaned in to place one on my neck instead, smiling up at me. I saw how her hair was all hanging in her face, how she blew an errant strand away to giggle. I guess it was charming.

I began to sit up, as if to force my way out of this situation. The sun was up, there was an itinerary to attend to. But she put her weight on my chest and forced me down. "H-hey," I began.

"Hey, c'mon," She uttered softly, less of a command and more of a plea, ever so subtly as I grunted. "We never do this anymore."

"What?" I was almost prompted to brashly utter 'cuddle after sex' as a joke, seeing as we'd only gotten this intimate once before, but didn't feel the need.

"Let's just… just feel the moment, okay?" Maybe 'cuddle' wasn't the right word for her either. "Just... be together."

A minute or two passed, until I tried to get up again. She did not try to stop me, though she silently stared at me- glared, perhaps, as I distanced myself. She sat up with me but did not get out of bed as I did, and I took one glance back. I saw her shiver, looking to the window. I sighed. I had an itinerary to attend to.

Finally back in the air, I didn't feel so restless. My legs stopped shaking, the world stopped being just light and sound, and my mind cleared. up here, in between those two great, powerful sets of sails beating, Lauren's streamlined form brimming with power and heat that shot us forward at incredible speed, everything felt so much more simple, like everything below could be explained more succinctly. On the ground there was so much to be done, so much to organize. But up here I could just draw a line through the streets leading north; it felt like I knew exactly how to solve every problem, and all the ones I couldn't solve didn't matter.

"Sooo, Noah," Lauren said, popping her lips, making quippy smalltalk as we glided along, evidently letting her giddiness take control "You're being pret-ty quiet." She paused for a long time after another pop of her lips, and I didn't speak, feeling this to be a segue, not to mention smiling at her cheeky prodding and hoping to receive more of her cute banter. "Checking, out... *The blockade.*" Her pauses, tone and enunciation were practically comical. "Hell of an *excuse*, huh?"

"Excuse?" I asked, finally, and she was ever eager to extrapolate.

"You know, your excuse for wanting to fly with me," She finally presented. I chuckled. "I know you *want* to fly. Hell, everybody should want to fly; that's why we're doing this. But *checking out the blockade*? What a lousy excuse."

"I can't just fly with you if I want to? I need an excuse?" I prodded through a smile, despite not really needing to, Lauren proceeding to banter anyways.

"Well, what are you gonna tell Maria?" Lauren said, her playfulness taking a backseat for a moment. "I mean, it's not like she trusts me."

"What's that supposed to mean?" I asked.

"Well... you know," Lauren said. "She thinks I like you. I- I mean, I do, but... you know. N-not like that, of course. She thinks I'll *steal you away* or something," She laughed.

"She'll be fine," I sighed. "...You seen the blockade yet?" I quickly spat out to change the topic once more.

"I've seen it. Lots of tanks, not much action."

"Who else has seen it besides me?" I asked.

"What, other people have?" She said. "I just caught a glimpse while flying in my warmup. I didn't get too close though."

"Was Gabriel with you?" I asked.

"No," She responded. I sat back. "Gabriel's seen it?" she asked, before pausing. "...Oh, who am I kidding. He's a savant. Of course he did."

"Yeah, idiot savant," I growled.

"You should give him more credit," Lauren said. "We'd be worse off without him."

"What, you forget all about him taking jabs at you?" I said.

"I think he's kind of charming," she mused. "I don't think he's really mean. Like, I think he just *tries* to be that way. He doesn't *mean* it."

"What, why? you think he thinks it's fun? Because I bet he does," I said.

"Well, maybe," she sighed, before going on. "But maybe he's just afraid of showing people he can be a nice guy. It... He kind of feels... tragic. I think somebody broke his heart once." I sighed in silence, and Lauren paused for a long time. "How long have you known him?" She asked.

"Second grade," I sighed, after counting in my head.

"So what, ten years?" she asked. "Was he any different back then?"

I paused for a long time. "Yeah," I finally sighed, almost painfully.

"How so?"

"He was... I dunno. Nicer. Friendly. A real dork. He used to be kinda... Kinda chubby, too." Lauren chuckled a little bit.

"You remember how you met him?" She prodded further.

"What, are you gonna ask how I proposed to him next?" I joked. She gave a tiny laugh.

"C'mon. You gotta remember," She said. I sighed again.

"...I dunno the first time we met. But I remember the day we became friends." Lauren was trailing off of every word, gliding along there slowly as she could, turning her head a little and gazing at me, blinking. The wind wasn't so harsh now with the speed she was going, lazily flapping her wings along but mostly coasting, listening intently. "I'd see him around, we might have ate lunch together even if he was a grade above me. One day a bunch of kids were picking on me for something, and just as they were getting rough and pushed me down... He came in out of nowhere and started swinging, like he was crazy. I was just as scared of him as the rest of them. He... he called me a pussy faggot and told me to get up and fight," I was laughing at this point in the memory.

"...Man, that's pretty much what I'd expect," Lauren laughed along. "...What a bad-ass. Hah."

"Not really, we still got our asses kicked," I uttered, glossing over her joking tone, still chuckling. "We got suspended for the fight and hung out after it all. I didn't really regret it. It was kind of funny." Lauren 'humph'ed along with me in the amusing thought, as I went on, reminiscing about him some more. "He, he moved here from California, with his dad. I mean, he was nicer back then, but he was still an ass. He'd get into fights all on his own, although he wouldn't win very many of them. He was always in trouble, mostly because he'd accidentally tattle on himself since he had such a big mouth. Eventually he kinda learned not to, I guess. Had to."

"Sounds like a fun guy," She responded.

"Yeah, well, at least he was like that until around highschool started. I mean, we're a year apart, so we spent a year in different schools between eighth and freshman year. We played games and stuff, but he changed around then, must've been from the Cartel around then. Until I learned the truth, I thought maybe he realised how weird and intense he was and he was trying to tone it down, but I always felt like he'd got some shit on his mind, never could have guessed that he got hired as a trained killer." I laughed nervously.

"Huh, yeah," Lauren cooed in awe. "Does... *Did* he have any other family?"

"All I know is he doesn't like his dad. I never met his mom, she died of cancer. But he always talked about how his dad was a dick. At first, it wasn't that much, we'd joke about it, but when the years went on, I could really feel some... Some real, animosity, between them or something. I'd met him a couple times- if anything, he just seemed really mopey and frustrated. Even though he was living with him, and knew how his dad was providing for him, Gabe never seemed to have any respect for him, and always shit-talked him behind his back. But Gabriel never blatantly tried to piss the man off, it just sort of happened, and after a while Gabe kinda couldn't help but do it. Like, he'd always be getting on his case to the point where Gabe just wouldn't even talk about his dad, it was just the norm for him to be in hot water."

"Did he have any siblings?"

"I never met any. I don't think so." Off, in the distance, I could see where the suburbs ended. "...We're coming up on the blockade now, looks like," I said. "Spiral around and sail past. Try and stick behind that cloud over there. Don't get too close or they'll see how you don't have an IR marker." Lauren beat her wings in unison a couple of times, gaining some altitude. We soared over the suburbs. Out here, in the very outskirts, it was very quiet. Back around our own base just barely in the quiet part of town there were some people, but out here nothing looked alive, save for the blockade in the distance, silent gunnery camps with the thin smoke of campfires rising above all.

In determined silence, I zoomed in on a pair of tac glasses. Lauren soared overhead, and I quickly clicked a couple pictures. I could see the trash-piled roads, a couple tanks in the fields, all inactive, their big gun turrets staring off into the northern distance with camped-out crews sitting idly by. they stretched not only across the highway, but across the nearby fields as well, dug in. Behind them all as added measure, sentry turrets were sitting there, scanning with quiet beeps every now and then. As we circled slowly around the latitudinal perimeter of the blockade, I took picture after picture of each blocked road and clearing, hoping that at least later I'd be able to find an opening when I took a good look. Whatever way there was through the blockade, I wasn't seeing it right now.

"Land over there," I said, motioning to an old house nearby, after a couple passes worth of pictures.

"So, how about your family? I know about your dad, but who else?" she asked now that the suspenseful business was mostly over, gliding us down on silent, misty wings.

"I... I've got a little sister," I said. "Rica. She's... Twelve."

"Aw, cute," Lauren responded. "Is she up with your dad?"

"Yeah," I sighed. a wave of emotions hit me that I was trying to ignore. Worried about everyone worried about me.

We touched down on the back porch of some quiet, uninhabited-looking house. For a very awkward, airheaded second as I'd vaulted off her saddle I almost asked Lauren about her family, before feeling incredibly stupid and somewhat douchey of even thinking of such a thing. I just felt stupid, standing there in silence as she said a few words, and I was still swimming in my mind to find something to say, some way to reciprocate the conversation.

"...I think I'd be good with kids," She was uttering, and I was pulled back out of my own stupor. "I mean, I'm good with Susan- but she don't really count as a *kid*, I guess... a teen or tween or something," She thought aloud.

"Y-yeah," I spouted. She looked over to me and smiled a little, emitting a silent chuckle as we paced. "I mean, you'd be great with kids," I quickly affirmed. "You don't look *that* scary," I said, and she let out a laugh.

"*Raar*," she growled in jest. "Watch out, the big bad dragon's gonna eat you!" She said, and I chuckled along. We paused together to gather our thoughts. "I mean, I don't really think I'm scary anymore… I'm not, am I?" she asked. "With the horns and everything? Er, horn, singular?" She muttered with a motion to her remaining horn, trying to keep things light with a faded smile, though I could tell her inquisition was reaching a little bit.

"No, no, of course not," I responded quickly, not really trying to keep the laughable atmosphere going. Lauren began to pace towards the house, lips furrowed, her head shaking a little to herself. She might've been looking at her reflection in the windows of the house.

"Yeah, I guess I'm more used to this body," She uttered before letting out a dry chuckle. "…Listen to me, talkin' like I've ever been in a different one."

"Hey, your wings are working again, that's good," I noted, and she sighed, trying to smile for my sake.

"Yeah. Yeah they are. I'm trying to appreciate that, I guess, it's just…" A worried sigh escaped her mouth. "I mean, I just… I'm wearing a *saddle*, Noah. I feel a *little* ridiculous."

"Would you rather be wearing a skirt?" I asked, as she walked into the house. I followed, through the living room as we made our way from the backyard to the front of the house. The house was cold, empty. some windows were smashed. Chairs were overturned, and the television was missing. The pantry, cooking cupboard and fridge were ajar and empty, ceramic dining plates had been tossed from the table setting cabinets and I crunched over them in my boots, Lauren's four bare feet gingerly rifling their way around them.

"You know…" She said. "Call me weird if you want, but… I've been working on a design for one."

"Huh," I uttered breathlessly, glaring over to her in subdued, playful antagonism.

"Don't laugh," she said playfully. "C'mon. I'm serious."

"I'm listening," I responded. She smiled and looked down, as we walked into the foyer. The front door was ajar, an X across it; the republicans had already fully sacked it of everything of value. A draft wafted through sending a shiver through my spine.

"I mean, it's just, put the same kinda fabric over my rear body," She said. "Kinda so, if I sat my lower body down, it'd look more like I'm norm… uh, y'know, not a 'taur. At a distance, at least. You know?" She inquired, somewhat awkwardly.

"Trying to disguise yourself?" I chuckled. "Sounds like it'd kinda work," I responded. She smiled again, more confidently this time. "Between that and your saddle… It's too bad the world is ending, or else I'd say you'd be the next big thing in fashion." She laughed.

"Heh, sure," She was quick to brush me off, but doubled back as she took in my words. "Wuh- was the pun intended?" She asked, still laughing a little, as we crossed outside, walking down the road, passing downed cars, long since burned out, not deemed worthy enough to be hauled off for scrap by the Republicans.

"Pun?" I asked, oblivious.

"You know… *big thing*," she said. "…Me, big thing, giant freakin' dragon-centaur,"

"Oh," I said, it dawning on me. "Heh. Sorry about that." She smiled, a little more bounce in her step.

"I... Your dad will be alright with me, right?" She asked, and I slowed a little hearing it.

"Didn't we already talk about this?" I asked. She let out a chuckling grunt, still smiling meekly.

"...It's just that... I mean, you guys were alright with me, and you let all the other hybrids into your, our group pretty easily... But what about the people at the citadel? I bet most of them haven't seen a hybrid before, it's still worrying me."

"Well, I never saw a hybrid before you," I said. "Aside from like, on the news and stuff. And I'm alright with you, aren't I?"

"I guess so," She said.

"...I think a few of the old guys might be a little wary about it, but I'll vouch for you. My dad's respected in there. and if they don't let you in, I won't go in either."

"J-jeez, Noah," Lauren said.

"What?" I asked. "We're a *family*. We've been through all this together. I couldn't turn my back on you, and I won't. If they don't like you, fuck 'em."

"...Getting pretty dramatic for big ol' me?" Lauren almost laughed at my sudden display of chivalry and I rolled my eyes a little, pausing. "I mean, don't get me wrong, I appreciate the thought."

"...My dad always told me about loyalty," I sort of began my soft topic change. "...and how important it is to choose the right friends... You know, my dad said a lot of stuff that I never really thought of. But... Heh. It took the shit hitting the fan for me to listen."

"I bet he never said anything about dragon-centaurs, huh?" Lauren said with a little introspective chuckle.

"He said a lot about expecting the unexpected," I answered. "Always bet on something you never planned for happening. That's what he'd say."

"Good advice," Lauren responded with an ample nod. "Hey, also," she began anew, patting her side. "Check it out. I know I said we'd fly light but I couldn't resist testing this out- That rifle scabbard Mr. Pendrew had was more for a lever-action rifle so ARs stick out of it some, but I got this buckle so it stays in more securely, Threw a couple magazine pouches onto the straps too. Cordura and leather don't really match but I think I can pull it off alright. Neat, huh?" I was looking over her work, smiling along, more than charmed, seeing I looked over, seeing the butt end of the old-fashioned A2 stock sticking out, the buckle clasped around the high end of where the pistol grip met the receiver.

"Huh, damn," I said. "That's pretty cool." She beamed in pride. "You know, I meant what I said about you and fashion, you've got a gift for this," I said, and she blushed a little.

"Oh, come on," she said, looking down with a big grin on her face. "I'm not trying to make things look pretty, that's more Selicia's bit. I make ugly things that work."

"Hey, if it looks ugly but performs beautifully, it ain't ugly," I uttered with a smirk, still trotting side by side with her and feeling the breeze waft through the neighborhood.

"You sure that's how the saying goes?" She prodded, and I rolled my eyes as she grinned, tilting her head towards me.

"...What other designs do you have?" I asked.

"Oh, I've got a few," She began, bridling her enthusiasm. "Mr. Pendrew also gave me some old welding gloves, I'm going to make... See, I don't know to call them shoes or gloves," She uttered, slowing, raising a foreleg, that hand-like frontal talon displayed. "Like, I walk with my front feet of course, but they look like... stubby hands. I'm barefoot- bare foothanded?" I laughed along. "Stop laughing! I'm serious, what do I call these?!" She laughed along, twiddling her toe-fingers.

"I just think of them as talons, like on a bird," I chuckled. "...So you need... bootgloves, got it. Gloveboots."

"Yeah, I'm gonna start with those, try and re-fit his welding gloves for my... talons, thicken the pads so if I step on a nail I don't get stabbed. I'm thinking some of the spare kevlar we've got from the police vest that... y'know." She stopped dead, trying to avoid bringing up Wilson, and for a moment my heart ached too, remembering his fate, shuddering. In retrospect it was almost weird how I'd sort of repressed him up until now. I almost felt bad for it. I guess it was the situation, that it wasn't quite the time to grieve with our adventure ahead of us, in spite of our current stalling. "...I've also got an idea for what to do with my back legs, though- they've got like, more traditional paws, y'know? Archie has some weird custom-made shoes for his own feet and he's got paws instead of feet, I'm thinking of copying that design, maybe taking them apart to get a better understanding or something while he's not paying attention," Lauren smirked. "After that I'm gonna work on body armor, see what Gabriel can't cough up. I'd like to work with soft armor but Gabriel tells me that stuff is no good against rifle rounds, and..." She stopped, again remembering Wilson. "I think I'll stick with the high-density polymer that Gabriel got for all of us since he has a couple spare plates from the run into the facility. Steel and ceramid don't really sound that great for flying, even if they can stop more bullets."

"Sure," I said. "Just don't go overboard. You try and cover your whole body with armor and you won't be able to fly, lightweight poly-armor or not." She smirked a little, nodding like she'd already taken this into consideration but was humoring me.

"Got any other pictures to take?" She asked, waving about.

"I got everything I needed to," I said.

"Good, because my wings are pretty tired."

"...We barely flew that much."

"Hey, how about I ride on *your* back next time," She snarled back, still smirking. "Doctor said I should take it easy, so I am. We've got legs, so let's... *leg* it. Capiche?"

"...I thought you only knew English and sign language," She shrugged antagonistically with a couple brief handsigns I couldn't make out, beginning to walk. I followed, not really pressing her further. Did I miss flying? I bet I did. I guess spending more time with her was anything but a punishment.

"...Got any plans yet?" She asked, and I ditzily wondered about what the rest of my life would entail, thinking she was asking what I'd do at the citadel. "...To escape the city."

"Uh..." I came back to the actual topic like a shock to my brain. "I mean, I've got one but it's not pretty. We could all just walk there through the forest and ditch the vehicles. We'd run out of supplies though and we'd probably reach the citadel half starved at the very best."

"Ooh, I can hear the groans and the complaining now," Lauren laughed and I laughed along, the two of us trotting on down that road, Lauren out in front. "Hey, guess who," Lauren began, reaching back for her braid of hair and tossing it out in front over an eye, the thing flopping onto her muzzle. "Ughhhh, that's likeee, an issue in the society that we live in today, uhhhhhh, tha's *problematiccc*," Lauren sulked, drooping her arms and wings and slouching.

"Selicia?" Lauren laughed with a roll of her eyes.

"It's Sam, you dork," Lauren chuckled on, flipping her hair back out of her face again and straightening out.

"...Archie would have been my second guess." Lauren let out a burst of a laugh at this as we shared the joke. It was fun not being serious for once. I saw her laughing and I felt a lightness in my chest, as she looked back at me mid-laugh. Like a sudden twitch, my hand, still being sensed by my hologlasses' haptic controls, made the camera motion and I'd taken a picture of her, shining in the sunlight that filtered through the humid mists in shimmering bands of gold, her big brown eyes bright and looking into me, happy as can be. A perfect image, a snapshot in time of pure bliss. My first instinct was to delete this mistake, but as I saw the image preview in the corner of my HUD, I couldn't help but feel I was doing the very universe a disservice to delete such a flawless moment, so I saved it.

I took off my glasses for the rest of the way, to forget about distractions, just to be with her. We turned down the blocks to walk back towards our base in relative silence, just enjoying the company, the sunlight warm but the breeze refreshing in its wake. Everything was just right. We could forget about the war, forget about the gravity of the situation. Forget about everything and just be.

It was a couple minutes of walking before we saw it.

Down the road, so distant he looked like a brown speck on the horizon, a deer stood alone, near a burned out car, chewing on some weeds spurting from the cracks nearest to the woods across the street.

"Oh, shit," Lauren gasped. Before I had even thought of it, her hand was on the stock of her gun. Fumbling only slightly, she drew it from the oversized holster, taking the grip and clicking the safety off. I got a good look at the gun, one of the full-length Armalites with a dot sight; Gabriel had took off the long flash hider and had installed one of those handmade silencers made out of an old flashlight.

*Crack*. The gun went off, the supersonic bullet piercing the sound barrier despite the silencer muffling the burst and flash of powder. The supersonic bullet screamed through the sky, and I saw the deer reflexively jump a bit, as through the humid air a steamy bullet trail traced its way towards and finally into its body in the blink of an eye. Like that, it was away with a shot, back into the forest, the snap echoing as the shell casing tinkered across the ground.

"Did you get him?" I barked quickly, grabbing for the shell on the ground, still looking up.

"I think so," She said, panting, as if the simple act of pulling that trigger took her breath away.

"Quick," I said, and we sprinted towards it. I saw, on the road, a splash of blood, leading away. "Yeah, he's hurt. Badly," I said, looking back to her. I looked up, seeing her holding her gun limp in her hands, eyes sparkling in apprehension and anxiety, yet willful determination, as she closed her mouth to gulp down. "Try and track him from the sky. I'll look down here," I commanded. she nodded hastily, spreading her wings and leaping into the sky with a burst of air. I weaved my way through the forest, following the blood trail. I could practically smell it, the smell of blood. And in a few long minutes, I found it, laying there in a tiny clearing, bloody and tired, with a wide-eyed Lauren standing over him with her gun still in her hands. I came up next to her, moving slowly, and placing my hand on her side, near where her lower body met her humanoid part. She didn't say anything, just gasping a little to herself. Her gun shook ever so slightly, like she didn't know what to do, weapon still pointing at the dying animal like an enemy. "Don't waste another bullet," I told her. "If you fire one shot, all anyone knows is that somebody fired a gun. If you fire two you're easier to triangulate." I noted.

"I-I'll remember that," She shuddered out as if still on autopilot, nodding her head.

"Knife?" I asked. She pointed to her side, near where she kept her spare magazines on her bandolier, showing a micarta handle sticking out of a kydex sheath strapped down with paracord. I pulled out the knife, a long, thick slab of metal- an old Junglas knife just like my old one, the finish on it far more worn down. "Come here," I said, as I knelt down. she drew closer, down near the deer, laying down on her lower belly, humanoid half still upright as usual. I held the blade, before looking at the deer. I could see panic and pain in its eyes, its chest heaving and blood bubbling from its side. I felt a little sick looking at it- I couldn't imagine how Lauren felt. She looked terrified.

"Here," I whispered, taking her clammy, almost limp hand from her gun and putting the knife in it, feeling her tense up. I took the rifle to place it aside and I pointed to a spot under where the entry wound was. "The heart is right here."

"Noah," she whispered in a whine. her eyes were welling up. "Won't you do it?"

I stared at her, long and hard. Even though I had been projecting him all this time, the next words that came out of my mouth felt as if they weren't even from me at all, but 100 percent my father. "You started it, you finish it," He told me, the first time I hunted. I think I was twelve. My father pointed to the heart. I held my knife in my shaking little hands. Tears were ebbing at my eyes, as I looked down at my prey, defenseless and terrorstruck. What if I missed the heart? I couldn't do it. I could shoot it, but I couldn't *stab* it, could I? There's a disconnect when you're 200 meters away behind a rifle pulling a trigger, but a knife? That was barbaric!

His words remained. Finish what you started.

The knife fell with a tiny growling scream of emotion from the wielder, puncturing the animal. It let out one last heave, before the wide bestial eyes fluttered and dimmed. Lauren's human eyes held a universe of difference speaking a million emotions. The color in her face drained, as she drew out her bloody blade with a sickly scrape through rib. Her empty hand stroked the fur of the dead animal, as her other clutched the little sword so hard it shook, having slain the beast.

"*G-god*," Lauren cried in prostration, her voice but a hoarse whisper, tears ebbing at her eyes. She said this in the religious sense, not as some expletive but like a tiny prayer. My hand came around to pat her, as my other went for her shaking, gripped hand, taking the blade away to wipe and put back in her scabbard.

"...Good job."

### Chapter 50

"So, uh," Lauren slowly began again as we wandered wordlessly beside the road, her eyes flashing about in weary apprehension, a little self-assuring smile on the corners of her muzzle. "We can have this for lunch, right?" She asked.

"Well, dinner, we gotta carve it up and cook it first," I replied. Both of my hands were carrying big plastic bags of entrails. She was carrying the gutted carcass on her back with the rifle back in its sheath, one of her hands reaching back somewhat awkwardly to keep it from falling off. She didn't say anything, looking down the road for a couple moments. We were close by to our place. "Good thing the Republicans don't think that plastic baggies are worth taking from the exed-out houses," I chuckled as I hefted the gross guts. "This stuff will make good bait. We can go fishing in the streams or in that lake."

"Let's remember to invite the Pendrews over for supper," She put forth. "They gave *us* food, they didn't rat us out- you know."

"Well, yeah, of course we're gonna invite them," I responded. I looked over to her, seeing her still staring down the road breathlessly. Our cul-de-sac was within eyesight. "Good idea."

"Mhm," she responded, and nodded to herself. "They're nice people. We could use more nice people these days." She paused again. "More... love for our neighbors."

I paused, turning to look at her a little bit. "Love for our neighbors, huh?" I asked.

"Y-yeah," she said. "You know. It's... It's the right thing to do. The... Christian thing."

"That sounds really corny." I guess my scoffing was inadvertent, and after I'd said it I felt sort of like a jerk, but Lauren was there to reprimand me with a quivering playfulness.

Lauren "tsk"ed. "There you go, sounding like Gabriel." And that was all it took for me to hold my tongue there on in- not that it mattered, seeing as our street was upon us, and we soon turned the corner. "Oh!" Lauren let out, seeing Mr. Pendrew sitting there in his usual chair on his porch, accompanied by his dog that raised its head when he saw us, a tiny whine barely picked up by my distant ears. "Hi, Steve!"

"That's Mr. Pendrew to you," He said somewhat sourly, glaring at her- at first in his usual cynical disgust, then his glare turned somewhat analytical, making note of my bag of entrails and rifle, and the fact that Lauren most obviously was carrying something on her elongated back. "what-" he paused. "...Were you two *hunting*?"

"Yep," Lauren peeped cheerfully, biting back her sense of pride.

"You stupid kids. You could have gotten yourselves killed, you know that?" He barked in exasperation. "If one of those thugs saw you with that gun you'd've been shot on the spot." I could only shrug and laugh, covering up my feeling of realisation as to what he'd said with humor, as if finding it funny. Lauren evidently did the same, nervously laughing at the danger we'd just been through. Not to mention her adrenaline must've still been in her system and it was like lazily coming down from a high. Mr. Pendrew grunted, less than amused, shifting in his seat. "At least tell me you killed it in one shot," He barked at me.

"Yessir, I did," Lauren pointed out, beaming, not even hiding her pride at this point. Mr. Pendrew scoffed, and I think for the first time ever, I saw him actually smile, if only unintentionally.

"No shit, huh?" He said, almost flabbergasted. "*You* shot him?"

"Musta been two hundred yards," Lauren boasted. I didn't know about *that* but I figured I'd let her have it. "He didn't make it half that far before giving up."

"So one shot, huh? You finish him off like you're supposed to?" He asked. She nodded, reaching back slightly to pat the knife on the side of her saddle. "Huh. Surprised you didn't use your claws."

"Yeah, didn't get those- I can't wait for the update to come out so I can get some instead of these boring human-y hands, you know?" she joked, waving her free hand again. Mr. Pendrew didn't laugh, but he did smile more, so I suppose he was being cordial. "Well, uh, *Mr. Pendrew*," Lauren began, adding slight emphasis to his name. "Would you like to come to dinner- er, lunch, or whenever we get this thing cooked?" she asked, and shrugged one of her frontal leg's shoulders and turning slightly, as if to show the deer off.

Mr. Pendrew grunted, leaning forward suddenly. "Well, I suppose," he said. "After all, you'll need somebody who knows what he's doing to skin it."

"Mr. Pendrew, I can assure you I'm more than capable," I spoke up, not exactly offended yet not exactly impartial to his snide comment.

Mr. Pendrew scoffed. "You? You're a kid. What would you know about that?"

"My father taught me all about it. I've done it before," I insisted.

"Really, city boy?" he growled.

"well, c'mon, it's not exactly like you're from the sticks yourself," I shot back, somewhat impatient and more than hungry and fatigued.

"Don't get smart with me, boy. I've been here since this town started. I remember when they started building apartment complexes here back in the '30s. I remember when being part of this community *meant* something," He growled on.

"Look, Mr. Pendrew," Lauren led up to, still smiling, despite her exasperated tone. "Wou'dja like to come over or not?" She asked, and he, grunting, finally got up.

"Yeah, yeah," he groaned. "I'll tell my wife. Be right over."


Going in, I was greeted by the gang, who all gazed wide-eyed at our catch. Lauren beamed and blushed all the more, breathing in heavily and slowly, trying to mask her pride. Gabriel came up and remarked quickly on her bounty, and I hung back, to let her take in her accomplishment in full. I stood there, watching, seeing the faces, as I scanned the room. I saw how Lauren glowed in the accomplishment as she slammed it down on the dining table with a laugh, radiating with joy despite how she smelled of deer guts and was covered in blood.

Gabriel butchered the carcass with a machete, going to cook it on the grill, seasoning the meat and chatting with Mrs. Pendrew who helped with the cooking. Mr. Pendrew and I sat together, working over the skin with knives after stringing it up, with Lauren sitting nearby. I did my best to teach her, and she seemed to catch on quick. Of course, Mr. Pendrew had plenty to say.

"See, you've got the angle wrong," He critiqued. "You're not doing it right. You're gonna leave too much fat and fuck it up."

"It's getting there," I responded. "I'm not done with it yet."

"No shit you're not done with it, you ought to do the whole thing over again," he snarled. He grunted, scooting over so he could work closer to my half of the skin. "Let me do this." I, somewhat worn down by his demeanor, let him do as he pleased, and he toiled away as I held the skin taut. He toiled away with those hands of his, somewhat arthritic with sores and large, blocky joints. He worked with the utmost focus, bearing down on it yet staying gentle, almost in a respectful manner. "Beautiful creature," he let out in a winded sigh. "This'll do nice when it's done." He continued on, if not to look up and see Abel on the grass in the edge of his vision, using the grass to scratch his back. "Good thing you ain't a dog one like he is, or else you might be doing that kinda stupid lookin' shit," He remarked to Lauren nearby. "Must be some kinda genetic thing that makes them dumber."

"Uh... Thanks?" she remarked, not particularly able to categorize what level of offensive the old man's words would be under.

"Yeah, yeah," he said, and there was silence for a long couple of seconds. "...I've got a question, Green. Do you sleep on the floor or in a bed?" He asked.

"E-excuse me?"

"What, you deaf?" he growled impatiently. "Pffft... Let me rephrase that. Do they make you sleep on the floor like an animal? And if they don't, where do you centaur-lookin' freaks rather sleep?"

"Uh... *They* let me sleep wherever I want," She said, shooting a glance towards me. "And really, I- I can make do with both. Either, I mean."

"No shit you can make do with either. Anybody can *make do* with either. Which do you *prefer*?"

"Uh..." She went on. "I... I guess the floor," she admitted meekly, trying to stay honest. "Beds are kinda too squishy for me." Lauren cringed, as if bracing herself with some form of derogatory, species-centric statement from the old man, some indictment of her physical condition, as if he'd infer it were some sort of stereotype.

"Huh," he nodded his chin out, pausing his work to put his knife down and wipe his hands on a rag, then the handle of the knife, sop away the sweat and nod at her. "That's good," he said, taking Lauren, as well as myself, by surprise. "Beds make you soft. You get too comfortable, you begin to lose sight of what's important." He paused for but a second, as if remembering some far-away place. "And if there's a mortar strike, you want to be as close to the ground as possible. I learned that in Afghanistan, back in the day, when I was a younger man. It might come in the middle of the night. Blow your face to pieces and leave your buddies to pick the rest of you up. Until I was forty years old I couldn't stand to sleep in a bed. It so much as ruined a couple relationships." he sighed. "Recently, with all the shit that's been going on, I've relapsed somewhat. Explosions waking me up at midnight. Can't help but get to thinking Al Qaeda's coming for me, that I'm back there in the Korengal."

"Al-Qaeda?" I asked.

"Yeah, don't you pay attention in history class?" he barked. "Old enemy of America. I guess now they're not much of a thing anymore. After the shitstorm after the Iranian Incursion, I guess they dropped off the map for good, along with the Islamic State. But I wasn't in the military by the time that shit went down. Not my area of expertise." He stopped, looking at me. "Son, do you know what people can be willing to kill each other over?" he asked.

"A bar of soap?" I answered, almost reflexively. He smirked.

"That's right. The littlest shit. Anytime a crisis happens, people turn into animals. I saw it in the forties when shit was getting grim, all those riots and fearmongering." He stopped, to glare at Lauren. "Now, I suppose the animals are turning into people," he remarked, and she looked down, avoiding his razor gaze. Slowly, his head turned, to look at Abel, who was in the process of scratching his rear against the fence, itching himself. "...for the most part," he said, glaring at him. He turned back to Lauren, before giving a little toothless grin. "You... You're alright, Green," He said slowly.

"It's L- T-thank you," She uttered, stopping herself on something, her body lurching for a moment. I think she didn't like the nickname, glaring over to Gabriel before the grin, watching Gabriel enjoying his task of grilling the many venison bits. I could see the corner of his eye turning, glaring back at us. Like he was listening. I felt goosebumps crawl over me upon seeing his gaze.

"Hey, in that case…" He began. "Why don't you come over. I think I've got something else you could use," Mr. Pendrew put forth, and Lauren's ears and eyebrows shot up. This guy, inviting her over?

"…R-really?" She seemed quite skeptical, drawing her eyes into a squint now.

"Yeah. Think of it as a gift. I never use it anymore, anyways, like my hydration bladder."

I couldn't exactly hang out as there was work to be done and more cuts to be prepared, though sooner rather than later I heard their two voices once more chattering in Mr. Pendrew's backyard next door, evolving beyond into hearing a twang of taut wood and a thwack against some further object repeatedly. My ears perked up and I excused myself from the work to go and walk over to the other side of the pool, towards the Pendrews' house.

"Ugh," Selicia groaned with a tip of her hat and glasses as she was in the pool below me, floating there, buoyant by everything that floated in the pool supplies bin sort of comically keeping her waterborne. "Trying to get some relaxation during all this noise," she growled from the pool, her spindly legs uncannily sloshing about as she looked over to me now.

"Why, what are they doing?" I asked, still walking over. She scoffed obnoxiously as I walked up to the fence, peering over, seeing Lauren next to Mr. Pendrew. Her wings blocked what she was doing, however I saw a little cubical bow target set up on the far end of the yard, stuck full of arrows.

With a twang, another arrow sailed into the hard foam target. I heard Mr. Pendrew's voice, much softer than it usually was, in some fatherly tone.

"You're a good shot. Let's back up again and see if you can still hit it," Mr. Pendrew said as Lauren went forth to collect her arrows, himself beginning to walk back towards the fence I peered out from behind. He saw me, looking me in the eye, as Lauren noticed and turned slower, having to step around herself to do so. She smiled, raising the bow in her hand a bit as if to show it off- it was a simple wooden recurve bow. It looked very old, but well taken care of. She was smiling in delight, and I smiled back.

"Check this bow out, Noah!" Lauren said in genuine glee. "Mr. Pendrew says I can have it if I know how to use it."

"Yeah, yeah," He growled, voice coarse once more. "I ain't got a use for it anymore. It takes strength to use a real bow, not like how they always show it in shitty movies where little girls with sticks for arms use them. Green here's got some meat on her bones, she can handle the draw weight. Me, now I'm too old that I can't hold it straight anymore. I'll stick to my Springfield."

"You used to bow hunt, Mr. Pendrew?" I asked.

"Eh, yeah," He sighed nonchalantly. "Only got around to doing it a couple times. Never was that patient. Guns were always more my thing. At least now, I figure *you* all can use a bow to hunt without making a lot of noise. Also the ammo's reusable." Mr. Pendrew turned back to Lauren. "Well, shoot 'im." Lauren nocked another arrow, drawing the bow with an ever so subtle strain of wood. She held the arrow at her cheek for a long while, taking a smooth draw upon the target before letting the projectile fly, hitting it square in the center all the way across.

"Yess," Lauren hissed in success, letting her excitement get the better.

"You want to try?" Mr. Pendrew offered to me.

"Sure, I guess," I said, pulling myself over the fence with a hop, looking back for a moment to see Selicia rolling her eyes before she dimmed her glasses again. Lauren handed me the bow, and I picked up an arrow lying in the grass. Nocking the arrow, I felt the lacquered wooden grip of the bow, hardly used but still a little coarse, aiding in friction. It was a simple recurve bow, it wasn't takedown or had any confusing mechanisms or even sights, it was just a plain, old-fashioned recurve bow.

I drew the bow firmly, looking down the shaft of the arrow towards that hard little foam box. It seemed so far away. On my exhale, I released. The arrow swished across, before bouncing off of the ground once and embedding itself in the fence behind it.

"Oh... close," Lauren said, trying to be uplifting. I looked over to the old man, who looked to the target then back to me. For a second, I felt him trying to say something in mean spirit, as he usually did, but it seemed he was blank. I reached for another arrow, hastily nocking it as if to beat him at his response. My hands shook a little, as I drew it. "Hey Mr. Pendrew, d'ya have a quiver or something for the arrows?" Lauren asked, as I released. Swish, the arrow flew over to the right side of the foam target this time, on the other side of my first arrow, thunking into the fence and glancing off, ricocheting and spinning wildly a couple times before falling still in the grass with a paft.

"Y-yeah, it's gotta be around here somewhere," He said, as my arms drooped. I felt the wind blowing ever so gently, and I breathed in slowly. Lauren looked back to me and smiled, almost to reassure me. I smiled back.

"...More of a gun person myself too," I reasoned, shivering in the breeze. I handed her the bow back, which she took appreciatively.


An hour or so later and the cooking was finished. We all piled around the tables- we had a table outside, and a bunch of them inside in the dining room. a screen door separated the group. Most sat inside, but Lauren, the Pendrews, Susan, Maria and I remained outside, eager to take in the view of the sunset and the fresh air. My mind was drifting, as if on the wind.

"Who would like to say grace?"

"May I?" Lauren's hand went up a little, laying there plainly, ears perked up.

"...This ought to be good," I heard Mr. Pendrew mutter behind an amused smile.

"Go right ahead, sweetie," Mrs. Pendrew sang back.

"Dear god," She began. I stifled a laugh, though Mr. Pendrew was not so disciplined. It was like she was writing a letter. It was cute, of course, Mrs. Pendrew smiling away, even Maria suppressing a smirk for an instant. "Thank you for keeping us safe here in Shortstone, and thank you for our good friends the Pendrews." The whole time, I was glaring over to Gabriel, who also had his eyes open, that shit-eating grin on his face. Like he was about to say something but didn't feel like interrupting this cute little moment. We locked eyes, and I watched his smug smile grow as my brow arced down.

"...And, uh... Amen," Lauren wrapped up. I'd hardly listened to her long spiel with how I was glaring intently at Gabriel. Even here, as everyone fished for their utensils to dig in, Gabriel's eyes lingered with mine, that eternal smug chuckle hovering just behind his lips, and it would stay there in my mind, haunting me until I was asleep that night.

**Chapter 51**

The morning light of the Sun bore down on the misty skies, mists clearing as the great trees shot forth unto the sky, lighting the forest in hues of warm amber and cool blue shade. The ground was supple and moist and gave with each step, a thick blanket of mulchy twigs and leaves underfoot.

Gabriel walked a couple feet from me, and Lauren followed behind. Her feet did not crunch the same way through the brush as us humanoids did, they seemed to quickly pitter-patter along, hand-like talon mandibles in front and ample wide paws behind feeling their way through the brush, holding her little suppressed AR15 almost daintily in front. She could be quite quiet should she put her mind to the task. Armor, ammo rigs and red cloths hanging from shoulder straps or pauldrons were donned by all of us.

"Maria, spread out," Gabe said, walking about to critique. "Anthony, remember to keep scanning. You spend too much time looking at your feet. Susie, keep your weapon at low ready," Gabe instructed. "Reina, Since you're taking point, you need to be scanning the most."

"God," Sam grumbled, pulling the red bandanna out of her pauldron and stuffing it in her pocket. "I hate having to pretend I'm one of those fucking shitlords." Gabriel's head turned and his feet slowed. Out of all of us, his bootfalls had to be the second quietest behind Lauren's. Now they became quieter.

"Sam, what the fuck do you think you're doing?"

"What, you see any fuckin' Republicans?" She snarled back. I looked over to Gabe.

"...She has a point," I said. Gabe sighed.

"If you're that offended by cosplaying as one, be my guest. But if you blow us, I'll make sure you don't even survive long enough to see their firing squads."

"God, you fuckin' busybody," Sam snarled quietly. "...And like I'd even let those neanderthalic fuckers take me prisoner." Hearing this admittance of fighting spirit seemed to brighten Gabe's mood enough to leave her alone.

"Anybody else object to our disguise?" Gabriel said on the radio. I saw Susan, Maria and Anthony pause to remove their bandannas. "Jesus, that many of you? Go easy, if we get spotted we might just get fucked."

"Gabe, we're in the middle of the woods. There isn't supposed to be anybody here. No Republicans and no Democrats," Maria retorted tiredly on the radio.

"Supposed to be raiders or renegades or something, maybe even a couple monsters," Gabe pontificated. "Who knows, we might run into them and get some real-world training in."

"Yeah, like they'll give a shit what side we're on," Maria sarcastically mumbled.

"...Didn't I like, literally just fucking say that?" Gabe snarled. "You can't just take what I say and shoot it back at me."

"Gabe, let's get back to the lesson," I interrupted. Gabe looked over to me and sighed. It wasn't a particularly dense area, but there was good aerial cover and it was dense enough to demonstrate some tactics.

"Alright," Gabe began anew. "So far we've been moving in formation. You all seem to have lesson one down, for the most part. But now we introduce the crucial variable-" Gabriel paced up to a big, sturdy tree, and jabbed his knife into one tree. "The enemy. For the purpose of this demonstration, the trees with a knife in them-" he walked up to another a couple yards away, jabbing somebody else's knife into it. "Will represent hostiles actively engaging you in fire. You all will respond as you think you should, then-" Gabriel stabbed the final tree with yet another. "-I'll correct your fuckups. Alright, everyone back up." The group walked back as Gabriel ushered them away, back to a position around 100 meters from the group of enemy trees. "Alright, again. You're walking in formation…" with great waves of his hands, he bid the group to start moving, in that staggered patrol formation. "BANG! BANG!" Gabriel screamed. "Contact!" Immediately everyone dove for a nearby trunk to take cover behind, kneeling or crouching. Everyone pantomimed firing their guns, each gun and magazine in every chest carrier currently loaded yet not ready to fire, in the express purpose of teaching each person what the weight of ammo felt like- not to mention if we got especially unlucky and were forced to use them. "Reina, too much of you is sticking out, use your cover more aggressively. Green, get lower to the ground, lean down. You need to keep your head down. Susan, you're good. Cover the side you're on; look left." A little while of this and the next lesson began. "So, you're engaging with the enemy. One of you gets hurt-" he walked over to Anthony, pointing. "Now you're hit."

"Where?" he scoffed with a slightly amused smile. "I'm all armored up."

"Not all of you. Maybe you took a round in the leg. Maybe the soft of the inner shoulder. Maybe it was an armor piercing round and it went right on through your plate. Maybe even it blasts through your jaw, and your face is now blasted in half like Selicia when she's getting freaky." Gabriel gently forced Anthony over, addressing everyone. "So he's on the ground. He's screaming. Who responds?"

"Me?" Lauren asked.

"Okay, how come?" Gabe put forth.

"…I'm a taur, I'm the strongest here," She responded.

"Golf-Bravo's still shooting at you," He said. "Moving now would be suicide. And if *you* get hit, we'll have ourselves a much worse problem on our hands as opposed to having a two-legged person get hit. So, once again, who should respond to Anthony's screams of agony?" Reina raised her hand tentatively. "Now, we're getting closer. Reina is one of the closest to Anthony. However, she's taking point, and was doing so when contact was established. She's the spearhead, and her first obligation is to tend to Golf-Bravo and suppress, not her fellow Indigoes. Instead, Reina, you open up on the enemy position and cover for…" Gabriel motioned ever so subtly to Anthony's next-closest comrade, Archie, a ways away.

"Figures," Archie grumbled.

"What now?" Gabriel demanded.

"…I go to him? Archie answered, Gabriel biting his lip with a squint and shaking his head a little, Archie glaring at him.

"First, communicate. Always communicate."

"Uh, Anthony, I'm coming over," Archie grunted.

"And?"

"And what?"

"You don't need to let Anthony know. You need everyone *else* to." Archie sighed and rolled his eyes.

"Alright, cover me," Archie worked it out, though not without exasperation as he got up from behind the fallen tree he was propped up against, finally making his way over to Anthony.

"Keep your ass down, covered or not you're still getting shot at, do everything you possibly can to not catch a round. Don't worry about getting there fast enough, focus on not getting shot while you're making your way over. Now, at this point, Anthony's panicked mindset will turn to concern, even if amped up by adrenaline. He'll start feeling for the wound and realise where he's been hit. Well, man?"

"...Fuck do you mean?"

"Just say it's your leg or something," I said out. Gabe shrugged.

"Argh, my leg," Anthony lazily grabbed out at his calf. Gabriel rolled his eyes.

"Yeah, You're a real fuckin' Ed Norton," Gabriel sighed as Archie, ducking between trees and shrubs, made his way over, pulling his rifle onto his back with a couple tugs of his sling, going for his frontal medical pack.

"Wait, who?" Anthony asked, in between his oh-so fake moaning and groaning. Before Gabriel could berate him on his lack of cinema knowledge, his train of thought was interrupted.

"...You know, he was the Hulk in the old Avengers movies?" Reina interjected.

"As the Hulk? Really?" Lauren spat, before Gabriel could get a word in edgewise. "*That's* what you remember him from? Not like, Fight Club? Or Birdman?"

"Ed Norton? He's not an avenger," Susan grunted perplexedly, as the vast majority of humans began looking to each other in stupefaction. Gabriel seemed amused.

"No, no, you're probably thinking of the recent one," Reina said. "This is from the series from the 2010's, the OG Avengers,"

"...Last I checked, they don't play movies on the propaganda channel," Anthony mused to Archie. "They play movies in those big hybrid facilities?"

"I don't know what the fuck they're on about," Archie mumbled. "I could've used a fockin movie once in a while." Gabriel rolled his eyes.

"ANYWAYS," Gabriel roared with a smile. "We've gone over combat medicine, but applied combat medicine just comes down to two factors- Do you stabilize him here, or do you move him to a safer location?" Archie paused to look around.

"Do it here?" Gabriel nodded his head from side to side.

"Eh, it's a matter of opinion, but I'd say you're not exactly in the open. You can take the risk. But while you're doing this, your teammates have to provide cover-" he paused, eyeing around at the hybrids, still off thinking about their collective whatevers. "And this means that surrounding Indigos advance to provide a better buffer for the current medical Work in Progress. So-" he stopped to motion to many of the skirting friendlies. "Susie, Sam, Maria, you advance and take cover, one at a time. Just pick a tree in front of you and move to it. While you're doing this, your squadmates should be suppressing Golf-Bravo with volumetric fire. In retard terms, this means you repeatedly press your finger thingy extra fast. First, Maria," He motioned to Maria, who sprung up to sprint a couple meters before falling back down to her knees into mushy moss before a great tree. "Then Susie…" The petite cat girl, with a screaming whimper, rushed up to a position adjacent to Maria's, near a big solid rock. Her little submachine gun's silencer clacked against the hard stone as she reacquired a sight picture, mimicking gunfire. "Then Sam." Sam followed suit. "Green, you stay to the rear and provide overwatch. You're further back, so you should engage targets more accurately rather than suppress. So," Gabriel sprang up. "We generally get what we're dealing with here, eh? Squad-on-squad combat. Next, we're going over covering a retreat."

"So," Gabriel went on, after setting everyone all up again. "Retreating isn't as simple as just everyone running away like little girls. That's how to get you and your friends shot in the back. Be like the porcupine, where when you are retreating, you are at your most dangerous. Don't just run, constantly lead your pursuers into repeated ambushes. Nobody likes getting ambushed, they'll fuck off eventually, and that's the goal. A covered retreat happens to be rather effective, and when used with large-squad tactics it can be used to lure enemy squads in to be absolutely destroyed. However we're just fifteen guns strong so it's not like we're going to be conducting troop warfare. However, what we're probably going to be doing is either dealing with others using troop warfare tactics, or running the fuck away, so it's good to know how exactly best to do so and how the other guy will do his stuff."

"Now, if somebody gets hit in a retreat, that's where somebody like Abel or Greenie can come in handy. In a rapid ground evacuation, a gurney isn't exactly going to be the most realistic solution to a casualty since we need as many guns in the fight as possible. 'Taurs, however, can adequately balance a semi-conscious person on their backs effectively enough to still be able to use a weapon. Matter of fact I bet a 'taur with somebody on their back would be an optimal retreat solution, effectively being able to have the passenger suppress the enemy while ol' fourlegs does all the exfil work. Still, if a 'taur gets hit, we're going to be having a major problem. That's why Green, Abel and Selicia are going to always take the most defensive position, and that's *not* up for discussion. It's not that they're more important than any of you, since you're all equally useless. However, I'd assume that a 'taur with a leg shot off is gonna be a lot more of an inconvenience than any of the rest of us minus a leg. A 'taur bleeding out or unconscious, even worse. You ever try to drag one? They're a tad *heavy*."

Gabriel went on, demonstrating a tactic he called "pepperpotting"- where half the team would move while the other half would lay down smoke grenades (or rocks that we pretended were smoke grenades) and covering fire. Once the moving half reached a defensive point, the other half of the team would then move while being covered by their teammates, and the cycle would repeat. It seemed to be simple enough.

"Alright," he finally said. Everyone seemed to be somewhat winded, as Gabe paced up to those trees, taking his knives back. "Pepperpotting works for both assault and retreat. The real idea is that, like what I explained, if you have no cover you make your own. If we were trapped in a flat desert it's what we would do- half of the team would shoot, half of the team would move, keep the enemy's heads down at all times. But here where there is feasible, dense cover, either in the city or in the forest, we're going to do this to maximize our defensive capabilities. When you're out of ammo, move and reload. When you're loaded, hit the dirt and start laying waste. Make your enemy advance through a wall of bullets at all times. One more time: If you're not moving, you're shooting. If you're moving and shooting, you're not going to be hitting that much. Don't multitask. Take good aim before you lay on the hate."

There wasn't much else to explain. We took that half of the group back once Gabriel, Maria and I figured they'd gotten the point, going to get the other half of the group just to do it all again. It was surreal, teaching our band of misfits military bounding maneuvers. Like Gabriel's mercenary allegory explained to Mr. Pendrew was something closer to truth than a lie. I'm sure Gabriel thought the same, but here it was really hitting me. I took one look at Maria and saw her reciprocating the feeling, this uncomfortable wind trapped in her chest as she watched and helped to teach, though she was more of an alumni student than an instructor like Gabe or I. I think that her uncomfortability was curbed of course, though a double-edged sword. Racked with memories of fleeing in terror from homicidal paramilitaries, like she was back there all over again, but her pragmatic overture of really understanding how vital this was, this training, kept her serious and lucid. I looked at her while we taught our little seminars, saw how her lips pursed, her eyes grew distant stares and her knuckles turned white around the grip of her rifle and there was some dried-blood vindication still in her, more than a decade later. She knew If we needed to use these tactics, she may be in fear for her life again. But at least this time, it'll be more than fear keeping me alive, she must have thought. We will make *them* feel that fear right back. I bet she almost wished she could have had the fangs the three of us were sharpening for the group right now, back when she was small and helpless and terrorized, so far and so long away, yet so vivid in her sparkling eyes and shuddering mind.

Like that, I was sort of there between the two of them, their experiences. Gabriel had no doubt seen these tactics used firsthand while Maria must have borne witness to a utilization of these skills without any means of defense. I knew the tactics, dad had made sure of that. But it was still a facsimile, something I knew the physicalities of but not the metaphysics, the emotion, the vigor, the horror of relying on, as Maria was the opposite.

Another evening of relative relaxation, spending time with the Pendrews, doing some crafts, tweaking and customizing things to kill time. In the night, Maria bid me to make love with her and I obliged. The whole time it was like she needed me for something else, needed an anchor, someone to rely on. Something I felt incredible sadness at the entire feeling of until we slept, and another dreamless night passed us before I rose again.

That weird feeling always stuck with me after I'd rose that followed me through the mornings, that weird comfortable disassociation. Like I could get used to this, like this was all normal. I chalked it up to dad's training, figured it was a good thing. But I wanted to fight it anyways just for the sake of progressing in our little adventure, going to sit at the table while Gabriel made breakfast before the stove. I saw him cooking away with what he had access to, eggs and tomatoes and spices. I saw how he cooked, how he knew I was here but didn't really acknowledge me. I looked over to the ajar pantry, finally noticing how it was stocked. It was beginning to look a little sparse.

"...Gabriel," I began, albeit groggily. "We need a strategy for provisions if we don't know how long we'll be stuck here before we can find a good way to leave."

"Well, Abel's a good enough shot with a slingshot," Gabe offered, and I rolled my eyes at him.

"You can't exactly shoot three square meals a day out of a tree."

"Not with that attitude ya can't."

"...That deer Lauren and I got was by chance," I advanced through his wit with a sigh. "I doubt we have that many chances left. If we can't keep everyone fed that's a big problem." Though he still faced away from me, I could practically see him rolling his eyes. Why wasn't he taking this seriously? Did he really think he had this under control?

"...Yeah," He finally sighed. "You know what, fuck it. Let's go for it. We've still got some red paint left."

"...What are you thinking now?" I snarked, maybe a little nastier than I should.

"Republicans haven't searched every house yet. Let's do some wealth redistribution of our own, huh?" At him saying this, I sucked inwardly, almost like I was admitting to myself that going out in search of supplies wasn't the best idea. I guess this was my idea anyways, couldn't bail now.

"...Gonna be risky," I said.

"Beats starving, huh?" He asked, pausing to finally look over his shoulder, barely peering back at me from the corner of his eye and I bit my lip, intertwining my fingers in a big fist as I sat there at that table. "...See who wants to come. Tell Green to stay home, air support's not worth much in the denser town."

Gabriel, Sam, Daniel, Archie and I rode in the truck. Gabe and I sat in the front, Me holding Gabe's MDR and Gabriel with his handgun, with Abel, Archie, Daniel and Sam in the bed of the truck. We had our rifles of course, but that rotary grenade launcher Anon lent us as well, just in case we had to disable any pursuit vehicles if we had to make a quick getaway. We drove in silence for the most part, looking about for mark-less houses. The longer we drove, the stranger the feeling got, like we were driving too close to enemies for comfort, though we would spend long stretches of time seeing nobody, much less Republican Guardsmen.

"So, again, exed houses," Gabriel re-explained. "Those've probably been totally looted. Government looks for empty-looking houses, trashed or busted up with the lights off. Raids 'em, takes what they can. Food, jewelry, nice clothes, guns and ammo. Spray paints that X on the front of the ones they've been through. But the single slash?" He said. "Means they found something in there, but mean to go back to get it. Maybe there's more food than can be carried in one car. Maybe a gunsafe bolted down, so they need to go get a roundsaw to crack it. You know. Marked houses also are a dead giveaway for squatters, hence why we chose the house we're based in, as it hadn't been looted before we got to it."

"Isn't this illegal?" Sam asked. She'd paused for a while as Gabriel took a moment for her question to really sink in, not for his sake but for everyone else. Her uncomfortability reached its peak and she spoke again. "I mean, as in, if the Repubs catch anybody in these houses scavenging, they'll kill us?"

"Yeah," Gabe conceded, smacking his lips in his own personal self-aggrandizement, not even bothering to look back at her, even in the rearview mirror. "...So don't get caught."

We started with an X-ed house, just for a baseline. For security reasons, we all covered our faces- Gabriel wore that ballistic mask of his, while the rest of us stuck with bandannas. Like we sort of expected, we didn't find any guns, ammo, jewelry or unspoiled food, but we found plenty of old clothes. Whoever had lived here was an older fellow and had a couple suits. "We can trade the clothes if we bother to set up a fence for the goods, a contact or something. Or we'll use them, maybe break them down for material, see if Legs or Green have any use for 'em," Gabriel said, rifling through.

"I'm keeping this one," Sam said as she tried on a business jacket, looking in the big mirror on the side of the room and pulling down her bandanna. "I look cool."

"You look lesbian," Gabe said and she shot a look at him. We carried the clothes to the truck, as well as a bunch of the sheets and blankets. We rode the car along to the next place. "So what made you want to come along this fine morning, Sam?" Gabriel asked.

"I think this is all pretty fascinating," She said. "Like, I think I could use the experience, y'know?" She said.

"Sam, are you saying you're using this apocalypse as a way to apologize for your privilege or some shit?" Gabriel said, and Sam flipped him off.

"Maybe I am, shithead," She growled with a smile. "I still think of this as a learning experience. I mean, there are people who go through this every day of their lives, it'd be nice to see into them, y'know?"

"Archie?"

"...I'm bored?" He grunted.

"Danny?"

"I, uh," He began, stammering a bit, looking down at his feet before looking back up at Gabe's eyes in the rearview mirror. "I kinda agree with Sam." Gabriel smiled to himself, letting his chest rock back as he laughed within himself. I guess it was good enough.

The day passed by as we cleared houses like this, bringing back our haul to go out again. We didn't find much food, but we ended with more than we started it with.

"Oh, shit," towards the end of the day when the sun was hazy in the sky, Gabriel retreated to a room in one of the houses while we rifled through. Gabriel was laughing as most of us were checking other rooms. "Arch, come check this out," Gabriel called.

"Wh- Oh Jesus fock, take that shite off," I heard him grunt. I peeked my head out of one of the other bedrooms, seeing Archie pace back outside the door. Daniel was watching too, as he stepped out of the bathroom after using the facilities, looking up to see Gabriel waltz on out with some sort of freakish facsimile of Archie's visage on his head, a big... Helmet? Mask? Like a hybrid's head, but made out of plush and with these big unblinking eyes, face warped into a big dumb smile. Gabriel was beside himself, laughing away as Archie looked away. "God, that's focking unsettling," He grunted, shielding his eyes, while Daniel watched.

"What? Come on, fellow furry! We're like siblings!" Gabriel's voice was muffled by the head. Gabriel pulled the weird dog-fox head off, seeing daniel there. He laughed once again, the head beneath the crux of his arm. "Here, you want to get close to your spirit animal?" Gabriel tossed the head to Daniel who fumbled a little and caught it. "...See, Noah? I told you people are *into* that shit. No wonder we ended up making hybrids. Some people just gotta get off."

"...It's not always sexual," Daniel grunted defensively, Gabriel's brow raising, still with that shit eating grin of his as he leaned back to intertwine his thumbs into the shoulder straps of his armor.

"Yeah, yeah. Whatever you tell yourself to function in society." Daniel, Archie, and now Sam were glaring at him. Gabriel didn't care. He just had to be a smartass. I think he knew he was always a bit too vicious, but kept himself from caring.

Back at home it was silent, Maria was attending to the apple tree in the backyard; she had a bit of a green thumb she'd picked up from her mother. I can remember their aquaponic garden in the backyard of their house in Vegas, where she'd been made to spend so much time as mother-daughter bonding. I always figured she was less than enthused by it, but it turns out she retained a lot of it, like me and my father's gun obsession. Susan was working on drawing, hanging out with Daniel and Sam again, whom the two of them seemed a little bit more at ease with, exchanging art tips.

In the evenings, Ms. Pendrew would come over and check up on everyone's health well-being. Aside from acting as a rehabilitation nurse for what was left of Abel, Daniel and Lauren's wounds, she would exchange small talk and generally lift people's spirits. Mr. Pendrew kept his distance, for the most part, yet occasionally popping in to critique our methods or decisions in this or that, often harshly; and as for Mrs. Pendrew, I think she was lonely; this war made everyone wary of each other and she must've hated that. She just wanted others to talk to.

The next day the cycle would continue. It was always me, Gabriel, and Sam. sometimes one or two different people would come along, often it included Daniel and even Abel, who especially seemed to take a liking to Sam, and vice-versa. But Sam was by far the most consistent. She wanted to see the suffering, and live through it. I'd see it in her eyes, she looked like she was constantly taking everything in for the first time, and at the same time trying to not let it get to her. I guess I could appreciate it. At nights we'd take people out, usually one on one to work with nightvision, get a feel for moving while wearing it and strategies to take. "Remember, nightvision isn't an invisibility cloak, but it does generally insure you'll see the bad guy before they see you, so you can fool yourself into thinking it is one. You have the luxury of being able to move slowly. Matter of fact, you *should* move slowly. Be methodical. In the dark if you move fast, you'll be seen faster by someone with no nightvision. You hold the advantage of seeing them first, but your field of view is cut down so you need to watch how you move, scan everything and plan your attack. Count bodies before you start shooting. Yeah, you'll be waiting on orders from Noah, Maria or me, but this is going to be what we're doing and what you should be thinking about doing. Count Golf Bravos, shoot Golf Bravos. Slow and steady."

### Chapter 52

More training, more scavenging. The day came along where the Pendrews invited us to church again. Gone to church twice, been at least a week here. It felt weird how we weren't really making any headway, but at least I could count the days like this. Took us this long to get this far, and here we were. Burning time, waiting for that next church session.

In the back of Mr. Pendrew's truck I found myself, with the usual group. Lauren, Maria, Katt, Anthony, but Abel joining us as well. Bumping on through the road at this subtle pace. It was kind of nice, after all. "...Yes, yes; this is all so fascinating," Mrs. Pendrew went on, evidently in the middle of something by the time my disassociation paused for me to focus, still gazing out at the countryside on this short drive. "I never could have imagined that we humans had created so many different creatures like you. No offense, of course,"

"Yeah, no problem," Lauren responded meekly, doing her best to keep smiling.

"Yeah, I agree," Susan was saying back, sitting up with the Pendrews. "I never knew about any of you, either. I was surprised too."

"Hm, of course," Mrs. Pendrew was doing her best to be polite.

"Yeah, well they could have done without making spider-ones. Eugh, always hated spiders," Mr. Pendrew grumbled, through the cab. "And... Giant spider women. This is exactly what the end of the world needed, as if... Dragon-centaur people weren't enough."

"At least we won't get bored," Mrs. Pendrew joked back, maybe to take the bite off of Lauren who sat there a little less than offended. "Imagine how sullen this apocalypse would be without hybrids!"

"Yeah. Lucky us." Mr. Pendrew paused, slowing for a stop sign, if only out of habit. "So Green, how do you feel that you're actually only the second-weirdest one?"

"Uh... I don't know about that," Lauren reasoned. "I'm still pretty weird."

"You're joking, right?" Anthony piped up, from the passenger seat of the truck. "At least you don't have four creepy glowy eyes. And like, spider-bits."

"Am I weird?" Abel asked.

"Heh, gotta ask?" Mr. Pendrew responded.

"Uh... yes?" Abel responded, the sarcasm lost on him as well.

"Don't worry about it, Abel," Maria offered less than enthusiastically.

"Hey, what if, like, Selicia could fly, too?" Susan said, sitting in the little half-seat between Anthony and Mr. Pendrew. "Now that'd be freaky."

"Don't make me think about that," Maria contributed to the ongoing conversation. "She's hard enough to smack while she's bumping her head into the ceiling."

"What if, like, she made a wingsuit using her spiderwebs and her legs?" Lauren pondered, thinking aloud. "And what if she strapped rockets to herself? That might work, Huh? heck, I ought to try and make that- I bet it'd work!"

"Start a company already," I said only half jokingly, smiling at Lauren. "I'm serious."

"Hey, the worst that can happen is she dies," Anthony joked. "Go for it."

"Oh, pssht, she's not that bad," Mrs. Pendrew hushed playfully. "She does her best to help around the place! And her web can make for fantastic thread," She defended.

"Yeesh. I can't believe you use that stuff for seamstressing," Mr. Pendrew scoffed.

"Hey, it works," Lauren also came to Selicia's aid.

"...If she's such a saint she ought to join us in church. Sleeping all day," He muttered on.

"I mean, it's kind of what her kind does," Lauren added.

"Oh, so now you're racist too, huh? Back in my day that'd be hate speech. Hah! Get a load of that, huh?" Mr. Pendrew's humor was a bit beyond the reach of the rest of us, who left him to chuckle at his own "joke".


Arriving at the church felt the same as last time, but this time, more formal, more familiar, more... normal. I'd seen all these sights before, all these people, the refugee camp, the soup line. We, along with so many other somber men and women, piled into the church, sitting in the pews. Abel and Lauren of course sat in the aisles, since the seats weren't quite designed for them. Maria was next to me, leaning into me even as I stiffly sat there, sighing. I was on the very edge of the pew, next to Lauren, seeing her in my peripheral vision. I felt myself leaning towards her every now and then.

We began by singing a few songs, about God and forgiveness and whatnot. I swayed and moved my lips along with the words, but I didn't feel compelled to really sing at first. I guess I was too tired to, or I didn't care enough. Might have even been Gabriel's words about singing being mind control or something rattling in my head. Even Maria, who was religious, didn't seem to sing that loudly or proudly, humming along plainly with the tune. But, over to the side, I could definitely make out Lauren's voice. I turned, to see her singing along with the rest of the congregation, arms raised. She had quite the voice, a voice that raised itself above the rest of the congregation, and in perfect tune. A voice to be proud of. I found that idiot smile on my face after a little while of singing along, watching her out of the corner of my eye. It prompted me to raise my own voice more, until there were no more songs to sing.

As it turns out, the pastor indeed was repeating himself, both last week and today. The sermon was nigh identical- about how waging war against your brother was self destructive, that you should put your trust and hope in God, all that goodness. Listening to it and knowing that he pretty much had nothing else to say, it kind of depressed me- probably because I already agreed with most of what he had to say. Preaching to the choir, I guess.

"Hmmm... " Maria sighed towards a quieter moment, maybe letting her mind wander, despite her manners telling her not to speak during the sermon. Wasn't exactly a catholic cathedral, maybe she was more comfortable acting out like this. "Well, this- this is a nice church, isn't it?"

"I guess," I responded to her, as she slowly rested her head on my shoulder, sighing again as a hand went up to grasp at the crux of my elbow, as if goading me to put her arm around her.

Goosebumps rose on me, though I let her lean as she did, not exactly knowing what to do and settling on finally grasping my arm around her. Her skin was cold and clammy. Maybe it was just my arm, tingling, like I was paralyzed there.

This long, awkward moment passed in a couple blinks and the service was over. I looked over to see us piling up to leave, Maria still there in my arm, droning with her eyes shut. She'd fallen asleep. Weird, I figured the stress took its toll on her. She used this time to feel safe, maybe here in a church she felt comfortable. Might have even been me. I woke her up to let everyone get up and out. I looked over, watching between the people leaving and walking about, talking, seeing Lauren in front of the pastor, her head bowed with his, as they prayed together. I saw the pastor raise his hand and place it atop her head, as she slowly rose her own hands in holy prostration as he gave her his blessing. I couldn't make out what they were saying, but I saw the contented smile on her face and somehow, this made me feel happier. She, beaming, received a meager little splash of water from where it sat in the standing basin up there by the podium. How she smiled meagerly, bowing over in front of this slender man to let the drops of water race down her face, eyes and muzzle, hands clasped together into a praying fist at her midsection, arms straight.

Huh.

"Yeah, time to go," Maria came to life a million miles away a foot behind me, taking me by surprise. She rose, oblivious to everything, taking my hand as if to drag me towards the door. I was standing there, blinking, seeing Lauren biting back her glee walking back up to us with the pastor smiling and waving her off- but her smile diminished quickly and as I turned,

And that was when I saw him.

He was wearing a nice button-down shirt and tie, tucked into his khaki combat pants, those unblinking tallow yellow eyes staring forward, holding the hand of his little girl behind him, her wings flapping a little bit as he walked behind the mother of his child, another dragon hybrid, a bipedal like him, but a dark orange hue to her scales, their little girl being a bright, happy sunflowery color, with eyes of sparkling aquamarine. That hybrid soldier who took my gun two weeks ago, Michael like he was dressed up in a costume with his family as accessories.

At first, I felt anger, seeing him here. After what he did last week, taking the church's food- but here he was, dressed in his sunday best, with his wife and daughter. It almost made me sick. But then, I was struck with a feeling of guilt and regret- this dragon, this creature and man I hated, had a family. I knew deep down that he was probably doing this, these terrible things, to support those he loved, no doubt. I saw his eyes, and for once, I didn't see them as lifeless- I saw them as sad, almost defeated, with bags beneath them, like his spouse's- but to be fair, she smiled more, looking back once at her little girl and smiling at her. I watched them go up to the pastor to talk for a little bit, thank him for the sermon, the pastor kneeling down to smile back and greet their little girl.

A quick egress and we were outside the church again. I sat on that same bench as last week, seeing the starving, hopeless people huddled in tents around the premises. Grunting quietly, I leaned back heavily on the cast-iron furnishing, as I watched the people, the members of my group intermixed in the little mob of well dressed, if not darkly dressed, hushed people.

I spotted Michael, emerging with his family in tow. He approached some people around somberly yet putting on a smile. *What is he doing here?* surged through my mind. I guess was just trying to give myself vindication to be disgusted, atop my racing heart, like my cover was about to be blown.

It was a while before his eyes caught mine. I did not look away, I did not change my face to a scowl or snarl: I simply met his gaze, in acknowledgement. He looked down and away, if only for a moment, and I saw his family stop behind him, taking note of me. His daughter clutched her father's hardened, leathery fingers of boiled cherry, her other hand clutching a little cookie the pastor had given her, a couple bites taken out of it. She paused her snack to stare awkwardly at me the way kids are prone to, and it was my turn for my stare to falter.

"Where's my gun?" I asked once he'd taken a step. I think I meant to sound sarcastic. I don't think I did a good job, coming off as bitter.

"It's safe," He said. "You're... you're not really with the Republicans, *are* you?" he noted, slowly. I didn't respond, staring at him. His lip smiled a little bit, not in indignation or vindication, but almost in a mournful, shared amusement without judgement.

"The Republicans? Not *us*?" I asked, prodded, interrogated practically, right on back at him. He sighed heavily, glancing off to the left, spotting Lauren, with the Pendrews and their other church friends.

"...You know, it's not personal, what I did that day," He said slowly, slowly meandering away from my little inquisition, a change of subject. I read the anxiety in his family's eyes. "I... I don't want you to think I'm a bad guy."

"Bit late for that," I droned. I saw his daughter's wings shake a little bit, and his tiny, almost-friendly smile was sucked once more back into his default deadman look.

"Hey, Reed, this guy giving you problems?" I heard Mr. Pendrew cut in on my behalf, at a distance. The little dragon girl quickly hid behind her father's leg, letting out a tiny whimper. The dragon man raised his gaze up, steadfast as he looked to Mr. Pendrew, those mournful eyes focusing finally. "Remember, buddy- you ain't got your friends with you now. You best watch yourself."

"I wasn't going to make trouble," Michael let his voice shake atop showcasing the fear of his family. "And I certainly don't need my 'friends' to 'back me up'."

"Cute, acting brave in front of your kid and wife," Mr. Pendrew snarled back. "They know you kill for money? That you're a murderer?"

"Steven!" Mrs. Pendrew barked out, coming right over. "Stop making such a scene! You know Michael only does what he has to!" She said, trying to get between them, but Steven didn't even give her the time of day, glaring at this sinner of a hybrid before him.

"Good thing you've got red skin, *Mikey*," He went on, spittle flying from his drawn face. "Makes it almost look like you don't got blood on your hands. Your kind makes me *sick*." Michael turned to lead his family away, as the pastor approached.

"Brother... Take pity on Michael. He's been through as much as any of us, if not more."

"Is that supposed to make me give him a free pass?" Steven hissed. "No. In fact, I think the opposite."

"Steven, you know I don't condone this war, but I think you two..." It all just faded into disassociation as I walked over to where the rest of the gang was. Lauren and Maria standing apart, yet nearby, watching over expectantly.

there was little rest to be found outside of the halls of the church, like the world paused itself inside, and only inside its walls. It was time to leave, and we left sooner rather than later. The ride back was much more silent than the ride to the church. The brief reparté with Michael had evidently taken its toll on Mr. Pendrew's mood, despite however cross he always seemed to be, as he grumbled incessantly on the drive back.

"Hey, Green," Mr. Pendrew finally spoke up, as we approached home once more.

"Yeah?" Lauren piped up, ears perking a little as her head came up from where she'd been watching off into the forest along the road.

"Ain'tcha got wings?" He burst forth.

"Uh... Yeah?"

"So what, you just gracing us with your presence right now, is that it?" He said. Lauren smiled a little bit, like some sudden metamorphosis resulting from the humor she found in his vicious words.

"Trying to spend some time with my friends," she responded with a shrug.

"...Or are you just being lazy?"

"Do you *mind* me being here?" she prodded on back, almost defensively.

"Yeah, weighin' down my back end."

"I'm sure your truck can handle it," Lauren responded.

"You break it, you buy it," He responded in a mutter, before we turned into our cul-de-sac, pulling up in front of his house. "Hey, Green... Lauren," He said again, growing more serious as he cleared his throat. "Seeing you in church and all, I think I've got something else for you," He said, parking and stepping out, as we all got up to hop off.

"Another present?" Lauren implored with a simple joke, and I watched as he reached into his pocket, swiftly producing a little icon on a chain. It was simple, a trinket. A little three-pronged star of sorts, sort of like a shuriken at a glance, composed of glittering stainless steel, well worn and scuffed.

"...Thought you might want to keep this close. Not exactly a cross, but it's a symbol of the trinity. God the father, the son, the holy spirit, you know." He flipped it in his hands some more, eyes glassed over for a split moment, maybe to past images, places and people and events. "A symbol of faith. I never liked jewelry, sort of always figured things needed a useful purpose." He took that little star, with two prongs sticking out he stuck the other prong between his middle and trigger finger. "Think of it like a little brass knuckle. I've got big hands, and you aren't undersized yourself. See? Fits you alright," He noted as she took and held it as instructed. "So. Somebody's giving you trouble, you can use this symbol of faith to make 'em meet Jesus real quick. Don't fuck around, you can cave someone's skull in with this thing." He took a second to have a morose little chuckle as she smiled back somewhat weakly, though without missing the ironies.

"...Gotta use me to get rid of your junk, huh?"

"Wouldn't call it that. I'm just a bit old for fisticuffs. Somebody's giving me problems, I go for my gun." He went to pull out the chain for it as well. "...Thread this through and lock it in like this. This is the sort of clasp where you can just yank it and it pulls right off and you can get to work; called a drama clasp."

"...Thanks for everything, Mr. Pendrew," Lauren uttered as he waved it off, shaking his head.

"Don't mention it. Keep up the good behavior and I might drop more kitschy shit on you. Oh, and Call me Steven if you want. I won't hold it against you either-other way." It was a nice little scene there that I felt like watching was prying a bit, so I finally re-entered the house, hearing Lauren and Mr. Pendrew's voices drone on in the distance until the door shut.

"Hey Gabe," I sighed as I came up upon the den, seeing him sitting at the table again, a whole salvo of twelve gauge shells sitting there like toy soldiers. Gabe smirked at me indignantly as I entered, as if judging me in his usual atheistic piety.

"Sup Noah," He said. "How's God doing?" I didn't respond, going past him towards the cupboard, before realising I wasn't hungry. I turned back to him, and he continued, even if only he was listening to himself by any means. "...Noah. What's your take on the training?"

"...We've still got to do some more nightvision exercises, everyone is still bumbling around a bit too much, especially the Shepherd siblings and Sam. As for personal tactics, Daniel and Selicia could use more one on one practice."

"Yeah, that's what I'm thinking."

"...Why'd you ask then?" I plopped down in a seat to glare at him.

"Eh, thinkin' out loud, y'know," Gabriel leaned back, looking out the window at the little garden in the backyard, seeing Selicia floating in the pool again, belly-up and wearing nothing but her swimsuit bra top and her glasses. "...Speaking of, you seen Danny try to reload? Dude shifting hands all the time like a game of hot potato. Damn near couldn't believe my eyes. Reminds me of the days before Sinaloa. Amateur hour."

"...*Before* Sinaloa?" I asked, and I saw a pause in Gabriel's whole being, his face going blank for a split moment- nothing that noticeable, but some part of my mind picked up on that instantaneous pause.

"Well, yeah," he scoffed, looking me in the eye. "You don't think the world's biggest drug cartel just picked me up out of nowhere, right?"

"...I guess so," I said, looking right through him, waiting for him to elaborate. "so how'd they do it?" I asked, and he smiled, trying to play it off.

"I was in with a small gang first, right?" He said, as if it were common knowledge, obvious.

"...You really never talked about this." I smiled. "You know Gabriel, you never struck me as somebody good at keeping secrets."

"That means I'm the best secret keeper, don't it?" He responded. "Sun Tsu had something to say about that. You don't need to be smarter than your enemy to beat him- just convince him you're more of an idiot than you really are and you'll have the upper hand. Get him to underestimate you."

"That's gotta be written right after 'don't clean all your guns at once', huh?" I mentioned, and he laughed a little. "Still, you know what would be more important than teaching them to shoot as a team?" I put forth the question. "Getting out of this place."

"...Working on it. Slow and steady. I think our best idea might be to just book it on foot, maybe requisition a vehicle at some point up north, but that means we'll have to leave a lot of ammo and food, we'll be vulnerable, can't move fast, and be extra-squishy. Wouldn't be pretty."

"Yeah, we'll probably run out of food by the time we reach the citadel. Hunting on the way won't do much." I sighed. "Hike will be a week on foot with fifteen some-odd people at our top speed. Moving that slow we'll probably end up in more than one firefight with our luck."

"Doesn't help that the place was built to be hard to find," Gabriel mused on back.

"...Sort of the point." Another long sigh. "Got any bright ideas?"

"Took a look at the Reds' stockpiles on my own time. They've got a bunch of the new Quantum-boosted helicopters- They may be becoming obsolete but they're quiet as a motherfucker. Seems that the dudes who know how to use them are old army, not exactly fanatics of the cause sprung up from the grassroots. Just military looking to pick a side to feed their families. Most of the military sided with the Republicans but it doesn't mean they're gung-ho about dying for the cause. See if I can't track down one and make him an offer he can't refuse. Turn off his radio on one of his patrol missions to come and airlift our vehicles down past the roadblocks."

"...Shit, you think you could get away with that?"

"Don't need to make it subtle. Just make it quick and move before they decide to investigate." I nodded, chewing on my own doubts. We didn't have much options, and though it was otherworldly creative, I didn't see a reason that it couldn't work. The pilot would be a loose end, but I guess it doesn't matter now that we'd be gone.

"Cool then. Let me know if you need help."

"Yeah, it's the idea."

### Chapter 53

Bored.

Well, maybe that's not the right word. But this feeling of restlessness, despite how I filled my time. The same old, same old. Nothing new could really satiate that uncomfortable feeling. We had things to do, things to keep ourselves busy with. Go scavenging, look around. Lauren did her scouting thing, working with Gabriel a little in the business of knowing the status of the roads. We'd be leaving soon, right? Couldn't be soon enough. Finding and coercing that pilot, though, was probably going to be the hard part.

At nights we'd start taking people out to work with nightvision in the woods, as you could only get so far with cute little exercises in the basement. Selicia made a few obstacles for a little training course and everyone would get to go one after the other. As it turned out, through a little experimentation we found out that Selicia's own biological nightvision capabilities rivaled that of a generation one NOD set while the rest of us had our Gen 4 sets, which she seemed a little insulted at, though at how heavily she relied upon her infrared illuminator in the pitch blackness of the basement and how prone she was to tripping over things anyways, Gabriel shared a laugh with himself at Selica's expense. Gabe also figured if he could get her a NV monocular he ought to, even at her protest.

The days passed in a haze. I couldn't put my finger on what it was that fueled my disassociation aside from simply everything and nothing all at once; the warmth of late summer, the nothing to do but go the motions, the full stop here maybe. We'd keep busy with exercises, quizzes about combat and medical. There was a blackout for a couple hours one day. Nothing serious much, but it would prove to be an omen of things to come. Here we'd sit, Gabriel going out on his own again. Not to scavenge, but for his harebrained idea about airlifting the vehicles.

Watching Gabriel address everyone with such bloody conviction was a sight to behold. How they were gazing back at him. I wondered how they could reconcile their memories of a him before this, and it set me to ponder. I knew Gabe was a killer, sure, I'd seen it up close and personal. But for once it seemed like I could see him like my friend again. But what about me? How many people have I killed? Up until we went into that facility I thought it would be like how they said it was in all the cliches. How I'd be able to count them, see every last face. But at this point they were all blurring together. The countless hybrids I'd gunned down in that facility, too hectic to remark upon the violence like I had with my first kill, that vagrant that felt like a lifetime ago. The democrat militia in Elko, how I'd ripped and torn while piloting a cruel metal beast. And that horror in the desert, where I knew the consequences well and harsh.

The dreamlike, lethargic state persisted into the night, where I'd walk, crawl, fly, run, burrow through images, emotions. Places and people. Things outside of the waking world. Could I even call it that? Maria was there with me, in the dark. Make love, they'd call it. Fucking was a more apt term. She'd kiss me and pretend everything was alright, but I was never there.

Rolling through the footage that I'd taken of the blockade, looking for some edge, something I needed to know, I would stop on that accidental Lauren picture. I don't know how long I'd be staring at it, hovering in my vision in my hologlasses. God, she was pretty. That bashful little smile. The way the rays of the sun filtered through her hair. She had kind eyes. I used to think that Maria's eyes and hers looked the same, but... Lauren's eyes could look into your soul and inspire a calm comfort, despite her anxious tinge. Maria's only rose haste; anxiety was the center stage with a splash of performatory killer-calm. Lauren was looking out in this snapshot of infinity, towards her life to come. Her world expanding before her, a captain upon her ship, her domain. Where she lacked confidence, hope found her. If she could move forward, so could I. Maria's eyes only inspired survival at any cost. They didn't look as alive.

I just wished I'd be out of this place, out of Shortstone, and out of my own head.

There was more training to be done. Something to help me forget, at least without absorbing myself in complete dissociation. In the black of night, where the world was still and only buzzed with the chirping of crickets, where the image of night stood long enough for it to not disappear into flashes of unrelated images and places. All of it was more manageable, yet not quite lucid but there was something to be done, something I could quantify as important, something that roused me. I was muttering out orders and advice in our training. "Alright," I must have been saying. Everyone seemed to be somewhat winded, how I could see their breaths in the infrared display. "Let's go over assault tactics again. So-"

*Snap.*

It was a sound I'd heard before. A dry crack of a whip, a flash somewhere in the night. I felt a sting on my shoulder, and I could see a vapor trail for a brief moment graze my arm, before it disappeared into thin air. Maria cried out, and my head turned as her body twisted, taken by surprise and now falling from her feet onto her side, like she'd been pushed over. All of it in absolute blackness in the readout of my NODs.

Boom, the gunshot echoed out after the crisp supersonic snap, filling the forest as birds left their perches around us, roused from sleep. I stood there, almost confused, like one of us had fired a shot. I was looking back, going to look back over. Like I was still dreaming.

Gabriel slammed into me, knocking me to the ground, cursing at my stupidity. "This is no time to be spacing out you retard!" he hissed in my ear. I heard a weapon being filled, and shouts in the distance.

 Sam began screaming, but soon her screams were drowned out as her carbine belched rounds, casings vomited out the ejection port as the weapon cycled automatically with rapid flashing that lit up this dark world, her mouth open in a scream as her weapon roared, every round of the thirty-round magazine a snapshot, an image in this black night. As she ran out of ammo she was already in the process of diving for cover, everyone else already down.

As the barrage of automatic fire echoed towards silence, the first sound I could make out was panting and breathing. Then, Maria's yelps behind us. "I'm- Agh, I'm hit!" She cursed.

"...You're wearing your armor, right?" spilled from my mouth. Seemed like the right thing to say at the time. In my nightvision I could see her glaring up at me for a short moment, before feeling behind her place carrier. I stared at her, Gabriel brushing himself off of me, seeing her armor plate's upper left corner emitting smoke.

"Y-yeah... I'm good," She huffed. "Didn't pen."

Then, in the distance, from where the shot had came, I heard multiple voices, cursing in surprise and exasperation. "What the fuck are you doing? Jesus christ," I could hear faintly in the distance.

"Yo, WHAT THE FUCK WAS THAT SHIT?!" Gabriel did his best to shout from his prone position as everyone readied their weapons from cover. There was a long, awkward silence.

"...Hey, yo, this is gonna sound weird, but I've gotta ask," a voice, quite possibly the voice of the one who'd just spoken in the black distance, called back. "You guys Republicans?"

"Why, you Democrats or something?!" Gabriel cried.

"Nah dude, we're antipartisan," The voice responded.

"We got something in common then," Gabriel responded. Another long pause. "...You shot one of us, what's the big fuckin' idea?!"

"...Shit, I hit her?" Another voice called, as other voices emanated in the distance, muttering almost concernedly. It was beyond uncanny. At least I was finally in the present again.

"Yeah, you owe us an armor plate," Maria responded breathlessly, in the way that she wasn't depleted of ire but the current air was more conducive to jokes than swearing. There was a quiet laugh in the distance as a response.

"...Yeah, sorry about that," The evident leader called out. "Paul here overdid himself on his trigger job, now it's got a half-pound pull." Gabriel chuckled, and even I cracked a morose smile, as the sniper called out his own apology with a brief, shameful "sorry".

"Jesus," Gabe muttered with a chuckle.

"We hit any of you?" I put in.

"...That bitch killed the fuck outta the tree in front of me," Another voice called. They chuckled.

"Yeah, well, how are we supposed to know you're not fucking with us right now?!" Maria interrupted.

"...Yeah," Gabe added. "Awful good shooting for an 'accident'."

"...Shit, you do have a point," The probable leader cried. "I mean, we can call parley all we want, but you're smart to not trust us." There was another pause.

"Well, you shot at us first. So you come out first. Then I'll come out. Just us, no guns."

"Where do you want?" The other man asked.

"See that big tree with the rock next to it?" Gabe commanded, shining his infraed laser on it. "Go there. I'll come out as soon as you're there. Bring a flashlight so we can talk without nightgear."

"...Better not fucking shoot me," He cried.

"If you don't I won't," Gabe said. I looked over to him.

"...You're gonna do this?" I muttered quietly, almost letting concern get the better of me, like I forgot I was in my usual haze for once.

"Hey, never pass up an opportunity to make some friends, especially in the middle of an apocalypse. Didn't daddy ever teach you anything useful?" Gabriel drew his Bren from his holster, dropping it in my hands, along with his unslung PDW. I saw the other man approach the parley point through my NODs, seeing a stout, darker-skinned fellow with a cheap NVG goggle set over his eyes, and Gabe got up. I sighed apprehensively, seeing Gabe walk over. There was a deathlike silence as each side watched and waited, the two there mumbling in distant silence, motions pantomimed like shadow puppets, shaking hands and conversing for long too briefly, before each representative cried back to their group that it was all clear.

Wearily, we approached, eyes darting about pensively. Through the shifting barrage of trees separating us, we saw other figures through the veil of that little clearing, three more men, all visibly armed with cheaper NODs and rifles- I counted an SKS with a 20 round integral magazine, an ancient-looking Galil 5.56 with two 45-round magazines duct-taped to each other, and a Mosin with a scope mounted, barrel still smoking and wielded by the most likely marksman, a short little human with a red face and a bashful, embarrassed smile. He caught Lauren's eyes for a second and shrugged. I stepped closer to her, and she edged up next to me, a wing brushing my back.

"Kommandos, Gabriel Noria," The leader of this little squad introduced. The three of them saluted with a nonchalant hand wave.

"Indigoes, meet Joe," Gabriel told us, and the squad leader waved. He was a tall, rotund man with a head and face that looked like they'd been shaved three weeks before; rough, ugly stubble all over him, hair hardly poking out from under a flecktarn boonie hat. Joe immediately went to elbow his sniper, pointing towards Maria.

"You gonna apologize or keep on oglin' her, Paul?"

"Hey, uh… Well, at least you know your armor works, right?" he attempted to joke. Maria didn't seem amused, lips still pursed, flaring her nostrils at him. Joe elbowed Paul harder. "Yeah, s-sorry, uh… miss..." He paused, as if asking her name.

"You're pushing it, dude. My boyfriend's with me," She growled, interlocking her arm betwixt my elbow after I'd given Gabriel his gear back. The sniper's eyes flashed to me and his smile disapparated. Before anything could get any more on-edge, Gabriel jumped in.

"He's got a point," Gabe said. "You ain't gonna take your armor for granted anymore, are ya?"

"G-gabe!" Maria fronted, and even Gabe's smile disappeared, growing stern.

"Look, we could be killing each other right now. We're not. Let's keep it diplomatic." Gabriel turned back to our previous assailants, keeping things cordial as best he could. Maria was inches from being beside herself but she held her reserve.

"Agreed," Joe said in response to Gabriel's expectant pause, hands on his hips. "I apologize for Paul's *lack* of *trigger discipline*," He snarled, turning his head to Paul, who simply fidgeted with the lens cap of his rifle and looked at his feet that shifted uneasily. "But things coulda been a lot worse. Look, you aren't Republicans or Democrats. We don't exactly feel vindication in killing fellow independents."

"So what, you're out here hunting Republicans?" Sam asked.

"...Or Democrats, what have you," He shook his head from side to side. "War profiteers, I guess you could call us."

"...Just the four of you?"

"Oh, nah, we've got a whole outfit going," He said. He motioned to Paul, who reached behind himself, taking Joe's rifle, an old Kalashnikov, handing it back to the squad leader. "Wanna see?"

"...I don't see why not," Gabe shrugged, looking back to us. I nodded apprehensively, somewhat curious.

"So," Joe began. "You guys were training, right?"

"We were," Gabe said, as we walked with them. Joe clicked his lips.

"At this time of day? Uh, night?" he asked in playful insolence.

"No better time to practice using the NODs."

"Hm," Joe muttered, like conceding a point, as we walked on further. "Now that begs the question, what're you doing teaching a bunch of draft-dodging peaceniks paramilitary shit?"

"Well, you know the saying," Gabe said, stepping over a log. "Si vis pacem..."

"Parabellum, brother," Joe responded in a show of kinship. "Still, what's your endgame? Stickin' around or exfil?"

Gabe looked at me, as if for confirmation to divulge the information. I weighed it in my mind for a second, before figuring that at least these people didn't seem particularly burdensome, nodding subtly.

"Moving north," Gabe said. "Noah here's got some relatives and friends in a survival commune up in the panhandle."

"No shit?" He asked. "We heard about a place like that about a hundred miles north of here. Big stone walls, whole Lord of the Rings-y shit?"

"Yeah, that's the one," I put forth. One hell of a secret.

"Aw fuck, nice," Joe said. "We've been trying to establish radio contact with 'em, try and get an invite. So far it's gone silent, we're just waiting around for a reply before we try our luck with a face-to-face introduction."

"Yeah, we can't hail 'em either," Archie put in.

"Probably trying to keep from drawing attention from the reds or blues," Joe theorized. "So what's keepin' y'all here?"

"Reds've cordoned the north road. Can't get the vehicles out."

"what, don't feel like walking?"

"I'm dealing with the uninitiated here, dude. We've got gear to hump."

"Don't look all that uninitiated," Joe responded.

"Well thanks, I'm working on it," Gabe said. "So what, you guys go out and ambush soldiers to take their shit?"

"Workin' so far," joe said. "rear guard troops are a piece of cake. We like to add some realism to their training sessions up here. Paul here's a real machine, don't underestimate him just cuz he's a sped. He stacks bodies like he's not even autistic. Or maybe like he is, you decide."

"300 confirmed kills," Paul laughed.

"See? He can only communicate in stone-age memes. Now, supply shipments, that's where the good stuff is. Lotta war machines down south at the border for the taking, ever since the Mexican intervention ten years ago. Up here at the northern bits of the US, it's mostly non-mechanized conflicts, and whatever heavy metal that either side does have access to, they're awful stingy about using it. Still, even the best and the most expensive tank will get fucked with a couple molotov cocktails in the ventilation shafts and cooling systems. Worked a hundred years ago, still workin."

"Well, the trick is to get the right amount of plastic, synthesize a little napalm," Gabriel amended.

"Sure, yeah, the materials may have changed a little but the basic principles still remain. The real trick is sneaking up on tanks. I find the best way is to dig a man-sized ditch, fill it with water and hide in it and wait for the tank to roll past. The water helps fool thermals. Get out, blaze the tank, and shoot the fuckers pouring out." A little silence as we walked on, before Joe found another topic. "So, just you guys?"

"Nah, we've got a foothold in town. Just training this half of us tonight, going over group tactics."

"Sounds about right, They're still moving in formation, that's good," joe critiqued. "So, what's the story with your hybrids?" Joe asked.

"Ran into 'em moving north from Vegas, Archie here was in charge. We took pity on 'em, I guess. Figured we could help each other out."

"Vegas, eh? Stick around to watch the fireworks?"

"Fuck, yeah, we saw the nuke," Gabe responded. "You heard about that, huh?"

"Yeah, fuckin Blues, man."

"Know anything else?" Gabe asked.

"Just rumors. Republicans nuked DC, Boston. Dems nuked Juneau and tried nuking Houston; Austin is Blue territory and the Republicans are purging 'em by sieging the city and shooting anyone who tries to escape. Then again, it's all rumors."

"What about Canada?"

"Heard the Quebecois are riling up shit and Ontario's a warzone. Western Canada isn't doing too well either, despite being cut off from any other conflicts. The West-Coast-Democrat-Alliance is trying to annex the Yukon, so I've heard, to get a defensive buffer against Alaska when they mobilize, which they keep saying they will soon. Meanwhile BC isn't taking their annexation too kindly, and there's a lot of pushback against the mostly Californian chain of command in Washington and Oregon too. As far as we can tell, Every dem that's not Californian on the west coast is showing signs of dissatisfaction with the Californian management of the war. But its not like anybody'd want to admit it and get gulagged."

"What else? Overseas?" Joe shook his head.

"That's where rumors get real sketchy. Some say Japan and China are fighting, some say China is starting a famine and having a coup at the same time. Some say loyalist communists from when North Korea was a thing are riling shit up. Haven't heard shit about Russia, but people are saying everywhere from Egypt all along the Middle East and Southern China to Australia is a radioactive shitshow. Europe too, their confederacy is all fucked. People are saying England, France, Germany are all fried to a crisp."

"How about Africa?" Gabe asked.

"Eh, no UN means most of the subsaharan going to hell, but New Rhodesia is keeping together despite all the invasions from the north, bless the crazy fuckers. South Africa's doing alright, but they're floating on Rhodie handouts. Think the only reason the Rhodesians haven't annexed them might just be because they're being nice, hah. Hell, I got family in Bulawayo. I'd try to get to Rhodesia but the east coast is a shitshow from New York to Miami so getting a boat would be hell. Still, way it's sounding, Africa sounds like the best place to be. Even South America is having problems, hearin' that Brazil's economy's tanked and all the Brazilian states are fighting each other over food and politics, just like us. Argentina's digging itself into a socialist coup and annexed Chile after they also went into economic collapse."

"Fuckin' A," Gabe said.

"Well, again, nobody really knows what's going on anymore. It's all rumors. There's a chance that we Americans could be alone in this shit, but the lack of international intervention makes me figure otherwise. To think we've got a bunch of furries wrapped up in the shit with us's kinda sad enough to be funny, y'know?"

"Fuck of a welcome to the planet," Gabe laughed. "Don't figure it was their fault, do ya?"

"Well, *fault's* a hell of a word here, but it's not like they didn't play a part. Eh, don't mean to sound Joneseyian or anything, but I figure they were a part of a bigger plan, y'know? All this don't sit well with me, with next to nobody getting off easy, everyone wrapped up in coups or civil wars or economic collapses. Who's probably at fault is ElTek. Think about it- it was all their technology that went haywire, it was their servers that went down and took electronic currency with it, and the hybrids all got 'Property of BioTek' on their fuckin' shoulders, so who the fuck do you think is at fault here?"

"...Sic semper tyrannis," Paul mumbled, practically off-topic, just saying something to fill the air. Gabriel smirked.

"For all we know it was Rhodesia's fault," Gabe said. "Since they're the only ones not getting raped as hard as the rest of us."

"Well what do you expect? They were the only economy set to survive the Standstill before those fucking ElTek globalists unfucked the world by giving everyone a free iGlass and paying everyone's bills. And Rhodesia only got founded like ten years before the Standstill. My question is, how come ElTek didn't do so good a job at trying to destroy Rhodesia? After all, it only took the CIA and the britcucks like 10 years to destroy the old Rhodesia."

"Yeah, and they managed to undo all the shit Zimbabwe fucked up in ten years after they reformed," Gabe said. "Fuck, Noah, why didn't your dad just plan on moving to Rhodieland to survive the apocalypse?"

"...He didn't trust passports," I responded, and Gabe laughed. Even Joe and his gang chuckled.

"Now, ain't that some Jonesyism if you ever heard it?" Gabe laughed. "You guys should see his dad, tho. Fuckin' fits the bill and everything."

I silently sighed, drawing closer to Lauren as we walked. I felt a sick feeling in my gut every time I thought of my family. I leaned a little on her, and the back of her elbow, with her rifle's buttstock right next to it, brushed against the very top of my shoulder. In my haze I almost forgot she was with us.

"Ah, here we are," Joe said. "Just up here." I looked forward to peel through the mists. My ears could pick up the faint sound of a guitar being strummed, a couple voices chattering, and machinery being worked. The closer I got, the more I heard. The faint crackle of a little fire. I could smell its smoke. Before we knew it, the forest broke into a clearing- a clearing wide and vast, beset by the ancient mountains to the east, broad, gentle slopes stretching until the eyes lost track of them into the sky, ancient lifts dangling in the wind, paint peeling off to reveal spotty rust; inactive for a long while. Before us, a massive three story building in the aesthetic of a cabin sat, surrounded by tents and people, some tables and fire pits. I was somewhat surprised by their bit of racial diversity, seeing a rather large horse-like hybrid playing that guitar, sitting before the fire. An ink black avian type stood in the dimly lit doorway of the cabin, and I counted more than a few canids and felinids here and there. Nonetheless, they were still outnumbered by humans, and I think I only saw a single human woman out of any of anyone.

"Check it," Joe said. "Place used to be a little ski resort back when it snowed half the year here. Climate change made it unable to turn a profit, and the Standstill is what really killed it. Makes for a pretty nifty motherbase, eh?"

The music stopped as we drew near. Joe and his boys were out in front, but everyone still took notice of us, and hands motioned towards weapons. Me and Gabe looked back to the rest of us almost simultaneously, motioning to sling our weapons across our backs rather than in front of ourselves. Tentatively, we did, Lauren putting her rifle in the scabbard beneath her rear-right wing.

"What the fuck is this, Joe?" one asked, not particularly threateningly. "Recruits or what?"

"Don't worry, guys, they're bros."

"Lookin' pretty strapped," One of them said. Joe chuckled a bit.

"Easy, guys. They're squared away and're partial to the cause."

"...What cause would that be?" Sam blurted, for clarification.

"Impartiality," Joe responded, to Sam's satisfaction.

"...It's a nice start," A voice came from above. Our necks strained as we gazed up to a man standing upon the upper balcony of the old place. He was flanked by a dragontaur who nonchalantly leaned upon his shoulder, a couple heads taller than the human who had spoke.

"Hey, Squid," Joe called out. "Got some-"

"Yeah yeah, I've been paying attention," 'Squid' responded. Before anyone could get a word in edgewise, He jumped up onto the rail, before springing off and mounting the dragontaur, who jumped the rail and sailed down before us, comically gracefully. "So-" He addressed, not bothering to dismount his hybrid friend, the both of them with their arms crossed as they indignantly looked through each of us like flipping through the pages of a book. "Fancy being part of the anti-party, or what?"

"We'd be more partial to a collaboration," Gabriel responded. "You shot one of us, after all." Gabriel thumbed back towards Maria, who hid a snarl behind unmoving eyes as Squid and his dragon eyed her particularly, before the draconic's eyes wandered. I saw the sly smirk invading that big red dragontaur's face, and with a cautious flip of my head I could see Lauren's gaze averted with a tiny blush, him staring into her. I felt my brow furrow and my feet dig themselves into the ground. My hands clenched and I felt my body shake. Where Lauren was still yet to look back in her bashfulness, I caught his gaze instead, mad-dogging him without even thinking about it. I saw him laugh in silence, blushing under his reddish-black skin, a hand going up to feign coughing as he smiled at me, purple eyes narrowing.

"Oh, shit," Squid said, as the dragontaur and I had our little nonverbal conversation. "...It was Paul, wasn't it? God dammit..." He barely had to affirm his guess, Paul visibly cringing. "Jesus christ, Paul."

"What? You should have seen that shot, it was a good ass-" he was immediately elbowed by his squad superior, Joe. Maria still glared at him, nostrils flared.

"Right, Duke-" Squid tapped his bareback mount on the shoulder as he alley-ooped off. "Thanks," he said quietly, as the dragon reciprocated thanks. Squid approached us, making a beeline for Maria. "I suppose you've heard sorry before, but y'know..." he paused to kick at some dirt. "Mi casa es su casa. Always glad to-" He'd reached out where he approached her to lay a hand upon her shoulder, that she deflected aptly.

"Don't patronize me. Speak English." He shrank back if only in pace, his flamboyantly confident pose remaining, how he formed his lips into a whistling shape for a moment, eyes scanning Maria's ferocity.

"-Well then," He continued on best he could beneath her iron gaze. "Pardon the humor. It's a bit hard to... switch off." he gave that charming, nearly flirtatious smile again and her eyes were on a runaway roll. "I mean it, though. I've got some extra supplies hanging around y'all can borrow."

"...Happen to know any helicopter pilots?" Gabriel was next to chime in, leaning up against one of the resort tables, where a game of cards was taking place between a lot of Squid's miscreants, these 'Kommandos'.

"Whoa, don't you think you're-" I began, petering off.

"We've got winged hybrids if we need air support. Besides, your troupe's got at least one yourself," Squid motioned to Lauren, and I caught the tiniest wink. My fists clenched once more. This 'Duke' dragontaur was also eyeing at Lauren again. I felt my skin crawling.

"...Not what I asked. I'm going to take that as a no."

"Hm, a man of plans and mystery, huh?" Squid remarked as Duke was looking down upon me as I glared at him again.

"We're in the market for one. We're on our way north but the roads are all impassable. We're looking to get our vehicles carried over to clear roads."

"Shame this fine specimen here can't do it," Squid sang playfully towards Lauren. "She looks just about as capable, though. Maybe Duke here has met his match."

"Maybe 'Duke' should keep his eyes up," I found spilling from my mouth, gnashing. An ample moment passed where the canter of the conversation stuttered, eyes falling on me and my indignance. Even Lauren looking down on me in couched surprise.

"...Jesus, man, what's your deal?" Squid said, taken aback. I saw Duke's hands go up to his mouth as he snuffed his laughter and my blood boiled. "I was gonna give you guys a couple weeks worth of free food." My eye twitched ever so slightly, especially to hear Lauren's exasperated, almost embarrassed-for-my-sake laugh.

"Wh-" Maria began, but Gabriel was there to save my ass and the conversation.

"-Honestly, we're good on food," Gabriel said. "However we could use a last-ditch trump card."

"...Ah, I think I see where you're going with this," Squid said as he leaned upon his dragon friend, reaching back to gingerly drape the dragontaur's red arm over his shoulder and chest, like pulling a window curtain over himself as the two of them swayed in unison, still rather amused in me and Lauren's direction. "You want us... To help you guys out in a tough spot, should said tough spot ever arise?"

"That's the gist of it," Gabe said.

"Why, just because we had a little friendly fire incident and that makes us owe you?" Squid put forth as a little pushback, as he began playing a little with Duke's hand and fingers in front of him.

"Well, that and..." Gabe looked over to me. "We heard you took some interest in the Citadel." Squid paused inspecting Duke's nails in boredom, as he looked back up, interest piqued.

"...Yeahhh," Squid said. "Seems like a place I'd like to hang out in. After all, this war's gotta end sometime. Don't want to turn to banditry after the profiteering business dries up."

"...Cheeki breeki!" Paul cried, and everyone eyed him and his stale reference sourly.

"Anyway, fun's gotta run low sometime. Being the moralfag I am, it'd be nice to do some PMC work for a legitimate, albeit tiny government. You sure you can get us talking with their higher ups?"

"If I can get the hybrids in, I'm sure I could get you in," I cut in, swallowing my pride and stammering rage.

"...Yeah, but can you guarantee that? What's your relationship with 'em?" I gulped.

"Uh... my dad's their primary electricity and civil engineer?" I said, stowing my ire long enough to put my reasoning forth. "He worked- works the solar emplacements and the hydraulics in the dam. Supplies the town with power." Squid rubbed his stubble of a beard on his neck.

"Well, it ain't town jester, so it's better than nothing," He said. "Would have been nice if he was something like a chancellor or a mayor or some shit, but it's worth a shot. And hey, any excuse to fuck shit up, right?" Squid walked forward, Duke's arm trailing off him as he brushed him off.

"One free fuck shit up coupon?" Gabe asked, hand sticking out. Squid took the hand and shook it.

"Eh, buy one, get one free," He laughed. Squid then approached me, hand out. "You're not gonna die on us, right?" He asked me. "Because that would fuck our shit right in the ass."

"I won't do it on purpose," I responded, taking his hand. He chuckled.

"Pack lube just in case." I released his hand, fighting the urge to go find somewhere to wash mine.

### Chapter 54

We wandered about the camp, having a look around. I stuck by Lauren if even at some distance, as she gravitated towards the little musical circle. That equine minauren hybrid played the guitar as another human sat ready with a harmonica, joining in when he could. The melody was a lukewarm thing, something that had a somber joy to it. I guess it sounded lonely, if only when he played alone. When the harmonica joined, it did not change; it only sounded lonely together.

Duke stood a ways away, now armed with his guitar that he'd gotten, evidently from his quarters within the resort, walking on towards the music circle. A lot of us were enjoying the music and the camaraderie-by-proxy, sitting there and resting from the training. I saw Lauren looking towards Duke.

"I've... I've never really seen another centaur-y dragon before," She said, and I froze a little. I looked to her and I could see the faintest blushing.

"*Really?*" He responded, squinting coyly as he put his muzzle up.

"Well, I- I for sure never really talked to one before." He smirked at this with a little "hmph".

"That seems kinda odd," He said. "We're supposed to be pretty common." I didn't like the way he spoke. Like he was hot shit.

"R-really?" Lauren asked. "I mean, I guess... I've seen others like us, it's just..." She grunted. "I dunno. I'm the only one in our group."

"Well, there's always me, now." He smiled ever more slyly. He flipped his guitar a little bit, letting it stop with a slap upon the wood that resounded. "...You got any songs you'd like to hear?" I could see the two other musicians roll their eyes and groan subtly in exasperation, easily heard by Duke but not reacted upon.

"Uh... I dunno, I don't listen to m-"

"Great! You can hear one I came up with myself," He plopped on down by that fire to get a better position with which to begin, crowding the human sitting with his harmonica, the music of the two stopping abruptly before Duke began.

"...The wizard! OuOOUHuhuUUUHhhhh... BEWARE!" For a centaurical, who were supposed to have deep voices, his singing voice was notably shrill, challenged only by the twangy simplicity of his chords, and even then, their utter imprecision. He demonstrated his inability to keep beat with his instrument quite well. "For un-be-known-st to the MANNN, in the great CASTLEEEEE... He can burn stone (burn stoneeee)!!!"

"...Yo, you get a homoerotic vibe from Squiddy or what?" Gabriel muttered closely to me.

"Dude looks like he'll fuck anything that walks," I muttered back, still amused at Duke's playing.

"Even this dork," Gabriel motioned to Duke, as Lauren was now eyeing around, pursing her lips with drawn brows and a raised hand like she was going to bite her nails to preoccupy herself.

"...Hey! Did ya like it?" Duke's voice radiated as his wailing slowed to a stop, after what he must have thought as a melodious wind-down.

"It sucks!" one of the other Kommandos blurted distantly. He was just beaming too hard to care.

"It's... Okay," Lauren put forth, letting her hands slap at her sides and nodding her head from side to side, giving a toothless grin.

"It needs a little work. Like love," He put forth with a grin, and I watched Lauren's brow arch with closed eyes, like taking a whiff of something noxious by surprise.

"Sure," She muttered, wandering off as Duke watched her go. She came right up to Gabriel and I. "I think we've made ourselves acquainted, can we go?" She muttered.

At least the encounter with the Kommandoes netted us some good stuff. Gabriel took it upon himself to get me and Lauren more gear to replace our old stuff, not to mention some various doodads.

There the next day, back in our own base as we stood around the table where Gabriel had been taking inventory, sat a large array of plate carriers and chest rigs, loaded down with ammunition and armor.

"One chest rig with a plate pocket, eleven by fourteen inch, polydynamid armor with a drop-down protective plate, ten by six inch. Camelback Mr. Pendrew gave you can fit into the back side, it'll interface with the molle on the straps, and with a bit of tweaking should work around your wings." Gabriel tapped the somewhat exposed plate with its upper edges sticking out, where it sat behind the many magazine carriers and administration pouches, that auxiliary plate swinging beneath by molle latches. "Dynamid weave to intersperse in your saddle," Gabriel motioned to the tough yellow fabric-like material piled on the table, looking like it was pulled straight from bulletproof vests. "And, just as a gift, I found one of these."

"A baseball cap?" She asked, before taking the hat he stuck towards her face. "What's this?" She noted of the concealed plate inside it.

"You can't exactly wear a helmet, but you're a seamstress, so I figured you'd figure something out with this. Bulletproof hat with a level IIIA trauma pack. I used to wear something like this on extra sensitive, gunfight-light ops where my full mask would be a faux-pas."

"Aw, thanks Gabe!" Lauren gushed, of her new gear. "I'll get right to work!" She scampered off with the new materials happily enough, leaving Gabriel and I in the dining room as I turned over my new cuirass.

"Don't tell the rest of the group," He said as I hefted it up with an "oof". "But I got some level four armor for you. It'll stop armor piercing rounds. Need you to stay alive all the way to the Citadel, y'know."

"Jeez, this is almost as heavy as my old stuff but an armor level down," I grunted.

"Yeah, well you'll tough through it. Front and back plates, side plates, shoulder pauldrons, level three polydynamid helmet with a applique plate in the front, raising it to level four in that area. Idea is to make you really hard to kill."

"Make me really hard to move, too," I retorted. Gabriel rolled his eyes.

"Whine less. I'm not the one who got your shit stolen," he snarled playfully, and I rolled my eyes right back at him.

"...Yeah. Appreciate it," I said in earnest, though it may not have fully come out that way. I realised how it sounded, reaching out to grip him on his own shoulder, looking him in the eye for one last "I mean it. It means a lot."

"Yeah, don't get sappy," He brushed me off, sighing.

"The Kommandoes give you any leads on a pilot?"

"Nah. Didn't expect it, to be honest. Gonna have to do things the old fashioned way. Stalk a pilot on his way home from work. Airport's got a good amount of dead man's land around it, which makes intel tricky. Nothing I haven't dealt with, though." I scoffed out a laugh.

"Well ask me if you need a hand."

"Bank on it."


Another couple of days passing by in a blur. Lauren chopped up the back end of the hat and sewn on velcro strips, to make holes for her horns. I saw her in her little tan cap and body armor and she looked so much more official. Like a real warrior. She'd train incessantly, absorbing as much information as possible and reading constantly, shooting her new bow at targets and going out to come back every evening with freshly killed and dressed small game. But most of all of her bid to improve, to move forward, she'd weigh down her saddlebags and chest rig with rocks and metal, whatever she could get, and go out to train her wings, always striving to make them steam, to work herself to that limit she'd experienced with me. I guess it was inspiring. I couldn't help but feel some strange secondhand pride upon watching her test herself, see her timing her flying speed, her overall stamina, how she stood a little straighter and a little stronger too, her hard work inspiring confidence. How her soreness never got her down, she just got a massage from Mrs. Pendrew or Selicia and kept moving. I was so proud of her, and everyone could tell she was proud of herself.

Another day at church came. More of the same, I was just floating along there. This session was different, with a ceremony they'd do once a month. Consecration, the Lord's Supper, they called it. Eating little scraps of bread and drinking a tiny cup of grape juice. I was rather surprised they still had any of this stuff, the pastor adding that they won't be doing this next month, probably out of it, more important things to get for those in the camps.

I remained seated for the quaint little ceremony, as the Pendrews got up to join in the line going down the central aisle- out the outerward aisle, of course, as Maria and Lauren directly joined them, as well as Katt and Anthony, to go recieve a little piece of bread and a tiny cup of grape juice. Sam sat in the aisle behind us towards the edge, where she'd be close to Abel in the aisle, those two also who didn't feel like going forward. as Maria came around to sit back down next to me, I watched Lauren quaintly trotting on back precariously ferrying the little cup and bread. The care she took to avoid spilling as if it were the very blood of jesus christ himself, slowly going to lay her lower body down after turning back forward. I did not break my stare even as Maria intertwined her fingers and clasped her off-hands so hard her knuckles turned white, avoiding everyone's gaze by barreling her eyes towards that pastor, just gripping me as she sat distantly up next to me.

"Here, I got some for you," Maria finally said as I looked over, shoving a tiny plastic glass and a piece of stale bread towards me, seemingly unmoved by me despite the emotions raging behind her glassy eyes. She impatiently motioned for me to take it, and I did.

I drank the blood and ate the body when the pastor gave the cues, and the session was adjourned to let us all meander outside. God, I could just sit and stare at that sky. The deep blue, almost spotless aside from a couple thick clouds, one of which blocked the sun completely. That dampening blue, how a cool breeze floated on by and I could sigh, feeling the crisp burn enter and exit my lungs. Was it pretty? I don't know. It was something.


It was pretty much a month since it had all started, and here we were. Gabriel was digging for intel, the Blue's armies to our west seemed to have came to a crawl just like we did. There was far more fighting to the south. Shortstone was quiet. Now that I was more able to withstand the thought, I was out scavenging again. We spoke with the Kommandos over comms, Gabriel obviously working through things. The news spoke of a heatwave coming, as well as how the Californian army was crippled by a new infectious disease spreading rapidly throughout their ranks. But when we went out, we'd see a much more somber reality beyond what was propaganda. We'd come across houses full of people, dead where they slept, various accoutrements of well-making around them. Like they died of a cold. It was eerie, sifting through them. Humans, all humans. Gabriel acted like he didn't seem bothered by it, more glad to have extra stuff, but he wore his mask with the filters on anyways, as I did similarly with a gas mask from the kit dad assembled for me. Archie or Abel would be worried about infection since they didn't exactly have masks, but Gabriel noted how it was always humans. Just humans in these circumstances, a family or group of humans alone dead and gone. The soldiers were wearing gas masks more and more in their patrols. We began to get concerned, the Pendrews checking up on us to make sure we were all healthy, in case any of us needed to be put in quarantine and helped before it was too late. But it was strange how it seemed to avoid us, as everyone around us seemed to be getting sick. The Kommandos didn't seem too bothered by it, either. But the mounting heat was different.

"Noah." Maria would be asking me, and there I was, with her in bed. So much stress, the two of us sitting there on our opposing sides of the bed after working all day to pull up each backyard to make room to grow crops. She'd sigh long, that heavy heart of hers. She needed something, some closure, some measure that yes, we were getting closer to our goal. Her goal. She'd touch me gently, like afraid to break me, like fine china.

"...It's getting hot these days," I mentioned back. It's June already, anyways. Isn't it? The thought sailed in and out of my head slowly, floating on through without a care. I couldn't get hung up on it.

"...Are you mad at me?" The conversation, if you could call it that, wavered this way and that. Like I was floating in and out of myself, in and out of this place. Maybe I was uncomfortable. God, she was pretty, wasn't she? Right?

I'd lean over to kiss her. It was like I wasn't hearing her, though I was speaking back. Another part of me. She'd lay there to flutter her eyelids at me, but it all felt like a stage play. Something was off. I was undressing her, watching her pretend to giggle. What did she want here? I was undressing myself, and we would make love. I think. The world came in and out. Until we were done, laying there, staring at the ceiling. Pretending to enjoy the other's company. Marriage. Was she talking about marriage? Sure sounded like it.

I let the world fade. It was all going to get so much further from lucidity, and soon.

### Chapter 55

During the heatwave, it felt as if the days all fell together into one muddled stream of thought. Sleep. Get up. Do stuff. Go to bed. Have sex with Maria, maybe. Sometimes. Often, more often than usual for sure. It didn't matter. The days were incomprehensible from each other. I'd go scavenging with Gabriel, talk about the pilot or something, maybe hang out with the Kommandos. Avoid Republicans. Go home. Lounge around. Gabriel played his games and I sat to take in the world all at once.

But it mattered little to me. Maria would come upon me, like a beast in the night. It wasn't like it bothered me, I just wasn't really... There, for her. Ever. I couldn't really. But where I lacked that primal reciprocation, Lauren would be there and my fog would clear, if only a little. We'd be laughing and joking, playing cards or billiards. She'd always be working, finding something to do, like she couldn't sit still. Admirable. An admiration that I lacked around Maria. Poor Maria.

In my stupor I felt frustration. Every emotion I felt for Lauren I tried to put towards Maria, and it always fell flat. I distanced myself from Lauren. I would look away when her gaze drifted towards me. before long I could hardly stand to be in the same room as her. I'd have my meals earlier or later than the rest. If Lauren wanted to come along with Gabriel on a scavenge run, I'd feign disinterest or make excuses. I started skipping church- Lauren was wearing her little trinity crux constantly. I could hear her praying at meals. I couldn't even look near a bible. That cheerfulness I felt around her, I knew was wrong for me to enjoy too, or something. Like a little trespass.

To deal with this, I made love to Maria, every night. Well, maybe not love. We certainly *fucked*. At first it was quiet, it was mutual, it was at its most genuine, even if at that early point it was all a performance anyways. But the shadowy disassociation would not stop, and my frustration grew, grew upon that shadow looming over me. Every day with my only respite the night, and I'd simply go at Maria harder, longer, more ravenously to fight the stagnation, the nothingness. I had my pleasure, but did my damndest to make her pleased. I wanted to hear her moan and squeal. Fuck being quiet. Fuck it all. And fuck the deafening silence in my head. I stayed up late, we'd make our facsimile of love for hours. I think I was trying to keep myself from sleep, to keep myself away from the next day's sick nothingness. But every day it was back, and there was nothing to do but weep in my own brain.

When I was beginning to make our nights of sex all the more intense, Maria began to ask me all the more for my commitment to marriage. Sure, she'd been asking for a while, but now she was trying as best she could to put the pressure on. Poor, poor Maria. I always steered the subject away. And, at that, I even found myself unable to look Maria in the eyes while making love. I'd see her beautiful, Brown mocha eyes, and I'd see Lauren's, see how much better they were to look at and wish I was looking at them instead. It was haunting. I'd look Maria in the eye and make love to Lauren all at once. I'd scream Lauren's name and Maria's would spill from my mouth. It was almost like I'd made love to Lauren every night, right alongside Maria. I'd wake up afraid I'd said her name in my sleep.

As time passed on and on, I grew to hate her, I hated her so much, And I hated myself. I hated the thoughts that plagued me, the sick sexual desire of sliding myself up against her big, beastial lower body and putting myself between her powerful thighs; looking up, up, way up to her great, mighty and supple visage towering over me as her lower legs' talons would grab me by the shoulders and back of the head, and she'd caress her own soft, supple breasts with her hands and moan for me, moan in holy, flawless pleasure, up there above me. I wanted her out of my head, out, fucking out of my head but every night she was back and every night I had no choice but to love her, so I hated. I hated and hated and hated. But it wasn't really Lauren I hated. It was a reflection of myself I poured my ire into, my loathing. What the fuck was I doing here? What the fuck am *I* doing?

I would wake, and Maria would lay there. She wouldn't look at me. I wouldn't look at her, either. She'd talk about marriage every breakfast, less and less because she wanted it but because she began to loathe me just as I did myself, my personality, everything, and she desperately wanted my atonement. It was no longer love. It wasn't even sex. I was venting my frustration, like a tantrum from a little boy. The orgasms grew weaker and weaker, no matter how hard I'd thrust- or how much I'd fiddle and finger, lick and kiss, as Maria's beautiful moans of pleasure turned into ugly, exasperated groans and sighs of disgust and boredom. Even if she did moan as I wanted, I doubt it would have helped my drive much. She was done trying desperately to capture my eyesight, and instead looked off to the side, like she was dead, and I was fucking her lifeless body. Both of us felt it. And at the end of it every night, I'd stop and feel *unclean.* Disgusting. My skin crawled, but I had no choice. I needed this to function the next day, even though what I was doing could hardly count as functioning. I was a zombie, shambling around. I only really lived in my dreams of Lauren. And even then, the beauty was gone, it was like pornography in my mind. A part of me longed for those simple dreams of happiness when Lauren and I simply stared and smiled. The flower had wilted. Lauren drove me mad. Maria was fed up. Goddamn Lauren. Poor, poor Maria.

Finally, one night, it came to a stop. No matter how much I tried, no matter how much I'd feel her beautiful breasts and supple hips and massage her clitoris and strain and jerk and squeeze, I couldn't get it up. I remember the look she gave me. It was one of disgust, it was one of pity and it was one of relief. That look she gave me alone made me want to cry. I think by this point she, and we, knew in our hearts it was over, even if neither one was strong enough to admit it. She hadn't asked me about marriage since yesterday, and even then it was sheepish. Maria, sheepish. I could hardly bear to think of how *unlike* her it was. I looked her in the eyes, for the first time in what felt like forever. I forgot why I'd even bothered to not look her in the eyes. I didn't see Lauren. I didn't see Maria, either. I saw nobody. I saw nothing. dead.

After trying fruitlessly for what felt like an eternity, I rolled off of her and we lay there in silence. No, I couldn't deal with this. I couldn't be there with her, and she understood. I was up and away, down to sleep on a couch or something.

For the rest of the night, I could not sleep. I lay there, in my own sweat and regret for all those hours, reliving that horrible session, no matter how much I wanted not to. But it plagued me, something in me.

I was up. My legs spurring me on. I got my holos from the kitchen table. I was telling myself to go and look up some technical manual to distract myself, to sleep, but no. I knew what I was going for, even if I didn't acknowledge it.

Her photo, from that day scouting. Those beautiful eyes, how she glowed in the wind, hair flowing behind her. Why was I staring at her? I couldn't look away, I couldn't shut my glasses off. I was entranced. I needed a distraction, desperately. Who was on guard duty right now? I'd help them. Not like I was going to sleep anyways.

Daniel.

There he was in the attic, sitting there to look out upon the road. He looked over to acknowledge me, then looked back. Like he knew I was so restless, like he expected this. For the first time in what felt like ages, my blood began to boil, but I made through with some small talk. With every one of his responses it was more and more clear that he… knew. Or something. Something was fucked. Wasn't this *on him* in the first place? Fucking freak. Slinking in the shadows. All those weird drawings, his little obsession, the first hybrid he met and here I am, a normal person with a real girlfriend, in complete shambles. Daniel had been all but invisible to me for all this time. Fucking coward, hiding from me. I felt stupid, like he'd been hiding right under my nose this whole time. But more importantly, I felt like asking.

"Look, Danny…" I began, once it was obvious that my mind would not clear with pointless small talk. "What do you think… About Lauren?" he stopped to straighten up some. Yes, he still moved slowly, somewhat in pain from his tender scar, but the pain went deeper than that. It seemed to emanate, to resonate.

"Lauren," he sighed slowly and tiredly, as if the very word moved his inner being. "You *love* her, don't you?"

The words hit me hard, like a monkey had thrown his shit at me and nailed me right in the mouth. It was so brazen and vulgar it practically took my breath away. "W-what?"

"You look at her some way. When you're talking with her, you've got this… look in your eyes, this happy look that isn't there when you're with… Maria. Even when you're not talking, you *stare* at her. I mean, you must," He spoke slowly and softly without a single stutter, but it felt as if he was screaming at me. The rest of the world seemed so quiet compared to his words, so loud in their truth, shaking me to bits. "Do you? Do you love L-"

"T-that's none of your fucking business," spilled from my mouth in an instant, making me only sound guiltier. My voice shook like my body did.

"And what I think of Lauren is none of *your* business. But you asked, so I guess I'll tell you. I don't care."

"Wh- what do you mean you don't care?"

"I mean I've told you before. I don't feel anything for her, that's what I mean," his voice rose in decibel and pitch, in frustration and anger. In turn, my own frustration and anger rose.

"You don't? You don't?! You fucking freak! You spend all day drawing dragon tits and you don't feel anything for a real-life dragon girl!?"

"No. no I don't. She's nothing like me. I figured all this out back in the car, when I was eating baby food and shitting in a pan. She's all upfront and confident and sociable and it only makes me nervous, and she spends all her time around me babying me like I'm some fucking child. She doesn't see me as an equal. That's all anybody ever sees me as. A child, and I'm sick of it. I got shot, doesn't mean I turned into some crying little kid," He said, voice beginning to tremble. To be honest, I never expected this sort of eloquence from him. "You- You're perfect for her. You're both brave- and reliable. And Maria makes you uncomfortable, even if you don't want to admit it. But you'll never break up, because people think staying a little uncomfortable forever is better than being really uncomfortable for a little bit, even if doing that, dealing with your problems and getting over them will make you happier in the end."

At this point, my rage was returning to me. Gabriel, I could understand. Mr Pendrew, I could deal with. Even Archie I could take. But Daniel, lecturing me? This sniveling little kid who could hardly handle a gun? I couldn't believe what I was hearing. How dare he turn down Lauren, I put her right in his lap. She was his wet dream, not mine. I swear, *not mine*. Why was I the one being analyzed here? Daniel, so stupid. He must be wrong. He *has* to be wrong. By turning Lauren down, he's forcing me to choose, this selfish little prick, I've got better things to be worried about. Not like I'd even choose Lauren, it's not natural. Her body. Her face. Her abstract mockery of the human form. How could he be right? *How?* My hands balled up into fists. Daniel didn't move an inch. I wanted to drive my fist into his belly, twist my knuckle in his tender scar.

So I did.

He let out a tiny, wheezing grunt and fell to his knees, crumpling up into a ball. He knelt there, falling over to sit, motionless with a look up to me, grasping my eyes with his. I saw not pain, not sorrow or anger, but *pity*. Pity in his face, his eyes. Pity on me. From timid, meek little Daniel, defeated before me, taking *pity* on me. His unstoppable judgement blew through me, a fortress rent by a single glance.

I stormed off. I would prove to him he was wrong. I knew I would. I was headed straight for the girls' room. Lauren was in there, and I'd make her profess her love to Daniel. I didn't care that I was going to wake the whole group. I didn't care if I'd been making a scene, I didn't care that I'd knocked the wind out of Daniel for no good reason. I didn't care that I was wrong, that the whole world was ringing in my ears. I didn't care.

I wrenched the door open, and stopped dead in my tracks.

In that singular patch of light streaming in from the hallway behind me, the first thing I saw was Lauren, laying there, her rear body hanging off of her mattress bed lazily. She was naked and exposed on this hot night. I saw her breasts, her dark nipples glistening like emeralds. And, faced straight at me from between her rear legs which were spread eagle, I got a look at her that took my breath away. There it was- she never wore pants, but I'd never really seen her vagina before. She was hairless, and it was clean and her scaly skin's pattern made it almost artful, like a symmetrical design about it, subtle. I couldn't help but stare. Not a single girl in the room was woken, and even if they were I don't think I would have even looked away for a second. I couldn't stop staring. I was mesmerized, and I memorized everything about it.

In the bathroom, with the door locked and my pants at my ankles, I sweat, I grunted and growled. It must've taken me only thirty seconds of vigorous pumping, gazing into my hologlasses, into that beautiful face of hers immortalized on that magical day so long ago. I didn't have tissues or lotion, but I didn't need it. In my other hand, inexplicably, was that shot-off horn of hers. Like it turned up, out of nowhere, and I stroked it, stroked *her* like I stroked myself. The orgasm almost took me by surprise- and what an orgasm it was. My eyes rolled back in my skull. I let out an inhuman, growling groan and my legs- no, my whole body- shook with each pulse.

Before I knew it, it was over. Like every orgasm I'd ever had, it was gone, faded quickly, replaced with the black, all-consuming void of self-reflection. I was left sitting there, in the quiet darkness of the bathroom, lights flickering softly just like they always did, with my right hand covered in the mess I'd made, dripping to the floor every few seconds, *drip, drip, drip*; derangedly slumped there as she watched me from that beautiful picture. Like her judgement reached out to me there, as my quivering left hand, still full of her horn came up to strip my glasses off, and let my eyes flow as the objects clattered to the ground.

I didn't cry because of the mess I'd made. I didn't cry because of how I'd given in and betrayed Maria. I didn't even cry because of the fact that I'd pleasured myself to the visage of an unconscious woman, much less an unconscious dragon centaur, how reprehensible I must look in this current moment, sitting there, dripping in shame, in regret, in utter rapture.

No.

I cried because for the first time In my life, I knew just how  alone  I really was.

### Chapter 56

A cool breeze was wafting down from the mountains. Storm clouds gathered once more on the horizon, and the humidity was spiking. It didn't feel like it was getting cooler. How long had the heat wave been over? Was it over? What day was it?

I found myself again, like I was prone to simply find myself from time to time in different places, caught somewhere between life and limbo, this time sitting quietly at the dining room table. I heard the sizzling of squirrel meat and fresh eggs on the stove, as Gabriel stood in an apron, toiling away, like he always did. He never let us go hungry, at least. Something to remark upon. My fingers intertwined as I leaned against the table, all fingers except for my indexes, which pushed the other back and forth, back and forth. My mind crossed over Gabriel and pondering just how he did what he did for the cooking supplies other than what we drudged up, barely keeping myself from falling back into disassociation.

No one else sat at the tables yet, people were up and about, some still asleep, some keeping guard in the foyer and living room. That was odd, that we'd keep such vigilant watch during the day, too. some early risers were waking up by watching the Republican news. The power was back on, for the moment, and everyone was taking full advantage of it, charging their appliances and devices and whatnot. The lights still flickered every now and then.

There I was of course, sitting alone, in silence, at that table. I'd blinked and the food was nearly ready, people rustling by. I sat there, motionless, watching my index fingers push the other back, and forth. Back, and forth.

"Can I serve you some eggs?" Gabriel stood over the table with a spoon, ready to scoop some onto my plate. He towered over me there, where I was folded in on myself.

"...Not hungry."

"Not hungry my ass, you barely eat anything these days," Gabriel said. "Look at the bags under your eyes. Have you seen yourself recently? You're losing weight."

I said nothing, looking away. he put some on my plate anyways. I heard the clicking of her nails, as Lauren circled around and laid down her lower half, sitting across from me. "Mmm, looks really good, Gabriel!" she said with a bright smile. She looked over to me, and my eyes wandered down and away from hers.

"Anytime, Greenie," He said with a wink. She laughed a little, taking the utensils and digging in. Maria came in and stood in the corner, taking her plate as she stood, like a statue, hardly moving as she ate. I didn't look at her, I just felt the room grow colder and knew it was her that entered. I looked up once more at Lauren, who was now eating her breakfast appreciatively and looking down at her plate.

"God, I hate this weather," Archie came in, smoothing his fur with his hands, it all sticking up. "You'd think it would get cooler by August. Or at least for the fucking humidity to stop."

"I think it's quite pleasant," Selicia said, coming up to the table. "...Just like your cooking, darling," She looked over to Gabriel, who lowered his head, shrugged a little and smiled in a gesture of humility.

August.

For a moment, it was like the word inspired panic in me. What the fuck were we doing? I had to wake up. No. But I just slipped back into my chair and into my sunken world as it hit me. The cool breeze. The dog days of summer passing us by in the blink of an eye. My panic was not strong enough to break me out. Nothing short of an act of god would be.

I'm alone with Gabriel now.

"Noah."

I didn't speak.

"Hey. Noah. Stop fuckin' zoning out for once." Gabriel was snapping in my face. I looked over to him.

"Wh-"

"You good?" He barked, brows arched. Less like he cared and more like he was trying to illicit a reaction. I guess I couldn't blame him. "You haven't said a thing all week. People are worried about you."

Where were we? All alone here, in a blackout. Lauren was in the corner, before the kettle of water on the stove, the old-fashioned one. I'd been watching her, but watching through her. She'd been out and back in. She looked so different. So much stronger. Her horn had a point again, though it was still stubby.

"Noah. Are you all right?"

"I'm fine. Fuck off," I muttered into my coffee before me, taking a sip. It's easy to forget, but room-temperature coffee tastes like shit. "...I'm not sleeping well." Like I needed a further explanation, muttering more nonsense. Gabriel grunted too, sitting down opposing me. I felt my world shrink as he did, like an interrogator sitting across from me. He was just... staring at me. A solid minute as far as I could tell. I could hear the drone of the telescreen in the adjacent room. Hearing a date mentioned. August twenty-first... was something going to happen then, an invasion, perhaps? Wait, are they talking about the weather? What time is it? What day is it? That can't be today, It can't have gone by that f

372

"Noah." Gabriel's voce ripped me out of my own head again. He kept needing to do it, so I looked back at him. "You… Worried about this guy?"

"...This guy?"

"The pilot."

"Oh." We found one already? He must have. Gabriel is always so resourceful. I could really respect him for

"*Noah.*" Gabriel was more insistent now in his pulling me out of myself. He almost looked more like an impatient father than my lifelong friend, the way he stooped there, the way he lurched in with his big protruding brow casting his frustrated, tired eyes in eternal shadow. "I'm going to need your help if anything goes wrong. Republicans are getting antsy. We're far, far overdue an invasion from the west. I need you," He uttered. "...At your one-hundred."

"...You... don't think he set us up?" I proposed in a mutter. It felt like I was reading off a line, like 'oh, that sounds like the right thing to say' in my mind. To get him to believe that I was listening.

"Could be," Gabriel sighed. "It never hurts to be too careful. Just keep your eyes out for anything suspect, alright?"

"...Are you worried?" Gabriel sighed heavily, tilting his head away but keeping those hunters' eyes of his dead square on me.

"Not as worried as I am about you." Another spacious silence. You really could fit the whole world in this void.

"...We've been here too long," I uttered. "I think it's… I dunno." I took another sip of the foul drink. At least it elicited a reaction from me. Gabriel's frustration was reaching its zenith, even if he wasn't the type to show it. Funny how your perception changes when you're living behind the film of your own eyes. Like it doesn't even apply to you. Like you're in a dream.

Like you can't be hurt.

### Chapter 57

*Whoosh.*

The bag was pulled off of my head, as my cranium bobbed in response from the violent yank. Light streamed in from screaming spotlights, as my mind ached, my head still swimming.

Was I asleep? I guess I was. But this wasn't a dream, at least not anymore. The smell, the pain- and the noise.

I squinted, the ringing in my ears subsiding to the sound of heavy breathing and grunting in pain, the mist haze before my eyes clearing to reveal its source: a dimly lit Gabriel, bloody and bruised, receiving blow after blow from a gauntlet of men around him armed with batons, with tanned skin crowing in a rustic language that my brain deciphered ever so gradually as distinctly spanish; harsh, guttural utterances and spitting only interspersed by the wet slaps of bloody flesh against metal rods. I could see the blinking LED lights of the cameras all around the hard concrete ceiling, the dim spotlights of the basement seeming intense and hazy, forcing me to squint as my head pounded, to cut through the mists of my eyes and of the scene before me. I leaned back a little, only to feel a cold, hard object prodding me in the back of my neck. I blinked again, trying to raise my hands from behind my back to rub my eyes, and as I did so, I noticed that they were bound together. I sat there near naked in my boxer shorts, and as I looked around, still feeling steely hardness poking me where my neck met my head, I saw everyone in a wide ring around the room, Gabriel's beating taking center stage as the black-clad men struck him over, and over, and over.

Circled around Gabriel's beating were we all, in our sleepwear, underwear. Sam. Abel and Reina. Anthony. Selicia. Archie. Daniel. Maria. Lauren. and even the quivering Susan, everyone, even three faces I didn't recognize at first on the far end. I blinked some more, seeing them. It was Michael, that red dragon from the church, sitting there, his family on either side of him.

With a rustling, bags once covering heads fell to the ground, and there I saw, behind every last person here, a shadowy figure, black armor and baclava-covered heads, and in their red-armband wearing arms, rifles. I blinked again, and, upon seeing the hazy, dreamlike terror in the faces of all my friends with a gun pointing at each one, I realised just what was poking me in the back of the head.

Back in the shadows of a far corner behind where that dragon Michael and his family knelt, I saw a man, his hand on the head of yet another. I couldn't see his face from the heavy shadow cast upon him by the dim lights, but every second my mind swam slowly and horrifyingly towards a revelation. but the hostage he was lording over, the last stranger in the room, I certainly didn't. Did I?

Of the droopy, yet confused and panicked stares lingering in our eyes, there were but two exceptions outside of our captors- Gabriel, who despite being curled into a ball on the ground, his gaze I caught and I saw naught but hate overcoming fear, his bloodied eyes rousing more and more lucidity into me as he grunted and shook from each strike like he was goading me to awaken, and that dragon Michael, who sat there on his knees, hands unbound unlike the rest, sitting and staring down at the ground in a sort of reverent pose and posture, like a samurai preparing seppuku.

"*Suficiente.*" The man in charge in that corner barked, slowly yet powerfully. His voice radiated and I knew exactly who it was. "*Esta listo.*"

Gabriel's crumpled form steadily unfurled itself as the Sinaloan ops surrounding him took step after step back, to retreat into the shadows behind where the republicans held all of us at gunpoint. The leader approached, stepping into the light. I blinked once, twice. That long face with drawn-in cheeks and cheekbones that cut out; pale skin and unkempt red hair above a well-fit fine suit. His footsteps echoed in this place as his shoes' heels clicked and clacked, filling this place with a dreadful rhythm. He stopped near the fallen Gabriel and silence returned for a second, suspense hanging in the air as Gabriel lay there looking up at him with his hands on his heaving chest and over his mournful, hateful face, wearing nothing but his undershirt and boxers. That leader of theirs fell almost frighteningly quickly to a squat with a vicious squeak of his shoes that made us jump, getting on Gabriel's level yet still towering over him. How he moved so inhumanly set the hairs of my neck on end. He whispered something, before looking up, and very slowly and deliberately looking every one of us in the eyes, a dead smile on his lips. His gaze went around the room, and as it met mine and lingered on me, I looked into the corner of my eye, avoiding this gaze. upon completing this, he let out a silent chuckle. "You've got quite the circle of friends, son," He proclaimed loudly, almost friendly-like, feigning impressedness.

"Fuck you, Red."

"Hm, I expected just as much from you," He responded. "I mean, now at least. What happened? I *raised* you. I've done so much for you, and this is how you repay me?" He said, speaking with a whiny voice as if hurt, even if it was all an act. "I mean, I could guess that you had a little discontent, but hey, that's what makes *un ejecutor, eh hijito*?" Gabriel just stared off to the side, feeling Red's gaze boring its holes into the side of his head. "A little... Edge to let you cut with, if you will." Gabriel didn't respond, and Red stayed quiet for a couple seconds. Suddenly he sprang back up in an instant of horrifying movement and another screech of his shoes, looking about. "I'm being so rude, aren't I? allow me to introduce myself," He brushed off his suit jacket. "I'm a representative of the Sinaloan Cartel- perhaps you've heard of us," He enunciated, pausing, as if waiting for some sort of rapport with his sickly humor. "Anyone?"

"...They already know."

"Oh do they?" Red leaned over Gabriel and whispered, yet did so loudly enough for all of us. "Do they really know everything?" Gabriel's face contorted for but a second. "Oh, you think you're above what you did, do you? The blood you've spilled in our name? You think if you just run away and forget about it, it makes it null and void?"

"...I've got nothing to say to you."

"Hm, not even going to go with the classic, *hijo*? 'you made me do it'? I mean, I suppose even you've heard it before, on many an occasion. Oh, you've stood behind cowards and traitors and heard them blubber those very same words before you pulled the trigger." Red stopped to reach into his coat, and there it was. A piece of silvered steel, shimmering in chrome and blackened ivory, adorned with the visage of death on every glittering surface. Red's pistol, which he looked over while he nonchalantly spoke. "How many people have you killed, son? You never were the type to keep a tally, but I'm curious- were you ever counting? or did you just lose count?"

"Just get to the point."

"Well, *you* already know, but for the sake of your friends, allow me to explain." He addressed to "us". "It's pretty obvious now who I am, but I'll give you a little more background, since I might as well. Not only am I part of Sinaloa's regional management in Idaho, I also happen to hold a second job, namely the commander of the northwestern garrison. Surprising how the Republicans are so quick to overlook Sinaloa's criminality when they realise how useful my power, my influence here is. Anyway, how this concerns your good friend, See, he was my... Protegé, of sorts, back in the day. I was his manager, I guess you could call it, and I work for the Sinaloan Cartel. He, of course, had orders to stay in Las Vegas. We had use for him there, while I got moved up north a while back, and-"

"Vegas got blown up, I would have-" Gabriel interrupted, before he was cut off, as Red turned to face the hostage here I didn't know and his pistol came up and went off. His body jerked for a moment before toppling over limp, blood pouring from his head as it hit the concrete with a loud, splashy thud. Every ear in that basement rung.

"Do NOT mistake my mercy for leniency! You know what *duty* means to us, do you not?!" He hollered, perhaps to only be heard over the ringing of our ears. "You've already cost the lives of those two older folks, and *now* your little pilot. Do NOT press me."

"W-what?" I heard Lauren's voice raise itself among the silence, her tone cracking in disbelief, and I reared my head. I saw her breathing more deeply, eyes flickering, her little trinity symbol hanging from that chain around her neck clinking, the only sound in this frigidly hot and heady place. Perhaps they didn't see any value in it, had yet to pry it from her unlike her clothes, naked save for that pendant and her bra top. The room went silent, as Red turned to face her, and I saw her entire body freeze, iced over by the cold glare, Red growing before her, an icon of evil.

"We haven't been properly introduced, unlike your rider and I," With his pistol still in his hand, he straightened out his tie with a cursory motion in my direction, and Lauren fought back a gasp. "But drastic measures must be taken when discipline is needed. I'm sure you can understand."

"You… You…" she struggled, but her four legs had been hogtied, just like her wings and her arms. he rose the gun at her, and the guard standing a little off to the side jammed the muzzle of his weapon into the back of her head so hard her entire head rocked down a little. With that, I shook. I was a moment from blurting out.

"Don't forget your situation," He said, before turning to Gabriel on the ground. "Son, you know what I've noticed?" Gabriel just glared up at the man. "Centauricals happen to be a lot tougher than most others- two hearts, four lungs, a whole lot more blood, you know. But if you hit one just right…" He pointed that gun right at Lauren's face, her eyes wide as saucers, her breath freezing in her throat. "…The trick is to hit the centerline. A *spinal* will do them quick, just like anybody else. And I don't really see why you ever bothered with that collector's piece of yours. Bren Ten," He scoffed, still holding Lauren at frigid gunpoint like he held our collective attention with our breath in our throats. "What a silly name. you said you got it from your grandpa, right? Found it in his things when you went rifling through them looking for it after your… parental figure made you mad. You took it to a bunch of idiot street urchins to impress them. They had you rob a gas station to get into their gang, you remember? You killed those attendees. Wasn't on purpose, they just didn't take kindly to getting robbed and you did what any good soldier would do. Then *we* found you in that gang and really gave you something worthwhile to do- oh, that's the best part, isn't it?" He stopped, looking back up, smiling brightly in amusement and some detached glee. The gun turned away from Lauren and she could breathe once more, as could I. "Oh, look at me. I'm rambling again. Where were we? Wondering about the survivability of a centaurical hybrid?" I was frozen as he turned back to her, yet to raise his gun again, glaring her down with the barrels of his deep, dark eyes. Everyone was frozen. Silence took over the room, as Lauren stared death in the face.

He chuckled after that dead silence, Lauren finally able to release her breath again, practically whimpering as she breathed as he chuckled on and on, amused to no end. "You should all loosen up. Stress is not good for the body," He turned around fully, to lord over Gabriel once more, and I swear could see a little piece of Lauren's soul float away as she was exhaling, silent tears cascading down her cheeks as she fought back her screams, pale as can be. "Still, son, I don't quite get why you're so into guns in the first place," He said, looking on the side of his own gun. "See, you always go on and on about personal liberties, saying more guns is better, makes crime harder. But, given your line of work, I don't follow. Maybe… I think you're guilty. You've always wanted someone to stop you, right? You've always prayed for a way out, huh? Some… Responsible citizen, being a hero, stepping up to put an end to you?" He stopped. "Think of all the things we've- that I've done for you. *Sacrificed.* Why would you be so selfish as to get away from all that? All you had to do was end a couple dozen lives here and there, burn down a few meth labs and whorehouses- be scary. You revel in being scary, my son. Don't tell me you don't love being scary. You live to piss people off and get in fights and make people afraid of you; you thrive in hate and pain. Why would you think even for a second that you weren't *made* for this job? Do you really think you have a conscience left, let alone had one in the first place?"

"Don't you fuckin' lecture me."

"Huh," Red responded after a brief pause, before pausing again, to feel the gun in his hands. "Perhaps you have a point. There's not much you can really come to terms with here, aside from *everything*. Just look at poor Carl over there- Just a man doing his job. You really didn't have to bring him into this, did you?" He motioned to the previously nameless corpse. "Man was a great pilot. Shame he was so easily… corruptible." Red's tongue clicked, as he finally holstered his pistol again, though the air of imminent danger persisted. "Perhaps the rest of your entourage might be able to take his example."

"We're all fucking dead already, don't lie to them."

"Now, now- keep optimistic, shall we?" he said with a smile, looking over all of us, clapping his hands once at which we all jumped a little.

"So what do you want," I heard Maria's voice. I reared my vision over to her, seeing her with an oddly calm look on her face, eyes somewhat drooped and her posture rather relaxed- it dawned upon me that it probably wasn't just the drugs keeping her so calm, but also a good dose of personal experience, and the thought rose my goosebumps even higher.

"What do I *want*?" Red smiled over to her like he was moments from bursting into laughter, a horrible look glittering in his soulless eyes. "Eager to get to the point, aren't we! Not that I blame you, your time is important, after all." He cleared his throat, redirecting his attention to Gabriel once more. "Leaving Vegas was a *bad move*, son. But then again, that nuke would have rendered you useless anyways, so I think that, if you came to me, I'd be able to forgive and forget, right? I might have even made you a captain of the Republican guard- an authentic one, that is, maybe even get you sent further inland to somewhere like Texas, so you'd never really have to kill anybody again if you chose so, if blood really makes you *that* uncomfortable."

"Don't bullshit me, Red."

"Now, now, hijito. I like to consider myself a reasonable sort, and you've more than made it up to me in loyalty back in the day. I mean, I don't think I'd be able to just let you off the Cartel since, you know, the only way out is…" he put a finger to his head and pantomimed a gun firing. "But still. coming all the way up here, and not even stopping to say hello- that's rude. But even that I suppose I would have been ready to forgive you for- that'd mean my good son wasn't fried to a crisp by the nuke, right?" He smiled, before pausing, his laughter growing in his misshapen chest. "...but the fact that before that you *impersonated* a Republican captain so you could get your friends out of jail? *Man!* I feel like I should just let you go because of that! What an exquisite display of gumption! Nobody even bothered to check for the longest time, since nobody thought anybody would have the gall to try to fake it! So, I must give you some credit." He stopped, clicking the final syllable of his last word with his tongue, also letting the echo ring in this subterranean lair. "So, you, your friends, that's 'you'. The colloquial you, the *vosotros*, if you will. Charged with conspiracy to murder and commit terrorism, identity theft, property theft, weapons violations, arson, and undermining the sovereignty of the Independent State of Idaho and the New American Alliance." He paused, long and hard, to turn around, facing that dragon Michael, who knelt there, cold sweat beading on his head, yet a deadly calm instilled in his candlelight eyes. "Then, there's this man- this dragon. a Mr. Michael Draco- I mean, I must say, hybrids just have the laziest last names, do they not? I guess that's what happens when you're born out of a test tube. Name's more of an afterthought," He stopped to laugh and gauge our reaction. We were all less than entertained by our horror. "Anyways, guess what crimes Mr. Draco has committed?" He smiled brightly. "He… He stole food for his family." Red proclaimed, making a mockery of misery. "He was only doing it for his little girl, who looked him in the eye and told him her poor little belly was hurting. Oh, it's tragic, isn't it?" Red said. "Isn't that terrible? Is that such a crime?" He asked. Everyone was too horrified to answer. "But as you know, discipline must be upheld. And unfortunately, in these dire times, the punishment for most any crime these days is... Death." Red let a pause sink into every one of us like a dagger through the throat. "But- I'm feeling generous today, that's the thing. So you know what I'm going to do with these criminals?" He said. "In the cartel, we have a tradition. A piece of my culture I share with you. *Trial by combat.* Old fashioned. So. here are the rules." Red reached into his pocket, pulling out Gabriel's old music player. "I'm gonna put this little iPod on shuffle, random song- and by the time the song ends, unless one of you two is a clear victor, everybody dies. Okay?" Red smiled fatherly towards Michael, then Gabriel. I caught his glare and froze over.

"Don't fuckin' do this to him, Red," Gabriel growled, and Red turned back to him, seeing Gabriel wipe the blood from his face as he sat up. Red smiled.

"He made his choice when he stole that food, just like you did when you betrayed your *familia*," Red smiled Red began to walk over to a little stereo.

"W-what happens to the winner?" Maria asked as he walked, heels clacking.

"Nosy, are you?" Red noted. "Well, I guess the winner gets to... *Find out.*"

There was a little static sound as he plugged it in, like lightning scraping aside itself. Michael rose, and Gabriel went to one of those supports, using it to pull himself up. Red clicked the button.

"Tonight... I'm gonna have myself, a real good time," The stereo spat, as Michael rose his clenched red hands and leaned forward.

"Queen?" Red said. "Gabe, why do you have Queen on your player? I thought you said Queen was bad luck," Red noted. "Oh well, I guess you just need some bad luck every now and then!" Gabriel was wordless, his own hands raising like the gun barrels of a firing squad, and the violence began. It was almost like this smirking Red nodded in place to the music a little to the music despite how he stood in stiff relegation, amid the slaps of fist and flesh. It was hard to keep up with- maybe it was the drugs, maybe it was the fact that I was still trying to comprehend that in about three and a half minutes I would get a bullet in the back of the head unless one of them *killed* the other. My mind dwelled on some quiet irony of this, Gabriel and Michael had never met before but I knew both of them by name. It was funny enough to spawn a tiny smile on my lips for a split second, if even that smile was but a stressful twitch on my face.

It was hard to get invested in the fight, and at the same time I couldn't help but watch- not because my fate and the fate of all my friends depended on the fight, nor the reason that my best friend was fighting, and getting his face punched in, hell, I hardly knew why I was watching, but I couldn't stop. Nobody could. Everyone, even Susan and Michael's little daughter were watching, in terrified silence, as this happy celebratory tune played loudly, oh so loudly under the ringing of our ears and the sounds of screaming, growling and physical violence. I began to look at all the faces, one by one. Lauren, Maria, Selicia, Michael's wife and daughter, Abel, Sam, everyone. They all seemed to morph into one, the same face, same look on each one. I knew for a second there, I had that same guise of sick, mystified terror on my face.

Gabriel's fists pummeled Michael's face. Or maybe Michael's fists pummeled Gabriel's face. Michael threw Michael as Gabriel tackled Gabriel. I wanted to shut my eyes but I couldn't feel a thing. Michael screamed, Gabriel had bitten off a couple of his fingers as Michael had been grasping at Gabe's face for a handhold to strike with. His scream was addled with gurgling blood. It would have made any lucid man sick. Michael roared, striking at Gabriel in furious anger, blowing blood from his mouth. Gabriel grabbed Michael's head, and slammed his own head against the dragon, knocking him to the ground. blood was streaming down Gabriel's face; grasping at Michael's head again, before driving his knee upwards into the muzzle of the dragon. A horrible wet crunch resounded and Michael sprawled back. Gabriel fell upon him, knees crunching his wings. Another gurgling scream that could curdle iron.

I blinked slowly, to hear the final throes of the song, amidst the pounding slaps of fist against cranium. it was almost in-tune to the beat. Gabriel, his entire body heaving with every breath and blood pouring from his head and wild frothing mouth, gasping, screaming and painful moaning amidst the melodious harmonizing of Freddie Mercury, Michael on the ground, arms and body now limp as Gabriel's fists roared through his head, battering it from side to side, smacking, crunching, splashing. I could hear Michael's wife and child screaming off in the distance. My eyes drifted away from the scene, seeing everyone else, equally distancing their gaze from the horror before them. As the song ended, so did Gabriel's two jackhammers, soaking in spattered blood. Red began to clap in applause, beaming in pride.

"Bravo, *hijito*! and in record time, no less! Oh, would you look at that. Oh-" Red knelt down next to Michael's wife, grabbing her by the hair and forcing her to look at Gabriel's bestial visage. "Would, you look, at, *that*. My, I think he's still breathing!" Red noted as she wailed in horror. Gabriel, kneeling over the body of the dragon, looked down, past his own shaking, throbbing fists and arms, seeing the bubbling blood in Michael's open, broken mouth, moving ever so slightly. Red reached into his coat as he got up, throwing Michael's wife's head as she wept, before walking over to Gabriel and producing a distinct, vicious knife from the opposite side where he carried his pistol. He stood above Gabriel for a moment, who looked up at Red slowly, eyes inching his way up to see past the steel he held, as Red flipped the blade, presenting the handle to Gabriel. An ornate bowie knife, silver steel and ivory grips matching his pistol, engraved images of death and all, notably the end of the handle terminating in a skull. "Time to claim another victory." Red spoke with vicious cheer and glowing eyes, evidently revelling in the situation, as Michael's wife screamed again, along with her child.

Gabriel's shaking, blood-soaked hand reached forward, and as it gripped the knife, the guns once pointed at all of our heads were now pointing at him. He picked the gleaming sliver up, before holding it to the limp red throat of the defeated Michael.

Gabriel grunted once, dragging it quickly and forcefully across the dragon's throat, and the wife and child continued to wail, still held back by the men in black armor, holding them by their bound hands behind their backs and below their wings. Their other hands gripped their heads, forcing them to watch.

"I told you, you've still got it," Red said, practically gloating, glowing in a sort of proxy victory. "No hesitation. A professional to the end." Gabriel's eyes lingered on the mangled corpse below him as he breathed, knife still held in his hand so hard it quivered ever so subtly. "Well, now that we've gotten the non-cartel related justice out of the way… Son, if you will," He said, motioning slowly. Gabriel looked up ever so slowly, still knelt there, and for the first time as far as I was concerned, Gabriel finally looked Red in the eye, and I could feel a threat in them. "Well? You know what comes next, *mijo*." Red demanded, his voice raising, almost as if taunting him to act, taunting him to be a hero. Sprint towards him, throw the knife, something.

But that didn't happen.

Gabriel breathed in slowly, before switching his knife to the left hand, and placing his right hand to the cold stone floor. I saw Gabriel's face wince in preliminary pain as he looked over the knife, still bloodied. With a sort of strange feeling in my gut akin to morbid fascination, I watched him lower the knife down to his hand, his fingers separating the index away from the rest, before raising it up quickly and letting it fall with a forceful flick of the wrist.

*Whack.*

Gabriel screamed, a short burst of air and spittle flowing from his mouth between his grit teeth. He growled and roared and hissed and spat, frothing, curling up as he fell to the side to writhe. The knife clattered to the ground as he went to grip his hand, gnashing there, blood splashing from where his right trigger finger used to be. I saw Red squat down as he reached with naught but a smile on his face intently towards the bits on the ground he was interested in- His knife, and Gabriel's former trigger finger, as Gabriel was in his throes of throbbing pain. He took a moment to wipe the blood off his knife with his red pocket handkerchief, putting it away ever so delicately in its sheath beneath his right armpit before taking the finger and flopping it about.

"*Esta es un dedo en gatillo de Sinaloa, no es tuyo,*" Red hissed in condescension.

"*…¡Hablas tu lengua propia!*" Gabriel wheezed. Red smiled.

"I hope you see the irony in what you just said," Red chuckled to himself, and finally got up, pocketing the finger beside his handkerchief.

"You're… You're nothing to them, Red…" Gabriel growled. "That's why I wanted out. You're, *we're* not one of them. You're a… a ginger, for fuck's sake, you think they'll ever have you… as anything but a puppet?!" Gabriel's voice began to crack as he grasped at his squirting vein.

"They were gonna leave me... out in vegas to fry, you f-fucking moron. Why... do you think you're here to make buddies with the R-republicans? It's because you can speak without a f-fucking accent!"

"Oh, and so what if that's all I am? What if they saw the end of the world coming and just needed somebody to play the right part at the right place? If anything, that makes me useful, more than you can say for yourself," Red said, before raising a hand to his head. "Ugh, my boy... You know, I always thought of you like a son. You had a lot going for you and you always delivered. this hurts me just like it hurts you right now, *hijo.*" Red snapped his fingers, and one of the black guards paced away quickly, up the stairs. "Of course, I guess I'll hold up the rest of the deal." He clapped his hands. "The part where you all find out what happens to the winners!" As he said this, I looked around the room, seeing the armor-clad, silent Republican figures behind every one of us produce a knife. I looked a little to the side and there I could see it, held in the grip of the man behind me, a shining piece of steel. I didn't think my blood could have ran any colder. "You all get to live!" He said with an ample, hearty, horrible laugh that would haunt me for so much time to come, and the guards reached down for our hands and cut our binds. Almost as soon as they did so, rather than let us get up, they kicked us to the floor; at least all of us humanoids. Lauren and Abel were tipped to the side and Selicia was shoved into the floor forcefully. I, from where I lay, looked up to see one of the Sinaloans return, holding a white-hot piece of rebar by its cooler side. A barbaric first-aid tool. He tossed it beside Gabriel with a quick grunt of some insult in Spanish, Gabriel taking it, shaking like mad, and used it to seal his own gushing wound. Gabriel screamed amid the sizzle of flesh. Red's laughter was hardly louder.

The guards retreated behind us, and that was when Michael's widow charged, or at least tried to, towards Gabriel, stumbling across the floor, half from pure overwhelming grief and half from the drugs she was probably still addled with, before giving up on Gabriel and simply grasping at her deceased husband's mauled head, weeping and sniffing and wailing and screaming, and screaming, and *screaming*.

The guards began to walk away, one by one ascending the stairs of the basement, before Red stood upon the bottom step.

"*Hasta mañana, hijito,*" he saluted, haunting eyes following Gabriel away, and his footsteps echoed as he disappeared.

### Chapter 58

Speechless.

There, in the hot, heady and dark basement of that closed-up bar, with just us there all woozy, our heads spinning and ears ringing.

Michael's wife was screaming and sobbing and crying in agony, as her child crawled up on all fours, as they gripped each other and shook and wailed and bawled. Gabriel sat a ways away in an abject, blank look, just breathing, watching her mourn. He'd since finished sealing his wound with the fiery iron, its brightness now dimmed and leaving him sitting there in darkness once more. There was blood all over him, his face was broken, swollen, and I could see past the blood on his hands to see the torn, bruised, and ripped flesh on his knuckles and over them, of bruises spattered in blood. Gabriel said nothing, watching her writhe in agony, a silence of an upturned scowl still on his face, reacting in pain and grief in his own way, eyes a little darker than usual.

The lights stayed on, glaring down from the low heavens, cameras still watching.

Lauren was the first to truly rise to her feet, stumbling a little bit as she advanced to Gabriel. Gabriel reared his head to her, their gazes intersecting as she slumped down next to him. It felt like she wanted to ask him how he was doing, if he was alright, anything at all to keep herself from thinking about this new, horrifying situation we were soon to learn, to accept we were really in. But she was speechless from the fight. We were all speechless, the noise and sound rising from Mrs. Draco and her child drowning out all else. But even they tired of wailing, eyes drifting over to Gabriel, who was the second to stand, rising as a lighthouse amid a calm black sea.

Rage, I saw rage in her eyes, Mrs. Draco. Utter contemptible rage boiled in her heart as she gazed at the bloody killer of her lover, towering in his own bitter victory. I saw words form on her lips, but nothing solid came out. No "fuck you"s, no "murderer"s, no "how could you"s. only singly spattered syllables in place of actual words, but the noises and emotions rising from her told a thousand veracious expletives of hate and anger and terror and accostation, and even Gabriel was swayed by them, his lip twitching and eyes glistening ever so slightly. His unmolested hand twitched, as if he wished to wipe his bleeding face again, but it stayed limp.

Gabriel began to walk. He limped over to the dead stranger, the pilot's brains strewn across the floor. "Let's go, somebody carry Carl's body," splashed out between the blood and the teeth rattling and gurgling in his mouth. Silence quickly resumed as the echo of bloody phlegm slapping the concrete resounded alone. "...We've got bodies to bury." He turned, to see Mrs. Draco, now grasping her child and cowering over Michael's corpse. I saw what she was saying even if she couldn't get a word out. *Don't you dare touch my husband, murderer.* "...If you don't think you can carry him, I'll do it for you." She said nothing, glaring at Gabriel with her jaw drooling slack, nostrils dripping with snot and eyes puffy and red and overflowing with tears. Gabriel paused again to take in what her stare communicated. "Your husband was a dead man walking. If he won we'd still all be dead. I had to-"

"Fuck… you!" She bellowed and screamed. *That's a lie, you're lying to me*, she reasoned through her expression, unable to convey it, too struck with emotion to explain. Gabriel saw this.

"We're still all dead, I guess…" He sighed. "Believe what you want to believe. But your husband was a dead man when he got found out, and me or him winning this wouldn't have mattered. But if you want to bury your husband, I think we should deal with that first. I owe you that much."

"B-but-" I heard Selicia's voice, and Gabriel's eyes drifted over to her, his expression deadly serious. Her mouth shut once more.

"...I can't say I'm sorry for this," he turned back to her. "And I can't make this right. And I don't want your forgiveness, I know I'll never get it. But let me do this for you if you want something, anything back."

She sat there, biting her lips as her eyes welled. Her mouth opened, to sob loudly and wail a little. I saw in this, her nodding a little.

We shambled forth from our smoky dungeon, out into an old restaurant's bar, it looked like. Gabriel led the way, laying Michael down on one of the tables before folding the tablecloth over him. I carried the pilot up the steps, with his brainey head sopping blood onto my arms and legs, also laying him down on one of the tables to fold the cloth over him.

"Hey, Lauren," Gabriel said as she made her way over to me, so I could hoist the corpse onto her back. Gabriel reached over to the bar, and I saw it there- Mr. Pendrew's bow, sitting there quaintly, along with a quiver of arrows, as he picked them up. Lauren's eyes widened in some macabre pleasure of relief, even if it was distraught with guilt and only lasted for a second, the wider implication hitting her. "...Red's got a bit of a sick sense of humor," Gabriel coughed, not even trying for a chuckle. "I guess this is yours, isn't it?" he walked up to her and gave them to her, and she took the bow and the quiver, looking down upon them. He coughed, going back to pick up Michael. I hoisted up the body of the pilot, looking over to Lauren, who looked over and shuddered, almost tiredly. "...The Pendrews are dead." The bow quivered in her hands as she held it, and her face contorted for but a second as she looked back at Gabriel. I could feel her rage, her tired disbelief. "The house is burned down, so is theirs. Whatever they didn't take, they burned. I'm not going to lie to any of you about it." We all stood, staring wordlessly at Gabriel. I could feel the stares accumulating around me, directed at my old friend, Gabriel, the man who as far as we, and even I were concerned, had doomed us all. *How could you*, our stares would say. I could feel doubt accumulating in my head, that the Pendrews were still alive, that this was some cruel joke. But the brains cooling and chilling my arm, and the fact that Gabriel picked up three extra tablecloths attested a different story, that this was all too real. I shivered, despite the heat of the humid, stuffy bar. Everyone looked cold, despite being sopped in sweat.

We stepped out into the cool night air, and I felt the weight of the stuffiness of the bar lifted off my shoulders, despite the oppression of the knockout drugs still clouding my eyes and head. Like that, we were walking, a literal funeral procession, step after step down the road, towards our fate. We groaned and moaned and stumbled but we kept on going, without pause or even anything to say to each other. Gabriel led us, the thin, wiry body in his arms wrapped and bound crudely by tablecloth, the dead one's loved ones following behind him closely. I walked beside Lauren, helping to hold the wrapped body of the pilot on her back with an arm, as she clutched the bow and quiver so hard her knuckles turned white. Time fuzzed together into one indistinguishable line as we walked solemnly. The way the night felt, how the crickets chirped all lent this more of that unbelievable feeling. Every now and then, we'd be stared at, maybe even judged by a local looking from a window, and we'd stare back. Step after step we walked, before we finally passed our court.

Every house on the street was well ablaze, black smoke pouring into a black sky. We all stopped to look for a second, before approaching.

There on their front lawn lay Steven and Nica Pendrew, their dog Sabre laying next to them, the old dead grass watered by blood.

I looked to the eyes of Lauren, who appeared as a ghost, speechless. Her eyes had no life, no hope, and only the faintest glimmer of a similar feeling to disappointment, like she didn't, couldn't believe it until now. As we drew near, her teeth clenched ever harder, seeing the vicious holes pockmarking their bodies. Nica's body lay with one hole in her head, but Steven was full of them and his blood trailed towards the burning wreck of his house from where his body had been dragged, his right hand curled and trigger finger somewhat extended as if he was gripping an invisible weapon.

When Gabriel laid down Michael to spread the tablecloths over the Pendrews, that was when something within Lauren broke. She charged forward with a snap of the quick-release clasp of her holy amulet, chain flailing through the air as she gripped her weapon, and Carl's corpse fell from her back onto the pavement as she lurched, as I was unable to catch him. Gabriel turned sadly towards her, to receive a green-skinned, steel-augmented fist in the cheek, swiping across his face. Gabriel stumbled back from the blow more than sufficient to render a normal man unconscious and then some, as Lauren screamed and wailed, tears flowing- yet not expecting Gabriel's fury to return to him, as he quickly and terrifyingly reached out and struck upwards, Lauren's jaws clacking together so hard it resounded in my own jaws from the sound alone as I watched, feeling the strike simply by seeing it happen. Lauren fell backwards, tipped up on her rear before crumpling to her side. She simply breathed in and out, sniffling, dazed, as she stared dumbfounded up to Gabriel, who stood with his face drawn inward and eyes fiery like a beast, fists quaking, like for a moment he was teleported back into that hopeless dungeon he'd been in mere minutes earlier, more than ready to slay another dragon with his bare hands.

To regain his resolve, Gabriel breathed ever so slowly and deeply a couple times before reaching into his mouth. He grabbed the tooth that Lauren had loosed, wiggling the bloody thing free and looking at it for a couple quiet seconds. He spat blood to the side, before walking closer, staring down Lauren, towering over her until she looked away. He knelt down slowly, taking her still steel-filled hand and depositing the tooth into it beside her symbol of faith, a macabre show of apology, or something. Really I didn't know why he did this. Don't think *he* even knew. He must've just felt like it was the right thing to do at the time.

Gabriel finally walked back against that burning wreck, staring down for a moment's respite, and to me, that moment could have lasted forever. The bitter stink of burning house, the sick feeling of death, the fuzz of the drugging and the hopelessness made the moment a macabre, almost comic moment of reflection.

"Let's get going," Gabriel finally said.

We approached the church, walking through the quiet, sleeping refugee camp and up the steps to the main hall, greeted by the thin-as-rails night watchman, who took one look at the wrapped bodies before nodding slowly, with a simple "I'll go get some shovels", a look of sad, tired formality shimmering in his eyes and radiating in his voice.

We looked upon the cloth-swaddled bodies lying in those three uncovered graves one last time. The remnants of the Draco family sniffled, as the night churchcarer drove the second crude wooden cross into the ground, as he was also in the middle of giving an extreme unction. I looked upon the little family grave of the Pendrews, seeing them one final time.

"...Care to say a few words?" He asked slowly, standing before the dirt pile. Nobody said anything, not even the widow and her daughter. He bit his lip, going to scoop some dirt. Michael's widow let out a sob, and held her petrified daughter close. I looked to Gabriel, as he sat, propping himself up against a different grave's cross, breathing deeply and staring upwards towards the stars; deep in thought, or maybe doing his best to not think at all. I could see his mouth moving ever so slightly, slowly and subtly, as he gazed into the cold, dark expanse of space. The ends of his lips curled upwards in a dull smile, eyes never blinking.

On the walk back to what was left of our house, Gabriel finally admitted defeat and propped himself up against Lauren as we walked. The bow stayed slung around her back with the bow threaded between her wings, one hand clutching the quiver and the other, Gabriel's old tooth. We looked behind us while leaving the church grounds, seeing the Dracos standing there before the fresh graves. We didn't ask them to come. Everyone probably considered it, but nobody wanted to ask. We left them be.

There it was, the smouldering, burnt remains of our neighborhood in those early morning hours, still pitch black and too early for even the earliest risers yet too late to be considered true nighttime anymore. It smelled like misty, wet earth and smoky, smouldering haze. Gabriel lay up against an old embered piece of wall of our house, almost using it to keep warm. Unlike the rest of us, he did not shiver. He looked upon the ground, seeing an old cigarette butt, probably from one of the soldiers who had worked to kidnap us and burn down our houses. Gabriel chuckled desperately, reaching out to it with a grunt and picking it up, seeing some tobacco left in it.

"I know I don't usually smoke..." he sighed, as I sat near. Everyone sat near, almost in a semicircle, with us lit by the smoky, smouldering embers of the house and Gabriel sitting in his own shadow. He grunted again as he turned a little bit to put the remnants of the smoke up to an ember, lighting it again, before putting it to his lips, sucking in, letting his face glow. He coughed quietly. "But it seems fitting right now." He looked up at us, and we held yet another a moment of cold silence.

That was when the sound of an armalite rang out, the bolt being charged back, before releasing with a clunk.

We turned, seeing Mrs. Draco standing there, shaking in rage and terror. Michael's rifle, my rifle, was in her hands, and like the sea, we parted. Gabriel sat there, staring down the three eyes staring death into him. He looked down sucking on the cigarette again.

"Figured it would come to this," Gabriel said. "...So how come you haven't shot me?" She shuddered, staying quiet and still for what felt like forever, that gun's barrel quivering ever so slightly as she breathed in and out.

"...W-were you telling the truth?" She broke the silence, her voice quite near traversing its own breaking point, still barely holding it together. Gabriel did not move an inch, his face, his eyes set in stone as she begged for the truth. "Or were you just lying? When you said w-we'd all be dead anyways?"

Gabriel paused forever, as he took a drag on his cigarette, not exactly like a prisoner awaiting his execution enjoying a final smoke, but not entirely *un*like it. Her gun quaked. We could have jumped her, grabbed the gun, but none of us did so. I think a good bit of each of us was on her side at this point. She walked right up to Gabriel, step after quaking step, the barrel of Michael's, of *my* AR15 staring him down, right up between his eyes, kissing close. Gabriel could have grabbed the barrel, knocked the gun aside and laid her flat with an uppercut, done anything, but he didn't. I think even he was on our gun-pointing side at this point.

"Yes and no."

"W-what?" The gun shook again, and her mouth drooped a little bit. Gabriel paused again, finally looking her in the eyes, and she froze under his gaze.

"Let's say Michael won the fight." Gabriel stared down at the cigarette butt. "I'd get my throat cut, you all go free. My old boss hunts you all down and kills you one-by-one."

"W-what?!" she cried, breaking out of her spell. "He... He let us go!"

"Of course he did. It's too easy to just do us all right then and there. As you saw, Red's got a couple new employees as of late, so they've gotta get initiated somehow before Sinaloa bothers wasting perfectly good Augs on unknowns. You wonder why Red was so happy? Logistic opportunities make him hard. That and watching good people suffer. He was made for the job." Gabriel stopped to chuckle, realising that statement to be somewhat more literal than he'd intended it.

"I... b-but-"

"The cartel doesn't work on promises. They work on fear. You, me, all of us, we disrespected Sinaloa as far as they're concerned and that's a big no-no. Wonder why Red was so forthright about being a Cartel big shot, too? Why he let you see his face, why you saw his personal detail's faces? He knows we're all as dead as Michael." He took another drag. "...I'm sorry for involving you in this." We glared at him, while Michael's widow wheezed and she stepped back a little bit. "All of you. I'm sorry." He glared up to her again. "But..." he continued. "If I wanted you all to die a sick death at the end of a machete, I'd sure as hell have let Michael win. God knows I deserved what he got. But he didn't know this. If I let him win, I'd be being selfish just getting my death over with quick, since you'd all end up dying horrible deaths too." He paused one final time. "Back there, in that basement... Remember when I said I can't do anything to make this up to you?" Gabe told her. She nodded, ever so slightly. "That basement was wired to hell. Cameras, microphones. I know he was listening and watching, even after he left. Hell, he's probably whacking it to you and your kid crying over your husband's body, but that would imply he can feel happiness. I couldn't tell you what we can do about this, do about this so we, you, and your little daughter don't get raped and shot by some beaner fuckstain. What I should have done half a decade ago."

"W-what *can* you do?"

384

Gabriel paused finally to suck that cigarette down to the filter, before he opened his mouth to let smoke and noise pour out as he flicked the butt.

**"I'll chop Red's fuckin' head off."**

### Chapter 59

It was silent for a while, as we took in what Gabriel had said. If anybody but Gabriel had said it, we'd be surprised, even shocked. But every one of us, or at the very least me, knew this was probably the route we'd have to take, but Gabriel was the only one with the balls to say it.

"Kill him?" Lauren said, doubt accumulating, giving voice to our hesitation. "B-but... What good will that do? You just made an enemy of the entire cartel."

"Maybe, maybe not. It's tradition for the manager of a traitor to deal with the problem personally. It'd be insulting for anyone else to deal with me- to deal with *us* but him, unless he was dead or in a coma, of course. He might've reported back by now, maybe, maybe not. But if I kill him that buys us enough time to get out of the area alive, and that's all we need."

"Gabriel, they'll hunt you for the rest of your life," Maria reasoned slowly.

"I'd expect nothing less. I guess I'll change my name when I get to the Citadel, maybe break my nose or jaw into a different position, change my face. And if they somehow find me and hunt me down, I'll deal with the problem alone. None of you have to get involved. But right now, we're all in danger. And I need your help."

"W-why don't you just go face him alone?" Michael's widow asked, maybe putting on the edge how she really felt, as she let the gun droop.

"You're all in danger. Trust me, I've done this more times than I'd like to say. Every last one of you is target practice. Or a rookie's first beheading. After a few years they should forgive you if you 'earn' it by surviving, but they'll always hunt me. When that time comes, I'll deal with it alone. God knows I deserve it, even if I never believed that would be the case until now. But I need your help because I've got a plan that requires some backup."

"Backup?" Lauren spoke up again. "We don't- we have a bow and one gun between us."

Gabe coughed through that dark smile. "I've got a small stash, but it's not gonna help that much. But..." he paused to smile darkly. "Remember those friends we made in the forest that one time?" He said. "Leader said he owes me one free fuck-shit-up token. Well, here's hoping he meant what he said," Gabriel raised his left hand, crossing the fingers he still had.

"So let's go call them," Maria said.

"Eh, not that simple," Gabriel said. "See, we need their little base as a backup spot, somewhere to bunker down in in case this shit gets any worse than it already is."

"So...?" The crowd waited.

"See, if Red's half as smart as he used to be when I was his underling, I know we're all tagged. There's a lot of us, so he's probably not taking much chances on us escaping. See, we've got these little sensors- little microscopic GPS beacons he probably sprinkled on us, and they're tougher to deal with than fleas, takes more than a shower to get em off you. We used this trick when we did this to big groups, and *we're* probably the biggest group of traitor-lovers that Red has ever had to deal with since the war down south. See, the beacons last a little under a week before running out of juice to emit their tracking radiation, and by then we'll all just be a bunch of rotting heads in a bag."

"And what are we going to do then?" Maria asked.

"I hid my EMP Net Generator as my plan Z. It's handy for purging nanomachines. A couple seconds and-" He paused to snap, the sound echoing like a gunshot. "...All those tiny bots are dead." He smiled smugly to himself, even if it was a hopeless kind of smug. "Now, I'm willing to bet that a 'taur gives off about twice the beacon signature as a human, so I'm gonna need someone to come with me and stand right next to me the whole way until we've purged the bots."

"W-why would you need them to think a 'taur is-"

"Because then they wouldn't think it's a human, *me*. we're gonna get this machine, come back, and we're gonna go wading in the creek. This'll make some of the nanobots wash off. While we're doing this, I'll use it to kill the remaining bots. They might think that we just washed most of them off and the signature got too faint, even though that cover story won't hold up under scrutiny but we can't be too obvious. Then again, Red probably expects me to have told you all about him, and expects us to run. He also probably expects me to try to take him on one-on-one, go slit his throat in his sleep or something. He's probably taken countermeasures against a one-man infiltration. He wouldn't expect a traditional assault, and definitely not from inside the city instead of from outside it." He paused, to collect his thoughts. "So, after I kill the trackers. At this point, we've got to move because they'll probably start wondering where the fuck we went and they won't want to lose us. I really don't know where Red expects *you* all to go, if you'll scatter, if you'll stay together. but he'll expect you to run and for me to try to kill him personally. So we'll contact the Kommandoes. any luck and that'll get us enough guns, gear and backup for a surprise assault. Then when it gets dark, we'll go fuck up Red and his personal guard. We kill Red and his little friends and we've got a chance to make it far enough away to the point where they forget about the rest of you."

"'Go fuck up Red'?" Sam asked breathlessly, voice peaking with worry. "...I hope you have an actual plan."

"I do. I'll go more in depth about it later. But we've got to move, and fast. Every second we wait is another second that Red briefs his new rookies for their first honorary mission. Noah?"

"Yes?" I said, coming out of the haze of information finally. He snapped at me, grunting as he slowly got up.

"Let's go get our little macguffin."

The sky lost its darkness, minute after minute, while the sun still stayed just beyond the grasp of the horizon. Gabriel and I stood, close to each other. In fact, Gabriel was limping, and I was lending him my shoulder to help him along, my rifle slung again on my back. To be reunited with it after so long under these circumstances. At least it was loaded.

We didn't say anything for the first few minutes, but it was as if the silence only weighed us down more. I noticed, after a long while, how we were still wearing our undergarments. I chuckled a little.

"...What," Gabriel groaned.

"Dude, they stole our clothes, too..."

"Probably might have burned them, fits their M.O.," Gabe said. He was wearing his boxers and wife beater, both sopped with sweat and blood. Gabriel sighed. "You know, I'd never *seen* the sun rise before," He said. "I mean, I guess I did some times, but I never really watched it, y'know? And would you just look at the colors of the sky," he hushed in awe, though the quiet, reflective pause ended all too quickly as he continued. "...When they were training me in their little elite training camp for sure. Sometimes they'd wake us up at the smelly ass crack of dawn with a bucket of water, make us run five miles and crawl another through mud. God... Heh. As far as my dad knows, it really was a summer camp. Guess it was, technically."

"...Do you ever think about your dad anymore?" I asked. He took a while to respond.

"...Eh, mean bastard's dead now... I guess I feel sad for him, y'know?" He said. "...Anyways, I never really stopped to watch the sun rise back then. Thought it wasn't worth my time, even if I never did it." He coughed. "God, the clouds really are beautiful around now..."

"...You ever think you could have done things different?" I asked slowly. "Like with your dad?" Gabriel paused a long, long time, shuffling next to me. I didn't realise I was trying to steer the conversation back, I guess I just wanted to know.

"Course I do," He finally coughed out, no longer trying to escape that thought. "Don't know what good it would have done. Bastard could never stand me."

"...You really hated him, didn't you?"

"I think I did... I suppose I don't really anymore. I've... had time to rest on it. Sure, he was always looking down on me, but at the end of the day I had a place to sleep, y'know?" Gabriel pondered. "Thought the cartel would help me bump him off or something. Turns out you need clearance with this sort of thing... you know assassins and enforcers aren't allowed to kill anybody but who the Cartel lets em?" Gabe said. "For a bunch of lawless fuckers, they sure had their rules. 'Each of you is an investment, and we don't want our investments serving prison time. Stay in school. You're not allowed to go to prison unless we let you.' Sometimes they force you to commit an obvious crime or set you up to go to prison specifically as a punishment. Can you believe those pricks? Honor among thieves is one thing, but all the rules really got to me. Easy to forget you were in a gang until you see some guy get beheaded in front of his own kid." I shambled in silence though not without letting out a little humph at Gabriel's morose humor, and Gabriel eventually cleared his throat when the words returned to him. "Really, I could have blown him away any time I wanted. Now that I think about it, I guess I never really wanted to. Maybe I always held that little piece of respect for him. Maybe I never really hated him."

"Gabriel," I said slowly. "You've been doing this... You've been with me, helping us all along, because my dad promised to help get you in the Citadel, right?" Gabriel said nothing. "You really wanted to just get away from Sinaloa, didn't you?" Gabriel still said nothing, only pausing to look me in the eyes, mouth furling in frustration. "So what am I? A ticket to freedom? How long have you even had this agreement, to 'keep me safe'? Am I even still your friend?" I stopped fully. Gabriel stopped too, and we stared at each other as our embrace ended, no longer helping him stand as he stood on his own, apart from me, glaring at the ground with his mangled fists trembling. I saw sorrow well in his eyes.

A hand came back up to grasp my shoulder. Gabriel coughed, spitting his own bloody phlegm at my feet.

"Noah," He said slowly. "You know I was always the weird kid. I never had many friends, but you and I go back longer than anyone else. You were by my side since, since before I'd even touched a gun. You..." He paused, if only to suck in bloody snot. When his head came back up, his eyes were red, and tears ran down his cheeks. "You mean more to me than anyone else in this fucking stupid world, more than anybody else who I've ever held a gun with and depended my life on. You've always had my back, and I'm honored to have yours, even if I fuck up more than a real good friend would. I'm not saying I'm a good friend. I'm not saying I didn't use you and your dad and everything. But I'm saying... fuck it, I've got your back 'till the second my heart stops beating. You're probably the reason I never went on a shooting spree or anything, god dammit…" He stopped to chuckle sadly, disguising his coughing, maybe even his sobbing in it. "…Let's get moving so we can take back our lives."

It was a short while before Gabriel ever spoke again, but it felt longer and heavier than it was as he mentioned the right place. We approached the house of Gabe's hiding spot, a plain old house with an X across the front door. We made our way around the back, going to one of the rear heating ducts. Gabriel pulled the wire cover off, reaching into the vent and pulling out that device I hadn't seen in what felt like years. Hard to imagine that first day of all this, with it. But instead of getting up, He simply slumped, turning towards me and sitting up against that wall.

"C'mon, have a seat," He said, and I sat across from him on the cold tile underneath the back porch's gondola. He sighed in tired pain. "Lemme have a moment. We've got about a day or two with our heads still attached to our necks anyways. No rush." He sighed again, looking across the way, across the dead lawn and to the fence of the backyard as we took our little rest, to think and ponder and talk away our worries, our situation. I stooped over, taking my gun to put between my legs and lean my arms against the magazine well. "Noah… What did you want to be? If this never happened. I don't mean some stupid office job you would have probably gotten shafted with. What was your *dream*?"

"I… I guess I… Haven't thought about it in awhile." A pause preceded my thoughts, searching through myself. "…Novelist. Always wanted to write a book. Books. Stories. Guess I sort of forgot I had a dream the older I got."

"Write books, no shit?" He chuckled to spite his, our sadness. "That's prissy as fuck."

"Fuck off. You asked." I spat. I guess it was kinda funny, though.

"Heh, yeah… But on the real, how come?"

"I dunno. I grew up with my *father* and his prepping. Something about constantly envisioning a world of adventure, about how the post-apocalypse would be all wild and adventurous. A new start where I wouldn't have to get a job in a fucking cubicle and piss my life away. Not to mention how I spent my vacations in a giant castle town thinking about the coming new medieval ages, remember?"

"Heh. Here it is, dragons and all," He muttered out a little chuckle, appreciative silence overtaking us both. "Hm… If my life never got fucked up. If I never got roped into this life, apocalypse or not. I always wanted to be a cook. A real high-class chef. I'd make the best food you'd ever seen."

"And you're calling me a fag? Heh."

"Yeah, yeah. The irony isn't beyond me."

"…You always did love food. You were the fat kid."

"Yeah, before the cartel got their scalpels in me. I can't get fat if I tried, now."

"Well, if it means anything, I think you're an excellent cook."

"Thanks."

"…I think you'll be a great cook when we get to the citadel." I smiled. "The best the town has ever seen."

"You're thinking positive. Like we'll get out of this alive." He was smiling too.

"That's the idea, isn't it?" Another barrage of silence as we sat there, burning our eyes into the Sun beneath this pale blue sky.

"...I'm sure you'll be a great writer, too."

"Got a lot to draw from. Won't even have to think much up." Gabriel chuckled out a laugh.

"Maybe someday you'll tell my story too."

"You know, Gabe," I uttered, looking to him, sharing a smile as we took in the warmth of the rising sun. "That sounds like a plan." He chuckled back, and we went back to watching the sun. But there was still something frozen within him he needed to expunge.

"Noah," Gabe slowly began again, still gazing into the burning orb hanging above, motionless as he spoke, though I turned back to him, if only to watch him speak, watch the way his lips, his face moved. "You ever dream?" He asked.

"Dream?"

"Yeah." He coughed. "You ever had a *recurring* dream?"

"Not really," I responded. Gabriel smiled a little at nothing, still staring off into oblivion.

"Yeah, well I do. I keep having this same fuckin dream every now and then. Sometimes it's the same, sometimes it's different. But it usually goes about the same way." He paused abruptly to prepare extrapolation, turning his head back to look into me and lock eyes. "I've always considered myself an atheist. used to, at least. Now I'm not so sure. Sure, I still can't be convinced of a god, yeah; but I dunno, being so close to death for so long makes me wonder what could be worse, hell or nothing. I'd wonder it ironically, as a little in-joke between me and myself, at least at first. But more recently it's a question that makes me shake. I'm fucking terrified, Noah," he growled. He didn't look terrified, eyes dull and tired, now focused far past me, a thousand-yard stare if I'd ever seen one. "Hell or Oblivion. Suffer for eternity or cease to exist. God, what a choice. I suppose the right kind of mindset would put them one in the same. Shit, maybe that's the punishment for nonbelief- for there to be no afterlife at all for you, good or bad." he stopped, to look me back in the eye for a quick second and wet his throat as he swallowed his worries. "I'm rambling. So I keep having this fucking dream. It's me, alone with God. I can see myself and I can see God- don't ask me what he looks like, because I can never really get a good look at him. I just know it's the one in charge. God. But I can see myself like I'm the third person there, watching myself like a spectator as I stand there, glaring at god."

I'm just standing there... indignant, I guess. I'm just looking at him, glaring, like I want to say 'fuck you God, you're a cunt and I hate you, I want to kick your ass', and he just stares back. It's quiet, as we look at each other. But as each second passes, I start to look less pissed and more- I dunno, I lose my stomach for it. My arms go limp, my fists uncurl, and before I know it, I fall to my knees and I'm sobbing like a little kid, as god watches. Nobody says anything. Sometimes I'm screaming, screaming like I'm being fuckin' murdered and god's watching, just watching, judging me while I writhe." he stopped one more time, if only to sigh. "If God's real, he's like that. He's not a force of good or evil, he just is, and he's sitting there, judging you. Judging me. Judging. And no matter how strong, how good, how independent we think we are, we're just a couple moments away from groveling at his feet and screaming in agony. There's a constant out there we will never be able to live up to, one you can't help but feel. I've always felt that shit." He paused again, lost in thought, while I watched his face scrunch in a deep inner extrapolation, smacking his lips to continue.

"Sometimes in the past, I'd feel bullets whizz past me, and I swear it's like somebody pushed my head back a little right before one skims my nose. Somebody's been preparing me for judgement, Noah." He stared past me again, petrified. "Is this my judgement?" He paused again, to look around the place, lit by the solemn rising sun in the distance, eyes squinting a little. "Hell, oblivion. Huh. I'd always scoffed at the idea, but the fact that I'm so fucking close to it all… I can't laugh anymore. I'm *scared*, Noah," His voice was cracking and I felt my own eyes water, goosebumps growing as I watched him, his convictions shattered there on the ground, this super-soldier trembling like a baby. "I don't want to just stop existing. I don't want to go to hell. And I don't want to go to heaven if it means some pompous asshole put me through this for me just to suck up to the big prick like some bitch. But it's happening. I guess this is it, then. Maybe I'm finally 'getting' God, because I feel bad for everything I've ever done, like somebody'd been watching me this whole time. Everything's coming full circle, even if I've been trying to fight all of it, trying to feel like I'm the one in control." He paused, one final time, to fiddle with the machine cradled in his hands. "I guess, from here on out… It's in the hands of god now."

### Chapter 60

We still held that funeral's silence as we worked, once we returned. Going over everyone with that machine's scanning net function, one by one. Double-checking. Wading in that frigid creek on this fall day. Nobody spoke, fear was in everyone's eyes. Everyone quivered, but Gabriel waded deep there, letting the cold chill him to his bones, taking the time to let the blood wash off of him. I was staring at that shrine to death himself plastered in the tattoo across his back. It seemed fitting, the longer I gazed.

"Lauren," He spoke suddenly once more as she lay there on the banks after her wash, staring out to the glassy water of the calm deep of the stream. Her head turned itself up with a slow, strong whisk, where she was clutching her little trinity symbol. "You been baptized?"

"Uh… Yeah," She began, maybe becoming a little curious as she glared, head and ears cocked ever so subtly to the side, letting her inquisition overtake the shock that had been plaguing her, her eyes brightening into the present once more. "W-why?"

"I dunno." He just floated there, until he finally caught her glare with his. "Do you think God is kind?" Despite his words and how they might sound on their own, he said it in such a way that all who heard it were momentarily disarmed, even Lauren herself, the authenticity of Gabriel's voice shining through.

"I…" She paused, not without fulfilling her need to fill the air with noise, as if to begin to speak, but she was struck dumb, throat parched, tongue made of stone. She closed her mouth to grit her teeth, just staring with an endless expanse between the two of them, before she found her words. "I… I have to," She began to explain. I caught Gabriel's tiny nod, almost intangible how he wanted her to go on. To extrapolate. "If God is kind… If I *believe* God is kind," She uttered. "Then I have… Hope."

"Hope." Gabriel let the word linger in the air as he spat it, though not entirely without reverence. "Having hope in a time like this… It's the bravest thing I can see anyone doing." Gabriel turned his head a little, looking to Maria. Giving her a smile. Acknowledging her pain. Her terror. That familiar place she'd been in before. "…Lauren," He began anew, finally looking back at her. "Do you remember what the pastor said when he baptized you?"

"I… Not really."

"Do you think you can wing it?" A little smile. Lauren's eyes grew wet by the second, as she rose. Knowing exactly what Gabriel was asking for. She waded deep into those waters, before where he bobbed, tiptoeing off of the stream bed. Her arms coming up under where Gabriel bobbed. That little symbol of hers in her hand.

"Gabriel Noria, Do you take Jesus Christ as your savior and accept His forgiveness for your sins?"

"Jesus is as good as any. But for what it's worth I always liked the guy more than any other ones. Yeah."

"Do you believe in God the Father and His Holy Spirit, Gabriel?"

"I can't truthfully say I don't anymore."

"I, Lauren Green, ordained only with what forgiveness that has been bestowed upon myself, christen you and... tell you..." Like she was fighting with her own soul, trying to say this. Say what was hurting her the most. Tears flowing freely now, fighting back sobs, her icon of faith shaking, rattling in her hand hovering above Gabriel's face. "...Tell you your sins are washed away."

Gabriel's head was submerged, and the last of the sopping blood on him drifted downstream as Lauren held him there, before bringing him up, back up into this world, into life, as cruel and beautiful as it is.

It was time to go soon.


"We've got to move as soon as everyone's done. They're probably going to check the place where we last registered once we stop showing up on their scans," Gabriel ordered as we did our best to dry ourselves despite our lack of any sort of drying equipment.

We moved through the forest ever so quickly, though Michael's wife and child lagged behind. I was hoping that they wouldn't be some sort of weak link, so I lagged as well, to walk closer to them. I think they recognized me, though the widow clutched her girl as I approached.

"Hey," I uttered, to begin. "What's your name?" She stared at me for a long while. I looked down, trying not to stab my bare feet with branches. "If you're coming with us, we need to be able-"

"Olivia," She uttered. "...This is Emily." I nodded appreciatively, reserving my urge to try and be accomodating. I could tell they would appreciate distance for now.

"...Thanks for holding onto my gun," I said, feeling the strap on my back. She didn't say anything, though I saw her eyes flutter, confusion beneath her deep layer of mourning. "See, your... This is actually... Never mind," I uttered, going over to Lauren who lead the way, Gabriel on her back. It looked like he was practically unconscious, barely slumped up against her humanoid back. How she held him gingerly, that sort of earned respect. It must have felt like the right thing to do for him. "...How is he?" I asked Lauren.

"Heavy," She grunted. Trying to joke. God bless her.

"...And awake," he muttered. "I'm fine. If I'm not you'll be the first to know, Noah." I sighed. This didn't feel as desperate as it was. Maybe it was easy to not think about it. Just a leisurely walk through the woods. I can't say I didn't appreciate the atmosphere.

"Hey," I was hearing. I turned back to see Susan drawing near to that little dragon girl, Emily. "You... I heard your name is Emily, right?" They looked at the meeker, younger, and arguably cuter member of our entourage with a hesitation that melted quicker than with us. "I'm Susan, but you can call me Katt if you want." She paused for a while to kick at a clod of dirt. She was still in her sleeping clothes, barefooted like the rest of us. "...If you need somebody to talk to, I can... I'll try to help. Okay?"

"Y-yeah." Emily must have been five or six years old. I still hardly understood the hybrid experience. Were they really a family? They didn't seem to have barcodes. Neither did Susan. Did Michael? I don't remember seeing one. They must have been socio chamber ones. It

would explain why they're not all on their lonesome, with an actual family; each other.
"...Thank- thank you."

Maria was off to the side. She watched that little girl, human or not, speak with her best and bravest face after... all that had happened. There was a twitch in her eyes, a boiling rage beneath a firmly shut lid, the way her fingers clenched. The cartel taking another little girl's loved one away, like it was some kind of game. I saw vengeance shining in her eyes. A reason to fight. How the spark of emotion was returning to her. I suppose it was returning to me too. For a moment there was guilt at my realization, at how, perhaps, there was a void there between us. No more love. No more nothing. And instead, shared vindication.

It wasn't relevant to the situation, though, so I walked on.

The Kommandos were immediately concerned about our bloodied status, not to mention the fact that we were all here, in our entirety, unarmed and hardly even dressed.

"...So," Squid was saying, as Gabriel and I sat in the commons, surrounded by both our group and his men. "...You really expect us to do this?"

"...A man's only worth as much as his word," Gabriel muttered, playing his swollen face off like he was squinting and nonchalant.

"Fucking shit up may be our modus operandi, but your operation might be a bit bigger than the scale we like to work with. I think this is too risky, to be honest," He scratched his little beard.

"...We'll take the vast majority of the risk in our offensive. Not to mention if you get traced back here, we're leaving anyways and you've planned on tagging along, trying your luck with Noah's citadel. You've got the offroad vehicles. We've talked about exfiling together, anyways."

"You're right, but we're in hardly any shape to move. We're short on vehicles for a full exfil. We need more off-roaders to get through the forest."

"There's a all-terrain depot at this specific barracks. Once the raid goes through that won't be a problem. Remember, we're just after Red. You get all the spoils you can carry, so long as we can have our original stuff.

"...Exfil to the point where we discussed, about fifteen miles up the road, right?"

"Yeah, where we can really move. That's the idea, at least before our pilot bit the bullet."

"...You know," Archie suddenly spoke up, everyone turning a little towards him. "I've been practicing some flight sims. I could double as one if you wanted. We already know where the Republicans' airbase is."

"...Let's keep things simple for now, Arch. Here's the deal, Squid. You pull off your distraction tonight at midnight, false flag so it seems like the blues are getting ballsy. After all they're way overdue for an invasion and the Republicans are getting tired of fighting microbes and would rather shoot at people instead. Once they take the bait we strike from inside the city, where their base has the least structural defenses. The majority of us will take up firing positions using LMGs, launchers and anti-materiel weapons from strategic points along the inner flank of the base, in houses still facing their garrison, while I lead a flanking squadron inside to take out the HVT. We'll mop up the defenders and the base and everything in it is yours until the Red backup arrives, which should be about twenty to thirty minutes from our initial strike. We'll aim for ten just to be safe and make it worth your while."

"...How do you know this 'Red' guy is in this specific one?"

"I've done my homework. He likes this one. Biggest base, seems to think it's the safest. I also bet he's expecting a one-man infiltration. This is the perfect place to hide if you're only worried about one guy slitting your throat in your sleep."

"...And you and your fifteen-odd personnel can do this."

"Supposed to be raining tonight, isn't it? Big storm, should help. Besides, not your problem. We're taking the risk."

"Yeah, aside from the gear I'll be loaning you."

"Consider it an investment." Squid looked around the room for a second.

"Guys?"

"Shit, we can't let them have all the fun," Some voices rose from the crowd.

"Let's do it!"

Squid turned back, sighing. "Looks like a deal. Joe?" Squid turned to a specific squad of his, the ones who'd shot at us back in the forest. "Get our 'honorary kommandos' their gear. And how about you and your squad join the fireteam? Doubt they can't use the help."

"Sounds good, Squiddie."

Squid turned back to Gabriel. "You'd better be able to deliver."

"Would this face lie to you?" Gabriel chuckled, motioning to all his swelling. Squid cracked a smile.

There in the deepest part of the old ski resort, the basement near the central supporting strut of the multi-story hotel was the Kommandos' armory. Ammo stacked to the ceiling. Guns, body armor, gear, all of it being fit. It wasn't the best stuff, but for what we were doing, it was sure better than nothing.

"You up to be on the strike force, Maria?" Gabriel asked.

"You're really gonna ask me with *your* face looking like that?" She joked without a smile or chuckle, frowning in endless somberness, fitting body armor and the chest rig over it, full of AK magazines. "Fuck that guy. I know you want to kill him, just save some of his personal guard for me."

"See what I can do. No promises." Gabriel smiled slyly, nodding his chin out. "Now, you," Gabriel suddenly reached out to grab Susan by the strap of her oversized body armor as she stealthily tried to pass him. "You are staying here."

"You fucking kidding me?!" Susan snarled with a viciousness that took even Gabriel by surprise. "You teach me to shoot at people but don't want me to?! That asshole deserves it!" She was inconsolable, whipping around as Gabriel held her by her wrist and she struck fruitlessly at his arm.

"Did you forget what I said?!" Gabriel roared back, and she was still for a moment, glaring up at him in fear. "You don't want to fight unless you have to."

"...And we have to; and I want to!" She reasoned, finding her courage again. "That's what we have to do! I'm coming with!" Gabriel sighed with pursed lips, taking a long pause.

"Don't get your head blown off," He released her and she felt her wrist, 'humph'ing. "What about you?" Gabriel turned to Olivia in a surplus chinese chest rig. "You know how to work an AR15, but can we depend on you? You're not going to shoot any of us in the back, are you?" For a moment she was almost inclined to snarl at him, but the kind way he spoke now was disarming, at least somewhat. She faltered, wings drooping.

"For now I just want that man dead. I'll deal with... everything, later." Gabriel clicked his tongue. As she spoke, shaking with cold rage as she did.

"...Yeah." Gabriel turned back to Maria again. "...Wait, did you only put a plate in the back pocket of your vest?"

"It's got soft armor all around," Maria reasoned. "And I figure bullets are like trucks. It's not the one right in front of you that hits you." She humped it up a little, getting a feel for the weight. "And it's a heavy-as-shit steel plate. I don't want to carry any more of these than I should. And this way it'll counterbalance the ammo I'm carrying on the front."

"Fair enough. Just remember to carry extra chest seals for when you get popped." Maria glared at him for a moment. It was almost like we were back in the natural swing of things. Preparing for the worst but joking around.

---

I found my way to the bathroom, maybe to just look at myself and think things through. I saw how I'd let myself go. God, it's like the months passed in an instant. Staring at my hair and beard all grown out again. I felt sore already, my muscles limp from lethargy. I got out the razor I'd been leant, cutting my hair slowly and intently, the incessant buzz drowning out all else and leaving my mind in silence. I took in my surroundings while I cut, It was one of those big bathrooms with a lot of sinks and stalls, the others coming in as well to cut their hair with the few razors we had on hand. Gabriel's words about keeping hair short for combat must have resonated with nearly the whole group. So many of us were here. Cutting with buzzing razors beneath these flickering lights. Preparing for battle.

"Here's the plan," Gabriel would say. "Maria, Noah, and Selicia are with me. We're limited on NODs so we're taking spidergirl. Lauren will be flying above, sending a thermal reading to our HUDs so we can observe troop movement. The rest of you will be taking up your firing positions and relaying any extra information you happen to pick up. We've only got one shot at this. Glory or death, folks."

Not much was certain, save for that there was a whole lot of anxious rest to be had before the battle. I laid down to try and get mine, but there was none to be had, the sky outside growing dark with angry clouds, thunder pounding like the torrent of rain falling down. I lay there on some cot, and all I could think of was the day I met him.

---

"I bet you think you're real special, huh *Noah*?" I can remember that fifth grader's voice almost exactly. How he sang my name, rife with condescension, and how that finally struck me that this wasn't a friendly interaction. His name escapes me, he wasn't particularly remarkable physically other than the fact that he was overweight and obviously thought his size made him strong. Towering there over my little self, far less indomitable than he was. "You think that's cool, saying you shoot guns and run around in the woods like a little fag?"

"Y-yeah," Even there I had yet to fully grasp the situation. He laughed. His cronies laughed as they advanced.

"You think you're some kinda super cool army soldier?" He walked right up to me and shoved me. I tried to stumble back, but one of his friends caught my heel with his foot and I tumbled over onto my bottom, sitting there. "Not so strong now, huh!" I tried to get up but he shoved me back down.

"You gonna go get your dad? Or are you gonna cry?!" Another crowed. I felt my face, my eyes growing wet.

"You're not strong. You're not cool. You're just a-"

Whack.

It was out of nowhere when this other kid, somewhat bigger than me but definitely not bigger than any of these fifth graders careened into that ringleader, with a sloppy fist right to the jaw. Their leader crumpled back.

"Wh-"

"GET UP!" He screamed. Was he screaming at the fifth grader?

No.


"GET UP AND FIGHT!"


This overweight, fourth grade kid with his dirty blond hair and square head with deep-set, haunting green eyes was glaring death into me. I was almost in awe for a couple seconds, the other bullies ganging up on him quickly as the head of their little troupe was getting up and swearing up a storm. They were pummeling this random kid, and he was just *taking* it, crouched with his arms over his face. But he flew back at them, striking one in the crotch and the other upside the face. It almost seemed superhuman to my awestruck childish mind, the strength this guy pulled from within himself. In retrospect he fought like he had no training, but that wasn't to say that he didn't fight like his life depended on it. Even if it was a silly schoolyard brawl, outnumbered or not, I was more scared of him than the bullies for a moment. I saw pure hellfire in his eyes.

*Boom.* Like a moment where there was a lull in the battle, he was above me, towering, fuming, nostrils flared, face red, nose bloody from a strike. His hand fished for mine and he pulled me up. "It's not right!" he whined. A whine of childish conviction. The strongest goddamn whine you'd ever heard. "You let these jerks walk all over you and you'll never forgive yourself!"

It was that day that I had enshrined in my mind. The triumphant struggle where good stood against evil, and two stood against giants.

But there on the ground after we'd received our final blows, there in the principal's office where we were punished for starting the fight, that lead fifth grader would look at me. Then the boy by my side would look back and he would look away. And in a way, it was as if I could look at him and he would not look back. His bruises were developing, he looked far worse with two black eyes, a broken nose, and bruises all over. It was as if we'd won. Looking over at Gabriel, I felt this was a victory. That kid and his cronies would never bother me again.

There on the time-out bench for the rest of the trimester of the school year recess-free, Gabriel sat beside me. I always envisioned him, canonized him in a suit of armor, a knight, a paladin standing against all evil. Somebody I'd grow to be glad to have as a friend. "You can't let these dickos walk all over you," He humphed in dour seriousness, swearing like the child he was despite the conviction in his voice.

"We… We got in trouble," I asked back.

"That doesn't matter. That shithead fucker will never bother you again. You think if you let a mean person just keep being mean, they'll ever stop?" He glared over to me. Maybe he always had that way of looking at people, that serious eye that froze your blood. Maybe it was my fading awe in that situation. Doesn't matter, I just remembered it that way. "You've got to fight these jerks or they'll take everything you've got. Not your stuff or your toys, but your *thoughts*. You'll think 'bout how you sat there and didn't do nothin'. You've gotta fight 'em or they win. Fight 'em no matter what. *Even if you end up losing.*"

---

### Chapter 61

The rain was oppressive.

Falling on my head, where I ambled there. I checked the bright red armband of my poncho, maybe making sure my disguise was still holding up.

The guard was antsy, given the attack going about in the far distance, hard to tell an explosion from a thundercrack. I was watching the dispatch going about, trucks full of soldiers piling in to race on out, one after another. There was still a sizeable garrison that remained.

"Watch for inspections. Guard's expecting me," Gabriel's voice noted in my ear. "What's it looking like?"

"…We're right on plan," I muttered into my mouthpiece. "Bravo, you ready?"

"…As we'll ever be," Archie muttered. "We count… three machine gun nests, a mortar, seven fire positions."

"The reinforcements have passed the threshold," Lauren's voice buzzed, full of detached calm, forced as it may have been.

"Showtime." I looked over, across the way to see a large figure enshrined in a mass of wool blanket wrapped from head to toe slinking forward, across the road, towards the soldiers standing guard at the head of the gate.

"Hey, you," One of the soldiers was yelling at that figure covered in a billowing cloak. "You're not supposed to be here. Don't you know there's a curfew?" I heard them fiddling with their guns, but I tried not to stare. I had my own role to play.

"I'm sorry, but I need a place to stay," Selicia's voice carried up as she held her hands up from the great cloak, the vast majority of her rather expansive body shrouded in darkness and fabric. Was she trying to sound destitute and desperate? She sort of came off as too dignified for her role. "I'm sure if you two gentlemen could help me out, I might be able to… Make it worth your while."

"What's that supposed to mean?" They asked, though their poses shifted and the atmosphere changed. I felt my weapon.

"It's got to get lonely, standing out here all night," She offered.

"Are you human?" One asked, maybe taking too close a look at her number of eyes, unable to really shroud half of them with her shawl. Lightning flashed, and I saw the shine of a gun barrel poking out from beneath her. The thunder cracked. And then it boomed again, and again, and they fell from their feet.

Gabriel emerged from beneath Selicia's many legs, in the process of loading his shotgun to replace the rounds he'd just spent. I watched him rise for a few seconds, rising above this sea of mud. A deathly calm showed on his face, unlike how I usually saw him. I only could have a couple moments to remark upon this to myself, until he spoke "Execute." Having received the go-ahead, off to our right, towards the city, a cacophony of rifles went off. Just shooting at the building, probing shots. Cries of the guard. An alarm being raised within seconds, as he passed Selicia her shotgun and drew his own weapon.

"Time set. Fifteen minutes," Maria uttered. I saw her to my right, in a disguise like mine. I looked down the way, seeing the garrison practically emptying as the red-marked soldiers piled into the battlements and trenches, bullets flying over their heads, cracking over like lightning.

Like that, we were gone into the chasm, the dark expanses of this cold building. It was unrecognizable for what it once was, until it hit me. The wide, empty rooms, the halls, the floors, the lockers- this used to be a school. We had the blueprints on our HUDs, so we had some semblance of direction. Red must have been on the top floor, given what Gabriel thought of the guy preferring to lord over others; Maria and Selicia splitting off to check the lower rooms, just in case, so we split up.

It was us now, advancing at our brisk pace up, up the stairs.

Blood flew. One of Red's personal guard caught at a flank in the stairwell, Gabriel uttering some expletive in spanish as he drove a knife into his side and back, wedging in the gap between his armor in his side. With a silenced pistol from the Kommandoes he proceeded to shooting another guard entering coming down the hall to investigate. "Clear," He hushed me in up the stairs, as I watched his back. Top floor. This had to be it, if anything.

It was hard enough to listen with that battle happening outside, bullets crashing through the building here and there. It struck me for a moment how one ill-placed shot could hit either of us and our whole operation would go up in smoke, and in that thought I was, and Gabriel distracted as well, heard a guard calling out in one of the adjacent classrooms. The lights slammed off up here, and we vanished into blackness. "NODs," Gabriel hushed, voice still brimming with professionalism. I flicked the ones on my helmet down, seeing infraed lasers tracing around the place, Gabriel as well. Gabriel proned out to poke under a window and through a door, firing his pistol into one guard who screamed out. There were shouts in spanish from the adjacent room, a guard proceeding out but I caught him on the way with my own pistol-caliber carbine with a homemade suppressor on the end, putting what felt like half a dozen rounds into him before he collapsed to the floor in silence. Maybe he gurgled as he lay there to die, I didn't hear it, only the loud clack of his rifle hitting the ground under the thump of his big body. Down the hall, more gunmen emerging. Bullets cracked over my head as one popped out after I'd killed his comrade in response, and I ducked away. Their muzzle-flashes lit up the world and my older pair of NODs, a first or second generation, suffered an immense image burn as I cursed, seeing my vision reduced to fuzz in them. I whipped them up, hearing a tussle commence up there. A wet, gurgling scream. By the time I was back up and turned on the visible light of my subgun, I only watched as Gabriel took a knife into his gut from the only guard still alive, Gabriel barely letting out a grunt as his own knife was firmly embedded in this man's neck, twisted once and his assailant twitched to fall, releasing the blade. I was upon Gabriel in concern.

"Jesus," I hushed, my hands hovering over the knife in his side as Gabriel leaned against the wall there, having brushed his own helmet off. Like I wanted to ask him if he wanted to abort the mission. He could tell.

"Do I look like some faggot that dies from a single stab wound?" I heard him grunt. Like it was nothing, even though the look in his eyes told a different story. "...It ain't squirting, he missed the Vena Cava. I'm fucking good. Just cover me while I patch up." He whipped that knife out with a wet sliding sound, picking his shirt up to stick a syringe of FastClot in the knife's stead and grunting as he injected a bit of it before throwing what was basically a giant band-aid over it, whipping his shirt back down.

"You've gotten a lot further than you should have," A voice boomed that froze me in my tracks, Gabriel stopping to take a slow look back to me. Red was here. "For that, I must commend you. Bravo."

"Come out, Red." Gabriel stood back up.

"Oh, but I'm a cornered rat," He chuckled. He didn't sound fazed in the slightest. "There's no telling what I'm capable of. That should make you scared." Gabriel was moving again, scanning each classroom, me right behind, covering him as he peeked. "You know, Hijito," Red began anew. "You always dogged Sicarios, but I think you would have made an exceptional one. You might just be the quickest-thinking Ejecutor I'd ever marshalled. You're a finer infiltrator than half of them."

"You can save the sucking up. You're not walking out of this place." His voice was a low growl, practically driving my goosebumps further. I truly believed Gabriel would tear Red limb from limb.

"...Maybe even too good," Red went on unabashed. "You know what you have that makes you an exceptional operator? You have that drive, that *spark* that most people lack." Red smacked his lips, chuckling. Like he knew something we didn't. At least, that I didn't. "...The lengths you went to to carry this little operation out truly proves you will pay *any* cost for *victory*."

I was chilled at the onset of Red's implications, here in this black place. The two of us spreading out as gunfire was crackling outside, lightning in the distance lighting the place in brief flashes. I really wished my nightvision was working.

"But you aren't alone I see, Hijito. Sir *Dragonrider*... Did you ever stop to question your *friend's* plan?" He hissed. "I don't mean petty tactics. I mean his goal, his purpose. Four people you may or may not have been close with lay dead from his actions. Here you are, having slain my men for the privilege to face *me*, Dragonrider. A man you have had no personal quarrels with a mere twenty-four hours before this very moment. But my protege, on the other hand... His quarrel, his gain..." It was odd how his voice fluctuated. Did he have some sort of PA system set up? It's like he spoke from a different hallway, a different classroom each moment. The shadows were relentless, even with our weapon-mounted lights.

"No matter what your role in this is, Dragonrider, you gain nothing from before we came to our metaphysical blows last night. Gabriel however, seeks to gain *vengeance* for his past. I know what he must have told you, to console you. That it was all *his* fault. *His doing*. That nothing he can do will make this up to you. Both sentiments are far from false." Gabriel was checking the rooms on the right side, one-by-one, stopping in a doorway for a quick peek. But as this revelation came to me, my feet slowed, my mind became sluggish in my search, and my eyes found themselves drawn to Gabriel. Drawn to read what he was thinking, what he was reacting. I saw his usual scowl having grown teeth, gritting them. Had it grown? Was it the pain? Was he becoming frustrated?

"Well, Dragonrider? Isn't there a feeling in your heart? An intuition you cannot deny? You've been *had*. You've been played. Those two grandparent types- you know what the woman told me, before I ended her life?" My grip on my weapon was tightening, glaring at Gabriel, head pounding. "Don't hurt them'. She *begged* me for your life as I put a bullet in her head. Her final thoughts were solely of your little group. That's more than you can say of your so-called *friend*."

"Gabriel." I uttered, in that hall. "Is that-"

Lightning struck. In that moment, I saw Gabriel turn. His eyes grew wide. His weapon was raising, moment by moment, but out of the corner of my eye I saw glinting steel coming around my neck. My carbine was spun from my grip as I was yanked forcefully back. "NOAH!" Gabriel's voice radiated. In another moment, there he was. Gabriel pointing his gun at me, and my breath froze in my chest.

"Drop him."

"You've used, and used, and *used* your little friends this far in your *thirst* for revenge, mi hijo. What's one more... *sip?*" Red's voice radiating in my ear, past me and into Gabriel's. Red tossed my weapon behind him, hearing it clatter on the ground. "Give me your gun."

"I'm not stupid."

"I know you're not. That's why you'll give me that gun." Bit by bit Gabriel complied, each inch he lowered that muzzle like a tiny defeat. Gabriel tossed the pistol, Red catching it with his knife-less hand right before my face, again tossing it over his shoulder. That open hand reached into his coat once more, shuffling to display his own engraved pistol. It would be quite the beauty to marvel at such a close range if not for the situation distracting the opportunity to admire it. I saw Gabriel snarling there, standing with his fists clenched at his sides.

"You've made it this far, *hijo*. I'll do you the honor of obliging you to your *Baile Ultimo*, even if you don't deserve it." With that, he released me to push me towards Gabriel. I stumbled on over, to face him, seeing him place his gun to the side, now only holding his cruel curved blade. "I must apologize however, my dear Dragonrider. For I fully expected Gabriel, however I did not expect you." He produced Gabriel's Ka Bar knife from a belt sheath, tossing it to him, as if on a course right for his face, Gabriel snatching it out of the air without a moment's thought. "However I won't be one to have left you with nothing." He next produced a large switchblade, with a flick of his wrist it flew out and was embedded in the wall beside my head, easily able to have pierced by skull had he chose. He smirked at my realization. I pulled it from the wall, noting for a moment how firmly it was stuck.

We faced him there, amid the darkness, the cracking of the lightning. The shining of his eyes, the devil in them. It was entrancing, the horror standing before me. Silvered steel shimmering in his right hand. Slowly he took on a fighter's stance, blade coming up, and we copied him in our own stances. Ready to kill.

His gaze cut through me, how he glared. That radiating stare. Though I'd been preparing for this, for a moment I froze up. I had to remind myself that I needed to be

"NOAH!" Gabriel cried. He was fast. Barely two steps and he was beside me. Smiling kindly with those razor eyes of his, his knife point on its course towards my face, death a quarter second away. A blur of movement, Blood hitting my face. Gabriel was screaming. I was thrown back from my feet, watching Gabriel be picked up by this thin, lithe middle aged man and tossed across the room, Red's knife firmly planted all the way through Gabriel's already abused right hand. I was getting up, watching the now disarmed Red move in on Gabriel on the ground, who still had his own Ka Bar in his left, lashing out towards Red's legs in a bid for Red's quadriceps, Red zipping back again in a blur, a gleaming smile on his razor face. This was bad. I brought myself to my feet to lunge towards him but his eyes turned. That gaze again. Was this piece of shit really going to beat me with his eyes?!

All he had to do was move like he usually did, zipping away with a single step but leaving enough of his leg to trip me coming forward. I had to veer off to avoid colliding with Gabriel, who was in the process of getting up, to charge back at Red. In retrospect, it was like he was trying to keep at least one of us off our feet at any given time so he wouldn't have to fight the both of us at once. I could remember martial arts teachers talking about fighting multiple opponents, how your goal is to move so you're really only in danger from one individual at a time, which Red certainly had down to a T. They never taught me how to take on a much superior opponent as numbers as my only edge.

Gabriel must've caught onto this, keeping his distance, still with Red's knife gushing blood from his hand. Red didn't seem to care that he was disarmed, fists pummeling into Gabriel as he advanced faster even than before, the footwork of a champion boxer, blows landing with utmost force, circling around Gabriel to strike at him and drive him out the door, a free hand reaching past my own knife and grabbing me by the chinstrap of my helmet, throwing me out into the hall with Gabriel as my helmet flew from my head, clattering across the ground. I scrambled to get up but he appeared before me, laughing in glee as he drove his fist into my stomach, throwing me onto the stairs. Up and up, always on the defensive. Trying to get up, get a footing he would not allow us to have. *Playing* with us, glee in his depraved eyes and flashing smile. Who and what the fuck was this guy?!

We were on the roof, in the pouring rain. It was almost like he had a statement to make, as In a moment he'd grappled Gabriel and sent him over the edge of the roof as I lay dazed some ways away, disarmed. Gabriel held on with his left hand, his Ka-Bar spinning from his grip down below into the battlements, the battle raging behind and below him, his hanging right hand ever pierced by that knife, his left hand gripping the roof corner for dear life.

"You never know when to let go, son," Red laughed, going to pry Gabriel's hand from the sill, before I found that switchblade in a puddle on that roof and lunged, taking my opportunity as quick as I could I swore that my placement was exactly into his heart- center and to the left. He coughed, moving again. He was no longer smiling as he turned with a backhand that caught my jaw, dazing me for an unfortunate second as I sprawled out, layed waste by his utter strength. "*¡¿QUIERES MORIR PRIMERO?!*" He gnashed. He was on top of me. Eyes bloody with rage, hands around my throat. His razor smile returned, for much the worst this time. Pure evil gazing into me. Choking me. I tried everything I'd been taught to do to counter this situation but he was too strong and too present, too smart. Years of jiu-jitsu, judo, MMA all undone by his force of will. He knew it all, and was here to be my end. Making the world go from red to black for me, the last thing fading in my vision, the face of a razor-toothed demon ending my life.

Blood.

Blood washed over me and I could breathe again. I half breathed in that blood pouring on me, looking up, seeing Red, my killer clutching, choking his own throat now, eyes wide in abject shock. I watched him turn, facing Gabriel, heaving, Red's knife clutched in his hand, removed from where it had pierced his own.

No words, nothing but pure, raging and terrifying emotion as Gabriel advanced over the bleeding Red, grabbing the scalp of Red's hair with what was left of his mangled right hand, and *whack, whack, whack.* Slashing, cutting, chopping into Red's neck blow after brutal blow, eyes shining in righteous fury as thunder roared above us. Red going slack little by little, soon left as a limp corpse with mouth agape and eyes rolled back into his head from pain and shock. In no less than thirty seconds his headless corpse fell, and Gabriel rose silently over the world, an icon of utter victory clutched, running over with blood in his hand. That head, displaying a face of abject pain and fear forevermore, lit by god's righteous and terrible lightning splitting the heavens above.

Gabriel walked to the edge of the roof, overlooking the battlements. Taking a moment to see the defenders' panic, their disarray below, given how the two of us had decimated their command structure even before taking on Red, a rout seconds from occuring.

Gabriel spoke. I could have sworn that the battle grew quiet just enough for his voice to radiate into every soul to bear witness. "YOUR BOSS," He roared like the thunder cracking in the distance, holding the head aloft to soak in the torrential rains. Eyes of soldiers turned to meet him, confused and scared. "IS DEAD!" He ever so gracefully tossed that head into the trenches, gazing down in cool rage at those still there. Like that, they began to scatter, any way they could.

The fort was ours.

## Chapter 62

We *won*.

Back at the Kommandos base we hugged it out, tears of victory streaming down our faces. We took on a cartel boss and every one of us survived. More than that, we *won*. It was over. We cheated death. Gabriel beat him.

Maria came up to me, smiling. Maybe a month or two earlier she would have embraced me, but she stood there in her own little partaking of victory. For the first time in a while, she seemed… content. At least in some way. Ever since this all started all those months ago.

We had all our stuff back. My old armor, high tech and fancy and all. Lauren had her saddle and her custom armor and chest rig, even her old trinket from Curtis she used to hang on her ammo rig before we got captured. And of course, my rifle as well, brought of course well before the battle by Mrs. Draco standing off in the corner, not fully able to enjoy herself here and now without her beloved, relegating her to look after her sleepless daughter who Katt now tried her damndest to bond with, coming to the girl and telling her about how it was all over now and the man responsible wouldn't be bothering them anymore, trying to make things a little better for the younger one. I could still see the two of them, Mrs. Draco and her Daughter's eyes haunted by the visage of a triumphant Gabriel, even as he curbed his victory in all that he had lost, guilt still assuaging him. The Kommandos had their reasons to celebrate, a decisive victory and a whole lot of new supplies. Asses kicked, names taken, all that jazz.

And Gabriel, that Gabriel. I saw him toiling away in their kitchen, organizing all the new rations, speaking boisterously about the feast tonight, before we all leave this place forever in our new all-terrain strike vehicles. Sure, I missed my jeep, and I know my dad would be upset, but *man*. I hadn't thought about dad in forever. For a moment I wondered what he was doing right now.

But what really struck me was Gabriel's overflowing joy, not letting a wrapped-up hand and a hole in his gut get in the way of his victory, even going so far as to show off Red's knife and gun, laughing at them and pantomiming the blade through his hand to the kommandoes who roared with laughter and hubris. He was finally *free*. He stood taller, moved with less hesitation, and breathed like the whole world owed him air. I couldn't help but smile back at his mirth. He beat fate and he knew it. Despite what he had done to earn it, he was free, and, watching him, I felt just as free.

"There's a phrase that I've always fuckin' hated," Gabriel began, in the midst of our initial festivities. "And while I really wanted to save this little spiel for our real party tomorrow night, but hey. It's been biting on my mind." Gabriel spun about as he took a stand on the table, waving along to the crowd of all of us, our friends, and the Kommandoes willing enough to listen. "Blood is thicker than water. It's a stupid phrase and I've always hated it until I found out that's not the whole thing." Gabriel paused, masking his coughing as clearing his throat. Wounded or not, he wouldn't let a mutilated hand, a couple broken ribs, a stitched-up gut wound and a bit of blood loss get in the way of his victory. "*The blood of the covenant is thicker than the water of the womb.* It's not the pieces of human trash you're born into, it's the ones that bleed by your side that matter. You're all more than any family could ever be to me." A cheer rose from the crowd, Gabriel receiving his standing ovation with raised arms and a bowed head. His victory. His freedom. Him.

The Sun rose, and though many of us took the time to take a well-deserved nap, many of us were still left restless. I found a good half of the group still in the mess hall after our impromptu victory celebration, walking in on those who had yet to call it a night here in this bare morning.

I caught Lauren there by the door, looking off into the sunrise above the misty mountains. Her wings were rustling like she wanted to go for a flight, the way she always got before one. Sighing slow.

"...Feeling underdressed?" I mused with a bit of a smile of how she was wearing her reclaimed body armor. Her head whipped around, throwing her ponytail about as her ears flicked, bright, attentive eyes drawing themselves on me as I leaned there.

"You're one to talk," She muttered, since I was wearing my old set too, that I hadn't seen in months.

"I missed how this one fits. Custom, after all."

"You and me both," Lauren brushed her rig's shoulder strap with her wrist, flicking past a trinket. "You wouldn't believe it, but I found Curtis' little space ship," She mentioned of the red and white rocket hanging by one of the molle loops now.

"Guess this means you're fated to find that spaceship of your own," I smirked and she let out a little chuckle, looking down at her feet for a moment before eyeing back up at me with her face low.

"...Ain't that... Mr. Pendrew's old rifle?" I stalled slowly, out of our mutual pain. Lauren looked down at the wood-stocked weapon, that big old M1A rifle with a variable magnification scope on top.

"Yeah," She sighed, hushed. Staring from me to it. "It's... I dunno. I felt like he'd be okay with me holding onto it."

"Don't exactly want any of the Kommando geniuses getting their grubby hands on it, eh?" I chuckled dourly.

"It's not that I don't trust them..." She glossed over the sad little joke, sighing ever more heavily. "I dunno. It's... I think he'd be okay with me having it." A long silence to breathe and take in the sentiment.

"...Always thought you sorta dwarfed an AR," I smirked. "Battle rifle suits you." She smirked back, ever ready to move on to the next topic.

"So, Noah, I was gonna go and... see where we were, one last time before we go. See th grave, too."

"...You sure that's the right thing to do?" I let out in hesitation. "It might not be good to dwell on it."

"It's not dwelling," She blurted, interrupting herself with a sigh, like maybe it was. "...I just feel like... With the time I spent there..." She was clutching another trinket, beside where her little rocket ship was hanging. Her hand came away and I saw her little symbol of faith, that trinity hanging there. Gabriel's tooth was hanging as well, her three little pieces of adventure. "Jesus, Noah, it was most of my life," She sighed. "I need to know what to think about this."

"...You're going back?" Maria was there, evidently having listened for a fair while, leaned there. Her eyes had begun to bag from lack of sleep.

"Y-yeah," Lauren uttered.

"We want to go and have a last look too," Selicia uttered, also stepping forward. Sam, Archie, Daniel and Susan advanced forward too. Olivia was in the corner, probably still stewing over her husband, before getting off the wall to approach to join in.

"Sleep fifteen hours a day and I catch you awake at five AM?" I joked towards Selicia.

"...Something like that," She muttered, sighing. "I... Noah, I was on watch that night. I..." I wanted to interject, to chide her in her regret that we won, but I held my tongue. "I was careless and they got the drop on me. I just..." She was looking down at where her legs were all clacking against the ground beneath her, feeling her coffee mug in her grip with brushing fingers. "I just wanted to say I'm sorry." I bit my lip, but nodded plainly in recognition.

"It's in the past now," I sighed. "What matters is that we move forward. And we finally are about to."

"Don't count me out," Gabriel was the last to step forward. It took me by surprise, frankly, knowing how unsentimental he was. But I guess all that talking about god really got to him. "I need to give my respects."

We set out on this misty morning, tying on our red armbands. The rains had just stopped, and we trudged through mud on our way to the old broken down road leading out of the ski resort. The forest was so still, uncharacteristically so. I supposed it was that the heavy rains had just ceased. The way the mists hugged the earth around u, how this world was quiet and serene. Peace at last. I did my best to take it in, appreciate it all. Breathe that free air. Gabriel sure was.

I took the time to notice little things that had passed me by earlier. My disassociation melting, my own freedom returning. I noticed the little differences between Olivia and Lauren, not just the obvious things like Lauren's green skin vs Olivia's orange, or bipedal versus centaurical, but how olivia had no hair that extended down her spine, how her tail terminated in a fin, her ears were far more like fins than cow-ears, and she had a couple more bony ridges around her face, her eyes had less of a squint, and her muzzle was more angular.

I noticed little changes that I could hardly remember, how Selicia seemed a lot less antagonistic. Humbler. Daniel stood taller and carried his weapons more comfortably. Hardly looked like a soldier but it was almost like I didn't really give him credit for how much more mature he was when I attacked him for saying those things that got under my skin. I wanted to apologize, but felt this wasn't the right place for it or something. Susan too was more alert and acting like a real adult, though in some respects it was still like she was playing an adult the way a girl too young to be called a lady would have. Archie seemed more comfortable too, less uptight, how he walked with a little bit more of a bounce and talked not trying to artificially deepen his voice, and Gabriel- perhaps it was just the fights with his boss, but he was all the more humbled. Despite his victory, he strode with less gusto and more purpose. Like something weighed down upon him. Freedom weighed upon him.

We saw the church, standing there before the countless graves in this overcrowded makeshift cemetery. We found those four graves, practically one by how close they were.

"...Anything to say?" Gabriel asked.

"I was always hard on the old kodger," Archie muttered, fingering the straps of his armor. "Maybe too hard. I'm gonna miss him."

"It's a shame it went down like this," Selicia strode forward to feel the cross, before looking up, losing herself in the vast place. "God, its like you'd lose track of the graves here."

"Really puts things in perspective." Gabriel's musings were dark and completely without his usual mirth. "It's all fucked, isn't it?"

"...Gabriel," Olivia, Michael's husband spoke slowly, as if recalling his name ever so painfully. "I... I said I didn't know if I could forgive you."

"Yeah."

"I don't know if I ever will."

"Yeah."

"I... I don't even know if I can really say goodbye," She uttered, voice only beginning to crack. I turned my head a little, seeing her eyes water.

"...I owe you more than anything I can ever give to you. But we'll start with freedom." She sniffled, Gabriel's face pursed in utter seriousness as he glared to her, nodding slowly. She nodded back. "Maria?"

"...What you guys said."

"Noah?" He asked. To be honest, now I *did* have something on my mind. But I bit into my own tongue. Was this the place for this?

"...Nothing," I muttered. Gabriel humphed a little. Not out of his usual antagonism, that was well and extinguished within him. But here he stood, and for a second, my blood ran cold. Red's words still rattling in my mind as everyone went to walk away they were going to see the remains of the house one last time, Olivia taking to the sky and going back to the resort. They left us, everyone but me and Gabriel, sitting there on a bench on the outskirts of the refugee camp, just thinking, Gabriel standing against a wall of the community hall of the church beside me.

"So," he said out of the corner of his mouth with a smack of his broken lips. "How's Lauren?"

"Lauren's... Fine," I responded, figuring it was small talk, though his eyes shifted over to me, I had this biting feeling that this was more than a simple check-up. He said nothing, simply staring at me a little with his chin nodding ever so subtly, as if expecting me to say more, as if there were some significance to that which he'd said.

"How about Maria?"

"What's this about?"

"Do you really love Maria?" In a moment my blood ran cold, colder than ever before as he glared at me with such intensity that I was forced to look down at my feet.

"It's..." It's none of your business, I wanted to say. But that uncomfortability was back. "We just won against your boss, can't I enjoy that without..." I trailed off, trying to think of something to say, as Gabriel just chuckled.

"...So something *is* going on." He leaned in now from where he was leaned against the, still looking over to me. He was smiling, but not for my sake. "All this time and I've been too much of a coward to tell you to face your own feelings. Noah," He glared on and through me. "You think you're only hurting yourself by pretending to love Maria, but you're hurting her too. A year or two down the line and you're going to hate what you've done. It's not healthy, to *any*one involved. Least of all you." Almost more than I'd hate what I'd already done. "Maria isn't going to be the one to realise that enough is enough, you know how she is. She'd fade to nothing before she'd let her heart break. She already is, Noah. You're *doing* this to her." His voice was rising to a stark crescendo. "And if you want Lauren's love instead, there's only so many bad things you can do to other people until Lauren can no longer forgive you."

"You think you can judge me?" I began defensively. "What about how you used the group to get revenge on your boss?" Gabriel's eyes widened out, for a moment he almost twitched, anger, or possibly that guilt, that weight upon his shoulders finding him.

"...Not judge," He found his resolve again to close out his own argument, through grit teeth. "Just give you the advice you need to hear." He then stood up to lean against the wall of one of the temporary buildings and cross his arms, facing me there where I sat. "...So. You really believed him."

"Was Red lying?" I spat. Gabriel finally looked away, biting his lower lip. Sighing.

"There's a lot I can say. But I know what he said and what it must sound like." Gabriel eyed me.

"...You *did* use us."

"*I tried not to, okay?!*" His voice rose for a stark moment, his turn to lose his composure, and my eyes widened and my face grew pale.

"W-what?"

"I messed up, okay?! I didn't want to involve you. But I underestimated him and it cost them their lives, alright?!" He waved towards those graves with a voice like for a second, I was the one making a big deal of things. With how he realised the tone of his own words, he paused, face flushing out of color as he cleared his throat. "...There's nothing I can ever do that will make up for it. I'm sorry. " Like an admittance of guilt shaking me to my core, I rose to my feet, shuddering. I fell forward upon him, grasping him by the straps of his body armor. Like I wanted to pick him up into the air in rage, though I was limped up against him in shock, too weak to move a muscle.

"Gabriel," I spoke, my voice no more than a hoarse whisper, drawing in close to his face. "*G-Gabriel-*"

"...If you knew what he did, *what he made me do*," I heard in a whisper, though he would not look at me. "You would have done the same."

"For *revenge?!*"

"*To make up for what I've done*, and *for a chance to make sure there was a little less evil in the world.*"

### Chapter 63

It was in that moment, a horn of a truck blew in the distance, drawing our eyes up to the horizon. A moment of clarity, enough to hear the roar of aircraft in the distance, something we'd missed during our little conversation. I released Gabriel, finding my feet to look over. Soldiers were shouting. A truck full of Reds was converging. Sparse gunfire popped off from where some of the soldiers fired their guns. People, refugees encamped here fell, some to their knees, others dead. A crowd being gathered by the Republicans at gunpoint under the furor of roaring aircraft. Like that there was a battle, and in a moment our squabble felt petty as refugees were being lined up and shot, the mass of people being forced towards and into the worship hall. The pastor taken aside and blown away by an impartial moment of cold rage at the orders of some cruel-faced commandant. I watched him fall and my hardened heart ached for a moment, only to boil anew. The two of us had hunkered down to the side for a moment. What terrible things were taking place. Executions. The Republicans cleaning house in the shadow of this sudden, looming battle.

"You two!" A man, an officer, stout and gruff, was approaching us. One look at his rotund size and it was evident that he hadn't spent much of this apocalypse with an empty stomach, as opposed to the refugee woman he had by the hair, who was whimpering in fear, human skin sucked down to the bone all over her. "We're rounding these freeloaders up! Get as many as you can into the hall right now!"

"W-what's going on?" I asked.

"Blues are coming!" He barked. "We're cleaning house since their interlopers hit us hard last night! We think they've got spies in this camp!"

"You're gonna lock 'em in the hall? And then what?" I asked, though the gunfire was a little more than disconcerting.

"Burn the fucker down! Save the ammo!" He snarled. "Get to-" He couldn't finish his sentence before my rifle was off safe. I barely watched his eyes widen and face wash out from color in the moment I pointed my gun at him, barely a pause on my part. Boom, He crumpled back onto his ass, only beginning to scream, gurgling with a sucking chest wound, as I shoved my rifle into his gut in a moment of flash rage, perhaps spurred on by Gabriel's sins, practically muffling the gunfire in his gut as I let several rounds through him, shock taking him as the woman screamed and my ears rung. She fell away, terrified at this sudden betrayal, blood and pieces of guts sprayed across my arms and smoking weapon as I towered over her. A moment of her witnessing my rage before she scampered off, terrified of her savior. I shot a look to Gabriel, in his own shock at my brutality. Gabriel, shocked. A look I'd never forget.

"We gonna let them do that shit?! Or do you want to save some people?!" I roared. He nodded, though for once he did not smile. I was the one to smile. And like that, we were off to kill. As they were barricading the doors and throwing molotovs through windows and onto the roof, we got into our positions before opening fire, moments after I'd taken a man to the ground with my knife as he stood before a soon-to-be execution. I glared in the eyes of the hybrid refugee he was seconds from executing, his terror mirroring his would-be executioner, this Republican turning slowly enough to see me and my armband with a breaking heart that I drove my blade through.

We opened fire. Gabriel flanked when he reloaded, I shot, I flanked when I reloaded, Gabriel shot. The unsuspecting Republicans had little in the way of vigilance during their little war crime, and we took them by the utmost surprise. It was different, this time. In Vegas and the desert, I was terrified to kill. In the facility, it made me sick, but I could stomach it. Against Red and his cronies, I felt nothing. Like I was a real professional. But here, blowing these men from their feet and lives I must admit in the moment I felt a sort of cathartic bliss. I hardly knew these people, but I suppose it was all the talk of god and forgiveness and vengeance in the name of what was right that fueled a sort of zealousness against evil, though in retrospect, perhaps at least some if not most of these republican guards simply took this job to feed themselves and their families. Just following orders. I could only think one thing in the moment. Two words echoing, screaming in my head. *Fuck 'em.* Maybe it was my rage against Gabriel. Or maybe I was just desensitized to all the killing at this point, and I was lapping up the idea of doing it for the right reason for once.

"Move this fuckin' beam!" With our enemies bloody and dying, stepping over bodies we came to the door bar, pulling it up and throwing it away, wrenching the doors open. I fired into the air for attention. "EVERYONE GET THE FUCK OUT!" I roared inside, and we stepped aside as they poured out, smoke pouring with them.

But like a spectre, one remained. A tiny canid girl, hardly four years old, light grey fur, like a tiny wolf on two legs, almost comically. Hanging there, haunting eyes as she stared at me.

Right at me. "What are you doing, kid?! Leave!" I screamed. Her arm raised, towards the choking smoke within, and she was gone, back into it.

"You see somebody?" Gabriel hushed, getting up to look as she disappeared. I was beyond words, gripping Gabriel's combat mask where it hung from his body armor, and I charged in without a word, throwing it on as I went.

"Thermals!" I spat for the internal computer to respond to, seeing the world lit up in bright splotches, fire as the building creaked, pieces falling. That little wolf girl covering her face with her shirt, as if bidding me to follow.

Another body on the ground, still warm. She hung over him, looking up to me. I stooped down, turning thermal vision off to see his labored breathing. Slinging my rifle I stooped over to throw him over my right shoulder, going for the little hybrid girl too, her fishing for my hand as if to walk beside me, though I knew there was little time for that, picking her up entirely to carry her and the similar looking canid who was presumably her brother out through the smoke, her in my grip, him over my shoulder.

As the building collapsed behind us, I lay him down in the grass, wondering for a moment how exactly his sister was okay, coughing it out now as she looked down upon her wheezing brother. I turned on the medical functions just to check his vitals, seeing him in rather stable condition. the eyes of this fourteen-some year old canid just barely beginning to open as I stood up, hefting my rifle to tower above him, backed by smoke and the blinding sun, the church splintering and collapsing behind us as the flames grew, consuming all it could.

"We've got company," Gabriel snarled, artillery booming in the distance. More trucks, more soldiers. The disguise wouldn't do it now, not with all the bodies around us and blood soaking us. I looked to the sky, seeing Lauren zipping along. "Hell of a time for an attack," he hushed in my ear. The canid teenager sitting up slowly, coughing, feeling his head. Taking one more look at my masked face before we ran, and Gabriel snapped at me and I obliged him with his own mask, him putting it on his face.

"You guys good down there?!" Lauren barked over the radio. "I saw a bit of the gunfight!"

"Yeah, don't bother lending a hand," Gabriel grunted in some morose humor.

"Sorry! I've just been carrying people back to H- Alpha Site! Let me know if you need a lift!"

"We're good. Do what you're doing, we'll link up back at base. Don't get shot d-" A bullet skimmed the strap of my body armor from behind, the vapor trail hanging in the humid air for a moment as the round careened past me. The supersonic snap deafened my right ear for a solid half-minute, though Gabriel spun and fired, catching our gunman who fell with a simple cry.

"Popping smoke!" Gabriel communicated. Though we weren't that close together, I could assume our cohesion as a unit would see us through. As Gabriel was messing with the grenade, I was covering. The forest behind us from whence we'd came, where we now faced in our return-fire during the retreat swarmed with shadows and voices at a distance. Gunfire all around. Hard to tell if we were being fired at.

"Eyes open!" Lauren's radio crackled. "You've got more than reds to worry about! The blues are coming in from the east!" I was hearing gunfire through Lauren's mouthpiece.

"Noah!" Gabriel spoke. "We might be able to slip past. You have your blue bandanna?!"

"I ditched it!" I hollered.

"What?!"

"I- I thought if we got searched it'd blow our cover!"

"Good enough! We'll make it work!" Gabriel was throwing live grenades now. Despite the billowing clouds, the smoke was less than enough to dissuade the more zealous reds. We made short work of those who poured through, the grenades Gabriel threw enough to gain us a moment of respite, Gabriel leaving frag mines here and there. "Setting shit to make them think twice about charging! Just-" Gabriel cried out as a bullet whisked his arm, rather too close for comfort especially given how he cried out, dodging down by falling onto his back, as another round that hissed through the smoke from some suppressing Red somewhere across the smoke caught him upside the face, mask exploding out sparks. He cursed as he went to whip it off, well and shot up. A Republican with a Mosin rifle somehow had traversed his flank rather quickly and was the one who'd blown out a piece of his deltoid with an ancient weapon somebody like either of us wouldn't be caught dead in a firefight with, hurriedly ejecting and chambering a cartridge, shouting something about getting one before Gabriel drew his pistol and I aimed at him and we both sent a handful of rounds through his chest and head, his legs still wheeling away as his rifle spun from his grip and he splashed into the mud. "*F-fucker!*" Gabriel wheezed, blinking a little bit. I was working my way back to him for a moment despite the mob chasing us, slinging bullets blindly through smoke and muddy dust. "Don't go for me! Spread back out!" Gabriel holstered his pistol and let his rifle hang to administer first aid as he ran, ripping enough gauze to hold his blasted right shoulder in place before emptying a quarter a tube of FastClot into the raw bits, tightening his bandage over the rapidly developing seal.

But in that moment, another bullet skimmed my leg, biting into my calf a little, sending blood out. I turned. A flash between the trees with just enough blue and a distinct lack of red. A democrat scout sprinting lengthwise with a pistol. Like we were being circled by sharks, both Red and blue. I followed him with my rifle's muzzle, watching him darting between trees before a bullet could catch him through the side of his chest. He dove for cover but I heard how he cried and gurgled, failing to see him get back up before another round struck the back of my armor, shoving me forward with a cough.

"GO!" Gabriel screamed, firing, evidently at my Red assailant.

"Fuckin' crawling with Golf-Bravo! Lauren! You-" At that, I looked up, seeing a whisk of green on its way back to the old base, darting between the trees. *Thump.* A grenade went off in the republican lines as she began to circle. *Thump, thump.* Two more explosions, a contingent of Blue scouts lifted out of their cover by violent pyrotechnics, de-limbed and screaming. *Thump, thump, thump.* Final three rounds from the revolving grenade launcher and Republican bits were spewed forth from gluches and ditches and close smoke.

"Read my fuckin' mind!" Gabriel laughed, advancing in front of me.

"You looked like you could have needed it!" She extrapolated in the radio. "Gimme a couple minutes before you get pinned down again! I'll load when I land and pick up more people!"

"Right! Let's move!" Gabriel waved to me, and I followed. "Covering!" Gabriel cried as he hit the dirt behind a tree.

"Moving!" I passed him, going for another suitable foxhole.

"Eyes up! Watch for blues!"

"Covering!"

"Right, moving!" He was up as I lay in my shooting position. An engine betrayed the stealthy advance of an ATV, two blues buzzing in from behind me. I was watching towards the reds at the time, fighting to turn over and fire as the vehicle and its rear gunner bared down on me. I sent round after round through the driver, 5.56 rounds cleaving straight through to the gunner, his shotgun going off and its pellets slapping mud that was thrown into my face from the impact. I cried out as the vehicle careened towards me, only able to open my eyes long enough to see Gabriel in front of me, sort of catching the vehicle and redirecting it with a shove before it did any damage to me. "You really about to get killed by a fucking ATV in a firefight?!" Another bullet as he quipped with rage, throwing him to the side as the round impacted his armor. I had to open fire again as he dove, watching another Democrat with an SKS rifle recoil from my rounds hitting him, diving for the dirt, yelping. I was empty now.

"You get him?!" Gabriel asked as I dropped the empty magazine. Just as he had, more shadows emerged from the misty, dank forest. Truly the place was too dense to really hold any expectations to a firefight, going from medium range engagements to whites-of-their-eyes terrifying claustrophobic skirmishes. I dove for my pistol, feeling my old glock back in my hands. I hadn't shot it in forever, especially after it had been stolen from me. But the feel was natural to me. Like shooting targets. Perhaps it was how far I'd fallen and how willing to kill I'd become, perhaps it was the familiar feel after ages without. Maybe it was a little bit of both. Four Democrats advancing brutally quickly. Bullets, pellets from their weapons falling all around me. Rather than like I was actually being shot at, now it was just an annoyance. Like I wasn't even in danger as I drew on them. Half a magazine later, four more lifeless bodies. I'd just brought the red dot of my pistol to each one and moved onto the next once they started falling. Gabriel was flipping over and crying out, gnashing his teeth, almost to the point where if he didn't have another bullet in his leg he would have remarked upon my newfound brutality. "Fuck! FUCK!" Gabriel lay his leg out, going for the rest of the FastClot syringe as blood gushed from his thigh.

"You think it's an arterial?!" I'd processed that he'd been hit and moved on to a more important question immediately, seeing the blood flow as he wrapped the FastClot with more gauze.

"Doesn't matter, FastClot will hold it for now. Let's get the rest of the way first," He ripped the gauze and I came up under his armpit, hoisting him to his feet. He really was heavier than he looked. Funny how I could notice this here. Still standing, if only weak on his left leg.

"We've got more," I hushed, finishing up loading my rifle, hitting the bolt release. Gabriel took one look to me before we set off again. "Let's try to take this a little slower, Gabe. We're definitely outgunned and we're taking too much fire as it is."

"You afraid of a couple mooks, Noah?" Gabriel chortled darkly, weaving through the trees.

"...Eh, lead poisoning," I huffed, noticing that despite his cavalier musings he wasn't at such a hasty pace anymore. Maybe the bullet in his leg, maybe my plan to take things slower. "We still need to evade Golf-Bravo."

"Means we need to pick up the pace, more like," Gunfire was echoing through the trees as Gabriel grumbled. Not directed at us, for once. Like we'd slipped the front lines. Battle swirling around us. At least I was in the moment, for good for now. We were knee-deep in scouts, it seemed. "We're taking a detour to evade," Gabriel relayed. "How is it at Alpha?"

"We- We're in some shit!" HQ relayed, though there was a lot of noise on their end.

"Is- is that gunfire?!" I asked.

"We're surrounded at the moment! Blues for about two hundred degrees to our west, a contingent of reds on the southeast! We're taking heavy fire! We've got people with holes here and it's not long before we start getting KIAs!"

"What's the status on exfil to our secondary position?" Gabriel uttered, though his humor was now extinguished. There was no spark in his eyes, no curl in his lips, no pep in his voice. This was bad.

"It's not looking good! We're pinned! They've broken their roadblock to the south and are bringing up technicals! We can't move!"

"I'm sure its nothing I can't handle," Gabriel grumbled as an aside, looking to me. "Roger. Nearly all Indigo Group is back at base. Soon as I get there we'll find a workaround. I bet we blow the red heavy metal and we'll be sailing smooth."

"I-if you think so! Maybe- FUCK!" another spat of explosions, gunfire, yells.

"You there?" I asked.

"I think he just got busy," Gabriel grunted. "Let's go. We're almost there."

"Guys," a worried, female voice huffed in our ears. Lauren, well and panting at this point.

"What's up, Lauren?" Gabriel uttered.

"I've got the last one here," She spoke as we advanced. "At least, my last run before I help with the fight at base. Noah, Maria opted to take it on foot. She's gonna be inbound to your position."

"Shit, that's suicide," Gabriel grunted. "Why would you just agree to that?!"

"She seemed dead set on it! She's good with a little skullduggery!" Gabriel couldn't help but smile with a chuckle.

"Always digging the new lingo," Gabriel uttered. "So you already got Selicia back too?"

"Yeah! Not as heavy as she looks, but I wouldn't want to fly with her for fun!"

"Heh, right." Gabriel coughed, still scanning as we slunk through the forest, a mist rolling in. "Hunker down at the base for now. We'll ring you if we need air support, so keep the MILKOR loaded."

"Right!" We advanced with that, inch after inch. Fleeing from voices, sitting in ditches and behind trees hoping the denseness of the foliage would mask our presence. I looked over to Gabriel, seeing him in determined pain, but in his eyes there was a different spark. Something far bleaker, something that shined when he limped or coughed. A distance in his eyes. Was he worried?

"Gabe?" I spoke. He didn't even look over. His lips moved for a split second, like perhaps he thought he'd spoken but failed to realise he hadn't. "Gabriel, you good?"

"Yeah, I'm fine," he relayed as we walked. But I was worried. Gabriel had been in this position before, hadn't he? Trekking through the woods, knee deep in bad guys. But something was off. Something that made me quiver.

Breaking through the brush, where we could hear fierce battle drawing closer, the resort somewhere before us. We didn't even have to use the usual navigation landmarks, we were just listening for fighting.

Another barrage of Democrat scouts before us, still more preoccupied with scanning towards our base. We had the initiative, knives ending a couple stragglers. A couple moments before being spotted for us to open fire. I saw Gabriel take several of them out, yet one of them with some bolt action rifle spun around, in the process of being gunned down, his trigger pulled and Gabriel was sent sprawling back with a puff of dust from his plate carrier and a cough. I made sure said gunman was dead with a couple ample rounds, making my way over to him on his side of our little pincer movement.

It was only by the time I was near to him that I knew something was wrong. "That was AP," He noted with glazed eyes, blood sputtering from his mouth. Horrible words that I wished I'd never heard, the gurgle of his voice completing the dire picture.

"Oh shit, where are you hit," I uttered, maybe not really realizing the severity yet. The tree line was close. We were almost to the no man's land, and there he lay. The beginning of the end.

"L-Left side, didn't pass all the way," He muttered as I undid his plate carrier's straps, first the shoulder, then his cummerbund. I saw his T-shirt soaking with blood that I cut off rapidly. Gabriel lay there with his pistol in his hand, glaring off to the side. Still scanning, trying not to breathe too hard to keep it from collapsing.

"HQ, this is Indigo Leader! We are inbound from the southeast! Two friendlies, one injury! We're about to breach no man's land, check your targets!" I whipped out a chest seal and threw the big adhesive patch on him and he breathed in, coughing a little bit. "Easy, eas-" I began, going for his plate carrier, but as I turned it seems that our quick spat with those red scouts attracted the wrong kind of attention. Gunfire erupted from the foliage in the direction I turned to get his armor, bullets trailing past me as Gabriel raised his pistol and fired, firing past my head. My ears began to ring as he emptied the magazine towards the repeating muzzle flash, the unforeseen gunman ceasing his weapon's report. I wanted to say good shot, thank Gabe for saving my ass. I spoke and no words came out, my ears ringing too loudly. But as I scanned towards the muzzle flash just to make sure he was done, I felt a sopping wet grasp on my side.

I looked again, seeing Gabriel there, face flushed. Hands full of blood. His leg had sprung a fountain, a round destined for me finding him, and unlike his earlier injury this was most evidently an arterial, dark black blood splashing out as Gabriel reloaded, only paying it mind with the grim gritting of his teeth. I was screaming obscenities as my heart raced. All I knew is that I had to stop the bleeding, as I pulled out the tourniquet and ratcheted it down. Gabriel raised his pistol again, having reloaded.

*Wham.* I was atop him, someone having pushed me. A bullet slamming into my armor from behind, the sonic thumps of Gabriel's weapon the only audio. A moment later and Gabriel was speaking. Mouthing things to me in that shocking silence as I lay atop him. My eyes were wet. He was speaking. Pleading. Something. Emotion in his eyes, grit in his teeth.

I picked him up over my shoulder. Whatever he was saying could wait. I was charging across that no man's land, that mud slopping around my boots but hardly slowing me down. I just needed a medic and everything would be alright. Bullets were hitting my armor. That concussive thump of his pistol behind my head. I ran, and I ran, and I ran. I just needed to get over there. We'll figure something out. We'll...

I burst into the building, some of the Kommandoes there ushering me forth. Gabriel felt heavy but the world screaming in my ears was heavier. Passing doors. Like I wasn't even in cover, like I was still in those killing fields as I laid him down on a table in the armory. Silence around me, even as my hearing was slowly returning to me here, if only distant echoes of voices aside me. Voices save for one. A voice just as distant as the echoing world grew as I stood there, feeling wetness on my shoulder and dripping down the back of my plate carrier.

My best friend of nine years, Gabriel Noria, at an age of nineteen years and a handful of months, was **dead**.

### Chapter 64

It was unmistakable.

When face to face with the death of a loved one, people often remark on the feeling of denial coming first. No, that was gone. Gone like the top of his head and his right eye blown asunder by an ill-fated bullet, and replaced with a deep, deep despair. Here he lay. Our only hope. My only hope. In my selfishness, for a moment I wondered how I'd be able to survive all the way to the Citadel without him- Without Him. It hit me. *My best friend is dead*. I fell upon the table where he lay to hold myself up over him, bloody, no longer twitching, no longer bleeding. *Butchered*. I wanted to touch him, to cry out. To ask him to repeat what he was saying back there in that ditch. What his final words were, drowned out by his pistol. His- his pistol. Where was it? He'd dropped it when he- I wanted to storm out and get it. Bring it back to him. His one birthright. Not what his stupid, neglectful father had to offer, but what he *claimed*. What he cultivated, what he made of himself. I couldn't think of him as a murderer, as the man who used us, used *me* for a personal crusade, as one who had been blowing people away just like I had been mere minutes ago. He's my friend. My *best friend*. He's the best friend anyone could have ever hoped for. He's self-actualizing, smart, witty, strong, brave, and dead. He didn't look peaceful here. He was in agony, final eye splayed open, almost quivering with the pain it felt in its last living moment. Please, I begged him, where I slumped up against the wall, glaring down at his corpse. What were you saying back there? I... I couldn't hear you, dude. You can tell me now. I...

I...

I drug my cowardice outside of the armory. Back in the external rooms of the place with their wide, coverless windows, where the Kommandos were fighting and bleeding. It was all distant to me. I wasn't here. I walked among them, stumbling. Like they didn't even notice me, shrapnel and bullets whirling past my face. I paid them no mind, my eyes lost out the front door. I wasn't particularly thinking of letting some sniper get the best of me and send me to my best friend's fate. It's just that grievous bodily harm didn't really cross my mind. I wanted to go get his pistol, something to really remember him by. But a Kommando grabbed me by the strap of my armor and dragged me back inside, screaming at me from the miles away where he stood. I was blinking again, watching his lips move. Who the hell was this guy to scream at me? *Did he know who we just lost? Did he know how fucked we were?!*

I was up the steps. Wandering. Like I was looking for him. No, I was looking for hope. I guess. Something. I watched Anthony firing there. Screaming about the vehicles crossing the no man's land, an oversized flare launcher loaded with homemade explosive shells in his hand as he fired with loud thumps. I took a moment to look out, seeing a BMP making its way across the no man's land to the west, blue stripes proclaiming its allegiance, hastily painted over the faded police markings. Grenade shells bounced off of it like nothing, until with a much more pressurized thump that filled the room with dust went off, a rocket streaking towards the armor and striking it with such force to blow through its armor. I watched people stream out of the back of it engulfed in flames, as the munitions of the light tank flared up and the whole thing blew, blanketing the battlefield in shrapnel and smoke, whatever windows left in this place shattering instantly. Reina a ways down the way dropping that smoking husk of an empty AT4 and scrambling back for her rifle to fire more and more towards the tree line.

"NOAH!" Anthony was screaming in my face, I just noticed. "W-where's Gabe?!" he asked as I finally looked him in the eye, watching him wince and duck at every errant explosion and bullet whizz.

For a moment, I knew I had to lie, to keep the squad cohesion. "He's... he's downstairs," I said, but my eyes betrayed my words. He was dead. I think that Anthony knew this, sitting back. "He's downstairs, taking a rest..." I moved on. Walking through this place. I saw my rifle hanging below me, and I finally took it back up from where it hung in my sling. I decided to fire a few rounds, maybe to help things out. Keep up a good show, that everything would be alright. God, how are there so many vehicles out there? It was kind of funny. Watching the blue technicals and armor limping their way across the killing fields, their soldiers ducking behind the advancing metal as rolling cover.

*Boom.* A louder weapon. Abel on a fifty, some semi-automatic anti-materiel rifle the Kommandos had procured, for sure. Sending white hot phosphor rounds that lit up the misty, smoky battlefield with each round that sailed into an advancing truck with what looked like a lift kit and plate steel sautered onto its front end. A couple rounds for one, a couple rounds for another. Firing to see if they'd stop moving, and if they didn't, by the time he rotated back to that particular vehicle he'd fire again, others lobbing grenade shells behind the stationary, dead-in-the-water vehicles now being used as cover. Selicia had Lauren's MILKOR. Why didn't Lauren have the rotary grenade launcher? Where was she?

I went over to her, tapping her on the shoulder. Her eyes shot to me, glasses dimmed enough to look to me. How she looked at me, as if I was an enemy sneaking up on her, her legs skittering beneath her for but a moment as she shifted.

"Where's Lauren?"

"What?!"

"Lauren! Where's Lauren!"

"She's-" Selicia began, an explosion rocking the building. "She's... Evacuating people!"

"What?!"

"She's working with the other flyers! Taking people to the extraction point!"

"That'll never work!" I spat. "Whoever gets left behind is gonna get overrun!"

"That's what I said!" Archie spat, a ways away. Then with a snap, I watched Abel tense up and fall over. I saw his armor on his humanoid chest smoking, but as I advanced, seeing the look in his eyes as he lay there, I knew there was a problem.

"I'm hit," he muttered blankly.

"ABEL!!!" Samantha hollered, going for the cannon, screaming as she loosed the rest of the fifty's magazine, probably missing but it wasn't really my concern as I undid his armor straps.

Blood hit me right in the eye as I did and I hollered and gnashed, blinded by squirting blood. Abel yelped in fear at this. At least he hadn't even been wearing a shirt when he threw on his armor, gave me one less thing to cut off at least; out of the center-left of his chest was the squirting wound that had hit me in the face. An inch to the right and he would have been paralyzed from the humanoid waist down, and by how all four of his legs kicked off to my left where his body rolled on the ground as I wiped blood from my eyes, I could tell that at least the shot wasn't a spinal, a moment's reprieve. In panic, I threw my hands over the wound, snapping my fingers for a syringe of FastClot from Sam. I could tell it wouldn't be enough, but I did it anyways, stabbing his open chest wound and pouring some in, but the bloodflow was too thick and it all poured out before it could solidify. I went to dig a chest seal out of my own aid kit, but like that, I heard three letters that stopped my heart, soon followed by a distant thump and hiss of a rocket.

"RPG!" Somebody screamed. I dove over the open wound to cover it from debris, hearing the roaring hiss grow loud until it was deafening in a couple moments, and then the world was gone into dust and shaking and stinging particles of concrete and drywall and shrapnel, chunks of wall being thrown onto and into me, slicing up the top of my head and face pointing towards where the explosion radiated from. I took one look up, and Anthony was slumped there across the way from the big hole that was previously absent from the wall, a dazed look on his eyes. In a single moment, he reached for what looked like a protruding piece of rebar stuck in his neck, and in horror he wrenched it out- a mistake by any stretch of what I'd been taught, and in my daze I said nothing to stop him. In retrospect he probably wouldn't have heard, blood guzzling out of the open wound as his other hand pulled his busted hologlasses off his helmeted head.

"H-help," he splashed, blood coming from his mouth, Abel still screaming and grasping at my shirt and armor with his outstretched hands. Before I could order, Selicia was upon Anthony with an utter, shocked concern on her face, going for gauze, FastClot and a rubber overseal bandage all at once. My mind reminded me I had a situation on my hands already, so I left Selicia to deal with Anthony on her own, maybe figuring in a split second her morose studying of medical techniques would finally shine, despite how she was seemingly petrified at working on one of her fondest teases. I guess she considered him a friend. Has she changed while I wasn't paying attention? I guess she did, remembering earlier today. Earlier today, Gabriel...

This really was no place to let the mind wander. Back into my programming before my thoughts could get too far. I threw another chest seal over the gushing wound and sandwiched some FastClot beneath it as he yelped and cried, doing my best to hold the substance in so it could do its job, Sam hurriedly administering an IV drip module to his arm as he was hollering questions, such as "what the fuck" and "am I gonna die" through screaming grit teeth.

"All teams, all teams, be advised Golf-Bravo has explosives and armor piercing capabilities, I repeat, armor piercing capabilities, and more than likely dug-in snipers," I uttered in autopilot into my chest-mounted radio as I worked. I sure as shit couldn't hear any response with the state my ears were in, but I did my duty to inform. Felt silly but I knew the armor-piercing sniper was rather pertinent. "B-be advised, over," I finished to go back to holding that seal to let the fastclot do its namesake, then going to roll Abel as his anesthetics kicked in after Sam had hooked up the IV machine, checking the other side, seeing a bent bullet barely peeking its way out of the fur of his back, the blackened tungsten core peeking out of the warped copper jacket all covered in blood, evidently stopped dead by his rear armor plate.

"D-do we want to remove that?!" Sam asked in a scream, evidently just as deafened as I was.

"We don't want it going back in!" I noted, going for my multitool. "He got shot through the heart! It'll end up somewhere we *really* don't fucking want if it does!" Sam gasped and Abel cried sickly.

"Ohhh fuck! Fuck! I... I don't wanna f-fucking die!"

"Don't worry buddy, you've got one left! Happy thoughts, happy thoughts!" I shouted over explosions that made him yelp, checking my pliers. "Sam, Put some morphine into his plasma drip! We need to lower his heart rate or he's gonna burst the seal!" I uttered, as she did, hurriedly reading off modules before finding the right one to shove into his IV machine.

"I... I don't feel so good," He whined sickly, as I went to pry the bullet beside his spine out. He cried out as I whipped it out, readying the FastClot syringe to stick back in, another chest seal over it as I held it, cursing his fur. It made getting a proper adhesive seal a bit of a challenge, though I left it to take a bandage to tighten around both sides and hold them. "I don't..." He uttered, the IV machine showing his pulse, his lower heart doing twice the work now. His eyes zoned out, as his pulse grew faint, jaw hanging slack as the septic shock of his upper heart shutting down, combined with the unfortunate necessity to lower his heart rate with morphine taking his second heart with it.

"Fuck! FUCK!" Sam screamed as he flatlined. "*ABEL!!*"

"AED! AED! WE NEED DEFIB ON THE THIRD FLOOR!" I screamed into my mic. Maybe Gabriel would be here with it. I couldn't think about that right now. He was just taking a rest, that's all. "AED! WHERE'S THE FUCKING AED?!" I got above Abel's lower torso's ribcage, hammering down on it in CPR. "Sam! Keep him breathing!" A Kommando collapsing beside me with the defibrillator kit moments later, dodging bullets as he ran past the exploded part of the wall, a little concerned at Selicia's current medical work-in-progress, Selicia at this point using her natural threads for bandage rigging rather than most of the medical gear. It looked like she was doing a pretty good job, in retrospect. Anthony was still lucid and everything.

"You think that's gonna work on him?!"

"Archie! You fucked with this one, right?" I called, as he was covering on the fifty, ducking ever so slightly as a bullet scraped past his helmet, taking a moment to fire back at the shooter. He looked over.

"Yeah! Overcharged it!" I slapped the pads onto his chest, going into its settings for the modded overcharge option.

"Sam! Get off or you'll get fucked up by the shock!" I ordered, as she was clutching his face, tears beginning to flow as his lifeless body stared motionless to the ceiling. "All clear?!"

"C-clear!" Sam backed away, looking as if she was moments from needing to be restrained. I took another look around before I hit him, his entire body pulsing upwards in a spasm. No effect.

"Check his bandages! We don't want his seal coming out with the returning pulse!" Sam was barely coherent, going for Abel's face again to give breath out of instinct. "Sam! BANDAGES!" She looked up, going to do as I ordered, rolling him to check both sides, feeling the chest seals.

"T-they're okay!"

"Right! Charged! Get clear!" I hit him again. He coughed, pulse staying for a moment, but he was gone again. "Sam! Get some epinephrine into his drip! Not very much, just a little bit! We want *this* heart going, not *that* one!" I motioned positively to his un-shot lower heart, motioning negatively to his pierced one. She complied as the thing charged, now babbling about not wanting to lose him. She stayed on his head, giving him breath, still proclaiming how she loved him and didn't want him to go, didn't want to be alone without him. Now that was sort of interesting. I must have missed this development when I was disassociating. I guess they always were pretty close. He was her big dork, after all. Love, though? I *guess* he was Sam's type. Huh.

But this was no place to be lost in thought. "Clear!" *Whump.* He gasped and curled again, coughing and sputtering, this time back to stay. Sam collapsed on his face, her arm coming up to her as she wept. I went over to his arm as Sam was preoccupied with crying over him checking his pulse, seeing it stable, pulling the adrenaline and morphine drips out just under the assumption he was stable now.

"S- Sam?" He uttered weakly. She kissed him right on his mouth and grasped him in a hug, her nails digging into his shoulders. Babbling about what she'd do without him.

"Abel!" I had to interrupt their little reunion. "We need to be shooting right now, so it's up to you to make sure you stay stable!" I roared, and Sam could barely divert her attention, eyes bloodshot with tears, Abel looking over to me, just as dazed and terrified as Sam in his own way, still reacting to the kiss. I took the two capsules. "Regulate your pulse! Make sure you don't go too high and burst the seal in your chest, and make sure you don't go too low and ghost out on us again! Sam, check up on him! We still need you in the fight! He's pretty done though, just keep talking to him and make sure he's awake! Call me if he passes out!"

"Seal?" Abel coughed weakly. "W-where did I get s-shot?" He must have been fuzzy about the recollection of the event, looking to me. I slapped the modules into his hand.

"Don't worry about it! Just do what the machine on your arm tells you to and take it easy! You won't do much good fighting in your condition!" I hefted my rifle back up to fire, checking the advance. Things weren't looking good, even if we held a stable defense. I knew we couldn't lose many more and it was a matter of time before somebody wound up dead.

"Selicia!" I called as I reloaded. "Is he good?!" Anthony himself looked over to me, an IV machine already on his arm, neck and jugular all bandaged up like an incredibly utilitarian bowtie. Selicia, almost as if insulted, motioned down to Anthony next to her, where he sat, propped up on his rifle, still firing, obviously good enough to shoot.

"He's shooting, isn't he?!" She screeched. Anthony didn't have much to say, only a plain thumbs-up from where he lay prone, firing his weapon out through the big blasted crater. Can't really say it was his enthusiasm keeping him going, more just the desperation of the situation.

"N-Noah?!" Lauren's voice. I wheeled around, seeing her walking towards this area of the defense, walking with her head bowed and body crouched, in the middle of sucking on the teat of her camelback, wings steaming, completely disarmed save for her sidearm. Man, she really did train pretty hard the last couple of months. She was practically all muscle at this point. Funny how I noticed this now. "Where's Gabe!?"

"He… He got hit, he's getting stitched up!" I said, a better liar the more I believed the lie, the more stress forced me to. "We need to make do without him for now!"

'W-what?!" Another explosion, and we all winced, bullets ricocheting around us. Like a little piece of that despair hitting her. "We… It doesn't matter! Who should I evac next?! Anthony?!"

"Lauren!" Archie blurted, pausing his action on the fifty to interject. "You really fockin' measure you can airlift him safely?!" He motioned over to Abel, who was staring at the ceiling, lips moving, blinking, Sam beside him shooting, the two of them talking. Talking about their soon-to-be life together. I can't imagine talking about something like that in the middle of a battle. Feels kind of unlucky.

"I… I can try!"

"Bloody bull*shit* you can try! This isn't working!" Archie snarled. "You know I've got a plan! We steal Carl's heli- or any fucking heli and we can get almost everyone out in one go!"

"That's at the airfield, that's suicide!"

"*This* plan is suicide!"

"What if it's not there?!"

"Then we die! It'll be there! It's a transport vehicle! They're not gonna use it in a battle, it'd get shot down!"

"Then what the fuck is happening outside?!" Lauren spat, losing her temper a little.

"God dammit, it's all we've got!" Archie turned to me. "You're the leader, aren't you?! What's your call?!"

"...The chopper!" I shouted over the din of battle and the rings blaring in my ears. "Glory or death, right?!" Archie pushed Lauren's shoulder a little.

"Fuckin' send it, coz! Let's go!" Archie hopped into her saddle, Lauren taking one last look at me. Worry. Worry about the raging battle. Worry about this plan. Worry about Gabriel.

"You've got this!" I uttered with an OK symbol for redundancy, simply to be heard. She replied with the OK symbol back. Sign language, her thing. Wasn't really sign language, to be honest, sort of a thing everyone knows. I don't know why I thought this. They careened out the explosion-made window to zip away before anyone could draw a bead on them.

"You really think they'll get their hands on a helo?!" Selicia spat.

"If they don't, we're fucked!" I hollered back. "It's in the hands of God now!" I took a moment for my words to sink in, before I realized our plan would need more meat on its bones. "Squid!" I shouted into my radio. "Squid, call back!"

"Whassup, Indigo Leader?" He sounded quite nonchalant for somebody knee deep in the shit of battle.

"Where's your friend Duke the dragontaur?!"

"Fuckers clipped my lovely. He's sitting over at extraction getting stitched up. We're down to your girl Green." Green. What Gabe used to call her. It stumped me for a second. But he was just taking a rest. I had better things to be caught up on.

"She- We're trying something new! Evac one-by-one ain't working!" I spat. "They're- Archie, one of our guys did a little… skullduggery, located a support chopper! She's taking him to get it!" Squid laughed.

"Y-you're not serious, right?" Concern he was burying starting to wear away at him.

"One-by-one ain't gonna work! We need mass movement! Start moving all your essential gear and your wounded to the rooftop! Top floor if you want, but we need to be ready for the airlift!"

"You fuckin' sure they're getting a chopper?! Making a run for the airfield?! That's suicide!"

"Evac one-by-one is suicide! You don't need me to tell you that!" He was silent for the longest time.

"...Your friends better be lucky as fuck!"

"Pray for 'em!" I joked back in utter, un-stuttering seriousness, going to aid Sam who'd been grazed deep on the arm, going for gauze, not even noticing the wound before I pointed it out. Better to save the FastClot, however little left we had.

"Right! This is Squid! Get the wounded to the roof! We've… We've got an airlift coming!" A couple moments of shouts and more sounds of battle. "...You heard me! It's all we've got!" I felt a little relief as Squid accepted my order, even if it still came down to Lauren and Archie. I may not have been religious, but I did pray. I put more mental credence into that prayer than much anything else I'd really ever put thought to, even here, shooting upon our countless enemy. Still trapped between reds and blues. Each one just throwing more and more personnel our way, but as we fought, it wasn't long until the Blues seemed to overtake the Reds, the battle seeming to go their way, at least between the two of them. We didn't exactly have a say in the matter, just firing to keep them off our backs.

I saw Squid there, wearing, to my slight surprise, my power armor. How I hadn't noticed this before was a bit beyond me, but I guess my mind was on… other things. I saw him carrying a hybrid Kommando, some felinid missing his arm and leg on his right side, correctly amputated and stitched up, muttering in his unconcious.

"You wearing my armor?!" I asked as he passed, ferrying that wounded kommando upstairs.

"Sorry, the situation called for a little borrowing," He uttered as he passed me, though he paused in his step for a moment to look at me. Looking around for another moment, assessing everyone else, maybe to make sure they were all too busy to eavesdrop. "Hey, Noah, you're sure they're coming with that chopper?"

"Yeah! Positive," I lied, staring him dead in the eye as he bit his lip amid the building shaking from ordinance.

"...How about... Your buddy downstairs?" He asked. "You... You want to take him with?" Gabriel. My mind spun for a moment.

"...Leave him, load up on ammo," I uttered. Like somebody else was saying it. How heartless, I thought in retrospect. My pragmatic side taking over. The survival of those who were left took over.

"...Right. Your call." He advanced on his way away, leaving me there to look out to the battlefield. It almost seemed... quieter. Despite facing the democrat side to the northwest, the side that was overtaking the other.

"...Guys, we got a drone up?" I asked.

"...Yeah, we've got one," A Kommando called back. "...Shit, looks like the Republicans are withdrawing."

"...Is that a good thing?!" I heard Reina ask, eavesdropping as she was.

"Why are they withdrawing?" I pondered. "What do you see?"

"Oh shit," He said. That couldn't possibly be a good thing. "We've... We've got blue armor advancing a mile out! We've got superheavy tanks tearing their way through the foliage, bustin' down the fuckin' *forest!* Two M3 Mattis Bolo-class tanks and some rabbit-class walkers for support! Think I see power armored infantry too!"

"How are we on anti-materiel?!"

"We're already low on launchers, but nothing we have will do shit against a fucking Bolo! Those things are fortresses on treads!"

"...Doesn't matter! Keep the evac up!" The blue infantry was keeping back too. "If we're desperate we can get sappers up on it, toss a bomb into a hatch, but that's fucking plan Z!" Despite the fact that it was practically the plan A given how the battle was going. The air was growing tense despite the relative lull, save for countersniping anyone taking potshots from the tree line. Abel and Anthony were helped upstairs, everyone else up here on the second floor with us, still bringing ammo and supplies up to the roof. I could see the dust in the distance. Practically seeing the trees falling, hearing trunks snapping with violent crunches. But I could hear the whirling blades of a chopper somewhere to the south.

"-one there? Call back, Call back Kommandoes, Indigoes," That familiar, weirdly british tinge.

"Archie?! Lauren?!" I laughed. "You... Did you do it?!"

"No pressure, gov. Left the keys in the ignition and everything," He joked sternly in his own way.

"...Sure know how to cut things close you fuckin' bong!"

"Slob my knob, tosser; don't make me turn this thing around!" The trees before us snapping, crunching, being rent by cruel, roaring steel. The Bolos emerging from the tree line, only for great rockets to stream from the south, shredding heavy metal, HEAT ordinance cutting through their tytanaceramid carapaces. Explosions we could feel, shaking us to our bones, watching the shockwave of the detonations ripple across the field and hit the building. Pure awe as he made a pass, the bottom of the dual-rotor heli lighting up in brief sparks as the troops below fired up as he briefly flew over the northwestern tree line.

"Watch it! They've got mechs, they've probably still got heavy firepower!" We were now firing for cover as well, shooting indiscriminately into the tree line. Archie brought the gunship around with rockets trailing after him from the forest, popping flares that blinded one's eyes as the rockets burst and exploded as he evaded, screaming in utter exhilarated terror as he evaded over the killing field, before circling back above us and turning that behemoth slowly to reveal the right side of the heavy gunship towards our adversaries in the tree line, strafing low, low enough to be scraping the tops of the heads of those standing on the roof, with the remaining blue troops screaming across burning forest and through the wrecks of the Bolos to fire upon us and our savior of an airship, the tree line sparkling with muzzle flashes like a long, glittering emerald.

"GREEN! GETT'AM TAE FOCK OFF!" Archie brought the ship to a hover, as I looked up. Seeing the gun turret poking out of the right side of the ship, a six-barreled minigun spooling up as Lauren activated the cannon from where she was presumably crouched before the gunner controls.

*BRRRRRRRRRRRRRRRRRRRRRRRRRRRRRRRRRRRRRRRRRRRRRRRRRRRRRRRRT.*

Glorious 20MM HEAT ordinance streamed out of the M61 Vulcan armament in what could be considered the sound of one continuous, deafening gunshot at six-thousand rounds per minute, blistering hot munitions sweeping a full one-eighty of the tree line to our northwest, where the majority of their force had been. Shells and links rained down through the big blasted hole above me, and I dove for cover to avoid the scalding hot cartridge casings piling up and spilling over into holes in the floor and walls, the sweet hellish scent of sulfur inundating my position more than it had ever been. I barely had enough time to look back up to the killing field, watching trees already engulfed in flames from where the missile pods of the chopper had struck crumble and splinter and fall from the glowing-hot rounds that lit up the battlefield, felling tree after tree, shredding wood, steel, armor and flesh alike with utmost violence, all just morphing together into images and silhouettes in the distance engulfed in smoke and dust, Lauren at the gunner controls waving her magic wand back and forth across the tree line, a spell, a ward even of utmost disincentivization cast out into the woods upon any soul wise and alive enough to heed it. Explosions behind smoke and trees as fusion fuel cells of power armor and rabbit-class walkers burst, perhaps even the scream of blue soldiers if you concentrated hard enough despite the sheer ringing of one's ears. It was one's mind filling in the blanks. Soon enough that white hot pack of cannon barrels finally went quiet, spooling down as they smoked and glowed, depleted of its full munitions capacity in what must have been seconds, the battlefield growing a little darker in the absence of that white hot stream slicing its way back and forth across the tree line, bright enough to light up the misty, smoky world for those few brief, horrible, glorious moments.

"GOD DAMN!!!" Squid was ecstatic. "William Tecumseh Sherman, suck my fucking dick, play with my balls and finger my asshole! Now THAT'S Hell on Earth!"

"I'm setting her ass-end down on the roof! Make clear, and get everyone in before one of the dafter cunts with a launcher gets back up'n wastes us! Don't get cocky!" A strange joy overtaking me, despite what a display of breathtaking destruction I'd just borne witness to. We were making it out.

"See, boys? THAT'S why you have air support! Those retards took some slow-ass bolo-classes to a GUNSHIP fight!! Haha!"

"Can we not talk about them shooting me down until we get to where the fock we're going?!" Archie responded. Everyone getting up to go upstairs. Here, where we'd won. Utter victory, despite that we were retreating, still firing to the southeast where the blues, despite their broken morale at seeing their strike force obliterated, still pestered us with small arms, bullets hailing dangerously close to the rotor junctions.

"Go, go, go, everybody on! Get us loaded!" People were shouting, crowding into the back end of this Chinook as Lauren bidded us in, wings not quite steaming but sweat beading all over her body, soaking into her clothes and even her little armored baseball cap. I noted how she whipped a borrowed headset off from where they crushed up her ears, whipping them about a little as I could see her earplugs within it. At least she was less deaf than I was, blinking through her hologlasses.

"Lauren!" I called, almost laughing. "I knew you could do it!"

"Noah!" She wasn't excited for such a sweeping victory. Only concern in her eyes after she'd scanned every last soul being loaded onto the Chinook. "Gabe's not here!"

"He's... He's dead," I uttered, the truth finally sputtering out of me. Not even my own words.

"W-Wh-" She stammered. "You... You can't- He's not-"

"He's *dead*, Lauren! We need to get the fuck out of here!" I put concern back into my voice. This was a topic for later. Something biting at me in our victory here. Soon to be discussed.

"M-Maria!" She went on. Her battle-shaken brain moving just like mine, skipping over the horrible news as soon as she could. Telling herself, willing herself to get back to it later. "What about Maria?!"

"She's... *Fuck!*" I spat. I'd forgotten all about her. I looked over to the southeast, the city belching smoke into the sky by now, sounds of continued battle from that direction. I'd forgotten all about her. What should we do? I just wanted to be out of this place. This deathtrap.

"We... We need to wait for her! Hey, gimme my rifle!" She called to those loading supplies onto the chopper, who tossed her the scoped M1A and its satchel of magazines. "She'll be coming, I know she is! Noah, we can't just leave her! I'll wait here and pick her up!"

"N-no, I'll... Can you carry two people?!"

"I've been carrying people three at a time, Noah! You want to cover with me?!" We were yelling under the roar of the chopper blades.

"You need someone to watch your back, don't you?! It just keeps going and going, y'know!" Lauren almost took a second to smile at my recollection of her own joke, a stupid look on her face. She looked so professional in this moment, a mere snapshot: hefting her rifle over her armored rig, glasses slightly dimmed on her face, braided ponytail of her scalp hair hanging on a shoulder, there with her mouth agape in an awkward grin for a second. Hell of an operator. Gabe would be proud. Probably was.

"Right! Guys, the two of us're gonna wait for our last guy to radio in for a pickup!"

"See you! Don't get killed!" Archie said into the radio.

"Wait up! NOAH!" Squid roared, one last time as Archie stalled the vehicle above us, his grunting in slight frustration coming through on comms. A titanium hand came up to flick an object toward me, throwing it gently, that I caught as he spoke. "Not all of our munitions are onboard! We got a *lot* of explosives out of that raid last night! Too many to take with us! Support strut for the whole building leads right through the armory!" I turned the object over in my hand. A detonator. "Leave them nothing, Noah! You'll definitely get overrun defending this place! Blow it when you finally bail!"

"War's hell, huh?!" I reiterated his little phrase.

"Fuck yeah it is! Spares your buddy a mass grave, too! Dude was a hell of a guy, deserves a better sendoff if you ask me! Go out with a bang! See you on the other side!" With that, the chopper took off, doors closing as he smiled at me. I stuck the clip of the detonator into a molle loop, checking my ammo.

Time to fight.

Down in the foyer. Our first defense area to fall back from once overtaken. Braver souls, perhaps spurred on by a blue commissar threatening executions were advancing across the smoky world to the southwest, the battlefield choked from the smoke of the hellish, smouldering forest to our northwest. Firing, covering for the other as they loaded. "Soon as things get dicy, we hold from the stairs! When they're all over the first floor, we hold the second floor stairs! When we lose that we skip the third floor, then we hold the roof until they're about to overrun us and we blow it!" I reminded.

"Right!" Lauren affirmed before firing, clipping some poor blue soul with a couple rounds as he cried out, body spasming upwards before he fell, weapon twirling from his grip. Some not as close as him were certainly better marksmen, chewing up Lauren's close cover as she ducked to reload and was back up momentarily, concrete and stonework exploding before her face as she popped up, distracted for a moment before I covered for her as she ducked back, depleted of ammo once more, loading. We were holding our own, no doubt, but they were getting too close.

"Lauren, time to fall back!" I noted the growing density and proximity of golf-bravo, topping off my weapon.

"Right! Ready to move!"

"Covering!"

"Moving!" Lauren got up to trot her way briskly past me and up the stairs. Blues popped out of cover to get a shot off at her and I sent them reeling with rounds through their chests and torsos, before I was soon out, ducking to load as they shot back and Lauren took her position at the top of the stairs, able to see out of what was once the big glass panes of the façade of the building, to see enough of me and the battlefield before us.

"In position! Covering!"

"Right! Moving!" I got up to run, feeling bullets nipping at my heels, Lauren suppressing with her rifle, hitting more than one who dared to try us. There must have been fifty of them making their way across the killing field. These weren't the riled-up rioters they called an army back in Elko. These were war-hardened killers, and they had more gusto than I'd hoped. "Keep your radio on! Maria will let us know when she's in range!" Lauren was too busy firing to acknowledge this reminder, running dry and going to reload, a bullet flying true and I watched her head splay back and she yelped out, sprawling to the side in full cover of the railing of the second-floor overlook as I, in vengeance, fired at her assailant, watching his pistol spin from his right hand and a machete spin from his left as he fell hollering, his body armor having stopped the rounds. I sent a handful more rounds towards his head as he was trying to get back up and his corpse was sprawled back out on the ground. "L-LAUREN!"

"I'm- I'm good!" She whipped her hat off, a big welt forming on her forehead, the plate in her baseball cap well and dented at this point. A little nervous laugh as she went for the magazine she'd dropped to reload her weapon. "Fucker shot me in the face!" I was too busy shooting to remark on this. At least she was smiling about it.

"Loading soon!"

"Back in!" Lauren let her bolt slam home on a fresh round, firing as the gutsier ones were now entering the building. Smoke grenades being tossed in, figures shifting through the hissing smoke. Those we could see we shot at, before we could tell they were within the part of the common area below us, under where we were standing. A couple grenades being lobbed up enough to let us know we were about to be overrun, as I hastily tossed each of those explosive presents right back down with explosions and screams below.

"We need to move!" I said.

"Right! I'm covering! Move!" Lauren affirmed. I got up to go back further into the hallway, towards the stairwell to the third floor, stopping in it to turn and aim.

"In position! Covering!"

"Moving!" Lauren got up to sprint her way towards me. I saw blues following her up the stairs, shooting as soon as I saw their faces. Soon enough bullets were whizzing past my head- in the direction behind me. Lauren popped out to shoot back, covering my back as I fired on those still in front of us. "They've got inside the building!" she noted after downing the flanking assailants. "They must be coming up the other stairs!"

"We need to move!" We retreated into the stairs as I dropped a smoke grenade into the hallway, giving us enough cover to dissuade them from advancing as we went up.

"At the top of the stairs, I got you!" Lauren called out.

"Moving!" I uttered, passing her as they were coming, pulling a pipe bomb from a molle pouch to toss into the smoke that they were slowly probing into. "Get into the next stairwell!" I commanded, Lauren already complying as the explosion rocketed up the stairwell, the two of us out of the way, now advancing upstairs.

"Noah, real quick," She spoke as we climbed. We passed the third floor's entrance, going up the stairs toward the roof as we heard voices of blue soldiers clamoring already on the third floor, evidently already having breached it. I dropped a tear gas grenade at the foot of this one, running out of ordinance. "One of them got a shot off on me just now. Armor stopped it but it took out my radio," She explained, huffing, sweat beading all over as she panted just as hard as I was as we emerged from the rooftop entrance, out into that black midmorning sky. "You'll have to listen for Maria."

"Sounds good," I huffed back, turning round and barring the door to the roof. I looked around, seeing the sky black from the smoke, the forest to the northwest still aflame and pouring soot into the sky. The former battleground below was deathly quiet in comparison to the din it had once been earlier. Taking a single peek to see the building being stormed. Almost able to take a minute to reflect on things, Lauren laying her lower body down for a second to breathe, putting her rifle on safe and shoving it into her saddle scabbard, sucking down more electrolyte water.

"You ready?" I asked, seeing her refresh herself. Hearing them already banging on the door.

"You pick up Maria yet?" We heard them thumping on the door, something different now. Voices changing. All of a sudden, bright sparks flying from the door with a roaring hiss, a thermite charge cutting its way through the barrier.

"Shit, time to fucking go!" Lauren sprang up and I hopped on her back, as she sprinted down the length of the rooftop before careening off, gaining enough speed and surprising a couple blues who were still advancing out in the field, able to see the dumb looks on their faces as we whisked barely above their helmets, guns coming up towards us as I dropped the rest of my grenades one after the other. Lauren was approaching the tree line, beating her wings furiously, practically roaring in effort. We'd slow down and be easier to hit once we start to ascend, so I took the detonator out and turned the key just before we did, and behind us the building went up, the shockwave radiating outward before hitting us, enough to use as an updraft as Lauren soared away with me.

"We need to circle back and look for her!" Lauren cried, despite the snaps of rifle fire following us. Maybe it was just the Kommandoes' munitions going off, fragments of bullets and shells flying every which way.

"You crazy?! Fire's too heavy!" I said. "She knows where the exfil point is!"

"You- We're just gonna leave her?!" Lauren shouted.

"Do you want to get shot down?!" I roared. Lauren took one last look over her shoulder with a worried eye towards me, before complying, turning to the northeast.

But as she did so, there was a voice in my head. No. Maria's voice. In my radio, my earpiece. I turned my head, and even despite the distance, I knew it was her. Waving there as she ran. Her radio voice muffled and scratchy as my radio's antenna was harshly bent and mangled on my vest. I took one look, watching her bolting down there, For a moment thinking to tell Lauren until I realized going to Maria would be suicide. Like I'd foreseen the truth, she fell suddenly with a flash from a soldier's weapon who had been pursuing her, and I felt a pang in my chest before I turned back around.

But the entire day's worth of riding had taken its' toll on Lauren's saddle, specifically, her right stirrup. The one that had been busted up months ago, repaired. Those repairs, the stitching was growing looser and looser, and before I could even tell…

*Snap.*

I was falling.

"LAUREN!" I screamed, reaching out to her, already far below as she looked down upon my free-fall in sheer shocked terror. Her arm reaching instinctually back out for me, as I fell below her. The lake, that very same lake coming up to meet me, Lauren rushing after me before I disappeared into cold, blue oblivion.

## ACT V
## GRADUATION

### Chapter 65

---

There he was.

My father, standing over me. I was submerged, watching him through a pane of water as impenetrable as glass. Air leaking from my lungs, where I writhed there. My little arms reaching up towards him, towards the man who raised me, who kept me safe, kept a promise to keep me fed and alive.

Watching my little body breathe its last.

I couldn't understand it at the time. A lesson, he was teaching me. I'd slipped and fallen into the pool. I must have been six or seven. Something like that. I didn't quite know how to swim yet. He stood there, to see what I'd do. What I'd do to survive.

My lungs are full of water. *Please, dad...*

*Please...*

A hand slicing through the cold oblivion after the very last of my fading consciousness, wrenching me up and out in a single motion. Flipping me over with his strong arms to let the water spill from my lungs as I coughed and let in that sweet, sweet air.

"Oh, there there," he pat me on the back, the water mixing in with my tears. "Daddy's here. Sorry, I didn't see you until just now, oh, oh... I need to pay more attention, I know..." He lied. I was six and he was lying to me. For my own good, I'm sure he thought.

I'd repressed the memory, perhaps it was his gaslighting. Perhaps it was my own love, my own idolization for him and all his cool toys and tricks and know-how. But I knew it *happened*. I knew my own father wanted to watch me dying to see if I had the strength to live.

But in the horrifying oblivion of wondering what he must have been thinking, a question remained.

Did I fail his test?

---

I was sinking.

I felt peace for a few, long moments. A day of cacophonous struggle ending here in this quiet, cool place. No more sweat, no more blood, no more tears. No more killing and no more dead friends. This must be what being dead is like. It's kind of nice.

I wanted to breathe a sigh of relief but nothing but water entered my lungs, shocking me to action. I was drowning. Sinking deeper. My armor dragging me down. This was no way to die. I didn't want to die. I had to take so many steps before I could float again, here in the deep, only being dragged deeper into the black nothingness of death below. Unsling my rifle to unclip my body armor. Shoulder strap, cummerbund, and there it went. Ten thousand dollars worth of state-of-the-art ballistic protection not to mention a fair amount of ammo and my radio falling into blackness. My rifle nearly drifted away, sinking, but I grasped it before realizing I *needed air*. God, don't let me die here... The light seems so far away... Just, swim... Swim up...

The choking, smoke-filled air is frigid in comparison. Stinging my eyes and throat and I gasped, coughing, sputtering. Thrashing there. Maybe it's just the combination of air and wet skin, where in the depths it was warm. It felt warm, safe, even if it would have been my grave had I remained. But saying the surface wouldn't be my grave either might be a bit of a stretch, still hearing the sounds of battle in the eerie distance, blazing, choking smoke rolling in from the west.

Had to find Lauren. She was thrashing over there, trying to swim. She looked like she was drowning too, despite being so close to the water's surface. Why wasn't she swimming? Was she hit?

I re-slung my rifle and grasped her body armor strap, dragging her stroke after stroke towards the shore. She fought and cried out for a moment before realizing it was me, limping back onto land, back into this smoky, cold world with a charred, choking sky, the floating embers practically more illuminating than the Sun itself, so far away.

"C'mon, c'mon," I uttered. Distant shouts in the forest and sounds of troop and vehicle movements putting my goosebumps on edge, distant explosions. As the two of us splashed our way to dry land, trudging through the mud of the banks, I was checking my rifle. I lost a lot of my ammo with my armor rig- I was down to three spare rifle mags on my belt and one in my gun. Maybe it was half-empty. Felt reasonably full. "You okay?"

"N-no!" She hollered, like momentarily forgetting to be quiet, the two of us trotting our way to a tree for cover. More shouts.

"Shh, shh, what's…" I took one look. One of her big wings was bent, badly.

"It's broken! I hit the water too hard!" She hushed with tearful eyes. Distressed tears, tears of despair. Maybe it was just the pain or the choking smog, maybe I was just projecting my buried worries at this point. I already knew if we couldn't fly out of here, things were going to be bad.

"It's… It's not broken," I hushed, reassuringly as she lay down there and I knelt there. She curled inwardly and fought to not make a sound, letting out these reactive little squeaks every time I touched it, her wing flopping out on the ground. "The joint just… jumped the socket." her wings were still steaming. "Lauren," I said. "I… We have to re-set the joint before your wings cool, or it'll cramp and make things worse," I said. Her eyes flushed out.

"We- Do you have any pain m-meds?" Her voice quaking in terror, eyes shining.

"I gave all mine to Abel when he got hit. Do you…"

"I left them all once I had to start flying people out," She cried. I looked down at the injury. It wouldn't be long before it started swelling. This was really bad.

"Okay… Lauren, you trust me?"

"M-mhm," She nodded slowly, lips quivering. "Y- Are you-"

"Here," I found a thick twig, a fallen branch. "Bite down hard on this towards the back of your mouth. It'll… It'll make it hurt less. Okay?" It wouldn't. It would just keep her from screaming. She took it with her arms shaking, lip trembling, already in tears.

"Noah," She began, as if to say something, stall. Even she knew she didn't have anything to say.

"Bite. I'll re-set it on three." I positioned my knee below the big ball joint. She whimpered intensely, shoving the stick in her mouth and clamping down. Nodding with horror to me as she began to bite into it. I looked her one last time in the eyes. "Okay... one, two..."

"NGGHHHHHHHHHHHHHHH!!!"

Birds alighted as the piece of branch splintered and she screamed out a growl and the sickly, wet slapping pop sound of re-positioning her joint radiated between my ears like the bells of tinnitus I was already developing. It would have made my stomach turn if not for the sheer horror of the rest of this bloody day. Lauren, sweating, eyes bloodshot, staring up into the sky with that splintered, crushed twig firmly planted between her molars, letting out breaths of "Gguh, nguh..." as her jaw finally unclenched and she breathed heavily in a pained sigh, her intense pain subsiding as she spat it out, her teeth having made heavy indents on the stick. By the time she could be mentally present again I was already using all of my autocasts from my medical kit to fasten the joint in place, securing her wing.

"I... I don't think I can fl-"

"You can't. You can't fly after you dislocated your wing like that. The ligaments need to heal," I spat out the diagnosis to her, as her mind hadn't really caught up to the fact that I was putting her wing into a cast.

"Will I... I'll be able to fly again, r-right?" Her heart practically breaking with her voice. Tears of pain still flowing, not yet replaced by tears of despair.

"Yeah, yeah. You will. Not today. You just need to heal, okay?" I secured the joint good enough, before whipping my shirt off to combine with what bits of gauze we still had to create a suitable sling for her wing. "We just need... To get out of here first. Okay?"

"N-Noah," She uttered. Looking me in the eyes. Those tears still flowing. "I'm... I'm sorry, I-"

"It's not your fault," I said. Not your fault, not your fault, it echoed in my mind. She embraced me where I stood above her, her head in my lower chest with her lower body still laying, pulling herself into my pecs. I embraced the back of her head and shoulders, holding her as she needed. Letting out a sob. It was nice. So nice.

"W-we need to move," She uttered after a little forever that couldn't last long enough, getting up. I pulled her rifle out of her saddlebag and shoved it in her arms after press checking it.

"...And we might need to fight. If it comes to it, we'll have to commandeer armor and extra ammo for me from a straggler," I hushed as we advanced to the northeast, towards our waypoint. I could hear soldiers everywhere just beyond the tangibility of sight and knew that things weren't looking good.

"I... I still have my bow and arrows," She remarked. I turned for a second, towards the blazing fire behind us. There were few sounds of enemy activity in that direction. "N-Noah," She began, reaching out to grasp me. "They're... They're coming!" She noted soldiers before us as I turned around. Shouts. Did they spot us?

"Get down," I hushed, bidding her towards that tree. I saw the worried look on her eyes. I may have been able to duck into any old bush rather quietly, but aside from having mostly dark green skin, Lauren was hardly built for stealth, getting down low, slightly angling herself so her unbroken wing that wasn't covered in bright cream-white colored cast and gauze would show more than her broken, brighter-colored one. They were about a hundred meters from us, but if a single one of them had thermals or any sort of identification sensor they'd have us dead to rights and I knew it. I was near motionless despite the embers tickling my bare back, singing my skin as they danced around me. I slowly got into a shooting position, singling out their capo, or who I could guess was as he shouted orders to his cronies and seemed a lot better equipped with power armor and one of the power-armor centric OICW weapons; noting his nigh-invincible body I put the very middle of his standard-helmeted head right in the reticle of my magnified sight, knowing the best way to kill him would be a bullet in the face, straight through the bridge of his exposed nose. But besides him, there were a lot of them. More than a dozen in plain view. Probably a lot more just beyond the threshold of visibility.

"Lauren," I whispered.

"Y-yeah?" She whispered back. Her voice and her rifle trembled, mine didn't.

"When I start shooting," I hushed. They were ambling closer. Eighty meters, my magnified sight's rangefinding module read out. They clearly saw the autocast and gauze packaging littering the dry banks, seconds from coming over to investigate. "I want you to run the other way. Towards the forest fire. Keep a line-of-sight on me. As soon as I run dry I'll make my way to you and you'll cover me. Pepper-pot our way out of here. We'll try and lose them in the forest fire."

"N-Noah-"

"*Okay, Lauren?*" I growled. I saw in my peripheral vision her nodding, before she must have realized I was too concentrated to have noticed and stopped.

"Yeah," She uttered awkwardly, swallowing her fear. I could hear their voices now. Too clear to mistake.

"We need to search this area!" They were crying. No shit, I thought. In my battle-weary mind I found it more of an inconvenience than a bodily threat to life and limb, as it was. Of course it would come to this, I was thinking in some emotion akin to frustrated exasperation. Some of his personnel were looking a little too hard towards our position, and I just kept my reticle right on that fucker's nose. We had seconds. I could feel it.

"SIR!" One of his underlings with a radio array on his LBE came up. "HQ says the fire caused by that airstrike is spreading this way! The wind's carrying it east towards us!"

"You think I care? There's been interloper activity in this area. We're not leaving until-"

"Sir, you have new orders. Ask them yourselves," He presented the phonepiece to his superior, who took it.

"Yes. Yes… Yes. Yes sir. Long Live the People's Democracy." He hung up after a short spat, frustration showing on his face through my 2.5-times magnified sight. "…Move out! We're heading to where that chopper lighted down, some weird muster point they set up for a flanking maneuver or something! We don't know what the Repubs are doing and why they didn't re-arm after the airstrike, but we know it's nothing good!"

"Oh, shit, they're going for our group," Lauren noted.

"Let's move," I said as they were leaving, disappearing into the smoky, misty woods. "We're going to cut through the fire and circle around to the north. If they're gonna exfil soon we'll have a better chance of catching them on the way out."


A world aflame.

I knew that forest fires weren't usually as apocalyptic as they appeared in movies, typically one could usually out-jog the raging flames. But here we stood just north of the mass of fire. We trekked through the tread marks of the Bolo tanks, where they'd already chewed their way through the forest. We could look in that direction, seeing the black skies turned blood red in that direction, still hearing the embers crackle and trees pop and snap and fall, like a little battle still raging before us. A battle that edged ever closer, feeling the heat far off, approaching slowly, a behemoth, a monster.

We were just skirting the edges, so far away from where all the death was, but Lauren was entranced, walking along with me there, rifle hanging limp in her arms.

"About another mile north and we can start heading northwest," I muttered, gazing down at my compass.

"Noah," She uttered quietly.

"Don't worry, we're making good time. They'll-"

"*N-Noah*," She stammered harder this time, despite her voice seemingly growing more hoarse. She stood there while I walked on, oblivious, and only an eternity later had I turned around, so far away from her. How she let the stock of her rifle hit the ground, holding it up in her support hand like a crutch to help herself up on.

"W-what's…" I took only a few shambling steps to know there were tears in her eyes.

"L-look at all that," She wasn't here. Her eyes said she was a million miles away, towards the blood red skies. "…Was… Did I…"

"Hey, hey no," I came up to her, putting my hand on her arm, as if to pull her back into the real world. "You did what you had to do. You understand? These people were going to *kill* us."

"I… I know, but…" She couldn't help but stare wordlessly into the burning forest, the embers wafting past us. That choking smoke, that brimstone, the embers that danced around her like fairies, getting lost in them, like stars in the night sky. Those tears staying. "Noah," She hushed, barely audible, as her legs collapsed under her again and she was on her belly again, barely holding her upper half up with her rifle's stock against the ground as a crutch. "Gabe…"

I shambled closer. Gabriel. Gabriel was dead. Like I had to keep reminding myself, reminding myself that there was no invulnerable hero here to whisk in and save the day. God, we were so *fucked*. What… No Gabriel, my *best friend* was *dead*. I was already taking steps towards her to comfort her but I felt my knees turn to jelly to land in the charred mud. My best friend's life was over. Our anchor, our solid rock was gone and he's never coming back. I could see the inside of his *head*. There was no denying he was gone. It was all stuck in my mind, echoing out into nothingness, a deep, deep despair on every level.

I had fallen before Lauren, originally intending to do as I'd done before and hold her and tell her everything would be all right. I had to be strong, didn't I? But here I was. My hero was dead. Our hero was dead. Lauren clutched me and I clutched her, pressed into her chest as she cried into my scalp, her muzzle resting atop my head. Don't cry. That's all I could think about as I pushed Gabriel's corpse out of my mind. Don't cry. Both of you can't cry, one of you needs to stay resolved. Don't you dare fucking cry, Noah. Just hold her and let her hold you back like everything is gonna be alright. Everything is gonna be alright.

Lauren was looking up now, done sobbing. Looking into the blackened sun above so far beyond the smoke, watching the embers dance around us. Getting lost, running from thought and memory just like I was. I felt the soft of her chin atop my head, her tender touch as she'd finished squeezing me like a lifeline. I embraced her and I didn't feel so alone.

"We need to hurry," I uttered.

"We… We do."

There would be time to dwell on all of this later.

Weaving through trees, around bushes and through the brush we trotted at a brisk pace. Listening for voices, snapped twigs, shouts, engines, anything. The forests here were quiet. It didn't sit well with me, and we still had a lot of walking to do. But the hunger was now getting to me. A pit in my stomach, biting at me now that the sickness, the adrenaline of combat was gone. I knew we were alone here even if my mind told me to keep alert.

My stomach was growling by the time we could see where the muster point was supposed to be. That field was burned, democrats swarming the area, the burned-out chopper and a couple ditched vehicles the only remains of our group where we watched from a point of concealment, against the clearing.

"We're too late," I noted.

"Wh- did they take them?"

"No. They must have moved on without us- the vehicles aren't there. They saw the Democrats coming and got out before they got surrounded. That's good." Good for them, I almost added. It only made our situation all the more grim.

"Where are they going to go? You're the one who knows where to go," Lauren put in. The situation was all the more grim.

"They… They'll probably move north and predict where we'll go," I uttered mindlessly. Made sense to me.

"Let's… Let's move." Lauren put her best face on, trying to keep her composure here. The growling in my stomach let me know that the day was going to be very long.

### Chapter 66

I didn't notice it at first, but our pace sped up the more the day wore on. We were alone again, so far away from any more soldiers, or so it seemed. But that hunger stayed in their absence, and grew ever more present. I was tired too, as the adrenaline was fading, finally taking its toll my body. How many hours of sleep did I have in the last 48 hours? Couldn't have been more than five. But it's like every time we slowed down, the despair would set in. Gabriel. The hunger. Being alone here. The dead tired feeling. I just wanted to lay down for a minute, but I knew I had to fight it. I couldn't stop. Not with the world screaming in my ears. Where do we go? Where did they go? Where can we go? Oh god… We're so fucked, aren't we? We were getting nowhere fast. The despair was getting to me. My head was pounding. I had to sit down. Think of a plan, maybe.

I collapsed onto a log, Lauren surpressing a surprised yelp and coming to my aid as she watched me tumble down there. Not quite the calm, collected move I'd have hoped for. She had yet to speak as I waved her off in a brief motion, flipping over, now on the ground, my arms slumped back against the log the way one would lean against a kitchen countertop. I was just staring into the sky now, blue as can be. the clouds had cleared, the sun streaming through the dissipated mists and those evergreen trees carving their way into the skies. It was so peaceful here, nothing but the gentle waving of the pine leaves from the wind rustling through them. No more battle, no more death. Just indifferent wilderness stretching as far as the eye could see. "Got any food?" I panted, to finally take stock. She shook her head slowly, her ears drooping, eyes wide. She knew the problem as well as I did from the grumbling of her own stomach. I just closed my eyes with a pained look on my face, digging into my battle belt. I had a couple carbo blocks on my emergency kit, nothing more than 5000 calories. Far less than a day's worth of food for the both of us, which I dug into, snapping her off the bigger piece. She held up her hand for a moment to refuse, but I waved it at her more insistently, as if telling her to listen to her growling stomach that even I could hear. She took the big piece and snarfed it down far quicker than how one would expect given how she acted near seconds before.

"I... I think... They..." She started slowly, never to finish her thought. Perhaps she knew what she wanted to say, but lacked the eloquence with which to say it, sapped by the tumultuous events of this black day.

"We need food," I uttered, sealing the wrap on what I had. "...A lot more than this."

"Noah, you're... You're bleeding," She was noting tiny fragmentation pockmarks I was covered with. The grazed bullet wounds seeping blood, now dried and ugly. How I narrowly cheated death while Gabriel got what was finally coming to him. Luck. Irony. Fate. It was all just shit at this point.

"...We're out of gauze," I muttered. "We need to push on."

"Noah-"

"I'm fine. We... We'll need more food than that." Lauren looked around again, worriedly, the silence chewing at her. My ears were ringing. They'd been ringing the whole day, but here in the silence, they were deafening. "Let's try to hunt." I hefted my rifle where it was drooping into the ground, clacking against the fallen, mossy log.

"Noah," She was a little more pertinent at this point. "I... I don't think there's any deer out here."

"What? Nah, nah... There's always deer around here, my dad used to take me hunting here all the... All the time," I muttered. I was sore. Everything was in pain, right down to my empty thoughts, aching stomach and my screaming ears, trying to blink the discouragement away. I couldn't stand the quiet. It was like I was missing something. Missing the sound of an ambush approaching, or just wishing that the world would grow loud again and my horrible, poisonous thoughts would shrink.

"Noah," Lauren was insistent. "E-ever since we got that first deer I haven't seen a single one. And I've been looking, Noah," There was a quivering horror in her voice. "Flying every day, looking- Noah, G-ga..." She was lost on his name. Like she couldn't say it, trapped in the abyss of her mind, of her despair just like I was. "...There was a thing a long time ago called the Great Depression," She began. "W- people hunted deer to near-extinction, Noah. And this is worse than that time a hundred years ago. A lot worse. I don't think there's any deer out here."

"It's... It's okay," I hushed. I couldn't even hear any animals, no birds, no barking of squirrels, nothing but soft, cool wind. Was I going deaf or was the forest really that quiet? My head swam. "We'll try for small game," I offered. "We'll... spend the rest of the day setting traps. Do... Do you have any wire or string?"

"N-no," She said. I breathed out slowly. That panic was setting in. I was starving. I needed to remain calm. "Just My... My bow," she said. "And I..." She didn't want to cannibalize the bowstring for traps, I knew that much. I knew what her trinkets meant for her.

"...We need to save the bow for firemaking," I added. Pragmatism. Keep our minds off of sentimentality. The mention of fire reminded me of how cold I was, my shirt already torn into pieces and fashioned into a sling for her broken wing. "We can make traps using heavy stones and sticks to prop them up. Let's start looking for heavy stones- We can use some of the carbo block for bait. We'll... Let's find some rabbit tracks. See if we can't find a wildlife trail to put it near. Keep your eye out for purple flowers, wild asparagus or stuff that looks like cotton. That should be edible." I knew we had no supplies, and that the rains last night would have made finding animal tracks a bleaker proposition. We were equipped to fight, not to survive. We were lugging all this gear but we barely had any survival equipment aside from my compass and canteen. I noted how thirsty I was, too. I tried not to dwell on it as I went about looking for stuff to gather. I was already swimming through plans in my head, possible escapes to the situation. Hitting a military convoy, blue or red might work if I hadn't ditched a lot of my supplies. A two-person ambush of even a single truckful of roamers was a dicey proposition, but at this point I just wanted something, *anything* to eat. I knew I was growing desperate, too, just from all the places my mind wandered. Dad had prepared me for this, I kept telling myself. I was competent, and Lauren wasn't useless herself. But it was the whole day that really got to me. How wrong this all went, how it was going. We did spend the rest of the midday and evening setting simple traps, but I couldn't help but feel it was all for naught. We'd collect some small plants and come back to base hours later for a paltry dinner, the only real meal, eating the rest of the carbo blocks and the edible plants, not even coming close to filling us up. I remembered Gabriel promising to cook us a feast before we left. Felt like a different world. Not even that long ago, but like it was fiction, a movie we'd have watched on the big TV in Frank's house. We were silent there. Knowing we should be resting for tomorrow but the world swirled around us.

Night came, creeping up as we lay in our little camp. Lauren had started the fire and built us a meager little cover against aerial observation but at the end of the day we were sleeping on the ground with open sky above us tonight. While Lauren set up the camp I checked on the traps. A few of them were tripped, unsuccessfully. Only a single rabbit was caught, that I brought back, skinning and cooking it up.

"Here, you gave me too much," Lauren finally broke the silence after the rabbit was served, offering a good piece of her portion towards me as I was there sipping improvised tea made from stream water and pine needles boiled in the cup of my canteen, my actual canteen sitting near the fire, more of this improvised tea boiling, the both of us sitting there.

"You need the nutrients to heal. And you burned a lot more calories than I did today flying," I uttered coldly, not even moving aside from looking to the haunch she offered. "Eat it."

"I'm not hungry."

"*Eat it.*" I was more stern. She looked at the little drumstick-like morsel for a moment.

"...If you get hungry you don't think as well. You're the one who knows this place and what to do, and my wings are going to be resting for a while anyways."

"Lauren-"

"*Noah*," she growled, like she snapped for a moment, frustration finding her before she scoffed it all away with a momentary furrow of her brow, clenching shut of her eyes and grit of her teeth. "Noah… Please. I want you to have it."

"I'm not hungry either." Lauren, who had been laying there mostly leisurely across from me at the campfire sprung up, circling the fire and advancing quickly, shoving it in my face down there, her forepaws stamping into the dirt as she huffed out. I slowly caught her eyes behind her flared nostrils. I could barely stand to look at her, especially now, with her glaring down at me in nothing but her sport attire undergarment, body armor off to the side, I couldn't help but be flustered as she wagged the food in my face. I was hungry, but I really felt sick. I might have said that it was out of some gross self-sacrifice that I wanted her to be satiated, but maybe it was a little bit more than being a gentleman. Could I have chalked my feelings back then to what the world, what *Maria* was to me at the time? Did I still feel that way? I think I did. God, was she just so charming, so powerfully adorable when she had some conviction in her. I suppose if not for the long shadows cast by the dim, shielded fire she would have seen me blush.

"Take it," She demanded. "Take the fucking rabbit leg, Noah." I finally obliged and she stood there, watching with her arms crossed beneath her ample breasts, trigger finger twiddling on her bicep and forepaw patting the ground, waiting for me to eat, and I did, With her standing over me the whole time, as if to make sure I did. She finally went back over with a huff from her nostrils, laying down again with the fire between us, it snapping and popping. "...you have a plan to find the group?" She asked morosely. Still trying to make small talk to fill the awkward space instead of her thoughts. I drew in a large breath, ready for a heavy sigh.

"They're probably trying to find us too. The blues might be hunting them down as well so they'll probably be covering their tracks."

"...Think anyone is following *us*?"

"We didn't leave that much in tracks," I muttered. "I think we're safe here from most people." A couple more moments of that silence, that horrible silence.

"...What about Maria?" A dagger of ice shooting through my heart. God, I wanted to forget about her, but there she was. Falling to the ground all over again in my mind.

"She's tough," I uttered my lies of omission. "She's been through… Stuff like this before. She can survive on her own. I'm sure we'll run into her again." I tried to play things off, tried to make my lie more palatable but that pain inside me remained.

"...Should we leave tracks for her?"

"The blues might track her," I uttered mindlessly, like a weird segue without even noticing it. Ignoring Lauren's apprehension. "She'll be busy avoiding them." I didn't want to talk about Maria. I would even rather be talking about Gabriel than Maria. Two ghosts in my head but here I was with the woman I actually loved sitting across from me. I needed to tell her. I had nothing left in my way but guilt, and what a tremendous hill that would be to climb. I did know tonight was too soon. It would seem ingenuine, wouldn't it? I had to bide my time. Ignore my guilt screaming at me and focus on what was to come. Finally free, with Lauren. Did she still love me or not? We always shared such a rapport. We were *right* for each other. This was practically fate, right?

Right?

I fell asleep so close to her, up under her bigger unbroken wing gazing into the milky way, and the world became a haze of thought. Finally able to catch up on the hours of utter exhaustion of the last two days.


I watched Gabriel, back there on that table in the armory, set to blow. Single eye twitching, mouth moving, words choking to come out but they were silent to me. I couldn't hear him. I wanted to hear him but his last words rang nothingness in my ears. I was so far away.

My hands curled around the detonator and my fingers pressed that trigger and his world became blinding light, and he was gone, and I was falling through space. Like I'd been pushed off a ledge. Lauren soared above me, barely looking down as I screamed for her help. I was falling down, down towards the clamoring monsters, towards a black forest of death as she glided along the golden blue sky, apathetic. *Why… Why won't you come save me? Don't you love me?*

*Please… I want you to love me… Why would you do this to-*

I was awake and the earth was breathing mist. I just sighed there heavily a few times, still dead tired but having hit the ground. For a moment I considered getting up but feeling my bones creaking and all my muscles fuzed into a single solid mass, I gave up in pain. I rolled my head over to Lauren, her big body drawing great voluminous sighs of air into both of her chests, the wing that once warmed me like a blanket was retracted, perhaps out of instinct in her sleep as she clutched her rifle, still in her own dreams, that look on her face of bloody discontent playing itself out. I wondered with a sigh what she must have dreamt about as I gazed into the final stars of the night dancing among soft misty clouds above. God, I barely had any good sleep, it felt. I couldn't help but think of that first night with her. How adorable she was with her noble struggle against nightmares of implanted memories and white walls and men in lab coats, a cold unfeeling labyrinth she was carted through when she was small, however brief her childhood was. Made into this thing, this woman with the imprint of an upbringing, not even memories but their faint residue. And what a fine one she turned out to be.

My mind was wandering as I lay there, the chill of the mists dancing around me penetrating my skin. I remembered Gabriel that same night when this all began, so long ago. How I bore witness to his brutality. I'd taken a single life that day out of self-defense and it drove me sick. Gabriel took three in cold blood like it was child's play. Horror, I felt. But in his absence now, a far deeper horror. I wondered what Gabriel would do in this situation. What his real survival skills really were like.

He'd probably check the traps, which is what I finally curled myself to get up and do, ignoring the screaming of my sore bones.

**Chapter 67**

Breakfast consisted of more boiled pine leaves for tea, some mushrooms and a couple squirrels we'd bagged. We were silent as we worked and ate, Lauren having risen by the time I'd gotten back. She gave me a meager smile as I'd returned, letting me know there was still plenty of fight left within her. I knew why she smiled, to let me know that she still thought we could handle this, that I had a plan worth following.

"Let's not get lost in the forest," I uttered. "It won't be soon until it's August."

"...Noah, It's been august for a while," Lauren uttered, after being taken aback for a moment. Huh. Time really does fly.

"Yeah," I muttered, backpedaling. "Of course. There… There are hot springs in the forest, ever since Project Pompeii ten years ago there are a lot more hot springs around here. See, they… There's this huge underground volcano called Yellowstone that we… kind of stopped from exploding by… spreading it out, y'know?" Lauren was glaring at me with a furrowed brow and lips, sort of noticing how I'd segued away from my own airheadedness. "Like we made it bigger but less dangerous. We'll find a lot of hot springs out here."

"...Okay," She sighed, then flopped over on her side again onto the grasses, kicking her legs a little before yawning, then flopping right-side up and springing up. I found it very cute, her fighting enthusiasm. "We should get moving."

"Yeah."

We were never really full. Not then, and not from then on out. We'd be satiated, you could say, but scrounging for shrubs and taking potshots at small game- or at least planning on it- didn't exactly pan out much. Lauren really couldn't use her rifle for any small game hunting, as the larger cartridge of her M1A would blow the critters to shreds, and even with my 5.56 I had to be dead-on with a head shot given that the result would be rather similar. There were our pistols, but the lesser accuracy inherent to a sidearm was troublesome; though my pistol was certainly finer, my customized Glock 34 with a micro dot sight on the slide. We traded pistols so Lauren could prospectively varmint hunt with my better weapon, me taking Lauren's stock Glock 17. After a heavy bit of delineation, we realised that we'd do better to ditch some of the ammo to lighten our load. We dropped everything but three 25-round magazines for Lauren's

M1A, keeping my ammo since I really only had three far lighter 35 round 5.56 magazines and a single half-full one.

Days passed as we trekked, figuring to crisscross the forest in search of the group. The hunger grew and grew. Nights were either dreamless oblivions or restless deluges of thoughts and memories and waking to hunger. But it really was pretty out here. God, was it beautiful. And here I was with the most beautiful woman in the world, but every step I took closer to her brought a deeper pang of pain within me that I fought to ignore. I knew I was so close.

"Ah- oh," Lauren uttered suddenly. Some evening as we'd neared the end of our marching for the day, putting her things by the wayside as she strode forward, dropping her rifle, armor, saddle and finally pulling off her shirt, the homemade sling for her wing coming off to be tossed to the banks just before splashing into the deep waters, giggling as the warmth tickled her and she splashed gleefully into the sparkling spring, steam rising from it steadily. "...So this must be a hot spring," she smiled, wading ever deeper, letting her casted wing float under its own buoyancy, relieved of gravity for once, maybe reminding her of the sky itself, rousing contentment within her. Despite the world bearing down on our shoulders, she could smile here, and the worry in my heart melted. I saw the look of bliss on her face and I only felt more enamored with her. "...This is so much better than a hot shower... It's so *warm*... C'mon, Noah," she giggled, waving me in. She was in nothing but her bra top at this point, going to stretch herself as best she could in the waters, relaxing amongst the bubbles from the cracks lining the stone bottom of the pool. Deep enough now, she flipped herself over to float on her back as I was undressing myself, down to my boxers and wading in. Soothing warmth like I hadn't felt in so long overtook me. It must have been months since I'd felt warm water, even back at where we'd been in Shortstone with all the blackouts it was uncommon to even get lukewarm. But here it was warm. Truly warm, with warmth to share. There with her, floating beside her. "Oh, look!" She cried up to the canopy, lightning bugs fluttering above like an augmentation of the stars themselves. "It's... pretty," She uttered. It was getting darker sooner, for sure- but here we were in the glow of the world. Together.

We swam side by side, floating here, nice enough to make us feel like the world wasn't as bad as it was. I bumped into her where I floated, and she giggled a little bit. Her joy was music to my ears. "Hey," I uttered once we'd been there for what felt like an eternity, happy together, just enjoying something for once, able enough to ignore the problems around us, down to the hunger in our stomachs. "Remember all that stuff you said back then?" I floated close, feeling like I was calm enough, that she was calm enough, that the world was calm enough to float through thought lazily and towards where I wanted to go.

"...Back then?" She giggled out, kicking a little as she splashed calmly there.

"Y-you know," I was blushing, but she wasn't exactly looking right at me so I could play it off. "About how when we first met you were in love with me."

"...I-I wouldn't put it like *that*," She said, stopping her giggling, but not necessarily running out of mirth, finally looking over to me just as I'd fought back my blushing, as I went vertical to float, still a good meter between the floor of the spring and my feet, just treading water. She kept floating on her back, head and ears angled towards me while she looked at me. "I was just confused."

"Am I confusing?"

"Noah, you know I'm... I'm not..." I came closer smiling warmly, putting my hand on her shoulder as we waded there, as if to persuade her that this wasn't confrontational. This was understanding, this was us growing closer. At least, that's what I felt.

"Back when we were first flying into shortstone, I should have said something when we talked about this," I sighed, my smile fading to be fully serious with her. "I think... I think I felt the same way you did back in Vegas, and... and just now I'm realising it."

"N-*Noah*," It was Lauren's turn to blush, before pausing to flip over, splashing as she stood upon the floor of the spring with her rear legs, standing before me, eye to eye. "Really?" She was looking down at herself in what must have been bashfulness. I reached out again to touch her, to feel her on the arm, to show I wasn't messing around.

"I think you're the most beautiful person I'll ever see," I admitted, and her blush grew. I swam closer to grasp the soft of her torso with both hands, feeling down into the hip-like formation of where her humanoid half met her animalistic one. Her forelegs kicked a little, like she was almost going to grip my thighs with them, to touch me back, but she was frozen as her glittering brown eyes saw through me with a distant stare for a second, her mouth agape just barely, lip quivering, as her hand came up to brush her free bangs out of her face.

"Noah," Those forelegs of hers came up to gently push me away by my hips, ever so barely. "W-what about Maria?" That goddamn spectre. My eyes must have unfocused for a second, my only tell as I fought my reaction away. I was *so close*. I just wanted her to love me like I loved her.

"...Maria and I never really had anything going between us," I spoke truth that hurt like a lie, following it up with a real little white lie. "We broke up a while back."

"Oh, gosh..." She let out, before looking down again. Like she was looking down at her submerged body. "...Did you- did you feel this way about me when you were with her?"

"Lauren," I uttered, before pausing, hearing my voice breaking. I couldn't seem pathetic. I had to show resolve. I couldn't fail when I was this close. "I don't think I *ever* loved her." Lauren attempted to disguise a tiny gasp in her breath, but her surprise, her shock bore through. "I thought I knew what love was, but I was wrong. What I feel for you... What I feel between *us*..." I gripped her softly again, maybe to get a reading on whether or not I was breaking through. She hesitated, but she did not push me away. I was trembling on the inside. I wanted her so badly. I wanted to forget about Maria, about pretending to love her for so long and using her and leaving her to die so I found the will to push her into the very back of my mind as I worked towards Lauren. "...That's real. It's the only thing I've ever been certain of in my whole life."

"N-Noah, I..." she didn't touch me back, but I could see the starstruck look in her eyes, how her lips trembled, how, even inadvertently, she was opening up to me, reaching out. I had to be insistent, strong, passionate.

"I wish I could have told you then," I uttered. "I wasn't strong enough then, but I am now. I love you, Lauren. We're more than just friends and we always have been. I want to stop pretending and start *living*." Her arms finally came towards me, forelegs hooking around my thighs as she let me draw close.

"Noah... I... I..."

"Shh, don't say anything," I uttered once she'd delineated enough, taking my index finger and placing it on her lips, drawing my mouth on the other side of my finger. "Show me."

And that night,

for the first time in my life,

*I made love.*

**Chapter 68**

It was blissful.

Alone, without the world, without anything but pure passion. Nothing mattered but this holy gestalt, the ultimate *us*. I let myself free and Lauren with me. There was nothing I wouldn't do for her, this was my admittance of that, my conciliation. I guess in a way, I wanted to prove I was genuine. Her hesitance at first only made me want to show that proof all the more, and she eventually melted into me and it was better than I could ever imagine. Finally, after all this time, we could be together.

Laying on the cool grass, naked save for a wing covering me, basking in where the rolling mists met the heady steam in this land of cloud and fire, woods so dense you could hardly hear anything but the rustle of leaves and the hiss of steamy pools. We were together. She was happy back. Was she waiting for this? It didn't matter. Like me she was enjoying herself, enjoying me as I enjoyed her. We'd been through so much, and here we were. Exactly as we should be, *together*.

In sleep, that dream visited me once again, the one without plot and only raw force of emotion, to be finally surrounded in love, acceptance. Her acceptance of me, my acceptance of self. It was bliss, wasn't it?

Wasn't it?

A spectre lingered. Doubt. Doubt of how the past had panned out inflicting its wounds upon the future. Fresh memories. Guilt. Disgust. I had what I wanted and I felt terrible, disgusting, like an addict coming down from a high. The world screaming in my ears. I-

"Mnhh..." Her hand slowly passing my pectorals, resting itself closer to my heart. She was still asleep here. The sun was yet to rise and I was already roused awake from a sleep that grew ever more restless. Did she wake me up? No, no she was still asleep. A smile on her face. A smile despite everything. God bless her soul, ever ready to see the better side of things. She glowed here, her big dumb smile grinning into me. Steam becoming mist near us from the spring, glowing in our brilliance here.

I guess I could lay here with her. Bask in her indomitable happiness as she held me. This was how it was supposed to be, I knew. No her and I, but us. Seeing her glowing smile, I was so happy. At least, I thought I was. I wanted to be. I was desperate. I didn't feel comfortable. I felt my skin crawling. Her touch stung. No, I wanted this. Please God, I just wanted this so much. Why the fuck can't I ever be happy?

I was up, folding her arm and wing back on herself. God, I was hungry. It must be that hunger, making me miserable. Making me think about bad things. I had to get up, dress myself, grab my rifle and Lauren's bow to look around for some game. We hadn't exactly laid traps, but it was early, and this part of the woods was so deep that I doubted many other people had gone through here and I could gather shrubs and mushrooms plentifully. It was very dense here, very quiet. Easy to get lost in the trees and the mist, how cold, how quiet it was. I hadn't been appropriately warm for a while now save for our dip last night, deprived of clothing for my torso for quite some time, and the chill of the morning was certainly upon us.

By the time the sun had risen and I got back with pouches full of edible plants and a single squirrel, Lauren already had the fire back up. She looked over to me, face still bright enough to melt the ice in my veins. I was cooking up the game and she came around behind me to drape her arms across my chest, kissing the top of my head. Her touch was enchanting.

"I'm glad that you're here with me, Lauren," I chuckled, pushing my darkness aside for long enough to let myself enjoy the world swirling around me, her wings coming around to aid in this little hug.

"You're a hell of a person to spend the apocalypse with, yourself." I let myself laugh and the world seemed a bit kinder than it really was. We stayed there like that, swaying back and forth with each other until breakfast was close enough to ready. I wished it took forever to be done, but even forever might not have been long enough.

"It came out good this time," I said with my mouth full. "I think I'm getting the hang of this."

"I'll say," Lauren giggled, but the laughter seemed to drain away the longer we sat there. The thought of good food, good cooking roused a topic in our minds we wanted to avoid. The subject needed to be preemptively changed. "You know," Lauren began anew after sitting on silence for far too long, sitting beside me so we could lean into each other as we ate. "I think I know why I gravitated to you first, back then."

"Oh?" I uttered.

"Yeah, you saved my life, for one," She explained. I scoffed playfully.

"I saved myself. He pointed his gun at me so I shot him, just did as I was trained. You're hardly a damsel in distress. Your kind are supposed to be the ones kidnapping princesses, y'know." Lauren chuckled back at this.

"...Dude would have shot me if you didn't come through then, y'know."

"Right place in the right time, huh?" I uttered, taking a good look at her, catching her eyes and making her blush. "Sure glad I was there."

"...I think," She uttered after a long delineating pause. "...It's more probably that you were the first person to be nice to me- to really treat me like a real person, y'know?" She took another look back at me, catching my eyes like I'd caught hers. "I mean, nothing against the rest of the group, they just took longer to really... Accept me. Sort of felt like the group mascot for the longest time, almost," She was huffing out awkward chuckles as she looked away, a weird embarrassed blush embellishing her face this time, going to scratch the back of her head just below a horn with her free hand. "But you were always there for me. Ever since the first night when I woke up and came to you while you were on guard."

"You remember that?"

"Why wouldn't I; It's... It's my first *day alive*," She hushed. "You named me after the freakin' brand of shirt I found to wear," She laughed awkwardly and I let myself smile, charmed. "I just wonder what would have happened if I'd flown the other way out of that facility. If I went to any other building, if I even managed to hide from that hobo with the gun. Where I'd be now."

"Guess it's fate," I uttered.

"Somebody's been looking out for me, I feel," She uttered. "Not you, but they led me to you. God made sure that things would turn out how they did." I smiled. What a quaint sentiment. God, it just made me love her all the more, her outlook on the crazy world around us. Though as I watched her thumb through her thoughts, I could see her face darken, going to thoughts of places and times and people who were no longer with us.

"You know, it's stupid," I laughed nervously, trying to push through those thoughts. "That first night with your nightmare... That's what really made me want to make sure you stuck with us. Damsel in distress or not, I saw you as a person with problems, problems that weren't as bad as you thought, but like, I've been there, y'know? I know that sucks. I wanted to help you through everything. I wanted to make sure you were alright."

"Felt bad for me, huh?" she asked me with a trembling smile.

"Like if I didn't stick up for you I'd never forgive myself." Forgive myself. The phrase lingered in my head, echoing until it was deafening, even if I meant what I said there. "Don't think I really fell in love with you until we went flying that first time. I'm glad you wanted to share the sky with me."

"Gets lonely up there," She smiled. "Kinda always felt like you liked it more than you'd ever admit. Guess I'm getting better at guessing people. So you love me for my wings, huh?"

"I'd be lonely if I could fly, and I flew alone. I'd want to share it too." She smiled on and on. We were long done eating by now, just basking in each others' company.

"Well, as soon as my wings heal, we can fly again."

"Maybe we could fly right to the Citadel and get some reinforcements. Get them to open their channels and hail our group. Simplify things."

"Mm, how romantic," Lauren was behind me but I could envision her rolling her eyes. "I was more thinking after this stupid war blows over we can fly right to the coast so you can show me the sea."

"You promise?" I uttered coyly. "You can't make promises lightly."

"You promised to take care of me back then."

"Yeah, and look how that's turned out." Lauren let the laughter in her heart burst forth from her as I said this, giddy little giggles finding me too.

"...Heh, I think you did a good enough job," She uttered, letting her laughter wind down. Really wasn't that funny, but she seemed unable to help it. I was smiling like an idiot too, it was contagious. "I promise. We'll fly every day and every night, too. Just us."

"I'd love that, Lauren." I turned my head upwards to peck her with a kiss her right on the nose, and she blushed as I smiled at her reaction, kissing her again, on the lips with passion. The day was just beginning and there was walking to be done, but it would have to wait for us.

Trekking wasn't so bad now, now that my soul felt a little lighter. We were hungry, cold, not that well rested, but we were together. Repressing all the awful things on my mind was a little easier than it had been the week or so before. And so, we kept on our search, days passing. I'd come back to that conversation in my head every now and then. Try to think of Lauren, our soon-to-be life together. Things are going to be good and things are going to be simple, despite everything. But that wasn't true. Even when I thought, I thought of what it would be like if Lauren or I hadn't gone in that building. If I just ran away in cowardice once I'd heard the first gunshot. If I'd abandoned everyone aside from Gabe and Maria. We'd… I'd be at the citadel by now. Able to slip right on past this stupid war. But complications arose. A beautiful complication now trekking beside me, but there were far more complications than just her. I'd left Maria to her fate back there. I knew it was on me. And so I could never free truly myself from the guilt. From what had happened. From Gabriel's shadow. Wilson and Holly, Kyle left to grim uncertainty, though doubtfully as foul as Maria's fate, whatever it was. The world was hollering at me. I couldn't stand it, no matter how I tried to lose myself in Lauren's eyes.

### Chapter 69

It was Maria's face.

Not Gabriel's, Maria's. Blown open. Raw and bloody, a squall of gore. Her remaining eye was staring at me. Weeping.

"Why?"

I didn't have anything to say. I couldn't have said anything. How could I?

"Why couldn't you love me?" No. I didn't want it to end like this. I wished I could tell her. I wished I could have let her down gently but I wasn't strong enough.

"That's right, you weren't," She said. But it wasn't her. No, it was... Gabriel. Leaned against the wall of my house on the back patio. I could hear Kyle and Wilson in the pool. Gabriel was smirking, just like he always was. Like he knew it all. He knew every last dirty truth. "Do you want to go back? Start again?" He laughed. Kyle and Wilson laughing, looking over to me. I could hear Lauren in the pool, splashing back at them just out of my vision, around the corner, in the deep end. I wanted to go over there, away from judgement, away from my problems. I took one step and a hand was upon my shoulder. I was forced to turn and there they were. Heads hanging open, gore spilling out. And it was all my fault.

**"YOU THINK YOU'LL EVER BE ABLE TO LIVE WITH YOURSELF?"**
**"YOU THINK YOU'LL EVER BE ABLE TO LIVE WITH YOURSELF?"**

I sat up in an instant, chest heaving. The ringing in my ears gone in an instant, and Lauren waking with a start after I'd thrown her wing off of me with my burst to life, laying there, watching me breathe. It was the dark of the morning, just beginning to get light, mists kicked up by my initial thrashing to life as I sat there, drenched in cold sweat.

"You okay, Noah?" Lauren's voice was sweet, like a songbird, but I couldn't feel anything but the bitter cold as I flipped over towards the doused fire, stoking the embers with new sticks to get it up and running again. I rubbed my eyes. What a shit dream. "Nightmare?"

"What, don't you ever have nightmares anymore?" I spat, though in retrospect this probably was a lot crueller sounding than I'd intended, even with my mind racing with guilt.

"...I didn't mean it like that," She uttered with a whiper, taken by surprise.

"Yeah, what did you-" I began, snapping at her, stopping myself. I loved her more than to treat her like this. God, I just felt like an idiot. "...Just get the fire up and running," I snarled, going for the bow and my rifle. "I'll find us something to eat. I'm just hungry, that's why I'm pissed," I grumbled, standing up to go and dress myself. I took a moment to look at my battle belt with its suspenders, contemplating to wear them but deciding against it. I didn't exactly need the spare ammo or pistol, anyways. I took one look back at her big brown eyes as I let the suspenders slip from my grip, gazing at her, orbs of mocha sparkling there above her mouth slightly agape, those eyes glittering as if a little afraid. For the first time in a while, I took in how she looked. She'd lost weight. Looking down, so had I. It's all I could think of as I set off to check the forest paths.

The silence of these deep woods was remarkable. Magical, you could even say. Trying to keep my mind off things, just imagining what Lauren was thinking about this place where the ground hissed and sputtered out steam, where hot met cold, a land of fire and smoky mist. If it wasn't for the hunger and the dirtiness and the cold I would have been enjoying myself. That, and all those other things rumbling away in my head.

A rustle. Sudden, startlingly quick and close. I'd let my focus wane far too much. I'd been out to find some small game, but... But this was different. Was there somebody here? I'd already nocked the arrow I'd taken, but my mind went to my rifle still slung around my back. No time now.

A creature was dashing through the bush, and an instant after I'd registered it as something other than a person, realising this was a deer, I let my arrow fly, catching it beautifully beneath the right shoulder, hearing the thwack of the arrow as the animal dashed on. No time to think.

No time to realise how rare this must have been, how I had probably just shot an endangered species. All the worries that had been plaguing me evaporated into the mists and all I could think about was my ravenous hunger. The blood, I was following the blood. I could smell it, that wet rust. That deer wasn't getting away. I followed the iron scent on the air, floating on the mists, and the red splotches, watching it sparkle on the ground and the leaves and the mossy trunks as I whirled by. God, I could *taste* it. More than a mouthful of meat at a time. Finally, I could be full. I would have been giddy if not for the sheer rage of the hunt within me as I ran, rifle in hand, bow slung around my back.

There it was. Still limping along. Some inconceivable amount of time tracking and it was so close. I didn't want to shoot it, some idiotic fervor in me made me know my aim would be less than true. My rifle tumbled out of my hands as I gained on the panicked, nearly exsanguinated creature and out came my knife. I leapt upon the beast, snarling and gnashing in rage. Stabbing the poor creature over, and over, and over until it finally ceased and fell dead, with I atop its lifeless corpse. Stabbing into a heart long stopped beating. All mine. I ripped my arrow out of it and put it with the bow, taking the bow off of myself as I worked. Couldn't spoil the meat, had to skin and gut it now. God, I could practically see the look on Lauren's face. Her hero. Me. I was giggling to myself as I worked, soaked in blood. But, like that, there was a subtle crunch of a twig and the world began to spin again and my tunnel vision disappeared, and in its stead, the hairs upon my neck began to rise. My head went up, like an inquisitive dog, and my blood froze in an instant.

At first glance it appeared as a human face glaring at me, but huge, monstrous, animalistic. Not like a human beyond the first moment of realization. Nose flattened like a dog and the wrinkled skin of its face disappearing into black fur, teeth of daggers, drool dripping from its razor maw. And its eyes- what horror it really was. Cunning orbs of ice blue. Eyes that pierced, that saw through you. Saw you as unwitting prey. I was frozen for a moment trying to comprehend it, but my instincts told me I was in utmost danger. This… thing was massive. Not a wolf, something far more dangerous. A monster here to devour. What the deer had really been running from. And my rifle, thrown aside in my adrenal state, laying at its feet.

I lunged for the bow and arrow as it charged. It let out a strange barking roar that sounded more like the yell of a man, something to make ones' blood curdle, confuse you into thinking this was a person screaming for a terrifying moment. I knocked the arrow and let it fly, but it dodged like it was effortless, dancing around the projectile. I had a moment before it was upon me, and in my foolishness I fell upon my back to kick at it to buy time to draw my knife. Blood was flying. I was screaming, the beast was gnashing. Those daggers driven into my leg, my ankle crunching beneath horrific razors as it whipped me around, my knee cracking with its dislocation as it whipped its maw with me in it. I was slashing at its face, across its mouth and finally over its eye but it refused to let go. I drove the knife into its eye and it screamed again, recoiling back, taking my knife with it as it retreated out of sight, yelping like a human. The pain was unmistakable. Any other time I would have passed out. Maybe anyone less strong than I would have passed out. But I knew it was out there, barely wounded save for its eye, and I had little time to prepare to defend myself. I was crawling. Crawling like a madman, trying not to let the yelps of terror come from me. I had to focus on my gun. I was bleeding all over the place. This was bad. This was beyond bad. My rifle, my fucking rifle, where the fuck was my rifle?!

That monster was here. Charging back, calling out to me. Its voice drove me faster. I wasn't going to die like this. No, not now. I was so close. Close to the life I wanted.

I fell upon my rifle, flipping over, my destroyed leg flopping as I did. There it was, stalking there, but as soon as it saw my rifle in my hands, it was like it knew I was about to shoot it, leaping away, blood still dripping down its face as it disappeared into the brush, its haunting eye following me from the shadows and I fired towards it, screaming. It was gone and I was alone, bleeding. The world grew grim and it was like every shadow was another eye. I was going to die here if I didn't get help.

I fell upon my back, pointing my rifle from whence I'd came. Towards where Lauren was. I fired three shots up into the air in that direction before letting the weapon spill from my grip, but not too far as I knew the beast was watching. Fucking thing stole my knife, as I pulled my multitool out to chop a bit of my pants off to gum into my wound. Felt hopeless, trying to stop the bleeding. Didn't think it was an arterial so at least I had a chance. Silver lining on that cloud, I supposed. Just screaming in my breath at my dislocated lower leg and my shattered tibia and fibula. I knew it was watching me. Waiting for me to bleed out, just as hungry as I was. In those long moments that felt like eternity, I had time to reflect on the situation. The horrible irony. So close and yet so far. How stupid I had to have been. Blindsided like that. Dad would have been ashamed. Heh, dad would have been ashamed at a lot. How Gabriel was dead, how Maria was probably too. He always liked Maria. Now he was the father to some incompetent weirdo with a thing for a hybrid girl- and not even one with just two legs. It was strange how despair seemed to leak out with one's blood. But despite how comfortable I seemed to get, how apathetic with my own demise I was, Lauren remained in my mind. I'd failed her. I could do nothing but fail her.

A green angel descended upon me. Time was inconsequential, there was only the singular moment at this time, in my hazy mind. It was probably before I truly passed out and let the rifle fall from my grasp. I was pointing at the deer, telling her to get it but she didn't seem to care. A twig stuck into my mouth inexplicably before

**Pain.**

The twig served its purpose, splintering and cracking and sundering to my jaws as I bit and screamed. Lucidity returning to me for a brief moment as adrenaline kicked back in, spurred by pain. My leg mostly back into place, Lauren securing a splint with branches and her own shirt, at least what wasn't used as a bandage. I was heaving, wheezing. I would have thrown up if not for my empty stomach. "Th… Th…" Lauren hefted me onto my back as I pointed at the deer. She went up to it to throw it over her back before me on her saddle. Her words sounded as if they were spoken underwater when they met my ears. "Don't… Don't let it spoil…" I was muttering. Where was my knife? It still needed to be gutted. The meat was going to be ruined unless we gut it.

I was there by the fire soon enough. The world going in and out as I was fed. I could see Lauren toiling over the carcass, pained look on her face as she carved away tainted flesh. I told her, didn't I? Couldn't let the meat be ruined. Had to be quick about skinning and gutting it. Man, she really wasn't eating much of what she cooked. Just giving it all to me. I guessed being full for once was worth it after what I went through. I wanted to tell her that. Tell her I loved her affectionate streak. I loved her. Nowhere I'd rather be than here.

What time was it? It was so dark. But for once I was warm, so warm. A heartbeat, not mine, somewhere else. Warm and wet. Steamy. The heat was unbearable. Was I sweating? Was this a fever? I could hardly move. Was I restrained? How much blood had I lost before I stopped bleeding? Time had definitely passed. The world was a blur and here I was, blind and senseless. Was it the fever? I felt trapped. Claustrophobic, but not in a bad way. It was nice, considering the circumstances. There was movement. Swaying. Going somewhere. I could hear her voice but I couldn't see her. Where are we going, Lauren? I must have been delirious. But I felt her concern, her love like it softly surrounded me. Time was moving so fast, days seeming to blend into one another in this cocoon I'd seemed to have made for myself. Was it in my mind? Whose heartbeat was that?

A ceiling.

I was awake. Gazing up at timber beams stretching across the room far above me. It was dark but my eyes were already acclimated, the embers of a dying fire glowing in the fireplace in the corner. It took me a second to realize that the numb, fuzzy feeling all over my body wasn't some eerie paralysis but a blanket, tucking me in. I let out a groan, trying to get up before feeling the pain surging through my right leg as I attempted to move, laying back down. At least it didn't hurt when I was still. I simply rolled my head to the right to see the rest of the room, and through a couple blinks I could see where she was. There was a mass curled on the floor before the fire, casting long shadows, wings and two horns, one long and the other stubby, yet to have fully grown back out. I could make out her disheveled hair that hung from her head and clumped its way down her spine. Her body circled around her rifle, just laying there by the fire, sleeping with that worrisome look on her face. I wanted to wake her up and tell her that everything was alright, everything was going to be alright. But she needed her sleep. Just like I needed something to eat. God, I was so hungry. I could feel the tightness of my body, wiry and fatless. Was there anything of that deer left? How long had I been out of it? It all felt like minutes ago. Like I'd stepped off a ride at an amusement park, how the world stopped spinning. But in my stupor, like I'd known this wasn't the time to wake up, I simply lay back down and blinked, and the sun was streaming in as a pot of water whistled. Morning was well and here now, and I was alone. I could hear the birds chirping outside. What was this cabin? At least this wasn't part of the dream. This had to be real. All the little things, not just the pain of my leg but the hunger and the dryness of my mouth and the scratchiness of the blanket. And the smell of coffee, real coffee brewing, not stupid makeshift tea made from pine needles steamed from a pot by the fire, a kettle beginning to whistle. Where was Lauren? I flipped my body out of bed, going to pivot my busted leg out of the bed. Maybe it hadn't felt like minutes, the more I thought, like the more I could remember the longer it got. Lauren… Carried me here. I think. A lot of that was still unclear to me. I was looking around at the sparse decor of the cabin, the ceiling leaking from rain last night while I slept.

Hobbling my way over to the kettle on mostly one leg and dragging the blanket with me for warmth, I spotted our rifles leaned in the corner beside the bed, crossed upon each other, mine cleaned up nice and good. It was sopped in blood and dirt the last I saw it. I took a moment to take in the image of our weapons leaned together like that, hers towering before mine and the both of them leaned together with her saddle upon the ground before it, as the kettle began to whine and took my focus back. I took the kettle away from the fire and placed it upon the pewter table, a draft through this musty old cabin making me take notice of how naked I was. I figured I'd get coffee later. God, I was hungry, but I could ignore it with the thought of where that coffee came from giving me some degree of hope, with this place feeling like a little godsend. A comfy little abode. I popped open the drawers, seeing an abundance of flannel, selecting some long underwear for my first layer, ever so carefully drawing it over my splint, but it seemed that the fellow who had once inhabited this place was quite a bit bigger than I was so it wasn't too tight of a fit even with this hobbled together apparatus on my leg. I did take the time to notice how nice the splint she made for me was, even if it was just whatever she could find in this cute little cabin. Lauren must have really paid attention during those medical lessons. I also slipped into a flannel shirt, mostly to ignore how I could see and feel my ribs through my skin. Getting up again, I took a look out the window, hearing a thunking noise. I noticed immediately the vast greenery of the clearing the cabin was built upon the precipice of, seeing this rolling field here in the swing of autumn, a patch of green among browns and waning greyish oranges. This place must look incredible during the spring, I thought to myself. The swaying leaves and the waves of the grasses and flowers as the breeze fluttered over them, the mists sticking to the forests as if struck by fear of the open air. The sun was taking advantage of the mists' absence to cast beautiful rays through the far thinner haze of the open air. It was so clear here, so beautiful.

Another whack. I could see her tail whip a little, her wing slung up as the head of an axe appeared behind what I could see of her from that corner of the window, hefted up before falling onto the chopping block, wood splintering, Lauren grunting as she took steps forward to gather up the pieces, walking back. Garbed in flannel with one armful of splintered logs and the other hefting the axe over her shoulder, she appeared there as one of her frontal legs came up to push open the door. Immediately, she saw me sitting there smiling weakly, my body facing away with me looking at her over my shoulder, and she fought for a second to not drop the logs, letting the axe clunk against the doorframe.

"N-Noah," She began, eyes wide. "You… You're awake."

"Yeah, well, I really woke up last-" Crash. The wood being tossed from her hands as she fell near me to come over me with arms and wings, gripping me. Silence overtaking the cabin as she embraced me. Not even sobbing, just holding me, holding me and holding the fact that I was alive. I let her hug me and put my hand up upon the top of her muzzle after a second, letting me hold her back as she just dug her head into the soft of my neck and shoulder from behind. "You miss me?" I let out slowly. She barked out a laugh, a counter to a sob, the two noises dueling in her throat for a second.

"Jesus," She grunted. "I… I was so worried…"

"You think I look bad, you should see the other guy, he-" One of her hands drifted up to my face, putting a finger upon my lips.

"Can you save the jokes for now?" She hushed, moving a little ways away to look me more in the eye, giving a weak smile behind glittering eyes full of saline.

"…I lost my knife," I muttered. "And the arrow." She sighed, resting her head back on the side of my neck.

"It's okay. I'm just glad I didn't lose you too." A long while sitting there. By the time we spoke again, the coffee was a little cooler.

"…So what's up with this place?" She finally reared away, an arm still trailing on my shoulder as she reared back. I noticed she didn't look quite as emaciated as I did. Must have been the blood I lost.

"See, I always knew no matter how bad it got," She walked over ahead of me. There was a little kitchen adjacent to the firestove, and she opened a door to a pantry and pulled out some cans of food, showing them, jumbling them in her hands, a little excited. "I knew if I just prayed, it'd be fine. We'd be fine. And…" She didn't finish her thought, throwing the canned goods back into the pantry. "Whaddya want for breakfast? Pears or peaches?" She took two of them out, plopping the cans on the table. "Tell ya what," She interrupted my words before I even spoke. "Let's mix and match. A little bit of both for each of us!" She produced a can opener, going for the peaches first. I noticed the wrinkled wrapper on it as she stuck the old-fashioned twist opener on the peaches can, laying her lower body down before the table to open the thing. I picked up the pear can, feeling over the brittle, faded wrapper.

"March 2022," I read the expiration date. "You sure this shit won't kill us?"

"So far," She chuckled dourly. "We've been eating this stuff for a couple days now, since we got here sometime last week. Guy who must've owned this place hasn't been here for a while and didn't have the place *that* well stocked, there's about a weeks worth of food, but we'll make it last. You… You were lucid enough to eat, but… it wasn't like I wasn't still afraid I'd lose you." I smiled meekly back, going to reach for a coffee cup sitting there to pour myself some.

"I lost a lot of blood; to be honest I still don't quite feel that great," I muttered, before motioning to my leg with the mug after I'd poured a generous helping of sugar in. "…Even without all that."

"Yeah, you must have gotten attacked by a mountain lion," She uttered after sipping quite a bit of the canning syrup out of the can so it wouldn't spill, making sure as little as possible went to waste before moving onto the pear can. I let my eyes widen, figuring it would be better to make her think it wasn't quite as dire a situation as it really was.

"Yeah, fucker caught me unawares," I let out my lie of omission, scratching the back of my neck as I sipped, tasting the bittersweet drink. It really needed cream, but sugar alone was a lot to hope for anyways. I was grateful for what I had, including my life and the love of my life to rescue me, now that I dwelled on it. "I shouldn't have gotten that excited. I don't think we'll find another deer out here. I was just hungry," She finished opening it, hefting it towards me, offering me the canning juice. "...I've got my coffee," I sipped the stuff. "Little weak, though."

"I think I'm getting better at grinding it. Gotta kind of wing a lot of it, you know I'm no G..." She stopped dead, whole body going rigid for a second as she avoided his name at the last moment. Dead air hung in the cabin like a solitary note played on a piano, of what was once a heartwarming serenade that froze uncomfortably in place. This paradise was nothing of the sort. The real world still swirled around us. Around me.

But despite all that, we were together and things were good, for the time being, and we tried to appreciate the fact.

**Chapter 70**

The days would pass as we healed. It wasn't as bad as it could have been, at least not at first. My biggest problem was getting to the outhouse with this leg of mine, which was kind of a silly problem, all things considered. Lauren would be out foraging during the days while I did what I could to make the place nicer with my limited mobility, if only to keep occupied. There were a couple books to read, clothes Lauren would clean in the river to fold. We kept pretty busy, Lauren going out no matter the weather, sometimes bringing back a rabbit or a squirrel but most days just mushrooms and edible flowers. This place really was a godsend, quite literally if Lauren had anything to say about it, as she often did. Every night she would read us to sleep with the bible. She stuck to the new testament most of all, enamored with Jesus. I guess he was a pretty great guy, and her giddiness for the messages hardly came off as saccharine to me. Maybe if it was anyone else reading me this I would have scoffed, the messages saved by Lauren's infectious love rubbing off on me like it did.

There was only one bed in here, a twin sized bed that we really couldn't share, and though I'm sure she did when I was in my comatose state, now she bashfully tried to work around how she was essentially sleeping at the side of my bed on the bearskin rug like a dog, usually by slinking her humanoid portion onto the bed by at first balling up the rug to raise up towards the relatively short bed like a ramp, until I realized that we could just put the mattress on the ground and use the bedpost as firewood, making her blush madly at her overthinking of the situation. I laughed to get her to laugh with me, pressing my lips against her frustratedly red blushing cheeks and finally getting her to lighten up and kiss me back, snickering at her own tremendous foolishness before we laid down together all wrapped up in each other. It was kind of a shame to use the bedpost for the fire, seeing as somebody put a lot of care into making it from what they could get from the forest. I supposed I felt bad about bogarting the whole place, but figured that whoever owned this place last, living or dead, probably would have been glad that somebody got some use out of it, especially life-saving. Lauren was sure to give thanks at every meal and before bedtime to not only god and jesus but also whoever our mysterious benefactor was. This place was probably some old hunter's hideaway, and given the age of the stuff in here and the disrepair it lay in, we doubted that he was still with us, especially not with this war going on. He could have died peacefully in his sleep ages ago, he could have been shot in the back trying to get here to wait the war out, who knows. Lauren prayed for his soul in heaven nonetheless, thanking him profusely, even apologizing for taking his stuff. I guess just thinking about him sort of gave me a mental image of a lumberjack santa claus, some invisible saint who probably unintentionally saved our skin when we needed it most.

Sometimes, when my leg at the very least didn't need to be bandaged any more, we'd go for walks in the woods. Not really to hunt but more to just be together, get some fresh air. We'd go to the nearby hot spring where we could freshen up and I could massage Lauren's healing wing, as her wing got to the point where she could discard her casts. "I bet I'm almost healed!" She'd say, before trying to move it and let out a little "ow", re-slinging it with a dour look, not without a sparkle in her eyes that spoke of the progress she was making. "When it's healed all the way," She spoke brightly, as we lay together one night. "We can fly right out of this stupid place."

"I like it here," I uttered back.

"I mean, it's pretty, but y'know. Got places to be."

"I like it because it's simple. There's not much to worry about. Not much to complicate. Don't you feel that?" I asked, looking her in the eye, able to see her just barely by the shine of the dying fire. "Feel like as long as we're here together, the world is alright."

"Yeah, but…" She trailed off. "You know our friends are out there. Worried about us." I sighed heavily.

"…Yeah. But… But we taught them well. I think they can make do for a little while."


But this paradise was temporary, just as I knew it would be. The food didn't last very long, even if augmented with what Lauren could find. I was ravenously hungry, and given my recovery, Lauren refused to let me go without. I did heal a good amount, and eventually Lauren constructed a better brace for letting me limp about once I'd healed enough, but it was anything but ergonomic and I needed a staff to get around, one that I whittled out of a branch with the knife the old man left here. The hunger would get to us even if we didn't say anything, and even with having this amount of food for this little while Lauren had still dropped a lot of weight from when we were in Shortstone. Neither of us had any baby fat left, and Lauren couldn't stand to see my ribs poking through my skin and would cover herself up as best she could to get me to eat instead, but I knew we were both hungry. She'd make jokes about how much easier flying will be with the two of us so much lighter, and though we gave weak smiles we knew it wasn't funny in the least. Her wing's healing slowed down with our food down to what she could scrounge from the forest, and the fact that she wouldn't eat sometimes just to make sure I was fed only exacerbated the situation.

One night, when that day all she could find were some mushrooms and algae, we laid awake amid the pain of hunger. I guess when physiologically you are miserable, the mind tends to follow. Like doom was just around the corner. Lauren's wing was hardly healing anymore and she was in no shape to fly, let alone take off the sling for her wing. Even my leg, the scars around my ankle looked like at any moment they would revert to bleeding again. Must have been that insanity. Even as we lay here amid the dying fire, our very bodies seemed cold. The wind was getting colder outside, new plants to eat were not even growing. Winter was coming, and so too was our demise. We could feel it.

"You know," I uttered, breaking the silence. Neither of us was asleep, it was heavy on the air. Doom was heavy on the air. "They say… Starving to death is blissful."

"D-don't… Don't talk like that," Lauren whined weakly, but by how she said it I knew she felt it too.

"It's…" I went on, as if she'd never spoke. "It's when you try *not* to starve. You keep trying to eat things even when you know it's not enough and you're going to starve… That makes it the worst thing you can do. It's agony." Lauren's eyes were shining at me in the darkness. "I don't want to go out like that, Lauren. Just…" I didn't know how to say what I wanted. I wanted her to just die with me, with dignity, but when I thought that I knew how ridiculous it was. Practically insulting.

"Noah, you… you have to pray," She uttered. She was weeping in silence, as when I looked back at her streams were flowing down her cheeks. "You… You must. God will… God will…" She knew what she had to say was ridiculous too, made ridiculous by the stabbing pains in her own stomach. God will provide. We just have to stay faithful. She believed, but not enough to say it.

"You know what," I said, as if starting anew. It didn't feel like a topic change even if it was. It was on my mind ever since I watched his lifeless eye screaming in agony. "G-Gabriel…" Lauren's eyes shut as her lips trembled, more tears flowing. Trying not to sob but she couldn't help it, letting out tiny whines as she breathed. I could feel my face grow wet despite how I didn't think I was crying. I didn't feel it. I just felt numb. "He… I couldn't even hear his last words," I finally burst out into a sob. "I just… I want to see him again."

"N-no," Lauren barked out of a sob. "Gabriel wouldn't want you to die here. He wouldn't just…" She trailed off, just laying her head on my chest, her outstretched arm coming to the soft of my side to grip me, but she couldn't help but feel my floating rib and my hips, my skin taut and fatless, only making her sob further.

"My best friend died and I couldn't even hear him," I hushed. "He was with me and he still died alone. He used us and… And he was trying to apologize," I couldn't believe the words coming from my mouth. Like a revelation, while really it was more just what really happened and I could finally bear to think about it, coming to terms with the fact that my best friend's death even *happened*.

"I… I miss him too," Lauren whispered to keep from sobbing. "And I miss his cooking too. I'm not nearly as good as him." She laughed out and I laughed too, chuckling to keep from crying more, but as our chuckles subsided only tears remained.

"You… you've never had fast food," I uttered in realization, maybe trying to keep things light with a joke, but food was very much on our mind.

"…I've had a burger when we made it out of that first deer," Lauren uttered.

"That's… Venison. You haven't had a real beef burger with everything on it, lettuce, pickles, tomatoes, onions- and, and with french fries. Lauren… you've never had *french fries*."

"I… Yeah, I haven't," She smiled weakly, trying to play things off, but now I was the one breaking down again.

"You haven't even had french fries. You can't die yet, born and raised in America and you've never had french fries," We burst into sad, sobbing laughter yet again.

"…They have french fries at the citadel?" Lauren asked.

"Yeah, we grow potatoes and fry them up. Organic style, not stupid synthesized potatoes all smashed up and shaped into sticks full of additives- *real* french fries. The best of the best, crisp on the outside, soft on the inside, heaps of salt and pepper, not too starchy, not too oily…" I realised talking about food didn't exactly make the agony of its absence subscede so I stopped, trailing off.

"…I forgive him," Lauren uttered. "I think I can forgive Gabriel now." I looked to her hand, where she clutched her little crux-baton hanging from its chain. Gabriel's tooth in a little capsule hanging next to it. All that was left of the bastard clutched in her quivering green hand, her knuckles turning white from the pressure. "I think I know why I hit him with this," She held up the crux, that symbol of the trinity, holding it between her fingers like brass knuckles like she did that night she blew his tooth out. "I wanted to hurt him. Hurt him because the Pendrews were dead and that nice dragon man just looking out for his family was dead and even that pilot was dead and it was all his fault. I could have punched him with my bare fist, but he's… It's barely like he was a human himself. He was a monster, bare hands can't hurt him, not like how I wanted to hurt him. I… I think that's what I really regret. I couldn't forgive him then, when he was alive, because I was weak."

"Gabriel... Gabriel didn't-"

"I know he doesn't deserve it, deserve forgiveness, but that's what I should have done. Because we were friends- We were more than friends. We were *family* and that's what we do. We don't... hurt each other on purpose. Even if they deserve it. We all deserved to die for being around him, according to some people. A lot of people. But we didn't. We don't get the horribleness that we deserve and that's how I know god is kind. We should always forgive."

"...Did Gabe's *boss* deserve... Should *he* have been forgiven?"

"Maybe. Maybe if I was in Gabriel's position I would have forgiven him. I'd like to think I would have. But I've never known anyone as horrible as him, at least not from Gabriel's point of view, whatever he did to him to make him hate him that much. I've only seen a sliver of what really happened and there's no way for me to know... Maybe, even, Gabriel *was* god's justice for that man. I don't know. I can never know. But..." She was looking off into the distance now, enamored by the stars outside the misty window. Maybe just zoning out, her gaze a million miles away. "God knows. And god redeems. I believe Gabriel is redeemed and I could never be happier for him. And if Gabriel can be redeemed... That's how I know God is kind, and He will see us through this." I just laid my hand upon her back, patting her. "I'm gonna find a deer tomorrow. I know god will provide. I just know it and that's how I know."

I couldn't be as certain as her, but the doom above our heads seemed to hang a little further away now, and I could sleep a dreamless sleep.

I woke up and Lauren was gone. Away in the forest with her rifle. I'd brew some pine needle tea for breakfast; I may have made all that song and dance about just letting myself blissfully starve to death but I guess I hadn't the willpower to see that through, or maybe it was that Lauren had inspired that survival-to-the-bitter-end mindset in me. I couldn't know. Just like I couldn't know she was wrong. I must say I was excited to see her return as I waited those agonizing hours alone, if she'd really bag a deer off of the providence of god. I told myself it was manic folly inspired by hunger, both in her and in me, but nonetheless I felt that hope in the air. God is good, isn't he?

When she returned, she was running. Bolting full-tilt across the fields, rifle in hands. She got close and I saw no deer, no foraged edibles. All I could see was terror in her eyes.

"Noah," She burst in, huffing steamy breath as she donkey-kicked the door shut, no time to turn and shut it with an arm, going for my rifle in the corner and shoving it in my arms. Terror in her eyes. Like this was the end, not two or three weeks from now when we wither away to bones, but that death was already here. I took my rifle, turning to the window as she locked and barred the door. She didn't even have to say anything, simply saying my name to shut me up and get serious. Maybe she meant to say something after that but forgot, occupied with paranoia. I didn't have to ask. I knew even before they broke the treeline. Figures moving across the open field at a brisk pace, a light jog. The hair on my neck was on end. "Noah..." She said again as they approached. A dozen, maybe more, a couple on horseback skirting the flanks and one all the way in the back, unarmed yet wearing power armor, full helm and all watching the proceedings with his arms crossed over his OICW weapon magnetically holstered to his chest, just having his arms crossed to watch the proceedings. I didn't know what he looked like but I sure as hell could practically see his smug grin as he stood there and directed his troops- and the fact that behind him billowed a ground-length purple cape twirling off his shoulders, his smug aura only grew. I was looking through my magnified optic and I saw a plethora of blue armbands, yet some of their soldiers weren't even flying colors, even if they all seemed relatively well armed and equipped. We weren't shooting our way out of here, outnumbered and outgunned, that was for sure. "I... I don't think I can fly us out of here," She uttered. She didn't seem as worried as she was supposed to be. Neither was I, For that matter. Maybe it was the hunger, maybe it was death already looming over our heads.

"Alright, come out of there and come with us. This doesn't have to be ugly," one of the higher-ranked ones said through his megaphone, though the power armored one in charge kept his pose. It didn't take us long to walk outside with our hands up.

All we really could hope for was a bite to eat.

The hunger would have to wait as we were... *escorted* to their base. It was strange how I could almost ignore how we were prisoners and it really felt like we weren't, we were just walking along there with them. All they really did was take our guns, not our knives or even our ammo. I could almost swear we were doing this of our own volition.

I was on one of the horses, being led along by the biter by one of the soldiers, some tough looking female canid. I noted how they seemed rather diverse, men and women of all stripes and shapes surrounding us. Lauren wanted to carry me but their captain had given an order through their comms, without letting us prisoners hear his voice. Strange, but they still took into account how I couldn't walk, putting me on one of the horses. We were still escorted close-by to each other at a low voice's distance, again, almost like they seemed to be taking our feelings into perspective, respecting our wishes to keep us together. Like we weren't even prisoners. Mind games, I figured. Good cop before the bad. The sickness of waiting for the other shoe to drop was what was really getting to me.

And there he was, their captain. The closest to the two of us, heading us up right behind. I could feel his gaze underneath his impenetrable helmet. When he spoke I could only tell because of all the personnel nearby reacting to his voice in their headset over the radio, silent to us, his active voice projector turned off, completely muted by his helmet and an enigma to us.

"Hey," I uttered, turned around in the saddle on the horse. "Hey. Buckethead," I grunted, trying to get a rise out of the hulking captain towering behind us. I could tell how his gait shifted and his head slightly turned that he definitely heard me. "What's the deal with being so nice?" no response. "You guys found us in the middle of the forest staying as far away from the war as we can get. I thought that was a capital crime to you people. You gonna hang us in the town square or some shit instead of just shooting us on the spot? Make an example?"

"Heh." he unmuted his ambient voice just to let us hear him chuckle. I saw Lauren's head turn to mine a little, eyes sparkling in fear. I only reciprocated the look, though in my mind I tried to analyze his voice to whatever paltry degree I could. It was modulated through the software of the helmet, but it couldn't hide how his voice sounded hardly deep. Like a boy, but reserved. Like he'd won, and he certainly thought a lot of himself, but he was hardly gloating. Something was going on that I was far from aware of and that was terrifying in its own right. The look in Lauren's eyes was simple and to-the-point. Fear, bewilderment. Bewilderment more than the other, at just what was to become of us, why we weren't being treated like criminals.

The journey passed with the day before we came upon an ancient mining pit, excavated deep into the earth a century ago where the forest ended abruptly to become this great crater, a sickly lake repurposed as an aquaponics garden at its pit and their encampment encircling it upon the spiral descent to the bottom. It wasn't exactly a fortress, more of a garrison, and even then it wasn't much. The beginnings of battlements were being erected, a wall of wooden logs encircling the compound yet so far from complete. It was rather sparse for a war camp, and it seemed there were more conscripts than soldiers about. Slaves, you could even call them, working in the gardens and workshops. Hybrids and humans alike in their ranks and their indentured servants, this diversity again being something I'd noticed in the unit that had captured us already. However, I took a quick notice that it seemed like the hard labor and militia units lacked female hybrids that weren't canids or felinids, female dragons being completely absent from these roles.

I hardly had time to turn to notice Lauren being escorted in a different direction before I was rushed into medical. Doctors were upon me, that power armored leader of theirs gazing into the hermetically-sterilized tent for a single moment before whisking away as I was rather forcibly laid down, a sleeping gas mask shoved on my face by the medical technicians before I lost consciousness. My dreams were tumultuous, like screaming into a pillow. Nothing but writhing against the black oblivion of nothingness until I was suddenly awake, and the real show began.

## Chapter 71

I, gasping for air, sprang straight up to sit in the bed, as the world's memories caught up to me and I recalled the last day through the haze of myself. Cognizant once more, I noted how I was hooked up to an IV and I had an actual self-propelled brace on my leg, with a pneumatic hinge and all. I retched, feeling a feeding tube down my throat that I slowly hoisted out. That explained why I wasn't famished anymore, even if seeing the grey-brown protein paste oozing out of its orifice made me want to retch, able to sort of forget about it and focus on my leg. It was almost like I felt like I'd healed a week's worth in that one night. I'd probably been given a metabolic inducer, and given how long this war had gone on and how rare that stuff must be by now, that felt like especially strange treatment. Were we really even prisoners?

Lauren. I'd noticed her laying by my bed on a mattress on the ground, kicking in her sleep beneath a blanket. Not some scratchy surplus army blanket but one that looked soft, well-tended. So did my bedding, too, only adding to my strange suspicions. She lay there, and I was bewildered. Had she demanded to sleep near me? What had she gone through? My blood ran cold for a solitary moment, but I saw her kicking in her sleep some more, muttering concernedly with grit teeth. Hardly having a good dream. I threw my legs out of bed, prodding her with my good leg and her eyes blasted open with a jolt of her body, the spell of her nightmare broken, looking to me and rising.

"You know what's going on?" I asked as she stood. She didn't look glad to see me, even if she was. She looked increasingly uncomfortable.

"W-what time is it?" She asked. It was still a little dark out. It must have been very early. I hadn't even been woken by reverie playing, it was just from sleeping a good 13 hours straight on top of a boosted metabolism. "N-Noah, we should probably… That guy…" She couldn't quite get the words out, pausing for a long while to work out her thoughts while rubbing sleep from her eyes and straightening out her blouse- a real, new shirt somebody had given her. I saw her wing sling, an honest-to-god wing sling. It looked like it was made purpose-built. "Noah, there's something weird going on with their leader."

"Yeah, I could guess that much yesterday," I limped out of bed and Lauren was upon me, wordlessly insisting I ride and I obliged her, as she briskly trotted towards the door flap. No guards, just open air as we exited. "Let's get our-"

"MISTER, NOAH, REED!" three shrill yells from above before I could hardly perceive anything else, as terrifying as the crack of a sniper's shot. I wheeled about where I sat to gaze upwards, seeing a figure leaning over the balcony. The field hospital was just below a large building on the edge of the spiral downwards into the mine, the oldest building here, an overlook over the entire mine. And upon its balcony was a man of pale skin, stark naked and leaned there against the rails, pale skin held taut against his lithe musculature, topped off by a head of flowing golden hair.

"You told him my name?!" I hissed in her ear, already surmising this was their eccentric, power-armored leader from yesterday.

"I didn't tell him; he already knew it! Something weird is going on!" She hushed back to me over her shoulder and goosebumps grew on my neck.

"Now now, I'm glad you two're awake! How's breakfast sound? Crepes good with the both of you? Crepes and bacon!" I heard the camp crier begin to play reverie from the guard tower on the opposite end of the pit, my eyes straying to see the mess hall's fires a ways away nearer to the barracks, its fires producing smoke and steam that rose into the air, breakfast for the troops.

"...You serve your troops crepes?!" I thumbed towards their mess hall.

"Don't be ridiculous, Mr. Reed! Only the good ones! Now, come on up here so I can introduce myself properly!" Lauren turned around some more to let one of her eyes look me in mine, ear flicking. I shrugged, confused.

"What's up with this guy? What does he want?" I asked again as we walked briskly up the spiral of the mine, to go up a level towards his weird little mansion.

"I dunno, he said he liked you."

"What? Why, because I called him a cunt?"

"I dunno, maybe? he didn't seem that insulted about that anyways!" She uttered. "I think he wants to like... hire you, or something," She explained.

"Hire me? What, why?!"

"I don't know! Don't act like I didn't ask; he just kept being vague! He wouldn't tell me!"

"Do you have any *ideas*?" She was silent for a while as she trotted along at her brisk pace, looking down at the ground as she went. I couldn't see her face but I could imagine she was quieted by her own thoughts and wondering.

"He... I dunno. It's weird."

"...Yeah?"

"No, I mean... The situation, he... I think he might want to hire you because of me, or something."

"...What?"

"He, uh... *Really* likes dragons. Us." We were approaching the building, Lauren slowing. I saw the two guards at the door there, stepping aside to open the two doors and leading us in, the doors slamming shut behind us in this foyer. It was surprisingly well-furnished, even so much as to roll out a red carpet for us. Art hanging here, pilfered from museums and galleries no doubt. I could hear the clinking of dining ware being set in a distant room.

"I give you a perfectly good self-propelled brace and you use your dear, beautiful dragoness as a beast of burden? Tsk, tsk." Our eyes were drawn up to a second-floor landing up two flanking flights of stairs, and there he was, their commander. At least he was wearing pants now, in addition to the flowing purple cape draped behind him, the one for his armor that he continued to wear. He looked ridiculous with the big thing trailing on the ground, descending the stairs as I carefully dismounted Lauren. "My apologies, you two seem to have caught me in the middle of my morning exercise routine. Need to stay fit, you know. I didn't think you'd be up so soon." He approached Lauren on the side opposite me, producing his hand. Lauren awkwardly took it, and he held her hand to his lips to kiss her just below the wrist, bowing as he did. "Good morning, my lady-"

"Hey- HEY!" I lunged forward, letting my hand fall on his caped shoulder.

"My my, possessive, are we," He murred. I was stopped just short from striking him as he stood aghast.

"*Noah,*" Lauren's voice fell upon me just like my hand had fallen upon him, weighting me with worry and apprehension. In that pause he shrugged my hand off of himself.

"Hmph," He spun as I teetered there, cape whipping around as he proceeded towards the dining hall of this strange place. "You said yesterday you are not a man of war, yet here you are quick to violence. Ho hum."

"Just who the fuck are you and what do you want? And why do you talk like that?" We were off, following him down the halls. More art, paintings strung up on the walls as we proceeded.

"Mr. Reed, as for the easier to answer question, I speak like this because it is *fun*. Just as you prefer scale to flesh, as it is more *enjoyable*- ah, a figure of speech, as the draconic hybrid technically has no scal-"

"*Excuse me?*" I spat as he came upon the large door at the end of the hall, putting both hands up upon its great wooden frame, leaning in.

"There is something tragically *mundane* about our species, is there not?" he whipped his head to me as he leaned there, smiling devilishly through only his shining eyes. "And what is not mundane is unsightly- noses like mountains rising inexplicably above the sands of a desert, ears like freakish craters blown out of their foundations- Nonetheless, our flawed forms do not excite... those of us with *taste*." The door was open and I really understood, for the first time today. Draconic women, a smorgasbord of them from wall to wall, seated around the table, dressed up nice- though a bit sultry upon any sort of critical examination. He turned with a wide smile beaming on his smug face to see my slack jaw, waving me over to a side of the long table. Our seats- well, my seat and an empty place for Lauren with dining ware set for her and I at the very corner of the table, this commander standing before us and bidding us to sit. I saw his set, or what I presumed to be his set to my left at the head of the table, before looking back at him. Rather than just walk around behind us he made his way in the opposite direction, counter-clockwise around the whole table, sure to name off each of his prized girls by name. Reds and blues and oranges and sapphire skins, unique patterns of horns and fins and great wings behind each. Each one would swoon, or simply feign it, as he came upon each, profusely blessing and kissing and groping as he pleased. I could feel the scowling frown on my face growing.

"Oh my, I can see you're not that much of a fan of him, Mister Reed," I heard a voluptuous, sultry voice proclaim. I turned my head, seeing an exceptionally well-dressed, blue-and-green dragoness without horns or hair slowly stirring the tea in her crystal goblet, a hand propping her head up on its side on the table, eyes not even looking up away from her mindless task, an ear more akin to a fin on a fish flicking. "And you- You poor beast. He really fancies a hapless creature like you?" She had that same sort of tone that he did. Maybe he'd picked it up from these dragons, as I heard a couple of them speak like that. Maybe it was the way he spoke rubbing off on them instead. Either way it was strange enough to notice.

"E-excuse me?" Lauren muttered confusedly.

"Oh, you could do *so* much better," She rolled her eyes back to me, nodding her head towards Lauren with condescension rife in her voice. "Brains to back the bestial body. I'd expect charming wit in lieu of beauty, but find none. You could do so much better than this *centaurical* pack animal."

"H-hey!" Lauren growled, brow furrowing. "Fuck you, you... bald bitch!"

"Yeah, *fuck* you, don't talk to her that way," I backed Lauren and this critic rolled her eyes.

"Well, you'll just have to do the thinking for the both of you," She sighed to me, completely unbothered.

"Yeah, well, at least I don't have stupid fins on my head," Lauren took another shot back. "Blue skin. *Shape of Water* lookin-ass."

"Yeah, shouldn't you go back to your *swamp*?" I snapped, throwing my hand out towards Lauren and she took it in our little show of solidarity, like a weird high-five handshake.

"Oh, would you like to go off of a base mocking of appearance now? Very well then; darling, you could win a nostalgia contest with that mullet, it's very twentieth century," Lauren paused for a second, hand going to her neck, feeling her spinal tuft beneath her scalp of hair, cognizant of how it ran all the way down her long back and tail. I saw her blush, jaw clenching with wild, frustrated eyes. "And flannel? Ugh. Are you sure you don't fancy your own gender with your telltale fashion sense?" This dragoness seemed to really be getting to Lauren now, too angry to really respond, her face more red than green at this point. "Look, you miserable idiots. It's pain enough sharing my husband with all these other, baser creatures. Let me have my moment of lament." Lauren didn't say anything, simply pursing her lip and furrowing her brow in notable frustration while this rather full-of-herself dragoness looked to her left, seeing the commander still giving his goodmornings to each dragon woman seated there. "God, he really fancies himself a womanizer, doesn't he? A spoiled child with power getting to his head."

"...You don't seem that enamored with him," Lauren snarled bitterly.

"Maybe not the man himself. But his power, however... I'm sure you can relate, given the supposed tactical prowess of your boytoy," She finally gave the two of us a little smile, winking rapidly with a little giggle as her supposed beau came upon her and interrupted that thought, wrapping his arms around her back as she feigned a swoon, receiving many a kiss to the top and sides of her head. She continued to giggle and let herself be charmed as his hands crawled down to her breasts for a quick squeeze and a vocal utterance of pleasure.

"And Tanya, my dear, *le piece de resistance*," He praised and this dragon girl, Tanya, let out a ladylike giggle, still smiling at the two of us as he slid away to take her by the chin and plant a kiss right on her lips, one of his hands still solidly placed on her bosom. "*Mon cherie sans égal.*"

"Oho, *stop*, daaarling," Tanya winked as he whipped away from her to take his seat ever so boisterously, before clapping twice. In came the attendants- more hybrids, this time serpentine types, those who had the lower body of an especially large snake rather than legs, and sometimes faces more like a snake than a human, sometimes more human faces and upper-body skintones, each one dressed in a rather ridiculous maid outfit coming in to bring us platters of food. My eyes went to Lauren's first, seeing her similarly perplexed and slightly uncomfortable look, then over to the captain who was beaming, looking his servants over with very, *very* attentive fascination.

"Looking excellent this morning, Anastasia! Maureanne, ever so voluptuous!" He would call to each of them as they slithered on out, each one polite enough to curtsey or nod appreciatively towards him, one or two of them getting into the performance a little bit, as the final one came out slithering towards us. The captain didn't bark out her name just yet, grinning devilishly as she approached, eyes low and avoiding all contact with them. She was one of the less humanoid types with a snout and bright cherry red scales covering her whole body, save for her sharply contrasting blue underbelly and accents lining her figure every here and there as well as bright blue eyes, her most humanoid characteristic- aside from the sapience evident in her eyes and face- being her shoulder-length curly fire-blonde hair, which was a bit strange given her phylogeny, and if it wasn't for the scales of her somewhat more snakelike face being that same fiery color I could have sworn she was blushing, and not in any sort of charmed way. Rather like she was genuinely embarrassed dressed like that, setting that platter down before us and taking the lid.

"Here you go, sir. I hope you enjoy it very m-"

"Here you go *master*," The captain corrected.

"Yes... Master. I'll remember next time."

"Yes, yes you will, Adrianne. I may have to discipline you yet," He was thumbing his lip as he glared hungrily towards her as she clutched the lid to her chest, almost like she was covering herself up, still avoiding looking at him, uttering a "yes master" as she turned, though as she spun about I could see her eyes flash to me for a sheer second before she was gone, slithering back away meekly. I could have sworn I read terror and helplessness on her face. "Ah, see," He uttered, swirling his own drink as he stabbed into a couple crepes and served himself the fresh fruits and a couple slices of bacon charred to a crisp. "Adrianne, Adrianne. Found her and her hapless imbecile of a lover scrounging around in the ruins of Colville just south of here. I got her washed and prettied up, gave her hopeless romantic of a boyfriend a job, and yet she walks- er, *slithers*, on eggshells around me. Like I am some comical, hypercapitalist villain. But I know I'll win her over. I'd rank up her boy toy from simple indentured laborer to a soldier to show my earnesty, but he's not good for much more than digging holes. Perhaps I should resort to a King David maneuver and get him disposed of. Suicide mission might do the trick, and if he comes back alive, then he well and truly does deserve a promotion," He uttered, bursting into guffaws, along Tanya joining in with the forced laughter, Lauren and I left with our lips curled up in disgust for a long while before he playfully knurled his knuckles into my shoulder as he leaned over. "Come on, I'm sure it's not been that long since you've heard a *joke*, Mr. Reed."

"I'm sorry, what exactly do you want with us?"

"Ah, the literal or *royal* us? There needs to be a delineation, because there are things I want with you, and things I want with *you*, the colloquial you, the *vous*, *vosotros*, if you will," He stuffed food into his face as he let his words sink in. "You and I- See, I believe you and I have something in common, that I've alluded to. Something I'm sure the two of us can bond over. I've a fondness for scales, and I've come to the rather well-founded assumption that you and I share this affinity. I'd like you to take a look around the room, take the look you've been embarrassedly trying to fight from doing. To ogle. Yes, your S.O. may be sitting right beside you, but let me assure you that this is an order, as your *captor*, if you will. Please, oblige me. Feast your eyes," He waved his knife like a magic wand as he chewed, and I took another look around the room, even pausing on his so-called wife Tanya who winked at me, smiling appreciatively and gawking down at my form through the thin, size-too-small shirt I was wearing, making me self-conscious for but a moment. I saw the maid-dressed serpentine girls lining the rim of the room, waiting to wait on us. Adrianne standing with her tail coiled beneath her right behind the two of us, hands cupped at her waist, still looking at a low level and to the right to avoid the commander's gaze. I returned my eyes to him as he sat there smugly. "See, Noah, I must admit that in some ways I wasn't the perfect *comrade*. For example I do this cute little show of racial favoritism out of my appreciation of the scaled aesthetic, admittedly rather... Colonial, but *sharing*- now that's an ideal worth holding onto. To spread the means of *reproduction*, if you would," He smiled smugly at his pun. "Take your pick of any fine individual in this room. They are as much yours as they are mine. Yes, even the servants."

"You tell this to anybody with a scaly girlfriend you kidnap? How about Adrianne's boyfriend slaving away down in that pit of yours?" He took a moment to laugh right on back.

"He's a nobody. I share just for the ones that are worth the fanfare. Besides, none of these women are exclusive to me. Each and every delectable creature here has their significant other under my employ."

"Save for me, darling. I'm all yours," His "wife" Tanya uttered dreamily, fluttering her lashes.

"And my, *are you,*" He grinned back at her.

"Worth the fanfare?" I repeated back out of curiosity.

"...Mr. Reed," He smacked his lips to draw his eyes onto me, ready to meet my inquisition with yet more delineation, leading me conversationally down a path I couldn't quite predict. "What was your opinion of the Battle of Shortstone?"

"E-excuse me?"

"I find it quite intriguing. I've heard the opinions from those involved on both sides, I like to document the happenings, the unfolding of history, the closing of an act upon this great stage that is the earth. I've heard many opinions on it, an episode in futility, a valiant last stand, so much deception on the others' part, so much blood and sound and fire for nothing. As undoubtedly one of the final throes of this stupid, pointless conflict, most would wonder if it was even necessary. To what ends, to whose goals. Thousands dead because 'we had to', while millions died that day from the pandemic alone. The world is shutting down around us and we had a ourselves a massive battle out of *obligation.*" He paused to take a sip, leaning back confidently in his chair. "The world shrinks around us. I couldn't tell you what happened with California's invasion of Arizona or the war in the east coast or midwest, let alone what has been happening in Mexico or Eastern Canada. The world becomes white noise out of our immediate vicinity. Countries, continents disappear entirely. I for one, can appreciate that simplicity. I can work with my men, not pointless orders to throw myself upon the bayonets of republican troops fruitlessly."

"...So the war's over and you work for yourself now," Lauren interjected finally. "You think you're some kind of warlord?"

"Feudalism may oppose itself to socialism my dear, the latter of which I happen to endear myself to, but at the end of the day in both systems those above you decide where you work, if you eat. At the very least I can attest to having earned what sits around me, rather than some oligarch sitting on high in Sacramento or Greater Vancouver. My men trust me, they trust my judgement. Take heed, one day tasteless capitalists will be putting my face on shirts, just like Che." He scoffed at his own self-aggrandizement, as if he was truly self aware and not dead serious in what he said.

"So you're the eccentric-yet-proud king of a gravel pit and you kidnap people to enslave, take their stuff, so you can build an empire. Kinda reminds me of a thing. You ever watched any of the *Mad Max* movies?" Lauren snarled. His lip quivered upwards in a little laugh, heaving his chest a little as he beamed at her.

"Quite the wit, I must say," He smiled cheekily at Lauren, Tanya rolling her eyes dramatically, as he let his elbows fall back upon the table, intertwining his fingers to stare over them at us. "You think of me as a ravaging warlord, and yet go on to speak truth to power without hesitation. My, I *like* you." His eyes lingered on her before snapping to me. "If such heroism is the company you seek to keep, Noah, I must say that puts a lot of your actions into context. What a noteworthy segue back into our topic. Mister Reed, I have gotten many testimonies of this battle from many sides, save for one. The antipartisan troupe that beheaded Shortstone's Republican chain of command- rather literally- and forced the Democrat hand into an attack of opportunity, spurring on this pointless bloodshed." He paused again, to point with as few motions of his body as possible, most of him not moving an inch as he pointed to the platters before us. "You should help yourself to some food, you know. It will get cold soon." He pointed, still letting his bombshell sink in. "Please. I insist. Eat." I obliged, if only to get him to get back to the topic at hand in a dreamlike fascination.

"So…" I said after taking a single bite. It'd been so long since I had hot food that hadn't come out of a can, let alone soaked in butter and fried to a delightful crisp. I really was famished just by the sight of the delicious food, but it was like now that something far juicer was before me it all just turned to grey sludge in my mouth. I needed to know, even if I tried to play it all off. "You think I was one of these… Antipartisans?"

"*Think*. If only. It is more than a thought." He let himself chuckle for a long while. "A fascinating case study. Trapped between two opposing forces as the battle commenced. Your only goal was evacuation, and by all accounts, your operation was a flawless success. Using your besieged rally point as bait to wait for the heavy metal with the means to jeopardize your evacuation to reveal itself, before piloting your support gunship out of the blue, and two priceless bolo tanks and hundreds of personnel- and their massive offensive- go up in smoke. Of any side in that battle, yours was the only one to have really won. Just get out alive, achieved with flying colors. Like god was on your side that day. But more than that, you… A much more direct *vous*, if you will. *You two* in particular wait to draw the remaining forces into the building to distract from chasing your evacuation, and detonate it as you fly away. What tremendous daring for you, an utter embarrassment for us. What a callousness for life on the parts of my fellow commanding officers, sending their men into yet another obvious trap. If it wasn't for you, the democrat forces would have never invaded and taken Shortstone, and yet if it wasn't for you, our offensive would not have been such a disastrous pyrrhic victory." He sipped again. "So, how about it? What was your take on the battle?"

I chewed slowly, swallowing. "*It was terrifying.*" He smirked smugly.

"Not much more to it than that, eh? A housecat trapped between two fighting lions. Lucky to get away with the skin on your back, but you must admit you got far more than that. You humiliated us. We would refuse to acknowledge that you in this incident were anything but republicans up until the chain of command broke down and this war finally ground to a halt mere days later. Blasphemy to think the Democratic Allied Armies of California, Oregon, Washington and British Columbia were bested by a couple dozen filthy fence-sitters, plucky or not."

"You don't seem that mad I killed a bunch of your guys."

"That was when this was a war, a war that practically died on that battlefield. Anybody left who gives a shit is too busy starving or dying of the plague to care. I'm in this for my own skin now, so we're on the same side, where I'm sitting." He smiled smugly and sipped again on his drink. "Now, my real question being- why did you do it? Why take out the republican general if your only goal was to stay out of trouble?" I froze. My mind went to Gabriel. For the second I paused, he could read me, read the twinkle in the wettening of my eyes as I looked down. He tipped back, my emotions betraying my thoughts, at least to the extent he could read. "Ahh," He gasped. "It was personal, wasn't it? Quite a story?"

"What makes you think you deserve to know?" My voice had risen to a stark crescendo, glaring up at him through eyes that grew bloody. He leaned in.

"*History, deserves to know.*" His voice starker than mine, as if he had a point. I stood up, my chair screaming. I was seconds from coming around the table to put my hands on him, strangle him, strike him, do anything, but he sat there, as if he knew I had no fight in me. I saw how his arms were crossed, watching me. Even if I was fully healed I would have just fell back down into my seat like I did, defeated by a smug gaze, my legs crumbling beneath me, almost collapsing to the side upon Lauren.

"…You know who that… man really was?" I let out like a long-drawn sigh.

"A cartel higher-up who wanted to play war, like back in the good old days of Intervention. A ghost of a leader, a true John Doe, Only known by his moniker *Red*; heavy ties to the CIA. Possible plant on their part, massive genetic tampering after we analyzed his cadaver, hard to really tell what *race* he even was, let alone genealogy and family history. Early generation, most definitely a prototype cartel *Aumentado*, small wonder he wasn't riddled with tumors. Statements from people who interacted with him pointed to him having a couple screws loose in his head and violent habits, but other than that we don't have much to work with. A lot of the pre-May data is gone with the hack, shutdowns, so we had to find out what we could with what we had. You know."

"Yeah. You're right. He was all that." A long, heavy pause. Satisfaction on his face for his predictions. Lauren's hand reaching over my back to hold me as I stared at my plate. "My best friend... Was a former, *employee* of his."

"Ah, a mister... Noria, was he?" I glared up at him as he nonchalantly cut another piece of his meal to eat. "That contextualizes things. So, you, the second in command from what I gathered from intel, go through with such a risky operation. You and the rest of your troupe must be fond of your commander, dare I say downright fraternal. Where is the prestigious tactician himself?"

"He... Gabriel's dead." I watched his face contort. Like sadness portrayed by a robot, his motions paused to run a program of mourning, watching me writhe in my memories.

"Ah. I was worried it was as such. My condolences." He still watched, analysed even as I sat there in silence, staring down at my food growing cold. I wished I could enjoy it, in a single passing thought. "You must have been close."

"He was a brother to me."

"I was an only child. Forgive me if I seem ingenuine. You've lost a great man, from what it seems."

"Yeah. We have." I looked over to Lauren, seeing her too tearing up. God; I really couldn't let myself cry now. Lucky that I felt nothing but numbness. I couldn't cry if I wanted to.

"So, you two, estranged from your group. Lost in the forest. Who was your third in command? Anyone particularly competent?"

"We..." I felt that numb hopelessness. Maria. My lies of omission, my letting her die alone and terrified on that battlefield, flying so far away, hoping to leave her and the troubles she brought behind, haunted by her spectre. "I... We, my friends, were attached to another group. If anything, the rest of us are following them."

"They probably aren't even looking for you in that case," He morosely noted, but not without an edge of smug accomplishment. My loss, his gain. I couldn't discern it at the time, too gone inside my own mind. "You've lost everything, it seems," He noted. "The lord and lady of a lonely log cabin, sure to starve through the winter if not for fortune giving me to you. You know, as it turns out, I could use an advisor myself. A resourceful second in command who has seen a hopeless, uphill battle and came out on top, and shares my unique... perspective. Won't piss me off with an errant comment or two like the lot of them. You very much fit the bill. Just agree to my reasonable terms and I think we can cultivate a lasting friendship, Noah."

"Yeah. Whatever."


I was walking dead, shambling about next I knew, breezing through one moment to the next. Everything sat ill with me and it was like I was back in Shortstone, disassociating my life away. Wandering about was enough that I could do to keep busy, what with Lauren being whisked away by the captain's day spa attendees. Pretty her up or something, treat her like a princess. Pointless, I supposed. She'd taken a look at me as if to ask to stay by my side but I was gone within myself, and she vanished soon afterwards. I had nothing to do but wander and keep from thinking.

I'd go down to the deep pit to see the workers there, sitting to watch them farm in the aquaponics garden that was set up. The "slaves" didn't seem that poorly fed, nor did they seem particularly miserable, so I guessed that was a plus. I saw the younger men, counting through them, wondering who Adrianne's significant other was, if he was one of the humans, one of the canids or felinids. There were a couple dragons, only a handful working in the shops, the rest mostly part of the Captain's infantry. I wondered if the mysterious boyfriend of Adrianne was at least happy that his beau was working in nicer conditions than him. I wondered how long they were permitted to spend time together. I walked further, seeing women and children toiling away in the mechanical shops and miniature factories, carefully pounding cast copper bullets into reloaded cases and working on guns and engines. It was a small empire, a war camp for sure. Still was one, given the Captain's new business model of miniature empire-building on the backs of those too weak to oppose him. Plenty of people here with plenty of tasks.

The captain's "mansion" upon the lip of the great pit had a domineering central spire and tower that terminated in a bulged structure that I assumed to be a room of some sort, a recent addition, like most of the furnishings of the place. It did seem to serve as a watch tower, but it seemed so much bigger than it had any right to be as one, at least while I was traversing the spiral staircase. The guard post was staffed by a couple soldiers with their rifles cruxed upon their laps as they watched, barely noticing me as I poked my head into the central post. I shrugged it off, going back, but seeing a doorway opposite me, near the far top of the place.

Opening it up, it quickly explained the great size of the tower's high room, as I saw what the girth of the tower was for. A great room, as well furnished as the rest of the place, with comfortable, bright, girlish decorations, tassels and frills and all, with a big opening in one of the walls, like a doorway that could be opened or closed at will, but leading out into the open sky. A creature lay upon the great bed there, barely able to contain its size. A long, scaly mass of tail and wings, a shimmering mixture of sapphire blue and aquamarine, before at once looking back to me as I stuck my head in the room. I noted, most prominently, how this creature the size of a small car wore a great steel muzzle on her face, as well as a technological collar of sorts on her big, long neck.

"H-hello? Ah! A new face!" She spoke, eyes brightening up upon seeing me shamble in. I bet she was smiling too, but I could hardly see the very tips of her lips upon the recession of her muzzle curling upwards. "You! You're not one of his guards, are you?"

"Uh… No. I dunno. He wants to hire me or something, but I don't know." It was still like I was talking to myself. Could this be the current status quo for me? Living here? A private platoon in service of itself?

"Well, I daresay it would be a foolish endeavor, my dear sir…?" She'd interrupted my train of thought, making me cognizant that I was in a conversation, not simply debating my inner monologue. It also should have occured to me that she was asking me my name, but I could only sigh in my everlasting exasperation while she got up. She was no ordinary dragon- at least, not like the Captain's wife, or even a centaurical like Lauren. aside from being much bigger than even Lauren, she also had only four limbs- two legs and a set of wings, as she got up to sit on her hind legs and cross each long, thumb-like digit on the crux of her wingspans like holding her own hands in one another, eagerly awaiting my answer with a charmingly cheerful smile behind her iron mask.

"…Jesus, does anyone here speak normally?" I uttered, far less than enthusiastically, sighing. I saw her bright eyes droop a little bit, her tailtip wagging nervously some few feet away from her as she sheepishly eyed around self-consciously with an awkward smile. "You don't seem like you suck up to that dickhead. How come you're taking on how he speaks?"

"...Taking on? Oh, you must be mistaken, I've always spoken in this fashion," I had to admit, her attitude was cheerful enough to be charming, at least if I wasn't in this mental state. "I am a daughter of the firestorm clan, our proud people-"

"Huh, no barcode," I noted aloud after scanning her as I took a little time to semicircle around her looking for it, and inadvertently interrupting her spiel. "You must be one of the brainwashed hybrids from the simulations."

"I beg your pardon, milord, for I am a *wyvern*. A proud drake of the conquered realm of "Mount Robinson", as you humans refer to it. I am not this 'hybrid' term you and many others speak of." She would proudly arch back to place her wing's mandible on her chest as if a salute of some sort, only inadvertently bumping her horns into the twelve-foot ceiling before coming to her full stature, letting out a decidedly un-proud "ow" and blushing embarrassedly from where I could see under her metal mouth restraint. Her horns were the same shape as Lauren's, I noticed, though she was hairless and had the more western-style frills that Lauren lacked and the Captain's wife bore. Something interesting that drifted through my mind in my sloggy state.

"...you supposed to be from the middle ages or something?"

"Uh… I must confess milord, you confuse me so. It is year 433 of the third era last I made sure." She seemed almost like she was lying. Pretending to believe what she said, like somebody else had already cracked the façade of the world she'd constructed in her mind.

"No," I uttered, letting my frustration overtake my depression for a few mere moments. "It's 2060. You were made by humans to run psychology tests on. You were probably made in a test tube. You might not even be the only "you" that's ever been made."

"LIAR!" She grew angry, coming down to all fours again and glaring at me, still a head above me as she huffed. I saw flames fly from the inside of her mask as she loudly snorted outwards, her fire redirected to the sides by her metal muzzle to dissipate harmlessly. "You speak to the one-and-only Idrid Blackmantle from the depths of the Great Mount, lastborn daughter of the Sky-Knight Kant Blackmantle the Indomitable! Young of seventeen summers I may be, but I am no damsel, houndish sir! If it were not for this blasted masque, I would show you fire and doom befitting your discourteous nature! Or perhaps gobble you up!"

"Oh," I muttered. It was strange how calm I could be, given that this sedan-sized dragon, or wyvern or whatever, was verbally and physically threatening me at this point. I guess it was the disassociating keeping me from any semblance of fear. "So *that's* what the muzzle is for."

"NO HUMAN HAS *CREATED* ME! WE DRAKES ARE THE PROUD DESCENDANTS OF AK'ROHN; CHILDREN OF THE SUN!" She roared, pausing only to beat her chest with one of her wings. I noted how she shook in place, well and truly angered, but an anger that only reflected her true feelings, a hopeless tinge to all of her ranting and raving. She was keeping her lie alive, it seemed.

"Jesus. I must not be the first person to tell you all this. Look, I'm sorry if I pissed you off. I'm sure you're a princess or something where you come from. I'm just dealing with a lot right now." She glared at me, huffing smoke from her nostrils again before turning away to walk up to and stare out of the big open door-like window, sitting there. I stood there awkwardly for some time to realise I'd been an asshole yet again, before opening my mouth. "…If you want to escape, why don't you just fly away?"

"The damnable warlock himself has enchanted this necklace with his arcane magicks." She motioned a thumb at the collar on her neck. "If I fly out of his ideal boundary, its curse kicks in and shocks me until I cannot fly and simply plummet to the ground. A humiliating weapon. He too uses it when I spite him or his guard."

"You can still fly, right? Why not just fly around? Flying always makes me- makes my- makes my friend feel a lot better."

"With this cursed chain, I can only fly above his camp for his amusement. I would rather my wings rot off than him take perverse pleasure in observing my power over the sky." She was sighing, staring away. "I too wish I could free my voice and sing, but I feel that he would have the same undeserved joy. I save my voice for the dead of night when I am sure he is asleep." Another long pause, as she looked over her shoulder where she sat, eyeing to me with bright red eyes. "You do not seem at ease here. Do you intend to stay in his employ?"

"I don't know. Do I really have a choice?"

"You're not wearing one of these, are you not?" She pointed her wing-thumb to her collar. I sighed yet again. "Even the slaves down in the pit do not wear them. He says these enchanted necklaces are complicated pieces of 'technology'. Expensive. But it is an excuse. They stay for the food, for the privilege of purpose. I do not want to stay for I do not need to stay. I suppose, in some capacity I envy those who enjoy their plight." The thought of the phrase hovered in my mind, a lasting afterimage burning through the haze. "I have the mountain my people conquered some time ago, to return to. I... I believe I know the way. Somewhere to the north of here. It is a simpler place than this, your land with its wars and famine and plague and razored magicks."

"Ah, your geodome must be easy to get in and out of. I doubt somebody as big as you can just crawl through tunnels like that." she turned again, eyeing me, confused with a tinge of insultedness as I muttered aloud.

"...We broke free of the spell of the great unholy mages to bridge your world with ours, our world that seems so deep within that mountain. We knew it to be an illusion once finding the edges of the sky. It is our people's great triumph, many months before."

"Yeah, May first."

"...Yes, t'was the day," she uttered, glaring back at me. "It is quirksome that so many of you outlanders know the date of our victory, yet not our story."

"Yeah. We've all got stories of that day." I was thinking back to the beginning of all this. When I met Lauren. Even there she was beautiful, mind simple, only looking to survive. Unlike me with so many responsibilities, so many people to please, duties to uphold. The wyverness watched me say this, huffing a little.

"...Perhaps it was a day intertwined into the fabric of fate. For every being with an immortal soul to share such a cataclysmic change to our personal worlds, and worlds at large."

"Yeah. Fate." I found myself having walked over there beside her, staring out the window with her. It really was a nice view, rising over the endless forests of the pacific northwest. "It was nice having someone to talk to."

"Indeed. I miss a true discussion." I didn't really give her one, but she was courteous enough. Again, charming. Or something. "I do not mind you humans. In fact, I find you and your ilk charming. Your bodies are warm and pleasant on the eyes. And, I must confess, my dear Man-At-Arms, I have not caught your name."

"...Doesn't matter," I muttered, turning. "I still don't know if I'll stay."

"P-perhaps I could talk you into devising a plot to free me?" She uttered, practically spitting it out as I made my way to the exit. I turned around again, seeing desperation in her pained eyes. She didn't like to ask, I could tell that much. A stain on her pride. I suppose I'd oblige her pride and turn her down.

"...I don't even know your name either," I uttered.

"It- It's Idrid Blackm-"

"Goodbye, Idrin. See you later. Nice to meet you." I proceeded to the door and left without even looking back at her.

**Chapter 72**

The day passed me in a haze, until I was finally seated there. Something in my mind about how I was there, seated here to "ensure fair play", seated in this room with low lights, almost darkness, listening to the storm far above, thunder cracking so far away in our deep dungeon. I took a slow look around, blinking. Frilly and red. Iconography of love, paintings and pictures and portraits of draconic hybrid women up on the walls. Provocative, sultry, almost pornographic. Really set the tone. His dungeon, his *special* dungeon, deep in his mansion rather than the dungeon down in the pit for average discipline for his non-special lackeys. Lauren lay her lower body there on the bed with her front talons drooping off the bed by their wrists, hands crossed, and I at once noticed what she was wearing. Pink lacey undergarments, her nipples showing through the translucent fabric of her brassiere, similar near full leg length socks on each of her four legs and gloves of the same kind on her hands. Her wing was freed of its sling, perhaps it'd healed, but that wasn't quite relevant. I saw her fancy, sultry uniform of sorts, with a pair of panties specifically assembled for her true lower body of the very same frilly, showy type. She sat there, that hopeless look on her face. Like she'd been looking at me, trying to get me to say something, but so far beyond that. She knew I was gone. I couldn't help her. What exactly was I doing here?

"...Why, hello," I heard that modulated voice, barely registering it in my zombie-like state. Thump, thump, thump. Robotic servos pacing as the great armor suit made its way inside the room, shutting the door. "Good evening, Milady," He approached around the couch where I sat to Lauren to take her hand in his great metal clasp ever so gingerly, tapping the side of his helmet three times and up came the faceplate of his helm, and he bent down to place a kiss upon her hand. She smiled weakly, still uncomfortable, sneaking another look to me as he turned back to me as well. "Well then. As you can see, I'm sort of a sucker for theatrics. The armor makes me feel… Chivalrous. You must agree, as somebody with armor training yourself." I told him about my power armor experience? I guess I did. Huh. He opened the armor up to slide out of. "See, she can act as our guard tonight. Working with the older system though, primitive protocols, so she'll only respond to voice commands. Isn't that right, Darling?"

"Yes, master." The auto-generated, decidedly female voice of the suit sounded eerily similar to a voice I'd heard before. I think it was his wife's voice.

"Thank you, Darling. Please, do not interfere until spoken to for the rest of the evening."

"Yes, Master. Commencing standby." He smiled back to me, a toothy grin. I saw what he was wearing, already in his bare boxers.

"Now, to get down to business. You know, Mister Reed, my offer was sincere. What we share is between us, you know. And I appreciate your lack of resistance to what I must do." I saw him waltz over to a drawer, sliding it open and producing what looked like a pink collar and leash for a large dog, thunder cracking again. "I hope you don't mind my tastes in theatrics, either. I like to… make my love *exciting*." He mindlessly tossed the leash and collar to Lauren, who caught it plainly, looking down upon the degrading tool, letting his gaze settle upon me and dwell for quite some time before looking back over to her. "Lauren, my dear… If you would be so kind," He turned fully to face her but I could practically see the razors in his smile as she looked only once to me in worry before unclasping it and putting it around her neck, clasping it again, letting the leash droop in her hands, eyes drawn down to it in repressed terror as her breath shook its way out of her. He approached Lauren as I sat there, frozen within myself in my hazy, dreamlike state, like watching through a pane of glass. I couldn't do anything. God, I could hardly watch as he took the leash, slowly making a show of pulling her close, yank by gentle yank before coming upon her to grope her breasts, smiling powerfully.

"...Lay down now," He commanded. His boxers were coming off as she snook a glance past his head to me. She was terrified, trying to play things cool, freezing up even worse than me. "Laurennn," He sang, 'tsk'ing. "Don't make me punish you," With his hand upon the collar and his knuckles digging into her throat, he whipped the clasp of the leash off to throw the leash behind him, before yanking her by the collar alone downwards and she slumped down, humanoid half still upright, his member ready to wag its way up towards her chin and lips. "You know what you have to do, now don't you? You little *slut?*"

It was all too much to watch. God, I was thinking. How did it end up like this? The woman I loved, swore to protect was about to be defiled by this creep. What was she thinking? Why did she agree to this? Why did I? She was about to be raped. We had no choice. Share his women with me. This fucking dragonfucking freak. Here I was, watching it all unfold. Powerless. Why was I powerless? My mind fell to the topic I kept running from. The dead howling in my mind with the storm raging far above us.

But in that great howling that culminated into paralyzing white noise, a voice rose above the others.

**GET UP.**

The voice, **his** voice took my legs and forced me on them. I wasn't even wearing my brace. Was I healed? I couldn't feel the pain. I couldn't feel anything except for that leash on the ground as I bent over to fish for it as the storm's intensity grew, thunder booming over, and over, and over until I could hardly tell that it wasn't in my own head. I felt the coarse nylon with both hands, snapping it held taut between them once. Barely a sexual object, a regular leash. Disgusting. Disgust. Nothing but disgust. My face contorting on its own into a demonic frown. Blood pulsing in my eyes as I stepped closer, feeling the storm above me, around me, *inside* me. He was about to do it. But not if **we** had anything to say about it.

I whipped around as I crossed the ends of the leash, forming it into a half figure eight. Throwing it over my shoulder, whipping around his head to tighten in an instant at his neck. He barely let out a sound before I bent forward with all my weight, picking him up like a burlap sack over my back held by the tightening rope. Gagging, choking, as my little emaciated, wounded body held him with all my enraged might. Gagging and clawing at his throat, kicking this way and that as I frowned into the ground, listening to the storm, feeling him die. He was trying to speak, to speak to activate his armor standing idle in the corner to save him. Fear gripped me as I looked to the side to the motionless suit, like the fear of being found out. *You aren't saying anything tonight, you piece of shit.* I held on with all my life, all the more until my hands bled against the rough fibers and his pitiful kicks and throes of death subsided, holding him there for another eternity just to make sure, before I let his limp, naked, lifeless body slump to the floor, once the storm had calmed itself and thunder no longer struck.

Lauren's eyes were at once overtaken by a glaze of horror, before fear as she truly looked into me as I turned. I must have still had that deranged grimace on my face.

"Wh- What," She uttered, all at once covering her bosom and her mouth with opposing hands. "N-Noah, wh-"

"I wasn't going to let him do that to you," I growled, but it came out more akin to a whine. "We're getting out of here."

"N-Noah... What the fuck are we supposed to do?! You killed him!" She all at once exploded, hardly able to figure which point to lead on.

"He was going to rape you."

"He was giving us meds! *Me* meds! Noah, do you think I can fly us out of here?! The doctors said I need at least another week! Oh god, we- we're so dead-"

"Hey. You wanted to do that? Suck his fucking cock like a *whore?!*" I growled, getting angrier. The blood dripping down my hands. "You're no whore. You take all that back. You didn't need to do that. I *saved* you. You-"

"*Why didn't you say anything!?*" She burst. "I *wanted* you to say something! You could have stopped him at *any* time! He said so!"

"You believed him?" I motioned limply to his corpse. "You said it yourself at breakfast. He's a *warlord*. A fucking walking cliche, straight out of a movie. He just *takes*."

"Noah, you- What the fuck, what the fuck, they're going to *kill* us," She hushed, still gripping her muzzle and chest. I could hardly stand it. It was my victory, my rescue of her. Why wasn't she thanking me? I felt nothing but spite. The evil in the room was dead but here I was, wishing to destroy more of it. Watching Lauren pace in circles, still holding her chest and shivering, heaving nervously. "*What the fuck do we do?!*"

"We've got the armor," I thumbed to his great sentinel, still silently observing even with its master lying slain upon the ground.

"You didn't even have a *plan?!*" she hissed. "You- You- Noah, you know what your problem is?!"

"What," I spat impatiently, still groveling there.

"You don't *fucking* communicate! You just sit around and act all reserved and mysterious but you don't even *think*! The strong silent type act is getting real fuckin' old!"

A knock upon the door. Lauren froze, springing upright like a coil. I could barely swing my head over to look. God, this was some shit, I was thinking. Until it came to me. "I've got a plan," I uttered as I bolted over to the armor, opening it up and slipping inside.

"Hey! Is everything all right in there, boss?!" One of his lackeys was asking.

"What's your plan?!"

"I've got one," I grumbled back as it closed around me, sealing me inside. Like it was too much of a bother to actually state it, at least in my numbed state that refused to leave.

"*What fucking plan?!*" she hissed.

"I know I'm not supposed to interrupt, but it doesn't sound so good, boss. You good?" He was uttering through the door.

"Hello," that familiar voice of his wife Tanya that the modulator spoke as greeted me. "Password, please."

"...Can I get a hint?"

"Your favorite things."

"Uh... Dragons."

"Incorrect."

"...Dragonesses?"

"Correct. Full control granted, Master." With that the suit unlocked for me and came to life. I could barely chuckle as I began making my way to the door. He was coming in, Lauren was hauling the Captain's corpse into the frilly bed to cover him entirely with sheets and lay beside him. I stopped the door from opening fully with my hand as the soldier, some fluffy grey-white felinid guy poking in to briefly look in before straining his neck to look up at me and saluting, surprised.

"S-sir-"

"You have interrupted my... Intercourse," I uttered, trying to take to his voice and his mannerisms, figuring the combat modulation for the voice would cover my tracks enough. I could see in the heads-up display of the helmet the reverse-image camera on the back of the armor and helmet, Lauren on the bed instantly looking over to me with a somewhat disgusted look on her face, as if to remark ...*Intercourse? Seriously?!*

"Apologies, sir," He snuck a look past me as if to check but I landed my great metal hand on his shoulder.

"Do not interfere with what is not yours," I growled. "The last man who looked to take what is mine- Died with nothing but his humiliation." Again, weird phrasing that Lauren visibly cringed at. "Fortunately for you, I... Require a break. Be grateful that you did not catch me in the middle of my... Business. Do not disturb my guest while I am gone. Is that clear?"

"Uh... Didn't that guy come in here with you also? S-sir?"

"Ah, he's just taking a break himself," Lauren ad-libbed like a pro, figuring my dumb ass was going to get us blown. I was halfway about to snap his neck with my heavy hand upon his shoulder already. "All tuckered out."

"That is correct. I must have misspoken." He finally stepped back and aside, waving me out with a hand. "Make sure to keep my... Treasure safe. Let no one enter this room and live. Not even yourself. Am I clear?"

"Yes sir," He saluted again, stamping his SKS rifle on the ground a little as he shut the door for me, looking up embarrassedly. As he shut the door, I could still see Lauren using her sign language to me from that bed in rage, screaming "WHAT PLAN?!" In utter pantomimed silence. It was okay. I had a plan... Sort of.

I made sure to mute my outgoing voice and that all radio channels were dead as I spoke. "...Do we have a map of our base?"

"Of course, Master." The overlay of the pit popped up in my HUD. I looked to the radio building. Comms, perfect. Long range. I stepped outside, water plodding on my great metal body rhythmically. It was calming. A short walk over and I was there, letting myself in as the guard outside the door saluted and I waved him off, stomping on inside.

There was no plugsuit I was currently wearing- apparently he only wore the plugsuit with his suit when out on sorties. In informal dress, the machine was a challenge to maneuver deftly, and very much a big pain as I snuck up on the radio operator asleep at her workstation, some felinid girl in a cot right next to the radio apparatus, dozing gently. She was wearing her headphones as she lay, seeming to be jacked into her personal music player as she snored, listening to some smooth, calming tune. I opened the hand to expose my real, flesh and bone hand to more accurately pick up the jack for the comms equipment, wrestling with the controls for utter silence after having tiptoed painfully slow in these great metal sabatons suspending my real feet quite a ways off the ground. I took the jack to plug it into the holoconsole on my other arm, seeing the modules. A real hail-mary about to go out, double and triple checking to make sure I was close-voice muted and that nobody in camp would hear the broadcast, and most of all that it wasn't a loudspeaker broadcast.

"Hey. Squid, if you're reading this, call back. Squid, tell me you're reading this. This is the rest of Indigo squad, call back, call back." I held my breath, as if expecting an instantaneous answer, if an answer at all, switching between the frequencies we liked to broadcast on for a couple minutes. "Kommandoes, this is Indigo Omega. Tell me you're-"

"Hey, buddy! Long time no see, huh?!" It was the Kommando radioman. I could barely remember what he looked like, but I knew his voice. "Yo- Yo Squiddie! You got a phone call!"

"Who's- oh shit, you're alive?! Noah! Ha ha! How was war, huh?!"

"It was hell," I muttered and he guffawed.

"Fuck yeah it was! Hey, you're probably calling for a pickup, huh?"

"...Would be nice," I uttered. "Glad to know you guys are alright."

"We're doing fine. For the moment, at least. Could use to get to that place you know. Y'know, as we were flying away, I was like 'dammit, who the fuck is gonna get us into that castle now?' By the time I made up my mind to ask you to get your ass over to exfil you blew the fuckin place! I felt it even in the middle of the shootout with the dems at exfil!"

"That's great, Squid," I uttered, more looking to get on with it. "Look, tell me all about it later, okay? Our coordinates are..." I looked on the tackboard for home base, which was labeled nicely enough. "48°42'27.3" North, 117°50'00.9" West. Comstock quarry."

"Oh, fuck, *that* dickhead got you? Damn. Well, you're on a real radio so I'm assuming you're springing your escape."

"That's the plan." The very word *plan* made me cringe. God, I was such an idiot. At least it was working so far. "We probably don't have that long. An hour or two tops."

"Yeah, we can work with that. We're in the area, kept an eye on that fucker, he knows us well enough. Weirdo kept gunning for my boyfriend's Duke's sister, tryna get her to defect."

"Boyfriend? you finally came out of the closet?" I uttered. "Congrats."

"...I was never in the closet, he's been my boyfriend as long as you've known me," He grumbled and I felt my cringe return. God, why the fuck did I disassociate so fucking much?

"Yeah, uh... How is he?"

"He's good."

"Okay after getting shot?"

"Yeah. He's healed. We have meds." This sure was awkward.

"Uh... See you guys soon, huh?"

"Yeah. We'll be heading in from the north and send your Indigoes in around through the south, flanking maneuver. That's where his mansion is, I think."

"Yeah, that's where we'll be, in the basement. Don't shoot the green dragontaur, or the guy in the power armor with the purple cape. That's me."

"Oh fuck, you stole that creep's armor?"

"How the fuck did you think I got to the radio? Needed a disguise," I explained.

"Heh. Huevos on you. Wait, what about Maria?"

"Huh?"

"So it's just you and Lauren. You pick up Maria?" Shit. My mind blanked out for a moment.

"She... She never made it to the rally point."

"Oh, geez man, I'm sorry," He uttered his condolences, but I was ready to steamroll past *that* conversation.

"L-look, I killed their captain too, so that might simplify things."

"Well," He sucked inwardly. "That's good. Dude doesn't have much of a chain of command, he's the only one of them with anything between the ears. Kinda think he couldn't stand anybody else with any sense of leadership so he could bask in the glory, personally. This is gonna be easy. A'ight, see you soon. Good fucking luck my guy."

"You too. Don't get too risky."

**Chapter 73**

I stepped outside of the place, receiving a salute from the door guard and making my way back to the mansion, thinking things over in my head, staying cognizant, letting the rain calm my mind. The plan was in motion. The Captain's little sex dungeon was in the deepest part of the mansion, so that was a plus. No errant mortar shells would threaten us. But as I walked, I could hear a sound emanating from the great above. A haunting, melodious wailing, a song penetrating the gale of the storm that I stopped to listen to. Slow and somber, full-ranged, in some strange tongue, with words too slow to really be able to recite, like a hypnotic sermon of itself. It was beautiful, this mournful tune coming from on high. I looked up to the tower as I walked step after massive step, knowing the wyvern girl was finally singing. Why exactly, I could never know. Was it a desperate call to help to any of her people who might hear? Was it a way to pass the time? Did she simply miss the feeling of letting her voice soar? I couldn't imagine that she would be any good of a voice with that metal mask on, but it seemed she more than made up for it in skill. What a nice girl, even if she was really weird. I sort of wanted to go up and set her free somehow, pull off her collar and mask, but I figured she would complicate the escape and that was hardly bound to work anyways. I just sort of hoped she would be okay. God, what was her name again?

Crawling down the steps into that dark dungeon, I detoured for a moment to gather Lauren's saddle and normal, non-fetishising clothing, noting the other cells about, only one of them closed, the rest open and looking rather cushy for a jail. I saw that dopey felinid guard sitting in his chair a ways away from the heavy wooden door at the end of the hallway leading into the Captain's "Love Suite" playing a game or something on his hologlasses, who bolted to his feet, saluted and let me in through the door, blushing as if he was worried I'd caught him in an act. Maybe I should have yelled at him, like the Captain did. I think he took notice of Lauren's gear in my hands.

There I was alone with Lauren and the lifeless Captain again, Lauren still laying there on the bed with the sheets curled over and around her in lieu of overclothes, covering the useless and chilly, overtly sexualizing clothes she was wearing, looking to me with shining, intense eyes, breathing heavy. Almost like she was sexually charged, if I didn't know any better. Instead, I knew she was definitely perturbed. She moved to speak, but I put my finger up, turning to the door, waiting to hear the guard go sit down. I gave it a good few seconds before plodding the armor over there, dropping her stuff and opening the suit up to let myself back out.

"What the fuck did you do?!" She hissed, doing her best not to screech out of pure anxious rage.

"Called for backup," I uttered. "Kommandoes will be here soon."

"...Y-you serious?" Like for a moment it surprised her that there was an actual plan now.

"Yeah. They were in the area watching this place." Lauren was silent for many seconds, blinking incredulously for an eternity before whipping out of bed, ripping the lacey, translucent fabrics off of herself, trying to gird her happiness at the revelation that salvation was on its way, focusing on the sheer unexpectedness of it. I sort of liked the thigh-high socks she had on all four of her legs and wanted to say something before she discarded them, but she interrupted me.

"...You know that was *blind luck*, Noah. What if they weren't?!"

"Well, they were. What'd you expect they'd do? They'd go back to Shortstone?"

Lauren snarled out a sigh as she threw an actual bra on, going for her shirt. "I swear to god, Noah," She snarled, but I came up to her.

"You know..." I grasped her arm, stopping her and she glared up at me intensely, though like she didn't really mean it, her glare soon subsided with a heavy sigh, huffing through her nostrils. "Look, you- you're right. I need to stop acting unilaterally. This was all stupid of me."

"Yeah, I'd say," She snapped, though she was steadily losing her taste for conflict.

"Hey, before you take those socks off," I said. "I just wanna say you look really good in them."

"...You're really in the mood? Now? After all that?" She thumbed over her shoulder at the bed, presumably where the Captain's corpse resided.

"I'm saying you should hold onto them at least." Lauren sighed and I laughed, and she glared right back at my laughter. "Yeah, kind of an... inappropriate moment. But we do have, like, an hour."

"Yeah. We do." She uttered. "You want to discuss any other details of your master plan?"

"Just to keep our heads down and not get blown up." we went back over to sit on that big showy lacey bed, Lauren walking over it to lay down beside where I sat. I sat upon the Captain's leg for a moment, before shifting uncomfortably, letting his legs lay between where we sat beside each other. "God, I can't wait to get out of here."

"Me too," Lauren said and I looked over to her. "I guess... I guess this works. Thanks for... stopping him."

"Yeah, I should have said something earlier anyways."

"...If he would have listened," Lauren uttered, and I let out a single chuckle.

"Damn, did we switch sides on this issue?"

"No- yeah, Noah, you were right. He would have just done what he wanted anyways."

"I'm just hoping that nobody gets killed trying to rescue us. I-"

"Boss! BOSS!" The felinid guard was slamming on the door again, and we sprang up. "I- I know you said not to bother you, but- Sentries are seeing a lot of guys headed this way! We need orders now, sir!"

"-That wasn't an hour," Lauren remarked hushedly as I made my way to the door to ambush the guard. Now that I was out of the armor and trying to move quickly, I felt the wounds of my leg, limping over there.

"Squid said they were close by! I didn't know they were *this* close!" I hissed back to her, as the felinid guard began to open the door. I pulled it further open and closed the distance to him, brushing the SKS out of his arms, headbutting him and grabbing him by the throat in a menagerie of swift, brutal motions, the rifle clattering to the floor. He fought against me for a couple seconds before I brushed him from his feet and slammed him onto the ground, yelping audibly as I held him on the ground, his radio and holos flying from his other, gun-less hand. Lauren dashed over for his SKS. "Y- Boss?!" He shrilly called over to the bed, with no response, his nose bleeding.

"He's dead," I snarled, reaching to grab the walkie-talkie in my throat-less hand. "Call it in."

"W-what?!"

"Call it in! We fucking killed him! Tell everyone to surrender!"

"You mean *you* fucking killed him," Lauren uttered, a little too nonchalantly for the situation. The felinid slowly took the walkie talkie. From me, fear quivering in his eyes.

"He- Those two killed the boss! They're gonna kill me, come over here and-" I gripped the end of his muzzle to shut his big mouth, whipping the walkie talkie away.

"Fucking moron!" I snarled, slapping him upside the face as he cried out. Hell of a soldier, whimpering where I pinned him. "You're pissing me off! Lauren! Gimme the gun!"

"What? No! We're not killing this guy!"

"P-please don't," the dopey felinid interjected.

"Fine, eat him!"

"Ex-*cuse* me?!" Lauren spat in revulsion. "*Eww!* Do I fucking look like *Selicia* to you?!"

"We've gotta restrain him, right?"

"Please, *please* don't eat me either," He whined softly.

"...We've got that bondage gear, don't we?" I motioned over to the corner drawer.

"Okay, let's use that," she said, going over there to pull it open and look inside. "Uh... Noah," She asked.

"You bringing it over here?"

"...Do you know how the fuck any of this works?" She brought out an entirely too convoluted harness, barely hanging onto it between her index and thumb, not really wanting to touch it.

"BDSM isn't really my thing!"

"Oh, but you like these tacky socks, don't you," She snarled, letting it fall from her hand as she brushed her hand off on her shirt, flicking at it on the ground with one of her toe-fingers.

"That's *entirely* different!" Lauren went back to digging through the drawer.

"H-here! These are easy enough!" Lauren produced a pair of handcuffs. "Man, not even, like, the kinky type," She jangled them.

"Good enough!" I cried, though not before I could hear bootfalls descending the stairs, dragging him over there and rushing to put them on. A couple moments of finagling and he was bound, but not before more guards on their way. He was hollering enough until Lauren settled on muffling the guard with a blanket over his head.

Gunfire was still erupting outside, though I could hear their approach, more bootfalls coming our way. Two human guards, one male, one female burst in. The man was easier to take- not necessarily because he was worse at fighting or anything, but once it was time to restrain the woman I was taken aback for just a moment. The man I chopped hard in the side of the neck. He, stunned, stumbled though I tripped him and his rifle fell clattering to the floor, his body following it. The woman behind him, a gruff sort began to raise her weapon, and I barely had time to step aside as she fired, my ears ringing as the shot cried out before I grabbed her sub-machine gun with one hand and punched her nose in with the other.

"J-jesus!" Lauren cried as I was upon the female, grasping her by the throat before she could get back up.

"Get that big fucker!" I spat back, Lauren charging in as the male attempted to get up, tackling him as he coughed at the weight now upon him. The female, now unconcious, I could drag over to the impromtu wall-shackles and string her up with what was to be had in the chest-of-naughties in the corner next to that felinid guard, still with that blanket over his head proclaiming out.

"...Not exactly what it was made for," Lauren was exclaiming as she tied him to the piping by way of a harness, re-purposed for the task. There was more than enough thread left on it to tie the woman guard's hands too, just barely. With them now awake again and glaring up at us, we just stood there blankly to listen to the sporadic battle above, until I heard a voice.

"Sir, someone wishes to speak with you," Tanya's voice met me and both Lauren and I jumped to turn towards the power armor, inactive save for glowing eyes.

"...Must think the last person to use the armor is always going to be the Captain," I grumbled to Lauren as I approached to see the holodisplay the suit's forearm computer emitted, seeing how the muted radio was going crazy. People begging for orders or something. I opened up one of the feeds, not looking like it was related to any of the Captain's soldiers, being an outside broadcast hailing us. "...Hello?" I asked, unmuting it.

"Noah! You're alive!" I heard... Who was that? Was that really Daniel?

"That was one fucking fast hour, man," I uttered.

"You're telling me! These guys are pushovers, most of 'em just came outside to surrender when they didn't get any orders! We're in the building now! You said you're in the basement, right?"

"Yeah, pretty much," I grunted.

"Hey Anthony! They're in the basement," Daniel relayed. A couple moments, and his voice was calling down the halls. Lauren, still with that SKS in her hands, peeked out the door.

"Oh shit, hey Anthony," Lauren uttered, cracking the door open.

"Man am I glad to see you guys. How's it been, man?" He croaked hoarsely. I noted the ragged scar near his throat.

"What's the deal up top?" I asked, going back over to the armor and following him out, leaving the dark dungeon step by step.

"Shit, Squid isn't kidding. These guys don't put up much of a fight without their leader. Sorry about my voice being hard to hear if it is. Kinda got…" He motioned for his throat and its big scar.

"…Man, metabolic inducers make you scar up, don't they?" I noted, leaning in to look at his throat wound.

"Yo Anthony, you got 'em?" His radio crackled.

"Yeah, they're both here, Danny. All clear, we're on our way back up. Noah and Lauren mopped up the mooks before I got there. What's the deal with the tower?"

"Bit of a situation ongoing. Back me up."

"Right." Anthony looked to me. "Ready to get back in the swing of things?" I reached down for one of the dropped rifles, opening the hand of the power armor to take the AK's pistol grip with my own hand.

"Let's move."

Ascending the tower, the battle wound down. I could hear less and less gunfire until it ceased completely, just before the door to that wyvern girl's room. Up here the rain was still pounding, any fighting left anywhere else was drowned out by the deluge. Boom. Gunfire in the room, in that room before us that I threw the door open to.

I burst in, ready to shoot, as I watched a power armored figure tussle with someone very close to him, ripping a shotgun away from the gunman and shoving him powerfully with his other hand, sending him sprawling from his feet, coughing and choking, wind knocked out of him for sure. Another bullet soared out of a rifle somewhere in the room, and I saw the power-armored figure wince, a round careening off of his cuirass, still facing away from me as I entered, and I spread out to cover our armored ally, going over to that guy on the ground, pointing my rifle at him to dissuade him from getting up.

"Get back!" The gunman shouted as the original power-armored figure in the room hefted up his OICW heavy rifle, the kind made specifically for power armor. There were two others in this room, across from us and backlit by the storm outside through that big window: the wyvern girl was hunched there, terror in her eyes as one of the Guards held her by the horn, his armalite poking into the side of her neck where it met her head. "Get back or I'll kill her!"

"Drop it!" The other armored figure commanded. He wasn't wearing a full powered helmet, but a regular infantry helmet with integrated comms and NODs- that was *my* helmet. Matter of fact, that was my armor, evident by the scrubbed red paint still clinging to odd nooks and crannies.

"I swear to god I'll blow her brains out!" The guard was terrified, inconsolable. He looked like he was bound to do it at any moment, The wyvern girl's face still pleading with us from beneath her iron mask, eyes shining in fear, tearing up. I could hardly line up a shot even with my flanking position, as working with the controls of this armor sans plugsuit was difficult enough, and the metal buttstock didn't quite stabilize off of the metal inner shoulder of the armor.

"Hey, listen to me now," The other man in the power armor called. I wanted to step around and see who that really was, but I didn't want to set off the guard holding that wyvern girl's life in his hands. "Look, man, you put the gun down and you'll be fine. It doesn't have to be this way. What's his name, you know his name?" He asked her.

"Alex! His name's Alex!" she remarked, and before her hostage taker, Alex, could respond, the armored figure spoke again.

"Listen to me, Alex. There's been enough bloodshed today. And you hear that?" He asked. "You really hear that?"

"Hear- hear what?!"

"There's no more gunfire. The battle is over, you're the last one holding out. You can't shoot your way out of this, Alex. Just drop the gun, man. C'mon." I could see the guard, eyes wet, begin to soften, lip quivering. "Jeez, what's she even done to you?"

"She... She..." He was breaking down, before the gun fell out of his hands. "God, I'm so sorry," He fell to his knees, weeping. She just sort of reached over slowly, picking up his carbine with the thumbs of her wings and tossed it over to us as he cried, clattering against our hostage negotiator's sabaton. "I'm so sorry, Idrid... You're always so nice to me, I... I..." She, awkwardly, went to use her wing to pat Alex on the back once before figuring he didn't exactly deserve it, looking over at us expectantly.

"Man, that was close, huh?" The power armored figure uttered over to me, turning his head, and I raised the faceplate of my helmet just to take in who it was. Daniel. The man himself, his calm mocha skin and wide nose. Maybe it was the strap of my helmet he was wearing, but his chin and jawline seemed so much more pronounced now, too.

"Danny?" I asked, but he was already striding forward towards the two of them. I looked down at the man Daniel had pushed off of himself, groveling there and coughing to himself.

"...Don't look at me, she's a cunt to me," He snarled, still holding his chest, probably a broken rib or two as he slumped up against the wall. "I would have shot her."

"Oh god... What came over me..." Alex was inconsolable as Daniel led him away, and he went to go sit down in the stairs outside. I watched him for a second, him staring blankly at the future he nearly came to, lost in the distance of his own eyes. He pulled out his pistol and knife and lay them on the steps behind and above him, out of his sight, not because we even ordered him to, but probably because he felt that bad about it all, letting his face fall into his hands to weep. Anthony still kept his eye on him and his beat-up, uglier buddy, who our prisoners now or something.

"Hey, you alright?" Daniel was asking Idrid, approaching her.

"Yeah, I'm... I will be okay. Thank you for your chivalrous wit, sir knight." Daniel chuckled once, his chest and OICW heaving as he stood before her.

"Knight?" he asked, smiling. "Well, I don't know about that."

"My apologies, I made a foolish assumption," She asserted, still brushing herself off mentally from the whole event, trying to hit the ground running best she could. "I mused, 'By what right can one bear such magnificent enchanted plate if not in service to a lord?' I forget in this realm such pleasantries are regarded as quaint." Daniel laughed now.

"Idrid, isn't it?" He noted, smiling wide. "I love how you speak. It's fun."

"Fun?!" She blushed, rearing back and up a little, raising her head above the towering Daniel. "I- I would thank you, I suppose? Sir... Danny?"

"Daniel, actually. I like the sound of Sir Daniel." She clawed a little at her face as if to hide her blushing beneath a wing, though she still had her muzzle on, which Daniel finally found reason to acknowledge. "You... Do you *want* to have that on, or-"

"Oh, no! If you could remove this and the cursed necklace I wear, I would be eternally in your debt. Well, in addition to reasoning with poor Alex." Daniel approached her and she took steps forward, his OICW magnetically locking itself to his armored back as he inspected the latch, snapping it off with the armor's fingers, the mask clunking to the ground. I saw her smile, opening her mouth wide in a happy yawn. "Ah! Free to sing again!" She beamed, as he also crunched through the locking system of her shock collar, it as well falling to the ground. Idrid laughed out, smiling wildly, feeling her neck and face with her wing-ends, Daniel stepping back to admire his work, her happiness. He was practically blushing harder than she was, as she picked up the smashed remains of her chains and tossed them out the open door-window leading into the night sky in glee, laughing as she stuck her head outside and let a powerful stream of flame burst forth from her maw, the rain steaming and sizzling and she laughed in freedom, turning back to Daniel, her wingtips gripping him by the pauldrons. "Oh, Thank you, Sir Daniel!" With her mouth still full of smoke, she kissed him on the lips in an instant, before whipping back around and leaping from the window, sailing off, laughing, practically in song. I watched Daniel's reaction, an armored hand coming up to his mouth and face, like still tasting the smoke on his tongue, letting it waft out of his mouth, agape in awe.

"...Sir Daniel, huh," I uttered, as he blushed on and on, practically quivering in joy, watching her zipping about outside, flames brightening up the world as she laughed and harmonized, soaring over the treetops until she disappeared from hearing and view, Daniel tantalized by her afterimage. "...You... you good?"

"...Never kissed anybody before," He whispered, feeling his lips, like touching hers all over again. I couldn't help but smirk, watching him staring out into the storm.

### Chapter 74

Coming back down, with the rain slowing, it was evident that the pit was ours. Nearly all of the Captain's soldiers sat huddled by kommandos watching over them with their guns, the indentured servants coming out to look and be counted in our weird little census, those of the Captain's harem standing beneath the awning of the mansion, the serpentine maids standing about as well. I paused for a second, watching one of the maids, that cherry red one throwing her stupid showy hat off and screaming "Mark!" and embracing one of the male draconic workers who came forward for her, his arms wide open. I noticed Tanya huffing to herself in indignation, her glare finding me. It was weird, to say the least, how she was singling me out here in her gaze. Like I'd spilled milk on the carpet.

"Oh, hey Noah, Lauren," A voice called brightly, a somewhat shorter combatant approached, face obscured by her NVGs that were soon flipped up out of the way to reveal it was none other than Samantha, a strand of faded, bleached pink bangs still jutting out beneath her helmet just out of the way of her eyes. "You guys are alright!"

"Where's Abel? Is he okay?" I asked, giving Sam pause.

"Oh yeah. He's back with the rest. The hole sealed up but his upper heart's still not back to beating yet. He gets kinda lightheaded because of it so he's taking it easy."

"Hey guys," Reina uttered brightly, approaching us nearby.

"Hah!" Archie chuckled grimly, also coming up, letting his weapon hang in its sling around him. "Gormless sons of bitches! If only shortstone was this easy!

Hey, it's Noah's fault they gave up; these guys didn't want to fight without their commander," Anthony nodded to me with a look over his shoulder towards Archie, Selicia also coming up to greet us, as I heard the Kommandoes' chuck wagon coming into camp, that big school bus the kommandoes had lifted, reserve kommandoes manning it, seeing Abel sticking out of a window on a mounted gun, waving as he saw us.

"Noah! Lauren!" He uttered weakly, though girding his strength with the joy of seeing us again. "Good to see you guys."

"Hey, Abel," I waved.

"Almost like the whole band's back together again," Archie grumbled with all of us standing here, and I was given pause.

"...Yeah. Almost." The silence took over, and at least the rain was stopping. I looked over to the mostly silent Daniel, lost in thought as he presided over the affair, for a segue. "You wearing my power armor?"

"Yup." He was still looking off into the black distance.

"You figure the controls on your own?"

"Gabe taught me." I smirked sadly.

"Yeah. That sounds like Gabe all right." We shared a long, morose sigh.

"Alright!" I suddenly heard, turning to see Squid dismount the bus, slapping his hands together as he strode out, the imposing Duke alongside him, the two of them smiling over their little band of PoWs assembled. "This all of 'em? Where's the pile of the dead?"

"Uh…" One of the other kommandoes delineated, approaching, thumbing over his shoulder to two of the kommandoes hauling the Captain's body over out of the mansion, laying him in the mud. I could see Tanya over where she stood, hardly fazed by her so called "Husband" being tossed there like so much refuse, simply sneering at the inconvenience. "...That's it. Rest are just wounded."

"Man, what a cocksucker," Squid laughed out to the census crowds, the PoW personnel herded there staring at the tossed, naked body, his neck crooked and bruised black, eyes bulging and tongue hanging about grotesquely just like his genitals were, Kommandoes going to lay an old blanket over his mud-soaked corpse. I felt a little self-conscious seeing him again, even if the feeling lessened as his face disappeared beneath cloth. Was it guilt? I don't think I could feel that anymore. "Welp, since y'all made this easy," Squid addressed the prisoners. "I guess we owe it to you to let y'all either join us or go your own way. If you dip, we'll make sure you've got a gun and a magazine's worth of ammo and a week's worth of rations tomorrow morning when you set out. Some of us are gonna stay here and some of us are going to a different place; who you're with is up to you. Just let us know and we'll get you sorted into the right crowd." Meanwhile, I spotted Sam over there with Abel still on the bus, the two of them sharing a kiss as he hung himself out of the window and she got on her tiptoes to receive it, their little conversation ceasing. I turned back around, seeing most of the prisoner pile sitting there patiently to be sorted, waiting for a Kommando to question them and figure out where they'll be going. The servants were also similarly sorted, and of all of them, it seemed that the lion's share of people there wanted to join us. It felt good, I supposed.

"...You worried about the Citadel and all these people? We're practically an army now," Lauren's voice met me, and I looked over. At least it wasn't raining anymore.

"Yeah," I sighed, staring up into the black night sky, before down into the pit, seeing the bunks filling up with people yet again, the halls of the mansion lighting up as kommandoes and fellow indigoes celebrated the total victory. I noted Adrianne and her boyfriend Mark, a red-skinned humanoid dragon teenager, his shade of red practically mirroring hers, with shaggy blond hair over on a patch of dirt. Mark up to his knees and the halfway point of his tail in the hole he was digging for the covered corpse of the Captain. I guess he felt, out of some sense of nobility, to do the right thing for the bastard that enslaved the two of them. Despite that, the pair seemed genuinely happy through simply being together, Adrianne sitting there and conversing in cheerful, playful tones with her beau. "...But I figure we'll cross that bridge when we get to it."

"I can't wait to see it," Lauren threaded her arm through mine, even if I was wearing power armor, doing her best to rest her head on my hard ceramid pauldron. Maybe that we stood at a closer height to one another with me in this suit, she liked it in some capacity. "I've waited my entire life to, after all." I smiled, chuckling.

"Heh, yeah." You'll love it, how it looks in the winter. With the-"

"-The big central tower covered in frost, sparkling like it's made of crystal?" She smiled, reciting what I'd undoubtedly repeated ad nauseam. "Yeah. I also can't wait to see snow. It sounds magical." I let out a sigh.

But I noted another presence, turning my head a little. Daniel stood there, now in casual clothes, staring off into the cold, quiet night with his hands behind his back. He shivered in the frigid wind, staring off into the distance. I sighed, popping out of the armor and quietly commanding it to go walk into the awning of the mansion, the voice, now back to a normal one, complied simply. "Hey," I approached Daniel.

"Hey." I looked him over. He'd grown in these months I'd been with him, for sure. He looked so much stronger, stood so much taller, more confident. It just hit me all at once, standing here. Here he was, staring off into the distance.

"You waiting for her?"

"I guess," He uttered. "Probably silly. She was locked up, here. Makes sense for her to want to go home."

"Yup." I didn't have much to console him with. "You know, it's real cold out. You should come inside."

"I think I want to be alone for a little bit," He uttered simply, a sigh on his lips. "I'll join you guys soon."

The mansion was so much more... Joyous, now that the Captain's dreary shows of fanciness weren't being upheld at the cost of everything else. The central dining room was converted into a mead hall of sorts, Squid and Duke and all the rest helping themselves to locally-brewed moonshine and various spirits, the kitchen fired up for a late-night feast. "...Happy Halloween Noah," Squid said as I took a seat beside him, as he was currently chewing loudly on a chicken leg cooked up for him. "Well, not really. It's midnight. Tomorrow night's Halloween, but hey, might as well live in the moment, eh?" He laughed. "Never know when you'll get garroted by your own prisoner." He laughed on, and I sat there in silence. I guess I was pretty hungry, too. "Hey, bro. Uh... Sorry about your girl being AWOL."

"W-what?" I uttered, for but a moment before I looked to Lauren. But as I turned, I could see other eyes drawn to me. Archie, Selicia, Anthony, Reina. I could even feel Sam and Abel's gaze from the corner. "Uh... Yeah." I seemed to distance myself from Lauren where we sat. She too shifted uncomfortably, genuine sadness in her eyes. Sadness not for me, but for Maria. "I... We..." Telling the lie I told Lauren was so tempting. That we broke up. But it felt more than simply ingenuine now. Downright distasteful. Lauren was gazing into me. We were together now, and not once did we ponder how we'd break the news to the group. She looked at me, maybe wondering if I told anyone else that Maria and I had broken up. Maybe even if I was telling the truth. But probably, she was thinking, seeing that distastefulness too.

"...She's tough," Selicia cut in, maybe doing her part to try to be supportive. Sure didn't seem her character. The time must have changed her and I was just noticing, again. "I'm sure we'll see her again." The words like daggers in my veins, slitting my wrists with my own sins. I could hardly stand it, as I picked up a goblet of some sort of booze. I couldn't stand the bitter taste but it was like I needed to cover my face with something, the cup the closest appropriate object.

"Yeah," I whispered into my drink.

"...Well, uh," Squid trailed on, grunting and shifting in his seat uncomfortably. "I know you must be going through some stuff with the thought of her gone or something, I don't mean to impose, but..." reached over to knock my shoulder with his knuckles, speaking more softly now. "Gotta talk business. About the citadel."

"...You go up and find it without me?" I asked dully, not entirely seriously, yet glad enough for a topic change.

"Well, sort of," he uttered, and I eyed him, waiting for him to continue. "Kind of didn't want to make an introduction without you. You being our voucher and all. Don't really think they'd take kindly to our militia-like appearance. Especially given how sustaining ourselves is harder now with no war supply lines to sabotage."

"Hail them at all?"

"Nope. Still radio silence. We thought it might be that pandemic that's killing a lot of people, sent Corvie for a fly-by," Squid motioned towards the raven-like hybrid woman in the corner tearing at some chicken with her beak, the chicken wing held in her two scaly grey hands, looking up to us at the mention of her name and blinking a little, black wings ruffling behind her. "Hey Corv, tell Noah what you saw."

"Shit looks pretty grim, boss," she uttered, swallowing. "Town's neat, but nobody's in the streets of the place. Soldiers and all on the walls, looked pretty ready to go to me. No piles of bodies or anything, like other settlements we've found that's been wiped out. Don't think it's the pandemic."

"Thanks, Corv," Squid uttered and Corvie went to tear another piece off. If my mind was present, I would have noted of watching this bird hybrid devour a cooked bird was macabre enough.

"...Pandemic?" I asked.

"Yeah," Squid uttered. "We stumbled across other survival hides with nothing but dead bodies in 'em. Scavenging off of 'em is sorta how we've been keeping ourselves afloat."

"...Y-you have biohazard gear, right?" I stuttered concernedly.

"Ah, that's the thing, lemme get to the real surprise," He noted, waggling his finger, completely unfazed for somebody describing a certain-death super-disease, grinning smugly enough. "Not a single hybrid body in any of the pits. Not a single hybrid anywhere." He smirked. "One of these places had a bunch of iconography about some 'Kingdom of Humans' or something stupid. Humans-only racial movement started up recently, you might've heard of 'em. Place just full of corpses."

"It doesn't kill hybrids?" I uttered.

"That's the shit," He leaned in. "Our medic Jimmy thinks it's part of whatever's 'ending the world' or something, that whole conspiracy with the 'Creators'. Kills too quick and dies off itself. Doesn't live long enough to really spread; just gets in your place and wipes everyone out before you know what's going on. Not only that; it doesn't just not affect hybrids, seems to Jimmy as if hybrids themselves act like a ward. He did some tests, seems to think that hybrids produce antibodies that start to sustain themselves in living creatures around them. The more and closer the physical contact a human gets with hybrids, the faster you get saturated with the antibodies. Enough of it and you'll be as immune to it as they are. Points to the conspiracy idea pretty blatantly if you ask me, but again, just a theory."

"...W-what about the citadel?" I cried, concerned, even if I was given the rather calming revelation that I was more than likely basically immune to this mysterious instant-death plague.

"Dunno. Like Corv said, no body pits, some activity ongoing. Doesn't look like they're letting anyone in at the moment, figure it's not that." I sat there with that grim look on my face until Squid slapped me on the back with a chuckle. "Chin up, guy. They're probably not all dead."

"...Dad always did say if they could find a use for hybrids they'd let them in," I chuckled grimly to myself in remembrance, to keep my spirits high.

"Well, here's hoping. So the weather looks like it's gonna be alright, but given how it's been cold as shit lately, I'm betting we'll get an early snowfall this year. The roads back are dodgy, practically foot trails, but we should be there before the weather makes them-"

"Hey there," We were suddenly interrupted, watching as a specific dragoness came upon Squid on his opposite side from where I sat, draping her arm gingerly over the back of his neck as she poured him some more booze. Tanya, fins fluttering, sparkling eyes flashing upon him. She'd gotten dressed rather quickly, in one of her more sultry, showy outfits. The kind with far too much lace. The high socks and gloves were a nice touch, though. "...You're the... big man, huh?" I noted how she practically moaned the words *big man*, playing him up.

"Excuse me?" He grunted uncomfortably, almost seeming insulted with the arm draped on him, an eyebrow arched back at her.

"Don't play coy, now," Tanya uttered, puffing her lips out a little, doing her best to keep things going. "...I hear you like *dragons*." Squid took one more moment to look her over, a laugh forming on his lips, before he simply stuck his arm up and his big mitt of a hand formed over the end of her muzzle, gently shoving her away. She cried out muffled as she shoved him off of herself, recoiling dramatically. "Ugh!" She sat there on the ground with her tail between her legs. "*Fudgepacker!*" Her showy veneer sure was easily buffed off, showing that deep down she was just as vulgar and hotheaded as anyone else. The rather verbose and arguably antiquated term made Squid laugh. I laughed too, despite my nerves.

"Fudge-packer?" He laughed vehemently. "What, *faggot* not enough? Gotta get fancy now? Fuck off, gold digger," Squid picked up and sipped the drink she'd poured for him and smiled, smacking his lips. "This is good shit, though. Get me another bottle, would you?"

"Fuck this! I'm going to Vancouver, where they have straight people!" She screeched, stomping out, red in the face.

"Good luck!" Squid saluted and she just screamed into her teeth as the door slammed in her wake. I looked over to Lauren, catching a shrug and a chuckle. "Jesus, what an idiot. I wouldn't want to be caught dead over there right now. The place is busy in its own coup, old party members being executed by their own people over mismanagement. I do hear they've got some ideas about re-branding themselves as Cascadia, we'll see how that turns out. Once the heads stop rolling," He chuckled endlessly. It was weird how we could laugh about this like we were. Almost like the conversation avoided a specific topic at all costs. That I avoided a topic.

"Hey- This party still going on?!" I heard a laughing voice, one that raised my eyebrows, a voice that, last I heard it was mired in melancholy, now utterly joyous. It was Daniel's voice, and I turned to take in his smiling gaze, full of glee. Another second of looking, seeing past him to the movement behind him and I understood why. Idrid herself, with her great blue scaled body followed him cheerfully, having come back apparently, much to my surprise and Daniel's utter elation, walking on all four of her limbs, doing her best to remain at our height despite her rather great size.

"Y-you came back," I noted dumbly as Daniel pulled up a seat next to Lauren, one away from I, Idrid sitting her rear down but rearing up some, noting the low chandelier of the dining hall directly before her eyes as if making a note to avoid hitting it with her head.

"Of course, I, Idrid Blackmantle, am honorbound to Sir Daniel twice over," She uttered happily, Daniel smiling over to her all the way, everyone else in the room gazing up at her, like she was the centerpiece of the night rather than the two of us, our spotlight stolen away for a brief time. "I do wish to return home, but none of House Blackmantle would be so boorish as to skirt our honor."

"She says that, but she really wants to see the Citadel too," Daniel laughed. People being told about the Citadel was sort of expected, at this point, so I could hardly be mad. Matter of fact I was kind of charmed anyways. I guessed I didn't mind Idrid knowing.

"Oh, yes! Master Noah, your Sir Daniel tells me of the realm you reign over, with its glorious battlements," She smiled with bright, imaginative eyes. "Sir Daniel and I have discussed the terms of my recompense. Before I return to my people and show Sir Daniel our great realm, I wish to visit yours. I can delay a reunion with my family for a couple more days, I am sure. Perhaps, though I am merely the lastborn of House Blackmantle the royal Sky-Knights of our holy mount, I may help broker an alliance?"

"...Yeah. sounds good." I turned around again. Man, I guess I was hungry. I helped myself to some food.

"Miss Lauren, I hear you are a leatherworker and saddlemaker," I heard Idrid discussing beside me to Lauren. "I have not the coin to compensate you at this time, but could you-"

"I mean, I sort of just made a horse-saddle work for... Me," Lauren interjected. "I... I've got a few ideas though. I can probably make you a saddle, sounds fun. And, uh. Real clothes, if you want. If that's your thing."

"Thank you, Lady Lauren! My fellow, er..." Idrid was given pause, looking Lauren up and down. "...Half-drake? No, you are more akin to a... Three-fourths? Drake and a half?"

*"...just stick with lady,"* Lauren growled as cordially as she could, squirming in place trying to mask her discomfort, a grit smile on her face, nodding, trying not to be insulted.

"Y-yes, of course," I looked back over to see the blushing Idrid squirming a little where she sat, her wing-hands up towards her face as she blushed and smiled, turning back to Daniel. "What fortune, Sir Daniel! Soon I can show you the majesty of drakenkind as we sail the skies together!" She huffed proudly with a blushing smile upon her face, a little smoke coming from her nostrils as she did that chest-beat salute she did.

"Heh, alright. But you don't have to call me Sir all the time."

"Oh- do I embarrass you, Sir- Er, Mister- uh, D-Daniel?"

Daniel was still grinning ear to ear, looking at her with nothing but love in his heart. "...You know what, call me whatever you like. You can't make me not love the way you speak, Iddy."

"Oh- okay! Daniel!" Idrid beamed. I wondered if she was even picking up the signals he was sending out, but she seemed receptive enough as Daniel laid an arm over the back of her big neck and she leaned in, giggling.

It was late enough, and I got up, walking out. Lauren was right beside me, following intently. "Man," She uttered. "You know, It's good seeing Daniel happy, y'know?"

"...You know, he's said that if he hadn't come off as such a wimp when he met you, he would have put the moves on you."

"Heh, yeah right," Lauren chuckled a little, before feeling a little bad for laughing like that, scratching the back of her neck. "...I mean, nothing against him, it's just... Yeah. I guess I still see him like when I met him. Sure, he's changed, I guess..." She couldn't find a way to justify it, just walking in-pace with me as we found an unoccupied bedroom in the mansion. "...I think Idrid likes him. Guess it's all in the first impression."

"...How about me?" I asked as we walked in.

"Well, you always did stand up for me," She uttered. "I didn't exactly have the greatest self-esteem back then. You could say I was easy pickings for you."

"Mm, if only I knew I was interested back then," I uttered, plopping down. Lauren crawled onto the big king-size bed, turning once as she circled herself to lay down beside me, flipping belly-side towards me to look me face-to-face. "Hey, you remember what you said about being the weird one?" I asked. "Biggest thing in the room?" She burst out a breath of a chuckle, closing her eyes to laugh softly.

"...Damn, don't even have that anymore," She chuckled. "Yeah. I could get used to being average."

"*Above* average," I uttered, turning to place my hands on her humanoid hips, where her lower and upper torsos met. "There's still a lot of you to love."

"Just keep going and going, don't I?" She smiled plainly. I kissed her right on the lips, a quick peck.

"Don't think I'll ever run out of you."

Love. That love was between us and it seemed like nothing we could do would ruin it. Even all this tonight. God, I loved her, and I loved proving it to her. Like consummating a marriage. A *real* marriage. I knew as soon as we got to the citadel, we'd march right up to the town minister. My dad, my family, the situation there, none of it seemed to matter. We'll deal with it when the time comes, we thought, we knew, with conviction.

But a ghost lingered. A haunting spectre hanging herself in the misty, smoky air of the Battle of Shortstone, standing there with her broken heart in her hands. She did this to herself. You wouldn't go away. You did this to yourself. Just leave me, okay? You did this to yourself. I never wanted you. *You did this to yourself.* It was obvious. **You did this to yourself.**

But why am I the evil one?

The world stopped spinning when I awoke.

**Chapter 75**

It was time to go.

"Y'know, if the Citadel doesn't work out," Squid's voice hung in my ear as I sat there beside him in one of the seats, the bus ambling down the road with the rest of our vehicles, the second to last in the column. I noticed how interesting the vehicle really was- everything jury-rigged, battle-worn. A ferocious biodiesel engine screaming from whatever fuel they could synthesize to feed it. Armor panels along the sides made from ceramic tiles torn from the furnishings of houses, the roof cut for machine gun and cannon nests, just like many of the vehicles in this convoy were. "...We've got the pit now as backup, so we can always go back."

"...Yeah, if they had enough food," Squid's logistics guy uttered plainly, some felinid engineer hybrid. "The dude running the place was eating himself out of house and home. Wasteful fucker's stores were already depleted to shit. Even with the growing operation he had going, with the amount of personnel we have here and there in total, we'll never be able to sustain our population."

"Yeah, yeah. Don't be a pessimist, Gary. Once we get a good deal with Noah's people, even if they aren't keen on letting us all in as citizens I'm sure they'd like having a small army to call upon, and we'll work something out." The conversation was interesting enough, even if I was still out of it. God damn, it was like I was the ghost. It was funny enough to chuckle at.

The roads weren't good at all, much to none of our surprise. Even with the weather staying stable as of late, it seemed that we weren't going to get there until tomorrow by any means, and we had no intention of traveling at night with the demands of visibility in the winding roads of the dense forest, nightvision or not. Lauren was next to me, and we kept close. It seemed like our skin was stretched a little less taut over our bones now that we had food to eat, people to be with. But we'd sit there, and feel the atmosphere change as our fellows took notice. Even the Kommandoes seemed to catch on that something was different, seeing the two of us closer than before. Even if it was simple things, leaning up against one another, speaking reassuringly in hushed tones. I saw Lauren's eyes, saw how they glittered beautifully at my sight. And I couldn't help but see how everyone else saw it. I sighed, casting my worries aside as I let myself melt into her. It didn't matter anymore. We were going home, finally.

But it still sat ill with me.

We made camp, and for the longest time I was still, and was watching. The weight was far from lifted from my shoulders, but for a moment it felt lighter, as I watched, perhaps a bit too voyeuristically Anthony and Selicia laying there. How Anthony slowly sat down at Selicia's request and lay down adjacent to her, staring up at the stars.

"...It's pretty, isn't it?" Selicia sighed long and hard, humanoid chest heaving as she unclipped her body armor and shrugged it off of herself for it to thump in the cool grass. I turned a little bit to eavesdrop.

"Yeah," Anthony responded. "You can really see the whole Milky Way out here, with no city lights or anything." The crickets chirped on and on as the two of them sighed together.

"...You have your night vision?"

"Yeah," Anthony rose a hand, as if to point to his headset where the helmet-mounted swivel eyepiece was, before letting his hand fall back down. *There was no need for motions, she wasn't looking at me*, he must have thought awkwardly to himself.

"Turn yours on and look again." Anthony took a moment in that silence to reach back up to his monocular atop his helm, flipping it down. He drew in breath again.

"W-wow," He uttered. "They're- *wow*," He was beside himself.

"...Really that much better, huh?"

"It's... beautiful," He hushed.

"It's what I see all the time," Selicia explained in yet another sigh. "I guess it really is special. I just had to stop and appreciate it." They were quiet for a while, Anthony just looking up there. "...If the stars only came out once every hundred years, everything would just stop. Everyone would go outside, a holiday would be called, everyone would turn off their lights, and people would just look up into the sky. World peace for a night." She paused to sigh silently, but it wasn't her pause. It was a charismatic, showman's pause that held the platitude balancing in the air, but not like the way *she* would have said it: it made it evident that this was something she was merely repeating. "...But instead the stars come out every night and we'd rather run around amusing ourselves with meaningless shit." Another sigh. Like each was a sentence or a thought of their own. She really couldn't run out of them. "...Gabriel told me that. One night when he woke me up for my turn to guard, but he took me up onto the roof and made me lay down and just... look at the stars with him. I..." She paused, letting it trail off. Rather than sigh again her breath hung heavy in her heart, teeth gritting a little bit. "...I really appreciate him doing that," She said as her voice cracked, Anthony finally looking over with his free eye, where she lay opposite him, the two of them head-to-head. They didn't say a thing, still staring up into the endless sky to sigh and let their eyes gather water.

For a moment there, I felt that weight grow lighter. How this world was spinning out of control, how I could just look up into the sky for a moment and simply exist. I looked up, just to pull my own helmet back on to flick down the NODs. God, it was really that beautiful. Why... Why did he never tell me this? What other things did he know, little bits that could make one's life just a little more magical? What else had he taken with him in his passing? Maybe he had told me, and I just ghosted through the conversation. I felt that sour pit in my stomach at the thought. Wishing to redo this whole stupid summer all over again. God. How could I have been like this?

"What do you think Curtis has been doing all this time?" Lauren's voice met me like a shark meeting a swimmer, dashing through the waters of thought to bear into me. I felt jelly in my gut for a moment, even as I was sitting down it was like I'd lost my balance as her voice hit me. "...Noah?"

"H-huh?"

"Y'know," She slowly delineated, an arm coming around my ribs between my arm, not yet my armpit or my hip, somewhere in between. Her grip was rigid. She was staring up too, with her tac glasses and its night vision module attached, gazing up as well. I could see the water in her eyes. Trying to distract herself with petty conversation, barely hiding her creaking voice. "A-alien guy, back in... Crystal Springs."

"...Yeah." I paused, not really realising it was a question. Still stargazing, into that bright blackness. "...Probably with... the bunker guy."

"You think he's looking at the sky right now?" Lauren asked. I saw she was clutching that little tin spaceship on a lanyard he'd given her. I saw her trinkets, that spaceship, that three-pointed crux, and a white molar tooth, pierced by wire to hang with the rest of her nicknacks as she rubbed the little rocket ship with her thumb. "...Thinking of aliens?"

"...Yeah. Sure." I wasn't one for conversation, still lost in myself, lost in the sky. Lauren leaned into me, her eyes also transfixed into the eternium. The two of us sitting there, trying to lose ourselves. Trying to flee from regret, from loss. We knew in a day all this would be over, but it wasn't that simple. There was so much to come back from. So much to have *survived*. Too much.

"...What do you think about aliens?"

"I dunno." We had nothing to say. This October night, a Halloween so far and long away from home. Here with our band of brigands. I didn't want to think of Gabriel, how gone he was from this world yet refused to leave my mind. His cheerful smile with its mysterious edge. The way he stood like a mountain, invincible. I'd see him and feel like any situation in the world could be made right. But he only remained in my mind, and with the thoughts of Gabriel and his lack came images of the situation that to me could truly never be made right. Maria. Her eyes wide in that betrayal, that piercing sorrow as she fell, still cemented in my mind. What have I done? I… I could never tell her that I never felt a single thing for her. That was what really stung, not her falling, but my… betrayal. She bet everything on me. I cost her everything. What could I truly enjoy with Lauren, with the one I loved, knowing what my inability to face my own feelings cost the one who loved me? What have I done? I wished Gabriel was here. I wish he'd tell me what to do. I wish he'd have told me earlier. I wish he'd have told me everything he knew, everything I should have known. I wished I could see that sardonic little smirk in these overwhelming odds and come back in the morning with some wild game to cook up for us, this starved army of rags, for him to laugh and tell us not to sweat it and that it was all gonna be alright. I wished I could have done that whole day, his last day differently. I wished he wasn't dead. I wished he was right here next to me. I *wished he wasn't dead*. And I wished I had never betrayed Maria. I wished I could have told her years ago. But here, it was getting harder and harder to deny my guilt. I was cursed.

God, why did you let me be so cruel?

"Noah?"

I couldn't stand the chasm widening in my mind. I embraced Lauren, and she reciprocated. God, loved her but I felt a million miles away. No way to tell her what I'd done. No way to confess. It was like I knew if I couldn't be with her, I would die. But if I remained, no amount of love could take away my monstrousness.

We went to our tent. Away from the rest a ways. Stripping down, embracing each other flesh-to-flesh. The frigid wind blew outside, even permeating the tent in here. There was only warmth in one another. But deep down I knew that as soon as her and I left this embrace, I would be hollow once more, like I would be hollow forever. I didn't want it to end. I didn't want to be a sinner anymore.

"Hey Noah!" I was hearing outside. Squid's voice. He sounded as jolly as usual, that unstoppable mirth of his. Not now, I wanted to say. I was busy. "Guess who's here! Ahaha!" Like an unexpected birthday guest. I could hear others outside. A crowd gathering.

I could hardly raise my voice, before Fate herself walked through the flap of the tent and my sins were made apparent.

Maria stood there. No, not an apparition. This was no trick of the mind, this was no ghost haunting me. What I saw standing there was *flesh*. Bones upon taut, scarred skin and rags upon them. This was not the Maria of my mind, Maria the Beautiful, a perfect ghost, but Maria the Punished, punished for loving one who could not love her back. The skin upon her face was ragged, aside from how she lacked all body fat, a garish scar extended from the side of her chin, through her lips before deviating at her cheek, one ugly tendril reaching out towards her shattered right ear and the other bisecting her right eye, no longer a clear mahogany brown but a faded, cataracted squint, the explosion scar resulting in more than a couple spatterings of fragmentation pockmarks scabbed over yet not truly healed, the scars burned into her flesh from a general lack of nutrition after the fact, bits of her scalp on the right side of her head raw and inflamed from the burns, hair missing and clumped in places. I saw her rags, a poncho improvised out of a plastic trash bag, the end of some rifle, not her own trusty AR15 but some wood-stocked bolt action piece scavenged or stolen poking out from beneath it, and her rifle-free right hand clutching a flat, black object, many fingertips missing, replaced only by raw bandages.

A smile was on her face, at first. A true smile of her soul, not a performative grin like posing for a formal photo; the smiles I'd been used to seeing on her. Something it feels like I'd never seen, more alien than everything else about here in the here and now. Like her pride was spilling over with how she made it. How she was strong, and how she would be received by the man who loved her. Not the man who left her to die on a battlefield alone, so far from home. About how she betrayed herself by believing vainly after all this time, the truth cracking its way through her edifice. That smile disappearing like a sun setting never to rise again as she saw the both of us embraced and naked. I saw through her rags how her knees turned to jelly, and I looked down, seeing only one boot-clad foot, her right foot gone and replaced from about mid-calf down by a stick, a twig tied to the remains of her lower leg with tight wire that dug into her raw flesh, an improvised prosthetic she'd walked a hundred miles on. This leg was the first to give out, falling to its knee and holding herself off the ground by the stock of her rifle, as she uttered a single word as her heart finally broke, unable to deny the roaring truth any longer.

"W-what?"

A broken-voice whimper that resonated like a scream. I could make out that object that occupied her right hand as it spilled from her grip to embed itself in the dirt like a dropped shield. A simple steel armor plate with a single, large dent on its front. More than likely, her rear body-armor plate. The one that saved her life while we sped away from her and a bullet struck her in the back and sent her falling to the ground, probably something she wanted to bring forth to laugh about. To say that it must have been fate for her to have been saved, for us to be together after all the tribulations she went through. The question as to how she survived, what terrible trials she'd endured to make it here to us hung for a single second before it all really hit me. Before her tears began to flow, her mouth agape. Sobbing without sound. It was like she would scream if not for her voice abandoning her just as it had abandoned me.

In a moment, I knew Lauren knew. I only had to take one look back at her and she knew, she knew it all from the look in Maria's single eye. She knew I never "broke up" with Maria. She knew of my cruelty. Perhaps she even could surmise that I left her there to die on purpose, Maria's horrified face enough proof of its own.

Maria's face was petrified into a grotesque, gaping howl despite her silence, clawing at her face with her mangled hands in an attempt to respond, to cover her visage somehow, before she forced herself up, up, like she had to flee from danger, or like she was a wild animal herself fleeing from a horror more vicious than she. Hobbling, shrouding her face with her raking hands like a witch, cursed. The sound beginning to flow. An awful, ugly howl, like the song of a banshee. Wailing into the sky as she limped out. I saw the people out there, looking in. The judgement. The awful judgement. I could hardly think. The noise in my head was deafening, and as I looked back to Lauren, the final blow was dealt.

*"How could you?"*

She stood there, trembling. Eyes red and tears cascading down her face. Whatever selfishness, whatever monstrousness still remained in control of me at that point wanted to hide myself in her bosom once more, go back to the carnal pleasures, worry about all this some other never-time. But one look down her trembling arm and I saw how her fist clenched itself white, knuckles clasped around her crux, just like when she struck Gabriel as she stood there in the silence of Maria's mourning wail outside. I knew there was no escape now. *"How could you, Noah?"*

Naked.

Even after pulling on clothes numbly, staring blankly off into the abyss, I was cold, and I was naked. Here, fully clothed, no rain or snow, I'd never been as cold as I was in that moment. There I was, naked, writhing at the feet of god whom I once rebelled against in vanity. My weakness laid bare, my bane staring too, blankly, into the crackling fires of the camp as Selicia, Sam, Reina, Susan all doing their best to share space with her as she lost herself in the fire, the hellfire surrounding her, single eye glittering with it. They could do nothing to console her. And as they looked back upon me with glares mirroring God's very judgement, I knew there would be no consoling me either.

I went back to looking at the stars, away from everyone else, and let the numbing cold bid me to a dreamless void of sleep.

### Chapter 76

Nobody spoke for the longest time.

The engine of the bus was incredibly loud. Given the paltry state of the fuel synthesized to make it run, there was little wonder as to why. I sat as far forward as I could, not merely in the seat, but in the very doorway of the bus, just to be close to that harsh, numbing noise. And to be away from everyone else. I needed solitude. Really, I wanted to be with Lauren. Of course I did. But I needed to be here, I couldn't not be far apart from everyone else. Just looking outside to the forest rolling by. Like I was out there. That roaring engine made things quiet. Made the sound of people disappear. Made me think I was running out there, in the woods. Perfect, horrible solitude. A solitude that I couldn't escape.

I knew that at the end of this journey, so close, I would have to explain myself to the Citadel so they'd let us in. I figured I was saving myself for that moment, but I couldn't escape the feeling of judgement, even as far off as I pushed it in my mind. God, just to look at Maria and see how we held ourselves now and everyone there would know. My parents would know. God, I hadn't thought of them in forever, and I could already feel their shame, their judgement. I was dreading it all.

Maria. Sitting there. Minus a leg, an eye, an ear, her beautiful face, the bits of her fingers and, finally, her hope. Or maybe she still had hope. She hadn't done anything drastic since our reunion. She was sticking with us, even if not with *me*. I saw her blank eye gazing into the forest just like I was, losing herself out in oblivion just like my love. Love. It wasn't love, it never was. She should have known better, I was thinking. A cruel musing to make myself feel better. I was done being cruel, I thought in an abstract lie. This was it. Nothing could top this.

I saw how she was clutching herself, wrapped in some scratchy surplus army blanket, the doc beside her. Looking down, holding his breath even, eyes wide. Maria was holding her belly. Not like it hurt, but rather like it was a burden. A burden she'd carried all the way back to me, for me, on my behalf. One look by the medic, that worried, awkward glare from him, too shocked to really be able to say anything and I knew. I was burdened with knowledge, just like Maria, just like Lauren, just like the whole group was burdened with my betrayal.

    She was carrying our child.

It wasn't even a shock, once I'd realized it. Just another... *thing*. Another piece of information that lost itself in the forest whirling by as I went to look out the window once more for the rest of this long, long day. A grand victory march this was.

Forest made way for green fields, endless green fields, the Sun casting its rays through the mist and clouds, and we could see, far off in the distance, great fields of wheat and farms about a single, shimmering icon atop a plateau that was once a hill. A great castle, walls of steel-reinforced concrete girded by battlements and solar arrays, and a central spire that reached towards the clouds that sat pristinely up a road of golden asphalt shimmering in the Sun, the edge of the lake on the other side of the hill barely peeking its way around like a bed of sapphire, the river and its dam far off, wind-turbines lazily spinning on the next hill far off, glittering solar fields interspersed with the farmlands. I ought to have felt relief at its sight, but I felt nothing but dread. This adventure of a lifetime ending on such a dour note, and it was all my fault. I wished I could have enjoyed it. I looked back to Lauren, hoping to revel in a fraction of the awe she felt, but she was struck dumb already by my actions, gazing to it with barely a smile on her face. She must have thought it looked like everything she'd ever imagined, but her soul was caged by regret, by sorrows. God, why did I have to put her through this? She loves too much, and her love would be the one to hurt her.

"...Shouldn't there be people working the fields?" I overheard the radio operator saying. "Man, they're still not letting us hail them."

"It's november, stupid," someone sitting close uttered.

"November *first*! Shouldn't they be, like, collecting the harvest or some shit?" He did have a point.

"Hey, take it slow," Squid was saying, walking up to the driver, standing above me. "Take it nice and-"

*Pop-pop-pop.*

The shattering glass was most distinct, then the supersonic cracks of machine gun fire with the echoing booms of the guns some three hundred meters away and the shouts of everyone around in surprise filled the air in rapid succession. The bus driver stomped on the screeching brakes and everyone dove down, but they seemed to be done shooting, inexplicably. I barely flinched, sitting there on the steps of the exit door. Not to say I wasn't surprised, I was just lost in myself.

"What the fuck was that shit?!"

"Squiddy? Max?" I heard Duke start to cry out, crawling on all sixes up towards me and where Squid lay. "Max?! MAX?!" He began to cry out. Squid wasn't moving. One look back and I saw his head laying open. God, it was like I could see Gabriel again, watching Duke cowering over him and crying out for the doctor as he cried Squid- no, Max's name. He was dead, the bus driver crouched there and looking back could tell him as much. Gabriel. Just like Gabriel. I could feel ice in my veins. I needed to run. They killed Gabriel. I was back there and they killed Gabriel.

I pulled the lever to open the door and piled out. People cried out for me, but all I could see was Gabriel's destroyed eye and the inside of his head full of red goop, his lifeless body. I needed to act. It's what Gabriel would do. Static filling my brain as I paced forward, unarmed. I unhooked my body armor inexplicably. I think I did it to show I wasn't a threat, that they just killed one of *my* friends. I was pacing quicker now, my hands up. It wasn't a surrender pose, it was a show of bravado. If you're gonna shoot anyone, shoot me, I was thinking. They sent rounds over my head once and I didn't even flinch. I could barely hear them yelling, the static in my head drowning out all else. I opened my mouth and roared. Not a scream, but a bestial

483

bellow of utter frustration, of rage. They fired in response, bullets kicking up dirt around my feet, and I finally stopped.

"WHAT THE FUCK WAS THAT SHIT?!" I screamed up those massive walls, standing before the towering behemoth before us. Barely like it was an actual friendly fire incident and another friend of mine was dead because of it, but more in the vein that somebody had bumped into my car. I guess it sounded right at the time.

"...Turn around and go back. You got your warning shot," I heard a crier yell from the hundred or so yards' distance, up on the wall by that smoking machine gun nest. I saw his face, some canid hybrid, and I knew things weren't what they seemed.

"Into my buddy's face! You fucking killed him!!" I bellowed.

"We'll kill you too if you don't turn around. Get back in your bus and leave, now."

"I live here, asshole! My name is Noah Reed! My father is Johnathan Reed!" I beat my chest. I heard them mutter amongst themselves, before another stood up. A human. I didn't recognize him.

"Not anymore you don't. We run this place now."

"What?!"

"We took this place over during the war. We sure as shit don't have anything to go home to now. This place is ours. Now get the fuck out of here!" Another barrage of machine gun fire around my feet and legs. I felt the hot dirt and rocks kicked into my skin, but I barely flinched, standing there. I didn't fear death. I don't think I would have felt a thing to get gunned down right then and there. All I felt was rage, that roaring frustration that had been building itself in me. I grit my teeth. There was nothing more to say. I turned around, storming back.


This was bad.

Sitting there, a ways away from everyone else, we knew it. Max's body wrapped up in a blanket further down, just like I was, sitting and watching people bickering. Those who weren't in the fray were silent, just like me, staring into nothingness. The argument was simple, where to go back to. Back to the Pit that we'd taken over. Not enough food there, all of it burned through by its last ruler. Back to Shortstone. Become raiders to make ends meet. But the longer people argued, the quieter things became.

I was watching Maria. Dead as I was, silent, laying back with her hands on our child growing within her, staring off into the sky, the dying of the light this dreary afternoon. It should have been beautiful, staring up into the sky, the puffy clouds not yet overcast, the sun shining the last of its radiant rays through a pink sky as the cold wind blew through the deep and dark forest. The darkness was encroaching, and that set the tone. No debate could withstand the awful truth that things could be no more grim.

I stood. I didn't even know it at first, like I was being lifted up. Forced to my feet among the dying of the cacophony of voices. Eyes shifting to me as I stood, and I approached the center of where we'd encircled our vehicles, seeing everyone there. All of the people I'd once called friends, before I let them all down. Nearly every Kommando and a good chunk of the Pit's militia and serfdom, the rest still back there, our backup. Maybe without us, those back at the pit would make it through the winter without starving. It'd be better for them if we all died, I thought morosely. It was bleak. We numbered just shy of a hundred, and it felt so insane. So pointless to try and make an assault. But it was our only option.

"...Listen," I uttered. Repeating myself in my head. I'd felt small, weak, pathetic and incompetent before this moment. Perhaps I still did, standing there, puffing my chest out, looking my friends and allies in the eyes. Ignoring it. Putting on the strong front. "What are you guys afraid of?" I asked. A legitimate question I was posing as they all looked to me. Murmurs abounded, but nobody really responded. "Some of you, I barely know. The rest must feel like you didn't know me at all, after what I did," I uttered, looking to my friends for a brief moment. "We've lost friends. Good friends. I know what you're afraid of." I paused, going to point. Point back, away from the great spire of the Citadel pointing skyward in the distance. "Back the way we came, back there- is nothing but death. Starve, and starve slow. Some of you may know hunger, and I know hunger. And we all know that's no way to go out." I then pointed the other way. All the way up that spire. "And that way... That's *my* birthright. It was my home away from home. It's what I came all this way for, and many of you did too. I don't know about all of you, but as for me- that's where I'm going to die. Either tonight, or years from now. Tonight, I'm gonna find the mother-fucker in charge of those cunts that took over *my home*, and I'm gonna rip him to pieces, even if it kills me." I was looking around as people watched, listened. Some Kommandoes nodding. My friends, eyes wide and receptive. Even some of the total strangers seemed moved by my bravado, or maybe even the bleakness of the situation itself. I had to say, even I was. It didn't even feel like I was the one speaking. It felt like my lips were being moved by someone else, my voice was deep and rolled like thunder. I believed every word I spoke, and it rang in the ears of those bearing witness. "I am the living dead. I shouldn't be here. I don't deserve help. But, if I'm gonna kill that mother-fucker, I'm gonna need backup, to make it a chance."

"...Have you got a plan?" A voice rose. Maria was sitting up now. She had yet to smile. I doubted my paltry apology resonated in her. It was too early for true sorries, but she spoke nonetheless. It almost made me fumble, having to fight through my shame to answer her.

"The Citadel has a secret entrance," I uttered, first to her, then to everyone else as I found my courage again. "When I was a kid, I'd always play in the tunnel. I know it by heart. The secret entrance leads right into the heart of the city, into the keep, and the tower. Beneath the tower is the armory, and beside it, the war room. If he's anywhere, he's there." I paused, looking over to our armor suits. "I'm gonna take a suit of power armor and go in alone while you guys assault the walls themselves. Just take potshots, snipe, send a bit of mortar fire. It'll just be me, and I'll get in and kill as many of the bastards as I can. Soon as I breach the surface and get back in radio contact, you should charge the walls while they're disoriented, and by that time their leadership should be out of the picture."

"Alone, huh?" Daniel was asking, leaned up against Idrid while she too listened in awe and respect, like she was bearing witness to the final battle speech of a legendary hero. Too kind of her to think of me in that light. Maybe it was the words I spoke. Who I was emulating. "We've got two suits of power armor, Noah. Maybe-"

"No," I uttered. "You'll be needed in the frontal assault. I need to do this alone. I can't be bogged down." Nobody responded, but I could feel the thought coursing through everyone. That I was embarking on a suicide mission. But the air permitted it. It was on all our minds, everyone ready for their own personal suicide mission.

"Beats waiting to die," Archie scoffed. "So what are we waiting for?"

"Get some rest," I ordered. "Five AM tomorrow, when the night is at its darkest, we'll strike, and we'll make 'em wish they never put eyes on this place."

### Chapter 77

Death.

It was like practicing for the real thing, waiting those long hours for the night to pass by. I took the time to shave my head bare, to feel the cold bite of the frozen wind upon my head, but even that didn't seem to faze me. A sublime period of time, not unlike the last time we all prepared for a hopeless battle at our lowest point. But this was different, so very different without Gabriel. I sat there, glaring into the armor I'd soon don and ruminated on it all. Like I was asking for his guidance, his divine providence. It couldn't have been all augmentation, could it? There was always something more to him. His spirit. His soul. A concept he would have scoffed at more than a day before his death.

No, I knew. This all rode on me. Really, it always had, but here it was most evident. If I failed to take out their leader, if my flanking maneuver goes up in smoke, everyone is doomed. But somehow, nobody seemed to want to stop me, and even Daniel's offer to back me up was singular, and he pressed no further after I'd refused his help. Maybe they all knew. Knew I needed to face my death on my own. Redeem my honor with a final, valiant charge.

I wasn't tired. I wasn't hungry. I didn't even wear my brace, just sitting naked there before the armor, the plugsuit folded neatly. Maybe this is how Gabriel felt on his own suicide mission to take out Red. I'd practically forgotten the day, the utter triumph dashed by the very next battle and his own demise. I smiled at that victory, so far away, practically lost to the ages. I was alone now, unable to escape back to when things made sense. When we had a leader, not a pretender. God, this was stupid. Pointless. But beyond that, this was necessary.

Good old Sentinel, full of dings and pockmarks and blast damage all the more. The Captain's helm placed on the suit, a fully-loaded OICW ready to go, the armor girded with AR10 magazines full of armor piercing munitions for the main gun and 30mm Vulcan rounds bandoliered for the top-mounted cannon of the armament.

It was a religious experience, hearing someone call to tell me that it was time, as I slowly stood up, stripping myself bare. I took a moment to look over my body. I barely felt the frigid wind that blasted through the trees, but I could hear so much. I looked up into the stars. The world was beautiful. I hope Gabriel thought the world was beautiful before he died, too. I slipped into the plugsuit, tightening it up, coming up behind the armor to climb inside. The claustrophobia melted away as the suit came online and came to my bidding. I felt light. I felt like a warrior. My wounded leg was no hindrance with the suit's power. I walked, step after thunderous step to our rally point, seeing everyone there. Body armor, ghillie suits, rifles and grim faces. I saw Maria, in battle dress as well, despite how she carried our child. I felt no reason to stop her. She, like me, sought to face her death as well, even with our bastard germinating within her. I saw Lauren, ready to fight. Her heartbreak paused for the battle, yet she clutched that religious knuckleduster of hers with her left hand upon the forestock of her rifle. She shuddered at the sight of me, inhuman, mechanical, cold, and her grip tightened upon her amulet. Glaring at me like the devil I was. Daniel too, in the Captain's suit sans full-helmet, wearing his own helmet, kissing Idrid on the nose as she smiled, set up with the thermal camera as she finally took off to ascend, up into the sky. Our HUD's lighting up with her imaging, a thermal readout of the area. We saw the heatmarks, the enemies on guard.

And like that, I was gone. Walking out into the black forest that I knew well, all alone. One sublime feeling after another, it seemed, in these eerie moments before the violence would begin. Soon I stood before the terminal, deep through the great cavern. I unmuted myself, opening ambient voice. "Wardrobe of Narnia." The great door shuddered to life upon the utterance of the password, the jaws of the beast falling, and I stepped in. That eerie silence. Hearing the battle commencing, echoing down the halls behind me. My steps, like the beating of war drums. I knew the sensors in here had picked me up. They were coming to oppose my advance. I could feel it. I could feel my fury being reciprocated. My metal grip tightened around my weapon, and I knew beyond a shadow of a doubt that I was the death of whoever would come for me.

They came, like waves crashing upon a mighty cliff. Bullets ripping up all around me, their panicked shouts carrying down towards and past me. Their screams as I, barely changing pace, fired, the armor-piercing .308 rounds ripping through the junk that there was for cover in the tunnel. Blood flying, bodies crumpling as I practically sprinted past, unstoppable. I was rage, I was fury. The death I spewed was impartial, coming for all who dared stand before me. Sparks flew off my impenetrable armor as bullets crashed against my hull, grenades thudding at my feet casting hot fragments into every which way of my legs and torso. For a moment, it almost struck me how strange it was. What side had they been on during the war? They were diverse, humans, hybrids alike. They all became red in my eyes. Not the red colors of allegiance, but the universal red. My vision was clouded with blood, and it did not matter.

The rage I felt could be no different if I was buck naked armed with nothing but my hands. But with my great, cruel armor, they could not hope to even slow my advance, the dead behind me, the dying around me, and terror before me. Mere guns and bombs could not slow me. My scanners picked up heavy weapons being deployed further down, and I loaded a phosphorous 30mm round to send roaring from the OICW's cannon to shake the very walls, ripping through the concrete and steel barriers where they set up a machine-gun nest, ammunition flaring up and popping as the phosphor round detonated the munitions, filling this place with smoke. A rocket streamed past me, in their desperation they employed AT4s even here, hundreds of yards beneath the very earth. *How dare you,* I was thinking. How dare you use explosives underground, how dare you come here and take over *my home* and go on to fight with such recklessness. No fear in my mind. Only spite, hearing the great boom far behind me, hearing the cries before me. The fear was all for them as my armament tore into flesh and bone, spewing up ichor. I could soon see that power armor of their own was coming to meet me. A worthy challenge at last, as I loaded the cannon of my gun again, the barrel swiveling out of position and spitting the smoking 30mm cannon shell out to allow me to replace it with a fresh cartridge from the bandolier loops of my armor, as I went for an explosive projectile this time around. The first hardly had time to fire his M2 machine gun before his head disappeared into sparks of his shredded helmet and a squall of gore, the machine's diagnostics keeping the soldier's headless body up and even walking for a couple feet before what was left of him collapsed, his headless shoulders belching blood and sparks. I had yet to reload before his armored compatriot's microgun ripped through the concrete divider I took cover behind, to pepper my armor and weapon. Though the 5.56 rounds of his gatling gun were hardly a threat on their own, in the flurry they were being sent at me my diagnostics in my HUD lighted up like a Christmas tree, alerting me of the damage steadily being dealt to my carapace. I didn't even have to think, I simply charged from my destroyed cover into the white-hot munitions stream, though my weapon was shredded I did not need it, I thought, even though at a glance one would think this would spell my doom. I was upon him quickly. All the diagnostics and gyrostabilizing support in the world could not save him as I swept his leg and sent him to the ground, to lay there as I towered above him and slammed my boot down into his helmet, the great helm crunching and exploding as I stomped once, twice, three, four times. He'd stopped moving like his microgun spooling down, the smashed helmet oozing blood and bits from its cracks at this point.

And that was when the EMP dart hit me.

I didn't know it at first, feeling the thunk upon my armor. I looked up for a moment, seeing men charging me there, that enraged terror in all their eyes. A dozen, it seemed, breaking cover. I went to raise my fists to fight these fools, only to find that the suit would not respond. I could barely keep myself standing, and then they toppled into me, screaming, yelling to shove me to the ground, immobilize me while my HUD flashed, beginning a reboot. The suit was hardened against EMP effects, but only to a point. And this was a direct hit from a localized EMP burster, the type of things cops use to kill the electronics onboard a getaway car in a chase. I slammed on the ground, gazing into the ceiling of the tunnel as they scrambled atop me, some even physically holding down my limbs, just in case. I knew I was safe in here, laying there, but for the first time I did feel fear. That apprehension. This was bad. I needed at least a minute to restart my systems. And that was when I saw the roundsaw being dragged up towards me, the great blade spinning a few times as a test before being lowered to my helmet and I was blinded by sparks, my helmet screeching and rattling deafeningly as I lay there, helpless.

The next few moments, by far may have been the most sublime of my entire life. I still didn't feel fear, but a strange disappointment as I watched the diagnostics come online, showing the entire body of my armor blinking in orange and red, my helmet growing steadily redder as those sparks flew. Soon they'd cut right into my head, and it would all be over. I'd failed, and here I was, to die alone, paralyzed, as helpless as an infant, trapped in my armor. Maybe I didn't even believe it. I just shut my eyes, my ears already ringing from the grinding of the saw etching right into the plate of my helmet. I guessed this was it, then. I guess I can give up now.

## GET UP.

It was as clear as day. He called out to me. Get up and fight. I must have imagined it, but I knew it came from deep within. Gabriel sat on high. Gabriel himself glaring down on me. *This is no place for you to die. Now.* **GET. UP.**

The suit still was without control, yes. And even then, they held onto my body, holding me down for dear life. I don't know how I did it, but with raw strength alone, I whipped. Rolling to the right with a great lurch, slipping my left out to bludgeon the saw-operator with my bare power-armor hand. I watched his skull cave like a crushed melon. I roared as blood and brains cascaded over me, still swinging onto those latched onto my right arm. Bones crunching and sundering. They screamed. I was the dead coming to life. My suit was still in the midst of charging up, but I did not care. I was up. I was heavy now. I felt every ounce of the suit, but all I heard was Gabriel screaming at me. He picked me up and shoved me towards death. Not mine, but theirs. The hands of the suit were offline, and even then they'd been mangled by that other power armored fighter's microgun. I could not use a weapon with them, I knew with a single glance to them, hobbling forward. But I did not need a weapon when I was wearing one. My arms were cruel cudgels, my body a battering ram. I found the one with the EMP dart launcher skittering away and I crushed him underfoot. Blood flew, guts and glorious ichor. Noah Reed wasn't there anymore. In this moment I was no man, but rage. At some point the suit's power did indeed turn back on, but I hardly felt a difference, save for finer motions I could finally perform. Ripping arms from sockets. Breaking necks with a single hand. Using my sharp, broken fingers to eviscerate, tearing guts from bellies amidst their owner's horrified screams. Even in here, I could smell their fear. A killing machine was coming, unleashing his pent up frustrations upon those who committed no sin greater than taking over the wrong place. My place. I saw how they looked at me, each of them in their final moments as I was upon them with cruel metal fingers to rip and gouge. I could practically see my reflection in their eyes. *Sentinel was painted red again.*

He was running. I could smell him, pursuing him up the ramp, the steps, through the armory. An older fellow, human, big bushy moustache, barely time to dress himself in his fatigues. I saw how some of his men threw their bodies in front of him fruitlessly and I knew this was the one. I would rip them to pieces and remark to myself how he must wish he never came to this place.

We broke out, up and out into the street, into the town square. He'd been firing his pistol at me fruitlessly, bullets bouncing off my helmet, only serving to enrage me further. He was a good shot, I figured. Some big, heavy revolver that must have weighed a ton and fired bullets just as weighty, each one causing my helmet in my readout to become redder and redder, before the HUD itself seemed to crackle and spark, well on its way to destruction. I noted how I could hear friendly radio chatter again, the battle at the walls, however garbled by the the damage dealt.

"...This is Noah," I growled. It didn't sound like my voice. It ought to have scared me. It didn't. "I've got him." I deafened radio chatter again. I needed to focus. You're gonna wish you never set eyes on this place.

He was babbling, screaming for help as he dropped his empty piece, slipping in the stone of the simple roads of the place, proceeding towards the town square. Houses all around.

Houses of people I knew. He was running, running as fast as an old man could, running for his life. I stooped over to pick up that gun, and I threw it with all my might. It collided dead center in the middle of his back, and he fell. How he crawled with his legs motionless, I knew instantly that his back was broken. I reached down for him. Punishment. Rage, misplaced perhaps. Though I did end him quickly, it was messy. Cruel. Cruelty befitting what state I was in. I picked him up over my head, and with him still screaming, I separated his two halves with a great sundering of what was left of his spine, skin tearing to reveal guts that cascaded and fell upon me, a fountain of blood and ichor pouring down as his screams became a sickly death rattle, and those soldiers of his stood around for a moment, before they ran. They all ran, leaving me alone there. Covered in blood. My helmet was belching sparks that stung as the blood short-circuited them, so I unlocked it and pulled it off, letting it fall to the ground with a thunk, embedding itself in the dirt with its weight. I looked to the sky and I roared, screaming, raising my mighty hands, my entire body emitting mist from the hot blood covering me, steadily cooling in this freezing november morning. It felt like the whole world heard me in that moment, that God himself gazed upon me in horror. I ought to have been satisfied. But as the blood cooled, it was evident that nothing had changed. My misery remained, even as the gunfire slowed to a stop and my allies stormed into the town square to see me, towering above the two halves of our opposing force's leader, with me just staring up and out into the dawn sky, feeling the cold wind whip my naked head, flakes of snow drifting on the gust and stinging my face and lips. They didn't cheer. Maybe they would have wanted to at first, after achieving such a tremendous, life-saving victory thanks to me, but seeing me there, pasted with blood and bone and guts, they lost their taste for it. Most of them were cheerful enough, seeing the state of the aftermath. Looks like their defenses were pushed thin enough as it was, and without a capable leader they fled. Well, the ones who'd seen me had fled in utter terror. Some of them on the walls no doubt surrendered as they'd been routed.

The locals were coming out. People I knew, people I'd grown up with. They looked upon us, their new conquerors with fear in their eyes. But to see my own father look upon me, eyes wide in horror, was beyond anything I'd been ready for. I knew it was him, I just did. Despite how battered, hopeless and terrified he looked with his slung arm and his limp with a crutch below his good arm, how he'd lost weight and seemed like a shadow of his former self, I knew it was him, and my goosebumps grew.

"Dad?" I uttered, and his terror compounded for a moment. He hadn't recognized me. The next moment, he seemed almost happy to see me, then it was like he remembered how I was covered in blood, girded in cruelty and violence, and he simply settled on shock.

"N-Noah?" He asked. Like he didn't even believe it was me. I supposed that I didn't even look like me anymore, my head lacking my usual thick tuft of hair and my face angular and fatless, with the eyes, the soul of a killer standing in the ichorous spoils of his victory.

Victory, indeed. In the end, we made it. 1200 miles and seven months of hell. I stood there, frozen solid, feeling the judgement. The judgement of my father and his friends and comrades, the people I'd known from my countless vacations here who were shocked to finally recognize me as their gore-soaked liberator. The judgement of the mother of my unborn child, having survived her own death charge, standing there in rapture, gazing into me. To have survived so much only to lose everything at the hands of the one person she'd so desperately and hopelessly clung to in her ultimately futile bid for love, for acceptance. I'd let her down, but deep down, she'd already known my love was only ever performatory. If you could call it that, call it love at all. It was only ever a face I put on that I didn't even know I wore until these last hopeless days preceding what should have been my ultimate triumph, saving my family, my friends, this Citadel. But I felt empty here, without Gabriel to share in reverie, and having turned down who once I erroneously thought to be the love of my life, in all my cruel sorrows. What sorrow it must be to have been Maria Delarocha, defiled by violence, the last and only of her family until our child is born, standing there to bask horribly in the greatest pyrrhic victory of her life, to stare into me and reflect my sorrows for a moment, before gazing down, down to the cold earth here, down to her midsection, our bastard child, never to look back up, frozen there with her rifle clutched, no more tears to shed. Mom, Dad, nobody here could understand how I looked upon her scarred, tortured body with such regret and remorse, and I knew nothing would make this news better when it came time to explain myself, explain that I never loved her, and the reason *why* I never loved her.

Now my eyes went to Lauren, that very reason. The woman I loved, who I was really fighting for all this time. To see her safe, to watch her grow into an incredible person and stay by her side, hand in hand. I'd already watched her grow into a person, but now here she shivered upon the cold wind of the first snow of her life, the tiny flecks of ice falling to deposit themselves in her mane, the Sun finally peaking its way over across the wall of the Citadel where we stood, where I stood over the piles of blood and death of our untimely enemies. Lauren gazed into me, mouth shutting and teeth gritting as she shuddered out a sigh. The stare of judgement. Not my father, not my mother, not any of my friends from before this awful adventure, not even Maria's eyes could compare to the penetrating judgement of Lauren's visage as I turned my head away from her in shame. Her face burned in my vision forever, a ghost of an image as I blinked away, gazing over to my father. A slow, careful nod. You could even call it respectful, though awestruck might be a better word for it. Like he knew just what I'd went through, or could easily imagine it from how unrecognizable I was, even past the blood I was soaked in. He saw me here, an icon of death. No longer his son, but a commander. a warlord, a man of action, violence, righteous cruelty. Lauren's face stayed in my mind as my father nodded to me, then him gazing over to Lauren behind and off to the side of me. Gazing at that strange hybrid woman as if taking in her exoticism, the one my heart so unequivocally yearned for. The woman I would rip an army of a thousand men limb from limb on her behalf. That freakish giant hybrid *thing,* like some vague macabre mockery of the womanly form that I could love like I could never love any human.

But I couldn't love her. Not anymore, not with this world of judgement bearing down on my shoulders. If I wasn't in this mechanized armor, this cold shell of mine, I would have fallen from my feet, my knees turned to jelly as it all hit me, Sentinel's software keeping me up like a statue, my titanium and dynaceramid sarcophagus forcing me to stand. Lauren was still gazing into me off to the side, and in my shame I could not look back. What have you done, she still thought. Noah. She wanted so desperately to forgive me, forgive me for what I'd done to Maria, done to her, done to myself. but she could not. Her mouth was dry, grit shut, her heavy breathing of the battle slowing before she huffed out a heavy sigh that hung in the cold air. And I knew there in that moment, the silence of our breath quieting that I would never forgive myself so long as I drew breath.

Here, at the end. That crumbling loneliness finally ever present to me. My very best friend unable to be here to see me through, to tell me what to do, to tell me it's alright with a laugh and a shove. My mind went to all the friends we'd lost, the bodies I'd stacked upon my terrible name. I was looking down to my metal hands, soaked in blood, as if to see the souls counted upon my mangled titanium fingers.

We'd made it. I'd made it. This journey was finally over, the adventure of a lifetime complete. But I could see that judgement. That sinking, crushing feeling. I'd made it, but at what cost? The cost of my humanity? No. I was still human. I was no monster and that was the real tragedy; I would still live with my shame and my regret and my sorrow. I was just an eighteen year old kid. Nineteen, actually. My birthday must have come and passed. But still I was here. Despite everything, I was and am still Noah Reed, Noah Reed the sinner. The liar, the manipulator, a man of half measures. Noah Reed the weak, the unlovable, the father to an unwanted child, a living testament to his weakness.

The story of the grand adventure, all its ups and downs, triumphs and victories, elated highs and bitter, bitter lows ends here. We made it. I made it, at the cost of everything. But my personal journey, it seems, has yet to end. Perhaps, standing here in the falling snow, I was tasting only the beginning of my most profound sorrows while I watched everyone leave, going to tend for the after-battle. My father, Maria, and Lauren lingering, before they too turned to leave me, like the statue I was, glaring into the frigid dawn sky, tasting my regret like the snowflakes burning on the skin of my face.

I was alone now, and alone I would remain.

# AFTERWORD

THE "INSPIRATION"

Jackal may have been my first book in all factuality, but The Prepper's Son is, to me, my true first story. Not only is it a much better introduction to my world (starting at the "beginning", per se, in 2060 and helming a human main character before introducing hybrids and weaning the reader on to the very concept of the hybrid as a character, while Jackal throws you into the fray with one immediately and expects you to buy the concept right off the bat, et cetera), but it was the first book I actually ever set out to write, in 2012. I was sixteen, and I'd been writing "unprofessionally" on deviantART for the last three years, but that year I set out to write an honest-to-god story in my newfangled universe. I wanted it to be a mid-apocalypse to post-apocalyptic story. The initial rendition was set in one place, rather than a journey across the country. Then, I read a book I hated, John Christopher's No Blade of Grass, or The Death of Grass as it was titled in its original release, and I realised that I enjoyed the basic plot, but everything else was utter shit, and I knew I had a real plot for my story now.

In my mind, people are usually a combination of two aspects: the critic and the creator, and nobody is completely equal 50-50, nor are people 100-0 in one way or another. I see myself as more critic than creator: 60-40 split, maybe 70-30. 65-35, somewhere in that ballpark, you get the gist. So when I read No Blade, I ended the book thinking of how I could have written it so much better. Characters did things that made no sense, the story was mired with cliches, even at the bleakest points the storytelling seemed too dry and impassionate to really understand the narrative that was being written, the very weight of the situation it was dealing with being completely mishandled, if not outright ignored- it's a shit book. Fuck that book. A dude shoots a guy in the head with a rifle and kisses him for some reason. As soon as the main group meets another group the resident badass (*No Blade*'s Gabriel, if you will) shoots their leader in the head and says "ok we're in charge now. Yall followin us now." That's retarded. I don't even remember that much about it other than the fact that I hated it. Might revisit it on my show and see if it's still as bad as 16 y/o me thought it was, but that's a topic I'll get to later.

I really hate a good lot of books, and that's what spurns me on to write, because I know I can do it better. My introduction to writing was when I was a child. I was (and still am, in a decidedly different direction) obsessed with dragons. I'd always be reading books with dragons in them, but no matter what I came upon, nothing really portrayed them the way I would have liked, and that made me take up writing, among other things. I'll tell you that film is a superior medium to text, because it absolutely is and if you don't agree you're a moronic contrarian living in the 19th century, and fuck you, idiot. Take, for example, Neil Blomkamp's District 9. That story would make a TERRIBLE book- the main character is an irredeemable asshole for no reason and inexplicably stupid and his ineptitude almost seems to be the driving force of the story(which is A BAD WRITING TOOL), but what does the movie have? Awesome stuff. Cool aliens, good, dare I say powerful imagery, great action, and badass weapons and a *fucking mech suit*. There's more to movies that can be appreciated as opposed to simple text- there's artistry in more places. there's more meat on the bone, so to speak. Even a bad movie can be enjoyed, but a bad book is miserable the whole way through. Honestly, I'd much rather make movies, but what can I do as just one man? So, I write books, because that's the budget I'm working with.

I fully admit I am a reactionary, through and through. I am more of a critic than a creator, and almost every one of my ideas has been inspired somewhere else or is a response to something. My entire universe's meta-narrative is a prolonged commentary on furry culture in some way or another. Jackal is arguably just furry Taxi Driver, and the driving force of Jackal, the main character's sleep paralysis is probably my most original idea, as it was inspired after I watched a documentary on sleep paralysis and thought "hey, I've never seen that done in fiction before". Sure, somebody must have done it at some point, but I've never heard of their work so they probably suck and their book will probably piss me off too. My next book planned follows the plot of one of my favorite martial arts films, with a few twists (that's all the spoilers you'll get though, be patient). As for other "inspirations", the setting of TPS was chosen by two elements- the Citadel itself inspired by a news story of a survival commune in north Idaho I'd read, and Vegas and its destruction by nuclear bomb a reference to Fallout: New Vegas. (kind of a stretch, but trust me, that's the reference.) The Crystal Springs arc being just a wackier knock off of *Tremors'* setting. "Squid" and the Kommandoes are a reference to the /k/ board of 4chan. Et-cetera, et-cetera. There's nothing new under the sun, and my work is no exception.

## THE CHARACTERS
### NOAH AND GABRIEL

Though more of a trope and less of an outside inspiration, the characters Noah and Gabriel are both reflections of myself. I know every character I write technically is, but Noah and Gabriel are by far the most, even moreso than the reflection of myself I poured into *Jackal*'s Jobe, who was meant to be a reflection of the toxicity within myself, being needlessly edgy and standoffish simply to be the center of attention, using big words to make himself sound smart but being a complete moron in actuality, never saying anything meaningful. Jobe may have been a far more distinct personality than Noah, but that was more because Jobe was meant to simply be sympathized with, while Noah is meant to be someone the reader can see themselves in.

Anyways, Noah and Gabriel share a dynamic inspired most heavily by my favorite movie, Fight Club. (which is a MUCH better movie than book. Seriously, I read the book and put the fucking thing down when Palahniuk started describing the "Silencer holes" drilled into the barrel of a pistol. I know it was written before Google, but like, damn dude. Libraries are free. Go to a gun store and ask somebody. If I wrote about cars, a subject I don't know, I'd at least make sure I wasn't writing down utter horseshit. Do the bare minimum of research, it's your fucking duty as an author. *Please.*) Although, Gabriel is 100% tangible and not a figment of Noah's imagination, Gabriel is my Mary Sue, or Gary Stu, if you prefer. Gabriel is myself, idealized- badass, invincible, unfazeable, quick-witted, resourceful, ice cold under pressure and terrifying once you get him mad- and ultimately, *comfortable in his own skin*. He is my, and therefore Noah's Tyler Durden, so to speak, as Noah is the me I am closer to, the weak me, a weak person who thinks he is only at his strongest when emulating another, or denying who he is. Noah is "in the closet" for the majority of the story, while Gabriel lacks a sexuality entirely. While Noah's plight can, and arguably should be read as an analogy for closeted homosexuals, the subtext I went for is far more literal.

When I was still yet to develop into puberty, I was already exposed rather irreversibly to what would affect my sexuality for the rest of my life; in my search for dragon-related stories I enjoyed as a child that ultimately led me onto DeviantART and introduced me to what I would become today. It's silly to talk about "coming out" as a furry, matter of fact it's downright laughable, only surpassed in ridiculousness by 'coming out as a brony' or an 'otaku'- but it's true, and that's what's saddest about all this. Perhaps me writing this, and writing all my stories with such melancholy is my response to myself, that even if I lived in my ideal world where I could finally be satisfied, I probably would still be miserable. After all, I am a reactionary. I write in reaction to what I have become, to what has been done to me. I would even go so far as to describe myself as a cautionary tale, a warning for parents everywhere- **don't let your kids go on the internet.** Force them to take sports, make real friends, grow up well adjusted so they aren't hopelessly miserable because what they want to fuck flat out doesn't exist and never will. That's my thesis to why god is cruel, after all. It's selfish, but I can never get what I want, and I live with it every day, hanging over me. I guess I *need* to believe in god, because I need someone to blame, and that helps me deal with what has been done to me. I just hope that he's doing this for a reason. That once my life is over I finally get a why. Or, I don't, and god is just a dick for no reason. I guess it doesn't matter, because after what's happened to me I'd never reciprocate by bowing down and accepting myself into heaven, and if there is a hell, I'd cast myself into it sooner than kiss the feet of the motherfucker who's *cucked* me my entire life. Go take my rage out by fighting some demons with an astrally-summoned sword. Sounds badass. Honestly, what I really hope I get is an answer followed by reincarnation. A chance to go again, get a shot at a normal, well-adjusted life where I'm not in anguish, or maybe to go where I'd be normal, into my "ideal world", so to speak. What I really don't want is for there to be no god, no heaven, no hell, no afterlife, nothing. Nobody to blame but the causality of the natural law of the universe itself, no transcendence, no *after*, nothing. Trust me when I say, *if there's nothing after I die, I'm gonna be pissed*. I need somebody to cuss out. And that's what keeps me stuck to religion. Even so, with all this unnecessary information in mind, this really is why I write, why I keep going, why I don't just shuffle off this mortal coil and go tell god to suck his own dick right to his face *tonight*. I know there are others out there like me, others who need to know that somebody understands them. I know that this speaks to them, and even if it doesn't speak to you, dear normal, well-adjusted reader who may or may not be reading this, take some pity. Reality validates your sexuality. For us, we have paid the price. Decadence of the modern world, you could even say, cursing us like this. We are the Rats of Utopia, the Behavioral Sink, those who have failed sexuality and now wait to die and be free of our un-indulgeable urges, a microcosm of our species. We usher in the end of this cycle of mankind, so heed our existence as a warning and learn from us, or go the way of Calhoun's mice.

Gabriel's asexuality is my answer to the question of "would you have preferred to be normal?" Yeah, I suppose I would, but that's an answer I can't give with full confidence. I grew up with this curse of sexuality. I have almost no concept of being "normal" so I can't really attest to wanting it; the difference between Noah and I being how Noah deceives himself into believing he is normal to uphold his toxic, if not downright corrosive façade, while I own up to my deviancy, as painful as it is to admit, in an attempt to reconcile myself. (and boy, do I *cringe* every time.) Gabriel, however, is free of his carnal urges. That I can truly understand, as I have experienced that state of being before my puberty. The answer to that question is that I suppose I'd rather be like Gabriel. No thought of sex or fetish to poison his judgement, to torture him with unattainability. But even then, he is tortured, and writhes before god. This is my reaction, my telling myself yet again that even free of my curse I would probably still suffer in some way or another.

MARIA AND LAUREN
But even with my curse, there are still things, namely specific personality traits I find attractive from a human female. Though I'd much prefer she have scales by a *wide* margin, the perfect woman is headstrong, has a goal and is working towards something, something tangible, yet profound in its own way. She's sensitive and caring, but she knows when to get real and lay the law down, and she's resourceful, not a wallflower or trophy; a doer, not a watcher. Maria was initially based off of my high school crush, who could be accurately described by all of the above. During the initial idea phase and beginning of the first draft of this book, her and I shared a class. I was in 11th grade, she was in 12th grade. At first, the inital outline of TPS sort of mirrored my own denials at the time- I wouldn't really truly come to accept what had been done to me until the very end of that school year in 2013. When I set out with the initial outline of the story, her and I were cordial, and the Maria I based on her was intended to spend the entire novel with Noah, Lauren instead ending the book with Daniel having finally won her favor. Obviously, that version of the story didn't pan out, and I never professed my infatuation to my crush, and never would. She and I had a serious falling out far before I could tell her how enamored I was, coinciding with how I finally worked out that I would never be normal with the collapse of an actual relationship I tried to cultivate with a different girl earlier that year, before I started to sculpt out TPS. I knew that permanent damage had been done to my sexuality and it could not simply be ignored, and that compounded with the bitter end between Maria's real-life inspiration and I gave me the true plot of the book; more than the actual journey to the citadel, but a plot of finding onesself, only to find that one's self is often more disturbing than you might like and doing everything but owning up to it until it is too late to fix the harm you have done to others. Maria's desecration towards the end of TPS is, in my mind, not indicative of any sort of spite I held for the woman who inspired her, rather, to me it is the sorrow of how I might have let her down should I ever have had a real relationship with her. I'd like to think I spared her the emotional labor of putting up with me, as melodramatic as that sounds.

Lauren's inspiration is far less personal, yet somehow more complicated. Lauren began the story's outline with the name Lauren, before I quickly shifted it in the initial draft to Tanya. The Daniel-Tanya paradigm was originally intended to be a reference to one of my deviantART friends and the main characters of their stories, but that friendship was steadily degraded as them and I grew in our differences. (if you want to have a wild ride, google Malatora. They were a part of it, and a true believer. Or something. I might get into all that at a later date, stay tuned.) I kept the name Tanya, as the true reference behind Lauren was... sort of a stranger tale. The name "Lauren" was, and I guess still is an inspiration by/reference to a green dragontaur girl original character of a very similar name from somebody who used to be somewhat infamous on deviantART back during that same era of my life in the circles I inhabited between 2009-2012, the joke being that TPS' Lauren's character is the almost polar opposite of the character in question despite aping her physical design quite closely. (don't go looking for her though. You're gonna find stuff you'll wish you never saw. If you do know the character though, kudos, you fucking degenerate.) The real reason I scrapped the "tanya" moniker is because I always felt like Tanya was a name for a Russian stripper and unbefitting of Lauren's character, the name Lauren holding a much more down-to-earth feel.

EVERYONE ELSE
If you read Jackal, Selicia should ring familiar as she's essentially the character Mary Lubo recycled from the Facility arc of Act III, only not texan, and black... Ish. Originally, Selicia was supposed to be a dragontaur like Lauren, but silver and black rather than brown and green, with western features like frills and less hair unlike Lauren's asian-dragon likeness. This was a reference to another Original Character from a deviantart user, but of course, this fell through because that reference was pretty dubious even in the original story, and the story required that Noah would obsess with only a single love interest and he's obviously physically attracted to dragontaur women, the original first draft of the story often having too many secondary characters that Noah would have taken interest in. I of course scrapped all of this once I'd realised that I wasn't exactly trying to write a tasteless harem anime. Another scrapped "harem" character being Adrianne, who was originally supposed to be one of Selicia's 'friends'/Anon's lackeys who "wanted to go on the adventure too". Of course, I recycled her character at the very end during the Pit arc, just as I re-used the name Tanya for the Captain's "wife" sort of as a little joke. Anthony is actually a random dude that I met on a ski trip during that fateful december/november of 2012, who when asking me what I was writing about on my laptop in the cabin and learned that I was writing a story, said I should make him a character, so I threw him in and he's stayed since draft one. Kyle isn't based off of anyone in particular, save for maybe a more athletic-minded friend from middle or high school, and Sam is actually based off of a girl who used to be really mean to me. I go out of my way to not use caricatures of people I know in real life for cathartic punishment. I see that sort of behavior not only as immature, but downright unlucky, like if you wish harm upon them they'll go on to win the lottery or everything that happens to them in your book just ends up happening to you. So I set out to write a more sympathetic Samantha than the real deal, maybe my way as forgiving her for being an intolerable cunt who thought colored hair is a replacement for personality. Archie's name comes from a music artist I used to listen to, an electronic producer by the same name who was big in the brony community, as I had a brony phase in 2011, and even if I didn't start TPS until way after I'd sworn that "fandom" off, I still enjoyed his music at the time. Anyways, Archie in the final draft ended up playing the role of two characters from the first- Himself, and the real leader of the hybrid group, A-L, or Al. Al was supposed to be this badass canid wolf dude who takes no shit, but I realised just how superfluous his character was. He was really supposed to be a parallel to the "badass" old man character from No Blade of Grass who dies in the final battle to take the survival commune in that book, their version of the citadel if you will. I really only wanted him for the ending where I'd copy the scene where said old dude's body floats down the river after he dies, him and the main character assaulting the commune from the river that runs through it. Also, AL had a kid at some point. Originally there were a lot of kids, until I realised that I could basically just consolidate all of their individual story beats into Susan and have the narrative run much more smoothly. Really, the original 2012 draft and even the paltry 2015 edit were mired in an excess of characters. Sure, TPS may have a lot of characters as it stands, but it was much worse before, trust me.

THE ORIGINAL DRAFT, AND MOVING FORWARD

Earlier, I mentioned a show. I'm in the process of starting a youtube series called JoelReads, where I'll read cringy stuff from my past, starting with the original draft of TPS, moving onto my old deviantart page, a couple stories on deviantart that used to inspire me, maybe even some "actual" publish books by other authors for me to rip apart. The driving force of the show being cringe, allowing you all to witness me reliving my hilarious adolescence in all its painful glory. That'll be a month or two off, but it'll be worth it. In the meantime, since I don't really have any social media for my stuff so far and intend to get into that once I've gained some traction, I do have a semi-personal facebook you can follow if you want to lose absolutely all respect for me through my intolerable shitposting. I only really use facebook and never use my twitter, so you can follow me there for """"""""""content"""""""""" if you so desire. Links to my facebook and my YouTube where JoelReads is going to be uploaded are in my amazon bio. As for my next book, I'm gonna go on a short hiatus while I get JoelReads up and running and make horrible attempts to shill my work through tasteless advertisement. Expect it in early 2020. As for a direct sequel to TPS, let me just say right now that it's not gonna be for a while. The sequel takes place some time after the end of TPS, so I'm gonna need to let Noah marinate in his own misery for a little bit before I get back to him. I've already got a basic plot outlined, but again, I need to be in the right headspace for it. There will probably be three other books out, all based on their own plotlines before I get cracking on TPS 2. TPS 2 will probably be the end of my first phase of stories, before I get into some anthologies for universe flavoring and finally get to the Creator plotline, my phase 2, if you will. Gotta build up speed, first. No sense to hype up an empty crowd. (tell your friends. Shill hard. I'll work faster if I get clout. I totally promise.)

So. Noah & Co. will be back. But not for a while, he needs some time. My next book will take a little time, since I know I'll be stretched thin between that, shilling myself and stealing internet clout through a terrible "Comedy" show on the internet and maybe a couple video essays where I can bitch about stuff and pretend to be an intellectual. Have some faith. It's gonna be a wild ride. Stick around.

    -Joel

**P.S. if you're reading this, you're holding a (hopefully) rare pre-cover art version of the book! I'm sure the collectability will make up for the lack of aesthetic! Cover art coming soon, but not to this one!**

Made in the USA
Lexington, KY
01 May 2019